LAV'RINTIR NEARLY RUINED US.

The mistake was bringing me into the room. Had they seen chaos alone, they would not have questioned.

I needed you there. For advice and support. A wave of jealousy washed through Dh'arlo'mé at the thought of leaving the staff for others to discover. *We belong together always.*

Indeed. A few moments apart won't change that. I convinced Lav'rintir and the humans that I belonged to you. I can convince anyone who touches me to leave me where I lie.

And the Staff of Chaos will corrupt the king?

It seems certain. It lies. It cheats. It follows no rules. As it comes into its power, it will find a way to ruin him. But we must prepare to interfere once mankind destroys itself. We cannot allow the elves to crumble into chaos' influence.

Do not worry for the power lost in Béarn, Dh'arlo'mé. We still control the kingdoms North and East. The roads in the West will prove more valuable than any kingdom. Let chaos rage amid mankind, and all the world will belong to the elves. . . .

Mickey Zucker Reichert

PRINCE
OF
DEMONS

The Renshai Chronicles:
Volume Two

DAW BOOKS, INC.

DONALD A. WOLLHEIM, FOUNDER

375 Hudson Street, New York, NY 10014

ELIZABETH R. WOLLHEIM
SHEILA E. GILBERT
PUBLISHERS

Map by D. Allan Drummond.
DAW Book Collectors No. 1038.
DAW Books are distributed by Penguin U.S.A.

First paperback printing, November 1997
1 2 3 4 5 6 7 8 9

DAW TRADEMARK REGISTERED
U.S. PAT. OFF. AND FOREIGN COUNTRIES
—MARCA REGISTRADA
HECHO EN U.S.A.

PRINTED IN THE U.S.A.

To birthparents everywhere
for making the most loving,
unselfish decision in the universe
and for caring about a child's future
in a way few ever acknowledge or understand.
No children are more loved.

ACKNOWLEDGMENTS

Many thanks to the following people: Sheila Gilbert, Caroline Oakley, Jonathan Matson, Jody Lee, Mark Moore, Dave Countryman, Jennifer Wingert, Dan Fields, and the Pendragons, each helping in his or her own way to make this a better story.

For patience, support, love, and example: Ben, Jon, Jackie, and Ari Moore. Also Sandra Zucker and Evelyn Migdol, always interested and always caring.

Contents

Prologue

Clouds embroidered netlike patterns across a sapphire sky, and muted sunlight glowed along their margins. The ocean lay calm as glass, a rare breeze chopping the water into stray bits of froth. Kevral Tainharsdatter stared over the taffrail, ignoring the elf captain who manned the tiller, singing his sweet, quiet song of the sea. Joy entwined inseparably with dread, and her inability to concentrate on one emotion bothered Kevral. Though only fifteen, she had achieved the sequence of sword training, knowledge, and mental control that signaled her passage to Renshai adulthood nearly three years ago.

The *Sea Seraph* glided through the Southern Sea despite the dearth of wind. Kevral's understanding of seamanship was spotty, yet it required little more than logic to realize the tiny craft should lie becalmed upon the wind-shy waters. Captain's millennia of piloting had gained him skills mortal sailors could only envy. She turned her gaze to the triangular wavelets and foam spirals the rudder churned in their wake. Her companions' voices wafted from the bow, their conversation distant murmurs carried on the intermittent breeze. The music of clamps thumping and clanking, the hum of lines, and the flap of canvas drowned out individual words.

Kevral had slipped aft to think, certain their elfin captain, unlike her friends, would not disturb her contemplation. She had maintained her position for more than half an hour, her mind distant but her senses keenly pitched for danger. By Renshai law, her people had become the guardians of the high king's heirs; and Kevral had protected Princess Matrinka from assassins for long enough to keep a part of her constantly alert even while she brooded. Insignificant details disappeared. Outside noises, however, always filtered through, processed by a finely-honed awareness, and discarded or retained without need for conscious thought.

At length, Kevral pulled herself from her musing. Unsorted

concerns remained so, raising an irritation that could not assist the problem but managed to usurp it for the moment. She spun to face Captain, deliberation reluctantly yielding to reality. Though hacked functionally short, her blonde hair had become ruffled into tangles by the ship's momentum. Salt stung large blue eyes that well-matched her rounded cheeks and the soft, childlike contours of her face. The Renshai racial tendency to appear younger than her age had never bothered her, but now that romance had blossomed, adolescent awkwardness undermined her usually unflappable confidence.

Captain broke the long silence. "Violence cannot solve every problem."

Kevral blinked. The comment appeared sourceless, and annoyance over unrelated matters nearly drove her to rudeness. Only then, she realized her fist had winched closed around her sword hilt. She released it, indentations from the knurling etched against her calluses. "I wouldn't have harmed you," Kevral felt obligated to reassure him.

To Captain's credit, he did not laugh. To do so would have besmirched her honor and might have sparked the very brutality she had just dismissed. "I wasn't afraid." The reply still bordered on insult, and Captain rescued the situation with a compliment. "Renshai violence is swift and merciless, but never without cause." The elf smiled, engraving the familiar wrinkles deeper onto his timeless features. Amber eyes, homogeneous as gemstones, studied her mildly from canted sockets; and the sun lit red highlights into mahogany hair faded from salt and weather. Rare silver wound through the brown, little resembling the gray of human elders. He wore his locks swept back and tied at the nape of his neck, opening the high-set cheekbones, broad mouth, and low ears and making him appear more alien.

Footsteps midship rescued Kevral from a reply. Four of her six companions headed toward the stern, Matrinka and Darris in the lead. The princess sported the massive bone structure that defined even the women and children of Béarn, especially those of the king's line. Thick black hair flowed past pleasant features and enveloped the calico cat, named Mior, so often perched upon her shoulders. Mior studied Kevral, wearing the smug expression cats had perfected. Darris held Matrinka's arm under the pretext of steadying her, though the gentle drift of the *Sea Seraph* threatened no one's balance. The love those two could never consummate had become too familiar for Kevral to pity any longer. At least, they had stopped denying their feelings for one another, though the difference in station between the princess and the bard would never allow them to marry.

Darris' gentle features had slackened since learning of his mother's death only a few days earlier. Grief softened his hazel eyes, usually peaceful and now nearly glazed. Brown curls flopped across his forehead, hiding the fine, Pudarian brows and drawing attention from the large but straight nose and broad lips. He wore a sword at his hip and his favorite lute slung across his back. His sorrow, Kevral guessed, stemmed not only from the loss of a parent but also from the responsibilities her death had heaped upon him. An ancient curse on the bard's line, passed always to the eldest child, imbued them with insatiable curiosity yet forbade them from passing on the knowledge this gained them in any form except song. In addition, the bard was always the personal bodyguard of Béarn's ruler.

Kevral acknowledged her friends with well-directed nods, then turned her attention to the young man behind them. Though only a year older than the Renshai, Griff towered over the others, his huge frame packed with Béarnian muscle and fat. His features contrasted starkly with his size. Cowlike, dark eyes looked out from a rotund face wearing a vast, friendly grin. Black bangs dangled into his eyes. Only the day before, Kevral and her companions had rescued him from the elves' dungeon, yet he looked none the worse for captivity. Griff did not even seem to realize the significance of his being the last untested Béarnian heir, the only descendant of King Kohleran left to pass a trial crafted by Odin to judge the neutrality and innocence of king or queen. But Kevral knew that, without the proper heir on Béarn's throne, the balance would dissolve and the world would fragment into chaos.

Rantire followed Griff, hand on hilt and gaze wary. Though a distant cousin to Kevral, she bore little resemblance. Her bronze hair and gray eyes broadcast her descent from one of the less pure-blooded Renshai lines, the tribe of Rache. Her face still bore evidence of her much longer imprisonment by elves. Unlike Griff, Rantire had been tortured for information, and Matrinka had spent the better part of the night tending her myriad wounds and scars. Kevral's private discussion with her cousin revealed that the elves had inflicted far worse than kindhearted Matrinka could know. Between sessions of brutality, they had magically healed the vast majority of Rantire's injuries.

Now, Rantire fairly shackled herself to Griff's side, his self-appointed guardian, at least until he took the throne. Kevral did not begrudge her cousin an honor won, with words, faith, and courage from Ravn, a young god descended from Renshai. As a token of his trust, Ravn had awarded her one of his own swords, a blade she wore proudly at her hip. Rantire's eyes zipped to every motion, never still; and her stance remained perpetually alert.

Kevral could not resist teasing. "Rantire, if you got any tenser, you'd explode."

Rantire's eyes narrowed, and she glared. "Perhaps, Kevralyn the Overconfident, if you became as serious about your charge as I am about mine, you wouldn't see a need for jokes."

Anger splashed through Kevral at the use of the full name she despised, the hateful nickname that suggested her self-assurance stemmed more from arrogance than ability, and the questioning of her loyalty to duty. Attributing Rantire's hostility to stress, Kevral forced herself to forgive it, resorting to sarcasm rather than blows. "I apologize for the affront." She curtsied, passing the victory to Rantire. "It takes more skill than I have to deliver three insults in one sentence."

Matrinka joined in before the dispute could escalate. Unlike Kevral, she could not see that a wild spar between Renshai warriors would probably do both participants good. "We were just discussing how much smoother things could go from here if we knew more about the elves." She walked to Kevral's side, settled against the gunwale, and faced Captain directly. Darris waited until she found her position, then took a comfortable one beside her. In contrast, Rantire placed herself between Griff and every rail until he finally sat with his back against the jib mast. Even then, Rantire violated his personal space, an imposition he did not seem to notice.

Captain clung to the tiller, though his features revealed no discomfort. "What would you like to know?"

"Everything." Matrinka glanced at Kevral for a reassurance the Renshai felt ill-prepared to give. Too late, Kevral wished she had directed the conversation to the facts necessary to stand against the enemy. Matrinka's book schooling would steer her toward history and details that little interested Kevral. "Like why haven't they had dealings with people before this? And why do they hate us?" Matrinka's face suddenly tightened into a painful grimace. "I'm sorry. Was omitting elves from 'people' insulting?"

Captain shrugged, taking no offense. "I never thought about it, really. The elfin terms and mind-concepts for humans and elfinkind are quite distinct. Common trading is your tongue. You decide."

Matrinka obliged. "I think 'people' ought to refer to humans *and* elves."

Worry about semantics seemed a waste of time to Kevral.

Captain smiled. "I like that. A word that lumps us together. It suggests the potential for cooperation."

Kevral believed Captain's choosing to work with them demonstrated the concept far more aptly, but raising the issue might only prompt a longer discussion about terminology. She waited patiently for them to continue.

Darris interrupted, and Kevral cringed reflexively. The bard's curse rendered his every utterance either an aria or paradoxically succinct. Although she delighted in listening to his peerless musical talent on most occasions, breaking for song in the middle of a conversation sometimes made him tedious. This time, Darris kept his comment mercifully brief. "If we're going to talk about something important, shouldn't Ra-khir and Tae hear, too?"

Matrinka nodded agreement.

"I'll get them," Kevral said, ignoring Rantire's disdainful look as she abandoned her charge once again. It was not that her guardianship had grown negligent; simply that she had come to trust her companions. The self-assurance other Renshai condemned as overconfidence stemmed from proven ability. Kevral trusted herself to handle any situation that might arise, no matter how sudden or unexpected. She headed amidships.

"They're below," Matrinka called.

Kevral nodded without turning or bothering to reply. Soon enough she could see if Ra-khir and Tae stood at the foredeck, and the tiny *Sea Seraph* left them no other place but the cabin to hide. The customary mixture of excitement and discomfort assailed her as she set to the task. In the months they had spent traveling together, both men had fallen in love with her and she with them. It had become a strange triangle, devoid of deceit. Everyone knew where the others stood, and both men had promised to wait for her decision. Even before this competition, the two had hated one another. Yet circumstance had intervened, and they had managed to become friends. That bond, too, ultimately hinged on her. Kevral shook free of the burden of responsibility for now. The choice would have to wait until they delivered Griff to his inheritance and saw him safely ruling.

Kevral reached the hatchway and pried it open. Sunlight filtered through the hole and into a single room sparsely lit by lanterns. Tae's voice funneled upward. "... saying you'd starve to death rather than steal to eat?"

"That is correct." Ra-khir's crisply enunciated trading tongue followed.

"Yeah? Well, what if it wasn't just your life? What if you had a wife and thirteen little redheaded brats? Would you let them starve to death, too?"

Ra-khir ignored the jab against innocent children who did not yet exist to focus upon the question. "I'd get a job, no matter how demeaning."

"We already said there aren't any jobs."

"Tae, this is a ridiculous discussion."

Kevral had had her share of honor arguments with these two. This one seemed particularly pointless. "If either of you are counting on me to supply those thirteen brats, think again."

Ra-khir rushed to the bottom of the companion ladder. Even the strange play of light and shadow could not hide the classic handsomeness of his face. "Tae was just . . . I mean, he wasn't trying—"

Tae interrupted, "Easy, Red. She was joking." He moved up beside Ra-khir, his Eastern features coarser and diminished by his companion's natural radiance. He winked. "Besides, I was talking about *his* future wife . . ." He jerked a thumb toward Ra-khir. ". . . not mine."

"Aaah." Ra-khir joined the lighthearted banter. His months with Tae and Kevral had developed a sarcastic edge he reserved for them. "But it was Tae who picked the number."

Kevral smiled, many quips coming to mind, but she shoved those aside for the more important matter of Captain's explanation. "Come join the rest of us in back." She jerked a thumb aft, ship terminology a second language she had not yet bothered to learn. "We're going to talk about elves and their motives. That seems far more important than speculating about how a Knight of Erythane would survive on the streets if he was a completely different person living in a completely different world."

"Apprentice Knight of Erythane." Ra-khir's sense of honor forced him to correct. He had not yet passed the tests required to take his place among the rigidly honorable and maddeningly honest knights. He headed up the companionway, each step steady.

Tae scrambled up behind Ra-khir, his motions comparatively quick and light. "Knight, apprentice knight. A matter of formality."

Ra-khir heaved onto the deck as Kevral back-stepped to give the men room. "Don't let Knight-Armsman Edwin hear you say that. He'll take it out of *my* hide."

"Promises. Promises." Tae scurried up beside the muscular redhead. Though seventeen and a year younger than Tae, Ra-khir carried far more height and bulk than the wiry Easterner. They seemed a study in opposites. Ra-khir's hair lay neatly combed around comely features, and his green eyes sparkled with affection. He always dressed in the colors of Erythane and Béarn, like all the knights, yet he somehow managed to bring together the orange and black and the blue and tan without it clashing. His every movement seemed poised and his every action polite.

The son of a criminal lord, Tae had grown up surrounded by thieves, thugs, and murderers. He looked the part. Shaggy black hair tumbled over his forehead and spilled into his face. Restless eyes seemed never still, and his simple garb did little to enhance his narrow, sinewy body. An edge of a scar peeked from beneath one sleeve, mute testimony to the night enemies of his father slaughtered his mother, stabbed him sixteen times, and left him for dead. Kevral knew most women would believe her insane for even considering a life with Tae after a proposal from Ra-khir. Yet his wild spontaneity and quick sarcasm attracted her every bit as much as Ra-khir's gentle kindness. Both had touched her heart with their honest openness and competence. There was more to Tae than even she would have believed and more to Ra-khir than most would believe possible.

"Stop staring at us and let's go," Tae cut to the obvious with a directness that made his companions blush. He headed aft without savoring the results of his words.

Ra-khir inclined, then raised his head toward Tae's back, the gesture plainly conveying respect as well as indicating Kevral should precede him. She obliged, and Ra-khir followed.

As the three fell silent, the voices of their companions at the stern reached them as whispers. Matrinka and Darris enjoyed a rising wind off the port rail, and Mior threaded between the gunwale gaffs as the wind ruffled her fur in patches. Captain tacked smoothly to take advantage of the wind. Griff remained in place with his back against the mast as the boom swung harmlessly overhead, forcing Rantire to shift position. Kevral hopped into a crouch on the gunwale, without supporting her weight against the rail. She chose the port side mostly to appease Rantire as it placed her in a better position for guarding Matrinka. Tae hunkered in the stern, and Ra-khir picked an attentive position toward starboard, one hand balanced on the rail.

Captain waited only until all of the humans had settled before commencing. A strand of his red-brown hair floated on the breeze, and his yellow eyes gazed out over the sea. "At one time the elves lived on a world called Alfheim, without worry or weather, without need for sleep or shelter. Our magic served no purpose except enhancement of play. We lived too long to concern ourselves with time, and the concepts of need and power held no meaning. Our language did not acknowledge any of these.

"The gods could reach our realm freely. Frey, our creator, lived on our world. Our only contact with humans consisted of rare visits by the Northern Wizard, he or she who championed the cause of good. The elves were his charge along with the Northern peoples, while evil claimed the East and neutrality the West. No magic existed among humans, so they could never find us, and the elves never thought to concentrate their magic or visit the world of mankind. I came at the request of a Northern Wizard to navigate the seas to the Wizards' Isle where they met for matters of import. I was considered ponderous and too serious by the others of my ilk."

Captain frowned at an irony too obvious to deny. He had become outcast for his wish to restore the elves to the lighthearted state they had once defined without need to question. "Elves had no laws, no conventions to govern behavior—such was unnecessary. Every elf did as he or she pleased. When Odin created our worlds, he took all chaos from man's world, believing they could not handle it. For whatever reason, he left the elves a balance of sorts, though the fulcrum falls far more toward chaos than the one eventually intended for mankind."

Matrinka cleared her throat, brows low in concentration. "But I've always heard chaos is the root of deception and treachery as well as idea."

Captain mulled the words, mouth tightened to a slit that scarcely lessened the broad lips. At length, he spoke "Thank you, m'lady. You've brought a detail into focus I'd never considered before. I've always accepted that Alfheim's balance falls farther to chaos while Midgard's shows a preference for law. It explains why elves never banded together in causes, never built dwellings, and never combined abilities until we came to Midgard." He smiled, his mouth appearing enormous in the wake of the pursed line it had previously formed. "Or, depending on your viewpoint, why humans did do those things. Think of law as structure and chaos as planning. Evil is self-interest and good a sense of brotherhood."

Kevral fidgeted, glancing around at her companions. Everyone seemed riveted. Aside from Rantire, who attended her charge, they all stared directly at Captain. Kevral forced herself to focus on the elf's words, though they had begun to seem more tedious than any song of Darris'.

Captain continued, "Long ago for you, but within my lifetime." Catching Kevral's eye, he winked. "And Colbey Calistinsson's. . . ."

Now, Captain gained Kevral's attention, too. She had modeled every aspect of her life after the legendary Renshai hero who had lived centuries before her time. No swordsman had ever neared his weapon skill, but Kevral set her sights on that goal. Once, she believed she had come close; but a recent meeting and spar with the Renshai-turned-immortal had proved her far wrong.

". . . Midgard contained law but not chaos. The Northern Wizard championed good. All Northerners, including elves, had no concept of evil. The so-called Southern Wizard championed evil and the East; and his people knew no good. Between them stretched the Westlands all but one of you call home."

Tae corrected the misconception. "The West is my home, too. Now." He did not explain further, but Kevral understood. Tae's father had sent him westward with the instructions to return East at the age of twenty, if he survived, to claim leadership of the underground, his birthright. Hunted by his father's enemies and disinterested in organizing criminals, Tae had no intention of going back.

Captain accepted the words without question. "*All* of you call home, then. The Eastern and Western Wizards championed neutrality, unaware that Odin planned eventually to give them charge of law and chaos. The Wizards maintained the balance for millennia.

Matrinka redirected the story back to her question. "So elfin chaos consisted only of genius because Alfheim had no evil and therefore no self-interest."

Captain nodded. "My assumption exactly."

Rantire added dubiously, "So adding chaos to Northmen could have turned them into elves?"

"Theoretically." Captain turned to look directly at Rantire. "Not physically, of course. Which might explain why our languages and religious beliefs are similar. But humans didn't start of a single mind, as elves did. There're many different types of people. As evil tried to persuade good and good evil, the lines blurred. That started fairly early on after creation, from what I've read."

"The point being?" Kevral's warrior need for swift answers made her impatient.

"An important one for me." Captain swung back to Kevral without disturbing the tiller. "Elves did as they pleased, which, essentially consisted of whatever felt good. Ultimately, they all carried the same deeply ingrained, innate sense of values. Elves always agreed."

Tae asked the significant questions, the ones that had initiated the conversation. "So how did elves get here? And why do they hate humans?"

"That's where Colbey Calistinsson enters."

Interest piqued, Kevral rose. Relying on holy tenets, she took up the tale. "Colbey unwillingly became the Western Wizard and brought chaos to the world." She corrected. "*Our* world. He championed law and the Eastern Wizard chaos. But everyone thought it was the other way around, and everyone was afraid of chaos, so they all tried to destroy Colbey." Finding every eye on her, Kevral turned the story back to Captain. "Right?"

"Not exactly." Captain sucked in a deep lungful of sea air. "Colbey did carry the Staff of Law and hand over the Staff of Chaos to the Eastern Wizard. And everyone did believe he had done the reverse. But Colbey never championed law or chaos. He believed ultimate balance could exist between law and chaos, as it did for good and evil. That view was shared by few, at best. Colbey gained more enemies, including the other Wizards, and the very gods he worshiped."

Darris twisted as if in pain, the need to question a brand for his bard's fiery curiosity. Matrinka saved him the stress of finding proper wording so as not to spark the requirement for song. "So the Renshai's twist on religion is correct?"

"From what I understand, in almost every detail," Captain admitted.

Darris finally found his tongue. "So the *Ragnarok* occurred?" It was the major point of contention between Renshai and others who followed the once only Northern religion, including Béarn and most of the Westlands.

"Of that, my friend, I am absolutely certain."

Kevral's heart pounded a slow cadence. Where once she found the elf's story a chore, now she would not have missed a syllable.

"The system of Wizards championing causes gave way to a balance that hinged upon the Béarnian ruler's neutrality. Colbey became the immortal overseer of balance, charging his people, the Renshai, with protecting the heirs. The Staves of Law and Chaos became the test by which the rulers are measured, and magic otherwise disappeared from man's world. Poised on the very brink of *Ragnarok*, Odin talked Colbey into joining the gods at the final battle."

"I'm sure that was difficult," Kevral inserted with a smile and obvious sarcasm. Death in valiant combat with its guarantee of Valhalla—the goal of Northmen for eternity. Heroic death established a place among the *Einherjar*, those souls who battled on the side of gods in the greatest of all wars. Even now, the Renshai still fought for that goal, believing a second *Ragnarok* would come. Kevral could think of no greater reward than a place among the gods during the *Ragnarok* while still alive. Nothing could please a Renshai more.

Captain grinned at the interruption. "Now, the gods entered *Ragnarok* knowing in advance who would live and die, and the means of their deaths. No one suspected Odin had groomed Colbey to rescue him at the final battle. Odin intended for Colbey to shift the tide of the war, to help him fight the Fenris Wolf destined to kill him. Together, Odin reasoned, they could slay the wolf, and Odin would defy his fate."

Kevral listened, rapt. She could hear the voices of the gods surrounding her, the rasp of sharpening weapons, and the clatter of warriors arming for battle. She savored the perfume of enemy blood, and the sweet cries of battle seemed to echo through her head. She could imagine no honor greater than exchanging attacks with the massive wolf and dying so that the gods' All-Father might live.

Captain chuckled at his own image of what came next. "But even Odin's power was not strong enough to stay Colbey from his own cause. Frey, the elves' creator, was fated to die on the sword of the fire giant, Surtr. The giant would then live to kindle great conflagrations on the worlds of man and elfin kind, destroying them. Setting his sights on saving humans, Colbey betrayed Odin and assisted Frey instead. Odin was killed, and the fire giant, too. But, in the moments before his death, Surtr still managed to set both worlds ablaze. There was no time to save Alfheim *and* Midgard. Frey chose the former and Colbey the latter. Neither could battle the fire alone, and they could not reach a compromise. Colbey won through guile and strength of mental will. Their combined efforts rescued Midgard, but Alfheim was lost."

Tae tapped the taffrail. "Which explains the elves' hatred for humans. But how did they survive? And how did they get here?"

"Dh'arlo'mé, now the leader of the elves, was the Northern Sorceress' apprentice when the system of Wizards was destroyed. Knowing the *Ragnarok* was imminent, he taught the elves to combine magic—a difficult task given the nature of elves. Eventually, they opened a gate to Midgard. Those nearest escaped in time, but most elves perished in the fires. Even those who survived got badly burned. Bitterness scarred them as deeply."

Silence followed Captain's tale as the humans considered the implications of what they had heard. Kevral tore her thoughts from the conjured images of *Ragnarok* to understanding of the elves' trials.

Griff broke the hush at length. "I don't understand."

The simple statement fit the heir's childlike innocence, though it required elaboration.

Captain indulged without patronizing. "Which part doesn't make sense to you?"

Griff rose, towering over his guardian. "I could understand why elves might not like Colbey, though surely they realized the difficulty of his decision." He scratched his mop of black hair. "But why do the elves hate us? We weren't even born when all this happened. We didn't even know they existed. At least, I didn't."

"None of us did," Rantire asserted, protecting Griff's feelings as well as his safety.

Captain gestured Rantire and Griff away from the jib sail. They complied. As the wind shifted over the starboard bow, he brought the *Sea Seraph* about. The boom swung through a perfect arc as the canvas took its new position. "Elves live centuries or millennia. The concept of generations means nothing to them. Also, remember, elves exist as a single, ethical unit." He lowered his head. "At least, they used to. They assumed humans do the same. It's only natural to apply your own experiences to others and expect them to react as you would."

Thoughtful nods joined Griff's.

The story meshed perfectly with Kevral's understanding of Renshai religion. Only one thing jarred, and that was a detail outside the story. All Renshai believed Colbey had died battling Surtr's fire, sacrificing his life for mankind. Some factions maintained that Renshai prayer and dedication to his causes raised him from the dead to live among the gods. Kevral, Matrinka, Darris, Tae, and Ra-khir had briefly traveled with Colbey prior to joining Captain. From him, she had learned that both interpretations were wrong. Colbey had survived the battle and now lived in Asgard with his wife, Freya, and his son, Ravn.

Ra-khir indicated a wish to speak with a gesture as formal as court. "Is it correct, then, to assume the sudden rash of assassinations of Béarnian heirs has some connection to the elves?"

It seemed obvious to Kevral, yet she still hung on Captain's answer. King Kohleran deteriorated, victim of a slow, terminal illness. One by one, his children and grandchildren died. At first, the causes had seemed natural or accidental. Then the pattern had become too strong and suspicious for coincidence until, through a mysterious process Kevral now knew was elfin magic, bear statues had come to life in Béarn's courtyard and murdered several of the youngest heirs. In desperation, the prime minister, Baltraine, had talked King Kohleran into an unprecedented staff-testing of all the remaining heirs, hoping to discover how to best concentrate security. In the past, staff-testing began after the king's death, administered to the heirs in proper ascension order until one passed. Those who failed often lapsed into depression, attempted suicide, or turned to the comfort of drugs or drink. Their despondency went far beyond the loss of rulership, for the king or queen treated family well and those siblings who did not undergo the test seemed as happy before as after.

Low in the king's line, Matrinka had never expected to become queen; yet her failure at the staff-test had left her battling hopelessness. When she surreptitiously discovered that no one had passed the staff-test, the gravity of the world's situation came to light for Kevral. The king's imminent death would leave only a three-month window to find a proper heir. Desperately, Matrinka and her friends had sought a solution and, eventually, had discovered the existence of an outcast uncle and his two sons. Uncle and eldest son had died accidentally, leaving only Griff.

"Yes." Captain answered a question Kevral's musing had forced her to forget. "The elves fashioned the assassinations. It was their belief that creating chaos in the high kingdom would cause all of mankind to fail. I was the lone voice on the council who argued against it."

"Their belief?" Tae spread his fingers, a gesture suggesting anything next spoken should seem too obvious. "They were right."

"Coincidentally," Captain admitted. "They didn't know about the staff-test or Béarn's ruler being the central focus of neutrality. They just assumed humans would prove as consistent as elves and that striking down the highest leaders might force the collapse of human society."

Tae whittled Captain's point to its simplest reality. "In other words, they didn't realize humans come in lots of different types, with different ideas and different beliefs."

Rantire nodded vigorously. "I'd gotten that pretty well figured out by the questions they asked me. I didn't think they'd ever realize they could get the information I wouldn't give them if they just found someone dishonest enough to betray mankind for money."

The implications of Rantire's words alarmed Kevral. "But they did? Eventually figure it out, I mean."

Rantire scowled. "A prince named Xyxthris sold out Béarn without remorse."

Matrinka gasped. "Cousin Xyxthris? He wouldn't." She shook her head so hard her thick black hair flew. "He would never turn against Béarn." She looked directly at Rantire. "Surely they got the name wrong."

Rantire shrugged, granting no more quarter than she would in a battle. "If you heard those elves bandying about their million-syllable names, you wouldn't consider the possibility."

Kevral rescued Matrinka from Rantire's ire. "Is there another prince with a similar name?" It seemed unlikely. The sibilance and coarse-sounding consonants would never become popular.

Matrinka lowered her head and shook it slowly. "None of my cousins would do such a thing."

"The staff-test," Kevral reminded. "It damaged you, and you've had a mission to concentrate on. There're people with a lot less inner strength than you, heirs included."

Matrinka said nothing, head still sagging.

Tae settled back into his crouch, eyes narrowed and gaze directed at Griff and Rantire. "What I don't understand is why they kept these two alive once they got a cooperative human."

Rantire answered first. "I was surprised, too. I think I got their leader convinced Griff was more valuable to elves alive than dead."

Captain pasted back strands of sea-wet hair that escaped his knotting. He studied the waters. "I quit the council and turned outcast over the issue of whether to keep or kill Rantire. No elf has ever done that before. Even those who most wanted Rantire executed appreciated my sacrifice. Besides, it's not the nature of elves to kill for any reason. Until they began disposing of heirs, no elf had ever done so before."

"They don't eat meat," Rantire supplied. "Or keep pets. Apparently, Alfheim had no carnivores of any kind."

Captain gave Kevral a brief warning look that proved unnecessary. Kevral knew another reason why elves never killed, one she had promised to keep secret. When elves died of age, their souls became recycled into an infant, stripped of memory though occasionally some remembrances slipped through from previous lives. Elves never sickened. When they died of unnatural causes, their souls disappeared. If humans knew of this process, they would slaughter all the elves so that no new ones could be born. Captain had confided this detail to wring the promise from Kevral that she would kill no elves during Griff's and Rantire's rescue. So far, she had kept both of her vows.

"Things have changed," Rantire warned. "At first, the elves' torture was laughable. They fed me food I didn't like or gave me scratchy blankets. Later, they got past whatever kept them from hurting me." She rubbed her forearms as if they were still in pain. "Far past."

Matrinka cringed.

Rantire finished. "I wouldn't count on their lack of experience with killing to keep them peaceful anymore." She glanced at Captain in an obvious attempt to separate him from the elves she despised. "At least not all of them. There seem to be good elves and bad elves, just like humans."

"Now, perhaps." Captain's concession was noticeably incomplete. During the battle on the island, the elves had organized a spell that would have incapacitated every being capable of sleep. It would have affected many elves and all humans but would have left enough awake to slaughter Kevral and her friends. Captain had divided the elves by calling for those faithful to him to withdraw from the combined magics. Kevral believed she understood the agony that disunity had caused Captain. He had weakened the very singularity he had intended to hold intact among the elves.

Darris paced, clearly wishing to summarize and needing details he could not phrase into simple enough questions.

Anticipating his friend's need, Ra-khir attempted to properly sequence the story and the necessary strategy. "Colbey told us Darris' mother is dead."

Darris' pacing quickened.

"She was the bard," Ra-khir explained for Rantire's and Griff's benefit. "The king's bodyguard. She wasn't sick when we left, so we have to assume there's been violence in Béarn."

Matrinka looked stricken, and Griff's face lapsed into horrified creases. Mior trotted back across the gunwale, rubbing against her mistress' hand.

Ra-khir continued, his somber expression revealing. He clearly hated acting as the bearer of bad news, no matter how easily deduced; but he saw the necessity for it. "Likely, that came on the heels of King Kohleran's death, in a scramble for the throne."

"But my cousins wouldn't resort to such a thing," Matrinka insisted.

Tae shrugged at the obvious naiveté of their companion. Though he clearly believed Matrinka wrong, he surprisingly chose diplomacy. "It didn't have to be your cousins. *We* figured out no one passed the staff-test. The council knew. Others might have found out also. With all the potential heirs unworthy, that leaves a free-for-all for the throne."

Even Ra-khir cringed at that. He had more reason than most to worry. Framed by Béarn's prime minister because of personal differences, Ra-khir's father moldered in Béarn's dungeon. A coup would catch him in the middle, loyal to Béarn and her proper ascension yet considered a traitor to his own side. "There's no way for us to know exactly what's happened. We'll just have to assess the situation when we get there and pay attention."

More nods of agreement followed, but the mood of the group had chilled noticeably. Matrinka looked away, Mior's attentiveness suggesting that her mistress cried. Even the excitement of coming battle did not penetrate Kevral's discomfort. Once they rescued the heir, she had believed all would turn out well. Yet their mission had only raised more issues and questions, discovered enemies where none once existed, with magic humans had no experience to face or counter. The war that, until that morning, she had believed ended had truly only just begun.

CHAPTER 1

The Summoning

The goal of a warrior is not to engage in a test of strength or skill; it is to kill the enemy.

—*Colbey Calistinsson*

Clouds darkened sky that arched over Nualfheim's forest, and the Nine of the elfin council waited for Dh'arlo'mé to speak. Excitement and rage warred within their quiet leader, dulled by a fatigue he had never known before he left the lands of elves to become the Northern Sorceress' apprentice. Now it fogged his thoughts, trebling his irritation. Tired or not, the Nine must act immediately. If Arak'bar Tulamii Dhor, the one who called himself Captain, reached the shore, humans might soon arrive to slaughter the elves on their island. The two hundred thirty remaining elves would stand little chance against hundreds of thousands of humans.

A breeze stirred air otherwise stagnant, and rising mist speckled the elves' hair. Dh'arlo'mé trapped his heart-shaped lips between his long fingers and fastened his single emerald eye on Hri'shan'taé, an ancient second in age only to Captain. Rumor claimed it took her fifty years to form or switch an opinion or a mood. She would prove the most difficult to goad to action.

"Fellow Elders," Dh'arlo'mé started, "I apologize for the hastiness of this gathering." The leader of the elves shortened the once-necessary amenities as he had done for the last dozen meetings. Once, the slowness that pervaded every action of every elf had seemed right to Dh'arlo'mé. Recently, it had become an aggravation; since the battle, it had receded almost to memory. In less than a quarter hour, the entire council had gathered and the conference began. "It is with great regret that I recommend renaming one of our own and borrowing a term. I cannot describe the crimes of Arak'bar Tulamii Dhor in our language. Words for such do not exist."

Sixteen gemlike eyes, ranging in color from sapphire to ruby, gazed earnestly from canted orbits. Each met Dh'arlo'mé's remaining eye, avoiding the socket empty since the battle during which elves had slaughtered Béarn's envoy.

"I am forced to borrow from Otherspeak and call it . . ." Dh'arlo'mé switched to the Northern human tongue for 'treason' and 'traitor.' ". . . *forraderi* and him a *forrader.* Among humans such is punishable by death."

Vrin'thal'ros broke in. "You're not suggesting we kill one of our own."

"Certainly not." Dh'arlo'mé lowered his hands and flicked back fine red-gold hair with a toss of his head. "Arak'bar Tulamii Dhor cannot have many years left. When his soul leaves him, it can only return to us."

Hri'shan'taé, She of Slow Emotions, smiled. A long time had passed since the birth of an elfin child, an event always preceded by a death.

Dh'arlo'mé swept another glance around the Nine. "I recommend we rename the outcast Lav'rintir." The name translated to "destroyer of the peace." "And that he be considered unworthy of trust or knowledge. I beg your forbearance in that I have already confiscated his belongings. What I found there may prove the answer to our dilemma."

The interest level rose immediately, expressions more suited to humans than elves for their loss of subtlety. Only Hri'shan'taé maintained her mask.

"As you know, long before I became the Sorceress' apprentice, Captain served her and her predecessors." Dh'arlo'mé used the eldest's chosen name since they had not yet voted on the change. He did not wait for acknowledgment. Captain's millennia on man's world had become common knowledge long before any of their births. Already on man's world, he had not suffered the fires of *Ragnarok,* a windfall Dh'arlo'mé could not help begrudging. Surely that accounted for Captain's sympathy toward humans. "I had believed myself the only one in possession of Wizards' books. His collection made mine look meager." The excitement flared again, finally overcoming fatigue. Without his own books, Dh'arlo'mé would never have found the passage that spurred him to teach the elves to direct and combine their magic and, eventually, create the gate that had rescued them from the *Ragnarok.* He had pored over Captain's library with a diligence that precluded sleep. History had taught him much, including the procedure and purpose for summoning demons.

The council's excitement went beyond facial expressions. Thoughts slipped through in a gentle murmur of *khohlar* or mind speech.

"I believe we all agree we cannot allow Captain's ship to reach human lands. To do so would condemn all elves, current and future, to death."

Tight nods met Dh'arlo'mé's dire forecast. They had observed humans for three centuries and dreaded mankind's swift violence. Every elf murdered left a hole never filled, a line of babies never born. Humans wasted lives like water, and yet their numbers only seemed to grow. A single elfin death was an intolerable abomination. "What would you have us do, Dh'arlo'mé'aftris'ter Te'meer Braylth'ryn Amareth Fel-Krin?" Vrin'thal'ros asked at length, using the complete name as elves always did. "We set the winds and waters against them, but they've sailed beyond range of our magic. We have only one ship of our own, and no one as well versed in sailing as Arak'bar Tulamii Dhor. Even should we catch up to them, they would attack us and slaughter more than one."

Dh'arlo'mé grinned. Vrin'thal'ros had presented the dilemma perfectly, leaving only the opening he had discovered in the Northern Sorceress' books. "We pursue them with one who travels faster than sea craft and whose strength exceeds their own. One more of chaos than ourselves. One whose ties to evil make him expendable should he fail."

The Nine met Dh'arlo'mé's words with silence. He suspected they conversed one to one. *Khohlar* allowed for broadcast to an individual or to everyone within range, nothing in between.

Finally, Petree'shan broke the silence with the obvious question. "Who could fit that description?"

"One in here." Dh'arlo'mé drew an old book from the folds of his cloak, the cover faded except for a vivid triangle where another book had rested against it. He stroked the cloth lovingly. Portions of the text described the Northern Sorceress' two personal summonings in frightening detail, along with the wards and bindings required to safeguard the summoner and shackle the demon to a contract. "One in here."

The drizzle strengthened to a cold rain that battered the common house roof and drenched the autumn night. Even after three hundred years of weather, many of the elves still chose to spend the night amid or beneath the long, serrated leaves of the island's trees. The clouds veiled stars that winked and sputtered as they never had on Alfheim, and their patterns shifted in the heavens with the changes in the seasons.

Dh'arlo'mé believed anticipation would keep sleep from him, but exhaustion wrenched away his burdens while he still studied a page of text. Nor did he awaken when others of lighter heart, who did not yet require sleep, gently slipped the book from beneath his arm to read the necessary passages. Soon, nearly every elf had weighed the danger of a demon against that of human violence. Not all might agree with their elders' decision, but none would challenge it. The nature of elfin society did not allow it.

The morning dawned bright and clear, burning off the glaze of clouds and sparking rainbows from moisture trapped on leaves and grass. The dull tan stretch of beach seemed to dance with fire in the sunlight. Dh'arlo'mé ignored the warm tickle of sand between his toes, marching directly to the gathered elves, his chosen. He had selected these for their inherent tendency toward magic and their ability to focus spells.

Dh'arlo'mé scratched absently at the scar tissue in his empty socket. Over time, magical healing would replace the eye, but it would take two centuries to complete the process. As green as sprigs of algae spiraling in the drifts, his other eye examined Baheth'rin at the center of the cluster. She stood with her head bowed and yellow-pink eyes closed, white hair like a shroud around her shoulders. She did not join in the myriad conversations surrounding her.

Dh'arlo'mé smiled, more certain of his choice. Baheth'rin had gained much confidence and self-control in the centuries since crafting the gate between Alfheim and man's world, barely in time to save any of them. The desperation of that moment returned to him now: the blistering heat, the acrid stench of burning flesh, and the hopeless certainty of death. He had forced himself past endurance, goading Baheth'rin, who had come closest to conjuring an escape. Desperately, he had placed the survival of elfinkind into her hands, boosting her with his own strength, shielding her with his own body, forcing encouragements past the raw, horrible screams that seemed far more natural. And she had succeeded. No individual elf had done anything so powerful or remarkable in the time since. Despite Dh'arlo'mé's training with the Northern Sorceress, his own abilities paled before Baheth'rin's. His power stemmed from authority and leadership, not skill.

Now, once again, the fate of all elves lay in Baheth'rin's small hands, and she took her responsibility seriously. Dh'arlo'mé placed an encouraging arm on her shoulder. "Do you feel ready?"

Baheth'rin opened her eyes and nodded. "I spent the night reading. I'm ready."

Dh'arlo'mé guided Baheth'rin to the shore, then gestured for the others to take their positions. The chosen ones settled into a grim semicircle open toward the sea and with Baheth'rin and Dh'arlo'mé as its centerpiece. Waves chopped the shore, foam glimmering through tide. Sunlight settled like a fiery blanket, disrupted by ripples, and the water appeared the same clear blue as the sky. The other elves gathered in a hushed crowd beyond the chosen ones, attention riveted on caster and guide.

Dh'arlo'mé turned his head to glance at the chosen. The twenty elves began a chant that rose and fell to the rhythm of the sea. It buoyed Dh'arlo'mé and, he hoped, Baheth'rin. The steadiness of the sound brought solace and sharpened focus. It would amplify Baheth'rin's spells as well as bolster her concentration. Again, she shut her eyes and lowered her head, one ear cocked to catch the first whispers of Dh'arlo'mé's guidance.

Dh'arlo'mé obviated her need to hear, instead choosing singular *khohlar*. Drawing the book from the folds of his cloak, he sent the incantation that would draw the weakest of demons to them. *Khohlar* worked best for concepts, granting means to send a paragraph of need or instruction in an instant. Now, he slowed the process to an unnatural crawl, enunciating each syllable with deliberate care. All that Dh'arlo'mé sent to Baheth'rin, she spoke aloud. He sensed her nervousness through the backwash of their contact and struggled to maintain an aura of unshakable confidence, in her and in himself.

Gradually, a dark blotch appeared above the ocean. Dh'arlo'mé maintained his contact with Baheth'rin but fixed his concentration on that point. Cautiously, he edged knowledge of its presence into his sending, careful not to break the flow of the enchantment. Baheth'rin's eyes flicked open, attentive to the hovering, shapeless shadow. Her head rose, her manner betraying no fear, though her mental contact told a different story. Anxiety balled beneath a thin veneer of confidence.

The chant swelled. Baheth'rin tapped its power from long habit, crafting ropelike bindings and wrapping them tightly around the darkness that was not yet a being. It seemed less black than absent of color, as if a hole had opened in the ocean sky, sucking in shadows rather than displaying pigment of its own. Suddenly, a vast sensation of horror slammed Dh'arlo'mé, upending reason. For an instant, he lost his contact with Baheth'rin. The world seemed to spiral out of control, dragging him into an endless, spinning void. Shape, form, and being rejected all meaning. He fumbled for them, sacrificing identity along with reason. Desperately, he scrambled for an anchor, finding it in sound where sight and touch had failed him. Using the chant as a lifeline, he scrambled back to law, battering Baheth'rin's mind with images of solid entities.

When Dh'arlo'mé regained his toehold in reality, he found the darkness intensified into a formless, ceaselessly moving object ringed by glowing bands of Baheth'rin's magic.

"Elf." The demon's voice crashed like the most violent storm against stone. "You called me to this world, and you will pay with your life and those of your kind." It strained against the wards, random appendages disrupting and retreating into the soup.

Dh'arlo'mé felt the chant weaken as some of the chosen fought the urge to bolt in terror. Having grounded his own rationality, he sent a general *khohlar* to brace flagging reserves.

The demon laughed at Dh'arlo'mé's efforts. "Your magic wavers. These wards are not strong enough to hold me."

Dh'arlo'mé returned to his single contact with Baheth'rin. *Focus.* With that one word, he sent a concept of absolute dedication. The longer they held the demon, the stronger it would grow; and magic only weakened over time. He fed Baheth'rin's next line to her, desperately fighting back his own concerns. Already the demon had alternately cowed Dh'arlo'mé, Baheth'rin, and several of the chosen. If too many wavered at once, they would lose control; and the demon would slaughter elves before starting on mankind.

Baheth'rin raised her voice, surprisingly steady. "By Odin's law I have called you here. You must answer my questions and perform a service to the best of your knowledge and abilities." The statement of a fact they all knew seemed frivolous formality, especially since they would not risk holding the demon long enough to bother with questions, but the books insisted on its necessity. Demons had no constraints and followed no laws except those thrust upon them.

The demon laughed, the sound as harsh and thundering as an

avalanche. "What use the laws of one long dead? The forces of chaos slaughtered Odin . . ." Its volume rose with each word. ". . . as I will *slaughter you!*"

Dh'arlo'mé felt the catch of Baheth'rin's uncertainty. For an instant, he thought he saw the bonds flicker, and the demon seemed to swell. It assumed human form, red eyes like fire against its sable head.

Dh'arlo'mé growled, fists white against the strain, as he channeled concepts of consolidated power to his student.

The bonds held, coiled like steel around limbs and abdomen. Baheth'rin replied with more assurance than Dh'arlo'mé expected. "The AllFather may have died, but his laws remain to govern this world I've called you to. And you must follow them." She assumed a commanding demeanor that tightened the bonds until they cut furrows into the form it had assumed. The demon howled, the sound raw with ancient pain. It flickered through a parade of animal figures, none of which granted it reprieve. As a bulbous pig with seven appendages, it hissed, "Ask as you will, elf. Only hope the answers are worth the blood I'll claim in return."

Dh'arlo'mé's reading had revealed the truth of its claim. If a Wizard lost control, the demon would remain on the summoned world sating its hunger for blood; and the summoner always died first. Even fully bound by wards, a demon claimed its payment for services in blood. Evil Wizards had sacrificed enemies or followers, dispelling the creatures while they consumed their proffered meal. Too compassionate to kill, the Northern Sorceress had offered her own blood, forced to battle for her life even as she banished the demon. This time, the sacrifice would prove no issue. The lives of the humans aboard the *Sea Seraph* would work as remuneration as well as service.

Baheth'rin returned her wards to normal, and the pig creature dissolved. The demon oozed and squirmed in its bonds. The elf's voice remained calm. "I'll not waste either of our time with questions. Demon, a ship recently here now sails to the west. All humans aboard her are yours, just leave the elf alive."

The demon assumed a parody of elfin form, its eyes grotesquely slanted and the graceful musculature bloated. "I will do as you ask," it said softly.

Dh'arlo'mé reveled in rising triumph and sensed a moment of joyous relaxation. The elves' chant scarcely wavered an eighth of a tone, but that proved enough. Suddenly, wind slammed the ocean into wild breakers that gobbled up the beach. The sky darkened to slate, and the sun disappeared. Dh'arlo'mé battled panic that turned his thoughts to liquid, too caught up in his own scramble to lend himself to others. As if in a dream, he saw the demon flex and the bonds bow like heated metal. Baheth'rin shouted something desperate, and magical syllables spewed from her lips. The chanting became distant background, a bare hum in Dh'arlo'mé's ears. Then, the bindings shattered, hurling hot shards of sorcery that glittered in myriad hues against the solid darkness of the sky.

The demon hurtled down upon them, all sable and claws. Seized with the urge to run, Dh'arlo'mé held his ground, though whether from paralyzing fear or courage he never knew. The demon crashed into Baheth'rin, pitching her into a wild spin. She crashed amongst the horrified chanters, most of whom scattered along with the observers. Blood splashed Dh'arlo'mé, then Baheth'rin's agonized shrieks shattered his hearing.

Dh'arlo'mé called a frantic *khohlar,* urging any elf still rational to continue or join the chant. His vision became a savage swirl of black splashed red as the demon's claws tore through its summoner's flesh. Need brought deadly logic. Dh'arlo'mé realized it no longer mattered that others cast magic stronger and better than he did. Few could have read the sequence required to banish the creature and its murderous frenzy, and none of those seemed likely to remember it now. The first few syllables rushed from Dh'arlo'mé's throat even as the demon shredded Baheth'rin and her screams became mindless. The third word peeled forth, then disappeared. The next would not follow. He dove for the book, knowing as he did so he did not have the time to scrabble for the page.

Dh'arlo'mé sobbed, beyond desperation. Even as his mind dismissed one strategy as hopeless, it clung to another. The banishment incantation would not come, the memory too distant in his hysteria. But another sequence flowed smoothly into conscious thought, the one of binding he had shared with Baheth'rin moments ago.

Baheth'rin lay mercifully still, tatters of skin and bloodstained clothing inseparable. The demon whirled toward Dh'arlo'mé, eyes burning, Baheth'rin's intestines wound like a rope around hawklike talons.

Dh'arlo'mé drew a shuddering breath. There was not enough time to cast in the moment between the demon's scarlet glare of triumph and its leap toward Dh'arlo'mé. Instead, he condensed the spell into concept, shouting *khohlar* at the demon. He kept the sending personal, directed at the creature, even as the semi-solid blackness descended upon him. The thought scarcely left Dh'arlo'mé's mind in time for him to tense in anticipation. He could smell its fetid breath, and a drop of its saliva burned his arm like poison. He screamed, imagining the nails rending him, his flesh yielding to their sharpness.

The hot wind of the demon's passage raised Dh'arlo'mé's hair, then the beast swept out to sea on leathery wings. It took the shape of a serpent, blood drizzling from its claws in pink-red droplets. Its words echoed in Dh'arlo'mé's head, though whether aloud or as *khohlar* he did not care to wonder: "Bound to my summoner's assignment, damn Odin's corpse. But when I'm done, I'm free. And you're next." Its laughter boomed across the waters, and the waves seemed to shiver in response.

Dh'arlo'mé lay still several moments, his body refusing to respond. His mind raced with all the vigor his limbs lacked. His *khohlar* had accomplished nothing. Only the demon's promise to Baheth'rin had brought it back under control. When it returned for him and the others, they must be prepared.

Dh'arlo'mé forced himself to rise, hid his terror behind a mask of false bravado, and headed off to gather his troops.

The *Sea Seraph* scudded across the Southern Sea, caressed by a gentle northerly wind. The breeze filled sails hauled taut that did not spill a puff of precious air. Blue water reflected blue sky, mirrored expanses interrupted only by white clouds above and eddies below. At the forward bow, Kevral stared out over the placid waters, enjoying Ra-khir's presence at her side and the occasional, casual brush of his weapon-hardened hand against her own. Wind swept red hair from his stately features, floating strands into streamers. His green eyes sparkled in the sunlight, and his lips parted slightly, bowed subtly upward. Their frivolous conversation meant little to Kevral, but their closeness brought a joy she had cast aside for days. Moments like this one seemed a haven in the tempest her life had become. She could study his face forever and never tire of it or discover a flaw. The masculine ideal stood beside her and, for reasons she could not discern, wanted her. The thought of losing him for the love of an Eastern crime leader's son seemed madness. Yet Kevral knew from experience that if she stood with Tae instead of Ra-khir, he would seem just as much her one and only choice.

Kevral's contemplation broke the thread of their conversation, and they slipped into a comfortable silence. The wind rose, scarcely ruffling Kevral's short locks but sending Ra-khir's longer hair into a wild dance. A shadow dimmed the sky's brightness suddenly. Rantire's voice rose in alarmed question from the aft deck. "Captain, what *is* that?"

Softer, Captain's reply scarcely wafted forward. "I don't know, but I don't like the look of it."

Kevral and Ra-khir turned. Beyond masts and canvas, a dark form blotted the sun. *A cloud,* Kevral guessed, though it moved too swiftly and its shapelessness seemed to stretch and pull as she watched. Ra-khir placed a hand on her arm, the gesture polite habit. A Renshai warrior needed no protecting.

"Get below!" Captain instructed suddenly. "Safer there."

Footsteps clattered toward Kevral and Ra-khir, interspersed with voices. She could not pick out individual words. They headed aft to meet their companions halfway while Tae climbed the companion ladder from below. Darris and Matrinka rushed toward them, Mior trotting in their wake and Prince Griff only a few steps behind them. Rantire guarded her charge's every movement.

"Strange weather," Matrinka explained.

Rantire herded the two Béarnian heirs below, forcing Tae back down the rungs.

A roar rolled toward them in a savage crescendo. Kevral looked up to see the shadow hurtling toward the *Sea Seraph* at a pace too fast for any cloud. A gust slammed the ship, rattling clamps and lines and flapping canvas crazily.

Kevral raced aft, Ra-khir matching every stride. Tae scrambled over his descending companions. Darris remained above, torn between Matrinka and the need to assist.

"I'll watch these two!" Rantire shouted, making the decision for Darris. Kevral ignored her cousin, without judgment. Renshai fought without pattern or strategy. Kevral had made her choice to remain at the heart of any danger and Rantire to tend their charges.

Captain shouted a wordless expletive, launching himself at the lines securing the main sail. Kevral skidded across the planks to the taffrail. The thing hurtling toward them howled noises that grated through her ears, like steel scratching slate. The blue arc of sky stretched above and before them. Aft, the blackness seemed to spread from thing to horizon, as if it poisoned clouds and atmosphere where it touched. Kevral drew her sword.

Abruptly, the thing struck, hammering the *Sea Seraph* with a strength that should have shattered the tiny craft to matchsticks. The timbers held, but the canvas tore. A sheeting sound screamed over the cries of the creature. The ship rolled, lurching suddenly to starboard. Kevral seized the rail, keeping her feet without losing a grip on her sword. Thrown sideways, Ra-khir crashed into the jib mast, then tumbled to the deck. Captain sprinted for the tiller, too late. The *Sea Seraph* yawed widely, thrown broadside into the trough of the sea. "She's broached to!" Captain shouted as waves hammered the strakes like drumbeats.

Kevral had eyes only for the dark form that had slammed into the ship. It seemed to flow like water, then solidified into a disproportionate man. Muscles clung to arms and legs like boulders, and red eyes flashed out from a bulbous, hairless head. *Demon.* No other word fit the creature, though logic, experience, and training defied the possibility. The creature bashed the *Sea Seraph* again, sending it into a wild, rollicking spin that knocked even Kevral to one knee. Ra-khir clung groggily to the mast. Darris scrabbled for purchase as he rolled across the deck. A wave smashed over the port quarter, plucking Tae over the gunwale and into the roiling sea. Water broke over Kevral's head, soaking her. Salt stung her eyes and slicked her grip. Receding ocean sucked at her hold.

Raising her dripping sword, Kevral screamed a desperate challenge while Captain fought a losing battle with tiller and lines. "At me, demon! Any coward can fight a defenseless boat. Dare you face a Renshai?"

Captain gasped out a sob of frustration as he raced by Kevral with impressive dexterity. "Nothing but magic holding her together. Even that will soon fail."

The sable bulk of the demon wound between the sails. A massive fist hammered the main mast. It bent and reeled but did not break. Then the creature alighted in front of Kevral. A snout grew from the otherwise human face, and a muzzle crammed with canines opened and shut with every word. "You're nothing, trifling human. Nothing would give me greater pleasure than crush—"

Kevral sprang, sword flailing. The blade cut the dark form half a dozen times yet met no resistance. Kevral's lunge propelled her through the demon, and she skidded savagely out the opposite side. Wet planks gave no purchase. Kevral scrabbled for balance, slamming into Darris as he finally regained his feet.

Both sprawled in a wheel of flailing limbs. Kevral rolled to a crouch, only to find the demon on top of her. Its jaws splayed open, and saliva dribbled from teeth like daggers.

Kevral jerked up and aside, shoving Darris out of the way. The bite grazed her arm, pinching without tearing, and its spittle seared her flesh into a blister. "Modi!" she screamed, the Renshai battle cry naming the god of wrath. The cry brought new strength and rage. Renshai fought not through pain but because of it. She swept, jabbed, and looped. A sword that should have torn the demon repeatedly sliced harmlessly through it. Finally, Ra-khir managed to draw up beside her. His sword accomplished nothing more than her own.

The demon laughed, the sound so rich with ancient evil it raised every hair on Kevral's body. Terror hammered at reason, but desperation and Renshai courage drove fear into oblivion. Catlike claws sprouted from the demon's fingers, and it swept at its attackers in a patternless frenzy.

Kevral dodged and leaped, returning strikes that cleaved the black form without consequence. Ra-khir retreated, his strokes comparatively slow and clean but no more effective.

"No!" Captain ceased struggling with the ship long enough to hurl himself between the claws and Ra-khir's face. A blow intended for the knight-in-training slashed the elf's tunic instead. Four, bloody gashes marred Captain's upper arm, and his sleeve hung in tatters. "Ten years each," the elf gasped, eyes glazed with pain. "I can afford it. You can't."

"I can't hit it!" Kevral shrieked her frustration as she circumvented the mast and drew the demon back toward the aft rail. The demon ignored the weaving steel that could not harm it. Soon, Kevral knew, they would tire of dodging. When they did, they died.

"Only chaos can hit chaos," Captain explained, drawing a figure in the air in front of him. Kevral stumbled on a slick board, crashing to one knee. The demon's fists galloped toward her, then slammed an invisible barrier that Captain had, apparently, drawn between them. A high-pitched tinkle like breaking glass filled Kevral's ears and the fists continued their plunge toward her. Captain's magic had gained her only the few moments she needed to scramble free.

Magic. The answer seemed obvious to Kevral, the solution less so. "Can you put some magic on the swords?"

"No." Captain built another barrier that the demon shattered effortlessly. "That's beyond any elf."

The demon's attack increased. Five more arms appeared from the mass, driving toward Kevral and Ra-khir with increased fury.

"Darris!" Kevral screamed, remembering the sword Ravn had given her cousin. "Get Rantire."

Darris scurried amidships. The ship rolled and yawed, violently erratic. Ice-grained wind battered the back of Kevral's neck, and she felt the gunwale touch her thigh. As three claws sailed for her at once, she threw herself sideways. The tiller gouged skin from her calf, tripping her, and she sprawled to the deck once more. The *Sea Seraph* pitched, ocean funneling over the stern. Water churned around Kevral, breaking her grip on the sword. Standing, she would have been ripped overboard. Now, the sea only heaved her against timbers that should have fractured long ago. *Nothing but magic holding her together. Magic!*

Kevral tottered onto rubbery legs, feeling the hot swish of a demon fist through the air beside her. Its roar deafened her. Her wet hands chilled to numbness, and wind tore beneath her sodden cloak. Her fingers closed over the tiller, and she wrenched at it desperately. Apparently second-guessing, Captain jabbed a latch at its back. The tiller jerked free in Kevral's grip.

The demon's fist caught Ra-khir a solid backhand across the mouth. The Erythanian flew over the gunwale, flailed for the rail, then plummeted into the ocean.

"Modi!" Rantire's battle cry echoed across the deck, and she charged the demon with a bellow of fury. Her sword plowed a gaping furrow through its belly. Its shriek combined pain and rage, and it turned its attention to this new threat.

Kevral sprang from behind, banishing images of loved ones dumped into the frothing waters. Until they destroyed the demon, she could not help them. The rudder thrashed down on the demon's head with all of her strength behind it.

The demon's scream intensified. It stumbled forward, onto Rantire's stop-thrust. Blood splattered from the demon, nearly as dark as its bulk. Kevral caught the beast three more blows across the head and back, driving it further onto her cousin's sword. The demon staggered. Suddenly, it lurched backward. Its massive form slammed her against the rail. Her head snapped back, banging metal. Consciousness swimming, she slid to the deck. The demon hurtled awkwardly over her, splashing into the ocean.

"Oh, no." Captain's quiet expletive did not prepare Kevral

for the tidal wave that followed. Water seethed, washing the planks from stern to stem. The *Sea Seraph* bucked and reared. As the stern smacked the water, the ship pitched over, tumbling aft over fore, dumping Kevral and her remaining companions into the sea. Kevral ducked, anticipating the weight of the craft on her head. Instead, she crashed into the sinking demon as the *Sea Seraph* finally surrendered to the sea. Something wooden bumped her hand. Without bothering to identify it, she jabbed, slashed, and hammered at the creature as it slipped deeper beneath the water. It did not resist. Still Kevral did not cease until her arms ached from fighting the thick constraint of water and her lungs demanded air.

Finally, battered, bruised, and exhausted, Kevral surfaced. The sky had returned to jewel blue decorated with white clouds that seemed impossibly fluffy after the battle that had taken place moments before. Stray hunks of wood swirled through the waves, but Kevral saw no sign of any of her companions. "Captain! Ra-khir! Matrinka!" Alarm flared to panic. "Griff! Hey! Can anyone hear me?" She spun desperately through the water, then bobbed, gaze blurred by salt. She saw only ocean, sky, and less rubble than she expected. "Captain!" Kevral choked seawater from her lungs, treading water and scanning in all directions. "Tae?" Her voice seemed to carry forever, without cliffs or forest to return the echoes.

Kevral looked west, the direction in which they had been traveling. The boat had flipped end-over-end across the bow which meant the remains, and the survivors, would have most likely gotten tossed eastward. The idea of heading back toward the elves rankled, but it seemed the most productive direction for the moment. She swam, strokes broad and strong, scanning for any sign of movement, any calls for help. Every fourth stroke, she shouted a name at random.

Afternoon glided into night. Moonlight sparkled through the swells. Clouds spread across the stars, and Kevral lost all sense of direction. She continued to swim, ignoring the aches that came as much from the battle as from hours of fighting ocean. She found no more pieces of Captain's shattered craft, wondered if she had chosen her direction poorly, and vowed to head west at first light. Images of her friends paraded through her mind's eye, worrying at her emotions and conscience. Placing the needs of the world before her own, she pictured Griff first, his raw innocence puppylike and occasionally broken by unexpected insight. His extra weight should help buoy him in the ocean, and Béarnian size and strength should serve him well for swimming. Yet those thoughts were scarcely reassuring. It was not enough to believe Griff might have survived. The balance of the universe rested upon his sturdy but naive shoulders.

Kevral pictured Ra-khir next, and her eyes brimmed with tears. She banished these with resolve. Until she knew the fates of her friends for certain, she would not mourn them. Instead, she imagined the knight-in-training struggling through the waves to rescue others. Tae came next to her thoughts, then Rantire, Matrinka, Mior, Darris, and Captain. For each, she conjured a steady, easy swim or a piece of the *Sea Seraph* to serve as a raft.

Fatigue caught up to Kevral in a wild rush she could not ignore. Lying carefully on her back, seeking stars through the veil of clouds, she drifted peacefully into sleep.

CHAPTER 2

After the Storm

Rigid laws do not make allowances for circumstance.
                                            —Colbey Calistinsson

In the wake of the demon's attack, wind chopped the water into foam and clouds enwrapped the night sky as if to cleanse it. Matrinka scanned the ruffled waters until her eyes ached, ears pitched to catch the most distant splash or cry for help. Gusts tore beneath her sodden clothing, icy agony against skin already enveloped in gooseflesh. Desperation did not allow her to care. Too many companions remained lost in the Southern Sea to spare attention for personal discomfort. She sat on a sodden, surviving chunk of the *Sea Seraph's* bow that bobbed in the restless ocean, buoyed by Captain's magic. She and the elf had discovered the makeshift raft soon after the ship's destruction, and a spell had located Darris, floating unconscious amid the debris. Now, bard and elf hunted amid the carnage for useful pieces of wood as well as friends. Matrinka listened, watched, and fretted.

"There. Over there," Captain said suddenly, finger jabbing the darkness to indicate something Matrinka could not see. His tattered sleeve flapped back to reveal the bandage she had placed over the wound left by the demon's claws.

Matrinka shifted to a crouch, hope rising guardedly.

Using a broken board, Darris paddled in the indicated direction. His lute lay on the raft, waterlogged beyond use yet too beloved to discard. Darris had lugged aboard a portable arsenal of instruments, all now lost beneath the surging sea. "What do you see?"

"Bit of canvas and a perfect piece for a small mast."

Matrinka sighed and settled back into place, unable to share Captain's excitement. She understood the significance of his find. Makeshift paddles could never get them to land in time to survive an utter lack of fresh water. Thirst had not yet brought that lesson home. For now, the lives of friends mattered more than her own. Though the situation had not changed, the dashed hope sent her into a fresh round of sobbing. Her lids felt hideously swollen, and salt tears stung eyes already raw from crying. A lump of lead seemed permanently lodged in her throat. Her mind refused to grasp the enormity of permanence. She might never see Kevral, Tae, Ra-khir, or Rantire again. If the last possible suitable heir to Béarn's throne drowned in the Southern Sea, no hope remained for any of them. And Mior was missing, too.

Matrinka gasped reflexively as sobs racked her. Guilt tainted otherwise innocent sorrow. If Griff died before he reached Béarn, their adolescent self-assurance had wholly destroyed the world's last chance for survival. She could no longer justify their mission with the understanding that the kingdom's scouts and envoys had also failed. At least they had not *killed* Griff. Other shame assaulted Matrinka simultaneously. She felt ugly for worrying as much for a cat as over her human companions. Mior had come to her nearly four years ago as a filthy furball that King Kohleran, her grandfather, had rescued from a sewer trough. From that moment, they had become all but inseparable, their relationship more than just pet and owner. A limited form of mental communication had developed between them, one those she told had dismissed as silliness. A world without magic could not support such an association. Even her friends had required an intensive demonstration to believe.

"Darris, over here!" Captain called suddenly, abandoning a dripping hunk of sail for some object to his left. "Steer this way." He made a broad gesture toward the focus of his gaze.

Darris paused, mast board halfway drawn onto the raft. If he let go and paddled, it would likely slip off into the water.

Captain trotted over, as light-footed on an unsteady chunk of boards as on the *Sea Seraph*'s unbroken deck. He seized the makeshift mast to steady it and allow Darris to attend to rowing. "Human. Griff, I think."

Immediately, Darris let go of the mast and seized the paddle. Rowing furiously, he headed in the indicated direction.

Though she knew it would assist him little, if at all, Matrinka scrabbled in the water with her hands. The raft skimmed over the sea, bumping bits of wreckage. Soon a dark shape hove into sight, unidentifiable shadow in the night. Captain shouted, "Yo!"

"Over here," Rantire's voice returned faintly.

Matrinka's heart quickened, and the tears gave way to excitement. She sat back on her haunches. "Who's with you?" Her higher-pitched voice did not carry as the elf's had.

No reply followed.

"Who's with you!" Matrinka repeated, louder.

Darris panted. "Save your breath. It's not worth shouting back and forth. We'll know soon enough."

Matrinka went silent, the trip to Rantire seeming to span hours. Suddenly, a presence touched her mind weakly. *Help me. Help soon.*

Mior? Matrinka scarcely dared to believe.

Heavy ropes. Can't fight any more. Help! Urgency pierced the words as well as a sense of desperate weakness.

Hang on! I'll get you. Matrinka attempted to identify Mior's position. Darkness confounded her vision, and only knowing the extent of their mental bond assisted. "Mior's over here," she called aloud. "And in trouble."

"We'll get her next," Captain promised.

"No!" Matrinka felt the cat's presence growing weaker, though whether because they shot out of range or due to the cat's condition, she could not tell. "She's in trouble."

Pain filled Darris' features. "Matrinka, people have to come first."

Though Matrinka knew Darris spoke truth, she could not allow Mior to die. Without another word, she dove from the raft.

"Matrinka!" Darris cried out.

The roar of water closed over Matrinka's ears, deafening her. She swam toward Mior's remembered position, foiled by the constancy of ocean and darkness. *Mior, I'm coming. Where are you?*

A long pause followed while Matrinka chose a direction nearly at random. Terror seized her as she swam. The possibilities for the cat's sudden silence pained. *Did Mior drown, or did I drift out of range?* Then, just as she prepared to mind-call again, Mior's answer reached her, *Don't know . . . wood under a claw. Rope I can't untangle.* Desperate need replaced the transmission suddenly. Words required too much effort.

Matrinka pivoted toward the direction from which the reply had come. *I'm coming! Following your "voice." Say anything as you can.* Spray slapped Matrinka's cheek, stinging. Chill water ached through her limbs, and currents under the surface battled against forward progress.

Can't hold— Mior started, call fizzling into a frenzied surge of panic. *Get it off me! Get it off!*

Matrinka did not bother to request details. The frantic leaps of Mior's thoughts would not allow such focus. She quickened her stroke, battling undertows like a mad thing. Mior's mind-voice cut out, replaced only by the fright leaking through the contact. Then, even that disappeared.

Mior! Matrinka scrambled through the water. Only one shape broke the ocean's surface, and she lurched for it. *Mior!* Matrinka reached the object, a scrap of planking, and hopelessness speared through her. "Mior," she sobbed. Her hands chopped the water as she switched from swimming to treading. Her palm slammed something solid, driving it deeper, and something soft and wet slid across her thigh. It took Matrinka's mind a moment to grasp the obvious. *Mior!* She dove for the cat, blindly plunging after its natural sinking course. She flailed wildly, fingers churning through the dark ocean.

The need for air hit Matrinka suddenly, and she cursed herself for not taking a deep breath before plunging downward. Her wrist touched something. She lunged for it. Both hands clamped around a solid, hairy object with trailing loops that tickled her legs. *Mior?* Matrinka dared not imagine it as anything else. Her lungs bucked against her control, hungering for air. She held the bundle tightly to her chest, using only her legs to kick wildly to the surface, afraid to release her hold with even one hand.

The surface seemed miles above her. Her lungs throbbed, gasping for a breath she dared not take. The thing in her arms remained unmoving. The need for air dizzied Matrinka, leaving her mind free to conjure images of what might lay pinned against her chest. Pictures paraded through her mind of long-dead sea creatures moldering, hunks of human flesh half-eaten and trailing intestines, unidentifiable objects coated with slime. Cold air washed Matrinka's forehead. Her throat spasmed open, breaking her control. Water trickled into her airway, followed by a rush of air. Her lungs sucked greedily, then she choked on the seawater. She sputtered, coughs shuddering through her, interspersed with gulps of air that drove the water deeper.

Only when her own body stopped hacking and battling did she gain the control to tend the object in her hands. Water matted black, white, and orange fur against a frame that now seemed fragile. A tangle of rigging lines imprisoned her hips and back paws. The eyes and mouth lay closed. Mior floated, still and lifeless in Matrinka's arms. "No!" Matrinka screamed. "No! No! No! No! NO!" She found herself incapable of other speech, her mind paralyzed by denial.

Darris' voice wafted distantly. "Matrinka! We're coming."

Matrinka did not care. Only the silent bundle in her arms mattered. But the cry did galvanize her thoughts, and her healer training reemerged. Without bothering to tear free the heavy ropes, she turned Mior upside down, squeezing her from abdomen to chest. Water dribbled from the cat's nose and mouth, less than Matrinka expected. She repeated the maneuver, gaining little more.

Matrinka sank dangerously deeper into the water. She flipped Mior into the crook of one arm, belly upward, and used her other hand to tread back into a more stable position. *Stimulate and give air.* Matrinka instinctively likened the situation to a limp, blue newborn. Every competent healer knew that even a baby who appeared far beyond help might respond to blowing and shaking long after birth. She huffed into Mior's pink nose repeatedly. *Live. Please, Mior. I need you. Live!*

"Matrinka!" Darris' voice sounded as wildly distressed as she felt. "Matrinka, say something. Where are you?"

Matrinka pounded on Mior's chest, her supporting hand and the cat tossing with every movement. The water did not allow her the steady surface she needed to work. Understanding Darris' need, she broke away from her patient to shout back. "I'm here!"

In the moment's lapse, Mior coughed.

Hope flared into a bonfire. *Come on, Mior. I need you!* Matrinka shook the cat.

Mior coughed again, struggled and twisted, then opened her eyes. *It's about time you realized that,* the cat sent back accompanied by an awkward purr. Though glazed, the yellow eyes met Matrinka's.

Thank you, gods. Thank you. Matrinka squeezed Mior into a viselike embrace. The interlude without kicking sent her sinking.

Mior scrambled from Matrinka's arms and settled into her usual position on the princess' neck, writhing through the lines still trapping her back legs. *Are you trying to drown me?*

Matrinka trod water with more fury, the imbalance of the cat's position costing more energy, though it did free her hands. *I'm trying to save you, you ungrateful little mouse-eater.* Salt stung superficial scratches the cat had accidentally clawed into her forearm.

"Matrinka!" Darris shouted again. "We can't find you if you don't talk."

"Here!" Matrinka called back, surprised at how fatigued her own voice sounded. "Over here! Here!" She did not bother to wave. The darkness swallowed her, and her friends could hear farther than they could see. Now that violent need no longer spurred her, she felt as if chains weighted her limbs. Every part of her ached, and the cold seemed to have seeped into her very soul. "Here!" She added wearily, too softly, "Please hurry."

Matrinka fell silent, too tired to bother gathering breath to scream again. Nor did Darris request another location call. Apparently, Captain had her position pegged with magic. Matrinka's mind slipped into a quiet fog that begged solace. Her movements became habit, arms weaving in arcs that seemed tedious and legs whipping back and forth in a pattern that no longer required concentration. The world drifted, first into quiet contemplation of the darkness, then into nothingness.

A sharp thought prodded Matrinka. *Don't go falling asleep on me.*

Matrinka jerked to attention, fairly certain she had done just that. *Sorry.*

You better be. They're almost here.

Now Matrinka could hear the cut of the paddle through water. "Matrinka?" Darris said, backpedaling as the raft drifted toward her. "Careful. I don't want to hit you."

"I'm right here." Matrinka attempted to swim toward the sound, but Mior's bulk and her own fatigue foiled the attempt. Instead, she kicked lazily to propel herself sluggishly in the general direction of the raft. Finally, her vision carved the raft's shape from the darkness, several figures huddled on its surface. Darris and Captain stretched arms toward her, and she reached for them. A hand caught each wrist. "Wait," she said. *Go ahead, Mior.*

The cat shifted position, then stopped. She waited until elf and bard pulled Matrinka nearer the raft, then bounded lightly to the deck. Matrinka went limp, allowing the two to haul her on board. Only then, she recognized Rantire and Griff, the Renshai still hovering over her charge like a new mother.

Darris drew Matrinka into his arms, ignoring the rivulets that ran down her clothes onto his own. He held her tightly, as if to transfer heat as well as emotion, but he managed only to soak himself. "You did a very foolish thing. You could have drowned." A catch turned his lecturing tone into a frightened one. "I love you, Matrinka. I can't stand the thought of losing you."

"I love you, too." Matrinka returned a sentiment that never seemed to grow old. They could not marry, but they could stay together always. And she would see to it they would.

Mior sat, sulking. *You save my life and he calls that foolish? Can I use his leg for a scratching post?*

Warmed by Darris' kiss, Matrinka did not bother to answer.

Carved directly from the Southern Weathered Mountains, Béarn's castle stretched its great spires toward the heavens. Prime Minister Baltraine stood on the balcony, watching the masses gather below. Their excitement seemed tangible, a sensation carried to him on the autumn breeze. They shifted and whispered, the whole blending into an indecipherable hum. Occasionally, an organized chant could be heard over the mumbled chaos, "King Kohleran, King Kohleran, King Kohleran!"

Baltraine sighed. So often, he had considered the peasants fools for their blind loyalty to an elf masquerading as their dead king. Dh'arlo'mé had selected Pree-han because his voice most nearly matched Kohleran's booming bass, and Baltraine had schooled the elf to enhance the match. Twelve years as Kohleran's prime minister had accustomed him to the king's well-balanced judgments, word choices, and patterns. His training and written speeches had allowed the substitution to work. Without him, the elves would have failed.

A page slipped quietly onto the balcony. He bowed to Baltraine, hands nervously entwined, then shifted to the front of the balcony and looked down on the people. "His Majesty, King Kohleran!" he announced.

Applause exploded from the peasants. The page scrambled aside as the procession entered. First, two Béarnian guards examined the balcony for danger. Pree-han followed, accompanied by two elves. Half a dozen more guards followed, fanning into a semicircle behind them.

This sight and the aroma of mold, dust, and bonfires brought memories of King Kohleran's reign rushing to Baltraine's mind. His conscience awakened, hammering at the many decisions he had made in the last months. During King Kohleran's three-year illness, he had named Baltraine his regent until an heir claimed the throne. Gradually, more of the tasks of rulership had fallen into Baltraine's hands. Always, he had convinced himself he worked only in Béarn's best interest even as the kingdom divided into factions and the unity, once taken for granted, crumbled around him. He had joined with the elves at Prince Xyxthris' urgings and without knowing exactly what this association entailed.

Pree-han cleared his throat, and silence replaced the noise below with unnatural suddenness. Baltraine knew from past experience that, when the Béarnides looked upon Pree-han, they saw King Kohleran's massive frame, gentle features, and mane of black hair. No matter how hard he tried to picture the same illusion, Baltraine saw only the slight, graceful elf he had trained. Red highlights sparkled from white hair hanging thinly to narrow shoulders that resembled nothing Béarnian. The massive mountain people hewed structures and statues from stone. Swarthy, hardy, and dark in hair and eyes, even relatively small Béarnides made peoples of every other land seem frail in comparison. The elves looked positively childlike.

Pree-han began with his usual opening. "Friends. Fellow Béarnides. I thank the grace of the gods for granting me a second chance at life and for the incomparable healing skills of Dh'arlo'mé." He stumbled slightly over the name, accustomed to speaking it in the lilting elfin speech and in much longer form.

Baltraine cringed, but the masses did not acknowledge the lapse. It only made sense for their king to mispronounce a name so foreign and strange, no matter how many times he had spoken it. Dh'arlo'mé, they believed, had come from the great trading city, Pudar, armed with the healing knowledge of the city as well as of his people, the *alfen*. Pree-han had convinced the populace that the lithe, cat-eyed elves were actually a tribe of southern barbarians. The populace bought it all, not from stupidity, but from trust. They loved their king enough to believe that their need for his guidance had touched the gods into restoring his health. A world devoid of magic held no basis for deception such as this.

Pree-han continued. "Since my recovery, I've come before you with news fit for sorrow and for rejoicing. So much has happened so quickly."

Baltraine glanced over the balcony. The peasants looked up raptly. The bulk of the castle spared their eyes from the morning sun, a thoughtful construction. The Knights of Erythane sat stiffly upon their white chargers, their tabards spotless and free of wrinkles, their swords all set at the same jaunty angle, their mail pristine. The Béarnian guards who kept order seemed ponderous in comparison.

"As you know," the false king said. "We lost our council to assassins." Pree-han lied with ease, but Baltraine's stomach twisted at the memory. He had called together a meeting of the council and all those who would demand a close physical association with the king. The poisoned feast, arranged by the elves had claimed them all. Only Baltraine had survived by design; nervousness about the betrayal had cause him to vomit, the perfect excuse for why he had not succumbed with the rest. Healers, pages, and nobles had fussed over him as the others died, branding guilt deeply into his conscience.

"Other concerns have filled my hours since then, pyres and consoling families among them." Pree-han added the tearful catch with impressive precision. "Being brought up to date on news and politics. Now the time has come." He lowered his head, his mastery of Kohleran's mannerisms becoming quite convincing. "There are traitors in our midst, those who slaughtered my ministers, some who killed my children, my grandchildren . . ." He lapsed into feigned sobs that held the populace spellbound with regret. No one spoke during Pree-han's lapse, waiting patiently for him to regain his composure and continue.

The two elves pretended to comfort him while the guards remained rigidly attentive. Under the guise of concern about traitors and loyalty, Pree-han had replaced the human council with *alfen*. Since that time, they had worked hard at showing this group in an excellent light, their decisions solid, impartial, and merciful.

Pree-han collected himself enough to carry on with his speech. "We cannot tolerate traitors in our midst, those who would destroy the kingdom we love to further their own ends. Any information you can give us about those who have done harm to Béarn or her succession will be rewarded. The guilty parties will receive swift, fair justice. Those who turn themselves in or are appropriately remorseful will receive lighter sentences. Please help us with this effort. . . ."

Baltraine tuned out the rest of the appeal he had written as well as the platitudes and bonding rituals that followed. Not since Morhane had usurped the throne more than three centuries ago had Béarn lived beneath the rulership of an unpopular king. Peasants and nobles alike had loved King Kohleran.

During a reign that lasted for over sixty years, he had never made a poor decision. Now, the elves counted on that glory to hold the trust of the populace while they slaughtered humans en masse. First, those who might ruin the deception had died. Next, those who had worked against Baltraine would die, execution the swift, fair justice Pree-han had promised. Baltraine felt no sorrow for these, men and women who had turned to trickery and murder to attempt to displace him. They and others, had turned against the true line of kings, as well.

As Pree-han switched from heavy business to gentle promises and a perfect copy of the wisdom King Kohleran had always displayed, the populace moved from a desperate hush to shouted admiration. Baltraine's thoughts shifted in more troublesome directions. The elves' agenda alternately worried and confounded him. Only his own input, and Xyxthris', added the human logic elves inherently lacked. Baltraine understood that the elves intended to destroy large numbers of humans. So far, he had managed to rationalize their slaughter with the realization that they had, thus far, concentrated only on those who needed to die. Now, understanding struggled for recognition. The elves' vow to allow Baltraine and his six daughters to live out their natural lives had helped quell his anxiety. When the populace turned their minds from the miracle of Kohleran's recovery to more pragmatic aspects of rulership, they would surely goad him to take a new queen and create more heirs. Baltraine doubted the elves could magically simulate human pregnancy, delivery, and infancy, even should they wish to bother. They would need his reproductive abilities, and he would be only too happy to supply them. Forever after, his line would sit upon Béarn's throne.

Baltraine smiled, his conscience again assuaged by anticipation. Below the balcony, the Béarnian masses cheered. The false king stepped back from his perch, and the prime minister prepared for the influx of traitors requiring punishment.

The damp mustiness of Béarn's dungeon had grown familiar to Knight-Captain Kedrin during the months of his imprisonment. He sat with his back against a stone corner, legs stretched in front of him and journal balanced on his thighs. His copper-blond locks tickled his cheeks, in desperate need of a trim. He brushed them away, fingernails rasping through a beard that itched for its unfamiliarity. Meticulous almost to a fault, the Knights of Erythane kept themselves evenly shorn and clean-shaven. Though he realized no one could fault his appearance in prison, he could not help feeling slovenly and uncomfortable. Months without changing had left his clothes brittle and malodorous, though still emblazoned with Béarn's tan and blue and Erythane's orange and black. A Knight of Erythane would never be caught without those four colors.

Footsteps echoed between the bars, headed toward Kedrin. Early in his captivity, he had found the deep reverberations difficult to decipher. Sound carried strangely, and movements that seemed near might originate at the prison's farther end. Now, he heard the familiar, swirling patterns that indicated someone approached his cell. Setting aside book and stylus, he rose, trying to identify the visitor by movement. The hard steadiness of the footfalls suggested a male accustomed to marching and formation. Yet a scrape of boot against stone revealed sorrow or regret. The walk did not falter, however; no nervousness or indecision here.

Kedrin had had few visitors during his incarceration. His son Ra-khir had come only once, the day after his trial. Then, Kedrin had urged his only child to find Béarn's last untested heir. Apparently, Ra-khir had left to do so. No other explanation existed for his absence.

Baltraine visited occasionally, at first contritely, then to elicit advice, and later in search of a safe confidant. The prime minister had engineered Kedrin's imprisonment, falsifying a charge of treason. True to his honor, Kedrin had not fought the allegation; to do so would have divided the kingdom at a time when it most needed unity. Kedrin had placed his trust and life in the hands of Kohleran's regent, respecting his king's decision. Baltraine had sentenced Kedrin to death; and only Ra-khir's desperate plea had softened the punishment. Not only had Kedrin's sentence been commuted to life in prison, he had kept his title and his authority over the Knights of Erythane. Once a week, a Béarnian guard named Denevier relayed the needs of the knights and delivered Kedrin's counsel back to his men.

Finally, the visitor drew near enough for Kedrin to pick a shape from the general darkness. Too small for a Béarnide, the man walked with a crisp posture that seemed more habit than intention. Only his hanging head and the shuffling step revealed his discomfort. When he at last came face-to-face with Kedrin, the knight-captain recognized one of his own. A young knight named Braison stood before him. Hazel eyes looked out from under straight, dark bangs; and Kedrin read anguish there.

Kedrin moved quickly to the bars, seizing one in each hand. "What's wrong, Sir Braison?" He kept his voice low, pitched to prevent the echoes that would open their conversation to every prisoner and guard in Béarn's dungeon.

"Braison, my lord," the other corrected, equally softly. "I am 'sir' no longer."

Kedrin froze in position, ignoring the rust digging into his palms. "You've lost your knighthood?" Pale blue eyes, almost white, sought the young man's gaze, but the hazel eyes dodged his.

"Lord, I did not lose it. I am surrendering it."

Kedrin was stunned. Never in the millennia of the Knights of Erythane had any renounced the title. He had trained Braison himself, and his mind filled with images of an eager student, brimming with life and honor. Though not naturally agile, he had given his all to his lessons, practicing even when the others had quit for the night. Rarely had Kedrin felt so unequivocal about granting a promotion. "Surrendering your knighthood? At whose recommendation?"

"No one's, my lord." Braison continued to avoid Kedrin's gaze. "It's my own decision. I'll turn my armor, sword, and tabard over to Denevier when I'm finished here."

"Look at me," Kedrin said, pain aching through his heart. He would never consider forcing knighthood on anyone, yet he could not let Braison leave without understanding.

Finally, the usually placid eyes met his, looking far older than the twenty-year-old face that housed them. Something had scarred him deeply.

"You need no reason," Kedrin admitted. "Yet it would help me if you gave one."

Braison turned the need back on Kedrin. "And it would help me to know if my Captain truly committed an act of treason." The eyes not only met Kedrin's now, they pinned him. "Yet you sidestep the question with vagaries about truth and the king's judgment being all that matters." His jaw set, as if he struggled to speak the words, but his gaze did not falter. "Captain, whatever you tell or don't tell the populace, I have to know your guilt or innocence. Not the decree of prime minister or king: the truth."

Kedrin sighed, stately bearing and handsome features strikingly out of place amid the dungeon's dank filth. Braison spoke forthrightly, and Kedrin had little choice but to do the same. "I did and would do nothing to jeopardize Béarn's king or kingdom. I would willingly die in withering agony rather than betray Béarn. In *any* fashion."

"Generalities," Braison shot back.

"Yes," Kedrin admitted, "but with a little consideration, you will draw the right conclusions." He loosened his hold on the bars. As Baltraine knew, Kedrin's journal contained an explanation of the incident and justification for the silence in court he had chosen. Written mostly for Ra-khir, it also contained a treatise on honor, including ethical traps and clarification for why he had allowed Ra-khir's mother to deliberately destroy the bond between father and son. Their marriage had failed early in Ra-khir's youth, and she had used her hatred and bitterness as a weapon against Kedrin. He had suffered her cruelty in silence rather than fight and inflict more harm on his son. "You're a smart lad, Braison. I believe you can recognize a moral dilemma and the path a knight must follow to stay true to his honor and kingdom."

Braison's face lapsed into pained creases as Kedrin, apparently, struck to the heart of the problem. "Smart, maybe. But I can't reconcile the tasks I perform for my kingdom with my honor." He wiped a clean, dry palm on pristine breeks, as if desperate to rid himself of a remembered stain. "That's why I'm resigning my position."

Kedrin knew of no terrible task assigned his knights. In fact, since the king's spectacular recovery from coma, he had been led to believe life had returned to normal for all Béarn's citizens. Except, of course, himself. "I don't understand."

Tears blurred Braison's eyes to muddy pools. He dabbed at them surreptitiously. Then, as the droplets coursed down his cheeks, impossible to hide, he sobbed unabashedly.

Kedrin's heart felt leaden. He wanted nothing more than to hold the young knight like a father, yet the bars would not allow it. He said nothing, allowing Braison to speak in his own time.

For several moments only tears emerged. Then Braison gathered his scattered composure. "I do not believe the Knights of Erythane were ever intended to become executioners."

Kedrin said nothing, the words explaining little. Although not specifically hired for such a purpose, he saw no reason why knights could not carry out such a sentence if the king requested it. "Did you have to kill someone?"

"Seven men, Captain." Braison sobbed. "Three women." He shook his head, eyes restless again. "I'm not afraid of death or killing. In a war, I would slay our enemies and take pride in bringing Béarn or Erythane one step closer to safety. But these . . ." His mouth splayed open, as if he would continue, but only hoarse gasps emerged. "I'm sorry," he managed, "for my demeanor."

Kedrin dismissed the apology as unnecessary. "I knew nothing of this. What crime did they commit?"

"Treason." Braison did not question their guilt. To do so would place the king's judgment in doubt and go against the honor ingrained in him nearly since birth.

"Ten at once?"

"I handled ten. The others handled their share."

At most, twenty-six Knights of Erythane existed at any time. They rotated twelve through Béarn while twelve stayed home in Béarn's sister city, Erythane. Two remained as alternates. They had lost six to attacks against envoys sent to fetch Griff. At the time, only one alternate existed. Three apprentice knights had recently completed training, filling some of the gaps. Ra-khir, Kedrin lamented, would certainly have been among them had he not interrupted his training to hunt for Griff, unofficially, with his friends. *A suicide mission.* Guilt squeezed and hammered Kedrin. *I sent my only son out to die.* Tears rose, unbidden. Kedrin held them at bay, forcing his thoughts back to the matter at hand. Ten knights currently held positions in Béarn. The math was simple. "A hundred traitors at once?"

Braison nodded.

"Gods," Kedrin whispered, chest tight.

"Sir," Braison started, then stopped. "Sir, I can't reconcile my loyalty to king and kingdom with my personal honor. When those two became separated, I no longer deserve the privilege of knighthood. I have no choice but to renounce my vows."

Kedrin wished he had some precedent on which to base his response. No words came, and his thoughts floundered. He had little choice but to agree with Braison's assessment; yet, clearly, the Knights and the kingdom needed men like Braison most of all.

Before Kedrin could speak, booted footfalls pounded toward him, steady and authoritative. The time for speeches and encouragements had ended; the slowness of his reaction had betrayed him.

Shortly, a stocky Béarnide dressed in mail and Béarnian standard drew up beside Braison. He glowered down at the smaller knight, his bravado ruined by hands that clenched and loosed repeatedly, betraying nervousness. The guards had always respected the Knights' elite position. "Sir, you'll need to come with me. Your clearance to visit was inappropriately granted." He glanced at Kedrin, explaining apologetically as he never would to a lesser prisoner. "Captain, he claimed kinship."

Kedrin glanced at Braison, for the moment more shocked by the ex-knight's lie than by the realization that men directly beneath his command needed unrelated reasons to receive permission to see him.

Braison's hazel eyes met Kedrin's white-blue, no shame there. "It's a true kinship, just distant."

Kedrin nodded, sorry he had doubted Braison's word even for that one moment.

"Come with me, please, sir." The guard became insistent. He anticipated trouble, and the idea of battling a Knight of Erythane clearly unnerved him.

But Braison followed willingly, as Kedrin knew he must. Even as the young man took his first steps, he called back softly to the man once his captain, "I believe those people innocent. And you, too." He disappeared into the darkness, his footsteps swallowed by the louder thump and rattle of the guard.

Kedrin slumped to the floor, Braison's last proclamation like an arrow in his heart. Knight's honor would not allow him to doubt the king's decision, and his personal respect for King Kohleran only doubled his certainty. Reconciling Braison's descriptions to the world Denevier and Baltraine had presented over recent months seemed impossible. *Baltraine betrayed me?* The realization was its own answer, undeniably true in at least one sense. The prime minister/regent had deliberately entrapped him with a crime they both knew he never committed. The memory returned in vivid detail. Baltraine had arranged for Kedrin to meet him in a hallway, then started an argument. Kedrin's knife, awarded to him with his captain's title, had disappeared days earlier. Baltraine returned it to Kedrin at that time. Then, as Kedrin clasped his knife to sheathe it, Baltraine revealed its presence to his guards and claimed Kedrin had drawn it to harm him.

Yet Baltraine had changed in the months since the incident. He had seemed genuinely sorry, confiding his fears and stresses and requesting advice from the knight-captain turned prisoner. Months earlier, he had even granted Kedrin his freedom, a privilege the knight-captain had reluctantly declined. He had done so for the good of the kingdom, to maintain the citizenry's trust in the king's judgments and choice of regent. King Kohleran had rendered the verdict against Kedrin. Therefore, in Kedrin's mind, he was guilty.

The foundation of Kedrin's understanding collapsed beneath Braison's revelations. The King Kohleran whom Kedrin knew would never have used Knights of Erythane as executioners nor slaughtered a hundred of his people at once. The support the knight-captain had insisted his knights sustain for Kohleran's regent might be based on lies and misconceptions. Here, Kedrin did find precedent where he had not been before. Some three and a quarter centuries ago, before the staff-test assured the king's naiveté and neutrality, Morhane the Betrayer had usurped the throne from his brother Valar and murdered all but one of Valar's line. The bard and the Knights of Erythane had supported Morhane, as their loyalty and honor decreed. Yet when Valar's youngest son, Sterrane, returned to claim the crown rightfully his, the knights and bard had assisted the proper king and turned against the uncle they had once protected.

Kedrin sighed, the coldness of the stone floor seeping through his clothing. He could draw few comparisons between that situation and his own. The king's recovery, a miracle, compounded the situation. If Baltraine still ruled Béarn, Kedrin might have considered turning Béarn's most loyal against him. The king's return, however, placed Béarn back into proper hands, those of a benevolent king supported by the gods and their test. It made no sense that Béarn should further succumb to chaos now, at a time when peace and propriety had returned.

Knight-Captain Kedrin mulled the problem over for hours, thoughts shattering always into paradox. Once he sorted the myriad ideas barraging him at once, he believed he would find the answer to a colossal ethical dilemma, the solution to which might confound scholars and knights for centuries. Yet the answers would not come.

Men of honor cannot draw conclusions when they are missing the facts. The thought trickled into Kedrin's head, wholly foreign.

Kedrin straightened abruptly, only then realizing how near his considerations had dragged him toward sleep. "What?" he said, before he could stop himself. Surely the words had originated in his own mind, from the boundary between awareness and dream.

You're missing the knowledge you need for enlightenment. No doubt about it this time, the source was alien.

Kedrin rose, then knelt. *Are you a god?*

No reply.

Kedrin cleared his throat, preparing to speak the question aloud. Before he could, the contact wafted to him again. *I am the voice of Béarn's castle. I give the sage his knowledge and have done so for his predecessors through the ages.*

The castle speaks to the sage? Kedrin had never heard such a thing, though it made sense. The sage of Béarn never left his tower, yet he'd managed to gather and hoard all the kingdom's knowledge. Even the king found access difficult. The sage's servants rotated through court and attended the decrees of nobles and king; others brought the sage information as well. If the walls spoke to him, the servants seemed unnecessary.

Kedrin had not intended to communicate his thoughts, but the voice apparently read them. *There is logic to chronicling perception and fiction as well as fact. Truth and honor cannot always be coordinated. Properly credited, lies serve a purpose, though rarely one the liar intends.*

No longer believing he conversed with a god, Kedrin returned to a sitting position. *And you give the sage?*

Truth. Only truth. For good or ill.

Do you speak to others besides the sage?

Until today, no. I am speaking with you.

Why me?

You are a man of honor, and you need enlightenment.

Not for the first time.

Nor the last, the voice concurred.

So why now? Kedrin asked.

My power is growing. Until now, I had little understanding of what I was or my purpose. I saw a need to supply truth to he who records Béarn's history, and I did so.

And now?

I'm still not sure, the voice admitted. *But I know I represent truth. And honor. As do you. Do you trust me?*

Kedrin considered, finding answer in his heart and in his mind. *Yes. I believe I do.*

Then listen closely. What I have to tell you may stretch your faith to its limit or beyond.

Kedrin refused to lie. *Then I will surely need time to think about what you tell me, to draw my own conclusions, and to question my confidence in you.*

A fair concession, the voice agreed. *At least, for now.*

Kedrin returned to a corner of his cell, resting his back

against the wall. He ran a hand through his hair, shuffling the too-long, red-blond strands back into proper position. Stunningly handsome features became lost to the gloom of his cell.

King Kohleran is dead. . . .

CHAPTER 3

Mountain Trails

All forces must have opposition to exist.
                                    —*Colbey Calistinsson*

Though of little help in the battle against the demon, Captain's magic proved invaluable to the four humans and one cat aboard the crudely-lashed raft. Their makeshift sailboat landed swiftly, aided by Captain's command of wave and wind. Familiar mountains filled the horizon, and trees stunted and twisted by rocky soil struggled to form a sparse, scraggly forest. Matrinka gazed upon the scenery while Rantire sprang first from the raft, scouting the surrounding area for evidence of danger. Apparently satisfied, she assisted Griff, leaving the others to debark at their own risk.

Single-minded, isn't she? Mior sent, while Darris and Captain steadied the raft for Matrinka's descent.

Matrinka explained away Rantire's behavior with a single word. **Renshai.** A trickle of joy managed to slip through her sorrow. She recognized the pattern of mountains. "We're only a day or two from Béarn."

Rantire shook back shaggy bronze hair. "Fields of Wrath are straight north." She named the Renshai settlement. "Two days east of Béarn. Three to four days if we go through the Fields and take the Road of Kings."

The longer route Rantire described held its advantages. At the Fields of Wrath, they could gather Renshai allies. Matrinka saw merit, too, in arriving via the legendary route by which King Sterrane was spirited from Béarn during his uncle's purge and by which he returned to claim his throne. It never hurt to invoke ancient faith and custom. Yet Matrinka's exhaustion and concern for her injured friends would not allow her to add even a moment to their journey. Colbey's interest in their mission suggested that the three-month safe gap between the king's death and the heir's staff-test might be drawing to a close. Need took precedence over a grand entrance. "I think we should get to Béarn as quickly as possible."

Nods bobbed through the party. No one relished a four-day journey on foot after all they had survived.

Grief assailed Matrinka again, this time at the thought of the grandfather she loved so dearly. She had visited King Kohleran regularly as illness coarsened and whitened his black mane, as his flesh withered, and as his skin turned a sallow yellow. Still, when she thought of him, she pictured the robust, gentle bear of a man who had bounced her on his knee and told her heroic tales of the great kings and queens who preceded him. Her mind mourned the loss of three friends: Ra-khir, Tae, and Kevral. Without a sail-raft or Captain to control its course, it seemed unlikely any of them could survive the ocean. Even if they did, making landfall before dehydration drove them to seawater poisoning seemed desperately hopeless. Her heart, however, refused to acknowledge their deaths. Until she saw their bodies, they still lived.

"There's a stream this way," Captain announced, pointing. He had drawn the raft to shore and tended it, surely from habit rather than any intention to reuse it.

Darris turned the elf a startled glance. "How could you possibly know that?"

"I hear it." Captain tapped his right ear with a long finger. He addressed the unspoken question next. "No, I've never been here before."

"Let's go." Rantire focused on fact rather than method. No curse bound her to wonder over Captain's knowledge.

They all scrambled in the indicated direction, stumbling over craggy ground. The need to watch each step hampered what would otherwise become a mad dash to water. At length, the high-pitched babbling of a stream reached Matrinka's hearing as well. Picking her way around a wall of stone that Rantire had already vaulted, she discovered a mountain stream twining through the rocks. Matrinka ran to it and knelt, dipping her hands and sucking down palmfuls of water. Its coldness seeped down her throat, aching; yet the pain seemed a small price to pay to slake a day and night of thirst. Finally, they all finished, water that had seemed too precious to waste now dribbling through their fingers or deliberately splashed onto salt-rimed faces. Then, casting about through pebbly terrain nearly devoid of vegetation, they discovered a trail heading in the right direction.

A quaver in Matrinka's chest revealed an excitement that embarrassed her. It seemed evil to cast aside total absorption with friends recently lost, yet the joy of returning home would not be wholly denied. Her first journey outside of Béarn had proved more formidable than she ever anticipated. She had watched friends slaughter bandits and assassins. She had nursed loved ones back from the brink of death. She had stepped between bickering allies even as their taunts nearly turned to blows, and she had suffered the burden of choosing sides in disputes without winners.

Immersed in her thoughts, Matrinka scarcely noticed the narrow path skirting the mountains. Rantire took the lead, Griff following a few paces behind her. Darris and Matrinka came next, accustomed to enjoying each other's company in silence. Darris' need to break into song for explanations kept him quiet, and his bard's-curse inquisitiveness turned his attention on every twig, leaf, and shift in the breeze. His songs revealed the intensity of his concentration. With a few flicks of his fingers over an instrument or wavers in the pitch of his voice, he could simulate nature with peerless competence. More often than not, his choices evoked images as strong as reality without exactly duplicating the sound. A word or two created an image. Matrinka's hush stemmed more from adolescent awkwardness, though the two had learned to appreciate their quiet moments together, communicating more with silence than most could with words. Mior rode on Matrinka's shoulders.

Captain chose the back of the party for reasons he did not share with the others, though Matrinka believed she understood. Tears glazed eyes that already seemed more stone than flesh. They sparkled in the sunlight, convex stretches of yellow without shading or line. Captain had much reason for regret. He had become outcast, hunted by his people who formerly knew nothing of dissent. More than once she heard him whisper a phrase to himself that Rantire had hurled at him in outrage: "There may well come a time, Captain, when you need to choose between what's right for your people and your loyalty to them. When that time comes, the world may rest on your decision." That time had come and gone, and Captain had chosen. He had helped the party to free Griff and, while that decision seemed simple and obvious to Matrinka, it had clearly injured the old elf.

As the party snaked through a narrow, high-walled basin toward a slitlike opening leading into another valley, Rantire stopped abruptly, shoving Griff against a cliff face. "Were we expecting others?" she whispered.

Matrinka froze, dread crawling through her. She knew of no town in this area, and travelers always chose the trade routes farther north. It seemed unlikely they would find anyone else stumbling through the mountains.

Darris stepped in front of Matrinka, instinctively shielding her. "Others?" he repeated, cautiously moving toward Rantire. She stepped aside to allow him a glimpse through the opening. Darris craned his neck around her, then stiffened.

Matrinka held her breath.

"Easterners," Darris explained, the word stabbing coldly through Matrinka. Their journey through the eastern part of the Westlands had been fraught with attacks by Easterners determined to prevent all travel. She shifted forward hesitantly. On tiptoe, she could almost see over Darris' head, and a jump granted her a brief panorama. At least a dozen men lined the pathway, dark-haired and swarthy like Béarnides and Easterners. Their smaller size fit the latter. They faced the opposite direction, understandably expecting any threat to come from the city—not an isolated stretch of mountains.

"Enemies?" Rantire asked.

"Probably," Darris returned. "I believe someone . . ."

Rantire needed nothing more than the confirmation. "Guard Griff." Her sword sprang from its sheath, and she charged the Easterners with an ear-shattering war cry.

Matrinka retreated, fear slamming her heart into a wild rhythm. Darris' hand clapped to his own hilt, but he did not draw or attack. Instead, he herded Griff and Matrinka behind him, blocking pass and charges with his body. Once, Renshai had ridiculed him as a coward for this strategy. Now, the differences once again became apparent. Renshai honor would not allow Rantire even to take advantage of surprise. Her battle howls sent every Easterner spinning to meet her. Nevertheless, two fell dead before their swords cleared their sheaths. The others raged toward her.

Matrinka shielded her eyes from the clash that followed, the chime of steel painful in her ears. Soon, the cadence of sword pounding sword turned from curse to need. As long as that sound persisted, Rantire lived.

"Captain, can you do anything?" Darris asked over the sounds of the battle. Though just in front of Matrinka, his voice seemed weak and distant beneath the din of battle.

"Nothing magic that will help much," Captain responded. "I can lead us back to the raft."

Matrinka opened her eyes. Darris shook his head vigorously. "No good." His jaw set. "I'm going to have to go in and help."

"No." Matrinka seized his arm, hoping she had not stopped him purely for selfish reasons. "There're too many. What good is it if both of you die and leave us defenseless?"

Darris glanced from Matrinka to Griff to Captain. Of the three, only the elf might know anything about warfare. He looked back at Rantire.

Matrinka could not help following his gaze. The Renshai slashed and parried, sword a silver blur, never in one place for longer than an instant. Bodies littered the ground nearby, yet the tide of Easterners seemed endless. Suddenly, Rantire gasped in pain. The call that followed galvanized Darris. "Modi!" Matrinka winced. Renshai saved that shout for emergency, when second wind became necessary. Either someone had broken through her defenses or exhaustion threatened to defeat her.

Darris broke free before Matrinka could stop him. He galloped toward the battle, his sword freed only an instant before Easterners closed around him.

"Darris, no!" Matrinka had raced halfway to him before logic intervened. Without weapon or training, she had no hope of survival.

Matrinka, stop! What are you doing? Panic came clearly through Mior's contact. The cat sprang from her mistress' shoulders and bounced several paces back the way they had come.

"MODI!" Rantire shouted again, with frenzied joy. Death in glorious combat meant more to Renshai than winning. She disappeared beneath a press of Easterners, several of whom collapsed beneath blows Matrinka could no longer see.

Beyond rationality, Matrinka gave Mior no answer. The concept of danger seemed remote and dilute, keeping her from rushing to Darris' side yet not strong enough to send her back. Restless, yet unable to move in either direction, she pranced a frantic circle.

STOP! The mental call slammed Matrinka's consciousness. It was not Mior.

STOP! The command came again, surely originating from Captain. Only elves could communicate in this fashion.

To Matrinka's astonishment, the Easterners obeyed. The crowd surrounding Rantire stilled, some heads flicking about, apparently seeking the source of the *khohlar*. Darris' opponents froze, swords locked with his. The bard kept his eyes on the Easterners, but he did not violate the momentary truce. Matrinka looked back. Mior sat between her and the crags that had once shielded them from the enemies' view. The orange-and-black-striped tail lashed furiously. At the opening stood Griff and Captain. Matrinka read concern in every line of Griff's face, and Captain's usually stalwart features clearly showed surprise.

The elf pressed his unexpected success. *Lay down your arms.*

The Easterners continued to glance around warily. Some fixed their attention on Captain. Others looked toward one of their own, apparently the leader, who nodded. Those on the fringes of the battle sheathed their weapons. Matrinka believed the count nearer to thirty now, of whom at least eight lay, motionless or moaning, on the ground. She still could not see Rantire.

Darris disengaged in a slow, nonthreatening manner. Eyes fixed on his opponents, he slid his blade into its sheath. Apparently reassured by this action, those fighting him did the same. The leader said something Matrinka could not hear. Easterners began to back away from Rantire, restoring their weapons as they did so. Finally, the last few stepped aside to reveal the Renshai lying quietly on the rocky ground. Swords and knives found casings. Hammers, axes, and clubs slid into proper position on hips and packs. The Easterners' leader approached.

Matrinka froze, her eyes on Rantire. As the leader drifted toward her, the urge seized her to run to the Renshai's side. Darris turned her a warning glance that begged her to remain in place. Mior verbalized the concern. *Too much tension. The wrong motion or word might see us all dead.*

She needs me, Matrinka had to return.

A moment is unlikely to make a difference.

Sorrow engulfed Matrinka, but the tears would not come. She had cried herself out over companions lost to the Southern Sea. *A moment could make the difference between life and death.*

It could, the cat conceded. *But it probably won't.*

"I'm sorry, Lord." The leader's heavily accented trading tongue came from so close Matrinka started. Worry for Rantire had caused her to forget the man's presence. "We didn't know *you* traveled with these." He indicated Matrinka, Darris, and Rantire with a broad wave.

Captain's amber eyes glittered in the sunlight, and his expression scarcely revealed emotion. Matrinka thought she read anger there. "Well, I do. And I'll thank you not to attack my companions." No one acknowledged the irony. Rantire, not the Easterners, had initiated the battle. Captain made a grand gesture. "Matrinka, tend her."

Matrinka did not hesitate for an instant but scuttled to Rantire's side, Easterners parting in front of her. Not a corner of Matrinka's mind turned to the danger they represented; they could have been trees for all the heed she paid them. When Matrinka took her turn at the staff-test, and it found her unworthy for queenship, she had pledged to discover another way to serve her family's kingdom. Swordplay had proved a foreign concept she seemed incapable of learning. All her knowledge of vital organs and their functions disappeared in the irrational chaos of battle. Herbs and healing came more naturally. Now, a protector of Béarn's heirs needed her aid. Nothing else mattered.

Blood splattered and pooled around Rantire. The closed eyes revealed nothing. Matrinka saw none of the natural deep rise and fall that would indicate breathing, although she did believe she saw a fluttering. *Handle active bleeding first.* Training surfaced mechanically. Her vision blurred, making the search difficult. If she did not staunch the bleeding, no other ministration mattered. Breaths and heartbeats accomplished nothing for empty veins.

Matrinka worked with swift efficiency, focusing on her craft to keep emotion at bay. To think of Rantire as the alert, healthy person she had been moments before might cripple Matrinka with grief. Using bandages and fingers to apply pressure to holes in Rantire's calf and side and a slash across the abdomen, Matrinka stemmed the flow to a trickle. The warmth of fluid and flesh was encouraging. Ignoring bruises, scars, and the swelling lump on Rantire's scalp, Matrinka turned her attention to breathing and pulse. Though unconscious and in pain, Rantire lived. It might strain Matrinka's skills to their limit to maintain that spark, especially when she no longer carried herbs or healing devices.

Rantire awakened when Matrinka had scarcely half finished. Gray eyes whisked open, and she grabbed for her sword faster than Matrinka would have believed possible. Startled, Matrinka darted back with a scream. The blade carved the air in front of her, then Rantire took a defensive stance.

Shock fizzled into anger. "Stupid woman! You'll reopen everything!"

"And kill your healer," Darris added, rushing to Matrinka's aid. "Lie still."

A shiver racked Rantire as she fought the pain reignited by her sudden movement. Matrinka suffered a flash of joy at the poetic justice and immediately felt guilty for it. She watched as Rantire scanned the pass where Captain talked with the Eastern leader and Griff stood beside the elf. Ignoring her need for continued ministration, Rantire limped to Griff's side.

"You're welcome," Darris muttered dourly.

Oddly, his irritation spared Matrinka any of her own. "She's Renshai," Matrinka explained away the rudeness. Kevral had served as her personal bodyguard long enough to assure Matrinka that Rantire would worry for her charge above all else. For Renshai, the preciousness of life came of spending it on a cause.

Darris grunted something unintelligible, took Matrinka's arm, and led her back toward their other companions. He worried, as she did not, that the Easterners' peace might end as swiftly as it had begun.

Captain's manner had become uncharacteristically commanding and inflexible. He pointed toward Béarn. ". . . and you will announce my presence before we are forced to deal with others of your men. There will be no more attacks. No more mistakes like this one."

"Yes, Lord." The leader bowed. "Sorry, Lord." He bowed again, then trotted off to relay the orders.

Matrinka inspected her handiwork as she and Darris drew up to the others. The bandages held, though dark blood had soaked through the one on Rantire's leg. "What's going on?" she whispered.

Griff shrugged. Darris had, apparently, heard enough to speculate. He cleared his throat and sang a cappella, scarcely above a whisper:

> *"The elves devised, would be my guess*
> *An end to travel, east or west.*
> *Easterners paid to prevent ourselves*
> *And let through no one but the elves."*

Matrinka nodded, horrified, though she had known of the Easterners' ambushes long ago. Then, she had believed they followed an agenda of their own. Now, the implications appeared much more far-reaching. "Why would the elves do such a thing?"

Rantire saved Darris the need for lengthy song. "They want to destroy all humans." She added, pain making her curt. "Remember?"

Matrinka gestured to indicate she sought the answer to a different interpretation of her question. "Why would any humans assist such a thing? And why attack people on the roads. Why not whole villages?"

"One and the same answer." Rantire kept her gaze on the Easterners while she talked. "Some people will do anything for money, and the elves probably lied about their purpose anyway. But not *everyone* will do anything for money so, at least I hope, the elves haven't bought enough people to attack whole villages."

"But they're magic," Matrinka said. "It wouldn't take that many humans with magic behind them."

Captain sighed deeply. "Let's hope they don't figure that out for a long time." He changed the subject abruptly. "Let's go before Dh'arlo'mé gets word to these men that I'm outcast."

The group mobilized swiftly, heading toward Béarn. Matrinka watched Rantire hobble, skin pale even for a Renshai and movements uncharacteristically awkward. They could not survive another attack.

Dh'arlo'mé awakened with a snort, startled to full awareness by no sight or sound he could discern. He raised his head from the Northern Sorceress' book and slid his arm carefully from the pages. Soreness stiffened his hips, left thigh, and buttocks where the hard, wooden chair had stamped impressions into flesh. His private room on the sixth floor of the elves' common house had filled with night's gloom, and only dollops of wax remained from his candle. Moonlight beamed through the window, splattered to a diffuse purple glow by the thickness of the glass.

Damn. The human expletive came naturally where the elfin language failed Dh'arlo'mé. He freed strands of red-blond hair plastered to his cheeks. The need for sleep had become a nearly intolerable curse that he could not wholly blame on mankind. Centuries ago, he had willingly become the Northern Sorceress' apprentice, and the demand for sleep had accompanied a level of worry and responsibility beyond what any elf before him had confronted. Now it had wrested away the burdens three days of desperate study had ceased to dispel. Nowhere in the Northern Sorceress' texts had he found further answer to ridding the elves of a demon bent on their destruction. Their only hope lay with the banishment spell that had already failed once.

Elves waited for the demon in double shifts, those most skilled at magic teamed with strong chanters. One group lashed ceaseless storms upon the waters in an effort to stop or, at least, delay the demon. The others prepared for battle. While his followers ground the banishment spell into rote, Dh'arlo'mé desperately sought the answers that eluded him. Yet the sleep he despised brought others he had not thought to seek. Having centered his study on demons and the chaos they embodied, he had learned much about both. Everything he read assured him that the demon would operate without strategy. Bound to the service Baheth'rin had detailed, it would home in on the *Sea Seraph* without need to hunt. It would attack until it either completed its mission or was destroyed in the process. Then, freed, it would devastate the elves without delay. Afterward, it might go on to annihilate the world; only magic could return it to the plain to which Odin had banished the primordial chaos.

Therefore, no logic could explain the time that had passed in peace for the elves. No human could survive three days and nights in battle. Only two possibilities existed; either Dh'arlo'mé had managed to dispel the demon with his final, crucial, spell, or the humans had killed the creature. The last thought sent a shiver through Dh'arlo'mé. If a handful of humans could slaughter such a creature, the elves could not hope to stand against all of mankind. He had sorely underestimated the enemy. And he needed a new strategy.

Dh'arlo'mé rose and walked to the window, his light step a mockery of the turmoil grinding within him. He glanced outside, more from habit than purpose. The darkness and warped glass combined to show him nothing, yet he stared outward, his mind too full to process vision anyway. Even had a map of the world stretched in panorama before him, he would have had to shift his concentration to notice it. Wild for a solution, he had discarded all readings not pertinent to the matter at hand. Sleep, however, had allowed his thoughts to wander. Now he found other details springing to the fore, ones desperation had forced him to ignore.

Toward the end of the Sorceress' narrative, one theme repeatedly reappeared. The word "chaos" always referred to the Staff of Chaos she believed Colbey Calistinsson, who was then the Western Wizard, had wielded. In hindsight, Dh'arlo'mé could see the insidious changes the Staff of Chaos had wrought upon the Eastern Wizard, Shadimar. The Northern Sorceress' books revealed a story only Dh'arlo'mé and the gods could properly conclude. The only other witnesses, Wizards and mortals, were long dead. Shadimar had believed he championed the Staff of Law, fooled by Colbey Calistinsson and the lies of the staff. After winning both staves from Odin, Colbey had voluntarily handed one to his wizardly opposite along with the warning that he had given the Cardinal Wizards the one thing that could stop him from loosing chaos on man's world. The Wizards had believed he'd turned over the Staff of Law, their vanity never entertaining the possibility that the only way they could stop him from releasing chaos was to wield it themselves.

If the Staff of Chaos could destroy the wisest and most capable, what effect would it have on humans already willing to betray, enslave, and slaughter for wealth or power? The possibilities seemed endless. The freedom that sleep had accorded Dh'arlo'mé's mind brought a connection he had not previously made. Prince Xyxthris had mentioned the staff-test for Béarnian rulers on more than one occasion. Dh'arlo'mé recalled Baltraine's description: two identical, unadorned staves given to mankind so that they could judge the worth and neutrality of future kings. *Could these be the Staves of Law and Chaos?* Dh'arlo'mé's heart pounded. He touched his hands to the glass, allowing the cold to seep into his palms. Someone, most likely Odin, had found a means to bring the staves together. Yet everything Dh'arlo'mé read revealed the deadly animosity between those powers. If he separated those staves, could he reawaken their supernatural power and desperate struggle to oppose one another? In the right hands, Dh'arlo'mé felt certain, the Staff of Chaos could destroy mankind from within, without need of elfin interference or risk. Analyzing the staves, he believed, would bring those answers.

Dh'arlo'mé whirled suddenly and dashed to the exit. His door whipped open onto a common room filled with elves. Some huddled in groups, discussing the situation in hushed tones so as not to awaken the many sleeping around them. Others sat alone in thought, and some huddled in miserable silence. Most looked up as Dh'arlo'mé approached, and some called *khohlar* or spoken greetings. He ignored them all, too fascinated with strategy to bother with amenities. Down the stairs he charged, through the door, and into the night.

Slender trees with serrated leaves swayed and rattled in the breeze. The elfin compound held few buildings, their shadows ugly against the natural beauty of the island they called Nualfheim. In the millennia they had lived without danger or weather, they had had no use for dwellings of any kind. They had copied man's constructions here, trusting humans to have developed those most appropriate for a world that, until then, had belonged exclusively to them. Little of human nature made sense to Dh'arlo'mé: their desire to shut themselves into boxes as often as possible; their fascination with shiny metals and colored stones; their individuality, and their desire for personal power and gain. It seemed strange that a race which spent so much time indoors would consider imprisonment a punishment. Working with humans over time had given Dh'arlo'mé rare insight into a system that had once seemed without point or purpose. Still, he relied on his human informants to handle much he could not understand.

Dh'arlo'mé avoided the beach where his followers gathered, some casting and others staring out over the turbulent sea in search of the returning demon. They would continue to guard in shifts, and he saw no reason to call them away. If he had misjudged, and the demon did return, his presence or absence would make no difference. If it had been killed, as he believed it must have, then it did no harm to ward Nualfheim with storms and elves guarding seaward. He had to assume Captain, and at least some of the humans, had reached the shore safely. If so, war might ensue.

The familiar woodlands rolled swiftly past, a welcome change from the suffocating interior of a building, though the broad trees and viny foliage little resembled Alfheim. At length he came to the magical gate. The first time elves had created this route into Béarn's castle, they had cast spells into the courtyard, animating bear statues that killed several of the king's youngest heirs. Once crafted, the gate remained permanently in place, a connection between Béarn and Nualfheim through which only Prince Xyxthris and a few elves had passed. To further protect against the possibility of accidental trespass, Baltraine had turned the fourth-floor study room onto which the gate opened into a bedroom for Dh'arlo'mé. No one, not even cleaning staff, had permission to enter.

Sensing the gate's location as a prickle like crawling insects against his skin, Dh'arlo'mé closed his eyes and passed through it. White light slammed his lids, visible even through the membranes. A moment later, he opened his eyes, to find himself standing in a corner of his room in Béarn's keep. Everything remained as he had left it. The bed was made, not from any penchant for neatness but because Dh'arlo'mé slept on the floor from habit. Aside from desks and chairs, elves had found little purpose to human furniture. Here, however, his room held matching pieces—a desk, two chairs, and a wardrobe crafted from cedar and patterned with sweeping bulges and spirals. The woven carpet felt stiff and unyielding beneath feet accustomed to thick, spongy grasses, yet it still seemed far superior to bare floor. Dh'arlo'mé paused only long enough to glance at his reflection in the full-length mirror that occupied the space between wardrobe and desk before whisking toward the door.

The image stopped him with a hand on the knob. Bare feet and rumpled clothing of scanty, elfin cut would ill fit the dignified image he had, thus far, given Béarn's help. Thin, disheveled hair did nothing to hide the high-swept cheekbones and canted, uniform eyes that set him apart from humanity. The Béarnides had already grown accustomed to his strange appearance, attributing it to the barbarian *alfen* blood he claimed; but Dh'arlo'mé saw no reason to raise doubts. The more he downplayed his differences, the longer the citizenry would trust him.

Reluctantly, Dh'arlo'mé exchanged his elfin costume for a tunic, robe, and sandals, wondering what shame caused humans to hide their bodies so completely. He combed his hair into the bangs that minimized his elfin features, though it went against all vanity and inbred custom. Only then did he open the door and step out into the hallway. The curtains over the room's single window fluttered in the draft. Near his door lay dishes smeared with a brownish sauce and speckled with stems, bits of roots, and chewed gristle, as arranged. It would not do for the Béarnides to learn that their king's healer regularly disappeared to another part of the world. A society wholly without magic for over three hundred years, and limited to four Wizards of dubious existence for millennia prior, could not accept such a thing. So the illusion of Dh'arlo'mé as a reclusive studier had been created and nurtured. Servants brought food to his door daily, and Baltraine saw to it that it appeared Dh'arlo'mé ate some of it.

Dh'arlo'mé closed the door and waited. Despite the hour, a

young page soon happened down the hallway, straight sandy hair combed simply, tabard flapping the Béarnian bear tan against a blue background. Catching sight of Dh'arlo'mé, the boy stopped short and bowed. "Good evening—" He corrected himself. "I mean, morning, Lord. Good *morning*. Yes, morning."

"Good morning," Dh'arlo'mé returned gently, trying not to intimidate the youth. The servants became notably nervous around him, more so than he could explain simply by the tendency of humans to broadcast their feelings with relatively exaggerated gestures and expressions. "Could you please call the prime minister to my quarters?"

"Now, Lord?" The page fidgeted. The hall sconces lit flitting highlights in the folds of his linens.

"Please," Dh'arlo'mé confirmed.

"He'll be . . ." the page started. "I–I mean, you don't . . ." He paused to gather his thoughts, growing obviously more uncomfortable. "Lord, do you wish me to awaken him?"

Dh'arlo'mé's elfin patience tolerated the stammering. Compared to She of Slow Emotions, the most sluggish human acted at a gallop. "If necessary, yes."

"Thank you," the page said unnecessarily. He darted down the hallway.

Dh'arlo'mé did not bother to watch him go. Opening his door, he went inside to await Baltraine.

CHAPTER 4

Damnation

*What good is a man whose worth derives from the courage
or competence of his ancestors?*

—Colbey Calistinsson

Prime Minister Baltraine raced through the corridors of Béarn Castle, as fast as dignity allowed. Dh'arlo'mé rarely called for him in the middle of the night, and he had little choice but to assume the situation was dire. The familiar paintings, tapestries, and animal-shaped torch brackets flew past, unappreciated. The light blurred into confluent streaks on either side of Baltraine's peripheral vision, creating the illusion of a never-ending tunnel. The need to descend stairs broke the sensation at intervals, which Baltraine appreciated. At length, he came to Dh'arlo'mé's door and knocked in triplicate.

When there was no response, Baltraine contained his impatience, accustomed to the maddening unhurriedness that characterized everything elfin. Finally the door swung open, and Dh'arlo'mé gestured to Baltraine to enter.

Baltraine obliged, and Dh'arlo'mé closed the door behind him. Patting the nearest chair, the elf sat on the edge of the bed. Baltraine took a seat in the indicated spot. "What can I do for you, Dh'arlo'mé?" His harsh, human tones mangled the musical elfin name.

Uncharacteristically, Dh'arlo'mé came straight to the point. "Has anyone arrived in Béarn recently?"

Baltraine shook his head. For months, no messenger or envoy sent by Béarn had resulted in reply, including those sent to recover the missing heir to the throne. "No one has come to Béarn in weeks." The obvious question followed. "Why do you ask?"

"Curiosity." Dh'arlo'mé dismissed the significance with a word.

Baltraine shrugged, attributing the seeming oddity of an apparently idle question to the early hour of his summoning. "Is that why you called me here?"

"No." Dh'arlo'mé's smooth, green eye met Baltraine's brown ones. "I need you to do something for me."

Baltraine nodded once in confused agreement.

"I need you to have the staves brought to me."

"The staves?" Baltraine's heavy brow furrowed. "What staves?"

Dh'arlo'mé studied Béarn's prime minister as if he had descended into madness. "The staves of the staff-test."

Baltraine could not stop his eyes from growing as round as coins. He knew Dh'arlo'mé appreciated subtlety of expression, but surprise would not allow him to maintain his calm demeanor. "You want the staff-test brought to you?"

"Yes," Dh'arlo'mé confirmed. "Is that a problem?"

"I don't know," Baltraine admitted honestly. "No one's ever tried to move it before." He considered his few experiences with the staves and their test. Historically, when the king or queen died, the heirs underwent the staff-test in order of seniority. The first to pass became the successor. Those who failed often became despondent, many to the point of suicide, addiction, or psychosis far beyond the despair ever reached by those heirs left untested. No one who had not undergone the staff-test knew what it entailed, at least to Baltraine's knowledge. Those who failed refused to detail their humiliation, and those who passed had never chosen to do so. Even the understanding of how the tested knew the end result was a mystery.

"Please have them brought. Move them separately or together as you see fit." Dh'arlo'mé's strange eye sparkled like a faceted emerald in the moonlight. "One caution. Choose the carrier or carriers well. They must be strong enough to resist temptation yet not so strong they grasp for power."

A shiver ambushed Baltraine. The supernaturalness of Dh'arlo'mé's knowledge seemed unclean. "I don't understand."

Dh'arlo'mé smiled. Though the expression fit the ancient creases engraved on his skin, it still seemed evil. "You don't need to understand."

Baltraine pondered Dh'arlo'mé's statement. "If I don't understand, how can I choose the bearer wisely?"

Dh'arlo'mé relented. "A worthy point." He leaned forward, the inhuman eye and the empty socket disturbing Baltraine as they never had before. "I will tell you this much. The staves do more than judge. They contain powers beyond human understanding which may try to subvert their wielders. The ones who bring the staves to me must have the discipline to resist the power they offer."

Baltraine licked his lips, despising his position. The world seemed to crumble around him. He could only guess what effect removing staves placed by gods might have. Yet disobedience to Dh'arlo'mé would not only ruin his chances to place his line upon the throne; it would ensure his death. "How quickly do you need this done?"

"As soon as possible." Dh'arlo'mé gave the obvious answer, without revealing the motives Baltraine had hoped to hear. The staff-test had existed long before elves had come to Béarn, and Baltraine could not help wondering why they had suddenly become important enough to Dh'arlo'mé to drag the prime minister out of bed.

"Very well," Baltraine said. "You'll have them." He tried to sound confident, even as ideas crushed in on him, demanding sorting. He headed for the door, the mirror reflecting his Béarnian bulk, black mane, and hastily donned silks. Opening the panel, he paused in the doorway. Too many questions came to his lips at once, so he discarded them all. Better to mull the situation in private before raising issues that might annoy the elf. Saying nothing further, he stepped into the hallway and closed the door behind him.

The click of the latch released a torrent Baltraine felt helpless to control. Memories rushed down on him, interspersed with myriad questions; and he stood, confused beyond action. At length, he managed to force his legs to move. He shuffled mechanically down the corridor, then the steps, headed toward the first floor. There, the staves occupied a central room, scarcely bigger than a closet. By the time he reached the meditation area, directly beside the Room of the Staves, his mind was still in a desperate muddle. He plopped down on one of many padded benches, staring at the swirling design that formed the back wall, its brilliant hues providing focus for his vision while his mind hammered out issues he would rather have forgotten.

Aside from Griff, lost to exile, every heir to the throne had undergone the staff-test at Baltraine's insistence. He had sent them in the best interests of Béarn and with King Kohleran's consent. The king's imminent death and the rash of assassinations had forced his hand. Baltraine had waited by the door while each heir underwent the test, a brief matter, though the participants always seemed certain the trial had lasted for hours or days. None had passed the test. *None*. Baltraine recalled the desperation that discovery had raised. Bard Linndar, Darris's mother, had brought Griff's existence to his attention. That remembrance jabbed pain through Baltraine. Linndar had died at the poisoned feast, like so many others of Kohleran's most faithful, and Baltraine had had a hand in her demise.

Baltraine squirmed away from the pain of memory, forcing his thoughts to the matter of the staves. Failure had brought despair upon the heirs, but each seemed to cope in his or her own way. Only one had abandoned Béarn; sixteen-year-old Matrinka had demanded disownment before leaving the kingdom, an understandable request given that assassins had slaughtered so many of the heirs. When messengers and envoys failed to retrieve Griff, Baltraine had acted in hopeless urgency, retesting each of the heirs. He had done so in good faith, as always in the best interests of Béarn. The second judgment demolished those tested. Suicide and murder had taken those not lost to wine or drugs. One heir, particularly unworthy, had died during the second testing. The image of her twisted corpse, ivory-white face, and bloodless lips haunted his memory.

Baltraine craned his neck toward the Room of Staves. The plain door gave no hint of the power that lay within, and the quiet surrounding this area seemed eerily inappropriate. He knew of no one he could trust with the task Dh'arlo'mé had given him. Baltraine had always determined worth and ability by bloodline, disdaining those ministers who had won their titles honorarily or who appeared contaminated by Erythanian, Pudarian, or, worse, Eastern ancestry. Enlisting a proper man for the job meant revealing the elves to another and risking the plans they and he had so carefully constructed. No mere servant or page could perform this task. To Baltraine's mind, any soldier would have physical strength but little of the brain capacity necessary for the mental resilience Dh'arlo'mé had suggested would be necessary.

Other concerns pressed Baltraine, more selfish in content yet every bit as worrisome. If Dh'arlo'mé tapped the power these staves apparently contained, he might no longer need the prime minister who had guided him through what Dh'arlo'mé called Béarn's "maze of incomprehensible behavior"—its formalities and its culture. Baltraine could become as dispensable as the humans the elves had blithely ordered executed. Baltraine dared not answer his own worries, yet his mind would not allow him to escape them. Until recently, he had complied with the elves because their intentions jibed with his own. Now, these threatened to diverge, and Baltraine needed to do something, anything, to stop them.

Baltraine was up and pacing before he realized he had left his seat. Remembrance proved unkind. Much of what he had done for the elves was born of fear. He had long promised himself he would oppose them if they caused harm to Béarn, yet he had already waited too long. The urge to run to the temple nearly overwhelmed him. The terrible awe it held for him had begun in childhood and remained with him even after he had gotten to know the priests as men. The massive teak doors had sported carvings of rearing bears, their eyes sapphires and their ear leathers shaven pearl. One door ring had simulated the sun, the other the moon, worn smooth by myriad grips over centuries. These rings slammed the wood as the door closed, announcing the presence of anyone who entered, the embarrassment virtually assuring no one arrived at services late.

Twice in the temple, Baltraine had met an armed blond man who appeared to be Renshai yet called himself immortal. He had denied being a god, instead naming himself the Keeper of the Balance. First, he had advised Baltraine. The second time, immediately after the poisoned feast, the stranger had condemned him. Burning down the temple had rid the prime minister of the blond's irksome, judgmental presence; but it had not wholly cleared his conscience. In his stronger moments, Baltraine followed the way of the elves with fanatical devotion. In weaker times, doubts descended on him; and the blond's words and manner returned to haunt him: "There is much of evil in you, Prime Minister Baltraine. And more chaos than law." He alternated between times when he worried that such might be true and decisive moments when he knew it definitively false. And the blond had said another thing Baltraine remembered now: "Urgent problems need urgent solutions."

Baltraine turned his pacing into a walk to the library. Ignoring the texts, all of which he had read, he scooped up a woven bag used for wrapping books removed from their sanctuary. He headed for the Room of Staves with a confidence more feigned than real. Without hesitation, he pulled a ring of keys from his pocket, inserted one in the lock, and spun it until it clicked. He removed the key and replaced the ring. When his hand touched the latch, his bravado deserted him. He froze in place, fingers

curled around the cold metal. Time seemed to stand still. He had
done nothing irrevocable. Yet.

For what seemed like hours, Baltraine's mind had been battered by endless conflicting thoughts and schemes. Now, when
he most needed his wits about him, his mind went blank.
Awareness of the passage of time pushed him onward. His hand
winched closed, and he pulled the door open.

Immediately, his memory conjured images of the last time
he'd stood in this same position. The worst of the heirs lay
sprawled on the cold stone floor, the staves still leaning in their
respective corners. Terror seized Baltraine. He blinked several
times, and the corpse disappeared. Light angled through the
partially opened doorway, and shadow touched every edge of
the tiny room. The staves angled harmlessly in the far corners,
their plain wooden constructions suggesting nothing of their
power. The scene appeared so quiet and peaceful, Baltraine
could scarcely fathom the wild pounding of his heart. Keeping
one foot wedged in the door, he groped along the corridor wall.
His fingers found a bracket in the shape of a wolf, and he gin-
gerly worked its torch free. Torch in hand, he stepped fully inside and closed the door behind him.

His light played over the tiny, square room, so much like
every other, aside from its size. Baltraine cringed, awaiting
some grotesque punishment from the gods for his effrontery.
Nothing happened. Gradually, he relaxed and studied the
staves; the room contained nothing else. They lay still, inani-
mate for all their legend. Their plainness seemed a mockery.
Baltraine found himself wondering if the whole had not been an
elaborate hoax from the start. *Perhaps the heirs decided among
themselves who would rule, and the staff-test served only as a
device to convince the populace.* Baltraine dismissed the possibility as swiftly as it materialized. The gentle, naive men and
women who had governed Béarn through the centuries could
never create or tolerate such deception. Dh'arlo'mé's desire for
the staves only assured their significance.

Urgent problems need urgent solutions. Baltraine could not
banish the thought from his mind, even as most other ideas had
abandoned him. He looked at the bag in his hand, then hurled it
to the ground. *I will not work for elves any longer. It is* not *in
Béarn's best interests.* Baltraine wanted to shout the words at
the top of his lungs, hoping the gods might hear and knowing no
other would. The room's walls and door, deliberately thick,
muffled sound into obscurity. He contented himself with the

thought. The self-proclaimed Keeper of the Balance had read his mind effortlessly. Surely the gods could accomplish nothing less. Baltraine continued to stare at the staves. He was descended from true nobility, without honorary titles or commoner's blood to taint his line. Like Kohleran and his children, Baltraine could trace his roots to Sterrane the Bear, the last king coronated before the staff-test. So many twists and turns in Baltraine's ancestry had nearly landed him on Béarn's throne. Had the old laws of ascension still applied, Baltraine would almost certainly sit there now.

Dizziness assailed Baltraine suddenly. Realizing he was holding his breath, he released it in a long sigh. He had read every scroll and text in existence, but none of these had brought him succor. Odin had decreed that only siblings and direct descendants of the king be tested. The gods had made no provisions for situations such as this: no suitable heirs in Béarn and the only one remaining to attempt the tasks unreachable. Baltraine stomped on the bag. His gaze returned, once again, to the staves. *Urgent problems need urgent solutions.*

Closing his eyes, jaw set, Baltraine reached for the first staff. His fingers closed over the wood, and it felt smooth and cold against his palm. Slowly, it warmed to his grip. Baltraine opened his mind, waiting for the contact Dh'arlo'mé described, for reaction from the gods who had created this test, for some indication that he touched other than ordinary wood. Nothing happened. His head pounded, and he could hear the blood flow through it. He forced himself to relax, and the pain lessened in increments, a product of his own tension.

Baltraine pursed his lips, uncertain whether to take solace or hopelessness from the situation. His heart rate quickened further, hammering a steady cadence. He sucked in another deep breath, then touched the second staff. When no reaction followed, he flicked his fingers over it in an undulating motion, rolling the sanded wood into his palm.

Pain exploded through Baltraine. The room filled with a scream that echoed through the confines in his own voice. The sound crashed against his eardrums, intensifying an agony that already seemed beyond endurance. He collapsed, torch sparking on the floor, muscles tightening at once, including his hands. The wood pinched his flesh, minuscule beneath the torrent that assaulted him, and he became frighteningly aware that he could not release the staves. The realization became desperate need. He channeled the stray bits of concentration that pain allowed toward ridding himself of the staves.

Sweat dribbled into Baltraine's eyes as clenched muscles refused to slacken, and a ceaseless dull ache joined the sharp agony lancing through him. He felt consciousness slipping and deliberately hurled himself toward that oblivion. Then, abruptly, his body loosened and seized up again. Convulsions racked him, frenzied movement he could not control any more than the screams that ripped from his throat repeatedly. He lost control of his bowels and bladder, but his thoughts remained mercilessly clear. The pain stabbed, seared, and hammered relentlessly, hovering toward unbearable, then losing ground as he gradually grew accustomed to its presence. Eventually, his mind refused to register it.

Baltraine's world went dark, though the clarity of mind remained. The pain became distant background, and he lost track of its presence. Believing himself alone, he huddled into himself as much as his twitching allowed and fought to gain control of a body that seemed no longer his own. The sensation of someone studying him cut over other ideas, and he sought dappled patterns in the otherwise limitless blackness.

The other's voice touched him first. "Baltraine Demekiah's son, why did you come here?"

Baltraine forced all attention to the voice, desperately needing his wits. The words he chose for answer would surely clinch his fate. The pain dispersed, though whether due to the intensity of his efforts to concentrate or from true recession, he did not know. His body seemed distant, still beyond his control. He could not tell if he still clutched the staves, though he savored a new lucidity. "I beg your forbearance for this question, but formality requires knowledge. You know my name, but I am ignorant of yours." He left the matter open, not daring a direct question. Already, he began carving shape from shadow. A being stood in front of him, though he could not yet discern its form.

The other obliged, "I am the voice of Béarn Castle."

The response puzzled Baltraine, not at all what he expected. "You're not the staves? Nor one who controls them?"

The other hesitated, apparently as confused by Baltraine's statement as the prime minister had been by his answer. "I am part of a staff. Yes." He spoke hesitantly, as if revealing the knowledge to self rather than Baltraine.

Baltraine's eyes finally grew accustomed to the darkness, or so he believed. His perceptions seemed bodiless. He had lost track of flesh as well as pain. Nevertheless, he could make out the form in the darkness. Though man-shaped, it towered over him. He could not define its features without light. "I can see you. You're a being."

"A being. A being, yes," the voice returned hesitantly. "But what being?"

Baltraine stared, scarcely believing what he heard. "Don't you know?"

It paused, silent for several moments. "I believe I do." Then it blasted Baltraine with a rumbling laugh, powerful as an avalanche. "I believe I do."

Terror ground through Baltraine at the sound. The voice remained the same, but its intensity changed. An inhuman confidence radiated with every word, and panic scattered Baltraine's thoughts. Had he legs, he would have bolted, but his bodiless form could accomplish nothing more than a horrified stare.

Baltraine could not see the other's eyes, but he felt pinned by them. It took a step toward him, and the urge to flee grew into obsession. "Prime Minister Baltraine, Demekiah's son, *why did you come here?*"

Baltraine squeaked out the answer he had forestalled earlier. "Lord, please, I came to rescue Béarn from ruin and to stand against those who would destroy her."

The being's hot breath burned Baltraine's flesh. He recoiled as the other spoke. "You turned against Béarn when she most needed you. You destroyed her most faithful and tried to sabotage efforts to rescue the kingdom you claim to love and serve."

"No!" Baltraine shouted defensively, then amended. "No, Lord, no. I have not always chosen wisely, but I have always worked in Béarn's best interests."

The other snorted. "You defined your own interests as Béarn's and rationalized everything you wanted."

"No!" Baltraine screamed again. The being's stare seemed to flay him open, exposing his entrails to the boiling steam of its breath. Thoughts he had buried in the deepest corners of memory paraded before him, justifications and self-deceptions stripped from them now. He stood at King Kohleran's bedside, the rancid odor of disease roiling his stomach, the jaundiced, wrinkled skin and sunken eyes stark contrast to the robust man the king had once been. The immense Béarnide had symbolized justice and balance, a king beloved and deeply respected. Baltraine relived the awe that he had always felt in Kohleran's presence despite his innocent simplicity. Baltraine had all but forgotten the feeling which had withered to revulsion as illness claimed Kohleran.

Thoughts hammered Baltraine with the speed of a runaway cart careening downhill. He could not stop seeing himself studying King Kohleran's medications and their effects, selecting ones that made the king tractable. He watched himself manipulating the ruler he claimed to follow with blind loyalty into pronouncing a sentence of death upon Knight-Captain Kedrin, a peerless leader whose only crime had been irritating Prime Minister Baltraine. Guilt thrashed him, leaving a bruised and battered hulk of shame and humiliation; but the judgment did not cease there. A myriad of mistakes flashed through Baltraine's mind. The being tore aside his defenses, opening Baltraine to the greed simmering beneath his every action. Measures once justified, above reproach, stood revealed for the indefensible cruelties they truly represented.

Baltraine howled, the agony of these revelations surpassing the pain he had once believed beyond bearing. The being showed him no mercy. Instead, it drew him to a feast and forced him to view every person there. Again, Baltraine confronted ministers dead for weeks: old Abran with his head cocked sideways, habitually lacing the fingers of his paper-thin hands; homely Limrinial with her wavy, uncontrollable hair and the clump that always trailed down her forehead; Weslin with the paler features and lighter bone structure that revealed Pudarian contamination in his ancestry. These, Baltraine faced, and others as well. They flashed into his mind in a parade he desperately wished to end. Each had died of poisoning, and he bore the lead weight of every death upon his soul. "Forgive me," Baltraine whispered as each passed through his memory. "Forgive me, please."

None forgave, and the agony built to a feverish crescendo. Regret and shame filled Baltraine's conscience until it stretched to its capacity and beyond. Death beckoned, an escape from the agony his waking mind could never jettison. As the procession continued, he doubted even the ultimate end could leave his soul at peace. One acceptance, one exoneration would allow him that solace, yet not one of the spirits could give him that reprieve.

"Never," the nameless being whispered over the visions. "Never in the centuries of judging have I met one so unworthy." The last word stabbed Baltraine. His conscience shattered, hurling shards like glass through every part of him. He found himself back in his body, lying on the staff room floor. Physical agony again joined the suffering of mind and spirit. The torch had ignited his clothing, burning away vast tracts of flesh. He howled, fumbling at his face with nerveless hands. Hair scratched his cheeks, matted with clumps of blood that smeared, warm and sticky, across his features. Screams ripped from his throat. Moment flowed into anguished moment, each passing like a tortured week. Unconsciousness refused to claim him.

Exhaustion swaddled Kevral like a blanket, and she bobbed, directionless, on the Southern Sea. Clouds, spray, and waves disoriented her. Dehydration weakened her further. The sea seemed to siphon fluids from her, and she could find nothing to replace her needs. The taste of salt became a hatred that swiftly grew obsessive. Odors mingled indecipherably, the whole coming to symbolize the ocean she despised. On the second day, the smell had disappeared into a familiarity her nose ceased to register. Now, on the third day since the demon's attack, the reek of bracken returned, overwhelming her senses and spawning nausea. Alternately, she cursed and blessed the cloudy dampness. It stole her bearings, but it soothed her stinging eyes and parched skin. The strains and bruises from the battle bothered her less.

Peace settled over Kevral at length. The sea rocked her like a cradle, and the splash of waves and calls of gulls became a lullaby. She rolled onto her back, arms overworked beyond weakness and legs too fatigued to churn water any longer. Her eyes drooped shut.

Suddenly, wind howled, slamming Kevral's cheek like a giant's fist. Kevral's lids jerked open just as the clouds opened up. Rain pounded her face, driving it below the ocean. Sputtering, she clawed to the surface. Water spilled from the heavens in impossibly wide sheets. *How?* Kevral did not ponder for long. She opened her mouth, catching as much fresh water as she could, cupping her palms to gather more. The droplets pelted her tongue and palate, stinging; but the pain disappeared in the wake of this godsend. She gulped and swallowed, letting the gale drive her where it would. For now, only the water mattered.

Liquid soothed the inferno of eyes and mouth, and the downpour supplied more solace than Kevral would have believed possible. Rain barrels took months to fill, and it seemed inconceivable for one storm to supply so much. She had surely stumbled into something unnatural: an instantaneous gale saturated beyond anything she'd ever experienced. *God-sent?* She could find no other answer. She tried to shout supplications, but the wind lashed rain down her throat, choking her. Wind and wave battered Kevral. Only as her desperate need for water slackened to natural thirst did she realize she was spinning in crazy circles, water crashing against flesh without the power to leave bruises.

Kevral gathered strength to fight the waves, thrashing a frenzied path in a random direction. Vitality drained swiftly. Exhaustion had already pressed her dangerously close to sleep, and frantic, directionless swimming threatened the second wind that new threat had gained her. Conserving her energy, she struggled only to keep her head above the surface, letting the winds carry her where they would.

Clouds blotted the sun, leaving Kevral in a blackness as thick and unfathomable as moonless night. The tempest funneled her into chaotic zigzags and spirals that left her without a clue to even comparative position. Blinded by dark and deafened by the ceaseless howl of wind, she concentrated on Renshai meditation techniques to rebuild her reserves. So long as she kept her head above water and swallowed as much fresh rain as the clouds yielded, the storm could only help, not harm her. The pain of its thrashing seemed minuscule in the wake of the blades and poison she had survived over the last few months. Tempest and ocean would not have her.

Something heavy bashed into Kevral's side, bowling her over. Water closed over her head again, and she tumbled through waves that slapped mercilessly at every part exposed. She regained her bearings, slashing savagely to the surface. Her foot hooked something soft. She kicked to dislodge it, which only entwined her further. Swearing, she groped through the darkness. Her hands tangled in something gossamer. *Cloth?* She followed its weave to a solid object, apparently a body. Excitement stabbed through her, and she lunged for the other.

Warning pressed Kevral's thoughts even as she moved. Likely, she had discovered one of her companions, but the body's stillness did not bode well. Alternatively, the storm might have churned up an ancient corpse better left undisturbed. Death did not frighten Kevral, but the idea of handling ancient remains sent a chill along her spine. In daylight, on land, it would not bother her. Now, a creepy, buzzing feeling stole through her. Steeling herself for the dead friend she might have uncovered, she explored her find.

Kevral's fingers roved along a well-muscled forearm to a thick shoulder speckled with gooseflesh. The face sported pliant stubble, not yet stiff. The solid chin, straight fine nose, and square cut face revealed a comeliness even darkness could not hide. *Ra-khir.* Kevral gasped, loss slamming her with the power of the gale. Survival had consumed her thoughts for the past few days. Now, grief seemed to punch a hole through her chest where her heart had once beat. She gathered him into her arms, his bulk buoyed by the sea, and his hair tickled her face. Beneath the vile stench of the sea, she caught a whiff of his familiar scent. He felt warm and solid against her.

"Modi!" Kevral finally shouted. Physical pain had not elicited a need for the wrath the call would bring her, yet emotional agony had. "MODI!" Only then, details seeped fully into her consciousness. Dead flesh did not grow bumpy with cold nor could it share warmth. *Alive?* Kevral's heart fluttered. She had become so certain of his death, the possibility seemed ludicrous. She berated her stupidity. *Why not alive? I'm alive.* She shifted his face so that his mouth touched her cheek, and warm breath huffed through the tempest's ice. "Hold on," she whispered. "We'll get through this."

Ra-khir gave no reply, limp in Kevral's grip.

Kevral unwrapped his tunic from her foot. Battling the storm became more difficult with her burden, but the presence of a loved one and the task of saving him became a rallying goal. She fought to keep both heads above water, riding a channel that drew them inexorably in a single direction. Abruptly, sand grated against her toes. She struggled to plant her feet firmly on the ground. Before she could do so, a wave overbalanced her. Clinging to Ra-khir, she could not protect herself. The water dragged her up the shore, sand shredding her sodden tunic and tearing at face, chest, and abdomen. She clawed farther from the water that plucked at her feet as if to reclaim them. At length, she flopped to the beach, exhaustion threatening consciousness. Only then, she realized she could see. Wind, rain, and waves no longer hammered her.

After the constant shrill of the wind, the quiet seemed deafening. Gradually, her ears picked up a stray sound on the wind. Soft chanting formed a solid beat, a musical voice droning melody atop it. For a moment, she reveled in the sound. Then realization intruded, and she jerked her head upward. She lay on a familiar beach hemmed in by trees whose trunks sported concentric circles of thickened bark. Elves lined the shoal, glazed eyes studying the castaways. Beside Kevral, Ra-khir moaned, coughing up a thin trickle of water.

Kevral leaped to a crouch, though dizziness hampered her balance. Sword or none, she would fight to the death against their enemies. Shielding Ra-khir, she glared at the elves. They remained in place, making no movement toward her. Their mental communications filled her mind, but Kevral trained her concentration on her own equilibrium instead. She would give this battle her all, as any Renshai must. She thanked the gods for this chance to die in glorious combat and find Valhalla rather than drowning like a coward in the sea.

The chanting resumed, steady as a drumbeat. Calm settled over Kevral, wresting away the burdens adversity had placed there. Too late, she recognized the elves' sleep spell, and her thoughts folded quietly into darkness.

CHAPTER 5

Elf-Captured

All I want is to hear the savage bell of swordplay, to feel the excitement that turns blood to fire in the veins.
—*Anonymous, attributed to Colbey Calistinsson*

After what seemed an eternity, the door to the Room of Staves swung open. Dh'arlo'mé and another elf Baltraine did not bother to identify stood framed against the hallway torchlight. While Baltraine struggled against an agony that pervaded every part of his body, gathering words, the elves studied him in silence. Their gazes flicked over his person, coming to rest on objects on the floor near either hand. Dh'arlo'mé shook his head, lips pursed and features stalwart. Normally Baltraine found the elf's expressions impossible to read. Now, disgust settled on the alien face, as obvious as any human.

"Help me," Baltraine managed to whisper.

Dh'arlo'mé inclined his head slightly. Responding to some silent address, the other elf hefted the bag and wrapped it around one of the staves. Handing the package to Dh'arlo'mé, he removed his tunic and wrapped the other staff inside it.

"Help me," Baltraine forced again. "Please, help me."

There's nothing I can do for you. Concept accompanied Dh'arlo'mé's sending. Elves never sickened, so they knew little of the healing arts; but even an elf could see Baltraine would die no matter his tending.

"You can kill me," Baltraine returned. "Please. Take away the pain."

Dh'arlo'mé remained in place, wrapped staff clutched in one hand, only the twitching of his fingers revealing any thought at all. As the other elf drew to his side, Dh'arlo'mé called *khohlar* to Baltraine once more, expressing idea without the need for words. Anger raged beyond outward calm. Baltraine's stupidity and vanity had lost Dh'arlo'mé his puppet. *Die in agony,* he sent. *It's all you deserve.*

Dh'arlo'mé closed the door on Baltraine's desperate pleas.

Kevral awakened to the damp, musty aroma of moss. She sprang to a crouch, assailed by a curtain of swirling, white pinpoints. Nausea roiled through her gut. She clung to control, of her stomach and her balance. Gradually, the spots faded and the queasiness subsided. She stared through a wall composed of mesh triangles into an empty corridor. Light flooded through a gaping hole in the ceiling, and hunks of wood and mortar lay in frenetic piles beyond her cell. That conclusively identified the elves' prison. Attempting to free Griff, Tae had hacked an opening from above. The strange, elfin creation, gleaned more from observation of finished human buildings than construction in progress, lacked the proper supports. The roof had collapsed beneath him, spilling Tae into the prison.

"Are you well?" Ra-khir's voice wafted softly from behind Kevral.

Kevral rescued herself from stiffening and casually turned to face her companion. She would not give him the satisfaction of knowing he had startled her. "I'm fine," Kevral answered routinely, though the words sounded ludicrous. Crusted salt stung the wounds the sand had scratched into her face, and she felt bruised all over. Her clothes hung in tatters, tunic torn open in front where the waves had plowed her across the shore. The fabric left her breasts and abdomen exposed.

Wedded to his honor, Ra-khir fixed his green stare on Kevral's face and never strayed. Wind and wave had whipped his fine, red-blond locks into a snarl that detracted little from his stately features. "What happened?"

Kevral shook her head, as if that might help her sort the memories rushing suddenly in at once. The battles seemed endless: first the demon; then the ocean; finally the tempest. All of those she had won. Yet the most important one of all, the one for which she had trained since birth, had beaten her before it began. The Renshai training centered most on war, glorious battle against armies and death in the glory and honor of the fight. The elves had bested her without a single strike in return. Had they chosen killing rather than imprisonment, she would have died a broken, unworthy craven.

For too long, grief had haunted Kevral, and the seemingly endless struggle that chance tossed into her path grew tedious. Driven beyond sorrow, she glared at the only target for her rising anger. "Damn it, Ra-khir. Look at me."

Ra-khir blinked. His brows beetled. Either her hostility or her words confused him. He leaned back against a stone wall painted with stripes to appear like wood paneling and shuffled a foot through the moss-carpeted floor. "I *am* looking at you."

"No. I mean look at *me*." Kevral made a grand gesture that swept her entire person, tiny compared to Ra-khir's bulk. A descendant of the Renshai tribe that retained the most original blood, she appeared younger and smaller than her nearly sixteen years. "All of me."

Ra-khir pursed his lips and shook his head sadly. He continued to meet only Kevral's eyes. "You know I can't do something that impolite."

"You can't let up on your honor just this once?" Kevral picked the topic deliberately, knowing it would spark verbal warfare quicker than any other. She could not explain her need to argue, only suffered a driving need to bait.

Ra-khir sighed. "Honor is not situational. I can't just abandon it because I'd like to." His eyes beseeched her, begging her to abandon animosity better aimed elsewhere. He knew what was coming and also that he was helpless to prevent it. Early in their travels, their arguments over honor had driven Matrinka to desperate distraction. Later, they had found compromises, places where Renshai honor and that of the Knights of Erythane overlapped. Eventually, their companions and Colbey had forced them to accept and appreciate their differences.

Rigid and inflexible. The tired old assessment came to Kevral's mind instantly, then died on her lips. The ancient war that once helped dispel frustration now only heightened it. "You'd like to?"

Ra-khir paused, clearly tensed for a different response. "Look at you?"

"Yes."

Pink tinged Ra-khir's cheeks, then stole over his face. He looked down, careful to turn his gaze from Kevral before doing so. His scruples would not allow him even to sneak a surreptitious look. "Kevral, I once asked you to marry me."

"Would you look at me if we got married?"

Ra-khir smiled, eyes returning to Kevral's. "Every chance I got." His face turned crimson, but he still managed to add, "And I'd do more than look."

Kevral felt her anger drain away, along with her need to hurt one she loved. She drew the tatters of her tunic together, turned, and sat beside Ra-khir. "What happens next?"

"I don't know." Ra-khir placed a comforting arm around Kevral's shoulders, drawing her closer. He passed her a full bowl of water she had not noticed previously.

Kevral accepted it, gulping mouthfuls that stretched her esophagus painfully before returning the bowl to his hands. Only then, he drank, and Kevral felt a stab of guilt for taking so much. Thirst must have driven him near to madness; but he had waited for her to awaken, and to verbally abuse him, before drinking.

Finishing the contents, Ra-khir placed the bowl aside. "From what I could gather of their conversations, they're holding us until Dh'arlo'mé returns."

"Escape?" Kevral whispered.

"I've tried. The walls are stone. The mesh looks flimsy, but I couldn't budge a single triangle."

Kevral recalled even Tae, with his street knowledge, had had to steal the keys to work the locks.

Neither voiced what they both knew. Had Dh'arlo'mé been among the elves at the time of their capture, they would both already be dead. Kevral snuggled deeper into Ra-khir's grasp, enjoying the warmth of his touch, especially the areas of skin to skin contact. She recalled the last time she had sat in a prison awaiting execution. Then, regrets had paraded through her mind, and she had vowed to die neither a coward nor a virgin. Now, both seemed inevitable.

Kevral considered a long time, but her mind always returned to the same conclusion. She raised her face to Ra-khir, and he gave her a gentle peck on the lips. A second kiss followed, then a third that lingered. Kevral savored the salt taste of his lips, the gentle cautious exploration of his tongue on her own. Excitement thrilled through her.

Suddenly, Ra-khir jerked away. "We have to stop," he said, his words incongruous with the hungry look in his eyes.

"Why?" Kevral balanced need against anger.

"Because . . ." Ra-khir started, face growing red again. "Because I might take . . ." He seemed unable to finish. "I might take advantage of you."

Kevral snorted, then immediately wished she had not. The gesture might erode his manhood at a time she most wanted it intact. "No man could take advantage of me. You know that."

Ra-khir nodded vigorously. "I'd pity the man who tried. And I certainly don't want it to be me."

Kevral feigned desperate offense. She knew Ra-khir wanted

her and that he refused not from lack of desire but because his honor shackled him. "You don't want to make love with me?"

As Kevral hoped, Ra-khir turned defensive. "Of course I do."

"Then what's the problem?"

Kevral watched the progression of Ra-khir's expression from shocked realization to desperate hope. "You *want* to make love? With me? Here? Now?"

Kevral resisted sarcasm, though many snide comments came to mind. "Ra-khir, I love you. We may die tomorrow. Maybe tonight. I don't want to die without knowing the joy of having a man I love as close to me as nature allows. I want to satisfy the passion I feel every time you touch me. I want to feel a part of you inside me."

Ra-khir stood, as if rooted in place. Kevral could only guess at the struggle taking place behind the grim mask he showed her. With guilty pleasure, she studied the handsome features and solid physique, the scrutiny intensifying her lust. "I want that, too," he finally said. "I want that more than anything." Yet he did not move toward her.

Kevral released her hold on the tunic's front. The fabric dropped back, baring her breasts again. "If you don't come here, I might rape you."

The insanity of her suggestion mobilized Ra-khir. He looked at her, eyes roving to the places honor once bound him to avoid. He caught her into an embrace that pressed her tightly against him. She could feel her nipples smashed to his chest and his hardness warm against her leg. The sureness of his actions convinced her. No doubt, Ra-khir had reconciled his honor to his need.

Matrinka and Mior, Darris, Rantire, Griff, and Captain reached Béarn as the first grayness of evening touched the afternoon sky. Craggy mountains filled every horizon, their bulk and familiar conformation welcoming Matrinka. Too long suppressed, her hopes soared, seeming to draw her heart along with them. The gentle breath of the wind caressed her face like a brother's kiss and ruffled her hair in playful greeting. She moved to the front, leading her companions through streets she knew by heart, past cottages crafted by the famed Béarnide stone masons. Statues graced the yards of even the smallest and poorest dwellings, most in the shape of bears. Other crafted animals and humans stood arranged into scenes. Stonework filled the yards of the artisans, cramped quarters and numbers robbing the individual works of their beauty.

The towering poles of quarrying equipment broke the background irregularly, lines pulled taut and beams like proud sentinels. The mingled aromas of livestock and Béarnian spices that defined the city filled Matrinka's nose, adding to the sensation of comfort that enveloped her. After months on strange roads, dodging or battling assassins, assisting injured companions and terrified for the time her ministrations might fail, hunting elves that held Béarn's heir prisoner, she felt safely swaddled in the security of home. Matrinka could not help smiling. Reaching to her shoulders, she ran her fingers along Mior's smooth fur.

The feeling of sanctuary did not last. Gradually, strangeness seeped through the refuge home promised. Few lights flickered in the cottage windows, and Matrinka met no passersby on Béarn's streets. The town lay flat and silent, as if some god had plucked out the inhabitants, leaving the high king's city an empty shell. Matrinka scanned for movement, discovering cows lowing in their pens, pigs snuffling hay for the choicest remainders, and chickens pecking seeds dropped by carts in the roadway. Nothing human met her gaze, and Matrinka's grin wilted. She glanced at Darris who inclined his head toward the center of town.

Matrinka followed the gesture. In contrast to the cottages, lights hovered in the castle windows. Attention directed, she finally caught the faint sound of voices borne on the wind. For a moment she felt incapable of comprehending the significance. Then, logic finally threaded its way through thoughts otherwise suspended. At least five years had passed since King Kohleran had perched upon the balcony to speak with his citizens. The image resurfaced from childhood memory. From the castle courtyard, Matrinka had watched, wide-eyed, as Béarnides gathered to catch every word their beloved king spoke. Their dress and demeanor had covered a spectrum Matrinka would not have believed possible: farmers in thick coveralls reeking of manure and hay; stonemasons with faces and arms smeared with a paste of sweat and dust; women with baskets clutching wet-nosed children in homespun; merchants wrapped in colorful clothing smelling of exotic fruits and spices; and nobles swathed in perfumed silks.

The scene returned vividly to Matrinka's mind, unforgettable. She conjured up every detail as she continued to wind along the roadways with her companions in tow. Soon, memory became reality. Béarnides thronged the square beneath the castle's balcony, the ones in front nearly pressed against the courtyard walls. King Kohleran held a regal stance on a balcony that, like most of the castle, had been fashioned directly from the mountain. Ministers flanked him, and guards formed a semicircle that seemed more aesthetic formation than threat. Knights of Erythane, mounted on their white chargers, held formation among the audience. Draped over armor, their tabards displayed the tan bear on a blue background that symbolized Béarn. Their mounts' flowing white manes lay braided with ribbons of blue and tan, and every sword hung at the same rakish angle.

"By . . . the gods," Darris whispered, stunned.

Matrinka stopped to look at him.

"It's your grandfather. King Kohleran is back."

Matrinka's brows lowered, then rose as she disengaged from reverie to look again. The king she had long assumed dead looked down upon his people, very much alive. Though slimmer than she remembered him being before his illness, he appeared robust compared to her last glimpse of him on his deathbed. His hair and beard remained white, only stray black locks betraying its original color. *Grandpapa!* Matrinka scarcely resisted the urge to shout aloud. The need seized her to dash into the castle and run to his arms. Only propriety held her back. Tutors had trained her since infancy not to disturb the king while he held court.

Conversation died among the audience as the king drew breath to continue a speech Matrinka had, so far, missed. Attention fixed on their king, the Béarnides took no notice of the newcomers at their backs. Still far from the balcony, Matrinka strained to catch the king's words.

Kohleran made a broad gesture over the gathered citizenry. "The self-confessed traitors were given the choice of imprisonment, banishment, or execution." His voice emerged astoundingly strong for one poised for years on the brink of death, though higher-pitched and lighter than Matrinka remembered. "To my surprise, guilt drove most of them to choose the latter. They could not be swayed." He bowed his head sorrowfully. "I feel the grief of their families, yet I believed the kingdom bound to honor their wishes. Béarn has lost some of our own, yet we can only become stronger by the ousting of those who would harm us."

Matrinka fixated on the word "execution." Never in the course of her life had King Kohleran ordered such a punishment. She would not do so, and she had always assumed her grandfather equally benevolent. Matrinka lowered her head, ashamed. Every difference between her style and that of the king only reminded her of the unworthiness the staff-test had affirmed.

The king continued, "I regret that the ugliness has not yet ended, for it pains me. But traitors still abound among us, those who fought the proper ascension and would have doomed Béarn, indeed the world, to chaos' destruction." He paused, allowing the significance of his words to seep into every mind, including Matrinka's. "I cling to the virtue of forgiveness and request that every citizen do the same. Yet Béarn cannot tolerate such a threat. Those who would turn against us once will do so again."

A murmur swept the citizenry.

Matrinka studied her grandfather, stunned. Her love had kept her close to him even after the effects of his illness drove other family members away. His appearance, the stench of sickness, the death that seemed always to hover over him only drew her closer. She had last seen him the day she begged him to renounce her title so that she could sneak away with her companions to try to bring back the last untested heir. Her request had wounded him deeply. In the end, he had agreed to announce a disownment he would not officially grant. The nobility and citizenry believed her no longer an heir, but the records showed otherwise. She recalled the look of him then. Sleep claimed him more often than lucidity, and he babbled without reason at times. His form had grown skeletal except his abdomen and legs, swollen with the fluid his heart could no longer pump. His skin had turned a sallow yellow, and the brown eyes bore a film that made vision nearly impossible. Every movement looked painful and clearly sapped the few reserves the gods still granted. Even the effort of speaking threw him swiftly back into unconsciousness.

The image defied the vigor with which King Kohleran addressed his people, yet the features, the form, and the bearing could belong to no one else. His mannerisms had changed slightly, understandable after such a long and agonizing illness. The differences, though minor, bothered Matrinka. The words he spoke more so.

"I do not wish to turn families and friends against their own, but the greater good of the world's survival demands it. The gods have spoken, and it's my mission to act as they direct. We need to find and punish the remaining traitors. We must see to it that we ferret out the last of those who meant harm to all of us, and mete out the proper punishment."

Grandpapa? Matrinka fairly sobbed. Her heart fluttered, and waves of excitement pulsed through her. She loved this man with every detail of her soul; yet, at the moment, he seemed a stranger.

That's not Grandpapa. Mior's message was so bizarre it took Matrinka's mind irrationally long to register it.

What?

The means of their conversation did not allow for mishearing, but Mior dutifully repeated, *That's not Grandpapa.*

Matrinka narrowed her eyes, studying the Béarnide more closely. *You mean it's not like him to say such things.*

Mior's tail lashed Matrinka's face. *I mean that's not King Kohleran. It's an elf.*

Matrinka blinked several times, as if this might change the vision she saw. *On the balcony?*

Yes, on the balcony. Where else would I mean?

Matrinka's mind still could not reject what her eyes told her. *In the middle?*

Mior planted her front paws on Matrinka's chest and swiveled her head so that the yellow eyes glared into her mistress' brown ones. *It's not Grandpapa. It's an elf. I can't be any clearer than that.*

The stare convinced Matrinka more than the words. Mior found eye contact distressing. Among cats, it nearly always preceded attack. Matrinka cast one more glance at the charismatic Béarnide on the balcony, searching for some telltale detail to validate the cat's assertion. Gradually, her vision found the more delicate longer-limbed frame, the canted eyes, and the thin, redly-cast white hair beneath the image she had once believed Kohleran's. Her gaze wandered to his companions, and she realized she recognized none of those she had first taken for ministers.

Matrinka lunged forward and seized Darris' arm in a pinching grip. The sudden movement overbalanced Mior who half-fell, half-scrambled to the ground, then sat stiffly in a pose meant to imply she had alighted on purpose.

Startled, Darris instinctively jerked away, then stumbled to avoid stepping on Mior. "What's wrong?" he demanded.

Matrinka dragged Darris back into an alley. There, amid the shadows, she whispered, "Elf magic. That's not the king."

"How do you know?"

Matrinka did not wish to explain. Although Darris now knew about her communication with Mior, their other companions did not. "For now, just believe me. And take another look."

Shrugging, Darris went to obey just as Rantire, Captain, and Griff joined them. "What's going on?" the Renshai demanded, her usually harsh tone softened by a weakness she would never admit. Two days of travel weighed heavily against her injuries; and Matrinka had frequently discovered her leaning on, as much as protecting, Griff.

Matrinka looked at Captain. "Can elves make themselves look like people?"

Captain returned the scrutiny without obvious emotion. "Not that I know of, but I suppose it's possible." The implications apparently reached him without need for specifics. Along with Darris, he headed back into the street.

"What's going on?" Rantire demanded again, her mind not making the necessary leap.

Darris and Captain returned almost immediately. "That's Pree-hantis Kel'Abkirk . . ." He trailed off. "The name goes on, of course. The important thing is that the king on the balcony is an elf disguised by magic."

As usual, Darris had to understand details. "How come we can see him, but the others can't?"

Captain turned to the bard. "I don't know for sure. I'd guess it's because we know the truth now." His brow furrowed. "Though I don't know how Matrinka figured it out."

Matrinka shrugged, turning Darris an "I'll explain later" look. "What do we do now?"

"We'd better tell the crowd," Rantire said.

"No," Griff jumped in next, his gentle features grave. "I don't think they'd hear us, except the closest ones. Even if they did, it would lead to chaos. Maybe even war."

Rantire turned on her charge. "We can't just let this go on." Absently, she massaged the bandage beneath her tunic, tight creases around her eyes the only betrayal of pain.

"Griff's right." Darris took the heir's side, though whether from trust or a natural urge to follow his future leader, Matrinka waited to surmise. Darris started to explain, then released his breath in a long sigh. "I'm sorry. This is inappropriate, yet necessary." Closing his eyes, he considered in a brief silence before

singing in a sweet voice scarcely above a whisper. Though unaccompanied, his words and tune dredged up love for Matrinka's grandfather. He sang of King Kohleran, of the awe and
affection the king inspired, and of the joy that surely followed
the heavy grief that had suffocated Béarn during Kohleran's
years of illness. The Béarnides believed in his recovery, not because of its likelihood, but because they desperately wished it
true. With the unwavering faith of the priesthood, they clung to
an impossibility that elfin images made appear real. Matrinka
understood, without direction, that a simple explanation would
not prove enough to unveil the deception. The Béarnides would
refuse to believe.

Sweat spangled Darris's forehead, the effort of instantly conjuring images from concept matched only by the struggle not to
project. His training, from childhood, forced him to wrestle the
strength of voice that might pierce the crowd and draw attention
to their tiny band at a time when they most needed privacy. He
switched to a primitive rhyme scheme, unwilling to wrestle
ideas or training any longer:

> *"Centuries ago, the legends claim*
> *There lived a fair king, Valar his name.*
> *His brother, Morhane, usurped the throne.*
> *Killing king, heirs, and faithful—every one.*
>
> *But the Eastern Wizard anticipated*
> *So a secret escape route he had created*
> *And told its location to only three*
> *The king, eldest heir, and a bard like me.*
>
> *Prince Sterrane was saved and then returned*
> *Via this route we much later learned.*
> *The tunnel, we know, was deliberately destroyed*
> *So that by enemies it would not be employed.*
>
> *Only bard, bard's heir, and successful staff-tested*
> *Know of the new tunnel King Sterrane requested.*
> *In secret was crafted*
> *In secret remains*
> *Now just one knows where that route is nested."*

Matrinka squeezed Darris' hand reassuringly. Listeners usually begged his talents, appreciating the practice and concentra-

tion involved in performances. At times like this, however, they found him irritating. Matrinka appreciated that the songs created instantaneously would prove far more difficult than those rehearsed, no matter how much less polished they sounded.

This time, Rantire needed no explanation. "There's a secret way in?"

Darris nodded, resorting to speech to outline his plan. "If we sneak into the castle, we can get Griff staff-tested. Once we have a confirmed ruler of the king's line, it'll prove a lot simpler to convince the populace. Plus, we can get a feel for the elves' power and intentions."

The idea seemed perfect to Matrinka, and she gave Darris' hand another squeeze. Her books did not reveal how heir or populace knew who passed the staff-test, but no one had ever challenged the claim. Matrinka had believed in magic even before meeting elves had proved it so. Faith in a test sanctioned and created by gods came naturally.

For several moments, the companions looked from one to another, no one voicing opposition to Darris' suggestion. Finally, Rantire broke the silence. "Lead on," she told the bard's heir, hand falling to her sword. "And hope no one stands in our way." To emphasize her point, she took a bold stride forward, wounded leg buckling suddenly beneath her.

Griff seized Rantire's arm, managing a stunningly graceful rescue of balance and dignity. She shifted between him and the crowd, inferring she had deliberately drawn him to her side for his safekeeping.

Doubts trembled through Matrinka then, and she placed her hopes on Rantire's literal words. Physical opposition would find them sorely lacking, their only warriors Béarn's gentle bard and a Renshai battered beyond usefulness. A few days or a week of rest would allow Rantire to recover adequately; but the threat of discovery and execution, their own and those of Béarnian innocents branded traitors, left them no time to spare. They had little choice but to rely on stealth; and, not for the first time, Matrinka wished Tae accompanied them now. Images of the quick, sardonic Easterner who had grown from loner to beloved ally filled Matrinka's mind. From necessity, she forced them away, along with the tears rapidly brimming in eyes marred by red lines as wide as rivers. She placed her faith in Darris.

The bard's plan had to work.

CHAPTER 6

Destroyers of the Peace

I will gladly give my life for anything I believe in.
— *Colbey Calistinsson*

Despite Captain's magical light, the catacombs near Béarn's dungeon remained as dank and gloomy as a cave. Walls slicked with slime seemed to crush in on Matrinka, and she followed Darris as closely as she dared. Touching him might disrupt his concentration and leave them wandering aimlessly until thirst and starvation claimed them.

For centuries the maze had guarded Béarn's prison, foiling escapes. Any criminal who managed to slip free of his cell and battle past the guards became lost in corridors that seemed endless and demonstrated no pattern Matrinka could fathom. Captain's light scarcely grazed the darkness. She suspected torches would fare worse, not only due to their inferior illumination. A breeze, thick with mold and damp, wound through the hallways, and no flame would survive its presence long.

Trapped in self-imposed silence, Matrinka had vowed to memorize their route. The chaos of the complex befuddled her within half a dozen turns; direction lost all meaning in the murk. She focused on Darris' footfalls, afraid to lose him and all hope of leaving. Griff's boots clomped loudly behind her, the quieter movements of Rantire and Captain disappearing beneath the echoes. Mior sprawled across her mistress' shoulders.

The walk continued, longer than two circles around the outskirts of the entire city. Even then, it did not end. The party snaked through corridors that zigzagged in ever-changing intervals and depraved loops. Matrinka had grown accustomed to long lapses in conversation. Darris' bardic curse kept him quiet in intervals that socially crippled him, though the two of them had learned to say more in silence than most did in conversation. A touch, a smile, a gesture spoke more, at times, than a dozen words. Awkward among her peers, Matrinka had always appreciated Darris' problem. Now, the hush, broken only by rare coughs, scrapes, splashes, and footsteps, grated on her sensibilities.

At last, Darris made a brisk gesture for Matrinka to stop. She obeyed, watching as he examined one of a million blind alcoves. "Light, please," he finally said.

Captain pushed past Rantire and Griff. Matrinka moved aside, and the elf wriggled by her to Darris' side. The darkness seemed alive, pressing in on the scant illumination so that it revealed only tiny areas before becoming eclipsed by a bend or overcome by converging shadows. Matrinka saw nothing special about this corner, but Darris continued to work vigorously, his body shielding her from his actions. At length, he made a quiet noise of triumph. A tiny square of light opened into the blackness.

Matrinka breathed a sigh of relief. "Is that it?" she whispered.

Darris nodded.

"Close it a moment, please. I just thought of something." The idea had sparked shortly after they entered the catacombs, and a deeper portion of her mind had worried the problem while she concentrated on the nearer danger of becoming irretrievably lost.

Darris obeyed, though he kept his hand in place, apparently concerned about losing the door in the gloom. The inlet disappeared, and even Captain's light proved incapable of revealing its now-known location to Matrinka. Though she had requested the closing, the plunge back into tomblike darkness left her longing for the meager promise of airy, open space again.

Rantire's irregular panting broke the expectant hush that followed. Matrinka cleared her throat. "This maze leads to the dungeon too, right?"

"Right," Darris confirmed.

"Could you get us there?"

A stricken look crossed Darris' face, perpetuated by the gloom. "Not directly from here." He grappled with words, obviously seeking ones that did not require him to sing. "We'd have to go all the way back and start over."

Matrinka pieced together the problem. It made sense for the bards to memorize the routes separately. Surely a connection existed between the two; but, fraught with twists and tacks it would require a whole separate learning that seemed unnecessary. She spoke her main thought, keeping details to herself so as not to sound too foolish. The others might discover huge flaws in her logic. Like the staves, they would find her unworthy. "Ra-khir's father, the captain of the Knights of Erythane, is there."

Silence ensued as Matrinka's companions pondered her words. Despite his inhuman patience, Captain broke it first. "His help could prove invaluable."

Darris frowned, brows drawn in, considering. "An excellent idea, Matrinka."

The princess smiled, desperately needing the praise, yet certain a "but" would follow.

"But . . ." Darris fulfilled Matrinka's expectation. ". . . remember the trial? Kedrin didn't defend himself from Baltraine's false charges."

Matrinka had a ready answer. "Ra-khir said his father preferred death or imprisonment to allowing doubt to fall on the king's chosen regent. He wanted the citizenry to continue trusting Baltraine because he feared doing otherwise would result in a chaos that might destroy Béarn." She glanced at their other companions, realizing they knew too little of the situation to add much. "The situation has changed drastically. Surely, he'll understand that."

Darris was still for several moments before shaking his head. "We don't know what those in charge have told Kedrin over the last several months. They may even have used magic. If Ra-khir were with us, or my mother, I'm sure we could convince him. But he doesn't know any of us."

"He knows *of* us," Matrinka persisted. "Surely he'd believe a princess and the bard. And Ra-khir might have mentioned us." She wondered about her own last assumption. At the time, they had tried to remain secretive, and discussing their association in a dungeon would surely have struck Ra-khir as dangerous.

Darris' head did not stop moving. "Kedrin may not know my mother's dead. That makes me the bard's young heir and you a disowned princess. Even if he believed our sincerity, he might think we're deluded . . . or just plain wrong. Remember, he's never seen an elf or sorcery. It'd be like convincing him we're actually wolves dressed as people."

Captain turned to the practical. "Won't a dungeon have guards?"

"I'll handle any guards," Rantire said, a catch in her voice betraying pain and reducing her valor to bluster.

Griff continued, calling upon his own recent experience,

"And won't this captain's cell have a lock? We had to send Mior for our key."

Rantire grunted. "And that only worked because I'd observed the elves for months, watching where they kept it."

Time still pressed them, and Matrinka obsessed over Rantire's words. Béarnian guards would prove their unwitting enemies. She could not allow Rantire to harm them, yet neither could she let them hurt her friends. The thought seemed abruptly ridiculous. *As if I could stop either from happening.* Yet, she realized, Darris could well find himself in the position of choosing between loyalty, friendship, and the best interests of Béarn and humankind. Once the staves found Griff worthy, and she did not dare to contemplate the possibility that they would not, they would have ample opportunity to free Kedrin. Until then, working quietly and quickly seemed their only logical choice.

"An excellent idea, Matrinka," Darris repeated, his transparent attempts to bolster her self-esteem ineffective but appreciated.

"Guards, locks, the unlikelihood of persuasion." Captain shrugged, his eyes like garnet beads in the scant light. "If the magic of the staff-test will convince the populace of Griff's right to rule, as you both believe, we won't need force. I think it best to press on."

"Me, too," Griff added, studying Rantire. Surely, he also worried for his mangled guardian's need to traverse the catacombs three more times, though he would not dare speak the words aloud. Rantire would vehemently deny it, perhaps insisting they go just to demonstrate her vigor. Her stubbornness might kill her, if not her savagery.

That thought quashed the last of Matrinka's tenacity. "And me," she finally said, only then thinking to worry for a different lock, the one on the staff room door. When she had undergone her testing, Baltraine used a key to open it.

Before Matrinka could speak of this new concern, the square of light reappeared at Darris' hand and Rantire darted through the opening. Mior leaped from Matrinka's shoulders, glancing after their impetuous colleague. *It's the big library. On the first floor. Nobody there now.* The cat trotted through.

Rantire returned a moment later, hunched at the aperture, eyes cautiously watchful. "All clear."

Matrinka let Griff precede her, as she knew Rantire preferred. Captain scrambled after, followed by Matrinka and Darris. The bard pulled the portal closed, fiddling with it for several moments. When he stepped away, the opening had disappeared as if it never existed. Matrinka stared, seeking a line or crack to reveal the door. She found nothing.

"Let's go." Darris caught Matrinka's hand, jerking her toward their companions who had already reached the exit.

Shaking her head in disbelief, Matrinka turned away from the vanished door. Though born and raised in Béarn's castle, the skill of her people's craftsmanship, now and in the past, still astounded her. She tried to imagine masons creating such a thing with only the crude tools available centuries ago, while quickly heading for the doorway where the others waited. Rantire crouched, watching the corridor. Griff, Captain, and Darris stood patiently; and Mior padded out into the hall, turning toward the closetlike room that held the staves.

Only then, Matrinka realized, she alone knew for certain the location and procedure of the staff-test. "Next door on the left." She pointed after the calico. "But I'm afraid it might be locked."

Without comment, Matrinka's companions headed in the indicated direction. Rantire circled the others in wary but awkward circles, eyes never still. Matrinka reached for the knob, praying as she twisted. Anticipating resistance, she pushed halfheartedly.

To Matrinka's surprise, the door yielded easily to her touch. Light from the corridor funneled inside to reveal Baltraine sprawled on the floor, his breaths emerging in crippled gasps. Scraps of seared clothing clung to his torso, and burns blistered exposed flesh. His scalp gaped in a wound still trickling blood. Gobs more matted his hair and smeared across exhausted features. His eyes were closed, deeply recessed into bruised sockets striped scarlet.

Dead. Matrinka's mind rejected the breathing before the belief that anyone could survive in such a state. Horror stole color from her. Her face drained bloodless, then her body responded in a wave of icy terror that spurred her to tend his wounds. Yet the idea of prolonging such hopeless agony kept her in place.

"In, in." Rantire shoved the others forward. Darris staggered into Matrinka's back. Thrust toward Baltraine, she loosed a muffled scream, leaping aside to keep from stepping on him. She could picture his limbs and body yielding like putty beneath the pressure, and the image churned nausea through her.

The tiny room was not built to accommodate more than one,

and the figure on the floor kept the others smashed into corners now noticeably devoid of staves. Rantire pulled the door nearly shut, positioning herself against the panel with an eye to the crack.

Baltraine's lids eased open in response to Matrinka's scream. The familiar brown eyes had lost their confident gleam, and pain glazed them like marbles. They flickered over the others and came to rest on Darris. "Please," he said, his voice an agonized rasp. "Please . . . promise . . ."

Matrinka finally knelt at Baltraine's side. "Don't talk. Save your strength. You're going to be all right."

Baltraine's gaze swiveled toward her, though his head did not move. "I'm going . . . only . . . to die. Let me . . ." He panted wordlessly a moment. ". . . say what I must . . . before I do."

Matrinka instinctively reached for a hand. Then, realizing he would not feel her touch there, she used a shred of cloth to mop his forehead instead. She would not argue. She could not help him, and the realization ached through her like poison. Her hands twitched, training driving her to do something, anything. So long as her patient remained alive, she had a chance to save him. Once he crossed that line, nothing remained. Yet logic told her he had already died. His mind just did not accept it yet. Matrinka had to believe that came of a desperate need to speak the words she had just interrupted. Distressed by her rudeness, she fell silent.

Baltraine returned his attention to Darris. "Free Kedrin . . . please." He stiffened suddenly, and his eyes dulled for a moment. Though surely coincidence, the relationship of Baltraine's plea to their discussion shuddered a chill through Matrinka. To her surprise, he managed to continue. "He is innocent."

Matrinka nodded vigorously. Once Griff became king, Rakhir's father would receive his pardon. They would see to that regardless of any vow to Baltraine.

Darris bowed respectfully, a difficult feat in the crowded room. "Lord, it will happen. You have my word as the bard and the gratitude of all of us."

Tears trickled from Baltraine's eyes, and the grimace on his face showed his pain had intensified. "No thanks, please. I . . . don't . . . deserve it." A brief light flashed through his eyes, then disappeared. "Bard, not heir? You know?"

"I know my mother is dead, Lord." Darris' tone went from

comforting to aggrieved over the course of the sentence. Matrinka rose, torn between making Baltraine's last moments comfortable and soothing the man she loved. "I know nothing of the circumstances."

Baltraine whispered something too soft and garbled to interpret.

Darris shook his head. "Lord, I did not hear that."

The words rattled from Baltraine's throat a second time, louder. "I killed her," he admitted.

Shock blazed instantly into rage.

"And . . . others as important." His gaze turned imploring. "Please . . . I need . . . forgiveness. I cannot die without it."

Darris set his jaw, teeth grinding. When he finally managed to open his mouth, the words had nothing to do with Baltraine's need. "Where are the staves?"

"Dh'arlo'mé . . . has . . . them." Baltraine answered the question, then fixed his dying gaze on the man who might hold the key to his salvation. "Forgive . . . please."

Darris studied the pitiful man on the floor, once Béarn's vibrant, brazen prime minister.

When no words followed, Baltraine launched into a tale of selfish actions rationalized as being for the good of Béarn. Soon the confession failed to surprise any longer. Each recitation only fueled the flames of Matrinka's anger. Baltraine had sacrificed kingdom and citizenry grasping for a power to which he had no claim or right. He had inflicted madness upon innocent heirs, including Matrinka. He had slaughtered Béarn's most faithful, and he had turned over the kingdom he claimed to defend to those who would destroy not only it, but all humankind.

Matrinka had modeled her life on a pattern of kindness and mercy, yet she knew she could never forgive the evil she scarcely dared to believe. For a moment, she relished the deserved pain Baltraine had poetically inflicted upon himself. She chased away the impure, afraid to lose herself to a fury without boundaries. Even then, she could not forgive.

Darris echoed Matrinka. He turned away. "I can't forgive you. I can't *ever* forgive you."

Baltraine glanced around the companions in turn, expression beseeching, desperate for escape from the conscience that would not let him rest. Matrinka had seen similar expressions on the faces of parents begging help from the heavens while their children lay dying in their arms. Pity became a cold trickle through the frenzied flames of anger. Her spirit could not forgive, but she wondered if her mouth might speak the words to quell his agony. She tried to think of it as an extension of her training, a verbal balm to assuage the suffering of one dying. The lie refused to leave her lips. She could not forgive him. Rising, she turned her attention to Darris' pain.

Griff moved in then, taking Matrinka's position despite Rantire's warning glare.

Baltraine looked at the newcomer, desperate hope taking shape behind the anguish. He studied Griff for several moments in silence, then his eyes widened in sudden recognition. "You're the heir. You're . . ."

"Griff," Griff finished simply, leaving off his title and parentage. "What you've done is evil. You've brought chaos and ruin, and every living thing will suffer for your crimes."

"I know." Baltraine's voice became a resigned wheeze. He closed his eyes, retiring toward an eternity of affliction the details of which only the gods who determined the afterlife knew.

"Nevertheless, I forgive you." The words emerged impossibly gentle from one so huge, with the innocence of a child.

Peace settled over the prime minister's tortured body, and a tiny smile replaced the grimace. "Thank you," he whispered with his last breath.

Griff sobbed.

Comfort settled over Matrinka as well, like a moist blanket absorbing the heat that had flared during Baltraine's confession. Had any other who did not know Darris' mother granted that reprieve, Matrinka would have found them callous; but the genuine grief displayed in Griff's demeanor would not be denied. She glanced at him again, seeing the bearlike form that so characterized Béarnides of the king's line. His soft voice seemed to hover in the chamber, not an echo, but a guardian protecting her from returning cruelty for evil.

Suddenly, the judgments plaguing her since her own trial in this room became clearer. The unworthiness the staves had proclaimed did not reflect on her value as a human being, a Béarnian noble, or a healer. Simply, she did not have the natural, naive innocence the gods had deemed necessary for Béarn's ruler. There was no longer any doubt in Matrinka's mind. Staff-test or none, Griff was the god-sanctioned king of Béarn. And he deserved the title.

Moonlight dribbled through the window of Dh'arlo'mé's room, its intensity stark compared to the warped purple that the elves' thick glass admitted. Finished with speech and appeal, Pree-han sat on the floor. The mirror threw back obscure images that mingled his reflection with that of the disguise. Gray hair superimposed over red-white. The beard clung like a sculpted shadow. The narrow elfin torso and slender figure became dwarfed by broad, Béarnian shoulders. Spooked by a magic created at his request, Dh'arlo'mé casually moved to a position near the window where he could no longer see the mirror. This brought him to the desk and Khy'barreth.

Seated in one of the cedar chairs, Khy'barreth glared at Dh'arlo'mé through keen blue eyes framed by tendrils of raven hair. One staff leaned near the window, wrapped in undulating billows of gauzy curtain. The other stood in the corner near Khy'barreth's right hand. The strange, predatory look taking shape in Khy'barreth's eyes alarmed Dh'arlo'mé at least as much as Pree-han's reflection. Honoring his instinct, Dh'arlo'mé kept Khy'barreth in the corner of his vision, though he did not shift position again. Displayed paranoia did not suit elves.

Three other elfin members of Béarn's new council occupied the bed. The females, Tresh'iondra and Vincelina, sat together. The older one, Tresh'iondra, studied Dh'arlo'mé through emerald eyes, her cheekbones set high even for an elf and her lips thinly delicate. Vincelina kept her head low, a yellow curtain of hair hiding her features, one long finger plucking at a design in the coverlet the only evidence of nervousness or impatience. The last male remained still between them. If not for amber eyes fixed boldly on the staves, Dess'man might have slept.

Tresh'iondra finally broke the silence. "Whoever wields those staves has ultimate power. We need to choose wisely. I don't believe we can do that in one meeting."

The male beside her came suddenly to life. "I still say we give them back to humans."

Khy'barreth tore his gaze from Dh'arlo'mé. "They can't handle power of this magnitude."

"Exactly!" Dess'man drove home his point. "It'll destroy them. That's what we want, isn't it?"

Tresh'iondra smoothed red-black hair behind her ears. "Nonsense. Humans have had those staves for centuries, and it hasn't destroyed them yet."

"They've been locked up!" Dess'man shouted. "Now they're free. Look at what happened to Baltraine."

"Don't judge all humans by one," Vincelina at last added her piece. "That's what we're learning, right? They're all different."

"The more I'm told they're different," Pree-han added, "the more they seem the same to me. Greedy, dirty, lumbering creatures who would sell their loved ones for gold and shiny rocks."

Khy'barreth glanced from one staff to the other. Dh'arlo'mé watched the blue eyes stray back to him. Finding Dh'arlo'mé returning his stare, Khy'barreth glared again.

The discussion quickly degenerated into bickering, with each elf espousing his favorite suggestion and giving little heed to those of the others. Dh'arlo'mé contributed nothing, certain the proper course of action would come to him at length, whether or not the others reached an agreement. Ultimately, the decision rested in his hands.

Khy'barreth touched the staff in the corner, running a finger along the smoothed wood, apparently curious. For several moments, Dh'arlo'mé watched in fascination as Khy'barreth drew gentle circles then, as the argument entered a fresh wave, closed his hand around it.

"What are you doing, Khy'barreth Y'vrintae Shabeerah Elborin Morbonos?" Dh'arlo'mé asked beneath the quibbling.

Khy'barreth looked up, expression innocent, and drew the staff between his legs. "I'm just looking at it."

"Careful," Dh'arlo'mé warned.

"I'm just looking at it," Khy'barreth repeated, gaze straying to the other staff. "It's not doing anything."

Dh'arlo'mé watched the other closely, more from curiosity than concern. Operating among humans had made him more leery of others' actions, but it seemed foolish to worry about an elf. Other than Captain, who had lived among humans longer than among elves, his people operated as a unit. Khy'barreth would do nothing that might harm them, and Dh'arlo'mé could not help wondering about the effects of elves handling the staves, individually or as a pair. If Khy'barreth chose to volunteer for the experiment, Dh'arlo'mé saw little reason to stop him. Together, they could overpower him if something went awry. The image of Baltraine dying on the staff room floor entered Dh'arlo'mé's mind then, easily dismissed. The untended torch had ignited Baltraine, and he had died of injury rather than through any direct intervention from the staves. Here, among colleagues, Khy'barreth could do himself little harm.

Dh'arlo'mé eased away from the second staff.

As if waiting for this signal, Khy'barreth lunged for it. "I'm tired of petty squabbling! An elf must wield the staves." His hand closed over the second. "Behold!"

Every head jerked up as Khy'barreth raised the Staves of Law and Chaos. Suddenly, his eyes jerked wide as saucers. A scream raged from his throat, merging into a continuous howl that pierced Dh'arlo'mé's hearing.

Dh'arlo'mé lunged for the second staff, trying to hammer it from Khy'barreth's hand; but the fingers tightened around the wood, unyielding. Dh'arlo'mé cursed. "Silence him!" he shouted, concerned over whom the sound might draw. "Quickly!"

Khohlar zipped through the room in an instant, strategy for a spell. A faint duet rose beneath the shrieks, and a louder voice sang magical melody to its beat. Khy'barreth's mouth remained open, but no sound emerged. Unable to slap the staff from Khy'barreth's bloodless fist, Dh'arlo'mé worried at the fingers. Nails gouged his flesh. A trickle of pink-red blood wound along the outline of his cuticle. At last, Khy'barreth's grip failed. The staff slid across Dh'arlo'mé's hand for only an instant, yet it seemed to possess him in that moment. He felt as if his spirit had been flayed open, then the exploration ended and the staff found him worthy. It promised him a partner without parallel, a brotherhood no one could sunder, power beyond his current ability to comprehend. Then it clattered to the floor.

Khy'barreth went limp. Dh'arlo'mé caught him as he collapsed, lowering the elf gently to the carpet. The other staff rolled from flaccid fingers and lodged between desk and chair. For several shocked moments, no one moved. Khy'barreth's eyes fluttered open. The gemlike eyes stared calmly at the others in the room, and he gathered himself from Dh'arlo'mé's arms.

Dh'arlo'mé sent single *khohlar* to Pree-han. *Get the staff and put it in the bottom drawer.* He sent the concept of caution along with his instructions.

Pree-han sidled up to the staff lying half-beneath the desk, as if he approached a rearing snake. Doffing his cloak, he wrapped up the staff, placed it in the drawer, then resumed his seat with an obvious gesture of relief.

Toss me a cloak, Dh'arlo'mé sent.

Pree-han obeyed.

Khy'barreth blinked several times, glancing about the room

with a childish sense of wonderment. "Doo-doo-doo," he crooned, like an infant learning to talk. "Dadadada."

Dh'arlo'mé set the cloak on the ground, cautiously using an edge to roll the staff to its center.

You need not fear me.

Dh'arlo'mé jerked away from the contact, and the elves shifted nervously at his back. He reached for the edges of the cloak, folding them over the wood. Hefting the whole, he headed for the drawer.

I won't harm you, the staff continued through the transfer. *I am law.*

The words told Dh'arlo'mé nothing. Law would speak truth and chaos lies, so either would identify itself the same way. He would not fall into the same trap as Khy'barreth or Shadimar. He dumped the staff into the drawer with the other, and the presence retreated from his mind. Pushing the drawer shut, he instructed Dess'man. "Make a box for those." He indicated the closed drawer. "Something thick with a heavy lock." He glanced at Tresh'iondra. "Do what you can for Khy'barreth."

Tresh'iondra shook her head. "I've tried to communicate. I can't. My *khohlar* seems to reverberate inside. It's as if there's nothing there."

"Lalalalalalalala," Khy'barreth crooned.

Dh'arlo'mé shivered, implications a jumble in his mind. He needed time to think.

Kevral felt eyes bore into her in the darkness, and she startled awake despite exhaustion. Moonlight through the damaged ceiling revealed shadowy figures shifting through the prison, the light occasionally sparkling from eyes like multicolored diamonds in a mine. Their steps made no sound on a mossy floor patterned to appear like carpet, and they did not whisper as humans observing prisoners might do.

Having discerned as much as possible from her position, Kevral cautiously wriggled from beneath Ra-khir's muscular arm. Immediately, she missed the warmth of his skin against her own; the faint, clean aroma of him, and the strong, loving draw of his embrace. Death would come as a whole new world opened before her, yet it would not find her a willing victim. She would never die a coward. She would haul every elf within reach to Hel or Valhalla with her.

Kevral rose, gaze fixed on the elves as she donned her sodden breeks. She did not bother with the tunic, torn beyond usefulness. If her bared breasts distracted the enemy, so much the worse for them. Her state of dress would make no difference to her corpse or to the gods. Only the ferocity of the war she waged would matter.

The pattern of the elves changed subtly, apparently in response to Kevral's awakening. They drifted toward her and into a more compact arrangement, though still beyond clear sight. Ra-khir continued to sleep, his breaths breaking the silence. Kevral let him rest. Her love goaded her to allow him to die in glory, but, unlike her, he had no need to do so violently. Knight's honor differed on this point, though it jibed on many others.

Tensed for battle, Kevral waited for the elves to act first. When they did nothing more than make minor positional changes for longer than she would have believed possible, Kevral surrendered to impatience. "I've grown weary of your stares. If you're going to kill us, have at us already."

Fidgeting followed Kevral's challenge. Finally, one elf shuffled directly in front of her cage, glancing nervously right and left for support. Inky hair dangled to skinny shoulders, red highlights sparked by the moon. Enormous yellow-white eyes met Kevral's blue, then skittered away. Despite his obvious anxiety, he maintained the flowing grace that defined elfin movement. He appeared androgynous, as all elves, yet something undefined told Kevral he was male. "Hello," he said, without malice.

Kevral kept her expression stony. "I believe we're way past greetings."

The elf blinked, thin lids lowering like a film over eyes that appeared as large as dinner plates in a too-small face. He continued as if Kevral had not interrupted, using the Northern tongue without accent. "I am Haleeyan Sh'borith Nimriel T'mori Na-kira. Your friend, Brenna, called me Hal."

Kevral recognized the false name Rantire had claimed during her captivity. Hope trickled past suspicion, and the expectation of an immediate battle receded. Rantire had mentioned that, toward the middle of her captivity, a few of the elves had befriended her, listening raptly to her nightly stories. For the most part, she had relayed tales of heroism, with Colbey Calistinsson as their focus. "My name is Kevral." She waved vaguely in the direction of her sleeping companion. "Ra-khir."

Apparently awakened by the conversation, Ra-khir completed his title in the common trading tongue. "Ra-khir Kedrin's son apprentice knight to the Erythanian and Béarnian kings: His Grace, King Humfreet, and His Majesty, King Kohleran." Clambering to his feet, he pulled on his britches, then held open his tunic for Kevral to wear. She allowed him to place the fabric over her head and worked her arms into the sleeves. It fluttered into place like a blanket, the hem dangling to her knees.

Another elf stepped directly in front of the cell, this one with sapphire eyes and hair the color of straw. Again, Kevral could not define the details that identified his gender. He wore a curved sword at his hip. "A name worthy of an elf."

Restive laughter followed from the sidelines, and even Kevral smiled.

"What did he say?" Ra-khir moved up beside Kevral, every muscle of his chest and abdomen defined. His closeness and the smell of him evoked memories of the previous evening. The pain of losing her virginity had proved less than Kevral expected, especially compared with the wounds she had taken in spar and battle. It had seemed to bother Ra-khir more. The pleasure that had followed made the brief discomfort worthwhile. In the end, she had suffered it gladly.

"What did he say?" Ra-khir repeated in a harsh whisper the elves could surely hear. He did not speak the Northern tongue.

Kevral's smile persisted as she switched fluently to common trading. In everything she did, she strove for perfection. "Basically, he said your name is as long as theirs. His is about fifteen syllables."

Ra-khir grinned, too, though sheepishly. "Something to be proud of." He added, placing the conversation back on a serious note, "So they're not planning to kill us immediately?"

"Apparently not." Kevral returned her attention to the elves and the Northern tongue. "What do you want from us?"

The blue-eyed elf glanced at Ra-khir, then said in trading, "I speak your language." His singsong softened the harsher consonants. "And we mean you no harm. My name is Eth'-morand . . ." He trailed off, not bothering to voice a sequence that would likely prove impossible for human memory. "I'm a follower of Lav'rintir, once Arak'bar Tulamii Dhor, the elf you call Captain." He made a circular motion that indicated every elf currently gathered in the prison. "We all are."

The last of Kevral's animosity faded. Apparently reading her moods by stance and attitude, more elves crowded closer to the cell. Now Kevral recognized females among them, though the visual cues that separated gender continued to elude her. Their long-limbed grace, large canted eyes, and soft alien features brought an image of beauty to her mind, though it struck her more as the attractive innocence of children. "Thank you for helping us rescue our friends."

"We did not help," Eth'morand corrected quickly. "We simply did nothing."

"That was enough." Kevral drew breath to quote Colbey: *There exists no such thing as a neutral warrior. By not assisting one side, you are, by definition, assisting the other.* Once, Kevral had found no sense in those words; now the meaning became clear. By withdrawing their voices and power from the elves' chant, they had effectively ruined Dh'arlo'mé's sleep spell and allowed Kevral and her companions to escape. In a way, their lack of action won the battle. Even as she analyzed it, Kevral chose to keep the quotation to herself. Raising guilt among creatures with little understanding of individuality might drive them back to unify as enemies.

A young, black-haired elf jumped in then. "Brenna said me Dhyan." He pronounced it "Zjon." Unlike the others, he came right to the point, still using the human trading language, though badly. "Help us Lav'rintir with, we out you." Eyes as blue and steady as Eth'morand's beseeched her.

Eth'morand translated. "He means we'll let you go if you promise to lead us to Captain."

Kevral would have given much more for her freedom. In fact, she had once done so in Pudar, vowing to train the king's soldiers in exchange for release from his prison. "Agreed."

Hal glanced to his left, making a high gesture with his right arm but saying nothing aloud. Kevral watched as the elves passed an object hand to hand, recognizable as an oddly shaped key by the time it reached Dhyan. He gave it to Eth'morand, who placed it in the lock and twisted. The mechanism gave with a hiss rather than the anticipated click. He removed it, and the door swung open. The elves skittered aside.

Kevral stepped out of the cell, Ra-khir at her heels. Her heart pounded as she observed the wave of elves standing or perched on chunks of broken construction, many of whom appeared torn between welcoming and running. Kevral estimated a dozen elves filled the area, some with swords at their belts. Her eyes were drawn naturally to the weapons, and the first stirrings of envy drove her to think of snatching one away if the opportunity offered.

Eth'morand followed the track of Kevral's attention easily,

then met her gaze with eyes that did not blink or waver. "It is we who owe you gratitude from that battle. You could have killed many of us, but you chose to wound instead." Reading her need, he unbuckled his belt and passed her his own weapon. His mind touched hers, relaying concepts he seemed unable to put into words. He communicated hope that her mercy would persist and a reminder that the death of an elfin adult translated to destruction of every infant destined to bear that spirit.

Kevral accepted the sword and belt, fastening it over the folds of Ra-khir's tunic. Eagerly, she closed her hand around the haft. Constructed solely of metal, it swiftly warmed to her grip, coils settling against callus. She would not have chosen a similar weapon in the market. The hilt fit her hand poorly, and it would grow slippery in battle, slick with blood and sweat. The guard held too little depth, and its reverse slant could allow her hand to slide onto the blade. She drew it only partway, disappointed with a balance too near the tip. Not wishing to threaten her new companions, she let the blade slide back into its sheath. Excitement thrilled through her despite the inferiority of the weapon. She held a sword.

Eth'morand's mental communication radiated trust and grew swiftly into a bond that came as much from the deep respect and ultimate faith that voluntarily handing over his own sword displayed. On rare occasions, Renshai still joined brotherhoods based on Northern custom. A tie created in that manner represented a camaraderie stronger than blood. Though they had exchanged no vows, Kevral could not help feeling similarly linked to an elf she scarcely knew. She tried to reassure him. "It would dishonor your weapon and yourself for me to use it to slaughter your kin. I respect you too much to allow that to happen."

Eth'morand smiled, his *khohlar* now a vast gratitude conveyed in an instant. Another sword found its way to Ra-khir's hand, though no one pressed him for a similar vow, at least not that Kevral heard. Out of the prison they spilled in a group, into the chilliness not yet dispelled by the dawning sun. Colors blossomed on the horizon, blues giving way to greens, then vast spectrums of yellow to red. Beyond the bands, pink sky disappeared amid the trees, the whole occasionally disrupted by fleecy clouds. The packed earth had absorbed the night's coldness, icy against Kevral's bare feet. None of that mattered. She had her freedom and a sword, and a Renshai thus armed could face any enemy.

As the last of Lav'rintir's followers filed from the prison, elves on the outside gathered in larger numbers. Some stared from the trees. Others banded together, forming a semicircle around the emerging elves and human prisoners turned companions. *Khohlar* bounced and echoed through Kevral's head, and she felt bombarded by conflicting concepts. Her human mind seemed incapable of deciphering communication at such a speed. She recognized alarm, anger, and question. Threat vacillated with vows of peace, though which group radiated which, Kevral could not tell. Tedious names flashed to her as a sensation that separated individual from group, yet bound them together simultaneously. Then the whole degenerated into an incomprehensible muddle.

One mind-voice cut over the others, demanding a silence that swiftly followed. This time, Kevral found a source, an elf larger than most of the others with an aura of authority and age. Silver hair swept back from his features, and violet eyes pinned Eth'morand. His *khohlar* demanded explanation from this one elf alone.

Eth'morand obliged, also choosing general mental communication. *We are leaving, Vrin'thal'ros Obtrinéos Pruthrandius Tel'Amorak.* The tone that accompanied his response conveyed respect for an elder that scarcely matched his words.

Kevral appreciated the method. Had they spoken in their native tongue, she and Ra-khir could not have understood them. The Erythanian placed his hand over hers where her fingers kneaded her hilt. With a touch, he conveyed the need for patience.

Only then, Kevral recognized that she perched on the brink of violence. Fatigue spurred irritability and robbed her of the mental control that was as much a part of Renshai training as sword work. She let go of the hilt. In a crisis, she could draw and cut in the time it took any *ganim,* non-Renshai, to perform only the former. For the moment, however, no one had done anything more violent than make vague, unspecified threats. If war resulted, she would hack a path through the elves, killing every enemy or dying in the effort. But she would not be the one who initiated the battle.

You may not leave, Vrin'thal'ros commanded. *You will escort the prisoners back to their cell and apologize to your brothers and sisters.*

No. Eth'morand did not waver. Elves on both sides stared

silently at the conversants, their multicolored, gemstone eyes eerie in the growing light. If they judged at all, they did so only in their own minds or with singular *khohlar*.

What madness this? Shock and anger tinged Vrin'thal'ros' mental voice. *You did not refuse. You cannot.*

Eth'morand's hands folded over his chest, a human gesture. *I can, and I did. Step aside.* Despite his demand, he still sent the deferential notion of a youngster addressing an elder.

You may not leave.

Eth'morand glanced back at his followers for support, which he received as a subtle sea of nods. Kevral kept her gaze fixed on Vrin'thal'ros, daring him to attack while Eth'morand dropped his guard.

Buoyed by the endorsement, Eth'morand continued, *If you oppose us, we will fight.*

Kevral deliberately placed her hand on her sword hilt to back up Eth'morand's threat. Many of the elves had suffered blows from the flat or hilt of her blade.

Don't let these humans addle you. Wait for Dh'arlo'mé's return. He'll undo the magic these evil creatures have cast upon you.

That's nonsense, Eth'morand signified. *We made our decision long before these two arrived. Humans have no magic. I, and these others, believe peace can exist between us. Dh'arlo'mé's methods guarantee the destruction of our race or theirs.* Strength replaced Eth'morand's anxiety, and his words became as much plea as explanation. *Probably ours. We are the* lysalf, *the light elves. And we believe elves should shed their bitterness and become the tranquil, compassionate folk we once were. We still believe in peace.*

Kevral could not help noticing how the swifter communication allowed long points to reach conclusion without angry interruption. A human in argument would never have let another say so much.

You are fools, Vrin'thal'ros sent back. *Serenely oblivious, you walk into a wolf's jaws bearing an apple as a gift. We cannot let you go. You deserve the deaths you bring upon yourselves, but we cannot tolerate the permanent oblivion you cause those whose souls you borrow. The future of our children rests on your mistake.*

Or yours, Eth'morand sent in *khohlar.* *Whether we are wrong or you are, one group of us will die. No matter how right you believe your stance, we trust ours as strongly. Surely, it stands in the best interests of elfinkind . . .* The rest of the concept degenerated into elfin experience. Kevral's best comparison suggested she finish the idea with . . . *to plow different rows*.

Vrin'thal'ros returned to absolutes. *We cannot let you go.*

Eth'morand sent a message of sorrow. *You can stop us only by killing us. We deeply regret the loss of ours, yours, and all of our children. Let history show you left us without choice.*

Vrin'thal'ros' eyes widened, a particularly emotional gesture for an elf. *Elves cannot kill elves.*

Eth'morand said nothing, and Kevral approved of the strategy. Silence here told more than words. Hal, however, broke the effect. *Once elves could kill no one. Dh'arlo'mé changed that. If you force our hands, we will attack.*

Now, *khohlar* sang around them again. Kevral recognized only horror from the voices, a grim realization that such action would violate history, propriety, law, and a philosophy as old as the world.

Vrin'thal'ros silenced his followers with a wave. *There will be no war among elves.*

A hush trailed his *khohlar*, stretching beyond human decorum, to impertinence, and finally beyond Kevral's endurance. She fidgeted, squeezing Ra-khir's hand to keep from resorting to force.

At length, Vrin'thal'ros continued as if he had never paused. *I have no choice but to let the traitors go with the following vow: that you will never reveal Nualfheim to humans nor pass them knowledge they could use to destroy us. You are elves no longer, but* lav'rintii, *the followers of Lav'rintir.*

Kevral caught the underlying message as well. The word apparently meant "destroyers of the peace" in elfin.

Eth'morand relaxed noticeably, and he conveyed gratitude for rescuing them from the need for violence. *We agree to the vow, but not the label. To our minds, we will remain the elves and you* bha'fraktii.* It meant "those who court their doom." *As compromise, we may wish to use the terminology of history:* lysalf *and* svartalf.*

The last two terms Kevral recognized from the human Northern tongue. The first meant light elves and the second dark elves.

Genuine regret assailed Vrin'thal'ros' projected thoughts. *Good-bye,* lav'rintii.* He ignored the compromise as if Eth'morand had never spoken it. *We will not assist you, but neither will we harm you. Your souls are too precious.* The method of communication refined the intention of the words, Vrin'thal'ros and his followers cared nothing for those they considered traitors, only for the future lives their spirits represented.

The *lysalf* headed for the beach, surrounded by curious *svartalf* who made no move to stop them. Nevertheless, Kevral remained at the back of the group with Ra-khir. Any threat to those who wished to leave would meet with swift violence. Whether from fear of Kevral's sword or some depth of elfin honor, no one attempted to stop Captain's followers. And, by the time they reached the water, their ranks had swelled to thirty-five.

CHAPTER 7

Ravin's Promise

I am more capable today than yesterday.
                                        —*Colbey Calistinsson*

Griff's sorrow haunted him long after his companions' conversations turned from Baltraine to security. The unforeseen loss of the staff-test had gutted their plans, leaving them little in the way of options. Returning by the means they had entered might buy them time but no information, and every day they delayed might result in more executions of Béarnian citizens. Remaining inside the castle would give them an advantage, yet it would place their security, and Griff's, at risk.

Even Griff could see the folly of trapping themselves with a corpse in a closet-sized room on the main thoroughfare. While the others turned their attention to finding a new base, Griff continued to suffer the grief inspired by Baltraine's revelations and desperate need for forgiveness. Soon the heir's thoughts wandered, sadness a fog that deafened him to his companions' discussion. He pictured his mother, her plump curves defining safety, her dark hair swept back into a knot, and her brown eyes moist with concern. By now, worry creased her face into wrinkles that might never fade. After the deaths of Griff's father and brother in a plowing accident, she had protected him with the fierceness of a wolf with a newborn cub. What little money the farm earned for them went to a string of laborers who took over any chore that might present a hazard to him. The last of these became his stepfather. And Griff was not allowed to leave his mother's sight except for one sanctuary beyond the trees, still well within the sound of her call.

As he considered the agony his disappearance had caused his mother, tears dripped from Griff's eyes. His mind shifted naturally to the Grove. He had gone there as often as possible, finding solace amid the ribbon of stream, the trees, and the deadfalls perfectly preserved in memory. There, too, he had discovered the only friend his protected lifestyle allowed. For years, Griff had believed Ravn a figment of his imagination. The blond's sudden entrances and exits, the fact that no one else knew of his existence, and his strangeness convinced Griff he had conjured his friend from need. Ravn had taught him the names of plants and animals, how to recognize birds by their calls, and trivial details about the animals on the farm. Most of these facts, Griff believed, had come from suppressed memories—details his father had explained before his death that grief had relegated to the deepest corners of Griff's mind.

Then the elves had come. First, they had tried to drown Griff. Only Ravn's lightning swordplay had rescued him from certain death. That was the first time Griff wondered about the reality of his "imaginary" friend. On the elves' second attempt, a black bird had swooped from the sky, chasing them from a Grove swiftly losing its comfort as retreat and haven. Griff's concerns for his own sanity drove him there one last time, and the elves had captured him without a struggle. His mother might find nothing to explain his disappearance, just as the blood and corpses had vanished before Griff dragged his stepfather to witness the results of Ravn's battle.

Griff's thoughts brought him swiftly back to the elves' dungeon where Ravn had guarded him with fanatical devotion. Rantire's conversations with Ravn had revealed the truth. Griff's "make believe" friend was the son of Colbey Calistinsson and his wife, Freya. The boy with whom Griff had tussled and competed, to whom he had confided his deepest secrets, and to whom he often believed he owed his sanity was a god. Bold words, commitment, and promises had gained Rantire Ravn's trust and his charge. Griff desperately missed his best friend and worried about his mother's health.

Need drew Griff from his self-imposed isolation. He found himself crammed in one corner, arms hugging his torso and legs drawn to his abdomen. Politely, he awaited a lull in his companions' discussion before adding his piece. "Perhaps there's a place of worship nearby?"

All eyes turned to Griff. Captain nodded thoughtfully. "That's not a bad idea."

"You mean going to a temple?" Matrinka supplied.

"Don't elves worship the same gods?" Darris questioned next.

Captain made an equivocal gesture. "The same gods, yes. Worship, no. Elves have a different sort of relationship with

Frey and the others." He glanced at Darris pointedly. "This is not the time for a long explanation."

The bard looked disappointed.

"It's enough to know elves don't pray. And they don't build temples."

Matrinka confirmed the choice with more information. "The castle temple's a secure place, too. Except on holy days, it's usually empty. No one's likely to be there now, and it's impossible for anyone to enter without warning. No matter how many times they're oiled, the hinges squeak. The heavy doors slam, and the handles crash against the panels louder than any thunder. My father used to complain that the priests made them that way just to embarrass anyone who came to services late." A bittersweet smile bowed her lips. "It's the only place my father was ever on time."

Cutting through the unnecessary chatter, Rantire inclined her head toward the door. "Let's go."

The others obeyed immediately, while night still covered Béarn. Matrinka had explained that servants wandered the halls at all hours, but the nobles and general staff would disappear at night. The few guards stationed inside the castle would concentrate in the sleeping areas, especially the king's quarters.

Though channeled through the hallways in quiet bursts and pressed into puddled shadow, Griff could not help noticing Béarn's finery. Murals etched and painted on the walls depicted scenes that did not break, even for doors. He recognized a few historical and mythical scenes from his father's stories. On the left wall, a massive, one-eyed being with arms like tree trunks and face a study in rage battled a formless force. Clearly a representation of Odin banishing the primordial chaos from man's world, it captured the terrible divinity of the god. The single eye seemed to glare at the dark, coiling winds, and the muscles bulged with a maximal effort captured for eternity. A face, more impression than reality, glowered amid the shapeless entity. The scene continued, its forms and colors absorbing Griff's perception and twisting his mood to share the gods' desperation. Repeatedly, Rantire had to drag him away from images he longed to study for days, and each movement made his eyes ache as if physically tearing his gaze from their fixation.

Finally, Griff reluctantly turned his attention to the torch brackets that broke the artwork at regular intervals. Fashioned into the shapes of animals, they held his regard without the intensity of the murals. Satisfied to glance at each, identify it, and move on, he paid no further heed to the beckoning stories that covered Béarn's wall. If he became the king, Griff assured himself, the pictures would fascinate him forever. Never would he take such beauty for granted.

At length, they reached the end of the corridor and turned into an alcove. A double set of doors appeared in front of them, little resembling the finery of the remainder of the castle. Black indentations, ridged with ash, revealed where fire had eaten at the wood. A bronze plaque drooped from one, holes still evident where it had held a door ring in place. A faded crescent marred the other in the same location. Apparently, once, these had represented the sun and moon. The colossal panels buckled and splintered where someone had clearly pounded a heavy object against them.

Matrinka and Darris stopped suddenly, eyes wide. Matrinka's hand clamped over her lips, and Mior padded a step backward before sitting on her mistress' foot. "Gods," the bard breathed.

Rantire signaled the others to remain in place, then poked her fingers into the holes that once held the ring. Bracing herself against the wall, she pulled the door. Sweat beaded her pale forehead, and her muscles knotted as much from pain as effort. When Griff came forward to assist, she frowned but did not challenge. Together, they inched the panel open, the hinges protesting every movement. At length, a crack appeared. Rantire looked through it, then waved the others to her.

Matrinka, Darris, and Captain came, slipping inside while Griff supported the door and Rantire stood guard. Once they'd all passed through, heir and Renshai followed, the door creaking closed behind them. Matrinka stiffened, anticipating a familiar crash that never came. The lapse made her visibly nervous. She fidgeted, glancing anxiously over her shoulder.

The acrid odor of charred wood and fabric smelled stale. The wreckage of what had once been padded benches lay in heaps on either side of a stone aisle. At the front, a dais black with ash lined the farthest wall. Glass speckled the floor, shattered from tiny windows near the vaulted ceiling. Moonlight filtered through the openings.

"Gods," Darris repeated.

The word galvanized Matrinka. She loosed a stifled scream, more like a sob, then ran around the room examining every lump and alcove. "Gods," she repeated. "Gods. Gods. Gods." All else seemed to have fled her vocabulary.

Griff did not bother to reconstruct the temple in his mind. Instead, he knelt amid the soot and prayed. Silently, he channeled his fear and sorrow into concept, reaching out not to the gods, but to the friend who had made his childhood bearable. He begged for his mother's consolation, for the chance to rescue Béarn from looming chaos, to bring peace to a shattered kingdom as he had done for Baltraine's soul. Griff did not ask for the strength or wisdom to pass the staff-test. For reasons he could not define, the test seemed more formality than barrier. He only hoped he would find the ability to rule Béarn with the intelligence, strength, and mercy it needed. The burden the world had placed upon him seemed unbearable. He did not want to rule, yet to do otherwise would condemn both mankind and elfinkind to ruin.

A familiar voice disrupted Griff's prayers. "I see I chose his guardian wisely."

Griff whirled, hopes soaring. Rantire crouched in the damaged hallway, sword drawn and stance offensive. Ravn stood in front of her, eyes fixed on the bared steel. He made no move to touch the swords at his hips.

"Ravn?" Tears poured freely from Griff's eyes, and he raced toward his friend before he could think to do otherwise.

Rantire had little choice but to scramble aside as the huge Béarnide charged past her and wrapped Ravn in a suffocating embrace. Griff had never touched the young god before. In his youth, he had not thought to do such a thing. As an adolescent, he had feared such action would prove the ephemerality of a friend conjured from imagination and need. Now, he savored the feel of small, taut sinews and the soft leather of cloak and tunic against his arms.

Ravn laughed, returning a squeeze before extricating himself from Griff's hold. "Easy, Griff. If you pin down my arms, your guardian might just kill me with my own sword."

"She'll have to answer to me if she does." Griff spoke in jest, though he did release Ravn and glance at Rantire to ascertain that she had no intention of attacking.

Ravn readjusted his clothing. "A lot of good that would do *me*."

Captain, Darris, and Matrinka drifted over, studying Ravn in the smoky light the high windows admitted. Griff prepared for introductions, but the doubts and sorrow that had assailed him in the Room of Staves returned in a sudden rush that stole his breath. "Please," he finally managed to say. "Let me talk with my friend alone." His eyes rolled to Rantire.

The Renshai frowned, shaking her head slowly. "I cannot leave your side."

Ravn's head tipped sideways, and he examined Rantire as if to assure himself of her sincerity. "I protected him long before he knew of your existence. I think I can handle the job."

Rantire crowded between Ravn and Griff. "A god placed him in my charge. I will not leave his side."

Griff lowered his head, burying his face in his hands. He appreciated Rantire's dedication and in no way wished to hurt her, but his need stung. He tried to empower himself with the realization that, soon, his needs would cease to matter as he bonded to the kingdom and lived only for its requirements, but the rationalization proved of little use. He needed time with Ravn.

Ravn stamped his foot, his blond hair as functionally short as his father's and his blue eyes as keen as a falcon's. "Damn it, Rantire. *I* am the god who placed him in your charge!"

The proclamation jolted Darris and Matrinka, who exchanged wild glances. Matrinka fidgeted in a lopsided circle, then dropped to one knee in deference. Darris seemed incapable of movement. Captain continued to stare.

Rantire hesitated a moment, but she did not sheathe the sword. Her eyes fell from Ravn's face to his hands. When she spoke, her tone granted no quarter. "It doesn't matter. I vowed to protect this heir from anyone. Colbey Calistinsson fought gods who stood against him. I will do no less."

Griff paced frantically behind Rantire, but he did not challenge her space.

"Colbey is my father!" Ravn spat an exasperated sigh. "Rantire, I appreciated your devotion then as I do now. But if you don't let me talk to Griff alone, you'll leave me no choice but to kill you."

Rantire smiled, the expression ghoulishly out of place. "I would relish the opportunity to fight. And if I lost, I would find joy in method and cause."

Ravn dismissed the bold words with a bored wave. "Yes, yes. I know that. A pity and a waste it would be, though you'd never see it as such. It's the Renshai's job to guard the heirs, not the king himself. Soon, you'll have no choice but to yield your guardianship to Darris. I hope, but doubt, you'll treat him with more respect than me."

Rantire shrugged, saying nothing.

Griff could stand the pain no longer. "Stop it!" Sobs stole all authority from the command. "There's been enough killing. No one will die over me. I'd rather suffer alone." Turning, he headed for an alcove, blinded by tears and not bothering to listen for Rantire's ever-present footsteps behind him.

Matrinka's voice wafted softly to him. "Shame on you, Rantire. It does you little good to guard him from friends if he dies of grief instead. I'd kill you myself if I had the skill or nerve to do it."

Though mired in his own sadness, Griff could not help hearing. He would never have believed Matrinka capable of even such a gentle threat.

Ravn's tone softened. "If I can't convince you as a deity, perhaps you will yield your charge to me as a fellow Renshai."

Griff heard no reply from Rantire, Ravn's sudden presence beside him the only confirmation that she had relented. Griff felt weak as a rag as his friend gathered him into warm, strong arms and rocked him like a giant's baby. "You can handle this. It'll be all right."

Griff wanted to trust his friend, but too many barriers lay in his path. "Please tell me my mother's well."

"She lives," Ravn told him, the answer too vague to comfort.

"Her heart can't take losing me, too." Griff's own chest felt as if it might explode. "Someone has to tell her I'm fine, but to send a messenger would condemn him to death." Griff tipped his face down to meet Ravn's eyes. "Please help me."

Ravn released Griff, perching on the lip of an alcove and shaking his head in disbelief. "You want *me* to act as a courier? You're dangerously pushing our friendship."

Griff understood the sacrilege. "I'm not ordering you to do anything, I'm appealing to you as a friend." He wiped his nose on a sleeve, battling for control of lungs that forced gasping breaths at irregular intervals. "Ravn, I . . . I don't want . . ." He abandoned the effort. "You were the only one I could talk to. Now I have no one."

Ravn closed his eyes, wincing. "My father was right, Griff, though no son likes to admit such a thing. He told me every tiny action of mine would spiral beyond control. After I foiled the elves' attempt on your life, I faced the beating of my life on the practice field. I gained permission to join you in the elves' prison only by besting my father in spar. You meant enough to me to try my hardest, and I won through luck, not skill." Ravn opened his eyes, the light of mischief that seemed always to fill them finally gone. "I shouldn't have come, but I knew you needed me. I came to tell you this: Trust your friends and in who and what you are. Your job may seem the most difficult, yet your natural instincts make it simple."

Griff wanted desperately to believe in Ravn's faith, yet it made little sense to him. "I have no friend but you."

Ravn glanced at Griff's companions. "Give it time. As things settle into a routine, you'll see another side even to Rantire. There's humanity tucked behind the mechanical dedication to duty. I can't read the future. I don't know if man's world can be saved. But if it happens, and you live to take your throne, you'll find love and happiness amid the loneliness that is a king's lot. And, one way or another, I'll always be with you."

"Thank you," Griff said, feigning a courage he did not feel. Ravn's words gave him scant hope.

Ravn's gaze held Griff's, and the young god sighed. "You win. My father will practice me into oblivion for interfering, but I'll find a way to let your mother know you're well."

A sad, lonely smile parted Griff's lips, and he gave his old friend one last bear hug. For a moment, he could imagine them back in the Grove skipping stones, without the weight of the worlds and kingdoms dangling like blades above their heads.

Finally, Ravn pulled free. "I have to go now."

Griff nodded a stiff gesture of understanding. A boulder seemed to lift from his spine, and he headed back toward Rantire. A moment later, he turned for one last glimpse of Ravn Colbeysson. He saw only the sooty stone of Béarn's ravaged temple.

Sunlight filtered through the branches of Asgard's bulbous trees, dappling the soft, blue-green sea of grass. Multicolored seed pods littered the ground like children's toys, tossed and bounced by mild breezes. Colbey Calistinsson paid their beauty no heed. He would never lose his appreciation for scenery that daily dwarfed the splendor of Midgard's finest landscapes and weather; but, for now, his sword practice took precedence.

Colbey's long sword cut the sweet-smelling air into perfect segments, weaving and arching like a second being. Every movement flung silver highlights that betrayed its position; its speed made it otherwise invisible. Colbey's feet skimmed over the velvety carpet of grass, never in one place long enough to leave an indentation. With the grace of an acrobat, he wove and gamboled, yet no one could mistake his lethal devil-dance for entertainment. His *svergelse* combined the deadly force of a whirlwind with the capricious brutality of fire. His blond hair whipped around his clean-shaven face, cut short enough that no part of it ever fell into his eyes. Of average height, yet small for a Northman, daily practices had honed his sinews, though he lacked the bulging musculature of most warriors. He chose his weapons for balance, not weight; the Renshai maneuvers relied on quickness, rarely on strength.

No movement escaped Colbey's blue-gray eyes, from the gentle rock of branches to the slightest shift of the sun's course in the heavens. The faint perfume of the trees, the delicate drift of the bubble-shaped pods, the glitters the sun sparked from every object became an integral part of the obsession that was sword work. Excitement thrilled through every part of his being even as the need for further refinement and understanding drove him to work his limbs past exhaustion. The pain and perspiration, the scream of overtaxed muscles, had become simultaneously his desperate lot and his greatest pleasures.

Colbey launched into a savage maneuver created just the previous day, polishing it into a repertoire that had gone millions beyond counting. Imagined enemies recoiled from the onslaught, then bore in with a skill and speed that matched his own. One by one, he dispatched them, never losing track of the others as they charged tirelessly into the melee. Experience taught him that no man or god could have dodged those lightning blows, yet he pictured his enemies doing so. Where reality failed him, the opponents in his mind supplied the challenge he needed to hone his skills.

As the warriors closed on Colbey en masse, double sword techniques became necessary. Usually he savored working himself to the utmost, forced to track not only enemies but weapons working independently in either hand. Here dwelt a fascination that familiarity could never quell. Forever, he had pitied non-Renshai for their adherence to shields or their inability to comprehend the use of a second weapon, except to block. The skills the Renshai used to coordinate such attacks were based on hard work, long-suffering practice, and techniques of mental control. Even most Renshai never reached this level of ability, yet the vow that prevented Renshai from teaching their maneuvers to any but Renshai had spawned rumors about natural dexterity, tricks, or magic. Colbey shook his head as he pulled Harval, the Gray Sword of Balance, from its sheath. So many centuries past his birth, the lazy would still rather discount the hard work they could scarcely comprehend and attribute others' ability to gimmicks.

As Colbey drew Harval, his usual joy became tainted by its weakness. Crafted to his specifications, the sword had served him well in his mortal years until a battle with a demon had broken it, though not a single blow had landed. The Eastern Wizard, Shadimar, had repaired the blade, at the same time imbuing it with magic so that Colbey could fight the demons their misguided enemies sent to kill him. Years later, Odin had brought the balance of forces together into the sword. Law and chaos, good and evil had become Colbey's charge, and he their champion for eternity.

Colbey launched into a vicious flurry of strike and counterstrike, intermingled with a defense that consisted almost entirely of dodging. Thoughts of Odin annoyed him viciously. The AllFather's proclamations, though unanimously hated, seemed fated always to reach fruition. Only once had Odin failed in his pronouncements, when he set up Colbey to rescue him from his own prophesied doom. Only then had Colbey managed to betray him. Even after death, however, Odin's decrees haunted his following. Colbey continued to champion balance, though not because Odin had placed the responsibility into his hands. With the unshakable faith Colbey had once devoted to the gods who were now his peers, he believed in the necessity of balance and the demand for a competent custodian. He simply trusted no one else to handle the charge Odin had given him.

Harval and its essence had become a nearly impossible burden. As the balance on Midgard swung dangerously, the sword in his hands became desperately unreliable. Colbey flipped it in a delicate arc, and it thrashed the air like a clumsy bird unused to flight. Seventeen times in half as many seconds, he adjusted his action to suit the sword. No onlooker would have noticed the difference, but the endless concentration that controlling the blade cost Colbey might also cost him his life in battle. Only if no other sword existed, would he have used such an inferior blade in combat during his mortal years. Now he wielded the sword as a constant reminder of work that required his doing and an imbalance only he could correct. Should he fail, humans, elves, and gods would crumple into annihilation. Now, as always, he gave his all to his practice, hampered only by the ceaseless need to adjust for Harval.

A figure appeared at the farthest range of Colbey's vision. For an instant, guarded irritation trickled through the exhilaration that naturally accompanied every *svergelse*. Interrupting a Renshai's practice spelled death, and he had given every denizen of Asgard rash enough to do so the only warning they would ever receive. The idea of battling gods or their minions raised both regret and pleasure. He despised the thought of harming one he respected yet, at least, they might supply Colbey with a rousing battle. Perhaps the god might manage to best him.

Even as the thought entered Colbey's head, he recognized the other from her impeccable form and graceful walk. *Freya*. Though ensconced in sword work, he could not suppress a shiver of delight at the vision of his peerless wife. Incorporating the subtle movement into his maneuver, he continued without interruption. Once his practice finished, he would give her some of the attention she more than deserved.

Freya drew nearer, revealing the details that made her the epitome of the feminine ideal. Muscles firmed by her own sword practices defined uniquely feminine curves, slender and perfectly proportioned. Her wide-set, blue eyes held a twinkle of mischief, and her heart-shaped lips remained pursed, revealing nothing of her intentions. Golden hair billowed in a cascade around a face as smooth as ivory and tinged with just enough pink to rescue it from sallowness. Though gauzy, her outfit left enough mystery to entice, and rawhide ties on arms and legs maintained its practicality. Only the sword belted at her waist ruined the sensuality of the image. This, she drew and charged her husband.

Colbey met the assault with a deft parry, returning a looping cut that Freya easily dodged. Ecstasy thrilled through him, a second wind not yet needed. Nothing pleased him more than the opportunity to pit weapon and skill against a woman nearly his equal in battle. Their spars had become all too infrequent in the last hundred years.

Freya bore in with a weaving attack that left her head open for a fraction of an instant. Colbey resisted the obvious killing stroke, reluctant to end the match so soon. He found himself on the defensive as Freya's sword flicked toward his chest, then his throat. Colbey retreated, then leaped back into the fray, cutting beneath Freya's sword arm. A concentrated sequence of withdrawal and sidestep rescued her from disarming. Colbey gestured his approval.

Freya did not gloat. Rather, she became a furious blur of attack. Sword crashed against sword, more like music to Colbey then the tinny chime of bells or the bard's lute. Back and forth across the grasslands they wove, their swords entwined. Twice, Colbey ignored winning openings to prolong the pleasure that had become too rare for his liking. Forced to reassess every subtlety of one sword, Colbey found the spar more evenly matched than in the recent past. The excitement blossomed into a rabid explosion, the battle as intimate and provocative to Colbey as sex. If the spar never ended, he would truly believe he had found a place better than Valhalla.

Finally, a miscalculated parry granted Colbey a killing stroke. Pulling it would appear too obvious, an insult to an opponent he so respected. Instead, he bullied closer for an in-fight, wrestling the sword from her grip an instant before he sheathed his own. Colbey bore Freya to the grass and pinned her, excitement blazing into fiery need. He kissed her with feigned viciousness, and she jammed her tongue into his mouth. For an instant, the great swordsman who had lost none of a million battles froze, paralyzed by a need so great he lost control of every muscle. A bonfire flared in his groin. He managed to clamp a hand over her breast, feeling like an adolescent newly wed.

"Enough," Freya whispered, the words like a dagger through his heart. "Someone might see us."

"So what?" Colbey did not care if the whole of Asgard watched, so great was his need. "We're married."

"Our son might see."

Colbey showered Freya with kisses. "We'll kill him and make another one."

Freya eeled free, laughing at his obvious joke. Even had Colbey not loved Ravn with the devotion of ten fathers, gods reproduced rarely. Likely, centuries would pass before another child was born among the deities. Now sixteen, Ravn would soon get his first taste of the golden apples of youth, and his puberty would span longer than a human lifetime.

Colbey withdrew, though he felt as if everything in his genital region had twisted into knots. "Why don't we do this more often?"

Freya stared. "Every day isn't enough?"

Colbey rose, then extended a hand for Freya. "I mean the sparring part. If we did *that* every day, too, I don't believe I could possibly ask for anything more."

Ignoring the proffered hand, Freya stood, straightening her clothing. "Isn't it obvious?"

Colbey studied his wife, never tiring of staring at the perfection she defined. "Apparently not. I have no idea what you're talking about."

"Why we don't spar much anymore." Freya shook back her hair, and highlights shifted like sunlight through running water. "I used to best you sometimes. I no longer can."

The words seemed nonsensical to Colbey. "Of course, you can."

In reply, Freya shrugged. "In theory, perhaps. If you discard who you are and who I am."

Still bewildered, Colbey tried to clarify. "You mean husband and wife?"

"I mean Colbey and Freya."

Colbey shook his head.

"Don't you ever get tired of this?" Freya made a broad gesture.

The question seemed ludicrous. Freya had lived here millennia before his birth. "Of Asgard?"

"No."

An even more ridiculous assertion struck him. "Of you?" He gave her no chance to respond. "I love you. Your intelligence and skill never cease to amaze me. If I could spend every moment staring at you, I would consider it a blessing. If I could spend every moment sparring with you . . ." He trailed off, unable to concoct a suitable comparison and basking in an image that rekindled the fire that had diminished while they talked.

Freya's long-lashed lids rose and fell, modestly acknowledging the compliment without releasing a point Colbey had taken along an erroneous tangent. "I mean the sword practices."

Colbey sighed at a question that had plagued him since he vowed, at age five, to become the finest swordsman his capabilities allowed. For years, his parents had hounded him to perform his share of the work tending gardens, sorting, and straightening to no avail. Every spare moment, he devoted to his swords. In a society that valued war skill above all else, they found it difficult to reprimand him. Eventually, it proved simpler to do the work themselves and let him practice. When combat took them both, the society eagerly picked up Colbey's share of mundane work in exchange for teaching. Those who did not despise the brutality of his methods thrived under his tutelage.

Colbey had long ago found his obsession impossible to explain; yet, for Freya, he would try. "Battle is the source of euphoria. Nothing short of dire injury has kept me from it for longer than a day, and even then I feel like a drunkard locked in the cold who can only peer through a tavern window where the wine flows freely. Every day I miss places me a day behind for the competence I could have."

Freya huffed out a laugh that stung after the depth of his revelation. Immediately, her expression turned repentant. "I'm not making light of your need. I just think that after four hundred years you must have reached your goal to become the finest swordsman your capabilities allowed."

"That's just it!" Colbey caught Freya into an embrace, hoping to convey his excitement. "I realized the most amazing thing!" He delivered the words he came to understand in adolescence, a brilliant discovery that had colored the remainder of his life. "There's no limit to capabilities. The more you work, the more competent you get."

Freya nodded, a slight smile playing across her alabaster features. Clearly, she appreciated Colbey's observation, but not with the same fervor. "You're saying competence is infinite."

"Exactly."

"As is your time here."

Colbey considered. "That remains to be seen. The apples of youth, I've noticed, don't completely stop aging." He conceded the point, wishing he had not quibbled. Time had done anything but ravish Freya. "But close enough. My time here is essentially infinite."

"So if you missed a day or two of practice?"

"I'd be a day or two less competent than I could be." The thought chilled Colbey. "I couldn't stand that." Concerned his intensity might bother Freya more, he quipped. "You didn't know you married a lunatic, did you?"

Freya smiled back, perfect teeth gleaming. "Yes, I did. But I ignored the warnings."

Colbey grinned back, drawing Freya closer carefully so as not to reawaken a passion she would not allow him to consummate. "Are you sorry you did?"

"Of course not." Freya did not even pretend to surmise. "What about you? Do you ever wish you hadn't married me?"

Colbey laughed until Freya's sharp look silenced him. "I'm sorry. I thought you were joking." His grip tightened, and he marveled at a realization that had escaped him until that moment. Even goddesses had vulnerable moments. "Every man from the time he stops thinking of girls as a separate species until the instant he breathes his last breath wishes he could marry you. Every woman gets compared to your standard, and every one must fall short. No matter how skillful my sword work becomes, it's marrying you that the others will envy."

Freya said nothing for several moments, having trapped herself into a difficult position. To agree with any part of Colbey's assessment meant displaying an uncharacteristic vanity. False modesty, however, would seem equally shallow. "There are stories about me."

Colbey nodded, head swishing against the gauzy fabric. He knew as many from the myths told in his mortal years as from the gods themselves. The word "freya" literally meant "lady" in the Northern tongue, but it had come to connote wanton. "Are they true?"

"Very few."

"Then why do they matter?"

Freya pulled away far enough to fix her sapphire eyes on Colbey's icy gaze. "I'm surprised that, after so long, you've never questioned me about any of them."

Colbey met Freya's stare squarely. "Why should I? I love you. I trust you. What else matters?"

"Curiosity?"

Colbey shrugged. Early in their relationship, before he had felt comfortable discussing such things, he had sorted through the rumors and used scraps of conversation to ascertain their veracity. Another demonstration of the differences between a mortal living on Asgard and a true immortal was that Freya had waited three hundred years to wonder about his silence.

"And there's something else I find it hard to believe you haven't done yet."

Colbey moved his hands to hers. "What's that?"

"You set Valhalla as your goal your whole life. Until you got involved in the Wizards' balance, you claimed nothing else mattered. Everything you did, you did for Valhalla."

"That's true." Colbey could not deny it. Even now, every Renshai and every Northman did the same.

"Yet, in the centuries you've been on Asgard, you've never visited it."

Colbey's brow lowered slowly. Freya was right. Ravn had gone to Valhalla and described the constant war of the *Einherjar* who battled through the day, then rose from the dead to eat a great feast every night. Once, Colbey could think of no greater reward. Now he had found one. An emotion flickered through him, one he could not identify. He could not explain why he had chosen not to look upon the place that had occupied the central core of his thoughts through his mortal years. Something held him back, perhaps concern that seeing the place he had aggrandized since infancy would somehow render it a disappointment. Nothing could possibly live up to the expectations he had ascribed to Valhalla. "You're right. I can't explain that except to say the time doesn't feel right yet." Only then, Colbey considered the possibility that, in his heart and soul, he still hoped or believed he would arrive there if his death was brave enough. In his mind, he remained mortal.

Vivid images sprang to Colbey's mind. The mingled perfume of sword oil, blood, and sweat replaced the fruit and flower scent of Asgard's air. His ears reveled in the music that thrilled him throughout his mortal years: the chime of steel striking steel, war cries echoing, and the moans and gasps of the dying. Highlights flashed from myriad weapons, like stars. Blades of every variety, clubs and maces, fists and shields flew toward him, every one a challenge, each the possible vehicle of the death in glory he sought even before death itself held meaning.

Colbey remembered plunging into every war as if no other mattered. Each, he believed his last; yet his own dedication proved his undoing. Every practice, every combat honed his skill. Every battle that did not kill him enhanced his ability with sword and dodge until Valhalla seemed a distant impossibility. Few Renshai lived into their thirties, yet Colbey had reached seventy and beyond without committing a single act that might brand him a coward. He seemed certain to die of age or disease, either of which would bar him from Valhalla.

These thoughts flashed through Colbey's mind in an instant, followed by an incident he had banished from conscious thought until that moment. He had first met Odin as a mortal, the gray garb and broad-brimmed hat making the god appear nondescript. The aura of power had given him away, and the single eye had radiated the knowledge of the universe. The words the father of gods had spoken returned verbatim: "You do still fear one thing. And although you wouldn't have any way to know it yet, that fear has been recognized. You will never reach Valhalla."

The rage that pronouncement had raised returned to haunt Colbey, a shadow of its former self. Nothing Odin had decreed mattered now, centuries past his death. Yet Colbey could not help wondering if the words bore any relation to his decision.

"I didn't come to talk." Freya's voice seemed distant, and it took Colbey a moment to make sense of her words.

He smiled, hand straying to his sword. "You came to fight."

Freya laughed. "I'd say you had a one-track mind, but that usually has different implications. Actually, I came to drag you to a meeting."

Colbey rolled his eyes, suppressing a groan. The oppressive dignity and infernal patience of the other inhabitants of Asgard made Colbey seem like an undisciplined puppy. The dry, formal affairs usually involved assigning him desperate tasks, binding him hand and foot with restrictions, then announcing dire consequences if he did not act in the same swift and bold manner they reviled him for on a daily basis. At least, he appreciated their means of tearing him from his practice, sending Freya instead of servants. Colbey preferred conversations with the gods' attendants over threats against them. The viewpoints and experiences of these once-mortals remained closest to his own. "Now?"

Freya glanced at the sun. "We wouldn't arrive first if we left now."

"Very well." Resigned, Colbey took Freya's hand and they headed for the Great Hall where Odin had once presided over the gods' gravest matters as well as their feasts. "Does Ravn know?" Colbey did not want his son to miss his second gathering.

"He's there." Freya squeezed Colbey's hand with affection.

"So everyone's either at the meeting or headed for it." Colbey glanced at the familiar symmetrical trees. Their many hues created a pleasing contrast.

Freya nodded absently.

"So we could have made love in the grass without anyone seeing."

Without missing a pace, Freya kicked Colbey in the shin. "I stand corrected. You have a *two*-track mind."

"Finally!" Colbey threw up his free hand as if in celebration. "Someone recognizes my profound depth."

Though colossal, the single-storied Great Hall reminded Colbey of a crouching animal. Silver walls supported a domed, golden roof. Inlaid gemstones represented every color of the rainbow, and the glitter of sunlight that caught different groups in turn gave the impression of watching eyes. The materials came from the altars of their followers, sacrifices of Midgard's greatest wealth, a collection of treasure unmatched by all of mankind's kings combined. All wasted, to Colbey's mind. The gods had no use for money, and the sheer mass of valuables here eclipsed the beauty of individual metals, stones, and objects.

As Colbey and Freya approached, Balder disappeared through the teak door. Light danced through the edging pattern of diamonds in crazed lines and spirals, then vanished as the panel snapped shut. Colbey appreciated the sight. Once dead, Balder had waited in Hel for the *Ragnarok,* only after which, the prophecies decreed, he would live again among the gods. The experience had imbued a patience even beyond that of the other immortals. If Balder had just come, the others had already taken their seats. Colbey relished the lateness that would keep him from having to exchange small talk. He gave Freya's hand one last gratified squeeze. She had deliberately timed their arrival perfectly.

Colbey released his wife and reached for the latch. Tripping it, he opened the door. Sunlight glazed through, mingling with the lanterns; and the inside betrayed all the austere simplicity the metallic and bejeweled exterior lacked. A heavy wooden table, bound with iron straps, filled most of the inner court. In the past, the gods and goddesses had left the chairs of the dead unoccupied, a chaotic arrangement that never failed to irritate Colbey. At their last meeting, he had deliberately perched in Odin's high seat, though he knew it bothered the others. Odin's terrible dominance had stretched even beyond the grave. Apparently, Colbey's gesture had broken the pattern.

The current leader of the gods, Vidar, now took his father's place. He closely resembled Odin with his harsh round face, broad nose, and strong cheekbones; but he lacked the air of ruthless savagery and mysterious wisdom that cowed mortals and discomfited gods. Short yellow hair and a well-tended sandy beard drew no attention from the bulky body trained to war. Vidar's blue eyes had hardened, and silver locks now ran through the gold. Otherwise, responsibility seemed to have changed him little.

At Vidar's right hand, his half brother Vali sat in contemplative silence. Balder, also Odin's son, took the open chair at Vidar's left across from Vali. The last surviving son of Odin, blind Hod, sat beside Vali.

Freya's brother, Frey, had taken the seat across from Hod, his handsomeness nearly as striking as his sister's beauty. Only the scowl that scarred his features since the near-destruction of his creation, the elves, marred the image. Beside him, the women had chosen to sit together: Balder's wife Nanna, Loki's widow Sigyn, Thor's widow Sif, and Idunn, the keeper of the golden apples of youth. The sons of Thor, Modi (Wrath) and Magni (Might), sat beside Hod and across from Frey and Nanna. Their father's hammer, Mjollnir, lay on the table between them. By blood, Modi and Magni were Colbey's half brothers, though he felt no particular kinship with them. The mortal Renshai who raised Colbey until their deaths in glorious combat won them their places in Valhalla were, in every sense that mattered, his parents.

Ravn sat at Magni's right, the fidgeting youngster looking vastly out of place amid the grim collection of deities. Emotions radiated to Colbey in a wild mix: worry, anger, disgust. His son proved the jarring piece. Something unnerved Raska "Ravn" Colbeysson. Colbey made no attempt to sort his impressions or to read further. The gods would make their concerns clear soon enough. Ravn's vexation could wait.

Colbey accepted the chair beside Ravn, and Freya the one beside him and across from the other goddesses. Ravn's discomfort heightened precipitously. Sweat spangled his brow, and the smile he turned on his parents was tight and strained.

Vidar waited only until the last two had settled into their seats. "It appears we're all here now. We can commence." He peered around the gathered faces, meeting eyes that ranged from the palest blue to the richest green. Most wore war braids, yellow except for Modi's and Magni's fiery red. "At our last meeting, we found the balance between the world's forces teetering." At last, his cold gaze found the Renshai, and eyes like diamond chips bored into Colbey's as if to read the thoughts behind them.

The irony struck Colbey, and he barely suppressed a smile. Experience had taught him that the gods could not read minds, at least not his. He, however, could violate their thoughts with impunity. Odin had placed the world's forces—good and evil, law and chaos—into Colbey's sword. To a Renshai, that did not differ from entrusting it directly to his hands. So far, the gods had agreed, most reluctantly, to let him handle the problem on man's world. Their influence would prove too massive. Their slightest action invariably snowballed to shattering proportions. Only Colbey and Ravn maintained the necessary sensitivity to act without destroying, whether from age or proximity to mortals. Like his father, Ravn preferred swift and violent solutions without need for deliberation. Ravn, however, lacked the maturity to realize this situation called for the latter.

When Colbey did not answer immediately, Vidar asked the implied question. "How are you faring, Keeper of the Balance?"

Anticipation filled the room, accompanied by a hefty skepticism. Every god awaited his answer.

"I'm making progress," Colbey said, vague from necessity. He walked a delicate line.

A sudden slash of anger pierced the gathering, and Colbey did not have to seek its source. Modi surged to his feet, orange beard bristling and face as crimson as Thor's in his wildest rages. "That tells us nothing! We're talking about the survival or collapse of Asgard! Whimsy will not suffice. Have you restored balance or haven't you?"

"I haven't," Colbey admitted, his calm like a whisper beneath Modi's shouts.

Vali mumbled something unintelligible, though his attitude, as well as his aura, revealed disgruntlement.

Colbey blinked, not bothering to explain himself further. The monstrous might of the gods had awed and, at times, terrified him. Thor's heavy stomp had shaken the heavens with thunder, and lightning shattered and crackled in the wake of his violent anger. Odin's single eye seemed to consume all knowledge and understanding, and he gave nothing of himself in return. Loki sanctioned the chaos the others disavowed, a dark presence of destruction that fragmented honor and severed alliances in wild explosions of betrayal and hatred. Tyr had personified honor, and Heimdall had served as the watchman. But the time for absolutes had come and gone. No human followed a path purely good or evil any longer, and the gods' time had come as well. *Ragnarok* had destroyed the unconditional and left behind deities with little of their predecessors' directed power. He respected them because his faith would allow nothing less, but he would not kowtow to their petty needs just as he had refused to do so for mankind.

Freya clarified for her husband. "We're asking Colbey to coordinate irrational creatures, none of whom can be wholly predicted, nor does one resemble another. They have failings I can scarcely comprehend and agendas that can vary from day to week and often make no sense at all." She leaned around Colbey and Ravn, placing both hands on the table. "A failing in the Balance isn't like a hole in a dam that can be fixed with a straw plug and a handful of mud. Too much interference, and the wall tumbles. Too little, and the leak continues to widen. Meanwhile, new openings appear all over the surface, and he has to decide, *correctly,* which depend on others and which to handle first. None of us can afford a mistake."

Vali cleared his throat and rose. "Which is why someone more skilled and experienced should work on this project."

Colbey's eyes narrowed and his nostrils flared, but Freya blocked this response from the others' view. Many times, he had wished the problem lay in any hands but his own. Yet, with a certainty that transcended vanity, he believed himself the best qualified for the job. Likely, he would fail, but he felt certain any of the gods would. Bluffing, he gestured from himself to Vali, indicating that Odin's son could take the job from him at any time and without resistance. If Vali chose to do so, Colbey would have little choice but to oversee and intervene as necessary.

Sif rose, metallic gold tresses fluttering around comely features and warrior sinews, flinging highlights no normal hair could match. Colbey fought the urge to kneel in supplication. He had dedicated every practice since birth as a prayer to this goddess of Renshai, more fervent than the most devout priest. "This is nonsense," she said, her voice, though at normal volume, as demanding as a shout. "We trusted Odin's judgment since time began. Why would we question his choice for Keeper of the Balance?"

Balder and Hod nodded vigorously. Vali's scowl deepened. Beside Sif, Idunn spoke next. "Who among us could think like mortals better than Kyndig?" She used the name the gods had given Colbey long ago. Literally, it meant "skill" and placed him with his half brothers, "wrath" and "might."

Sigyn disagreed with her seatmate. "Just because we're working with mortals doesn't necessarily make thinking like one a positive thing."

Vali grinned.

Colbey relaxed, letting the others carry the conversation. When a group of personalities this strong came together, they could never all agree. Ultimately, he believed, it would come back to him. For good or ill, the group always gave less acknowledgment to Sigyn's opinions; marrying Loki placed her credibility in permanent jeopardy.

Sigyn continued, "Times have changed since Odin created the task for the Keeper. Perhaps the test is no longer valid."

Vali snorted, taking the point one step further than good taste. "We would have the Wise One's judgment still if Kyndig had assisted his battle as Odin intended."

Frey interrupted, his scowl deepening and his handsome features a study in rage. "Whatever your opinion of Colbey's actions at the *Ragnarok*, don't state it in my presence. He chose to help *me* instead. I believe that decision expedient for more reasons than that he spared my life instead of Odin's. Without Colbey, we would have no Midgard to balance."

Colbey gave his brother-in-law a nod that he hoped conveyed respect as well as gratitude. They had agreed on few matters since that day. Frey's demand, that Colbey kill no elves, had placed more constraints on him than any other. So far, however, he and all humans he employed had complied.

Vali relented, presenting an opinion Colbey had never heard before. "In all deference to your life, friend Frey, I'm afraid Odin may have known what was best even then. The *Ragnarok* was Midgard's scheduled time to fall. I'm afraid Kyndig's actions, however much you might believe in them, may only have delayed the inevitable. Only now, when Midgard falls, she will drag Asgard down with her."

Varying emotions turned to blank and open-minded consideration. Colbey glanced at Ravn, pleased to find his son still mired only in anxiety. He had not given the suggestion any more thought than the other bitter nonsense the gods spewed forth at intervals. Colbey only hoped Ravn's lack of reaction came of common sense and not adolescent disinterest.

The answer came sooner than Colbey expected. Speaking for the first time in a gathering, Ravn drew upon his courage. His voice emerged in a thin quaver, yet it rose over the hushed contemplation. "If that were so, if the world had a master plan even the gods don't know, why bother to live at all? And why would Odin have made a system of Wizards with the purpose of keeping the balance and making prophecies come true? If things happen no matter what we do, why should we do anything?"

Ravn had found the point well enough, but Colbey added the current practicality. "I believe I've made it clear I don't believe in fate. Not even my own. Those of you who do can hide in your halls and do nothing. I'm going to do my best to save the Balance, for our sakes and for the sake of my people."

Vali recoiled as if slapped. His pale eyes narrowed, and he glared at Colbey. Before he could inflame the issue any more than Colbey already had, Vidar stepped in to restore order.

"Let's not argue, please. There's no time or place for that." He sat up straighter in Odin's chair, finally taking the role he had held, in name only, since the *Ragnarok*. "Odin is gone, but we're not leaderless." He turned Vali a hard, calculating look as if he expected his half brother to challenge his command. "*I'm* the one who assigned Colbey to this task, and I stand by my decision."

Vali lowered his head, a silent gesture of capitulation. Nevertheless, he challenged Vidar's decision as he had not done his position. "You realize you place our fate into his charge as well?"

Vidar's reply followed without hesitation. "Yes. That would be the case no matter who I chose. The situation, not the man, determines that."

"But he's not even one of us!" Magni blurted, an attitude Colbey knew many of them shared.

Vidar grinned, turning his attention to Thor's son. For a moment, the ugly gleam in his eyes resembled Odin's. "That may well be his greatest asset."

Magni's eyes snapped wide, and his hand went to his beard. He said nothing further.

"Odin gave over regulation of the Balance to Colbey despite the fact that he expected to survive the *Ragnarok*. I condone his decision. And I uphold it."

Colbey remained silent. He would not stand accused of influencing Vidar.

Freya held no similar compunction. "Colbey's methods may be . . . unconventional." She paused just long enough to unintentionally broadcast "weird" to Colbey's mental talent. "He's done fine by the Balance in the past, even when certain of us tried to sabotage him." She glanced pointedly at Thor's sons, though they had not participated in the mistake.

The corners of Colbey's mouth twitched into a smile at the memory. Believing Colbey sanctioned chaos, Thor had blustered down from Asgard to kill him. No matter the winner, the battle between biological father and son, neither of whom knew of their relationship, would have instantly sparked the *Ragnarok* both were trying to prevent. Luckily, Freya and Loki separated them in time. Colbey knew Thor had meant well; the God of Law and Storms truly believed his actions would work in the gods' best interests.

Freya finished with a warning. "Vidar sent my husband to teeter on ice too thin to hold anyone and told him to repair cracks in its surface while the world's forces bombard him with wind and flying rocks. I won't have him dodging divine but stupid sea monsters at the same time."

"Meaning what?" Vali shifted his attack to Freya, a reprieve Vidar probably appreciated though Colbey did not.

Freya leaned forward, not shying away in the least. "Meaning if you or anyone else has any thought of interfering, speak now."

"There's no need for threats," Vidar asserted calmly. "We all understand there's no such thing as a 'small' act of gods on Midgard. Anyone may talk to Colbey or question his actions, but no one will intrude. No one." His last words took the burden off Vali. "Not even me."

A hush followed, as Vidar's command settled over the gathered gods. Colbey read discomfort and dissatisfaction in the silence, even a hint of fear. No one would directly challenge his actions, at least not until the stakes became intolerably high. Unfortunately, he realized, that might happen soon.

Balder's musical tone seemed a welcome relief from the tension. "What disturbs me is that we seem to have lost control. When did the forces of the universe become more significant than gods?"

When no one else deigned to answer, Colbey did. Not being a god gave him a vantage none of the others seemed able to fully comprehend. "That's always been the case."

Every face whipped toward Colbey, and a sea of cold eyes pinned him. Hostility flared, the fires of resentment burning through all other emotions.

Colbey explained, "The primordial chaos existed even before the gods. Odin banished the chaos, leaving a world wholly lawful. For good and evil, he struck a balance, assigning Wizards to guard it. But even Odin's powers could not contain chaos indefinitely. Gradually, he released small amounts to mankind, like a spout on a teapot. Ultimately, he knew, law and chaos needed to strike a balance, too, but he waited until he found guardians capable of properly championing them."

"You," Modi inserted.

"And the Eastern Wizard. Right," Colbey confirmed. "But even Odin can misjudge, and it soon became clear that the system of Wizardry he created could not handle law and chaos as it had good and evil. So he destroyed his creation and placed one being in charge of the Balance."

"You again," Modi said.

"Right. My point being that even the oldest and most powerful of the gods could not fully contain even one of the universe's forces forever."

"And you think you can contain all of them?" Vali laced his fingers through his beard. "Does your gall know no limits?"

"Gods, no!" Colbey immediately cursed the unintentional blasphemy. Even after three centuries, he still lapsed into mortal patterns of speech. "I know nothing of magic. I can scarcely contain my adolescent son, never mind an entire force. But I'm not trying to contain them, just restore the natural balance. I am capable of that." Colbey allowed no doubt to tinge the statement. "And Odin believed so, too."

"Which brings us full circle." Vidar reclaimed the floor. "So if there are no further questions . . ." He paused long enough to allow anyone to raise additional concerns. ". . . this meeting is adjourned."

Gods and goddesses rose, filing from the Great Hall. Some remained behind, presumably to discuss the events of the last few moments or the future that did or did not await them depending on Colbey's success. The enormity of the task awed even Colbey, and he harbored no wish to remain trapped in a room with deities assessing his abilities. Even if they kept their discussions to a whisper, the height of their thoughts and emotions would surely drag the gist to the mental gift that often seemed more like a curse. Leaving Freya behind, he funneled out the teak door with those who chose to leave. He sensed Ravn's presence directly at his back. The boy definitely needed to work on his timing.

The sunlight seemed dim after the vast array of lanterns in the hall that sparked a web of rays from metallic walls. Colbey found the change a welcome relief. His doubts did not stem from his ability to correct the Balance. If the task was possible, he would see it done. If not, it would prove an honest failure. He had lived a full and honorable life that could satisfactorily have ended in his thirties.

Colbey waited only until those who left the hall fully disbanded before turning to confront his son. Keen blue eyes studied him from beneath a tangled fringe of bangs just a bit too long for his warrior senses. Freya's straight nose and high cheekbones settled comfortably over a thin-lipped mouth so like his own. At sixteen, Ravn had already surpassed his father's height, not surprising given that most of the gods towered over them both by half again. Though the boy stood firm, nervousness still hovered around him like a mantle.

Colbey had no difficulty guessing its source. "You interfered, didn't you?"

Ravn heaved a deep sigh. "Sometimes I wish I had a normal father. One like Griff's."

"You mean dead?"

"I meant his stepfather. One who doesn't read my mind."

Colbey frowned. "I don't read your mind. You know I set strict rules about that. I don't invade the thoughts of anyone I respect, though I can't help what you send me. You're feeling guilty about something."

"You respect me?"

Colbey refused to be sidetracked. "Sometimes. Whether I do right now depends on why you're anxious."

"I interfered," Ravn admitted. "Does that mean the whole world will crumble?" His straightforward tone denied the possibility. His concern did not stem from this eventuality, more likely from his father's potential reaction.

Colbey folded his arms, brows arched. "Maybe," he replied calmly, lacking the knowledge to reassure. "What did you do?" He reserved his judgment, and anger, for the facts.

Ravn avoided his father's gaze, shuffling a foot through the thick carpet of grass. "Griff was worried about his mother." Ravn fell into a long pause that seemed unnecessary.

Though Colbey felt no conversational need, he filled in the opening to encourage Ravn to continue. "Understandable."

"So I promised to give her some reassurance."

Another pause into which Colbey inserted an impatient, "Go on."

"So I did." Ravn did not look up.

Colbey studied his son. He let the silence hang. Ravn's discomfort grew in increments, then burst suddenly to full alarm as his mind turned to concern over his father's lack of response. Finally, he met the icy blue-gray eyes.

Colbey doubted such action would affect the Balance, though it depended on Ravn's methods. The boy's devotion to Béarn's rightful king had grown dangerous, and Colbey only hoped his lessons on how to interfere had finally taken root. Ravn had paid dearly for defending Griff in the past. "You chose a vow to a friend over one to your father?"

"I'm sorry. I know I should have asked your permission first."

"I would have forbidden it."

"I know. I guess I figured if I didn't ask, I wasn't really disobeying."

"Ah. Adolescent logic."

Ravn did not dare to defend his action, only his methods on Midgard. "I was subtle. Like you taught."

"What did you do?"

"She made a prayer bargain, you know the way people do: 'If Griff is alive, give me a sign.' She was standing under a tree, so I had the branches kind of close around her a bit. Gentle, like a hug. And I whispered that Griff was all right with the breeze." Ravn's apprehension lessened, replaced by a quavering hope. A trickle of pride wound through him.

Colbey would have liked to boost his son's self-esteem, but the situation did not allow it. "I don't think your actions will harm the Balance this time; but you still have a lot to learn about subtlety." His hands dropped to his hilts. "Your lesson begins now."

Knowing better than to argue, Ravn braced himself for a spar that would leave him bruised, aching, and leagues past exhaustion.

CHAPTER 8

Death on the Roads

Distraction is not a substitute for learning to deal with reality.

—Colbey Calistinsson

Salt-crazed and achingly dry, Tae Kahn remembered nothing of his beaching. His senses returned as he lay with his face in a puddle, slurping what seemed like buckets of water, like an animal. Finally sated, he rose to his haunches, turning eyes and ears to his surroundings. Mountains filled both horizons, steep jagged monsters with rare vegetation twisting from their crags. His tiny valley pooled enough moisture to support a stiff undergrowth, a handful of trees, and a vine that crept snakelike along the branches.

Another wave of thirst seized Tae like a convulsion. Dipping his mouth back into the water, he sucked greedily, this time noticing the bracken and mud that accompanied it. The dull suffering of his kidneys spread into a net of pain along his back. His stomach felt bloated with liquid that only temporarily appeased his hunger. Soon, he hoped, the water would diffuse into the proper places in his body. Thirst would return to its normal baseline, his skin would no longer feel doughy, and his tongue would quit sticking to the sides of his mouth. Until then, his natural wariness remained hopelessly blunted, and he had little choice but to remain in place and hope no man or animal came upon him.

Gradually, Tae's discomfort waned, as did his irresistible craving for water. He clambered to his hands and knees, his snarled mass of black hair falling, as a single clump, into eyes nearly as dark. He flung the whole back, wishing he still had his knife to shear the mess to stubble. He envied Kevral's short locks for a moment before his thoughts turned to her welfare and dread dropped him back to his stomach. Tears stung his eyes, abnormally salty; for once, he did not fight them. He had learned never to show weakness of any kind because it invited predators, even goaded them to a frenzy. Now, he ignored the lesson years on the street had ingrained. His sorrow overwhelmed even instinct.

Reuniting with his companions, including the woman he loved, required Tae to head toward Béarn. He had traveled to and from there only once before, hidden in Western woodlands for which his city upbringing had ill-prepared him. Hunted by enemies of his father, he had learned swiftly, his best strategy to parallel roads and head as far from the Eastlands' border as possible. At least, the forests had supplied ample vegetation, moisture, and wildlife. Now his survival instinct drove him north from the rocky, barren terrain toward the wooded and more populous portions of the Westlands. These posed more danger, but at least he would not want for food or water nor could he trap himself against impassable crags. Ultimately, though he would cover more ground, he would reach Béarn far sooner.

For two nights, Tae traveled through the Western woodlands around the city of Almische, while voices wafted to him from the roadways. Occasionally, brush rustled and snapped near him; twice he caught sight of weaponed Easterners patrolling the routes. By day, he huddled in thick copses, sleep stolen by the jab of branches and thistles, or he huddled on the ground and hoped his still quietness would become lost in the normal stripes, patches, and movement of the forest.

Tae reached the Road of Kings during his third night. Moonlight revealed hulking forms that he at first mistook for larger clusters of enemies. Then his senses registered the unnatural stillness of many of the figures, and he recalled the many statues that graced the ancient route. Those stood in tribute to King Sterrane the Bear and the Western Wizard who spirited him from the castle as a child during his uncle's bloody coup and returned him to his throne as an adult. The statues' purpose mattered little to Tae. He noticed only that his days had become more restless. Dodging the Easterners who prowled the Western roadways had grown familiar while he traveled with his companions. Now, the enemies seemed to have trebled, their scouts spiraling deeper into the woodlands. The previous night, the feeling of someone watching had prickled through him twice, requiring a change of sleeping space. Exhaustion still weighted him from his battle against demon and ocean. Dehydration had weakened him; he found slim opportunity for gathering food. The need to remain hyperalert granted him little rest.

As dawn painted the eastern horizon in shades of pink, Tae scavenged desperately for a hidden place to camp. Fatigue crushed thought into a hopelessly dense fog. His muscles ached, and his slender body seemed to have doubled in weight. As if to mock him, the forest grew more open, providing scant cover. The sun rose higher, splashing oranges, yellows, and greens across a background of rose and dark sapphire. Need turned his search for a sanctuary to any spot not glaringly open. The shade of thickly-leafed oaks and the acid of their nuts kept them widely spaced and devoid of undergrowth. Tae's vision blurred, and his lids drooped shut against his will, further hampering the search. At length, he found a clearing hemmed by squatty, bushlike *jufinar* trees. He wiggled between two, then sprawled to the berry-speckled ground to catch his breath before securing camp. He fell asleep an instant later.

Tae Kahn awakened to the sharp snap of a breaking branch. He leaped to his feet, and dizziness washed his senses to a weaving spiral of dots. Consciousness wavered. He backstepped without intent, the instinctive movement all that rescued his balance. For a moment, his senses retreated behind a roaring, black wall. Desperately, he fought for control and regained it, only to find himself facing a semicircle of seven Easterners brandishing weapons.

Icy terror gripped Tae's chest. He whirled and ran in a single, fluid motion. Within two steps, the *jufinars* loomed in front of him. He dove without wasting time to judge the best path. Branches clawed his face and neck. Like an animal, he wriggled through, tasting blood. Fire seemed to score his flesh, and a limb snagged his hair. His own momentum jerked his head backward so hard a flash of white light slammed his vision, and agony lanced through his neck. Hands closed around his ankles. His feet went numb. His grip winched closed around the largest objects he could find, a trunk and a branch of *jufinar*. The strangers hauled him backward, sticks jabbing rents through already tattered clothing.

Tae stifled a cry of pain. *Show no weakness*. Sweat stung his eyes, and he threw all concentration into his holds. If he let go, he died. He wet his pants, and the self-directed rage that followed his loss of control fueled a second wind. Abruptly, he kicked, freeing one leg, and surged forward simultaneously. He tore his other ankle free. *Free!* Tae sprang for the opening. Branches parted around him. Then agony flashed through his scalp, and the limb entwining his hair jerked him backward. For an instant, pain incapacitated him. The hands closed around him again, pinching and bruising his flesh. A string of the foulest words in the Eastern language assaulted his ears, all directed at him.

Effort and pain brought tears to Tae's eyes. Panic assailed him, and he lost all ability to fight it. He exploded into a reckless flurry of attack: kicking and punching, twisting and clawing in undirected fury. The Easterners dragged him into the clearing, repeatedly flinching into retreat then rushing back in to work around his crazed defense. One by one, they pinned each limb until he lay spread-eagled on the ground.

Rationality returned to Tae in a rush, and he went suddenly still. His eyes flitted from enemy to enemy, registering nothing. Closing his lids, he forced slow, deep breaths and inner calm. Panic had shattered composure into a mindless frenzy that had accomplished nothing more than tiring him further and enraging men who held his fate in their hands. Carefully, he opened his eyes and took in the situation.

All of the Easterners sported black hair, and eyes that ranged from deep brown to dark hazel. Two were clean-shaven while the others wore beards without mustaches. Swarthy skin and coarse features completed the picture. Five riveted him to the ground. Blood ebbed from one's nose, thickened with snot, and his eyes held a glaze of homicidal fury. Apparently, at least one of Tae's crazed blows had landed.

The injured man seized Tae's tunic in a filthy, callused hand and tore off a jagged patch of cloth. He swiped it across his nose, stared at the smear of blood, then hurled it back onto Tae's chest. "You're dead."

Tae's gang training finally blundered through surprise and exhaustion. He stared back dispassionately, saying nothing. The longer the other raved, the more likely his companions would grow careless and Tae would find the opening he needed to escape.

The other man who wasn't holding Tae down reached for his hilt. A sword rattled free, blade notched and steel gleaming dully in the sunlight.

New blood trickled from his companion's nose, and the injured one raised a hand. Though he addressed the man with the sword, his gaze never left Tae's. Tae read nothing human in the dark orbs, just a predatory hunger only his own death would satisfy. "Please, Usyris, I want this one."

The eyes of the holders shifted to Usyris, clearly the leader. His lips pursed in a tight line. Sheathing his weapon, he nodded and stepped back. "Don't take too long."

Disappointment flickered briefly through the injured man's eyes, but his grin revealed only sadistic pleasure. From peripheral vision, Tae noticed that the man at his right wrist looked away. The one at his head flinched, and the one at his left leg lowered his face as if in prayer. Clearly, their companion's cruel joy bothered them, and Tae wondered if he could exploit their discomfort, if not their mercy. Cautiously, he tested the hold on his right hand only to find it steady.

Still fixated on Tae's eyes, the man drew a long knife from his belt sheath. Dried blood etched irregularities in the blade.

Tae's attention flicked from man to blade and back to man. *Show no fear.* The words started to lose meaning. Memory pressed in on him, though he struggled valiantly to stifle it. He could still feel the punch of blades through his chest and abdomen, the tear of flesh and the suck of steel withdrawing audible even beneath his screams. The blood in his throat had choked him, and its sickly odor filled his nostrils once again. The more he fought, the faster the stabs had come. Unconsciousness had claimed him willingly, blanketing the pain, the terror, the unfulfilled need to rescue his mother from a similar fate. At ten, Tae had not understood the outrage that accompanied the agony of his mother's screams. Now he knew they had raped as well as killed her.

Don't strain. Don't scream. Don't give him the satisfaction. Save energy for any openings they give for escape. Though sound, the advice defied reality. Tae felt his control slipping again as the knife filled his vision and remembrance lugged him back to his childhood.

The blade traced a cold line along Tae's cheek. The man's dead eyes betrayed no hint of compassion. To men like this, mercy was a weakness. "Perhaps I'll start with your eyes." The tip of the knife pricked Tae's lower lid. "You won't be needing them any more."

Don't blink. Tae kept his expression stony, testing the holds on his limbs and head with minuscule movements. Not one granted him quarter.

"Nacoma," Usyris reprimanded softly.

A slight smile twitched onto Nacoma's features, but he did grant his leader a promise in the form of a threat against Tae. "Given more time, I'd make this as slow and painful as possi-

ble. You should thank my commander for his kindness." The
grin widened into a rictus. "I'll have to make do with only
painful." The knife jerked suddenly downward.

As Tae recognized the target, he could not stop a convulsive
heave. The abrupt movement strained every contact point, and
ten sets of fingers gouged his flesh. Pain shot through his head,
and it felt as if his ear had become detached. Then the blade tore
a line above his loins, and all other pain lost meaning. Cold air
washed over his flesh, pleasant contrast to the heat of his fear.
His brain naturally assessed the injury: superficial, designed to
cut clothes and frighten him, not to maim. The smooth stroke
had sliced open tunic and breeks, fully exposing him to his murderer.

Tae recognized the technique as a panic-inspiring gesture.
The knife would pierce vital organs as easily naked or clothed,
but Nacoma had found one more way to embarrass his victim
and prolong his agony.

Usyris drew breath, presumably to hurry as well as discipline
Nacoma.

The knife, and Nacoma's fingers, found the depression between Tae's left second and third ribs. Steel carved through
flesh to muscle with an unbearably familiar ache. One hard
shove would drive the blade through his heart and end his suffering. Thrown back to childhood tragedy, he closed his eyes
and embraced oblivion.

"Wait! What's that?"

The knife froze in position, and Tae whipped his eyes open.
The man at Tae's left leg pointed frantically at him. Every eye
studied his exposed chest and abdomen. He could only assume
their interest stemmed from the sixteen scars.

Nacoma's blade withdrew, and the fire left his eyes. His
death mask grin became a jagged line of uncertainty. "You
don't think. . . ."

Usyris waved the killer silent, and his hazel eyes found Tae's
for the first time. "What's your name, boy?"

Tae swallowed. Blood trickled down chest and thigh in
warm, sticky rivulets. He cursed the fatigue and fear that fogged
his mind, wishing he knew the best answer. Likely, they knew
who he was. They had already made it clear they would kill a
stranger. Identifying himself as a known enemy might spare
him. Perhaps some rival crime lord had instructed them to bring
him back alive, either as ransom or to torture him for information. Neither of those options sounded appealing to Tae, but at

least they might gain him time. "Tae Kahn, Weile Kahn's son." His voice emerged as a thin croak, and he despised the weakness. He recited his full name. In the East, shortening names was deliberate insult, relegation to the status of an inferior.

Tae tried to read the silence that followed, without success.

"Let him go," Usyris finally instructed.

Tae waited only until the grips had eased slightly before twisting free and sprinting for the clearing's edge.

"Tae Kahn! Wait! We won't hurt you." Usyris' voice chased Tae to the *jufinar*. He sounded impossibly sincere.

Tae struggled between the stubby trees, this time thrashing his way to the opposite side. Movement widened his wounds, and blood spilled between his ribs in a steady stream. The loss, though minor, sapped the last of his reserves. He staggered a single step farther, then dropped in exhaustion.

Usyris said something to his men, too soft for Tae's hearing, then headed alone through the brush. He selected a path behind them, where some gaps remained between the *jufinar*. Deliberately drawing his sword, he made a grand gesture of tossing it over the trees and into the clearing. Hands empty, palms exposed, he approached Tae. "I'm sorry we hurt you. I swear we didn't know who you were."

Tae clamped a hand to the larger of his wounds, trying to staunch the bleeding with his fingers. He had nothing better to use; his clothes lay in the clearing. He back-stepped, the movement causing dark, intermittent breaks in his consciousness.

Usyris stopped. All the sympathy Tae could not find in Nacoma's eyes softened Usyris' expression now. "Your father will be happy to see you."

My father? Tae tried to concentrate on the thought while his awareness flickered like a failing candle. He studied the Easterners in this new light. He had become so accustomed to eluding Weile's enemies, it never occurred to him that those who attacked him might be his father's own men. Rarely, Weile had performed his business in Tae's presence. Now he thought he recognized the man who had pinned his right hand as one of the shadowed hoodlums who visited his father. Tae attempted to rise. The movement proved his undoing. His wits and senses gave out, and he collapsed into oblivion.

Tae awakened to a memory blank that bothered him as much as the realization that he was not alone. He remained still, eyes closed and breathing regulated, refusing to reveal his awakening until he recalled the others as friends or foes. Remembrance hovered, frustratingly beyond reach. Cautiously, he opened one eye to a slit, hoping vision would spark the proper pathways. A man sat far enough away to assure Tae that he was not a prisoner yet near enough to remain a threat. A sword rested across his knees.

Tae focused on the weapon, then on the man. Black hair hung around the profile of a clean-shaven, dark face. *Easterner equals enemy.* Tae launched himself for the other. He dove, catching the sword, then rolled to a crouch.

"Tae Kahn." Startled, the man rose quickly and retreated beyond sword range. "Easy, Tae Kahn." He held out his hands in a gesture of peace.

Nausea churned through Tae's gut, and memory slammed him in a wild rush. He remembered now he faced Usyris, a leader of his father's entourage who had six men at his command, including an uninhibited assassin named Nacoma. Tae lowered the sword.

"How are you feeling?" Usyris smiled nervously, still attentive to the weapon in Tae's hand and the swiftness with which he had claimed it.

"Fine," Tae lied, unwilling to reveal weakness. *A lot better before I did that.* He remained still while vertigo and pain receded. An unfamiliar tunic dangled nearly to his knees, and a loose pair of britches covered his legs. Though eighteen, he had not yet completed his adolescent development, and his beard still grew sparsely and slowly enough to allow shaving on an irregular basis. Every man in Usyris' entourage was broader, older, and taller than Tae.

"Again, I'd like to apologize for the way we treated you."

Tae was not in a forgiving mood. The wound ached, deep but too narrow to hinder respiration. Scant fingers' breadths further, it would have impaled his heart. Aborted, it would prove little more than an irritation and a seventeeth scar. The scratch on his lower abdomen, though superficial, reminded him vividly of Nacoma's intent to torture. "I know. You didn't know who I was." Tae rose to a normal posture but did not relinquish the sword. Instead, he glanced around the woodlands. Two men, one Nacoma, worked among the oaks. Tae saw no sign of the other four.

Usyris nodded confirmation.

"Presumably, you have some purpose for waylaying strangers and torturing them to death?"

"Killing them," Usyris corrected. "Or, more often, chasing them back the way they came." His brows rose, indicating an inability to answer, though he did not condone the behavior. "You'll have to ask Nacoma about the torture."

Tae took a deep breath, then wished he hadn't. Pain spread from the hole in his chest. "I'd rather not."

Usyris shrugged. "Suit yourself. I'm sure you'll find other things to talk about while he's escorting you to your father."

The pain became internal. "Excuse me?"

"I said I'm sure . . ."

The repetition flowed past Tae, unheard. "And by 'escorting,' you mean . . . ?"

Usyris smiled indulgently. "I mean escorting. You're not a prisoner, if that's what's worrying you."

"So I'm free to leave."

"Of course."

Tae considered briefly. "I don't need an escort."

"Maybe not, if you think you can survive eight hundred more traps." Usyris clearly exaggerated, though he made a good point. "They may kill you before you can tell them who you are, but they won't attack you if you're with Nacoma."

"What if I'm with you?"

"I can't leave my command." Usyris headed off the next obvious question. "Weile Kahn isn't exactly easy to find. You'll need someone to take you to the people trained to reach him. Nacoma's the only one we can spare." Usyris turned Tae a sympathetic look. "I'd hate him, too, in your position, but he's really not that bad. Before we got assigned to this project, he'd never killed anyone. He's just got a bad temper and a cruel streak. He's not going to hurt you now that he knows you're on our side."

Am I? Tae kept his doubts to himself and mulled his options. He had no interest in seeing his father; but his first thought, to refuse Nacoma and continue toward Béarn alone, broke down in the face of logic. Even if he managed to arrange safe passage for himself, every other innocent who traveled Westland roads would have to fight his father's men, including any of his companions who had survived the *Sea Seraph*'s destruction. He had little choice but to meet with Weile Kahn, discover why his father was involved in such an evil undertaking, and convince him to recall his men. Tae doubted he could accomplish such a thing, yet he had to try. Otherwise, he condemned all the Westland peoples, and ultimately the world, to their deaths.

Is it possible the future of humanity rests in the hands of Tae Kahn, Weile Kahn's son? Tae barely held back a laugh. *The world is in deep trouble.*

Swiftly, Usyris prepared a pack of supplies, discussing Tae's preferences over his shoulder as he worked. "All right. You've got the food, water, clothing, blanket, cleaning rag, utility blade, and fresh bandages." He laced the leather shut, then turned. "We'll get you a horse from the captured ones. Probably be lighter-colored than you'd want, but that's not necessarily bad under the circumstances. You want our men to see you."

Tae nodded, resigned. When it came to stealth, traveling on foot served him better, but speed seemed far more important now. "Thank you."

"Want some weapons?"

"Certainly." Tae grabbed at an offer he had not anticipated. "A sword would be great. And a couple of knives, if you've got them to spare."

Usyris smiled. "We've gained ourselves quite a few spares." He made a gesture indicating that Tae should stay in place, hefted the pack, then headed deeper into the woods.

Finally alone, Tae sat on a deadfall and tried not to think about his situation. The wound in his chest throbbed in time with his heartbeat, while the other bothered him only when he moved too quickly. Thinking about the pain only worsened it, and his mind slipped back naturally to his dilemma. He had never expected, nor wanted, to see his father again. The idea raised an ire stronger than that he felt against Nacoma. The first stirrings of hatred trickled through him, hot and ugly. At least, he could leave Nacoma once he no longer required an escort. Weile Kahn would never leave him. The elder's advice, his mannerisms, his dealings with people haunted Tae like a shadow, unshakable. Visually, they did not closely resemble one another. Like nearly all Easterners, they both had blue-black hair and irises scarcely differentiable from the pupils. Tae sported his mother's straight hair instead of his father's curls, and he had not yet attained Weile's size. Nevertheless, Tae saw vestiges of the father he loved and despised whenever he looked in a mirror. Though vague, the similarities were still apparent: the shape of his face, the set of his eyes, and the narrow nose.

Tae had much to tell his father, none of it kind, but the need to reestablish travel in the West would have to temper the words

he used. Tae cursed the urgency that tied his hands. Part of him
wished to avoid Weile forever, to punish his father with desperate wondering about the fate of his only child. A deeper, meaner
part reveled in the chance to confront the old man who had
brought agony and death to his mother and turned his life into a
constant, desperate struggle.

Tae had expected Usyris to bring the last of his supplies, but
Nacoma guided a brown mare and a dappled gray gelding
through the foliage. The pack lay secured behind a simple, battered saddle, a sword and belt sheath thrust through the bindings. The bridle looked as if it might fray into oblivion if he
tugged too hard, but Tae did not begrudge the gift. It was more
than he had expected.

Tae approached the massive murderer, his steps uncon-
sciously slowing as he drew nearer. His hands shook, and he
cursed his loss of composure. He kept them low, refusing Nacoma the satisfaction.

But if Nacoma noticed Tae's discomfort, he made no sign.
The ruthless fire that had seemed so much a part of his eyes the
previous day had disappeared, leaving unexpected compassion
in its place. He released the gelding as Tae approached, politely
moving his mare so that it did not interfere with Tae's inspection.

Tae examined horse and equipment, holding Nacoma always
in his peripheral vision. First, he jerked the sword free, fastening it to the too-large belt sagging at his waist. The arming fueled his boldness tenfold. A closer look at the tack showed a
reasonable attempt at repair. Though homely and simple, it
would not break as easily as his initial glance suggested.

Nacoma approached before Tae mounted.

Tae's heart seemed to spring into his throat, pounding madly.
He hid his anxiety behind a stony, expressionless mask.

Nacoma clasped his hands, a sure sign of nervousness and
one Tae had not expected. "These are yours, too." He thrust a
beefy hand in his pocket, emerging with an unmatched pair of
knives in sheaths. He held them awkwardly in the middle.
Though he offered similar instruments to those of his torture,
his manner and presentation did not spook Tae, who took them
without a word of thanks. Arranging one on the belt near the
sword, he flipped the other into ready position as he considered
the best hiding place for it.

"Cut me," Nacoma said, his voice still deep but without the
booming menace and deadly edge it had once held.

The words seemed nonsensical. "What?" Tae returned.

"Cut me," Nacoma repeated. "With the knife." He indicated his torso with rapid movements of the fingers of both hands. "Anywhere you want to."

The idea enticed. The image of plunging the blade deep into Nacoma's breast filled Tae's mind's eye, and the satisfaction that would accompany the wrench of steel tearing his enemy's flesh seemed euphoric. *Don't tempt me, you bastard.*

"I'm sorry what I done to you. I'm real sorry." The sincerity in Nacoma's tone could not be feigned. "We'll both feel better if you cut me."

The invitation pleased Tae, yet something stayed his hand. Nacoma's invitation seemed madness. Weile always forgave accident, and Tae doubted his father would hold any grudge against Nacoma for actions taken before he knew Tae's identity. In fact, Weile might see the incident as one more trial that strengthened his son. "Trust me. *You* won't feel better."

"Yes, I will." Nacoma spoke like a man who knew from experience. "My mama teached me that. She was nice most times, but she had a temper, too. After she'd whaled on me for something and she'd calmed, she'd make me hit her back once't. Then we could go on like nothing'd happened. Works for me, too. I've tried it."

Tae said nothing, the explanation ludicrous. He recalled a description his father had once given of the men with whom he worked on a daily basis: *There are important distinctions between men who sin from necessity, from loss of control, and for the pure joy of it. Have faith in the former; they are good men in bad situations. Avoid the latter, they can be used but never trusted. They have no conscience and will do and say anything that harms others and benefits themselves. With finesse, the middle group can become your most loyal, and a leader who steers them well can help them and, ultimately, himself. Over time, you can teach them self-control. The key is to choose your punishment wisely. Herein lies a secret I have learned.* Weile had leaned in close, his whisper conspiratorial. *Punishment absolves them of guilt. Instead, subject them to the horror of their own regret. Strange as it seems, it's a torture stronger than any you could inflict.*

At the time, Weile's narrative had meant nothing to Tae, though he had remembered the words because of their significance to a father he had emulated as a young and stupid child. The current circumstance colored his understanding. If Weile spoke truth, and Tae reluctantly trusted his father's judgment when it came to evaluating criminals, Nacoma would suffer more if Tae refused to return injury for injury. His heart still screamed for retribution, yet his rational mind dismissed the possibility. Even if Weile assessed men like Nacoma wrong, even if vengeance eased Tae's animosity, Tae doubted Nacoma's temper would allow for the penalty he had demanded. Tae might well find himself battling Nacoma for his life again.

Tae stuffed the knife in his boot and seized the upsweep of the gray's saddle. "Let's go." He swung into the seat.

Nacoma lowered his head, standing several moments in contemplation. He cast one last longing look at the knife in Tae's belt, shrugged, and headed for his mare. A moment later, he clambered aboard. The ease of the dismissal and mounting convinced Tae his father's advice had steered him wrong. His hand tingled, and he could feel the impression of a hilt against it. Just the fantasy of dealing Nacoma back his own appeased some of Tae's rage, and he realized he probably could not have dealt the blow. Whatever his faults, Weile had not been or raised a killer. Though Tae had struck down enemies without remorse, he had done so only in self-defense. He could no longer consider Nacoma a threat.

Nacoma glanced back at Tae. "Ready?" Disappointment tinged his tone, and the dullness of his eyes made Tae reconsider. Perhaps his father had understood men like Nacoma.

"Ready." Tae kicked his horse into a walk, prepared to go wherever Nacoma led him. Without the regretful assassin, he would never find his father.

The ride through open roads and fields brought a joy Tae scarcely realized he had missed. Early on, Easterners stopped them frequently, and Tae occasionally recognized fringe members of his father's entourage. Soon, word of his presence preceded them, and Nacoma's conversations became shorter and more directed. Tae grew accustomed to the wary prickle that came of eyes studying him from the sidelines. Most of his father's men had never met him, and their curiosity seemed only natural. Even the rain that pelted them on the second day seemed a blessing after the constant need for stealth and battle. They traveled northward, toward the great trading city of Pudar, yet they stopped on the second evening a few hours shy and west of its gates. This time, Nacoma brought Tae to a farm cottage lost amid the fields and forest. He tapped a halting pattern on the door.

A few moments passed in silence. Then, the door creaked, and a woman's face poked through the crack. She passed a few words with Nacoma, then flung the panel fully open. Nacoma gestured to Tae to dismount and followed the woman inside. Tae ground-tied the gelding and trailed the others to a spartan common room, strangely devoid of windows, and containing a rectangular table with four chairs as well as a shelf stuffed with crockery.

"Sit," the woman said. Her dark hair lay piled on her head, and a homespun dress fell to her ankles. He found her nationality impossible to guess. Though darker than most Pudarians, she could pass for a small Béarnide, an Easterner, or a mixed breed Westerner baked from the sun. "Kinya will be with you shortly."

Tae sat, recognizing the name. A jowly, friendly-featured man, Kinya was an old and trusted member of Weile's organization. They had met on several occasions, and Tae guessed the other man would serve not only to lead him to his father but also to definitively identify him.

The woman disappeared through a doorway. Shortly, Kinya entered. His well-tended locks lay flat, closely-cropped to his head. His bald spot had expanded, and a few silver hairs sparkled amid the black. Otherwise, he looked no different than when Tae had last seen him. Another man, an enormous stranger, stood in the doorway with arms folded. Kinya looked Tae over, grinned a welcome, then nodded to the other man, confirming Tae's suspicions.

"Hello, Kinya," Tae greeted.

"Hello, Tae Kahn." Kinya took the chair to Tae's right while Nacoma remained standing. "What have you been doing?"

"This and that," Tae replied vaguely. "Mostly avoiding trouble, until I ran into this . . ." He paused just long enough for Kinya and Nacoma to fill in derogatory terms. ". . . gentleman."

Kinya's dark eyes flicked briefly to Nacoma, then returned to Tae. "How's your brother?"

A test? "Unless a half brother has come along in the last few years, I don't have one."

Kinya looked slightly abashed. "My mistake. Your father talked about naming a child after a close childhood friend who died. I can't recall the name."

Another test. What's wrong, Kinya? Paranoia or blindness. "Curdeis."

"Right. That's it." Kinya's smile widened. "I guess it was just talk." He gave the thug in the doorway a more definitive nod, then turned his attention to Tae's escort. "Nacoma, return to sparrow hawk sector. I'll take care of Tae Kahn from here."

Nacoma turned Tae an oddly motherly expression. "Goodbye, Tae Kahn. And I really am sorry."

"I know," Tae returned, unable to forgive yet. "See you around, maybe."

"Yeah, see you around." Nacoma spun on a heel and strode through the door. He gave Tae one last, plaintive look, one last chance to speak forgiveness.

Tae said nothing, leaving Nacoma to the mercy of his conscience.

The door slapped closed behind him.

Kinya continued to smile at Tae. "Sorry about the necessary formality."

Tae shrugged, neither excusing nor condemning.

"It's been a long time."

That's what happens when your father tosses you away. Tae rose. "Yeah. Not as long as it was supposed to be." Though he suppressed the thought, he could not keep sarcasm from tainting his tone.

"You may not believe it, but I haven't seen your father this excited for a long time. Maybe ever."

Tae refused to comment. "Let's get this over with."

"Tae Kahn!" Kinya's clenched fists were so tight, his fingertips blanched. He studied the boy in the sparse light leaking in from the farther room. He bore the expression of a father pushed to the boundary by a toddler's tantrum.

Tae turned Kinya a fierce look of defiance.

"Never mind." Kinya shook his head. "Let's go." Whirling, he pushed past the massive figure in the doorway, whisked through a pantry, then headed out the back exit into the last moments of twilight.

Kinya led Tae on a winding course that took them alternately through forest, meadow, and pasture. They walked in silence at a pace that taxed Tae's shorter stride. Pride did not allow him to fall behind or to request a slower gait. The nearer they drew to his father, the stronger irritability and outrage grew. The safety of friends and Westlands seemed to lose significance to the relationship that could and should have flourished but had collapsed into hatred. Desperately, Tae scrambled to dampen his emotions, to play the necessary game with his father that would restore Westland travel. Yet the rage proved more tenacious.

Clouds masked the sunset, and only the world's plunge into darkness marked the day's passing. Kinya's circuitous route lost Tae all sense of direction. He felt certain they looped and doubled back, probably covering half or less of the straight distance they would have gained with the same amount of time and effort. Repeatedly, Kinya paused, head tipped to catch sounds through the blackness. Apparently satisfied, they moved ever forward.

Finally, when it seemed they could have reached Pudar and returned twice, Kinya stopped. He paused again, eyes restless, head swiveling. Tae scanned the darkness, seeing nothing but the bowing of weeds and branches in the wind. He heard their rustling and the rising and falling cadence of night insects. A rare whirring bark broke the stillness, answered by distant foxes. Finally, Kinya knelt, pressed a shoulder to a boulder, and rolled it aside. Brushing aside moss and dirt, he revealed a filthy board otherwise lost beneath the overgrowth. He rapped a fist on the wood in patterns: one-pause-three-pause-two-pause-one. A muffled answer returned from the opposite side, a single tap. Kinya moved the board aside and ushered Tae ahead.

The procedure did not faze Tae; he had become accustomed to his father's secret haunts. Lantern light funneled upward from below, barely revealing a stairway. Tae scurried down, testing each tread in an instant and leaving Kinya far behind. The momentary reprieve released little of the emotions pent-up nearly to a boil. At the bottom of the staircase, the tunnel opened into a room. Its natural coolness chilled him through clothing still damp from rain. Shelves lined the irregular walls, filled with books, journals, and bric-a-brac. Weile Kahn relaxed in a wooden chair softened with pillows. He wore simple linens, tailored for comfort rather than style. A man stood attentively at his side, surely the one who had acknowledged Kinya's code. Two other cushioned chairs completed the decor, and an archway led to another room, presumably sleeping or eating quarters.

The instant Tae entered the room, Weile Kahn sprang from his chair. A smile split the too-familiar features. Soft, brown eyes lit on his son, and he ignored the dark curl that fell into his eyes. He reached for an embrace.

Tae wanted to feel nothing except in control, but conflicting emotions hammered him into motionlessness. He let his father envelop him, but he gave nothing back except a cold stare.

Tae's lack of response cut short his father's exuberant greeting. "Kinya." He inclined his head toward the exit. "Daxan, wake Alsrusett and take him with you. I want to speak with my son alone."

Kinya opened his mouth, presumably to warn Weile Kahn of his son's hostility, but something in his leader's expression stopped him. Turning, he headed back up the stairs. The stranger, apparently Daxan, marched through the archway. After several moments, he returned with a yawning, sleepy-eyed man in tow. These two followed Kinya. The board shifted, admitting moonlight. Shadows partially blocked it, then the board moved back in place. Dirt splattered over the wood, simulating hail, then Tae heard the quiet thump of the boulder returning to its position.

Only then did Weile speak. "I've missed you, son."

"Have you?" Tae made no attempt to hide the sarcasm.

"Of course." Weile back-stepped, restoring Tae's personal space. He waved toward an empty chair. "Terribly."

Tae ignored the invitation, his father's last word remarkably apt. Tae met Weile's gaze directly, with blazing defiance. Anything less would have made him look weak. For several moments, their dark eyes, so much alike, locked.

For once, the father looked away first, turning his entire body for a paced step, then returning for another round. "Why did you come?" The voice lacked its usual authority, quiet with a gentle touch of pain.

Tae refused retreat. "Had I not, your men would have killed me."

Weile's lids separated further, and his chin sank slightly in question. "That's the only reason?"

"Yes," Tae lied emphatically.

The eyes returned to their normal size. "I'm your father, Tae Kahn."

"No." This time, Tae broke the contact as a deep sting warned of welling tears he would not dare display. "You ceased being my father the day you sent me away. It only took me a few months to realize it."

"You can't just decide . . ." Weile's voice boomed at Tae's back, then he dropped the argument as suddenly. It would get him nowhere. "I did it to help, not hurt you."

The ridiculousness of the comment chased away the tears, and Tae spun back to face his father. "Set me into an alien, hostile world with murderers at my heels?"

"Yes." Weile did not bother to correct the suggestion that he had commanded those murderers. They both knew the killers were enemies of Weile's, not Tae's.

"That was supposed to help me?"

"It did."

Now it was Tae's turn to stare in wide-eyed disbelief.

Weile explained. "Look at you. You're a strong, competent young man. You survived by your own wits and wile, and you're not afraid to face anything lesser." He smiled, his admiration genuine. "My enemies couldn't kill you. And my men said you gave them the chase and battle of their lives."

To Tae's mind, they had greatly exaggerated, but he would not voice such self-deprecation. He clung to resentment. "So you would take credit for my hard-won abilities?"

"Absolutely not." Weile returned to his chair, sinking into the cushions. Though he looked relaxed, Tae read balance. Weile could mobilize swiftly, if the need arose. Tae attributed the position to habit rather than any specific concern for his current welfare. "Your effort, your genius, is everything. I created only the need."

"Your *need* almost killed me." Tae turned his back again. "How can you claim to love me and do this? How can you claim to be my father?"

"I am your father."

"Only in name."

"I *am* your father."

Images avalanched down on Tae, accompanied by a feeling he equated only with Weile Kahn: nights when the wind howled, and a callused hand replaced blankets knocked askew in the early night; days when he sat alone with his father discussing frivolous details and learning advice that made little sense to him at the time; the gentle kindness Weile always displayed toward Tae's mother, so unlike the brutality and shouted cruelties most Eastern men inflicted on their wives; the love shining in otherwise hard eyes when Weile looked upon his wife and child. Tae could not stop the sobs that followed, but he could hide them. Finally, he took the proffered chair, burying his face in his palms.

Though Tae's turn to speak, Weile clearly sensed his need to regain control. Without action or comment to indicate he recognized Tae's fragile state, he took the burden of words onto himself. "Fathers make mistakes, and I've made more than my share. There's no instinct for parenting. You can only learn from the skills and follies of your own parents and hope you do better." He sighed deeply. "If you learn nothing from me but how not to treat your children, then you've learned a valuable lesson."

Tae did not trust himself to speak, and the lapse rankled. So often, he had used his father as the negative example for parenting. Yet, he suddenly realized, he had forgotten or trivialized the good. Without Weile Kahn's lessons and examples, he would never have survived so long. Without his father's closeness growing up, he would not have found himself capable of, even craving, the intimate friendships with Kevral, Matrinka, Darris, and, eventually, with Ra-khir. And, had he not followed his father's teachings about finding the best in the worst of men and organizing them into a cohesive unit, he could never have orchestrated the escape from Pudar's prison. King Cymion would have executed Tae in the most painful and bloody manner possible for a crime he had not even committed. In good ways as well as bad, Weile Kahn had taught him much.

Tae heard the hiss of a chair leg moving, then a soft footstep. Weile's meaty hand clasped Tae's shoulder firmly. "Son, I'm sorry."

"Why?" Tae's voice emerged thinly from between his fingers. "Why?" Somehow, they both knew what he meant. He did not question the apology, nor even the method of Weile's fathering. He had to know the reasons his father chose an occupation so fraught with peril, not only to himself, but to those he loved.

"The answers lie in my own childhood, with the skills and follies of my own parents. To this day, I'm not certain which were skills and which follies." The hand disappeared from Tae's shoulder, and Weile's heavy tread thumped against the floorboards as he paced. "I was the oldest of five children."

Even that simple fact caught Tae by surprise. Weile never spoke of his growing up, and Tae had always assumed his father an only child, like himself.

"Born with a deformed arm, my father could not apprentice in any of the standard trades. The army would not have him. His pride came from his family, and he often bragged of his ability to keep all of us clothed and fed. Early on, I did not question how." Weile reached a wall and stopped, not yet bothering to turn. "One day, they arrested my father."

"Theft," Tae supplied, taking advantage of Weile's back to wipe away the tears.

"Right." Weile turned, though his gaze was focused beyond

Tae. "They hacked off his good hand, and with it his will to live. For years, my belief in his return served as my determination." He paced back toward the center of the room. "He never did, of course. He died before his sentence ended."

"I'm sorry," Tae said and meant it. No matter his bitterness, he would not wish such sorrow on anyone.

"Not a day passes that I don't resent the time I didn't have with my father." Weile sighed deeply. "But that's a different story. More importantly, all five children wanted a revenge that my mother denied. Despite everything, she clung to morality, condemning violence. Scarce food turned our family to chaos. Widows never fare well in the East, especially wives of criminals. We lost our mother to violence within . . ." Weile's words caught in his throat, and he finished in a whisper. ". . . two years."

Tae thought it only fair to grant his father the same courtesy he had shown, yet he could not help staring in amazement. He had never seen anything rattle Weile Kahn. He had always believed his father as emotionless as a stone. Yet now Tae saw his father only as a blur. The tears had returned to his own eyes, spurred by memories of his own mother's haunting screams.

Weile quickened his step, striding beyond Tae's chair, then resumed his careful pacing. "The mad scramble for food that followed dissolved family ties. A brother and sister abandoned us to die. Ironically, the three of us who clung together lived, and it was they who died. From that agony, I learned a valuable lesson about loyalty and sharing. For the rest of my life, the streets became my parents and my tutors. Assassins, thieves, lunatics. Desperation and need. Starvation, cold, and disease. Lessons from brutal teachers are learned fast and well. An orphan who pays attention learns more than just survival."

Tae's mind slipped back to his own years on the streets. The knifelike pierce of icy wind through sodden clothes had become firmly entrenched in his mind. Fear flickered through him, tightening every muscle; and he clung to the deadly aura of competence that had bullied him past thugs seeking any excuse to slaughter him. For years, he had not dared to allow that facade to crumble, making it a part of him until it fooled even himself. That life had come to him much later, at his father's insistence, while Weile remained in the haven Tae and his family had once called home. A fresh wave of bitterness churned through him.

Weile whirled again, oblivious to his son's stony glare. "I developed a strange knack for organizing gangs. Children lasted longer on the streets by sharing their skills. We were a family, but, like all families, we reached an age where we grew up and separated. Only then, I lost Curdeis, my best friend." He met Tae's angry gaze. "My brother."

This time, the revelation did not catch Tae so off guard. He nodded stiffly for his father to continue.

Weile continued pacing and obliged. "That night, with Curdeis' blood trickling down my arms, *it* came." He paused, leaving Tae an opening for the obvious question he did not bother to ask, then went on. "I can liken it only to the calling priests claim to receive, whether they follow Sheriva or the Northern pantheon. It was an obsession that seized every scrap of my being, including the deepest portions of my soul. If children could unite, why couldn't adults? The streets need not take another brother. I lost choice in what I would become. Those whom law and propriety had dismissed needed me, and I could not refuse the calling even had I wanted to do so."

"So you became the king of crime." Disgruntlement drove Tae to demean. The story had qualified much he did not understand. Experience had shown him, in vivid detail, that his father did not lead criminals for the money, though it was there. He shared his wealth freely, without hoarding, and his tastes ran toward the simple. The challenge of uplifting the broken, of valuing men and women so despised even they believed themselves worthless, of cultivating loyalty in the lawless was met with an ardor that never faded. Weile had sacrificed his freedom and, ultimately, all he loved for a cause. Whether or not Tae believed in that cause did not diminish Weile's accomplishment or faith.

"In a manner of speaking." Weile took the faint praise in stride. "But I made one enormous mistake." Again, he faced Tae directly. Earnest eyes looked out from beneath a jumble of dark curls, and he gauged Tae's interest in the confession.

Tae nodded once, bland encouragement that did not reveal his deeply burning curiosity.

"I fell in love with a girl in the gang." A slight smile crept across features otherwise foreboding. "She was beautiful and brilliant, kind and soft-spoken. Her wit was immense, but never biting like mine." Weile's eyebrows rose, wrinkling his forehead. "And yours." Realizing the apparent connection, he amended, "Falling in love wasn't the mistake, of course. That was only natural. The wonder is how every other man didn't battle me for her."

Gradually, with a slowness that made him feel stupid, Tae came to the realization that Weile was talking about his mother. Though he had loved her immensely, he could not fathom how his father could call her beautiful. He pictured the deeply-set eyes, the too broad nose, and the almost lipless mouth. Years of scrounging for food had made her frail and stolen the rich, Eastern darkness.

"I didn't know the life I inflicted upon either of you when you were conceived and I married her."

Tae had already performed the arithmetic that proved things had happened in the order Weile just mentioned.

"No one had ever organized criminals before. I anticipated rivalry, but never to the extent that . . . that . . ." Weile could not continue. Instead, he broke down into wild sobbing so uncharacteristic it stunned Tae.

All of the hostility washed away in the flood of his father's tears. For a moment, the urge seized Tae to comfort, but he found himself unable to move. The memories that had tortured his dreams returned: the salt odor of his mother's blood, her anguished shrieks, the rancid stench of their attackers, and the cramping agony of blades tearing through his own flesh. Again, helplessness assailed him, and he alternately hated himself and circumstance for the terror that seemed endless. He had managed no action that spared his mother or himself.

"If I hadn't married her, there'd be an empty hole where my heart used to be. But she would live."

Tae doubted his father's assessment. Most Eastland men showed their women less kindness than cattle while his father had always treated his mother as an equal. "And I would never have been born."

Weile said nothing, trapped into a corner. Pregnancy would have sealed Tae's mother's fate. No good man would have married her.

Tae pressed, "So my existence was your mistake?"

"I don't know, Tae." Weile used the shortened form of his son's name as a familiarity rather than insult. He sat in his chair. "I love you, and your mother did, too. I can't imagine my life without you. But I sometimes wonder if you wouldn't have been better off."

"Not being born?" The rage Weile's story had dispelled sparked again, superficial and raw.

Weile made a noncommittal gesture.

"Now the truth comes out. You don't care about me. You never did!"

Weile flashed to life. "That's not true!"

"You wished I wasn't born!"

"That's not what I said. Listen to me!" Weile half rose, then dropped back into his chair. "Please, listen," he said, no longer a commander but a father. "That night when I came home and found you . . . and your mother . . ." His mouth worked soundlessly for a moment before he managed words again. "I just wanted to die with you. Had I mustered the strength, I would have killed myself before I discovered you were still alive. Bringing you back against impossible odds was the only thing that kept me going. I vowed that, if I lost you, I'd go with you. Does that sound like a father who doesn't care?"

"No," Tae admitted, but he could not help adding. "It sounds like a man who's lying."

The pain that bunched Weile's features was undisputable. "Ask Kinya."

"Kinya would lie for you."

"He's the only witness I have."

"How convenient." Guilt flared at Tae's own words. About this, he knew his father spoke the truth, yet he could not banish the need to hurt. "If you really cared, we would have hunted down those bastards. Together."

A light glimmered through Weile's eyes and disappeared. He hesitated, clearly fighting a battle within himself. At last, he spoke with a strange hesitancy. "I've told no one this before."

Tae gave an encouraging look.

"I did hunt those animals down, filled with all the fires of vengeance." Weile's expression went distant. "I slaughtered them, too. Brutal, bloody murder without a shred of remorse." His hands started to tremble, and he hid them in his lap. "I'd never killed before. And never since." He sucked a lungful of air, held it, then released it through his teeth. "It didn't make me feel any better. I still felt shattered into a thousand painful pieces. I vomited until my guts ached, and I howled my sorrow like a wolf. To this day, I still don't feel whole, like a statue broken on the floor and glued awkwardly so that every seam shows. It didn't make me feel better, but I didn't feel worse either. And, for one glorious hour, I savored my revenge."

A chill shivered through Tae. Sometimes, the promise of revenge had dragged him through days otherwise impossible. He had always believed a day would come when he would avenge his mother's death . . . and his own stabbing. Then, he felt certain, the nightmares would leave him in peace. His father's words brought home the truth. The victory would have proved hollow, and the remembrances would have lingered. Let his father suffer the horror. In truth, the vengeance was Weile's to savor, never his own. Finally, for the first time ever, he let Weile off the hook. "Mother's death was a tragedy, not your marriage. Or my birth."

A grin split Weile's face, jarring amid the dark agony of his revelations. He rose, extending his arms cautiously. "I love you, Tae Kahn."

This time, Tae joined the embrace, speaking the necessary words for the first time in many years. "Father, I love you, too."

CHAPTER 9

Lav'rintii Parley

*There is no such thing as a neutral warrior. By not assisting
one side, you are, by definition, assisting the other.*
                                        —*Colbey Calistinsson*

Alone in his sixth-floor study in the main common house on the
island of Nualfheim, Dh'arlo'mé sat cross-legged on the floor
with his face cupped in his hands. He did not know how long he
had remained in this position, but the floor had etched wrinkles
into his clothing and the air that he sucked through the cracks
between fingers tasted stale. The other elves had left him to his
thoughts. Once, his slowness would have seemed natural. Now,
he suspected, human-quick actions had become more character-
istic of him, and his long silence surely bothered his followers.

Despite Dh'arlo'mé's time in Béarn's lavish castle, he found
the elves' sparse furnishings more comfortable. His eyes did not
register the few scattered tools and the simple furniture. Only
the oaken box near his feet weathered his scrutiny and that a
dozen times in ten times as many moments. Repeatedly, he re-
viewed his readings, experience, and knowledge. No tiny detail
escaped his remembrance to hide in a quiet corner of his mind.
He considered everything, yet the answer to a question that
would decide the fate of elfinkind would not come.

To Dh'arlo'mé's undying relief, the Staff of Law did not contact him again. He did not know whether to attribute this reprieve to its inability to transmit through wood or whether it
wisely chose silence. Had it tried to influence Dh'arlo'mé's decision, it would surely have biased him against it. Now he contemplated the infinite possibilities, trusting only the facts and
his interpretation of them. The Béarnian sage's notes had
proved more difficult to read than he anticipated. The strange,
pudgy man who chronicled Western history protected his
knowledge even from the king and prime minister who commanded him.

Nevertheless, Baltraine had managed to secure accounts of the tested heirs. Apparently, the staff-test consisted only of clutching both staves, one in each hand. Several reported that the wood had seemed "empty" at first contact; the wizardry had not appeared until they held both staves. No heir would detail his experience, though the consensus seemed to be that magic transported the tested to one or more places where the staves created ethical scenarios that required proper solution. On one thing they all agreed. Only those chosen to rule Béarn emerged with their self-esteem intact. The others reported residual effects ranging from hollow uncertainty to unbearable self-hatred. Most became more contemplative and detached. Suicide, drug addiction, and mental illness afflicted several.

Dh'arlo'mé's thoughts drifted back centuries with little more difficulty than a man recalling his breakfast from the previous day. In his mind's eye, three of the four Cardinal Wizards, mankind's only link to magic, desperately contemplated the destruction they had caused in the name of deliverance. The fourth, the Western Wizard, Colbey Calistinsson, looked on sadly. As the Northern Sorceress' apprentice, Dh'arlo'mé had watched in horror as Odin condemned the three to death for their role in bringing the *Ragnarok*, and they had taken their own lives gladly. In those days, the Staves of Law and Chaos had promised nearly infinite power, and the Wizards had succumbed to the lies of the latter. Dh'arlo'mé could not risk a similar mistake.

Dh'arlo'mé compared the staves then and now. Visually, they appeared no different: smooth wooden sticks without the adornment worthy of their might. The staves' function in the staff-test also furnished no clues to their specific powers. Apparently, they worked weakly when in concert, their proximity canceling one another. Separated, they might prove more than any man or elf could handle.

Dh'arlo'mé dropped his hands and turned his attention to the staff box once again. His single, gemlike eye fixed on the wood, memorizing every line and knothole. Grand ideas took shape behind that otherwise bland expression. Together, the staves did him little good. He would heed the lessons of Baltraine and Khy'barreth, who had lost life and sanity attempting the staff-test. The Staves of Law and Chaos would serve Dh'arlo'mé, thus elfinkind, better separated.

The realization brought more than its share of danger, and Dh'arlo'mé could not afford a mistake. He walked a narrow boundary in a game with stakes that included the remaining worlds and the lives of men, elves, and gods. To act in ignorance would be folly of the worst kind. Yet no one had as much experience with the matter as Dh'arlo'mé'aftris'ter Te'meer Braylth'ryn Amareth Fel-Krin. No one. Not even the gods. The *Ragnarök* had taken Odin, as well as those who represented extremes. For knowledge and understanding of the Staves of Law and Chaos, Dh'arlo'mé believed himself peerless.

A plan formed gradually, every stage carefully considered. Slowly, Dh'arlo'mé studied the room, confirming a seclusion his followers would not dare violate. Rising, he moved toward the box. He flicked the metal hook clear of its loop. It spun through a semicircle, then fell into its unlatched position. Dh'arlo'mé sucked in several deep lungfuls of air, regulating his breathing into a calm cycle. He contemplated and discarded wards against magic. They should prove as unnecessary as they were useless. Seizing the lid, he shoved it open. The heavy oak thumped to the floor.

The staves lay still and silent in their box, their quiet simplicity betraying nothing of their power. Dh'arlo'mé studied them, seeking some difference in construction that might protect him from the Cardinal Wizards' fatal mistake. He found nothing helpful.

I am the one to your right. The familiar voice touched Dh'arlo'mé tentatively, as if it feared disrupting his concentration. *The Staff of Law.*

The identification did not reassure the elf. Dh'arlo'mé frowned. He delayed, glancing first toward the one that had contacted him. Study and experience suggested both staves would vie for his attention, competing forces each requiring a champion. Yet the other did not speak.

The staff anticipated Dh'arlo'mé's question. *Odin drained away nearly all of our power. My spark has grown back faster than chaos'.*

It can't speak to me?

Not yet. Now is the time to strike, while it remains weak. Destroy the Staff of Chaos, and Midgard will become yours to do with as you please.

The promise had undeniable appeal, yet Dh'arlo'mé had seen the results of single-minded devotion to a power. Once, the gods and mankind had supported a world wholly devoid of chaos. Ultimately, the need for balance had destroyed extremes, even among the gods. He pondered the staff's words. Unlike chaos, law could not lie. Untruths would clinch its identity, but honesty told him nothing. *You're the stronger power?* Dh'ar-lo'mé baited, believing chaos would confirm the words while law, though it would like to, would have to admit equality.

My staff-essence is currently stronger. If you wait, that may no longer remain the case. There will never be another chance like this one to destroy chaos ultimately. Even Odin failed to accomplish such a feat, though he tried. The staff paused momentarily, then addressed Dh'arlo'mé's question from another angle. *Stronger or not, I am the better power. Chaos is destruction and betrayal.* It drew out the last word, as if to remind Dh'arlo'mé of his current troubles with the *lav'rintii*, the followers of the first traitor elf. *I am structure, loyalty, truth. Vows kept and faith. Reality. All that is and has been.*

The staff's words did not convince Dh'arlo'mé. Its line of reasoning, though exactly what he would expect from the Staff of Law, was also exactly what he would expect from the Staff of Chaos posing as the Staff of Law. More than any human, Dh'arlo'mé understood the importance of chaos. Elfin balance fell more toward chaos, for it also served as the source of creativity and magic. With it, the world might shatter into ruin, but without it, it would stagnate into oblivion. Dh'arlo'mé had chosen to wield only the Staff of Law not because he wished to annihilate chaos but because history had proved it easier to control and a more faithful servant. The trick, he believed, was to think of himself as master rather than champion and never allow the staff, or its needs, to rule him. He required the staff only for the power it would render to him and to regain control of the world after the humans devastated their own. The beauty of Dh'arlo'mé's plan lay in its simplicity. Given the Staff of Chaos, humanity would annihilate itself.

Unable to assure himself of the staff's identity, Dh'arlo'mé passed the burden of proof directly to it. *How do I know you're law, and not chaos?*

The staff seemed appropriately affronted, its pause accompanied by a combination of outrage and understanding. *Take me in hand. Or it. Or both.*

The idea sent Dh'arlo'mé's nerves jangling. *Baltraine and Khy'barreth did so.*

Both exceptionally unworthy. And I was just coming into my power—testing. Historically, you'll find that the staff-test never killed until Ethelyn.

Dh'arlo'mé recognized the name of King Kohleran's daughter, the last of those heirs twice tested. *You killed Ethelyn and Baltraine?*

Yes.

Not the other staff.

I told you. Chaos has not yet regained enough power even to speak with you. Now is the time to destroy it. An opportunity like this one will never come again. Frustration leaked through the contact, easily interpreted. Though the staff could contemplate matters few mortals had the depth of understanding to consider, it lacked the body and hands necessary to act. For all its wisdom, it depended entirely on its champion for accomplishment of its goals.

And if I hold both of you?

You will know which of us is which.

You won't destroy me like you did Khy'barreth?

You are worthy. And you have no designs on Béarn's throne. It hesitated, apparently realizing it had made an assumption. *Do you?*

No, Dh'arlo'mé answered honestly. He harbored no wish to rule humans, only to destroy them. Though cautious, he believed the staff. Whether of law or chaos, it could find no better champion than the leader of the elves. Human mortality and lack of magic would hamper its freedom nearly as much as the wooden container that held it. Colbey had carried both staves with impunity, and he had made it clear he deliberately placed chaos into the Wizards' keeping. Reaching into the box, Dh'arlo'mé seized the left-hand staff first, tensing for a rush of magic he had no means to control.

The staff gave him nothing. It felt like ordinary wood in his hand, and its weight seemed unremarkable. He clenched it tighter, concentrating. A vague tremor passed along the arm that clutched the staff, so tiny he could not tell whether his intensity or the staff initiated the movement. A hint of sentience brushed his mind so lightly it seemed an impossible threat. It hummed, directionless and unformed. Like an infant, it seemed helpless, innocent, and utterly harmless. Yet, like an infant, its potential bore few limits. Dh'arlo'mé knew too much to be fooled. The right-hand staff had told the truth. He now held the Staff of Chaos.

Despite the baby gentleness of the staff's presence, realization overwhelmed Dh'arlo'mé. His fingers spasmed, and he nearly dropped the staff. He would not underestimate the bonfire this spark would eventually kindle. Already, the longer he clasped it, the stronger it seemed to grow. Dh'arlo'mé seized the other staff. In comparison, it seemed filled with vibrant stability. It promised magic of incomparable strength and near-infinite wisdom to share with its champion. This was the Staff of Law, though a weakened version of the force Colbey had wielded.

Dh'arlo'mé dropped the staff of Chaos back into the box, wrapping both hands around the Staff of Law. And smiled.

In the root cellar of Davian's cottage, Matrinka had grown accustomed to the odors of mustiness and mold beneath the sweeter perfume of stored tubers. Seated on a chair in the northern corner, she sewed patches onto Griff's britches and tried to imagine the rightful king of Béarn on his throne. The injustice that stabbed ceaselessly at her mind did not seem to bother Griff at all. Near the center of the damp, airless room, he played cards with Captain at a rickety table while Rantire remained restlessly at attention. Though two chairs lay empty, neither she nor Darris chose to use them. The bard sat on the floor, tuning a battered lute too warped for clear sound.

Matrinka alternately appreciated and despised the quiet passage of days that gave her too much time for thought. The danger of discovery had forced them from Béarn Castle. Fearing recognition, Matrinka and Captain had remained hidden. They had kept Griff from the streets as well, not only for his safety, but because an unknown Béarnide would surely draw attention. That had left Darris to act as their only contact. He alone had reason to walk Béarn's streets. The bard could come and go as he pleased, and the unnatural curiosity that was the bard's heritage had led his predecessors to do so on an irregular basis. The possibility existed that he would be dragged to the castle to serve as the king's bodyguard, his duty as Béarn's bard. The companions had seen possibility as well as concern in that strategy. It would allow one of them near the false king, perhaps able to infiltrate the elfin plot; but it would also place Darris in grave danger.

Yet, to Matrinka's surprise, the Béarnides paid Darris no heed, and he bought their supplies without harassment. Citizens ignored him with an uncharacteristic apathy, as if something had squashed all the vigor from them. Over a period of days, Darris discovered a populace cowed by a government turned gradually cruel and restrictive, their faith in King Kohleran strangely undiminished despite their condition. The people remained massive and robust, the market still bustled with activity, but the aura and attitude had grown bleak. In the midst of plenty, the people failed to thrive.

Eventually, a cooper named Dalen recognized Darris. Cautious questions and answers from both sides had revealed a hidden core of disgruntlement. Initially, it consisted of Béarnides who had turned against Kohleran's weakened line and the corrupt prime minister/regent yet had managed to escape the false king's "justice." Here Matrinka found allies mistrustful enough to look through the magic to the elf beneath the king's disguise. And, where this band of renegades had once condemned the royal line as no longer competent, they swiftly became avid advocates of Griff.

A fold of the britches flopped toward the ground, and Mior batted playfully at the fabric. Matrinka managed a tight-lipped smile. Gradually, the underground movement gained support, but the vast majority of Béarnides remained loyal to the false king and his *alfen*. Every person added to their cause became a potential betrayer. The renegade band was still too weak to face Dh'arlo'mé and the others. Every moment meant weighing the benefit of acquiring allies against the risk of detection. Eventually, the right moment would come. Until then, she could only wait and fret.

The scrape of the boulder rolling aside disrupted Tae's reunion with his father, and a wild hammering of a fist against the board followed.

"A moment." Weile Kahn darted into the other room.

Tae crouched into a shadowed corner, silent and nearly invisible in a gloom the lanterns scarcely penetrated. The chaotic sequence ended, replaced by a methodical pattern of taps.

Weile emerged with a sheathed sword and a row of daggers on his belt. "That's Daxan and Alsrusett. There's trouble." He stopped, glancing around the room, apparently seeking Tae. Without clearly locating his son, he sprinted up the stairway and returned a single, loud knock. He withdrew as the board scratched aside, and the pair of bodyguards scrambled in. Both sported the standard Eastern black hair, deep brown eyes, and swarthy coloring. Leather jerkins over linens revealed the broad, deeply-etched musculature of trained soldiers. Though Alsrusett towered over even Daxan, both stood taller than Weile and his son. Daxan had a sturdy compactness to his build. A sword hung at each man's left hip. Simple sheaths hid the blades, but the leather grips looked well-worn and darkened by old sweat.

Daxan did the talking. "*Aristiri* sector found the *lav'rintii*." He mangled the obviously foreign, last word which sounded Northern in origin. His voice and features displayed the evident wit of which few believed soldiers capable. Tae knew his father well enough to expect kindness, loyalty, and intelligence from any subordinate allowed so near self and family. "They're clearly headed for Béarn."

Weile made a wordless sound of irritation. "No trouble, I hope?"

Tae did not move, even as Alsrusett's gaze swept the room twice before fastening directly on him. The bodyguard smiled.

"Not with the *lav* . . ." Not wishing to stumble over the word again, Daxan chose the more common term. ". . . elves. There're two humans with them, at least one a Renshai. She tore through six before they got her under control."

" 'They' meaning the *lav'rintii*," Alsrusett clarified.

"*Starbird*'s got them cave-cornered at the sector border."

Tae tried to make sense of the conversation. The elfin language closely resembled Northern, so it made sense that *lav'rintii* was an elfin term. *But what's my father's involvement with elves? And why would humans, especially Renshai, accompany them?* He crouched in silence, hoping the details would become clear without need for direct explanation.

"Kinya?" Weile asked.

"He's awaiting your order, sir."

Weile glanced toward the exit, face lined in thought. "We're going." Without further command or recommendation, Weile headed toward the stairs as his bodyguards scrambled into position around him. "Daxan, forge ahead. Tell Kinya to get horses ready for . . ." He glanced over his shoulder at Tae. "You coming with us?"

"Yes." Tae would not miss this opportunity.

"Four horses, then," Weile finished as Alsrusett thundered past him. The bodyguard slipped outside, his inspection cut short by Weile's sudden emergence. Daxan headed through next, leaving Tae to trail in his wake.

A waning moon added a sheen to the forest's highest branches, and a glaze filtered to the ground. As Tae's eyes adjusted from lantern to duller natural light, he hurried after his father and Alsrusett. Daxan remained behind to seal the entrance. Moments later, his footfalls crashed after the others, and the squatty guard sprinted up beside them.

Questions plagued Tae, mostly those he had planned to discuss with his father before such an emergency arose. He had wondered whether Weile and his gangsters worked for the elves, but this incident suggested otherwise. He doubted his father would stand for an interrogation now, even if they could hear one another over the crash of movement; but he saw the need for a warning. "Careful. Elves won't stay cornered. Magic."

Weile glanced back, nodding acknowledgment. A quizzical expression slipped onto his features as he continued his walk. Surely he wondered as much about his son's knowledge of elves as Tae did about his father's.

Daxan dashed ahead. Possibilities assailed Tae as he accompanied Weile and his other bodyguard to Kinya's cottage. The close darkness of the forest hampered vision and direction sense, and they found a comfortable balance between silence and speed. Soon, they reached the cottage where Kinya had readied the horses. Mounting took moments. Tae, Weile, Daxan, and Alsrusett rode toward the stalemate.

Excitement plied Tae long after fatigue and the steady rhythm of the horse should have lulled him to sleep. Forced to an irritatingly slow pace by the darkness, Tae felt chased by a restlessness that apparently bothered the others as well. After a brief discussion with Weile, Alsrusett lit a lantern, suspended it on a pole, and bobbed it over his horse's head. His bay mare shied at its sudden appearance. Alsrusett calmed her with pats and praise. She soon tolerated its presence, though occasional shifts in shadow sent her skittering sideways. Alsrusett kicked the horse to a trot, then a canter. The other horses followed her in a line, tracing her steps and thus not requiring light of their own.

Dawn crept over the Southern Weathered Mountains as the horses broke from forest onto sparser, rockier terrain. An Easterner met Weile and his party at the transition, scarcely waiting until they drew up their horses before speaking. "The elves put our men to sleep. They're headed toward nighthawk."

Weile gave Tae an admiring glance, though he addressed the newcomer. "How long ago?"

"High night, sir, but they haven't gotten far. They didn't take our horses." Apparently finally recognizing Weile, he granted the commander a respectful bow. "They must have made a mistake, because their spell put some of their own to sleep, too. Carrying and dragging slowed them."

"Our sleepers?" Weile asked.

"Tern sector's watching them."

"Let's go!" Weile commanded. The man joined the group, and they headed southwest, along the mountains. With the help of a few more guides along the way, they discovered the elves trapped in a high-walled valley thick with trees. Tae looked down on the scene from horseback, counting nearly two dozen moving figures below and a few lying still amid the greenery. The array of hair colors would have clinched their identity as elves; humans traveling in such numbers would surely span only a race or two. But with color vision lost to darkness, Tae found it impossible to distinguish them. Easterners spread across the ledges above the valley. Weile rode them around these until he pulled up beside an obvious leader. "What's going on, Chayl?"

On foot, the man addressed as Chayl tore his gaze from the elves. He glanced at Weile, then looked back into the canyon. Gradually, his brain registered appearance and voice; and he gave his commander his full attention. "We've got the traitor elves surrounded. We lost six at *aristiri* sector, and there're fourteen more asleep there."

"I heard about that." Weile added in a threatening voice, "No elves hurt, right?"

"Right," Chayl confirmed. "Other than the sleep magic, which seems harmless, they haven't attacked. They have weapons, but only one of the humans has resorted to violence." He glanced into the valley and back again. "The man hasn't caused much trouble. The wild one's a woman. Renshai, I think."

"Have they tried to escape here?"

"Not yet. There're thirty-seven, counting the humans. A dozen or so are still sleeping. Including the humans. I think that's who they're waiting for." Chayl made a broad, sweeping gesture over the valley. "Obviously, they don't know much about war strategy."

Tae smiled. History recorded that the Easterners had made a similar mistake during the Great War more than three hundred years earlier. Attempting a sneak attack on the West, they had hidden their massive troops in a quarry where forewarned Westerners found and slaughtered them.

Weile studied the situation. "Tell the men to ready their bows but not to fire unless given a direct command. Remind them we're not to kill any elf. The humans, especially the woman, must die."

Chayl rushed to relay the message. Weile cupped his hands around his mouth and shouted into the valley. "*Lav'rintii,* can you hear me?" The cliff face shattered his voice to echoes.

Silence followed.

Weile waited several moments before repeating louder, "*Lav'rintii,* can you hear me?"

As the reverberations faded, nothing returned but the rustling of branches in the wind and the rising and falling cadence of insects.

Weile tensed to call again as a thin, musical voice scarcely rose above the other sounds. Tae could not discern words.

"*Lav'rintii,* answer if you value your lives at all!" Irritation entered Weile's tone. He had made it clear to his men he would not kill elves, but he would let the elves believe otherwise.

"They did answer," Tae informed his father.

Weile looked at Tae. "They did?"

Again, a lyrical sound floated up from below. This time, Tae thought he heard *lav'rintii* with the light syllables properly restored. The other words still blended into a jumble that even context could not sort. He suspected whoever answered used the common trading tongue with appalling syntax.

"What did they say?"

"I'm not sure," Tae admitted. "It's a lot harder to holler up through trees than down into a cavern. And it's possible this particular group doesn't speak trading, at least not well."

Weile's dark eyes fixed on his son. "How do you know so much about elves?"

Tae relived the moments of terror as he raced across elfin territory while they tracked him with magic. He had climbed their dungeon roof, hoping to create a hole for an escape route, rescue Griff, and slip them both to safety. But the elves had learned construction by viewing human buildings through magic, not by mastering the necessary mechanics. The roof had collapsed beneath Tae. The elves had captured him with magic, then tortured him unmercifully for information. Now, a brief sharpness twinged through him, and he appreciated the mind's inability to accurately recall pain. His current wounds bothered him enough. "I've dealt with them before."

"Have you?" Clearly surprised, Weile put aside curiosity for the moment. "We'll talk about that later. Can you speak their tongue?"

The question might have seemed strange to any other, but Weile had always pressured Tae to learn every language. Tae could not remember when he had not spoken at least four fluently. As an infant, his father had used Eastern and trading interchangeably, and they had hired a Béarnian maid to use her home tongue and Western around him. Whether because of his early exposure, or just a natural gift, Tae learned languages with an ease that made Weile's studies seem clumsy. Tae understood eight of the nine known human languages, barring only Renshai, spoke at least passing amounts of each, and could read and write the original four. This talent had served him well, not only in situations when others talked freely believing he could not understand them. It had allowed him to scan the sage's notes, written in Béarnese, to find the name and location of the missing heir. During his run from Weile's enemies, Tae had come to the realization that his father's insistence probably stemmed from the intention of turning his son into a spy rather than from any altruistic, fatherly reason. Now, he decided, the original purpose did not matter. Whatever Weile's intention, Tae had gained an invaluable skill. "They've got a language all their own. It resembles Northern. They seem to mostly understand Northern, too."

"Tae . . . ?" Weile started hesitantly.

Tae anticipated the question. "You want me to go down and talk to them?"

"It might be dangerous."

Tae doubted his father's concerns. The bits of information he had received from the various men suggested otherwise. The elves he had faced would have slaughtered all of his father's men while they slept. They would never have tolerated humans among them. Chayl had called them elfin traitors, a phrase Tae had, at first, believed a redundancy. Now he put the sequence together differently and, he suspected, correctly. When he considered *lav'rintii* as the elfin word for "traitor," it placed a whole new light on the situation. These elves would then represent Captain's followers, perhaps accompanied by the elder himself. *The Renshai could be Rantire or Kevral and the man Ra-khir or Darris.* Tae's heart pounded at the realization, and suddenly the mission seemed nothing less than dire necessity. "I'll talk to them." He dismounted and headed toward the edge, seeking the best route into the valley.

"Wait." Weile stayed Tae with the word and the sudden imposition of his horse. "Before you parley, you have to know the terms."

Tae nodded distractedly.

"Convince the elves we have enough arrows to kill all of them from here. Assure them they can go free if they change course away from Béarn. And, no matter what else gets settled, the two humans die."

Horror fluttered through Tae's chest, reawakening the pain of the injury Nacoma had inflicted; but he nodded grimly. He had to know the identities of those below. Plans would have to wait for knowledge. As Chayl returned, Tae slipped down the wall of the valley. He climbed well enough not to bother seeking the simpler access the elves must have taken, careful only to ascertain that he had not condemned himself to a fall. As he disappeared over the side, he caught his father's soft words to Chayl. "That's my son down there. If any man shoots, it'll be the last thing he ever does."

Tae clambered down stone that softened to a gentle, tree-lined slope, requiring no more attention to negotiate than a romp through the forest. He kept an eye on the pattern of trees as well as roots and other obstacles in his path. The lower he got, the more his gaze strayed to the bottom, seeking movement. The changing pattern suggested the elves had noticed him. As sunrise turned the horizon pink and light slithered down the faces of the cliff, they gathered to study him, then slipped quietly to a site near a clump of bushes. Tae directed his hearing to catch the first whisper of a chant that would indicate they had begun a *jovinay arythanik*, a shared spell.

"We've sent a man to talk!" Weile's unexpected shout startled Tae into a wary crouch. The sudden movement reawakened the pain of his wounds as his cautious climb had not. "Don't harm him, or you all die!" The warning should have been unnecessary. It was unlawful in every human society to kill a messenger or a mediator. Elves might not follow the universal convention.

Having been indicated by his father, as well as already noticed by the elves, Tae made no attempt at subtlety. He walked openly to the valley floor, resisting the cover of outcroppings and tree shadows to place himself fully into the growing sunlight. This had the added advantage of forcing the elves to look into the light to see him. He studied them between the trees. Ten had gathered beneath a spindly *binyal*, prodding someone he could not see between them. Their hair ranged from red-black to elder white, and he could now recognize their fragile-looking forms as elfin.

Tae used the Northern tongue, "I mean you no harm."

All of the elves turned to stare, their strange eyes reflecting light like faceted sapphires, emeralds, and topaz. The two nearest him rose and edged forward. The taller shook a mane of mahogany hair from his angular face. Heart-shaped lips parted to reveal straight rows of incisors and molars. Tae blamed nervousness for his own heightened senses. For the first time, he realized elves had no canine teeth, a detail that fit well with their vegetarian diet. He also spoke Northern. "You know Otherspeak?"

Tae hesitated. "Is that what you call what I'm using?"

"Yes."

Tae saw no reason to give an answer that had become self-evident, but the elves seemed to expect one. "Not very well, but I'll do my best."

The shorter elf seemed to sport every feature that typified elves, more alien-appearing than his companions. Grotesquely high cheekbones hovered over a small nose and lips so broad they seemed a caricature. Wispy, white-blond hair curled around a gently tapering chin and yellow eyes as pale as his hair watched Tae without emotion. "Why are you threatening us? Why are you chasing us? We didn't bother you."

Tae had hoped to assess the elves before committing himself to a cause. The straightforward queries stole the time he required. He weighed his options, his thoughts retarded by fatigue, sleep long overdue, and the dull ache in his chest. It seemed best to meet bold forthrightness with equally direct questions. "*Lav'rintii*." Tae seasoned the word with proper elfin pronunciation. "What does that mean?"

The elves exchanged unreadable glances. The taller one answered. "It means 'destroyers of the peace,' but we are not that at all. We call ourselves *lysalf* and the others *svartalf*."

Tae needed nothing more. He grinned. "You *are* Captain's followers." He amended, recalling Captain's elfin name. "Arak'bar Tulamii Dhor."

A groan emerged from beneath the gathering, deep and certainly human.

Tae felt an airless flutter in his chest, as if his heart had momentarily stopped. Terror naturally followed. Then the normal beat resumed, leaving only an excited tingle. "Which," he started, at once desperate and fearing to finish the question. If the Renshai was other than Kevral, he might not survive the sorrow. ". . . human is that?"

The elves scurried aside to reveal Kevral scrambling to her feet. She charged even as her sword cleared its sheath in a swirl of silver highlights.

Tae dodged from her path, not for the first time. "Kevral, it's Tae."

Kevral halted, blue eyes restless, sword sinking back toward its sheath. He hoped his father could not see the attack from the top of the valley. Kevral returned the sword to its proper place, sprang forward, and grabbed Tae in a wild embrace. "Tae! You're alive."

Tae wrapped his dark arms around Kevral, reveling in the sweet musk of her hair, the warmth of her presence, the pleasant, natural smells of her clothing and skin. The press of her body against him also aroused a desire he would not have believed possible in such a tense situation. His mind galloped off in a swirl of images that revolved around levering her down in the grass, despite the stares of the elves and Easterners, and making fierce, passionate love. Instead, he contented himself with a kiss that went from joyful to torrid in an instant.

Kevral's muscles loosened almost imperceptibly; if he had not held her, Tae could not have discerned the change. A moment later, she stiffened again, jerking her head aside and shoving him free. "Where's Ra-khir?"

Not exactly the response I wanted. Tae released Kevral and staunched embarrassment with humor. "I don't know. Was he supposed to be with me?"

Kevral gave Tae a measuring look. He had chosen a bad time for jokes. "He was with me. Is he all right?" Kevral did not await a reply to a question Tae clearly could not answer. "Ra-khir!" she called.

Brush rattled, then half a dozen elves emerged from the valley foliage with the groggy apprentice Knight of Erythane between them. Ra-khir's red hair trailed in strands down his forehead, and his clothing consisted of a crudely sewn patchwork of unmatched fabrics. Heavily muscled, he could not possibly have fit into any single tunic the elves might have spared him. His chin carried three days' growth of beard. Yet his wild hair, scrappy clothes, and dirt-smeared features only enhanced his attractiveness, and the bags beneath his eyes refined their striking green. Though more important matters plagued Tae, he suffered pangs of irritation at the realization that he could never compete when it came to looks.

Ra-khir shook his head to clear it. His gaze shifted from the ground to Kevral and finally landed on Tae. A smile glided across his lips, and he met Tae's brown eyes levelly. "Tae!" The excitement in the greeting sounded genuine, and the smile clinched the image. "Do you know if any of the others are . . ." He stumbled over the obvious "alive." ". . . safe?"

"I don't know about the others, but we're not safe at all." Tae glanced toward the crest.

Ra-khir followed Tae's gaze to the tiny, dark figures at the lip and groaned. The corners of his mouth sank back into a neutral position, and his eyes narrowed pensively. "How did you get here?"

Tae doubted Ra-khir currently wondered about how he'd survived the Southern Sea, so he addressed the more significant issue. "Those are my father's men."

From the corner of his eye, Tae saw Kevral nodding knowingly. Ra-khir's brows rose, and his forehead creased, as he made the obvious connection. Tae tried to focus fully on the situation he hoped to defuse, but he could not help noticing how close to Kevral Ra-khir chose to stand and the more relaxed posture he assumed around her now. Few would notice the difference, but years of guessing human intention and reaction, as well as the significance of this particular union, told all. Their relationship had drastically changed. *I've lost Kevral.* Though uncertain, the belief stung, even through Tae's concerns about his friends' lives. His new relationship with his father put the latter concern to rest. *Why couldn't I have been the one washed ashore with Kevral?* Tae did not ponder long. Luck and chance had rarely proved his friends.

The story of Kevral's and Ra-khir's beaching could also wait. For now, Tae needed enough information to make decisions about the elves. He switched to the Western tongue, one he knew both of his companions spoke but the elves most likely would not. "Can we trust your companions?"

Ra-khir glanced around at the elves who peered at the exchange from around trunks and low branches. "Implicitly."

Kevral nodded agreement. "What do your father's men want from us? Are they working for the dark elves?"

Tae shrugged, taking the questions in reverse order. "I haven't had time to ask yet. The elves have nothing to fear, but they want to kill you."

Kevral's blue eyes blazed, and her hand returned to her hilt. "Let them try. I'll send anyone who attacks to Hel."

"Maybe the first hundred." Tae chose a sufficiently high number to keep from insulting Kevral's skill. Attacked en masse, he doubted it would take more than ten to bring her down. "But that's not going to do you, Ra-khir, me, or Westland travel much good. Better I take you two up there and talk things out with my father."

Ra-khir made a subtle gesture of agreement that Kevral could not see.

The Renshai nodded grudgingly. "Let me just explain to Eth'morand, if he's awake. You two go. I'll catch up."

Tae measured the cliff wall with his gaze, choosing a gentler slope for the sake of his companions. He headed toward it, Ra-khir at his side. "Are you well?" The small talk felt grindingly out of place after a demon's attack and a near-drowning, followed by an unofficial sentence of death.

"We're fine," Ra-khir returned, readily guessing Tae had asked about Kevral as well as himself. "Bruises, gashes, scrapes. Nothing time won't fix. You?"

"Same," Tae said, catching his hand sliding to the wound over his heart and forcing it back to his side. "Got washed overboard before the demon could hurt me."

"Me, too," the future knight admitted.

Sudden fear clutched Tae. "It's dead, isn't it?"

"Yes," Ra-khir said emphatically and with profound relief. "One enemy at a time."

Tae smiled. "Be nice for a change, wouldn't it?"

They started up the slope, veering around trees already thinner and more twisted than those in the well-watered valley. The best soil washed to the bottom, leaving ruggedly arduous terrain for those seeds unfortunate enough to land on the sides.

Kevral joined them shortly. "I gave Eth'morand the general gist. He's keeping the elves quiet below until we or the Easterners give him reason to do otherwise." She looked at Tae. "So how are you?"

Tae chuckled.

"We've been through that," Ra-khir explained.

Kevral glanced from man to man. "So because I missed an instant of conversation, I don't get to know?"

Tae lowered his voice as they approached the Easterners. The nearer they drew to the top, the more the funneling effect of the valley might project their words upward. "I'm fine physically.

Emotionally, I'm drained. Meeting my father after all those years was more difficult than I expected."

Kevral managed to suppress a well-deserved "I told you so." She had encouraged him to make peace with Weile Kahn.

Unwilling to discuss details now, Tae waved his friends silent. He did not fully understand the acoustics of canyons but felt certain their whispers could carry farther than they realized. He would not risk embarrassing himself or his father. The three clambered quietly to the crest, a feat that required no particular skill, and a score of Easterners met them at the top.

Tae glanced at the semicircle of broad, dark figures, finding no mercy in the men nor in the weapons they wielded. He stepped in front of his two companions, the instinctive shielding surprising him. Nothing in his survival training taught him to make such a suicidal gesture, yet logic directed the action. His father's men would not attack as long as he stood between them and their target. Behind him, he felt certain, Kevral and Ra-khir stood as ready as the Easterners. Only Tae felt completely disarmed and anything but prepared.

Weile Kahn stepped up behind his men, his somber expression scarcely hiding a pride Tae wished he had seen more in his adolescence. Things could have turned out so differently, and he would not now stand between friends and family. "You've done well, Tae Kahn."

Tae dodged his father's dark eyes, so like his own. "Father, these are my friends, Kevral . . ." He indicated the Renshai with a glance that revealed her crouched and restless. ". . . and Ra-khir." The knight's hand also rested on his hilt, his expression hard.

Weile looked from one to the other, then back at his son. The pride disappeared, replaced by studied caution. "Tae Kahn, we need to talk privately."

Tae's gaze skimmed the gathered Easterners. If he removed himself, a battle would surely result. "Thank you, Father, for the offer. Anything you can say to me, you can say in front of my friends."

Weile's nostrils flared. Unaccustomed to disobedience, he considered in an unreadable silence that showed no failing. "Not appropriate, Tae Kahn. We will talk in private." The eyes brooked no further backtalk, and the anger there seemed to spear through Tae. Suddenly, he feared for his own life as well as for his companions. Further argument in this vein would gain him nothing good, yet he dared not step aside. "Father, I mean no disrespect. I just . . ." He inclined his head toward his companions, hoping Weile would understand.

The crime lord deliberated a moment longer, then lowered his head slightly, giving ground without seeming to do so. "So long as they are not threatened, my men will not harm these people without my direct order."

Tae hesitated, only partially reassured. The killing of several of their companions by Kevral might require retaliation. They would keep their definition of "threat" broad, accepting any excuse for a fight. Nevertheless, Tae knew he had received all the concession he was going to get. To refuse now would condemn them all. He whispered to Kevral and Ra-khir, "Stay calm," hoping they would read all the connotations in the few words he dared to direct at them. Then, breath held and emotions well-hidden, Tae headed toward his father.

Weile led his son out of earshot. Weeds partially blocked Tae's vision as well. Only then, Weile allowed his face to purple, and his words, though soft, held a knife's edge. "Tae Kahn, guard your tongue! My men are predators. Challenge their respect for me, and I could lose control of them."

Rage boiled up in Tae at the attack. He gave his father nothing verbal, just an insolent shrug.

Weile shook his head at his son's obvious ignorance. "Perhaps you want them to kill me?" He did not wait for an answer. "Well enough. But don't delude yourself into thinking the world would benefit from such a thing. Without leadership, or following another, those men would indulge in a spree of theft and slaughter that an organized army might not stop."

"Isn't that what's going on now?" Tae challenged.

"No. Not at all. We have reasons for all we do, reasons I'll eventually find time to explain. And we've harmed no one willing to forgo their travel."

Tae sucked in a breath and loosed it slowly through his nose. Anger would not serve him now. Anything he shouted in rage would only return to haunt him. "I did my best to show respect. I just couldn't leave without knowing my friends would stay safe."

"Don't you understand? It doesn't matter. Whether they die now or a few moments from now makes no difference."

Waves of heat and cold passed alternately through Tae. "Father, you can't kill Kevral and Ra-khir."

Weile remained in place, stance habitually wary. "I believe we can."

Tae lowered his head. "Then you leave me no choice. I'll fight on their side."

"You'll die, too," Weile warned.

Tae met his father's gaze squarely. "Yes," he said. "I will."

"These friends are worth dying for?"

"Yes."

Weile considered a moment, finding a solution. "Will they join us?"

Tae recalled his many conversations with Ra-khir and the knight's honor that would keep him from stealing morsels of bread from a rich man's feast even to feed his starving family. "No. Ra-khir would rather die. Kevral would sacrifice herself for him." Tae refused to blink. "She nearly did so once for me."

Weile found the flaw in his own hastily constructed plan. "She killed too many of my men. The others would murder her in her sleep."

They'd try. Tae did not bother to express a threat more appropriate from Kevral. To him, the only answer was obvious. "You're going to let the elves go, right?"

"I have no choice."

"Why not let Ra-khir, Kevral, and me continue with them?"

Weile's look turned even sharper, if possible. "You?"

The suggestion had seemed obvious to Tae. "They're like family."

"And I *am* family," Weile reminded. "I will not lose my son, powerful clients, and my self-respect. You're asking me for everything. It's not an option."

Tae suspected that if he considered carefully, he would understand his father's point. "All I'm asking for is mercy for my closest friends."

Weile turned his head but not before Tae thought he caught a glimmer of tears.

Tae pressed while he held the upper hand, no matter how tenuous. "Don't expect me to make all the compromises either. Give me an offer that doesn't involve killing my friends. Whatever the cost, I'll take it."

Weile stiffened, then turned. The strength had returned to his eyes, and Tae wondered if he had imagined the moment of weakness. "Join me, fully and irrevocably. Let me groom you to the position that's yours by right of birth. Only then will your friends go free."

Tae blinked, scarcely daring to believe the words came from his father. Every fiber in his being wanted to finish the mission he had started with Kevral, Ra-khir, and the others. His promise would place him firmly on the opposite side, and he would miss them terribly. Even if he could explain his position to his friends, and he doubted Weile Kahn would allow that, he would certainly lose Kevral to Ra-khir. *Fool, you've lost her already, and it should have happened long ago. Ra-khir has always clearly been the better man.* "Would you truly want me unwilling?"

"Tae, you have all your mother's intelligence, which was considerable. Over time, you'll understand the gift I've offered you. Time with you is all I need."

Tae did not know whether to dismiss the words as foolish or to fear them. "That's my only choice?"

"The only one that allows your friends to live."

Tae pursed his lips. "I'll take it."

Weile smiled, placing a strangely protective arm around his son. It bothered Tae that the contact pleased him.

CHAPTER 10

The Origins of Faith

Attempting to cut too fast can cause you to lose your balance. Using more force than is needed shows a weakness in technique.

—*Colbey Calistinsson*

The mingled odors of leaf mold, sap, and greenery had become familiar to Tae since the day he crossed the border into the Westlands; but now it became just another irritation. He lay on his back, staring at the vast pattern the stars sprayed across the sky. Insects chirped and whistled in cyclic harmony, and the distant calls of foxes interrupted their song. Occasionally, one of the horses snorted, and their hooves stomped irregular tattoos, thwarting flies. Daxan and Alsrusett took turns guarding their leader's camp, leaving Tae to his restless lack of sleep.

Tae waited until nothing remained of the sun and the moon hung low in the sky. He rose, making no attempt to hide the movement. Daxan would notice him missing no matter his means of leaving, and it seemed better not to draw suspicion. His father would trust Tae to return, just as Tae knew Weile Kahn would not break his word and secretly order Kevral and Ra-khir slaughtered. That sort of deceit was not what bothered Tae; he worried about the opinion his friends had formed of him. His father's arrangement had allowed only a pointed promise to allow the *lav'rintii* and their companions to reach their destination unhindered. Weile had left them with the understanding that any future travel went beyond the boundaries of the agreement. As the elves headed toward Béarn, Kevral had looked askance at Tae. Too far for a verbal reply, he had found himself capable of nothing more than a sorrowful shake of his head.

Tae brushed through trees and foliage without explanation to his father's bodyguard, hoping the short Easterner would assume he had left to relieve himself or to walk out concerns. Tae did not care about Daxan's opinion. So long as Tae returned before Weile's awakening, he felt certain he could concoct a reasonable excuse to explain his actions to his father. For now, his need to see Kevral one last time took precedence. Talk would suffice, but he also hoped to collect on a promise.

A random search of the woodlands would never reveal his companions' camp. Instead, Tae relied on memories of past travel. Ra-khir and Kevral would prefer the trade routes, especially since they no longer feared discovery. The elves, however, would temper that alternative. Tae had learned enough of their habits, from observation and Captain, to know they would feel edgy outside of the forest. When he had led the party, he paralleled the open pathways that usually represented the shortest route to the West's many cities and villages. Trusting Kevral to mimic his strategy, he found the elfin camp without difficulty.

For several moments, Tae scanned the camp. Now he counted nearer to three dozen elves, coinciding with Chayl's report of thirty-seven, including humans. Nearly half sat, slumped but clearly awake. The others lay in positions and locations Tae would have found impossibly uncomfortable, such as high amid branches. He wondered how they kept from falling. Ra-khir slept toward the center of the group, near the base of a tree. He lay sideways, in an awkward repose that suggested he had leaned against the trunk before sleep overtook him. An unoccupied blanket spread beside him surely belonged to Kevral.

Tae traced the edge of their camp, seeking recent passage and finding it near a clump of itchweed. Bent and broken stems, disrupted leaves, and sprung seed pods revealed someone's ragged passage that Tae followed in a cautious hush. At length, the swish and rattle of movement grazed the barest edge of his hearing. The sounds came from just ahead, too irregular to indicate forward progress. Tae faded into the few shadows brush and trees afforded, approaching with quiet anticipation.

In a clearing formed by the pound and stomp of her own feet, Kevral practiced sword forms with the Renshai exuberance that never faded. Moonlight painted shifting highlights through her short golden locks, and each strand seemed to fly with a life of its own. The keen blue eyes measured enemies that existed only in Kevral's head, and they sparkled like stars in the pale expanse of her face. Her limbs and sword sculpted arcs through the darkness, and the astounding grace of every movement turned her plainness into unrivaled radiance. Tae shook his head, amazed at how perspective could change a deadly art into picturesque beauty. In the heat of battle, he had experienced the heart-stopping instants before certain death on Kevral's sword, and the idea of repeating it sent a hot flood of adrenaline through his system. He would wait until she finished and sheathed the sword before calling to her . . . from a distance. He knew better than to interrupt a Renshai's practice, even had he not so enjoyed the view.

An end to the *svergelse* came too soon. Kevral sprang into a wild flurry of movement that hacked or skewered all of the imaginary enemies who remained. She stopped then, holding a stance only a Renshai could consider defensive. Fond of quoting Colbey Calistinsson, Kevral had once said that the best defense was to have your opponent bleeding on the ground. Glancing around to ascertain no enemies remained, Kevral jabbed the blade into its sheath.

"Kevral," Tae hissed.

Kevral stiffened and turned toward the sound, eyes probing the darkness.

Tae would not let her suffer. He stepped directly in front of her, yet beyond range of her sword. She could charge him easily enough, yet he hoped distance would give her time to recognize him.

But Kevral did not attack. A smile glided across features that bore a gleam of perspiration, and she turned her attention directly to him. "I knew it was you."

"How?"

"No one else can sneak up on me."

Tae was not at all sure he liked the woman he loved remembering him for that. "Well, don't count on it, or some quiet assassin's going to murder you while you're greeting him as me." He grinned at his own words. More than once, his secretiveness had gotten him into trouble with Kevral. Crazed by battle wrath, she kept track of companions but rarely paused to identify those who appeared suddenly. He had dodged more than one of her lightning assaults. "Considering the cold steel welcome you usually give *me,* that might not be so bad."

Kevral laughed briefly, then went abruptly sober. "What's going on, Tae? Are you back with us again?"

Tae would have enjoyed a few hours of friend-talk first, but he did not have the night to spare. "I just came to say a proper good-bye."

Kevral ran a hand through her hair, and it fell in damp feathers around the makeshift part. "You're abandoning our cause?"

"Only from need." Tae met Kevral's gaze. She studied him, withholding judgment. "The only way my father would agree to releasing you was if I promised to stay with him."

Kevral blinked once in slow thoughtfulness. "So your father used the threat of your friend's deaths to get you to join him."

"Right."

"You didn't have to do that."

Tae did not agree. "I did."

"We would have fought for your freedom."

"You would have died."

"Maybe."

Tae refused to argue prowess. Kevral would not have considered her death a certainty had she faced the Pudarian army carrying only a stick. "Ra-khir and I would have died."

"Maybe."

Tae searched for an answer that would circumvent Kevral's ego. "I wasn't willing to take that chance."

"And now?"

"I'm still not."

Kevral sighed. "I won't leave a friend imprisoned so I can go free." She added pointedly, "Especially you, Tae."

Tae caught the reference. After he had escaped Pudar's dungeon and Kevral agreed to take his place, Tae surrendered himself to rescue her. At the time, he had not known that Kevral had already bartered her release by agreeing to train the king's soldiers for a year. "I'm not a prisoner."

Kevral stared. "You can leave when you want?"

Tae dodged the question. "I'm not a prisoner."

Kevral kept pressing. "So you're there voluntarily."

Tae winced, but he would not lie. "Yes."

Kevral continued to stare, though she lost whatever words she intended to speak. Her mouth opened, nothing emerged, and her lips sank into a puzzled frown. Apparently finding nothing better, she simply repeated, this time as a question, "You're there voluntarily?"

Kevral's study became unnerving. Tae broke the gridlock, turning his gaze to the ground. "Mostly, I am."

Kevral's voice turned accusatory. "You said you didn't want

to see him again. You said you'd never have a hand in what he does."

Tae met Kevral's glare again. "And you told me to give my father a chance. I might find he cares for me more than I realize." He sighed, sliding from past to present. "And I love him, too."

Kevral noticed the change. "You do?"

"I do," Tae admitted, having no trouble meeting her eyes now. "I've learned a lot, and there's a lot more to learn."

"Why did you have to start listening to me now?"

Tae smiled at the mild self-deprecation. "Because you happened to be right."

"No," Kevral whispered. At first, Tae believed the word a directionless denial. Then she repeated it louder. "No, Tae. I was wrong. No father who loved his son would force him to stay against his will."

Tae had already considered that. "You might be right again, but my father does everything strangely. He means the best in the worst he does. I'm just beginning to understand that."

Kevral shook her head, disbelief obvious. "So you're going to join the rogues who tried to kill us, who poisoned me, who murdered innocents, and destroyed overland trade?"

Tae gave the only answer he could. "Yes."

Kevral glowered. Her hand glided to her hilt, as if she saw no reason not to slay one more enemy. "Are you going to do those things?"

"No." Tae did not waste a moment in consideration.

"Not even if your father commands it?" The question showed ignorance of organized military operations, which fit Kevral's upbringing. For all their skill, Renshai fought without group hierarchy or strategy.

"My father wouldn't do that. He doesn't kill, and he wouldn't expect it of the one he's training to replace him."

Kevral's expression softened slightly, and her hand loosened on her hilt. "And you're going to replace him?"

"I haven't thought that far ahead." Tae took a step toward Kevral. He had come for a gentle parting, not an argument. "All I know is I was unwilling at first, but now I want to give my father a chance. It's not going to change who I am."

"Yes, it is." Kevral spoke so softly Tae scarcely heard.

Finding no basis for arguing future events, Tae pretended he had not.

Kevral cleared her throat, hand finally slipping away from

the hilt. She could not harm Tae. "You're going to help your father order innocent deaths?"

"No. Not at all." The threat removed, Tae drifted closer and reached for Kevral's hands. She did not resist, though she made no active move to take his either. "Word of the danger has spread through the West. Only a fool would attempt travel now." Realizing he had just placed Kevral and Ra-khir into that category, he inserted, "All right, and people shipwrecked on the Southern Sea by a demon. How often do you think that happens?"

Kevral tried but failed to wholly suppress a smile.

"My point is it's just scaring, not killing anymore." Tae massaged Kevral's callused fingers. "And a battle is sometimes better fought from the inside. We haven't stopped my father's men by attacking them, but I might convince him to call them off with words."

Obviously at least partially convinced by the argument, Kevral squeezed Tae's fingers fondly. "You know, if and when we get a proper heir on Béarn's throne, I'm going to have to travel to Pudar and fulfill my arrangement to train King Cymion's men."

"One way or another, I'll see you safely there," Tae promised. He looked down at Kevral's hands, clenched in his dark grip, and tried to gather the proper words for his next request. "Kevral, do you remember that night we talked." He kept the question deliberately vague. They had spent many evenings in quiet conversation. "And . . . um . . . you agreed that if you chose Ra-khir . . ." He glanced up carefully to discern Kevral's reaction. His usual imperturbable composure stripped away to reveal the stammering adolescent he thought he would never become.

Pink traced a path along Kevral's cheeks, and she became as uncharacteristically nervous as Tae. "I guess I did sort of choose him. In all fairness, I thought you were dead."

Tae felt the first sting of rising tears and swiftly blinked them away.

Kevral added hastily, "But now that I know you're alive, I'll stick to what I said. I won't make a decision until *after* we've finished our mission." She used a euphemism for placing Griff on his throne. Neither wished to consider the possibility that Béarn's only heir had drowned.

Tae's eyes sank to their hands again. "Kevral, I can't help with that mission any more. We may never see one another again. Or we may be on different sides . . . and . . . well . . . I was thinking . . . maybe . . ." He cursed the discomfort that made speech nearly impossible. He had never felt this nervous about anything before.

Kevral regained her equilibrium more swiftly. "I promised if I chose Ra-khir, I'd sleep with you once."

"And it has to be before you two marry. He may not like it now, but he won't tolerate it then."

"It would be wrong."

Tae held his breath for clarification.

"Then, I mean," Kevral said. Her look was willing.

Tae needed no further encouragement. He pulled her into a tight embrace that crushed her breasts against his chest, and the gawkiness left him. All the joy in the universe seemed poised for this night. He would savor every moment of what he sincerely believed would be his last evening with Kevral.

In the austere room that served as his study, Dh'arlo'mé sat on the floor with the Staff of Law across his knees. For the last day and night, he had pored through the books in his library. Though he had read all of them before, the staff added a depth of understanding he had never believed possible. A whole plane of genius opened before him, an unexplored world, and he chased every nuance like a child in a field of butterflies.

Rest would do you good, the staff suggested.

The idea of stopping rankled. Exhaustion dulled the intensity of the experience, and its newness kept Dh'arlo'mé reading long past his body's needs.

There will be other days. Knowledge is endless. A thousand sessions as long as this one will not dent the surface.

The concept of family did not exist in elfin society. Sex was a freedom performed for pleasure and unbound by any custom resembling human marriage. Elfinkind raised its rare children communally, scarcely acknowledging the mother's contribution and never bothering to identify fathers. Dh'arlo'mé had no convention to define the fellowship he felt with the Staff of Law, no concept of love and closeness. He knew only that he felt omnipotent in its presence, and he thrilled to the touch of the wood against him. For the moment, the power it promised was the only thing in the universe that mattered.

Tae returned to his father's camp in the pallor of the false dawn. Alsrusett nodded stonily, condemning Tae's long absence without challenging it. Too excited to care, Tae still reveled in the perfume of Kevral's perspiration on his clothes, and the faint musk of her arousal still clung to him as well. A childish urge to never bathe stole over him, easily banished by need and logic but momentarily comforting. Blissfully exhausted, he fell asleep almost instantly.

By the time Weile, Tae, and the bodyguards returned to the cottage, Kinya had created a new hideaway. The direct ride they had taken to handle the *lav'rintii* opened the possibility of discovery. So they circled and quietly backtracked for nearly a day to the underground dwelling that closely resembled the other. Even the furniture seemed nearly identical: four of the cushioned chairs his father favored, two desks instead of one, a shelf of books, and a barrier that separated the main room from others. Further inspection revealed two bedrooms, instead of one, and a well-stocked pantry. Escape holes, secreted beneath straw ticking, finished the sleeping areas. Kinya, it seemed, had thought of everything.

Tae slept well that night, images of Kevral sweetening his dreams when the heavy burden of sleep did not drag him into its blackest, quietest corners. The security of Weile's bolt-hole allowed Tae to enjoy a depth of sleep he usually did not dare to explore, and the following morning found him torn between excitement and dread. His stomach felt knotted and burning, sensations food only worsened. The time had come for another discussion with Weile Kahn.

Tae sat in one of the chairs, leafing through a book that detailed the strategies of generals through the centuries while Weile scribbled the day's orders on parchment with a stylus. At length, Weile handed the paper to Alsrusett to deliver and turned his attention to his son. Daxan slept in another room, leaving the two alone for the first time since their conversation in the woods.

Weile hauled his chair away from the desk to sit in front of his son. Curls dangled over his forehead like wayward children, and his dark eyes contained the shrewdness of a king. Middle age had coarsened his features and added a few streaks of silver at his temples. "Did you give your friends a proper send-off?"

Tae did not allow his startlement to show, instead concentrating on the train of Weile's logic. He felt certain no one had followed him to Kevral and Ra-khir; his life had too long depended on noticing pursuers. More likely, the bodyguards had mentioned his absence; and his father knew Tae better than he would have guessed. "One of them," he answered casually.

"Good." Weile did not press for details. "Tae, I'm sorry I resorted to such a desperate measure."

"So am I." Despite his bold words to Kevral, Tae punished his father's method.

"Do you ever believe a bad action can justify a greater good?"

"It's possible," Tae said grudgingly. Having used such methods, he found it impossible to condemn them. He had once shadowed his companions when they had forbidden him to do so in order to keep them well-provisioned.

"That's what I was trying to do. I thought if I could make you stay, I would gain the time to convince you to do so willingly."

"I'm not totally unwilling," Tae admitted.

Weile smiled. "I can teach you a lot."

You already have. Tae kept that to himself. *Too much too quick. Besides, much of it was bad.* "Father, I've learned things I want to teach you, too."

"All right." Weile's tone did not patronize. "Why don't you go first?"

It was what Tae wanted, yet he did not know how or where to start. To change his father's intentions, he needed a solid foundation for understanding. Instead of explaining, he questioned. "Why are you working for elves?"

Weile hesitated, as if confused by the query. "Why not?"

"Doesn't it bother you at all that their goal is the destruction of mankind?"

Weile narrowed his eyes and drew his head back. "Who told you that?"

"An elf."

Weile waved in dismissal. "And you would believe everything one elf tells you?"

"I trusted this elf."

"And I trust the ten others who tell me otherwise. Would you put your experience judging motivation and sincerity over mine?"

"No." Tae could not argue that point. "But I put our experience judging *elves* at about equal."

"How many elves have you spoken with?" Weile seemed genuinely interested in the answer, though not in changing his mind.

"A few." Tae did not bother to separate those who had threatened him from those with whom he had conversed. "How many elves have you been tortured by?"

"None," Weile said. "What's your point?"

"My point." Tae leaned forward, hands clasped in his lap to hide anxiety. He knew the words he chose now might make or break the argument. "My point is that I've seen the bad as well as the good side of elves. Have you?"

Weile shrugged, a partial concession. "Men have hurt me before. It doesn't make me understand them better. Just hate them." He considered his words a moment while Tae scrambled to ready a better argument. "It would explain, however, why you don't think we should work with elves." He rocked slightly in a long silence. "Why don't you tell me what happened?"

Tae described the story of rescuing Griff, clinging only to the necessary details and careful not to define the heir's significance. Clearly, Weile had a trusting relationship with the dark elves who did not need to understand the damage killing Griff might inflict on mankind.

Weile listened without interruption, flinching at the brutality Tae described. When he finished, Weile summarized. "So you sneaked onto their island, where no human had gone before. They tortured you to find out where you came from and what purpose you had there."

Tae went still, realizing his father had described the situation aptly but not from a perspective he had considered before.

"Tae Kahn, in the same circumstances, I know of no human king who would have treated you any differently."

"What are you saying? Torture is reasonable in certain situations?"

"How about understandable," Weile compromised. "If you choose your associates by whether or not they've ever employed torture, you'd rule out every kingdom in every part of the world."

Tae dropped the point. "The fact remains that an elf I trust told me the others plot the destruction of mankind."

Weile held his son's gaze, hands motionless on the chair arms. "When you take counsel from traitors, you must weigh the information you get. Believe me, that's one of the first lessons I learned. Those who betray their own will twist information to their gain."

The idea of arguing which viewpoint constituted betrayal passed swiftly. Even Captain believed himself renegade. No matter the side of right, he was undeniably a traitor to the elves.

Weile did not await a response. "It's difficult to believe the elves plot the destruction of mankind when they won't even allow us to harm their own troublemakers."

Tae had no choice but to concede that one. He could not explain the elves' mercy at a time when execution seemed more logical. He could only assume that the elves' nonviolent policies still extended to others of their kind, though not to humans, in much the same way humans naturally ate meat but didn't practice cannibalism. The analogy stretched only so far, however. Tae could never imagine humans consuming elf flesh, yet it made more sense for elves to war with humans and, eventually, among themselves. "How do you explain the elves slaughtering so many of the high king's heirs?"

Weile loosed a snort that covered what might have been a laugh. "You believe the elves responsible for that?"

"I'm certain of it."

"Did you see the elves harm the heirs?"

Tae dodged the question. "I helped rescue one they'd captured."

"Captured from the castle?"

"No," Tae admitted.

Weile remained relentless. "Do you believe the elves responsible for the political upheaval in the East?"

Tae hesitated. He knew nothing of the problems in the East. "It wouldn't surprise me. I do know they're responsible for the death of the elder Pudarian prince."

Weile settled back in his chair. "How do you know that?" he asked, genuinely interested.

"I was there," Tae fairly growled, irritated by the remembrance. The odor of unwashed flesh remained strong in his nostrils, and the childlike chorus of chanting elves wound softly beneath the snarled curses of his father's enemies. The Easterners had pounded and slammed him in the Pudarian alleyway that day, but it was the elves who cornered him with their magic and blanketed his mind, and those of others, with a confusion he had sorted out only much later. The prince and his entourage had attempted to assist the strange, young Easterner smashed beneath a pile of men who clearly wished to kill him. Tae had swept his knife in frenzied, blind arcs, striking flesh more than once. Even he had not known at the time whether one of his strokes was the one that took Prince Severin down. "They pinned the crime on me."

Weile stared at his son, as if meeting him for the first time. "You escaped Pudar's justice?"

"I escaped Pudar's *dungeon*."

Weile smiled, clearly delighted. "How did you manage that?"

Tae feigned casualness, smiling only inwardly. He could not recall the last time an action of his had diverted Weile from an important discussion. "I did what you would have done," he admitted, almost grudgingly. "I organized my cell mates, the rattiest bunch of loners I ever met. But when they merged their skills in a cause . . ." He trailed off, avoiding the end of the story. The guards had killed or recaptured all except one of the other prisoners.

Weile grinned with pride.

Tae redirected the conversation back to its original track. "My point being that the elves had a hand in the slaying of Pudar's prince, so why not Béarn? Or the East for that matter?"

The smile got swept away in Weile's reply. "An elf killed Pudar's crown prince?"

"No," Tae admitted. "They just cast some sort of spell that confused those present enough to believe your enemies . . ." He emphasized the "your" slightly, just enough to instill guilt, ". . . when they claimed I killed the prince. At least, that's how I finally put the whole thing together."

Weile rocked in his chair, obviously contemplating Tae's words thoroughly. "Was that before or after travel became difficult?"

"Before."

Weile made a thoughtful noise.

"What are you thinking?"

Weile's attention drifted back to Tae. He paused longer than appropriate, obviously unused to sharing ideas. Then, realizing he could not train his son to his position without explanations, he said, "It seems the elves must have chosen to work with my enemies first. They must have rejected that association and come to me instead."

Tae blinked, his father's logic too clear to require such intensive consideration. "It seems that way."

"Either that, or my enemies hired the elves. That association left a bitter taste, so the elves came to me when they needed assistance."

Tae narrowed his eyes, attempting to track his father's intentions and believing he needed more information. "Does it make a difference who hired whom?"

"All the difference," Weile replied. "Who had more to gain from that scenario?"

"The elves," Tae replied.

"The enemies," Weile inserted, nearly simultaneously. "They had you dead and me at least desperately embarrassed, perhaps hunted by one of the strongest kingdoms in the world."

Weile's gall astounded Tae. "You would consider us more significant than the crown prince of Pudar?"

"To a rival crime leader, yes." Weile rose, walked beside Tae, and placed an arm across his shoulder. He spoke directly into Tae's ear, as if to reveal the greatest secret of the universe. "Tae, I swear I never did it for the fame or the power. It would scare you to know just how much authority you stand to inherit." He stepped back, clearly expecting the skepticism Tae knew his expression revealed. "My bodyguards." He jerked a thumb toward the back room where Daxan and Alsrusett waited. "The best and most loyal anyone could find. They worked for Stalmize's king before every noble with a taint of royal blood started warring for the crown. Disgusted, they came to me." Weile raised his brows, point only partially made. "Tae Kahn, princes battle for thrones all the time, and they slaughter one another with no more remorse than starving predators on the street."

The analogy unsettled Tae. He had always envisioned royalty as being above the deadly squabbles that those who lived by their wits survived on a daily basis.

"Right now, Tae, it's common knowledge among soldiers and town guards that the most stable group in the East is mine. We may not follow the official laws of the kingdom, but we can be trusted. That's more than any castle in the East can claim."

Though it seemed obvious, Tae had to ask. "So many of the men who are involved in this . . ." He made a sweeping gesture intended to include all of Weile's broad flock.

". . . once served Eastern kings as soldiers, guardsmen, elite fighters. Yes. Do you still think I'm aiding the wrong side?"

Yes. Tae thought it better to avoid an answer. "You believe the elves assisted a rival in order to . . ." The argument broke down. ". . . in order to what?"

"Test them," Weile inserted. "Calculate whether they would best serve elfin purposes." He returned to his seat, emitting a barking laugh. "Your escape made them look incompetent, so the elves came to me instead."

"And now you're essentially running the East."

Weile shook his head. "No. I'm not doing that. I could if I wished, but I never wanted a kingdom. You know that's not why I did this." He mimicked Tae's earlier gesture.

"Maybe not. But if the kingdoms have fallen to chaos, and you command this much respect, perhaps it's your duty to become king."

Weile's eyes widened, then he laughed again. "You're playing with me."

"I'm not." Tae's own words surprised him nearly as much as they did Weile. "You could always establish another king later, but if you have any loyalty to your country, you'll reunite it. If that means becoming the king, then so be it."

"I don't believe it."

"What?"

"It's not enough I'm offering you power? You have your eye on a kingdom?"

Now it was Tae's turn to laugh. "I don't even want the power, remember? I'm talking about you, not me." For an instant he contemplated the possibility that greed did drive him to recommend such an action, but the thought practically discarded itself. He had spoken the truth. His father had a strong sense of justice and an astounding ability to unite even those who seemed adamantly self-devoted. "And why are we talking about kingdoms anyway? I'm still trying to get you to understand that you're on the wrong side."

"Meaning criminals? Or the elves?"

Tae knew Weile would never listen to arguments concerning the former. "I mean the elves. They're planning to destroy mankind."

"I believe," Weile said in a bland monotone indicative of rising anger, "that you have now stated that four times, without a shred of proof."

Frustration plied Tae. "I can't bring you a signed confession."

"How about just a logical argument."

"All right." Tae sought the most convincing point, hampered by the nervousness stemming as much from the likelihood this might prove his first, last, and only chance to gain his father's trust as to rescue Westland travel. "Give me something to work with. Why do *you* believe the elves want to stop travel in the West?"

"They're trying to befriend humanity. They've met with

some understandable hostility. They want the chance to show their harmless intentions before humans amass armies."

"So they hire humans to kill other humans?"

"No. They hired humans to prevent travel. We chose the method." Weile added quickly, "I instructed my men to use the least violent methods necessary to accomplish that goal, though I did give them permission to kill." He shrugged, a gesture that neither excused nor condemned their methods. "Sometimes violent men press their limits. And sometimes travelers press their rights to the roads to the death."

Tae did not dispute the last point. Kevral, Ra-khir, Darris, Matrinka, and he would not have allowed anyone to stand in their way as they escorted the last heir to the throne of Béarn. "But why would elves who only wish to befriend mankind take the last true heir to Béarn prisoner?"

"I don't know, Tae," Weile said, his tone impatient. "We could ask them. I'm sure there're a thousand possible reasons, not the least of which would be his own safety. Gentle giants, the Béarnian kings. They would fall easy prey to warring cousins."

His own safety? Tae could scarcely believe he had heard the words. "Starving him doesn't seem protective to me."

"You think they wanted him dead?"

"Yes."

"There are faster ways than starvation. If the elves wanted this heir dead, they certainly wouldn't have wasted time doing it slowly so you could charge in and rescue him in the meantime."

Tae had to concede that point. Rantire had explained the elves' method by stating that she had partially convinced Dh'arlo'mé that Griff's death would herald the destruction of the universe. *If you knew a man's death could bring the* Ragnarok, *would you lock him in a dungeon?* Before Tae could speak the question, he anticipated his father's response. *If it was the only way to protect him.* The ease with which Weile, and now he himself, could counter every argument unnerved Tae. *Is it possible I'm looking at this from the wrong side?* The thought felt ridiculous, yet he sensed a grain of truth beneath the discomfort. Fatigue closed over him in a wave, and he cursed the blunting of his thoughts that even a full night's sleep had not dispelled. In a quiet corner of his soul, he knew, without need for proof, that he sanctioned the correct side in this dispute. Yet doubts nibbled at that certainty as they had never done before.

Details did not fit his image of the elves as demonic creatures totally dedicated to the ruination of mankind. If the elves could pin *Ragnarok* on mankind and despise them through generations, how could they so easily forgive betrayal among their own? Tae turned to the only argument left in his arsenal. "The gods themselves sanctioned our mission against the elves."

Weile stared, without blinking, far longer than decorum allowed. "Excuse me?" he finally said.

"Colbey Calistinsson directed us to the island of elves and told us to trust the elf they now call Lav'rintir."

"Colbey Calistinsson?" Weile frowned. "The Renshai warrior who killed the Eastern general in the Great War *three hundred and twenty plus years ago?*"

Tae realized how ridiculous he sounded. "Yes." The single word emerged almost as a question.

"Hmmm." Weile pretended to accept the absurd. "So what does a four-hundred-year-old man look like?"

"Amazingly spry," Tae played along for the moment, but sobered an instant later. "I know how weird that sounds, but it *was* him."

"You examined his teeth?" Weile referred to the usual way of aging livestock.

"He had an aura of power about him. He fought with a skill beyond any mortal's. He read minds and talked without words. He helped bring Kevral back from the edge of death."

"He read your mind?"

Tae winced, but he would not lie. "Not mine, but my friends told me he read theirs."

"And talked without words?"

Tae sighed. "Not me again." He defended those details he had witnessed. "I did see him practice with his sword." He shook his head, the sight still lingering as an image of flashing gold and silver, without detail, and a speed and competence unmatched by any mortal.

"A sword practice? That was enough for you to believe in immortality?"

"Yes," Tae said, without a hint of skepticism. "And Lav'rintir identified him, too."

"The traitor elf he brought you to."

Tae did not bother to respond. Again, he floundered, and frustration drove him to speak from the heart. "Father, even though I slept well last night, I'm still very tired. I don't know whether more sleep will clear my mind enough to find the necessary words. I don't even know if those words exist, but I do know I've worked on the side of right." His voice gained the unwavering boom of the staunchest priest. "There is the staff-test, sanctioned by gods. The wrong man or woman on Béarn's throne will result in the destruction of mankind . . . and the elves." His voice lost its authority, to turn almost pleading. "If we don't divert the elves from their petty vengeance, we will all pay with our world and our lives."

Weile applauded. "Beautiful speech, Tae Kahn." Then, his features drew into a tense knot of disappointment. "I taught you to think for yourself, not to believe the pretty words of some golden-tongued, self-proclaimed prophet. I didn't raise you a fool to fall prey to so-called truths whose only proof lies in the faith of its followers." Weile leaped from his chair, clearly agitated. "Hunches, intuition—only tools. I will support any cause you follow so long as it's based on reality and you understand its strengths and its weaknesses. I lead criminals. I make certain my interference does more good than harm and never try to convince myself that I represent goodness. Please, don't dedicate your life to words and unsupported concepts."

Tae lowered his head, pride dashed in an instant. His father had attacked the very foundation of his trust, and he wanted the words to enrage him. Yet he felt only exhaustion. The hot boil of anger would not come, and that only placed his beliefs further into question. "I can't talk about this any more today."

"Fine," Weile said softly. "I understand."

The conversation shifted to reminiscences, mostly happy memories of Tae's mother. Soon daily business replaced any chance for personal discourse. The give and take of men accustomed to working together lulled Tae into a calm routine. The discussions between his father, his bodyguards, and, at intervals, Kinya closely resembled a general conferring with his soldiers. Had he not known the nature of their business, he could never have guessed it from their discussions. To Tae's surprise, Weile occasionally asked his opinion of a particular strategy, with a nonchalance that suggested long association. Kinya smiled at intervals when he believed neither father nor son could see.

Tae discovered himself reveling in a closeness he had never anticipated. Their long talk about the past coupled with his father's direct, sincere attention to his suggestions regarding tactics filled the gap of bitterness between childhood and the present. It seemed to Tae as if they had never separated, in person or philosophy. He had not realized how much he missed his family, its traditions and its methods. He had changed so much, yet even this short time with his father brought back the Tae Kahn he had nearly forgotten and never realized he missed.

The day passed faster than Tae realized. Underground, night looked the same as day, and only the occasional openings of the door revealed the rain and the passage of time. The rich array of spices in the evening meal brought back a fresh round of memories of his mother's cooking and of a culture he once believed he could abandon without a backward glance. Western food tasted bland in comparison, and he had forgotten the vast spectrum of tastes that his friends had never savored. The Eastlands traded their gems and spices for Westland lumber, meat, and vegetables; yet the Westerners had never learned how to properly season their food.

But the sense of rightness quavered in the hush that followed the evening meal. The morning conversation returned to Tae in snatches, a wound that spoiled an otherwise auspicious day. His concerns upset his gut as well. No longer inured to the spices, he suffered stomach acid churning back into his throat and gas pains that knifed intermittently through his belly. Perhaps, no matter how right it felt at times, he could never return to his past.

Weile had avoided the morning's topic through the long hours, yet he returned to it one last time in the cool damp of evening. "Tae, it's been my experience that the side of right is whichever one you're on, and usually that's determined by circumstance. No matter how much you hate your opponent, if you can see through his eyes, you can realize his hatred, too. The time of extremes passed long before our births, when a man's morality was solely determined by his race. Then, good clashed with evil and both with neutrality. You took the side of your people and never questioned. Now, our world supports nothing wholly right or wrong. We pick our positions based on the knowledge we have. When it all comes from one viewpoint, we can't make a valid choice."

Tae smiled tiredly. "So I can keep presenting my arguments?"

"Of course. I'll always value your opinion, even when I don't agree with it." Weile grinned back. "And I'll state my case." He studied Tae. "Tomorrow. Right now, you need your sleep." Weile waved toward the right-hand archway.

Tae started in the indicated direction, then stopped. Need drove him to ask, "What if we never agree on this?"

Weile's grin broadened. "We will, Tae, eventually. Trust me."

Tae nodded stiffly. For reasons he could not explain, he did not feel reassured.

CHAPTER 11

The Bonds that Break

I can be there for you when you need me, like now. But I can't not be there when you don't need me . . . I'm afraid you're stuck with me.

—*Colbey Calistinsson*

Tae tossed and rolled on the thick straw ticking Kinya had provided, sleep an all but impossible goal. Every drift toward slumber brought images of objects breaking: church windows, statuary, and delicate carafes. He would awaken, startled, wounds aching, the explosion into fragments and the sprinkle of shards on stone ringing in his ears, only to find he had scarcely closed his eyes.

Restlessness churned through Tae. Throwing back his covers, he rose and paced the cramped confines of his room. Aside from the mattress, it held a dresser with a few items of clothing only one size too big. The top drawer contained parchment, a stylus, and a shaving knife. A washbasin perched on the surface beside a comb he would not dare to run through the colossal snarl his hair had become. Tae passed these items forty times without denting the anxiety that plagued him. Before he realized what he had done, he shifted the mattress aside to reveal the escape hole beneath it.

You can't leave. You made a vow. Tae stiffened before he recognized the voice as that of his own mind. He cursed the guilt that made him believe otherwise. His loyalty to his friends had caused him to make the promise, and that same bond had driven him to visit them and risk his father's wrath. The force that goaded him now went beyond friendship. If he remained with Weile Kahn much longer, he would lose his identity, be shaped into the perfect son by a man who had spent a lifetime chiseling the worst mankind could offer into devotees. He loved his father, yet he feared that emotion grew not from inside himself but from his father's ability to twist him. Tae had always believed himself strong enough to resist any man's interference. But the foundation of his faith was wavering, threatening to fall. *Is it because he's controlling me or forcing me to think?* Tae knew that, in order to decide, he had to leave Weile's influence. If he remained, he would gradually become whatever his father wished him to be.

Still, Tae could not shake the satisfaction and sensation of rightness that had settled over him throughout the previous day. That had come from himself. No one could change another that swiftly, no matter his skill. Yet, Tae realized, his own love and confusion would become the best weapons in Weile's arsenal. *If I do this thing. If I become my father's successor, I have to do it willingly. It has to be on my terms, or I'll find myself trapped into something I can't sustain. I'll never have control of those men. And I'll lose everything I could have been.*

The world closed in on Tae, and the cool touch of earth surrounded him. He smelled the fresh clean aroma of turned soil and realized he had crawled halfway through the escape tunnel. He froze there, torn between his word and his need. For several moments he engaged in a mental argument that would have seemed foolish under other circumstances. *I gave my word, yet who could better understand vows broken than a man who organizes criminals. But even my father won't abide men he cannot trust. My father. It was a vow to my father.* Tae shifted backward, wriggling carefully through the tunnel and emerging into his sleeping chamber. Resigned, he reached for a corner of the ticking and tensed to slide it back into position. It was not his own struggle, but Kevral's words, that stopped him: "No father who loved his son would force him to stay against his will." She had insisted his time with his father would change who he was. And, like so many times before, she was right.

Glancing at the dresser, Tae found his compromise. He reached it in a stride, yanked open the top drawer, and removed parchment and stylus. Sitting on the bed, he tried to compose something that could make his father understand the betrayal. He sought the words to define the need to find freedom before he could truly commit himself to his father's path. Seven languages failed him, and the eighth gave him only two words. He scrawled those in Eastern, their native tongue: "I'm sorry." It seemed woefully inadequate, but he could manage nothing more. Leaving note and stylus on the ticking, he headed into the tunnel. And never looked back.

* * *

Weile Kahn found the note in the early hours of dawn and crumpled it in a bloodless fist. He stared at the escape tunnel beyond the crooked ticking that had once covered it. The dark hole seemed to look back at him, unwinking, unfeeling.

A knock shuddered through the hideout, the pattern code unmistakably Kinya's. Weile remained in position while Daxan attended to the knock and, moments later, his most trusted confederate stood beside him. Kinya touched his leader's arm with a casualness that made the motion seem accidental, but Weile knew better. He appreciated the comforting. His bodyguards would notice the contact; their job required it. But they would not read the caring conveyed by such a simple gesture.

Weile let the fragments of parchment flutter from his fingers. He looked at Kinya, forcing regimented hardness into his expression. "Tell the men to find him." He managed to keep his voice from breaking. "And to kill him." Lesser punishment for betrayal would only make him appear weak. The ruthlessness of the men he led would not allow it.

Kinya pursed his lips. A glimmer in his eyes revealed a compassion his face would never show and his lips would never speak. He understood. "Right away, sir." He responded as crisply as he would to any command. "I'll return afterward to deliver the daily report."

Weile nodded. Ordinarily, he would have courteously allowed Kinya to report before relaying an order, to save a commander who was also a friend a long, arduous trip. This time, however, he needed some time alone. Kinya would understand that, too. Security could grow lax this once. They would need to create new quarters anyway.

Alsrusett escorted Kinya out while Daxan handled the morning rituals. Alone, at least for the moment, Weile kept his back to the door and silently wept.

Woodlands thinned, giving way to sawtoothed crags that swiftly turned from distant skyline to reality. Lit red against the dusk, mountains swallowed the three dozen *lysalf* and two humans, and excitement plied the usually placid apprentice knight of Erythane until he could scarcely contain the urge to sing. Doing so would besmirch his dignity, as well as draw potential enemies, so Ra-khir resisted. Long practice and training made the restraint simpler than the fluttering in his gut and the waves of exhilaration suggested. He turned to Kevral, only to find her crouched at the edge of a scraggly cache of trees and weeds, more like an out-of-control garden than forest. Her hand kneaded her sword hilt, and her expression seemed strangely sullen for their nearness to Béarn. "What's wrong?"

The concern in Ra-khir's voice drew the attention of several elves. These studied him through jeweled eyes of varying hues.

"We've been noticed." Kevral spoke quickly, head cocked to catch the last rustles of movement. "Youngish male. Béarnide by size and coloring."

Ra-khir considered the words, feeling foolish for his need to ask, yet unable to sort likelihoods. High emotions, an exhausting swim that would have proved impossible without the *lysalf's* magic, and constant battles had left little time for speculation. "Is that bad?"

Kevral stepped back, finally turning her attention to Ra-khir. "I don't know," she admitted. "Depends whether Griff made it to Béarn. Depends on what happened while we were gone. And it depends on what the *svartalf* have managed." She made no move to follow the spy. "He wasn't wearing colors."

Ra-khir nodded. *Not a guard or official.* "Should we keep going?"

Kevral sucked in a deep breath, loosing it slowly as she considered. Renshai politics gave her no insight into strategy or intrigue, but her time with the party, and especially with Tae, did. "Béarnides don't usually scout their borders, especially citizens. If he's willing to risk fighting Easterners by coming this far from town, he's got a reason."

Ra-khir had more familiarity from which to speculate. "Which suggests there's some sort of division, most likely involving the throne." He glanced around at the elves, most of whom watched him, unblinking. He would not drag them into a dispute which might not involve them. "For the moment, we seem safe enough here. Better to let them come to us."

"Night doesn't seem the best time to enter a contested kingdom with a group this size." Kevral opened her arms to indicate the elves.

Especially when most don't fight. One of the great disadvantages of the *lysalf,* Ra-khir had noticed, was that they tended to encompass the most peaceful of the elves. Violence did worse than appall them; they seemed almost unable to comprehend it. "We'll have to watch in shifts." Ra-khir motioned to indicate the two of them. The elves would provide scant assistance in this situation. "See who comes and what we can find out from them. We've got a definite stake in this. We'll have to be careful who we affront or befriend." He spoke casually, so as not to offend Kevral yet still get across the need for guarded courtesy in all dealings. He did not so much worry that Kevral might fall prey to the wrong side as that she might attack an ally for no worse crime than eavesdropping.

"I'll take first watch." Kevral nodded, giving Ra-khir only this scant reassurance.

"All right." The order did not matter, but it seemed likely that whoever had spied before would require time to report back or to gather companions. That might assure he did not return until Ra-khir's watch. *Or, perhaps, conflict will force them to muster more quickly.* It seemed useless to surmise, so Ra-khir gathered a blanket, bunched it into a pillow, and sought sleep.

Kevral yielded her watch to Ra-khir after the sun disappeared from the sky, leaving the mountains looking like giant's teeth against the blackness. Shortly after, a man stepped carefully from a stand of crooked trees, wearing a gray cloak with the hood drawn over his face. Had he come from any other direction, Ra-khir would have assumed him an Easterner. Despite Kevral's description, the stranger stood shorter and narrower than himself, certainly no Béarnide. He moved with a caution bordering on fear, though he made no attempt to hide. The overt approach held Ra-khir from immediately summoning Kevral. For the moment, he watched in silence.

The newcomer's head turned in tiny increments as his gaze swept the gathered elves. Then, his eyes found Ra-khir, and his attention remained there. He made the undulating gesture that passed for distant greeting in the Westlands, then picked his way toward the knight's apprentice.

Ra-khir made a crisper, brisker motion, more acknowledgment than welcome. He waited for the other to draw closer, gaze scanning the area for hidden threats.

At length, the newcomer drew up just beyond sword range. He shook off the hood, spilling light brown hair, in curls, to his shoulders. Bangs spiraled across his forehead, hiding his brows, but the keen hazel eyes, large nose, and broad lips were unmistakable.

"Darris?" Ra-khir dropped all pretenses and swept his friend into a warm embrace. Joy forced a quiet laugh. "Darris."

"These *are* Captain's followers." Darris nodded, apparently having handled his own question and not requiring answer from Ra-khir. "He was right."

"Captain's with you?" Ra-khir hoped the question would spur more than the obvious.

"Not at the moment." Darris glanced behind him, as if to confirm his own words. He made an exaggerated beckoning motion with both hands. "He's back at the safe house with Matrinka, Griff, and Rantire."

Ra-khir grinned, hopes further buoyed by the realization he could now account for all of his companions and could turn his attention to the situation in Béarn. "What's going on?"

"Wait." Darris needed his own reassurances first. "Kevral's with you, right?"

A Béarnide stepped from the brush where Darris had appeared. Also swathed in cloak and hood, he headed toward them.

Ra-khir fixed his gaze on the Béarnide who seemed a bit too small and definitely too confident for Griff or Matrinka. "Yes."

"So that leaves only—"

Ra-khir finished the thought. "Tae. He's well." Ra-khir's gut churned at the mention.

"He's here, too?"

"No." Ra-khir folded his arms across his seething abdomen and pursed his lips. "He's joined up with his father. On the dark elves' side."

"Oh." Darris looked carefully into Ra-khir's eyes, as if to read something unspoken.

The intense scrutiny snapped something. Anger wilted to sorrow in an instant, and tears pooled against Ra-khir's lids. The reaction startled even him.

Darris caught his old companion into another embrace, this time more comforting than exhilarated. "I'm sorry."

The dam finally broke, allowing a wellspring of questions. "How could he do that? How could he choose the company of criminals over us?"

Ra-khir could feel Darris' swallow against his shoulder. "Ra-khir, we *are* talking about Tae."

Ra-khir loosed a small, snorting laugh. "Of all people, I should understand that." They had first met Tae when he spied on the party, without even Kevral's knowledge, and learned about Béarn's dilemma. They would have killed him had he not managed to elude them in the woods. His motivation for joining them had seemed nonsensical, and Ra-khir had refused the companionship the others had finally forced him to allow. Even then, he had never trusted the Easterner, withholding information from him, waiting for the moment when Tae betrayed the party. That time had finally come when Ra-khir discovered Tae's real reason for assisting was to hide among them and use the armed party to dispatch his own enemies. Twice Ra-khir had tried to goad Tae into a duel, and twice the Easterner had refused a challenge no man of honor could. Left without options, Ra-khir had driven Tae away, which upset every member of the group: some because it left an enemy alive to interfere and others because they liked and forgave Tae. Since that time, Tae had proved his loyalty in so many ways, Ra-khir not only trusted him, but considered him a true friend. Now, all the old suspicion returned, accompanied by a bitter sadness that weighted the knight-in-training like poorly constructed armor.

"Kevral says Tae's father made him choose between staying or killing us." Ra-khir shook his head, glancing over Darris to the waiting Béarnide and keeping his voice low. He refused to share such information with a stranger not yet introduced. "But I think she's covering for him. No man would inflict that on his son." He thought of his own father, Knight-Captain Kedrin, whose honor had forced him to silence while Ra-khir's mother first denied his existence for a stepfather, then defended her substitution by denigrating Kedrin. That same awesome honor had condemned Kedrin to Béarn's prison. Ra-khir's train of thought raised concerns that dedication to duty had thrust aside for longer than seemed possible. He hoped desperately that his father still lived and would somehow find freedom from the very justice he had pledged his soul to protect, though it had wronged him.

The tears came faster, and warped images stretched through the blur Ra-khir's vision had become. He saw his mother, the freckles on her face adding character to the beauty of her large eyes, long lashes, and pouty lips. His love for her had turned gradually to hatred as he uncovered the lies and cruelties she had inflicted upon Kedrin and on her only son. Her ultimatum had severed the last of their ties: when he turned seventeen and finally managed to recreate a relationship with his father, she had demanded that Ra-khir choose between her and Kedrin. That decision had been the simplest of his life. He had scarcely thought of her since, yet her image came to him now, bringing a raw and unsortable mixture of emotion.

As memory assailed Ra-khir, he realized why thoughts of his mother rose now. If Kevral spoke truth, Tae's father closely resembled the mother Ra-khir wished only to avoid. Sorrow burst into sympathy as well as rage. He pitied Tae's choice, at the same time cursing his friend's concept of honor. The father should never have forced such a demand, yet neither should Tae have yielded to it.

Darris released Ra-khir, then glanced past him. Ra-khir did not bother to turn. Several elves were probably studying Darris, their gemlike eyes gleaming in the moonlight an unnerving sight to one not yet accustomed to them. Fourteen of the *lysalf*, like Captain, did not require sleep. Darris seemed relieved to have cause to focus elsewhere. He looked at the Béarnian stranger, touching his arm and drawing him nearer to Ra-khir. "This is Baynard. He comes from a long line of Béarnian soldiers, but he left his position due to politics."

Baynard tossed down his hood to reveal a boyishly round, pudgy face. His black hair clung to the cloth, and strands stood on end as the hood fell against his back. Ra-khir estimated he was in his early twenties.

Probably because of the length of his title, Darris left Ra-khir to his own introduction.

"Ra-khir of Erythane, son of Knight-Captain Kedrin and apprentice knight to the Erythanian and Béarnian kings: His Grace, King Humfreet, and His Majesty . . ." Ra-khir nearly said "King Kohleran" from habit, but Darris' frown and head shake stayed him. Instead, he looked askance at his friend.

". . . Griff," Darris supplied, "but don't say that around anyone but us. Leave it as Kohleran."

The words surprised Ra-khir. "King Kohleran still lives?" Colbey Calistinsson had led them to believe otherwise.

Baynard glanced at Darris. "He's safe, right?"

"Undeniably."

Accepting that, Baynard addressed Ra-khir. "That's what the elves would have us believe. It's a long story, and it's best to get all of you to a safe place first. Then, we can talk."

"All right." Ra-khir had no difficulty with the logic. "Where would you have us go?"

Baynard took over the preparations, leaving Darris visibly relieved. So far, he had stuck with simple details that did not require his bard talents to describe. Plotting or discussion would drive him beyond speech and into music. "A group this big would attract attention, if it hasn't already. We'll have to break it down to bunches of two to six. We've got a supply of scarves, and darkness will help hide the elves. They're too slight to pass for men, so we'll have to make them look like ladies."

Ra-khir nodded.

Darris headed back toward the trees for equipment while Baynard finished elaborating the plan. "Ra-khir, we thought you'd come with us on the first run. The Renshai can stay and guard the elves."

The idea of hiding out in a safe house while Kevral remained vulnerable rankled, despite the knowledge that she was the superior fighter. "I can help with each group."

"No." Baynard ran a hand through his hair, shuffling errant strands back into place. "You don't know enough history to talk your way out if we get caught. You're anything but the first volunteer. Darris and I can handle this. Any more bodies just makes the job harder."

Ra-khir conceded reluctantly. "All right. I'll let Kevral and the elves know what's happening. Let's get this started."

Baynard whispered, softly enough that Ra-khir questioned what he heard, "And may the gods be with us."

By the time dawn paraded its colors across the mountain skyline, no one remained at the border camp. Most of the elves huddled quietly in various basements, attics, and lofts. Each group contained at least one who spoke the common trading tongue. The humans congregated together along with half a dozen elves, including Captain. Ra-khir sat at a rickety table, nostrils assailed by the odors of must and damp. Baynard, Darris, and Captain took the other positions around it. Matrinka perched on a nearby chair, stroking Mior. The cat sprawled across her mistress' legs, head upside down to expose her neck, limbs extended to utilize the entire expanse. Kevral hunkered at Matrinka's side. The elves occupied various places on the floor. Three Béarnides, all strangers to Ra-khir, knelt, stood, or leaned near Baynard and Darris. Griff rested on a pile of sleeping rags in a corner, Rantire ever vigilant at his side.

The positioning injured Ra-khir's courtly sensibilities. It bothered him that the King of Béarn sat on the floor while others had furniture, but he did not voice his opinion on the matter. Griff seemed happy in the place he had chosen. Too much lay at stake to argue details of order and manner now.

The oldest of the Béarnides, a middle-aged, scar-faced carver named Davian, spoke first. "Our work last night won't go long unnoticed. We're going to have to make our move today."

Aerean, the only woman among the strangers turned him a shrewd stare. "And what, exactly, is 'our move'?"

Davian had a ready answer. "We rally as many Béarnides as we can and go right for the front door."

Baynard finished, "And get pounded by Béarn's army, the citizens who believe they're defending the king, the Knights of Erythane, and elves."

Elfin heads swiveled toward him at the mention.

Baynard amended. "The *dark* elves. Oh, and some Renshai if we seem like a potential threat to any heirs, and I imagine we certainly would under the circumstances."

Ra-khir was still grappling with the difficulty most of Béarn's citizens had discriminating between an elf and their elderly king. Faced with a situation his friends had had the opportunity to consider for weeks, he remained silent.

Davian frowned, creases scoring his cheeks. "I'd rather die in the confrontation than be dragged out of my home and executed."

The third stranger, Friago, chimed in, "No one's arguing we need to act quickly." He picked at a scab on his Béarnian-hairy wrist. A few years older than Baynard, he kept a massive ax leaning against the table by his hand. Though notched and dull, it carried no dust or stains. "But if we can delay a few days, we might gather some powerful allies." He turned his attention to Kevral, brows rising.

Davian followed Friago's stare. "Renshai?"

Friago shrugged. "Why not?"

"Why not, indeed," Baynard boomed. "More importantly, why didn't we think of this before?"

The oldest Béarnide muttered under his breath, so that only those nearest could hear. "We couldn't get our only one unglued from the king."

Ra-khir disliked the plan. "You want Kevral to travel to the Fields of Wrath? Alone?"

"Not necessarily alone," Friago said, clearly missing Ra-khir's concern. "What's the problem?"

"There're Easterners about, paid to kill anyone who travels." Ra-khir managed to refrain from adding, *Or hadn't you noticed*. Snideness did not become anyone, especially a future knight.

Friago's brow furrowed. "They let you go before. You think they'd stop you now?"

"They'd try," Kevral inserted. "I can handle them. Especially if my cousin assists."

All eyes turned to Rantire, who scowled deeply. "I'm not abandoning my charge." Her gaze went directly to Matrinka, a distinctly obvious gesture. She condemned Kevral's separation from the object of her own guardianship, at the shipwreck and now.

Kevral defended. "I didn't abandon my charge. You agreed to watch her while I fought the demon."

"I fought that demon, too," Rantire reminded. "And still managed to stay with both our charges."

An artery throbbed at the side of Kevral's jaw. Ra-khir winced as he imagined her drawing her sword and challenging Rantire before anyone could move to stop her. But Kevral had learned more self-control than even the man who loved her realized. "We can discuss the difference between dedication and luck later."

Rantire opened her mouth to protest, but Kevral continued over her. "Or my lapse, as the case may be. Right now, I'm asking for your help. You can come or not. I'd appreciate your company, but I can handle the situation alone."

Ra-khir read between the words. Kevral would not request assistance unless she believed she required it. She would happily die in combat, but doing so would suit neither their cause nor their relationship. Ra-khir intended to volunteer, but not until Rantire's role became certain. Two Renshai could sway Renshai better, and Rantire's experiences might help her find the words to convince. Kevral's confidence and perfectionism had not made her popular among her own.

Griff spoke his first words of the meeting. "Rantire, please. I'm in far more danger from never gaining Béarn's respect than from sitting among competent friends. What good do you do guarding me at the expense of my throne?"

Darris shook his head hopelessly and shared a wordless moment with Ra-khir. They both knew Rantire would remain loyal to Griff's person over his word, or even his best interests.

"That's it," Kevral said suddenly, as if putting together a puzzle that had confounded wise men for eternity. "Rantire, you don't *want* Griff to become king."

"That's absurd," Rantire shot back. "I'm just guarding his life. That's my job."

Kevral nodded sagely, ignoring Rantire's denial. "If Griff becomes king, Darris guards him. Your job is over. You think you need to do more to earn the respect Ravn Colbeysson gave you. No wonder you don't want him to become king."

"I *do* want him to become king," Rantire argued; but, despite the challenge inherent in such a serious accusation, she made no move toward Kevral. Apparently, the suggestion bothered even her. Ra-khir doubted Rantire deliberately intended to sabotage Griff's ascension, but Kevral's theory made sense, at least on a subconscious level.

"Then go with Kevral," Griff returned softly, but with a solidarity bordering on command, "and it might happen."

Rantire studied Griff for several moments in a silence that no one broke. "You really believe I should go?"

"Yes," Griff replied without hesitation.

Rantire froze, betrayed by her usual loyalty. Twice she had faced down a god for him, and the idea of simply leaving surely rankled. No one interfered as she crouched in quiet contemplation far longer, Ra-khir guessed, than she probably realized. "All right," she finally said. "I'll go." She glanced at Griff fretfully, as if she feared armies would sweep into the safe house the instant she no longer graced his side.

Now Ra-khir felt free to volunteer. "I'll go with them. Just to help with the Easterners."

"No," Darris replied softly.

Brows arched, Ra-khir turned his regard to the bard.

"We need you to gain us other powerful allies."

"Me? Who do I know?" Ra-khir considered, the answer coming swiftly. "You mean the Knights of Erythane?"

"Of course."

Ra-khir frowned, shaking his head sadly. "I'm just an apprentice. My word has no sway."

Darris stared pointedly, clearly not wishing to sing an argument that he believed should be obvious.

"Even being the son of the captain doesn't give me any particular . . ."

Darris shook his head briskly, though a slight smile playing at the corner of his lips told Ra-khir his words contained a glimmer of Darris' idea.

Finally, the proper thought slid within the boundaries of understanding. Ra-khir's eyes widened with incredulity. "You want me to convince my father to do it?"

Darris' lips spread into a broad grin. "Exactly."

"But my father is in prison."

"Exactly."

Ra-khir suspected Darris' intentions should seem stunningly obvious, but he still could not interpret the details. Baltraine had left Kedrin his command, even while he'd incarcerated him for life. "You want me to visit my father and convince him to is-

sue orders against the current regime?" His face pinched into a
skeptical grimace. "Don't you realize who relays my father's
orders? They'd kill him." He resisted adding the natural trailing
thought. *If they haven't already.* The superstitious fear that
speaking the words might make them happen kept him silent.

By now, others had pieced together what Ra-khir's honor
made difficult to comprehend. Davian said, "Ra-khir, I think he
means we break your father out of prison."

Darris nodded vigorously. "If by 'we' you meant Ra-khir and
me, that's just what I mean."

Ra-khir sat perfectly still, the suggestion an affront to his
own honor as well as his father's. "We can't do that."

"It won't be easy." Darris clearly misunderstood.

Ra-khir ran his hands along the tabletop, grainy dirt rolling
beneath his fingertips, disrupting its smoothness. "That's not
what I meant. Breaking someone out of prison is a crime."

Every eye at the table jerked suddenly to Ra-khir. Davian
couldn't help but snicker. "Of course it's a crime," Baynard
said, "but a necessary one. We need the Knights of Erythane to
restore the proper king."

Ra-khir shrugged, unswayed by the argument for two reasons. Need never justified sin, and not having the Knights' support would only make Griff's coronation harder, not
impossible.

Darris rose, knowing Ra-khir well enough to find the proper
justification where the others had failed. Crossing the room, he
plucked a battered lute from the corner behind Matrinka, reclaimed his chair, and placed the instrument into playing position. The humans at the table settled more comfortably,
resigned to the bard's curse. The elves watched him curiously,
unaccustomed to the oddity.

A short introduction flowed from the strings, the tones surprisingly pure for an instrument of such low quality. Then the
bard launched into a familiar song that chronicled the history of
King Sterrane's return from the viewpoint of a knight. Ra-khir
had heard the song before, but never from the lips of the bard.
Darris' voice, and the complexity of harmony, added a beauty
that made word and mood transfixing.

Darris sang of his own famous ancestor, Mar Lon, whose
name had become synonymous with peace. He sang of an escaped slave, Garn, a friend to the rightful king, who had
sneaked into the castle to assassinate the usurper. Ra-khir's
heart pounded as those two good men fought, one to kill and

one to protect a king who had obtained his throne through murder. He could hear the ring of steel, feel the ache of the blows through Mar Lon's muscles, and read determination in the actions of both. Each man fought with honor and for right, though their causes pitted them on opposite sides. But as the battle progressed, Mar Lon's certainty wavered. The now long-dead bard had wrestled with a decision not unlike Ra-khir's own. Law and propriety condemned him to defend the current king, but right placed him firmly in Sterrane's camp. Though he won the battle against Garn, he lost the one against his conscience.

Ra-khir knew the rest of the story from his books, yet Darris' timbre and pitch added the emotion written facts had never evoked. Mar Lon had freed Garn from the dungeon sentence to which his own actions had committed the one-time slave. He had promised assistance and delivered it in the form of the Knights of Erythane. These men of honor had pledged themselves first to the proper ascension of Béarn and only second to Béarn itself.

Darris' singing stopped, but the music continued in a slowly unwinding spiral that held the mood long past the words. Ra-khir conceded his friend's point. His situation seemed much more clear-cut than that of the Knights of the past. They had betrayed one heir for another, turning against the king they had faithfully served to band with the one who should have ruled in his place. Yet Ra-khir had never questioned the need to dethrone the false king. His problem lay with freeing his father.

Ra-khir waited until Darris finished before speaking. The others, humans and elves, remained in an expectant hush, convinced, waiting for Ra-khir's reaction. "I have no problem opposing the dark elves nor with helping band the Knights to assist. It's the breakout."

Darris slumped over his instrument, beaten. "So you won't help?"

Ra-khir wrestled need against right. "I'll help. I don't believe a false accusation by a deceitful prime minister and a verdict handed down by a spurious king constitute law. Therefore, violating the terms of sentencing is not really a crime." He considered his own words, hoping he had not simply rationalized the actions he wanted to take.

The room seemed to sigh collectively. Baynard and Aerean smiled.

"But," Ra-khir continued, and the grins wilted. Several people winced at the words that might follow. "I don't think my father will be so easily convinced. Remember, he refused to defend himself at the trial because it might damage the citizens' faith in their government. He may not come with us."

"You'll just have to convince him." Darris stated the obvious, making the impossible sound simple.

"I don't know if I can." Ra-khir's doubts became a desperate roar of uncertainty. "I don't know what to say."

Baynard offered no sympathy, summarizing what everyone surely felt. "Ra-khir, you'll just have to find the words."

CHAPTER 12

The Catacombs

*A warrior who dies fighting with his principles intact
dies in glory.*

—*Colbey Calistinsson*

Ra-khir blamed anxiety for the relentless feeling of unseen eyes watching him from the darkness. His discomfort began as they approached Béarn Castle and remained as Darris uncovered the secret entrance. Ra-khir had scanned the darkness a hundred times, seeing and hearing nothing to corroborate his fear. Even as they descended into the depths of the castle's dungeon catacombs, the sensation remained.

Damp air washed Ra-khir's skin into goose bumps, and the reek of moss and fungus became lodged in his nostrils. He followed Darris through impenetrable blackness, the tiny thump and occasional sheeting scrape of the bard's boots against stone guiding him long after his vision failed. Every few moments, Darris touched him to ascertain that they had not gotten separated.

Soon, the spirals, gradual twists, and sudden turns became too engrossing, and the sensation of another watching disappeared. Only the bard and his or her heir learned the difficult maze that warded Béarn's dungeon from escapes and that, Darris assured Ra-khir, took years of concentrated study. If not for the god-determined damnation that ceaselessly fueled bard curiosity, even Darris could never have memorized the details.

After what seemed to Ra-khir like hours, opacity softened to gloom. Stone walls fuzzy with growth became visible as dark, irregular shadows. Then, suddenly, Darris jerked backward, reaching for Ra-khir in silent warning. His hand found Ra-khir's chest, restraining.

Ra-khir peered over the bard's shoulder to a semicircle of torchlight. Apparently cautious because of its presence, rather than any direct threat, Darris inched forward again.

The passageway opened into a dank, murky room filled with cells. Scattered torches illuminated ghastly shadows, mostly long lines running from floor to ceiling. Many brackets held only charcoal stubs. Shapes shifted, animallike, in the darkness. Occasionally, the rattle of a pan against stone or a clink that might represent a sentry's armor broke the stillness. The air reeked with the stench of human excrement, disease, and unwashed flesh. Ra-khir gagged, turning away. If he vomited, he would need to do so quietly and mindful of his companion.

Ra-khir managed to hold down his meal, clutching his sword as Darris edged toward the light. Nothing changed in the sounds coming from the dungeons to suggest discovery. Carefully, in silence, Ra-khir followed.

Darris dared a whisper, cupping his hands to direct the sound into his companion's ear. "You saw him. Which way?"

Ra-khir racked his memory, trying to rethink direction. He had visited his father only once, coming through the main entrance and escorted by a guard. He had not traveled through the famous catacombs that had foiled escape from Béarn's dungeons since long before Mar Lon directed Garn. He chose a direction from intuition alone, gesturing for Darris to follow.

Again, the sensation of hidden eyes watching assailed Ra-khir, and he cursed the nervousness that made normal caution impossible. He guessed the entrance lay nearly in a corner of the dungeon, directly left. His father occupied a cell toward the far end of the first row. Any guards would cluster toward the main entrance to keep prisoners from escaping back into the palace. Therefore, it only made sense to circle right.

Ra-khir led Darris down the farthest corridor. To his right, cold radiated from the dungeon wall, deep beneath the ground. Cells lined the left, the first several empty. The next held a single occupant or a lumpy pile of blankets on the floor. Sound echoed in eerie disorder, the acoustics indecipherable. Tiny scrapes of movement reverberated, and rare coughs or sneezes shattered the stillness like explosions. Breathing originated from so many places it became a constant, easily mistaken for the puff of wind meandering through corridors.

Reaching a corner, Ra-khir turned, now pacing a course parallel to their entrance. The arbitrary lighting wore on his vision, as his eyes adjusted and readjusted to the constant changes. Rows of bars blurred into one. A prisoner sat up abruptly as they approached, startling Ra-khir into a hasty crouch. His boot squeaked against a worn spot on the floor, and he damned the noise. Other prisoners shifted to examine them in the dim light.

Ra-khir cringed, their passage now marked by the attention of curious prisoners. Though none spoke, he worried about the change in routine that the guards would eventually notice. He turned to Darris, silently requesting suggestions that the bard did not offer. They could sneak out and start again, probably with no better results. Time was a luxury they could ill afford. So far, the guards had not responded simply to differences in movement. The prisoners would not likely give them away intentionally; they held no love for Béarn's guards.

Sweat beaded Ra-khir's forehead as he crept forward. *One more corner.* Excitement plied him as he approached the corridor he believed held his father's cell. A day of rest had brought him only vague concepts with which to sway his father. Desperately, he hoped the proper words would come when he looked upon Kedrin again. He stepped into a ring of torchlight.

Darris' hand seized Ra-khir's cloak suddenly, hauling him backward. Startled, Ra-khir lost his balance, crashing to one knee on the stone floor. Pain shot up his leg, and he bit his lip to stifle a cry.

A gruff voice from ahead called. "Hey, you there!"

Ra-khir froze, blood like ice in his veins. Darris whirled and ran, feet thumping on the hard floor.

Shouts erupted from every corner of the dungeon, from guards and other prisoners. Footfalls slammed the stone, their echoes bewildering. Ra-khir drew his sword, torchlight flashing from the steel, only to face a dilemma he had not recognized until that moment. *I can't fight Béarnian guards!* He jabbed the blade back into its sheath.

Four men approached warily, Béarn's familiar blue and tan fading into the gloom. Two clutched poleaxes and the others swords. The tallest glared. "Don't move."

Ra-khir rolled his gaze down the corridor, seeing movement but unable to differentiate friend from guards. He realized his mistake then. He had believed the maze opened onto the wall directly right of the main entrance and now understood it was catercorner. Rather than working around it, he had dragged them directly to the main entrance. Darris' extensive knowledge of the catacombs had proved of little value when it came to negotiating the dungeon itself. Apparently, the simple layout was not part of his training. The irony rankled. *Like a general lead-*

ing armies in intricate strategies without learning how to wield a sword. Ra-khir held out his weaponless hands in surrender.

At the first sound of a guard's voice, Tae had shinnied up the bars of an empty cell. Height gave him vantage as well as security. The guards would focus on Ra-khir and Darris, unlikely to search above their heads, at least not until they had subdued the others.

Tae remained still, well-versed at subterfuge and effectively hidden among the smoky shadows. Unlike the massive party of elves, he had entered Béarn with his usual quiet caution, searching for signs of his companions. The difficulty he encountered warned him of their need for caution. He had finally discovered Darris and Ra-khir as they slipped toward the castle under cover of darkness. Brief snatches of conversation, and their bearing, revealed their intentions well enough. He had kept himself concealed, afraid of Ra-khir's reaction. The circumstances of their parting would have required extensive explanation that would have delayed or sabotaged this mission. Now, Tae wished he had confronted his friends. Either they would not have come or, at least, they would have had his expertise to draw upon and might not have gotten caught.

As the guards led Ra-khir and Darris through the corridors, their official calls to one another announcing their every move, Tae silently worked his way along the cells. Most of the prisoners had awakened, watching guards march through the hallways, some escorting their new prisoners. Caught up in the distraction, they did not notice as the small, quiet figure worked his way above their line of sight. He did not need to go far. Within a few cells, Tae identified the broad, red-haired Erythanian who was Ra-khir's father. The captain sat, listening more than watching, obviously awakened by the commotion. Ra-khir and Darris had passed him in the gloom, without either party noticing it.

The noises of prisoners and guards grew more distant as they hauled away a quiet Ra-khir and a resisting Darris. Tae did not wait, using the distraction to his advantage. Seeing no prisoners in the neighboring cells, he lowered himself cautiously, trying not to aggravate his wounds or startle the knight-captain into revealing his presence. Finally, he clambered to the floor, his face scarcely above the level of the sitting Erythanian's. Even more than with Ra-khir and himself, the difference in their heights was tremendous.

Calculating the pitch of his voice by the resounding echoes around him, Tae addressed Kedrin. "Follow me. Quickly." He jabbed a homemade tool into the lock, twisting until he felt the satisfying jolt of its unlatching.

"Who are you?" Kedrin asked, his voice reaching only Tae's ears. Clearly, he was familiar with the pattern of sound and echoes.

"A friend of Ra-khir. Talk later." Tae swung the cell door open in a manner designed to minimize squealing. It made less noise than he expected and even that was lost beneath the sound of a cell door slamming. He left an opening just wide enough for the knight-captain to slip through.

But Kedrin did not follow.

Tae's heart rate quickened, acknowledging the danger inherent in every passing moment as well as every word. "Hurry, please. The fate of Béarn depends on you."

Kedrin shuffled a single step, then stopped, shaking his head sadly. "I can't."

Tae gaped, scarcely able to believe he had heard correctly. "Are you hurt?"

"I can't betray my country and my honor. King Kohleran sentenced me here, and I won't disobey him."

Tae conveyed his frustration with a groan. "We don't have time for this." He glanced about, licking his lips though the pervading dampness kept them moist. *Remember, he's Ra-khir's father. Think like Ra-khir.* Precious seconds ticked away as Tae recalled his many sessions discussing honor with Ra-khir. *Think insane.* "Look, we both know you were framed. I can prove I had a hand in that. So if you don't come forward with the truth, I will." Tae stared fiercely, defiantly. Ra-khir had explained Kedrin's reasons for not defending himself at the trial, and the information Tae could reveal would destroy Baltraine and the hierarchy Kedrin had sacrificed himself to maintain. Like Kedrin, Tae had no way to know his knowledge threatened a prime minister already dead.

Kedrin's eyes widened. For the first time, Tae noticed their color, a blue so pale they appeared nearly white. "You're lying."

Inwardly, Tae cringed at the next words he had to speak, though he showed no outward sign. Kedrin had named the wrong action bluff. "Baltraine paid me to steal your dagger." He watched Kedrin carefully for evidence of coming violence.

Kedrin stiffened, but his expression seemed more shocked than angry.

"I'm sorry. It was wrong." Tae did not elaborate his motivations further. Time constrained him to as few words as possible. "Come on."

Kedrin lowed his head. "I can't."

Tae tried another tack. "King Kohleran is dead."

"I know. And an elf impersonates him. But it was the king who sentenced me, before his death. Not the elf."

Tae knew nothing of the deception, but he did not reveal his surprise. Ignorance would make him look weak at a time when he needed strength. The noises at the other side of the prison lessened, and he had no experience on which to predict future actions. Obviously, the guards would need to report to a superior and make decisions about Ra-khir and Darris. That might wind up bringing more enemies into the dungeon. He never doubted his own ability to escape; Kedrin, however, would have absolutely no knowledge of stealth. One thing seemed certain: Tae measured security in moments that swiftly disappeared as he wasted them trying to convince a knight overburdened with honor of the obvious. The necessary logic refused to come, so Tae turned elsewhere, to the mystical bond between fathers and sons. Hostility left a bitter taste in his mouth as his relationship with his own father rose to his mind, unbidden. For now, he shoved that aside. "Do you trust Ra-khir?"

"What?"

Tae dove for the jugular. "Do you trust your son? Your only son?" He did not wait for an answer, but tenaciously attacked, never leaving Kedrin an opening to consider. The answer, he made clear, should require no thought. "Because if you don't, you cast aspersions on yourself." A dull ache pounded through Tae, and he continued through gritted teeth. Images of his own father paraded through his mind's eye, and he fought down the emotion that might taint the only words he had to convince. "On everything you've ever taught. If you can't trust your son to uphold your honor, then, Sir Kedrin, you have no son."

"I trust Ra-khir." Under the circumstances, Kedrin could answer no other way. "Why?"

"Because that man the guards just caught . . ."

Kedrin nodded warily, then went still in mid-motion as realization dawned. "Ra-khir?"

"He came for you," Tae explained. "You know he wouldn't have done that if it violated his honor. Or yours."

"Ra-khir." Kedrin drifted toward the bars like a man entranced and gripped them, though his gaze sought details through the darkness behind his cell.

"Béarn needs you free. I'll explain when we have the time." *Once I figure out what's going on.* "Right now, you just have to trust Ra-khir. And, now, me."

Kedrin remained desperately silent.

Tae had run out of strategies, as well as time. "Are you with me?"

A long pause followed, during which the consummate man of honor weighed options with an integrity Tae could scarcely comprehend. "I'm with you," Kedrin said, at length, gathering a book and stylus. "And I hope my son recognizes the loyal friend he has in you."

Tae smiled at the irony.

Tae led Kedrin in a quiet sneak around the wall of the cell block, cringing at every heavy fall of the knight-captain's feet. The whispers of the prisoners and shouts of the guards drowned any noise they made, but he worried for the tromp of boot against stone or the betrayal of prisoners envious of their freedom. Under other circumstances, Tae might have released them all. The diversion they could create for him, as well as the loyalty the act would inspire, could serve him well. Yet the realization that his father would have done exactly that, organizing those he released into his band, made the idea unpalatable. Nor would Kedrin's honor have allowed such a thing.

Having relegated the stylus to his pocket, Kedrin held the book, safely tucked against his left armpit. Tae quickened their pace, breath catching in his throat with every noise. The guards' shouts remained mostly indecipherable, but he still managed to glean information from phrases plucked from the whole. They had imprisoned Ra-khir and Darris in central cells, having identified the former but not the latter. Tae guessed Ra-khir had recited name and title while Darris remained more circumspect. Some of the guards had left for reinforcements. Questioning would surely follow; and Tae hoped that Béarn, now beneath the rule of elves, would not turn to their methods of obtaining information. The thought of Ra-khir and Darris being tortured made him wince.

Boots pounded suddenly through the prison again. A chill invaded Tae, and he went abruptly still. Despite the odd acoustics of Béarn's dungeon, he still managed to separate individuals and determine location. Guards raced up every aisle, surely seeking other infiltrators. *Like me.* Tae forced himself to move, heart slamming like a blacksmith's hammer. Kedrin would not fight guards, so escape lay in his own barely competent hands. He dared not fight, and Kedrin's presence made evasion impossible.

Tae grabbed Kedrin's arm and pulled. The Knight of Erythane lowered his head to his companion's level.

"Run for the catacombs," Tae hissed.

Kedrin stiffened, though he continued walking briskly. "The catacombs? That's sure suicide."

"Trust me," Tae returned, with as much forcefulness as a whisper allowed.

Then the time for argument ended. Two guards pounded around the final corner and directly into their path. Tae did not wait for their presences to register and the guards to slow. He flung himself at their feet, jackknifing his body between one's ankles as he seized the other's legs. The first collapsed, momentum sliding him down the hallway. The other teetered, regained his balance, then stumbled into his companion and tumbled to the floor as well. A flailing arm crashed against Tae's head. He blundered sideways, careening into a wall, his thoughts spinning. Agony slammed through his chest wound. He sensed more than saw Kedrin dart past.

"Intruders!" one of the downed guards yelled, twisting and lunging for Tae simultaneously. "Aisle seven."

Tae jerked his legs, avoiding the grab but losing his own balance in the process. He scrambled toward the corner, betrayed by his own wild movement. He plummeted to the floor, impact aching through ribs and limbs, old injuries protesting. Desperate, he scurried blindly, throwing his lower body sideways to avoid capture. No resistance touched his legs, but unexpected hands clamped suddenly on his wrists.

Guards' voices echoed through the confines. "Seal the exit! Block seven!"

Hauled abruptly to his feet, Tae stared frantically at his captor. Kedrin's blue-white eyes met his. "Come on." He freed Tae's wrists.

Thank gods. Tae barreled down the hallway and around the corner, the clomp of Kedrin's feet a reassuring constant at his side. They careened around the corner, desperately scanning the darkness ahead.

Figures blustered toward them, too late to corner them in aisle seven. Tae saw the gaping blackness of the entrance to the catacombs to his left. Straight ahead, the guards raced toward them. "Row ten!" one screamed, voice reverberating into spooky, unintelligible sound.

Tae calculated as he ran. The guards would surely beat them to the exit, but he could think of no better plan. He sprinted toward freedom, praying.

Footfalls seemed to come from all directions. Tae lowered his head, tensing for a tackle and prepared to battle in a savage frenzy. Twice imprisoned, crammed into cells that seemed airless, anticipating the agony a vengeful king and bitter elves could inflict upon him, he would never survive another capture. If Béarn did not slaughter him, his own terror might.

The guards ahead tensed, fanning out to barricade the corridor with massive, mailed bodies. Anticipating a run for the main exit, they stopped well before the opening to the catacombs.

There's our miracle. Tae rushed the guards. Need drove him to turn as swiftly as possible, but years of covering his intentions allowed him to bluff. He waited until he came fully upon the opening before diving inside. Kedrin followed on his heels.

"You'd better know what you're doing," Kedrin mumbled as they scuttled through the first three turns.

Gasping for breath and suffering reawakened pain, Tae gave no reply.

"They're in the maze!" a guard exclaimed, his bass voice magnified to ear-splitting echoes by the tunnels.

Tae jerked to a halt, sweat clammy on his limbs and trickling down the back of his neck. He paused, pressing his back against a wall and allowing his breathing to settle to a quiet pant.

"You, you, you, you, you, and you stay here. If they come back out, kill them."

Kedrin's fingers touched Tae's arm, then seized it. His breath huffed warm against Tae's cheek as he spoke. "Was that your plan?"

"To sneak back into the dungeon?"

"Yes."

"No," Tae replied.

Kedrin remained quiet a few moments, clearly considering. "Then what *is* your plan?" He continued to clasp Tae's arm, apparently concerned about losing him in the pitch-black corridor.

"Forge on."

The grip on Tae's arm tightened nearly to pain. "Are you

aware it's a hopeless maze? No one has ever successfully negotiated it. The few prisoners who tried to escape died there."

"I know," Tae returned, though he did not. He had surmised
it easily enough when he followed Darris and Ra-khir. The
memory returned in a vivid rush of terror. Once his eyes had
failed him, only sound could guide him. He listened until his
ears ached. When Ra-khir and Darris spoke, he had trailed them
easily. Mostly, however, they had moved in uneasy silence. He
had staked his life on the occasional scuff of a boot against
stone or the faint rustle of fabric and, at times, worried that he
chased rats instead of companions. "The man captured with
your son is the bard of Béarn."

"The bard?" Joy entered Kedrin's tone. "Darris?"

Tae nodded, realizing an instant later that Kedrin could not
see his response. "Darris," he confirmed aloud. "And the bard
always knows the way through the catacombs."

"Really." Kedrin did not question, nor did his tone imply
doubt. "If anyone would, the bard would." Tae sensed movement through the knight's touch. "But how does that help us?
Surely, he didn't teach you." He emphasized "teach" rather than
"you," clearly trying not to imply that Tae was personally unworthy, simply that security would not allow the bard to explain
such a thing to anyone. Even trapped in an impossible situation
and hunted by guards that he would, ordinarily, consider peers,
Kedrin would not forsake his manners.

"No," Tae admitted, doubting he would have the patience or
memory to learn, even if Darris did deign to teach him. Breathing came easily now, and the anguish in his chest settled to dull
throbbing. "But we came in this way." The darkness swallowed
his grin. "And I marked the way."

Kedrin stiffened, the moisture on his palm washing cold
against Tae's skin. "You've opened the way for criminals to escape."

Tae snorted, as much at the idea that his handiwork could do
so as at Kedrin's concern about the future of Béarn's dungeon
when so much more lay at stake. "A week or so from now, my
slashes through the moss will have disappeared; and I plan to
pick up the things I dropped along the way. I don't own enough
not to find every bit precious."

Kedrin released Tae's arm. "Let's go . . ." He paused, apparently waiting for Tae to fill in his name. When he did not,
Kedrin finished lamely, ". . . friend of Ra-khir."

"Tae," Tae supplied, groping the wall for any sign of his

work. He had scored the passage in desperate haste, afraid to lose track of Darris and become irrevocably lost. Now, he worried that he might already have condemned himself and the knight-captain to that fate. No one could find them if they strayed, not even Darris who, presumably, knew only the correct route. After negotiating it once, Tae realized even learning that would prove beyond any other human he knew. "To get us out of here, I'm going to have to pay full attention to looking and feeling. I can't chat. I tend to move quietly, so you may want to keep close to me. I can't go as fast as Darris, so I doubt I'll lose you. Better be careful, though."

"I'll save my questions," Kedrin promised, his intonation implying he had thousands.

The journey through Béarn's catacombs stretched into an aeon. Cold air twined through the corridors from a source Tae did not consider, drying the sweat that seemed determined to coat every part of his body. Kedrin followed wordlessly, occasionally touching Tae to ascertain his position, rarely calling out when he lost all evidence of the Easterner in the gloom. The tedium of trailing through a maze at a snail's pace surely irritated the knight, but he made no sign. Tae envied the Erythanian's boredom. The effort of searching floors, walls, and ceilings for hasty scratches and discarded belongings kept his mind empty and his emotions in knots. Five times, he feared he had lost his way completely, and panic surged through him in a wave that drove him to choose a direction at random. Always, he resisted the urge, bullying through shock to reexamine small details. Guessing would seal their doom, and the hours wasted hunting for marks would prove well worth the frustration.

Long after Tae believed he should have negotiated the caverns twice, he funneled into a dead-end. He collapsed in a despondent heap, prostrate, tears stinging eyes already sore from a million desperate attempts to find clues in hopeless darkness. Repeatedly, his fingers explored the walls finding only more wall. No passages radiated from this corner. They were trapped.

Air stirred over his back as Kedrin's seeking hands swept the darkness. "Tae?" His boot thudded down on Tae's leg, and pain jerked the Easterner back to reality.

Kedrin withdrew immediately, replacing foot with hand. His fingers ran across the fabric of Tae's breeks, conclusively identifying. "Tae? I'm sorry. Did I hurt you?"

"No," Tae said, suddenly realizing the obvious. He laughed. "We're here."

"Where?"

Tae reached over his head, working loose the trapdoor wedged into the opening, amazed by the Béarnian construction that had left him no seams to see or feel. He pushed carefully. Though the tunnel opened into a secluded area, he had long ago lost track of time.

Sunlight filtered through the widening crack, but Tae did not falter. He would rather someone discovered him than remain another moment in the stale dankness of the catacombs. With a heave that taxed shoulders tensed into anxious balls, he shoved the stone fully aside.

Light blasted Tae's eyes, and he blinked repeatedly to clear them. Floating dark circles scored his vision. He caught blurred glimpses of trees, cottages, and less obvious shapes as his lids fluttered open and closed reflexively. At length, he gained a warped picture of surroundings he had barely glanced at when he crept into the caverns behind Darris and Ra-khir, squinting to widen his focus. Grass carpeted the ground, scarcely disrupted by a portal the color of earth. Figures filled the area, and Tae froze in place, certain the guards had discovered them. But the grayness of the manlike shapes defied life, and some clearly stood on all fours. Memory kicked in. *Statues.* Tae exhaled a long breath. A fence enclosed the area, and a nearby cottage stood like a quiet sentinel.

Kedrin waited politely while Tae scanned the locale, body blocking the exit. He studied each piece of stonework.

Bears outnumbered the other works, lumbering or rearing, their features fierce. Tae's mind immediately filled with the image of elfin magic drawing them to life, fangs and claws tearing through Béarn's youngest heirs. He shivered, pitying innocent Matrinka the sight she had suffered. If elves truly ruled Béarn now, a stonecutter's yard could prove one of the city's most dangerous places.

Other objects met and passed Tae's scrutiny: hawks perched in chiseled treetops; tiny *wisules*, cowardly rodents, tensed to flee from danger; and humans engaged in various activities. One of the latter held Tae's focus far longer than the others, a stocky figure swathed in gray robes with the hood pulled so low it nearly hid the entire face. Two eyes escaped the covering, along with an edge of nose and lips. Though deeply shadowed, the eyes reflected a glimmer of life.

Living, breathing human. Tae's mind raced, freed by the cool comfort of air bathing sweat-slick limbs. The other had certainly seen him. The catacombs held no escape, especially now that he had collected his markers. His best strategy lay in surprise. That this meant leaving Kedrin in ignorance did not concern him; he was accustomed to working alone. Levering himself out of the hole, he stepped aside, keeping his face toward the hiding human. Wanting his hands free, he did not assist Kedrin's ascent.

Suddenly, the still figure in the statue court rose, throwing back the hood to reveal familiar feminine features. "Tae?" She headed toward him, at first hesitant, then running in obvious joy. "Tae, it *is* you."

Matrinka. Tae barely had time to brace himself before the princess hurled herself into his arms. He held her tightly, and her joyful tears left a wet spot on his shoulder.

Kedrin emerged, watching the sight in silent curiosity. He did not interfere.

Finally, they both pulled free, and Tae spoke over Matrinka's inevitable questions. "Sir Kedrin, this is Matrinka."

The knight-captain executed a deep bow. "Princess. This is an honor."

"No. Please." Matrinka despised formality. "Just Matrinka. And it's an honor for me as well." Only momentarily distracted, she plied Tae with questions. "Where're Darris and Ra-khir?" She did not wait for a response before curiosity and need goaded her to question further. "How did you get here?"

A tense, short whistle faintly touched Tae's ears. He whirled toward it, crouching. Matrinka turned her head, as did Kedrin. Between two trunks, a shadow shifted.

"That's Baynard," Matrinka explained. "He's a friend."

Kedrin recognized the name. "Right now, Béarnian soldiers might not count as our friends."

"Baynard is," Matrinka assured. She drew breath to say more, but Tae silenced her with a subtle gesture. They would have to guard every word in front of the Knight of Erythane or risk offending his honor or losing his support. Matrinka continued in a different vein, "We'll have to talk later. In a safe place." She drew off her overlarge cloak to reveal another beneath it. Handing the first to Kedrin, she turned Tae an apologetic shrug. "We weren't expecting you."

Tae nodded his understanding. His own dark clothing would hide him well enough, if such became necessary. "Let's go."

Matrinka led Kedrin and Tae over the fence to a sturdy, robust Béarnide. Then the four slipped carefully through alleyways to a cottage. Baynard opened the door and waved the others inside. Even then, no words passed between them. Matrinka led them to a trapdoor, opened it, and gestured Tae through.

Tae balked, the damp coolness and odor of mildew wafting upward returning vivid images of catacombs he would never again attempt to negotiate. Looking down, he saw a single room with milling figures. The sight helped to dispel the comparison, and he finally trotted down the steps. Kedrin, Matrinka, and Baynard followed.

Half a dozen elves watched their descent through steadfast eyes that never seemed to blink. Captain rose from a chair near a table, gesturing for the newcomers to sit. Béarnian strangers rose simultaneously, opening spaces for the others as well. Kedrin, Baynard, and Matrinka accepted the sacrifice, though the knight remained standing. Tae moved to a dark, quiet corner. The man who had vacated his chair for Tae approached and inclined his head respectfully. Black bangs fringed hazel eyes, and a lean figure revealed him as a non-Béarnian Westerner. Though lanky and not more than a few years older than Tae's eighteen years, he bore none of the typical adolescent clumsiness. "Friend of Béarn, you may have my seat."

Tae shook his head and made a gesture of dismissal. "Thank you, no."

"As you wish." The man returned to his seat, but he did not sit. Instead, he bowed to Knight-Captain Kedrin and executed a grand flourish usually reserved for kings. "Greetings, Captain."

Kedrin smiled. "Greetings, Braison. Your gesture is appreciated but unnecessary. I am no longer your commander." He reached for the youngster, and they exchanged a brief, strong embrace. Both sat. Only then, Kedrin returned to the matter at hand. "Braison, I hope you can explain the situation. Tae's been understandably circumspect." He tossed a friendly look in Tae's direction to show he meant no offense.

Tae watched in silence. The light of day had surely revealed his tattered dress, hard eyes, and disheveled appearance. In the dungeon's gloom, Kedrin might not have recognized him as an Easterner. It had become inexorably clear that men like Tae and Kedrin did not often work together, yet the knight had said and done nothing to indicate his superiority. Tae appreciated Kedrin's acceptance but did not delude himself into believing their differences would not affect whether the knight joined their cause.

That thought raised many others. Kedrin's initial refusal to leave the dungeon clued Tae that knight's honor might prove more indecipherable than he expected. He hoped he had not ruined Griff's chances of becoming king by his presence alone. His throat tightened as he suddenly realized the prince and his annoyingly devoted bodyguard did not sit among them. *Are we fighting for any cause at all?* Ra-khir's presence assured it. The apprentice knight would never have attempted to free his father without more motive than desire. As he had assured Kedrin, neither father nor son would have allowed it.

Braison's explanation laid to rest many of Tae's more recent doubts. He spoke of Griff, apparently somewhere safe among them, and of the false Kohleran and his politics. Tae learned that all of his friends had survived the demon's attack and that the two Renshai had gone for assistance from their own. Braison spoke from the heart of the citizens' resistance, of the purgings that seemed random, and of the elves' apparent intention to utterly destroy mankind. He described the emotional state of Béarn's citizenry and offered to escort the knight-captain through a town whose people he might no longer recognize.

Kedrin listened quietly throughout Braison's narrative, the tightening set of his lips the only visible sign of emotion. Only after the one-time Knight of Erythane finished did Kedrin finally speak. "You believe in the rightness of this cause?"

Braison nodded, hazel eyes fastened to the blue. "With all my heart. I have met the proper king of Béarn, and we need his judgment and guidance. With or without the Knights of Erythane, I will see him on the throne." Stiffly sober, his features became a study in defiance.

Kedrin's mouth twitched to a smile without a hint of mockery, only pride. "I trust your honor, Braison. I always have. Even when it interfered with your knighthood. Once, I despised your decision to relinquish your title, though never your person." He glanced about the room, gaze falling first on Matrinka, then Tae. "At my suggestion, my son risked his life, and those of his friends, for this same cause. Then, I suffered the guilt of believing I sent him to his death. Now I know he's alive, but I still may lose him." He lowered his head, the words clearly more painful than his tone implied. "In this, we are all allied, no matter our background. Without the true heir, Béarn, and eventually the world itself, will fall. I will support this, and the other knights will as well." He winked at Tae. "Had you mentioned Griff when you came to me, I would have come without hesitation."

Tae saluted to acknowledge the more dangerous and desperate path he had chosen. The idea had not occurred to him at the time because he did not know whether or not Griff had survived the shipwreck.

Kedrin returned his attention to Braison, to Tae's infinite relief. He had spent too long on the streets to weather the stares of city officials comfortably. "It is my pleasure and my honor to assist King Griff's return, yet I still ask one favor." The intensity of his focus made it clear he wanted something from Braison, not the group. "When the proper ascension is restored, I want you back where you belong, among the Knights of Erythane."

Braison smiled, his youthful features aglow, and a light flashed through his eyes. For a moment, Tae thought he might wiggle like a praised puppy, but he contained the excitement his face betrayed. "You'd have me back?"

"And believe us the better for it."

"Captain," Braison started, his next words so predictable, Tae mouthed them as he spoke. "It would be an honor."

CHAPTER 13

Scepter of the Elfin Kings

*Like armor, magic is a crutch. Crutches are easily lost, and
their wielders with them.*

—Colbey Calistinsson

Colbey Calistinsson sat upon Odin's massive throne, *Hlidskjalf*,
the stone warming to the heat of his body. Inset gemstones on
the arms flashed and sparkled in the light. In the centuries since
the AllFather's death, the chair had mostly lain empty. Others
came, at times, to look out over all the worlds; but to them it
still seemed a guilty pleasure. Through the millennia, few but
Odin and his wife sat upon the high seat. Respect and an awe
that reached beyond the grave kept the gods away, though Colbey believed they had all come at least once since Odin's death.
Curiosity goaded even the deities.

Colbey watched Dh'arlo'mé. For hours, the aging elf sat on
the floor of his private chamber on Nualfheim, clutching the
Staff of Law. His red-blond hair hung like a curtain over his
eye, and a smile seemed permanently etched against his cheekbones. Colbey's frown had become nearly as lasting. Like gods,
elves did not concern themselves with the passage of time; the
length of their lives precluded it. Yet, in the last several months,
Dh'arlo'mé's actions had become little distinguishable from
humans. It made no sense for him to commune so long with a
staff emptied of power.

A deep sigh rumbled from Colbey, and he tapped his fingers
against the rubies, sapphires, and diamonds set into *Hlidskjalf*'s
arms. Emotion and thought wafting from Dh'arlo'mé told more
than Colbey wished to know. No doubt, the Staff of Law contained more essence than Odin, the forces, and circumstances
had led him to believe. The grim, gray father of gods had made
a grand show of draining the staves of their power.

Colbey leaned forward, devoid of options. Continued superficial study would gain him little more information. The time

had come for him to invade Dh'arlo'mé's thoughts, no matter that the effort would desperately weaken him. He should remain safe here. Even the gods seemed unlikely to bother him. Yet the idea of exhausting his endurance at a time when so much lay at stake bothered him. The need remained, ugly and urgent. Resigned, Colbey lowered his head and let his consciousness ease toward the leader of the elves.

Constrained by his own oaths not to enter the thoughts of allies, Colbey had never deliberately read an elf's mind before. The thought processes seemed alien, tied in unfamiliar loops and sparked by ideas that humans might never consider. Excitement struck him as a warm wash of color tainted by greed. Giddy with power, Dh'arlo'mé had bonded to the Staff of Law, embracing the knowledge and influence it promised. Already his mind filled with concepts once beyond his comprehension, and the space devoted to the wild chaos of magic enlarged at the expense of instinct and feeling. Another presence swirled among racing thoughts grasping for understanding. Colbey approached it hesitantly.

The raw power radiating from the being blasted him, stronger than he expected. He had never withdrawn from a physical battle, yet his mind reflexively recoiled from the thing in Dh'arlo'mé's head. It seemed familiar and strange at once, nothing like the entity that had unsuccessfully coaxed him to become its champion in the months when he had carried the Staff of Law. Without need for direct challenge, he sensed it would attack at his slightest touch. Colbey feared nothing, but no good could come of battling or joining the unbridled representation of law. Always he had chosen the course of balance. Colbey withdrew.

Fatigue weighted the Renshai's limbs and blunted his thoughts like one too many servings of wine. Even after five lifetimes, he still underestimated the effects of his rare explorations. Something followed him back to *Hlidskjalf*, a faint buzzing that hinted of coming warfare and a duel hungrily anticipated. Colbey's hand tightened around Harval's hilt; and he leaped from the throne, prepared for battle. The whisper of presence disappeared, leaving nothing to indicate it had ever existed.

Colbey drew Harval. The sword listed to the right, ungainly in his hands. Alarm prickled through his hand, then filled his head. He had grown painfully accustomed to the unpredictable shifts in balance that recently had rendered the weapon all but useless. Now, the savage, capricious changes became a constant that should have soothed but only rattled him more. Despite his best efforts, the balance teetered suddenly and dangerously toward law.

Colbey returned to the chair. Dh'arlo'mé still sat, attention focused fully inward. An army could have entered that room without his notice. Colbey felt equally engrossed in thoughts of his own. *Where did the Staff of Law get its power? Why hadn't Chaos paralleled its growth?* The natural proclivity of the worlds toward balance should have assured it. Only one explanation seemed to fit. *The Staff of Law consumed someone or something of astounding power.* The source eluded him, clearly not Dh'arlo'mé who retained his own personality. The change had come before the binding of a champion.

Ignorance of magic hampered Colbey's speculation. The urge to slaughter Dh'arlo'mé passed swiftly. It would prove a temporary solution that accomplished little more than angering Frey. He had promised his brother-in-law not to kill elves, and he had every intention of keeping that vow, not only to maintain goodwill. A god killing a lesser being, even a god who still considered himself human, would create repercussions beyond his imagining. It always did. Once before, gods and Wizards believed they could rescue the balance by slaughtering the Staff of Law's champion, then himself. *Ragnarok* had resulted, and Colbey had branded those who had assailed him fools. No matter how prestigious, he would not join their ranks.

Colbey paced, seeking another option and finding it unpalatable. Someone would have to wield the Staff of Chaos, someone of great morality and power. For, ultimately, it would destroy him.

Clouds blotted the morning sky, and lightning wound through the gloom unaccompanied by rain or thunder. The turbulence seemed proper background for the confrontation between Béarn's chosen and its usurpers. The Knights of Erythane rode at the head, Béarn's rearing bear banner raised high. The white horses walked with their triangular heads proudly aloft, manes braided with blue and gold ribbons, and their riders like lordly statues on their backs.

Immediately behind the knights, Kevral rode at Griff's left hand, amid a semicircle of guardians that included Braison, Baynard, and Rantire. The elves followed, riding two abreast. The Béarnian renegades came next, in ragged ranks that seemed a mockery of the Knights of Erythane's precision. The remaining Renshai trailed. The entire tribe of three hundred had come to restore Béarn's king and guard its heirs, sparing only those under the age of ten and a disappointed few to watch the children. The Renshai filed in the wake of the procession without any pattern to their location or movement. As always, they would fight and win—or die as warriors, not soldiers.

Tae and Matrinka hung back, the Easterner for purposes unexplained and the princess for better access to the wounded. Kevral did not believe either of them necessary to win this battle, and she appreciated that Matrinka's decision placed her in a position of relative safety. Once the battle started, the chaos of violence would claim the inexperienced first. She suspected, however, she would eventually discover Tae in the center of combat. *Or maybe not*, Kevral amended the thought. Tae had too often found himself the near-target of Kevral's sword to practice his usual stealthy tactics among so many Renshai.

The citizens stopped their work as the procession wound past, some dashing ahead to warn the castle, others begging information, and still more hiding inside cottages or shops. Kevral noticed the ranks of the renegades swelling, and a warm flush of satisfaction suffused her. Centuries of incorruptible reputation preceded the Knights of Erythane. No matter their own loyalty to king and country, Béarn's peasants would trust the knights' honor more. Despite their long commitment to the heirs of Béarn, the Renshai would never receive the trust that Kedrin and his knights inspired. Renshai had long endured a love/hate relationship with kingdom and populace, their infamous savagery and dedication to violence holding them always at a distance from the people their swords protected.

The march to Béarn Castle slowed as the infantry enlarged far quicker than the cavalry. All of the knights, Griff and his escort, and most of the Renshai owned horses. Equal numbers of renegades rode or walked, but the peasants who joined them either did not own, or did not bother to ready, their mounts. Some of the walking renegades paused to explain the situation to Béarn's citizenry. Although they would have little effect upon the coming battle, their support would make a smooth transition for Griff once the confrontation ended.

During the ride through the city, Kevral loosened her swords in their sheaths a dozen times. Instinctively, her senses remained keyed for threatening movements, freeing her mind for the thrilling inevitability of battle. Once again, she had promised Captain to avoid killing elves; but even he seemed to doubt the possibility of leaving Dh'arlo'mé and his closest followers alive. He had asked that the humans allow the elves to handle their own, magically and otherwise. Though the leaders had agreed, including Thialnir who represented the Renshai on Béarn's council, her people would ultimately do as each saw fit. While readying for battle, some may not have bothered with such details. Kedrin, too, had voiced his preference, that the combatants spare every Béarnian soldier possible. The need to kill even one, he had stated, would be a tragedy.

Kevral turned her full attention to the castle as the spires and turrets hove into view. A massive stone wall, cleared of vines and moss, surrounded the courtyard. Kedrin rode directly to the gate, where two guards clutching halberds stood guard on the opposite side.

Kedrin dismounted, and the two regarded him with jaws set stoically and fingers blanched around their polearms. Kevral sensed nervousness about their movements, though she could single out no specific action that triggered the impression. They certainly had reason enough for concern.

Knight and guards conversed for several moments, then Kedrin turned back to his men. Kevral read puzzlement on his features. She waited until he finished explaining to the knights and moved on to Griff and his guardians. "Dh'arlo'mé has requested a meeting with our leaders. He promised a peaceful discussion and a solution that would please all of us."

Griff grinned broadly. Rantire's eyes narrowed to slits. Kevral felt more confused than suspicious. "We'll need to discuss this with Captain."

Kedrin nodded once, authoritatively. "I'm headed there next."

"How many leaders does he want?" Baynard asked.

"Five or six. He said he'd have a like number." Kedrin did not await more questions but kneed his white stallion and rode off to relay the message to the groups farther behind.

"It's a trick," Rantire said as the knight-captain headed away.

"Maybe." Baynard shrugged, turning his gaze to Griff. "Then there're certain people we don't send. But killing five or six of ours, especially leaders, won't gain Dh'arlo'mé anything but a pack of enraged followers."

Braison joined the conversation. "Unless he's got magic to turn our leaders against us."

Baynard turned to the ex-knight. "That's why Captain has to

be among the ones we send. I trust him to identify any magic he can't handle."

Kevral did not know the best combination, but she definitely wanted to attend that conference. "Who decides who goes?"

"Davian and Kedrin, I suppose," Baynard said. "But first they have to determine *if* we go. . . ."

Baynard continued speaking, but Kevral heard none of it. She spun her horse around and headed for the renegades' elder, intending to influence the decision before representation of the Renshai fell naturally to Thialnir. He had the experience when it came to diplomacy, but Kevral had attended this matter from the start. She wanted to see it finished, and believed her companions, who crossed the entire Westlands for this moment, would feel the same. As that thought surfaced, it accompanied a better idea. Scanning the growing crowd of Béarnides, she searched for familiar faces. She located Davian long before the ones she sought, engaged in conversation with Knight-Captain Kedrin. The knight's pristine uniform and familiar silk tabard, bedecked in front with Béarn's symbol and behind with Erythane's orange and black made a brilliant contrast to the rebels' homespun.

Torn, Kevral hesitated. Her plan would work better, but not if the leaders decided their course of action before she prepared. *Continue looking or join those two?* She had just made the latter decision when a hand caught her mount's bridle. She glanced over to Tae who gave her a sweet smile of welcome. Readying plans had kept her too busy to chat with him. The moment she and Rantire returned with the Renshai, the group had prepared its assault.

Tae became instantly defensive. "I didn't trick you. I really meant what I said that night. And I love you."

Kevral had never considered the possibility of deception. "We'll talk about this later. Where's Matrinka?"

Tae raised and lowered his shoulders, displaying his ignorance. "I can find her."

"Quickly, please." Kevral turned her attention back to Davian and Kedrin, still together. "I'll meet you both here. Go!"

Apparently reading Kevral's urgency, Tae rushed off without a reply. The Renshai fidgeted, and the horse echoed her impatience by pawing divots from the ground.

True to his promise, Tae returned almost immediately, Matrinka riding at his side. Mior curled on the horse's rump, with no more attention to balance than if she slept on the pillows of her mistress' bed.

"What's the matter?" Matrinka rushed to Kevral. "Is someone hurt?"

"No." Kevral had planned to explain, but she feared the leaders neared a decision. "Just follow my lead." She kicked her horse into a trot toward Davian and Kedrin.

The men looked up as Kevral, Tae, and Matrinka pulled up beside them. "Are we going?" the Renshai asked before her horse even stopped moving.

Kedrin frowned at Kevral's rudeness but did not chastise. Davian asked, "You mean the contingent?"

"Yes," Kevral confirmed. "Are we going?"

"Griff is in favor. He thinks it's worth a try, as long as the ones who go understand the danger."

"We understand," Kevral returned, leaving no opening for the men to deny her personal role in the undertaking.

Kedrin smiled, clearly recognizing Kevral's ploy. Davian's brow furrowed around his dark eyes, and his mouth became lost in his beard. "We've only decided on the general constituents, not specifics: a Renshai, an elf, a renegade, a knight, and one other."

Tae grinned also, following more quickly than Kevral expected, though he had always proved quick-witted in the past. "The three of us." He indicated Kevral and Matrinka with a subtle gesture. "Plus Captain and a knight, perhaps Sir Kedrin."

The knight-captain nodded in acknowledgment.

"That is," Tae continued carefully, "if you wish to consider a Béarnian princess renegade. Otherwise, you might want to find one more from among yours."

Davian stared, mouth bowing downward and features darkened by Tae's presumptuousness. "And what makes you believe I would send any of you?"

Kevral met the dark eyes without compromise. "Because it's our dedication that brought Griff here, and we will see this through. What makes you believe you could send anyone other than us?"

Davian recoiled, blinking, obviously unaccustomed to such impudence. A tense silence ensued, Kedrin rupturing it almost as it began. "They have a valid point, Davian. They managed to accomplish what our envoys could not. They have a right to see this safely finished."

The leader of the renegades turned on the knight now. "I'm

not denying their skills, just concerned that diplomacy is not among them."

"I'll go with them," Kedrin assured, glancing carefully among the three. Kevral acknowledged the unspoken question with a discreet nod. She would control her own urges for the good of Griff and Béarn. Kedrin continued, "And you can send one from among your men who can speak as well as fight." He added, without offense, "Yourself included, of course, though I believe our cause better served with you continuing to lead this group in our absence."

Davian pursed his lips, glancing from Kedrin to Tae to Kevral to Matrinka. As his dark eyes rolled over the last, he started over, examining each in turn. Finally, he heaved a deep sigh. "My lord, I trust your judgment in these matters, even over my own. I still believe a parlay would fare better with experienced spokesmen and politicians as our representatives. But, if you endorse the group you described, I will send Baynard with it. Good luck. Gods' blessings. And please remember that at all times you represent the kingdom of Béarn."

Kedrin glowered at the obvious insult, though Davian clearly intended his warning for the others. The chosen ones reined their horses around, and Kevral whispered to Tae, "Let's go before he changes his mind." They headed toward the front of the crowd, pausing only to add Baynard and Captain to the group. While Kedrin explained the situation to the one-time guard, Kevral tossed Rantire a victory salute.

The older Renshai rode to her cousin's side. "You're going?" Rantire's tone lacked wistfulness and the pride Kevral expected.

"Isn't it grand?"

"Another way to abandon your charge." Rantire dismissed the honor by belittling it.

"I'm bringing her with me."

Rantire stiffened a moment, then glanced at Matrinka. "Worse than I thought. You're dragging her into the danger. Do you also shove her into the center of combat?"

Kevral threw up her hands, realizing she should have said nothing to her cousin. Her friends had always found Rantire overprotective to a fault. No harm would befall Matrinka that did not kill Kevral first; the Renshai's confidence in her own ability left the heir free to do anything she wished, short of suicide. When first assigned to protect the princess, Kevral had refused even to exchange names. She had worried that a personal

relationship would hamper her ability to guard or, worse, drive
Matrinka to her bodyguard's aid when running would serve her
better. Experience had taught Kevral that friendship only enhanced her loyalty to her charge, and it had allowed her to understand the needs beyond simple survival. Without a will to
live, without a sense of self-worth, breathing and a heartbeat
meant nothing. "As a matter of fact, I have dragged her to the
center of combat when I could protect her better there than in a
camp beyond my sight." Kevral shook her head, her cousin's
single-mindedness maddening. "Someday, you'll understand."

"No," Rantire also shook her head, but with a slow sadness.
"You're the one who will understand, and I regret the cost will
be Matrinka's life."

Without time or inclination to argue, Kevral returned to the
contingent, grumbling, "Stupid, bullheaded . . ." She struggled
for an insult without resorting to profanity.

"Renshai?" Tae suggested.

Kevral jerked her head to the companion, now at her side.
She flushed. "I didn't mean to say that out loud."

"You didn't," Tae admitted. "You whispered. I was eavesdropping."

"Bastard."

"Or that might have worked." Tae raised and lowered his
brows, wearing a cocksure smile. "But I like 'Renshai' better. It
more suits the narrow-minded inflexibility you once represented and now curse."

Kevral stared, as astounded by Tae's verbal dexterity as his
words. He had a point she could not deny. Early in the group's
association, she had condemned Ra-khir for his staunch devotion to an honor that differed from her own, even as the knight
despised Tae for completely lacking honor. Time had brought
tolerance and understanding to all of them. Tae had changed as
well. Fresh from his experience living on the streets, he had
measured every word so as to sound deliberately low-class,
composed, and in control. Eventually, the group had learned of
Tae's vast repertoire of languages. Kevral realized it should not
surprise her to learn Tae had mastered the long words and adroit
phrasings he chose to avoid in the past.

Kedrin waved aside the contingent for a short discussion.
"Captain, do you have any particular sense of what might happen here?"

The elf's head rotated back and forth in a sluggish, inhuman
rhythm. The amber eyes fixed, stonelike, on Kedrin. "I don't

think my speculation can add much. Once, I could at least have assured no killing, but Dh'arlo'mé has become more man than elf in action. So long as their contingent matches ours, however, they cannot harm us with magic. To do so would require a large group of elves merging voices. Six would allow only minor spells that this group could easily counter, and I will warn you of sounds or actions that appear suspicious."

Captain's description soothed only the edges of Kevral's worry. The elves could amass groups to catch them in the court-yard or the great halls of the castle. Yet she saw no reason to concern herself with such possibilities. Harming the contingent would gain Dh'arlo'mé little, only enraging the troops still growing outside the castle gates.

"Thank you, Captain," Kedrin said. He inclined his head in the direction of the gates. "Let's go."

The others followed unquestioningly. Three warriors, an ancient elf, and a crime lord's son had nothing to fear from death. Only Matrinka fretted, hands clenched whitely and expression taut. Kevral considered releasing the princess from a service she had never had the opportunity to choose or deny, then discarded the thought. The Renshai understood Matrinka well enough to know that she would insist on coming despite her fear.

The two guards in Béarn's blue and tan remained as rigid as their halberds just beyond the wrought iron gates. At their backs, Kevral saw the familiar gardens and benches, interspersed with paths and statuary. Proud bears and stags stood sentinel over multicolored fields of blossoms shaped like animals and banners or in simple geometrics. Some sported a single color while others mingled hues into patterns that demonstrated the gardeners' talents, not only as plant handlers but as artists as well. Less aesthetic, vegetable gardens sported melons the size of her head, clambering vines with crisp, colorful beans, and the leafy tops of varying tubers.

"Gentlemen," Kedrin addressed the guards with a courtesy that seemed misplaced. The oddity of pitting Béarn's finest against Béarn's soldiers struck Kevral then as it had not in simple theory.

"Captain," they said as one, heads bobbing in respect.

Kedrin brushed aside a strand of freshly cut red hair. "We have assembled our contingent as requested by those you serve." He chose vagary rather than insult. He would not call the imposter King Kohleran, yet neither would he antagonize with words such as "false" or "charlatan."

Kedrin's tact reminded Kevral why he had accompanied them. She resolved not to speak unless violence became necessary or she needed to impart information Kedrin did not know. She would not allow the elves to antagonize her into words she, or others, would later regret.

"Very good, Captain," said the right-hand guard. "You'll need to leave horses and weapons. You may do so here or inside."

Kevral stiffened, already prepared to fight. He might just as well have demanded she strip naked.

"Understood." Kedrin turned to relay the command, though they had all heard it.

Before he could speak, however, the guard added. "There will be no weapons at the meeting. On either side."

The words did not reassure Kevral. She had no reason to expect the *svartalf* to keep promises.

Without hesitation, Kedrin unbuckled his sword belt, passing it to one of the knights at the head of the procession. "It's routine."

Kevral believed Kedrin. Aside from Renshai, guards, and the occasional heir, no one carried weapons in Béarn Castle. She drew solace from Colbey's words: "A Renshai is dangerous so long as he shares a room with a sword." Kevral had proved the truth of that adage in Pudar's courtroom. When the need arose to defend Matrinka, she had drawn a guard's weapon faster than he could think to stop her. Though bothered by the request, she wordlessly joined the others. Soon the leading knights had collected a sizable pile. Renegades took charge of the horses, and one guard winched open the gates while the other protected the opening his companion created.

The contingent entered, Kedrin leading. Matrinka followed, Mior curled on her shoulders. Kevral took a position at her charge's right hand, and the others filed in behind them. The gate crashed shut, and one of the halberdiers led them along the straightest courtyard path. He asked the obvious question of Kedrin. "Why, Captain?"

Kedrin explained the situation for what seemed to Kevral the millionth time. She concentrated on the sights and sounds around them: the trickle of water through manmade streams and gutters, the creak of the lowering drawbridge, the glittering colors of the gardens, and the brackish water of the moat. Sentries on watch tossed the contingent suspicious stares as they passed. The halberdier led them directly to the front of the castle, then paused, listening to Kedrin in silence, while the drawbridge fell. Once it did, he wasted less than a second leading them inside.

The clinging warmth of the castle assailed Kevral, and sweat seemed to burst from her skin with the first few steps. The familiar tapestries and frescoes seemed eerily strange, spanning walls and ceiling, incorporating doors and archways into the pictures. Historical scenes paraded before her, centuries revealed in vivid images. Golden-haired reavers, clearly Renshai, slaughtered Westerners, heroically battling to their final breaths. In the next battle, the few Renshai assisted the West against waves of Eastern warriors in armor of black leather. One brilliant tapestry displayed four Wizards, their hair gray, their coarse faces defining age, and their eyes shrewd with wisdom beyond mortal understanding. Animals surrounded them, representing the realms of earth, water, and air.

The guard led them to the council's meeting room rather than the court, as Kevral had expected. The choice confounded her, but Kedrin nodded sagely. Another guard awaited them at the door, this one dressed in the uniform of the inner court and armed with a sword instead of a polearm.

The halberdier explained, "Prime Minister Dh'arlo'mé believed you would feel more comfortable here."

Prime Minister Dh'arlo'mé. Kevral quivered with disgust and rage.

Kedrin's nostrils flared, and his hands closed to fists. Otherwise, he took no notice of the insult to Béarn's nobility. "He is correct. Thank you."

"Good luck," the halberdier hissed. "Please don't think too harshly of those tricked by magic." Without awaiting a reply, he swept down the hallway.

Kevral shook her head, impressed by the respect a fallen knight-captain still commanded. The guard's words had bordered on treason, and it seemed ludicrous to expect him to believe such an outlandish story on faith. Kevral realized she had no way to know how suspicious those who worked inside the castle might have become. Distance might make the populace easy to fool, but the guards and courtiers had surely noticed some changes.

The guard opened the meeting room door and ushered the renegade contingent inside. Kevral peered around Kedrin's broad form to a semicircular table. An elf sat at the head posi-

tion, red-blond hair hanging to his shoulders and a single green
eye studying the knight-captain. He clutched a staff in a casually loose grip. A burning hatred started low in her stomach and
crept through her like a poison. Two elves sat at either hand,
their eyes glittering in the torchlight and their expressions
wholly unreadable. Kevral scanned them for weapons, finding
nothing other than the leader's staff, which seemed more walking aid than armament. So far, it seemed, the elves had dealt
with them honestly. That did not reassure Kevral who believed
the candor only an attempt to lull them. She sought hidden enemies in a room too small to hold them and finally realized why
Kedrin felt more comfortable here than in the court.

"Dh'arlo'mé's the one in the middle," Captain whispered unnecessarily.

Kevral glared as her companions filed into the room. A three-
chair gap remained between the last elf on each side and the
first human. Kevral placed herself nearest one of the elves, a
white-haired, blue-eyed male, keeping Matrinka and Mior beside her.

Dh'arlo'mé remained seated, quietly scrutinizing each member of the contingent. When the last, Tae, had finally entered,
Dh'arlo'mé signaled the guard to close the door. The swordsman obeyed, leaving himself outside.

Matrinka nudged Kevral with an elbow. "Staff," she mur-
mured.

Kevral's attention slid back to the only one in the room, in
Dh'arlo'mé's fist. It looked no different than before, remarkable
only for its absolute plainness. It posed no threat she could not
counter. Kevral gathered breath to reassure Matrinka. Understanding registered then, leaving her wordless and suspicious.
"Is it one from the staff-test?"

"Don't know," Matrinka returned in a nearly inaudible hiss.
"Couldn't be sure without holding it. Might need both to tell."
Her eyes revealed the terror her tone did not. Leaving Béarn to
search for Griff had spared her the second staff-testing that had
ravaged those few of King Kohleran's heirs who had survived
the elves' assassinations. Taking both staves in hand now could
drive her to the same insanity.

Kedrin frowned at the whispering girls and shook his head, a
quiet plea for decorum. Kevral and Matrinka fell silent.

Dh'arlo'mé looked first to the knight. "Captain, your escape
caused quite a stir in the dungeon. Many of the guards will wish
to hear how you negotiated the catacombs."

Kedrin acknowledged the words with a nod but made no reply. Kevral admired his control. In the same situation, she would have taunted.

Dh'arlo'mé next turned to the *Sea Seraph*'s captain. A smile touched the leader's features, so subtle only Kevral's experience with elves allowed her to notice it. "Lav'rintir, you have caused more trouble than I believed you capable of doing."

Captain imitated Kedrin's nod. "Dh'arlo'mé'aftris'ter Te'meer Braylth'ryn Amareth Fel-Krin, I cannot wholly deny the aptness of calling me traitor in that I voiced, and later acted against, the evil you proposed. If that is the act that earned it, I bear the new name proudly."

Kevral glanced swiftly at Dh'arlo'mé, anticipating, and so reading, anger. Yet Dh'arlo'mé's voice sounded more contrite. "You have a valid point. We may discuss it if other matters do not too far outweigh it." He glanced at the remaining humans in turn, without addressing them individually, although he did recite their names. "Baynard, Tae, Matrinka, Kevral. None of you have met me, but I know of all of you."

"We know of you, too," Tae said.

Kevral winced at the impropriety. Kedrin frowned, shaking his head judiciously, a warning to leave the speaking to those versed in the art.

"Not surprising," Dh'arlo'mé returned. "And I fear not all that you've heard has been good."

Kevral had no difficulty resisting a strong urge to verbally label the comment understatement. A hint of sorrow entered Dh'arlo'mé's tone, closely akin to guilt. The fire in her guts seemed to falter, though whether from interest or suspicion, she did not know.

Dh'arlo'mé rose, leaning on his staff as if desperate for support. "I made a terrible mistake." He kept his jeweled gaze on the tabletop.

Though the situation demanded her attention, Kevral could not help noticing Dh'arlo'mé's empty socket. Her thoughts turned to the brilliant green gemstone that Tae had given her. He had discovered it clenched in the palm of a slain Renshai warrior, a member of a Béarnian envoy. With Colbey Calistinsson's direction, they had learned that clutching it revealed Dh'arlo'mé's general location. Now Kevral knew for certain the nature of that item: it was the *svartalf* leader's missing eye. Although experience had given her no reason to believe it performed any other function, for her or for Dh'arlo'mé, she dipped a hand into her pocket and gouged her fingers into the stone, hoping the pain transferred to its one-time owner.

Dh'arlo'mé took no obvious notice of the maneuver. "Once, I allowed hatred over *Ragnarok* to consume me. I believed destroying mankind would serve the elves, and we claimed Béarn as our own. Now, I understand the truth." His head snapped up, and he met Kedrin's gaze. His single eye reflected nothing, as always, but his expression seemed sincere. "If the true heir does not sit upon Béarn's throne, we will all die. Elves and humans alike. And, perhaps, the gods as well. I made a mistake, and I'm sorry."

Kedrin nodded, as if he had expected to hear nothing else. He was not in a position to accept or deny the apology. The words stunned Kevral, the last thing she expected from Dh'arlo'mé. Still, she did not drop her guard. She studied the staff again briefly, finding nothing on further inspection. If it was from the test, it made little sense for Dh'arlo'mé to carry it. Everything she knew suggested the staves served no function separated. Together, they only identified the proper heir to Béarn.

"I would like to make an offer," Dh'arlo'mé continued. "First, please understand that my only intention, then and now, is to protect my people." His eye flicked around the gathering again.

Kedrin took the hint. "Our goal is to place the proper heir on the throne and oust those who plot against him."

"If I offered you a way to accomplish both goals without bloodshed, would you consider it, Knight-Captain Kedrin?"

The tension grew tangible as Kedrin prepared an answer. "Yes. King Griff . . ." He paused, waiting for the significance of the words to become clear. ". . . has granted the power of decision to his cousin, Princess Matrinka, daughter of Talamaine Kohleran's son, an unchosen and newly reinstated heir to the Béarnian throne."

Matrinka sucked in a sudden breath, then choked desperately. Both Kedrin and Dh'arlo'mé waited politely for her to finish, while Kevral prepared to assist should Matrinka stop breathing. At length, she caught a whooping gulp of air, though the sudden movement dumped Mior unceremoniously to the floor. "I'm sorry," she managed hoarsely, tears filming her dark eyes. "Carry on." Though her voice emerged calmly, Kevral read panic in eyes that seemed wide as moons. It was not the reinstatement that bothered the princess; Kevral knew the sage's records would show the king had secretly refused the disownment. Matrinka dreaded the overwhelming responsibility that Griff had heaped upon shoulders she believed ill-suited.

Kedrin finished, "She may accept or refuse any terms." He added, clearly for Matrinka's benefit, "And seek counsel as she so chooses."

"Very well," Dh'arlo'mé returned to his seat, turning his attention now to Matrinka. The princess' hands fidgeted beneath the table, but she performed a satisfactory job of looking self-controlled. The elves remained in position, rarely blinking and never moving. They could have been statues for all the heed they seemed to pay the proceedings.

Kevral gave Matrinka's thigh a comforting squeeze. The staves had found the princess unworthy of making decisions for the kingdom, and it seemed unfair for the capable one to place the burden on her. Kevral recalled the hollow-eyed stares of the princess to whom she had been appointed guardian, the crippling self-doubt, and the indecisiveness that characterized even the simplest choices. Matrinka had regathered her courage, dedicating herself to her people in other ways. It had quickly become clear that following the path of a warrior would only get her killed, and she had finally settled on healing instead. During their journey, she had grown comfortable with her skills. Now, weighting her with the very responsibilities for which she had been found unworthy seemed a cruelty beyond Griff's understanding.

Dh'arlo'mé threw Kedrin a questioning glance, obviously reading some of Matrinka's turmoil by her expression yet without means to understand the details of it. "My proposal is simple. We return Béarn Castle to its proper king, and you allow us to leave without violence or punishment. Furthermore, we become subjects of King Griff." His hair slipped slightly closer to his eye, Kevral's only indication that his brow furrowed. "I'm not good with human politics, but I know other faraway places handle that somehow."

Matrinka nodded toward Kedrin, and the knight assisted. "Béarn is officially the high kingdom of the West, meaning all other kingdoms ultimately answer to our king or queen. For the most part, these others govern themselves and come to us for military support or with problems they consider unresolvable." He added for obvious reasons. "Of course, in matters of disagreement between kingdoms, they must obey Béarn's decisions."

"Of course," Dh'arlo'mé said.

Captain's features revealed confusion to the point of startlement, his expressions more pronounced and human.

Dh'arlo'mé clearly noticed the change. A true smile appeared, an expression the elves seemed to have perfected by their facial wrinkles. "Don't look so surprised, Lav'rintir. The elves have had kings before."

"Not to my knowledge," said Captain.

"I've done a vast amount of studying over the past few . . ." Dh'arlo'mé fumbled with the word, time concepts rarely invoked by elves. ". . . months?" He shrugged. "Months, I suppose. Long before my birth, or even yours, elves had kings. In fact, I've discovered an artifact I never knew existed: the scepter of the elfin kings." He made a slight gesture toward one of the elves who rose and headed from the room. The door banged shut behind him. "To seal this agreement, I would like to present the scepter to the new king. Or his agents—I understand if you still don't trust us near him."

Something tickled Kevral's hand, and she jerked it from Matrinka's leg before recognizing Mior settling back into her mistress' lap. Kevral left the comforting to the cat, exploring her own reactions for the first time. She still did not trust the elves; no competent bodyguard would. Dh'arlo'mé's easy surrender both thrilled and disappointed. She would have to forgo the battle she had gathered the Renshai to fight, yet Griff, Matrinka, and the others would get exactly the result they wanted.

Dh'arlo'mé again addressed his question directly to Matrinka. "Does this sound like an agreement Béarn would like to enter?"

Matrinka swallowed hard. Her hands trailed over Mior's fur in mindless circles. She spoke slowly, a trait that did not seem to bother the elves at all. "It . . . sounds . . . good." She held the gemlike gaze only a moment before rolling her eyes toward Kedrin for assistance. "There . . . would be details . . . to work out."

Dh'arlo'mé gave a single, deliberate nod. "And those would be?"

"Well . . . first . . . we have to know you won't . . . do something like this again."

Nods confirmed Matrinka's choice, and Dh'arlo'mé's head bobbed with the others. "Understandable. The elves wish only to be left in peace. There are too few of us left to battle." He glanced warningly at Captain, who shook his head.

Of the humans, only Kevral could understand the exchange.

Necessity had forced Captain to tell her about the elves' birth/death cycle, but he had otherwise kept it secret.

Matrinka accepted the answer, finally pressing the detail that had bothered her since entering. "We get back the staff-test."

Dh'arlo'mé stared at her with his single eye, his face even more blank than usual. "I don't follow that."

"The staves that test the heir to Béarn," Matrinka clarified. "They belong in the room beside the downstairs library. Baltraine said you took them."

Dh'arlo'mé glanced around his colleagues who remained immobile. "I have no idea what you're speaking of. And I regret to inform you we found Baltraine dead." He paused thoughtfully. "In the room next to the library, in fact. But he had no staves." He glanced at the staff in his hands as if for the first time. "I made this one on Nualfheim, but you're welcome to it if it's staves you seek."

"That won't be necessary," Matrinka said politely, but only after Dh'arlo'mé had already passed it down the line toward her.

Kevral grinned at the subtle diplomacy.

Dh'arlo'mé glanced longingly after the object as it moved from hand to hand, then his face again became a mask. "We will look for these staff-test staves. If they're in elfin possession, they will return to you. I promise."

As the staff came into Kevral's hands, she examined it for any evidence of danger to Matrinka. Lovingly sanded, the smoothed wood did not even appear capable of leaving a splinter. A placating intuition allayed her earlier suspicions. Reassured of its harmlessness and certain it bore no relationship to the staff-test, she passed it to Matrinka. The princess held it in a fist only a moment, then smiled and passed it to Tae.

The elf who had left returned with a long, narrow case inset with rubies. He placed it on the floor beside Dh'arlo'mé, then returned to his seat.

Dh'arlo'mé ignored the case, politely keeping his gaze on Matrinka. Kevral suspected the princess would have preferred him to turn his attention anywhere else. "Anything more?"

"Yes," Matrinka said, then paused. Apparently, she had nothing specific in mind yet. She brightened suddenly as the proper idea came. "Who's going to tell the populace about King Kohleran?"

Dh'arlo'mé's head slipped sideways, and the fine hair hung in a curtain over his right ear. "Why, I thought you would want that honor." He specified, "You meaning your group, not necessarily you personally."

Tae stepped in to assist, though Kedrin frowned at the impropriety. Though best suited to speaking, the knight had resisted stealing a floor rightfully Matrinka's. "Your magic is convincing. It may take more magic to undo what you've done."

Captain spoke next, making an apologetic wave toward Kedrin to reveal he understood the procedural lapse but found it necessary. "The *lysalf,* or *lav'rintii* as Dh'arlo'mé calls them, can handle that. We only need Pree-han." He nodded toward one of the elves to Dh'arlo'mé's right. "That's the false King Kohleran."

Pree-han fidgeted, his first movement of the meeting.

Dh'arlo'mé's stony, one-eyed gaze found Captain. "We will agree to this only if you promise Pree-han's safe return to us. We will not allow your humans to harm him."

Though irritatingly phrased, the request seemed reasonable to Kevral. Once revealed, Pree-han might suffer the punishment due all the dark elves. Béarn's citizens would not weather the deception, purgings, and loss of King Kohleran kindly. She disagreed with Matrinka's easy forgiveness of Dh'arlo'mé and his *svartalf,* but she believed Griff would have done the same. Kevral would have inserted a stiff penalty against the elves; if it resulted in war and bloodshed, so be it. Most of the corpses would be elfin.

"All right," Matrinka said carefully. "Knight-Captain, can you think of anything more?"

Handed the floor directly, Kedrin seized upon the opportunity. "Humans helped you acquire Béarn." It was a statement, not a question.

"Yes," Dh'arlo'mé admitted.

"We get their names."

Dh'arlo'mé nodded without much need to consider. His loyalty to elves clearly did not extend to humans. "You'll have them."

Matrinka flinched. "Can't we forgive all and start over?"

Kedrin frowned at the naiveté. "We should know our betrayers, no matter how the king chooses to handle them." He returned to his conditions. "Everything that belongs to Béarn remains here: staff-test, money, property, art, writings, and anything I might have forgotten to mention."

Dh'arlo'mé nodded again. "I had assumed that."

Kedrin paused as Dh'arlo'mé's staff reached him. He took it, made as if to lean it against the table until he finished, then passed it back to the elves instead. "There're small things I'll see get into the agreement, but nothing else major I can think of at the moment. How about you, Captain?"

"Just one. We close all the magical gates."

"Yes," Dh'arlo'mé said emphatically. "And the *lav'rintii* stay on this side."

The Captain made a thoughtful noise. "We're not welcome back?"

Dh'arlo'mé pinned the elder with his eye. "We can forgive the humans their ancestors' crimes and their protection of their own."

"How enlightened," Captain returned, his sarcasm evident. "Months ago, you couldn't see either of those things. That's the reason for this split."

Dh'arlo'mé did not quibble. "The reason is immaterial. Whether our actions were right or wrong, you chose to work against your own. And so did your followers. You are no longer elves nor are you welcome among us."

Kedrin made a sign to indicate he had relinquished the floor, though hyperalert Kevral believed herself the only one who saw it.

A flush crept over Captain's face. "Your whim does not determine nature. You can't make a dog a cat because you wish it, nor an elf a human. No matter your change of heart, you are still the *svartalf* and we the *lysalf*." He half-rose, tensed as if to lunge over the table at Dh'arlo'mé.

"No," Dh'arlo'mé leaned toward Captain. "You are Lav'rintir and your followers the *lav'rintii*. Betrayers all. And we are the chosen ones of Frey, forever the *dwar'freytii*, the true elves."

Kevral watched the exchange, fascinated. The length of elfin names should have cued her to the significance of semantics among their people, yet it seemed odd that the heated discussion focused on terminology while the fate of the universe remained so tenuous.

Captain drew breath to argue further, then glanced left and right. He settled back into his seat. "Will you take back any of mine who disavow me and wish to return?"

Dh'arlo'mé did not consider long. "Yes."

"I will send any such back before the gates become permanently closed. I trust you will send any who wish to join us?"

"I would have no use for them."

The civility that followed arguing that had bordered on violence amazed Kevral. *Will I ever understand elves?*

Knight-Captain Kedrin made a subtle gesture, repeating it twice more in the ensuing silence before accepting its uselessness among those unused to Béarnian politics. "May I speak now?" Every eye turned toward the Knight of Erythane, though no one seemed certain who should grant him permission. Apparently taking this as an affirmation, Kedrin continued. "What about my son?"

Kevral cringed, irritated that the need to guard Matrinka and politics had kept her from requesting information about Ra-khir and Darris sooner. It had probably shredded Kedrin's heart to settle agreement terms before knowing whether his only child lived.

Dh'arlo'mé reclaimed his staff, leaning it against the wall. "Your son is in the dungeon, as is his friend. You'll get the prisoners back with the rest of the castle."

Kevral smiled. Kedrin fought valiantly not to let his joy show, but his lips twitched beyond his control, and he eventually succumbed to a tight-lipped smile. Nevertheless, he did not allow relief to taint his dealings. "I'll put the details in writing, as we discussed. For now, we'll let the others know that we've reached a peaceful solution. Thank you for sparing lives on both sides."

Kevral smothered a growl, despising the idea of thanking Dh'arlo'mé after the destruction he had reaped on Béarn. She bit her lip, true to her promise to allow Kedrin to handle diplomacy.

Dh'arlo'mé hefted the case his companion had brought and set it gently on the table. "This is the scepter we plan to give King Griff as both apology and goodwill gesture. You're welcome to examine it, handle it, deal with it as you feel necessary." He unlatched the hinges and flipped the lid. It thunked against the table, and a musty smell washed up from the contents.

Everyone in the room rose in order to see over the edges. The scepter rested on a bed of spongy moss with sparse tendrils and blue-green color like nothing of this world. Longer than Kevral's height, the scepter looked more like a staff, and an emerald half the size of her fist glimmered from wooden fastenings attached to the base. Though the scepter itself seemed unexceptional, the gem added a monetary value that well-suited a king.

As substitute for Griff, the task of examining it fell to Matrinka; but the fear stealing the color from the princess' swarthy features drove Kevral to act in her place. Carefully, she reached for the staff, waiting for a command to desist. No one stopped her from taking it, though Kedrin's smile disappeared, replaced by a hard glare of disapproval. Kevral did not care. She would weather a knight's irritation every day if it meant sparing Matrinka reminders of the staff-test. Her hand closed around the haft, and the wood felt smooth, comfortable in her grip, like a long-used hilt. She braced for an attack she could not guess how to counter and hoped the mental control all Renshai learned would prove enough.

At first, Kevral felt nothing unusual. Then, as she held the scepter several moments, bracing for the danger it might pose to the new king, a tingling touched her mind. At first, she attributed it to the intensity of her concentration. Then the presence groped aimlessly, staggering and falling like a toddler learning to walk. A gentle whisper begged for kinship and promised assistance, its being desperately innocent and needy. Kevral conjured images of a baby bird grasping blindly for the morsels its parents carried, wholly dependent on the one who loved and fed it. "It's magic," Kevral said.

Dh'arlo'mé seemed surprised by Kevral's need to announce such a thing. "Yes. Otherwise, it would have rotted ages ago. I used magic, too, to call it up; and that may still permeate it."

Baynard watched closely, having not spoken a word through the entire meeting. Tae nudged Captain. "Is it safe?"

"Is it harming you?" Captain asked Kevral, and Tae rolled his eyes. He could have done the same.

"No," Kevral admitted. "Do you want it?"

"Yes." The eldest of the elves took the staff from Kevral. As the wood left her hands, it left a lingering desire, like a tiny hole in her chest. Faced with a decision between lovers at an age well before she ever planned to marry, she had given no thought to children. Yet, when she released the staff, she knew a wisp of longing for the smell, warmth, and touch of a baby. She shook her head, dismissing the thought as foolish. She was, would always be, a warrior first.

Captain examined the scepter for several moments before raising it in offering. Baynard held the item briefly, while Tae and Kedrin declined. Then the staff returned to rest in the box.

Captain waited until that moment to speak. "Items imbued with magic are rare. All of the elves together could not have created this. When they lived, the Cardinal Wizards could; but static magic was unpredictable even in their hands. Whoever created this lived long before my birth and, I venture to guess, any others in this room. The fact that I've never heard of it troubles me, but it does lead me to consider that Dh'arlo'mé spoke truth."

Dh'arlo'mé's nostrils flared, his only sign of offense.

Baynard's first words of the meeting were an obvious question, "Do you think it could harm the king?"

"Unlikely." Captain refused to speak in absolutes. "If it could, it would have harmed Kevral. Dh'arlo'mé does not have the power to change its effects."

"So the answer is 'no'?" Baynard pressed.

Captain smiled at the renegade's insistence. "The answer is still 'unlikely.' As I said, magic is never wholly predictable. But the danger would come from the nature of magic in general, not from any property of the staff . . ." His eyes narrowed as his mistake cued him to a train of thought he had not previously considered. ". . . I mean scepter." He looked at Matrinka. "Princess, would you be willing to hold this?" He plucked the scepter from its rest. "And Dh'arlo'mé's staff?"

Kevral glanced at the *svartalf*'s leader and thought she saw a slight flare of his nostrils. Nothing else about him changed, however, and he passed his staff back willingly, without awaiting Matrinka's answer.

"No," Matrinka said, her voice soft yet still betraying fear. She hefted Mior to her shoulders.

Kevral's hand twitched, though she did not allow it to fall to her belt. That would only remind her of the swords she had surrendered at the gate.

"Humor an old elf, please," Captain insisted gently. "You're the only one here who has undertaken the staff-test. You're the only one who could recognize the staves."

Dh'arlo'mé shrugged, already humoring. Kevral discarded the concern as ridiculous. *If Dh'arlo'mé had the staves, why would he give one back to Béarn? Besides, Captain would never have suspected, nor could Matrinka test, if he brought only one to the meeting. Nothing forced Dh'arlo'mé to bring his staff here.*

Matrinka lowered her head, hiding her features, but her

hands shook frantically beneath the table. Mior rubbed against her cheek.

"No." Kevral turned an icy stare on Captain. "She doesn't want to, and she won't."

"I do want to." Matrinka's voice emerged as a thin quaver, yet it managed impact. "Pass them here."

Kevral accepted Dh'arlo'mé's staff from the elves as Captain handed over the scepter. "No. If these are the staves, they will harm you." The insanity the renegades had described for the twice-tested heirs returned to her thoughts in Béarnide voices: homicides, suicides, catatonia, and addictions. No one had survived the double testing intact. "No."

Matrinka studied Kevral, relief returning the color to her cheeks. The Renshai's refusal spared her the need to decide. Then, suddenly, her gaze flitted to the cat, their faces so close their eyes nearly touched. Determination set her pretty features, stealing emphasis from the oval face and broad lips. "Give me the staff, Kevral."

Kevral hesitated.

"It's the sacrifice I've lived for and would gladly die for. My contribution to Béarn. Kevral, if these are the staves from the test, we have to know. No one else can answer that. No one."

Kevral knew she spoke truth. Those heirs who had undergone it were either dead, untrustworthy, or steeped in madness. She stared at Matrinka until the princess quit looking at the calico and finally met the Renshai's gaze. For once, Matrinka's kindly, dark eyes held the blaze of a Renshai charging, mortally wounded, into a final combat. She wanted this as much as a Renshai needed death in battle. And Kevral would not deny it. She handed over the staff.

Matrinka took it into her other hand. Clutching both, she closed her eyes and waited. A bead of sweat trickled from beneath her black bangs, twining along the edge of her nose before dripping to the tabletop. She opened her eyes. And smiled. Handing Dh'arlo'mé's staff back to Kevral, she replaced the scepter in its case. "King Griff will accept your gift and your following." She looked at Kevral. "The staff and scepter did not affect me."

Kevral looked at the adolescent who had been her charge for months. Though large, the uncertainty of her movements and tender guilelessness of every action made her seem delicate and frail. Now a new confidence swept in, clearly visible in her demeanor. *You're wrong. The staff and scepter did affect you.* Yet Kevral knew no magic had caused the change. Matrinka had faced her greatest fear, the doubts about self-worth that had plagued her since the staff-test, and won.

CHAPTER 14

The Dark Elves' Legacy

The brave dead should be glorified, never mourned.
— *Colbey Calistinsson*

On Nualfheim, wide-trunked *doranga* with concentric rings of bark bowed in the heavy, intermittent breezes. Branches rattled over Dh'arlo'mé's head, and occasional fruit pattered prematurely to a floor spongy with rotting, serrated leaves. Though cloying compared with Alfheim, the damp natural odor of forest proved a welcome relief from the cleaners, spices, and perfumes of Béarn's castle. Shadows dappled with flickering sunlight possessed a beauty no torchlight glazing uniformly over muraled walls could match. The wind shifted the pattern, and sun rays sparkled like stars on the woodland floor.

Even the elves who had once formed Béarn's council understood Dh'arlo'mé's need for solitude. They left him alone with his thoughts and with the Staff of Law. Dh'arlo'mé clutched the wood in a hand that seemed birthed for the purpose of holding it, and he knew its precise position without the need to look. It had become an extension of self, wholly and irrevocably his. *Lav'rintir nearly ruined us.*

The mistake was bringing me into the room. Had they seen chaos alone, they would not have questioned.

Dh'arlo'mé believed his mentor, yet he defended his decision. *I needed you there. For advice and support.* A wave of jealousy washed through him at the thought of leaving the staff for others to discover. *We belong together always.*

Indeed. A few moments apart won't change that. Though Dh'arlo'mé returned nothing intentional, the staff read his unspoken concern. *No one could come along and take me.*

It's not as if you could run from them. Dh'arlo'mé finally articulated his concern.

Amusement tainted the contact. *I convinced Lav'rintir and the humans that I belonged to you, and the Staff of Chaos to the* *new king. I can convince anyone who touches me to leave me where I lie. Any fool who refuses hints, I can deal with as I did Baltraine and Khy'barreth.**

A shiver traversed Dh'arlo'mé. Anticipating sorrow, his own cruel amusement surprised him. *Can you fix Khy'barreth?**

*No.** The staff radiated a sense of disinterest as much as impossibility. *His mind is ruined, and good riddance to it. But I did not slay him. His soul will return to the elves at the natural conclusion of his life.**

Appeased, Dh'arlo'mé allowed the smile he had suppressed. Ultimately, nothing mattered but the soul. *And the Staff of Chaos will corrupt the king?**

*It seems certain. It lies. It cheats. It follows no rules. As it comes into its power, it will find a way to ruin him. But we must prepare to interfere once mankind destroys itself. We cannot allow the elves to crumble into chaos' influence.**

Dh'arlo'mé attempted to express his determination. *We will lead them with a loyalty all of the primordial chaos together could not budge.** A dribble of regret wound through him, so thin it barely touched his consciousness.

The Staff of Law discovered that thread. *Do not worry for the power lost in Béarn. We still control the kingdoms North and East. The roads in the West will prove more valuable than any kingdom. Let chaos rage amid mankind, and all the world will belong to the elves at length.**

Dh'arlo'mé's grin broadened, and he clutched the staff in a grip so tight his fingers ached. The euphoria fluttering through his chest usurped all worry. *Teach me more!** He chased knowledge with the vigor of a hungry infant at its mother's breast. And, with the love of that mother, the staff complied.

Griff perched on the bed in the king's master chamber, legs folded beneath him, alone for the first time since Rantire had won him as her charge. Wooden braces and posts, carved into bear forms, supported a massive square mattress that could have comfortably held his entire family. The coverlet was intricately woven into a perfect replica of the royal crest. Matching emeralds topped each of the eight pillars, scarcely smaller than the one at the end of the elfin scepter beside him. Bureaus, still stuffed with King Kohleran's clothing, lined every wall. Twin wardrobes occupied each far corner, and a chest lay at the foot of the bed. Crafted by artisans at least as talented as Béarn's stone carvers, all pieces flaunted chains of rollicking bears with tiny gems for eyes. A desk, a thick soft carpet, and three windows with gauzy curtains completed the furnishings.

Griff had noticed these details as he entered, the grandeur lost on a simpleminded farm boy without designs on power or money. The whole of the situation seemed too overwhelming for contemplation. He sat motionless, paralyzed beyond any but basic thought and function. Even the natural act of breathing seemed to require attention. One moment, dizziness warned him to slow down and shallow the nervous gasping. Soon after, yawns forced him to suck air more deeply and quicken the rate. Griff had known from young childhood that he descended from Béarnian royalty, yet the idea of becoming king had never entered his mind nor even his play. His mother's overprotectiveness had kept him friendless, except for the imaginary playmate who had turned out to be frighteningly real.

Thoughts of home sickened Griff. He pictured his mother, her whaleboned frame sinewy from farm chores and her dark eyes deerlike against prominent ridges. Though not a small man, his stepfather, Herwin, stood spare fingers' breadths taller than his wife. Other Westerners always seemed tiny compared to the Béarnides who so nearly resembled their bear symbol. Need washed through Griff at the thought of those two, and the room glided into a muddled blur pierced at intervals by the glimmer of sunlight off gemstones. He understood his duty, and could not forsake it; but he would have traded all the riches and authority to reunite with his family. *Ravn, where are you when I need you?* He laid a heavy hand on the elves' scepter.

I will help you. A sympathetic voice touched Griff's mind. The heir stiffened, worried for his sanity.

I'm your friend, your adviser, and I will never forsake you. I will long outlast you and your children. I will always be with you, your guide and your power. Though wholly internal, the voice soothed, its promise as gentle as a mother's lullaby.

Nothing in Griff's personality or upbringing prepared him for deceit. He did not question the scepter's sincerity, only its presence. "Who and what are you? How can you talk to me like that?"

I am the guardian of kings, a force locked into your staff. My power will become your power. My wisdom your wisdom. You need not speak to me in words, your thoughts in my direction will suffice.

Like this? Griff tried.

Exactly.

Distracted from his sorrow for a moment, Griff furrowed his brow. *This is weird.*

Weird? the scepter returned, along with the wave of confusion Griff might expect from a stuffy, elder statesman confronted with adolescent slang.

Weird, yes. Don't you think talking without words is weird?

No.

Griff conceded. He supposed he would not have found it so either if he only communicated in that manner. The thought raised a host of considerations he did not bother to ponder now. If humans, like elves, could talk to one another this way, it would change diplomatic negotiations drastically. *You're offering me friendship?*

And much more, the staff assured, excitement rising in a radiating crescendo. *Wisdom, knowledge, guidance. Help with the most difficult decisions.*

Griff shrugged. He had never found decisions difficult, only circumstances. He doubted the scepter could help with the latter.

Apparently, the scepter could not read thoughts not directed at it, for it ignored the vagaries currently floating through Griff's mind. *Nowhere could you find a stronger, more competent adviser.*

I thought the bard would advise me.

On procedure. Protocol. Formality. None of those things matter. It turned to unformed ideas concerning the jumble that currently faced Griff, a kingdom cut adrift. Having lost its council, its ministers, and all of its top officials, Béarn contained little of its once-famous order. The staff reveled in the chaos the elves had left Griff to sort, and excitement thrilled through Griff's hand where it came in contact with the wood. *There's an artful, natural beauty to the way things have become. Why spoil it with regimentation?*

Griff chuckled, and the scepter responded with a tangible flare of offense.

What's funny?

The question baffled Griff. *Weren't you joking?*

No! The scepter's conceptual demeanor went from irritated to explanatory in an instant. *Think of the possibilities, the genius in keeping people unbalanced. The power.*

Power, Griff repeated. *That's the third time you've offered power.*

The scepter quivered, its emotion now one of generous joy. *I have much power to offer you.*

Griff laughed again. *Would you also offer a drowning man a mug of water? What use could I possibly have for more power?*

What use? For power? The scepter's confusion battered at Griff. *The possibilities are staggering. And I can give you more than you could imagine existed. More than anyone could ever want.*

We're talking want *now? I've already gone way beyond that.*

The scepter's radiation intensified, stark incredulity. *What kind of being* are *you?*

The question surprised Griff only for an instant. *I'm a man. You're used to elves, aren't you?*

Not really, the scepter returned but did not elaborate. It tried a different tack. *All right, then. No power. I have other wondrous things to offer. How about the power—* It amended, *I mean the ability to see details mortal eyes overlook. I can show you the world in intensities you could never imagine, the full spectrum of colors including variations in hues that now look the same to you.*

Interesting, Griff replied politely. *But—no. A lifetime of study may not yield all the beauty of the murals and tapestries that fill the castle hallways. If you give me another dimension, my goal of seeing all will become unattainable.*

I can make you a genius.

Griff shook his head until the whipping, dark hair stung his face. *It wouldn't suit me.*

You'd be better. Smarter.

I'd be someone else. Not me.

Frustration trickled through the contact. *I could teach you magic.*

I have enough trouble managing the skills I have.

The scepter seemed to swell, its strain now clearly perceptible. *You're one of a kind, Griff Petrostan's son.*

Griff did not question how the scepter knew his name. *Thank you,* he said, though the scepter's annoyance did not suggest it meant the words as a compliment.

Surely there's something you want.

I want to make the right decisions for Béarn. I want to be the best possible king.

I can help you with that, the scepter made the task sound easy.

And I want my family and my best friend at my side.

The scepter had no immediate answer.

Griff lowered his head with a sigh, thoughts of his parents a dull ache in his conscience. He trusted Ravn to have brought solace or, at least, reassurance to his mother. For now, that would have to do. Eventually, when the roads became passable again and he did not fear for the lives of messengers, he would escort his mother and stepfather to Béarn.

So simple. So concrete. What I offer spans levels you don't even know exist.

Thank you, Griff shook his head, though he realized the eyeless scepter probably could not fathom gestures. *No. I have enough to handle on levels I do understand. All I need right now is a friend.*

I can be that friend, the staff promised.

Griff doubted the claim but appreciated the offer.

Someone rapped boldly on the door. The sound startled Griff, and he jerked away from the scepter with a suddenness that disrupted the contact. "Come in."

The latch clicked, and the door swung open. Rantire's voice wafted through the widening crack. "Come in, he says, without bothering to ask who. He still needs my—"

"Hush!" Darris commanded. Then the panel swung far enough to reveal the bard, now dressed in the blue and tan uniform of the inner court guards, and Rantire in her usual loose-fitting leathers. Darris bowed. "Majesty, I'd like to report."

Griff scarcely resisted looking beyond himself for the object of Darris' address. "I'm not the king yet, Darris. There's still the coronation."

"See," Rantire jumped in. "Not king yet. He's still my charge."

Darris' coiled limbs and flushed features revealed dangerous irritation. Though he clearly wished to put the Renshai in her place, he followed the proper convention of speaking first to the king's statement. "Sire, there's nothing remaining but the formal ceremony. In the eyes of your subjects, you are already the king." He glared at Rantire. "Since when do Renshai stand on formality?"

"It's my job to guard the heir," Rantire insisted.

Darris grated under his breath, so low-pitched and -volumed

that Griff had to strain to hear. "When one's born, we'll call you."

Griff stepped in to relieve the situation. "I'll hear that report, Darris, and thank you. Rantire, why don't you continue to guard outside?" Griff held his breath, awaiting the results of words more recommendation than command. The idea of others following his every suggestion had not yet sunk into understanding.

Though Griff no longer touched the scepter, it managed to waft a soft thought to him. *Let them argue. It gives them the feeling of accomplishment they crave.*

Finding the suggestion ludicrous beyond comment, Griff ignored the staff. Rantire hesitated, as if to argue, then quietly returned to her vigil. Darris closed the door behind her. Only then, Griff noticed the bard's brow creased in worry and the dullness of the familiar, hazel eyes. "What's wrong?"

"There's much that needs doing, Majesty." Darris' nod displayed more tired formality than respect. "You'll need new ministers, a master healer, and an inner circle of guards."

"Inner circle?" Terminology evaded Griff who had grown up as a farm boy. Healer, he understood, and the renegades had discussed the council and ministers previously.

"The dozen guards you trust to protect you when you hold court and in other public situations."

Griff blinked, cocking his head sideways while he considered. "Isn't protecting me your job?"

"I'm one man, Majesty. Competent, but no Renshai. The bard has other duties to attend as well. I can't be with you always."

"Oh." That news both bothered and pleased Griff. Rantire's presence, though it made him feel safe, had become suffocating. He wanted someone he trusted always available for consultation, and the scepter clearly would not do. He had finally adjusted to the realization that he liked Darris, trusted his boundless knowledge, and had never yet chosen the opposite side of a decision. He covered his disappointment as well as possible. "Of course not."

Darris studied the huge Béarnide with a quiet sympathy that revealed Griff had not hidden his disillusionment as well as he believed. "Majesty, there're many lower positions to fill as well. Servants, soldiers, even the number of nobles has slipped low. You have the choice to reaffirm or oust anyone you wish to as well."

"Oh." The task seemed daunting. Griff had no idea where to begin.

"I can help you." Darris and the scepter said simultaneously, the latter without words. The bard continued alone. "It's not as difficult as it sounds. Once we have trustworthy officials in place, they can handle the selection for all those posts." He smiled wanly, clearly plagued by other matters than those they had thus far discussed. "It's called delegation. Once your staff is in place, everything will come swiftly together. You'll see. Sire, the day-to-day decisions are not yours to worry about, unless you wish them so. You'll direct diplomacy and make judgments. The rest will fall into place."

"Good," Griff said because it seemed necessary. He knew Darris would remain with him, at least until he felt comfortable ruling. He had faith in Darris, yet he could not forsake the longing for Ravn's calm competence and friendship. He had relied on his only playmate for too long to feel quite right about any other arrangement. The scepter seemed positively imbecilic. "Darris, what's troubling you?"

The bard stiffened. "Is it that obvious?"

Griff widened his eyes, encouraging explanation. His answer did not require speaking.

"Sire, things are missing," Darris explained. "Gems, money, a few tapestries. We expected that. Much will need mending, and we'll need to put apprentices to work early to supply necessities for the populace, mail for the new guards, and so many other things."

Griff nodded. The renegades had led him to expect all Darris described. Darris still had not spoken his concern. "The elves left us a mess."

"Shambles would better describe it, Sire." The attempt at usual conversation fell flat, spearing Griff with abrupt terror. He hoped all his growing friendships would not become lost to the courtesy and homage they felt obligated to show him.

The scepter fueled Griff's new worry. *It's the curse of rulership, I'm afraid. A loneliness no other human can comprehend.*

This time, Griff sensed a truth to the scepter's words, though he despised them.

"Sire . . ." Darris' words seemed to catch in his throat, and it took him inordinately long to finish his sentence. ". . . I don't know why." He shook his head, as if to imply the explanation lay beyond human understanding. "Before they left, the dark elves poisoned some of the food."

Shocked wordless, Griff could only listen.

"We caught it before any of the staff or citizens ate enough to cause damage. Our elves are finishing a final inspection to assure no one else gets harmed."

"Else?" Griff pressed. "If not staff or citizens, who was harmed?"

"The prisoners, Sire."

Griff's heart felt frozen in place, and raw, cold terror swept him. "You?"

"Queasy. A bit dizzy. I ate very little. The healers say I'll do just fine."

The reassurance barely seemed to melt the dread. "Ra-khir?"

"He's in the best possible hands, healer and elfin. Matrinka's there, too. And his father."

Panic mobilized Griff. He leaped to his feet, leaving the scepter, forgotten, on the bed. "And us. We're there, too, in a moment. Let's go."

Darris sprang aside, though Griff took care not to trample his adviser. He would never miss every bauble, treasure, and gem of the kingdom; he would trade them all for the life of one friend.

Mattresses interrupted the usual straw that covered the weapons training room floor. Lanterns lit the room like day. Light elves and healers scurried between bedsides, carrying satchels, pastes, and herbs or removing basins of urine or bloody fluid. Driven to distraction by restless determination, Griff found the pattern of movement impossible to discern. Darris blocked his natural sprint for the doorway, saving king and a burdened healer from a collision and adding the necesssary delay for details to become clear. By the time Griff recognized the talent inherent in making a deliberate attempt to herd the king look innocent and accidental, order appeared amid the chaos.

On the left-hand side of the room, teary-eyed servants loaded five lifeless bodies, lovingly wrapped, onto carts. To the right, a dozen patients lay frighteningly still, tended by the bustling elves and healers. Two others sat amidst their blankets, and a third remained prone but chatted weakly with a young male attendant. Griff's eyes went naturally to Knight-Captain Kedrin, crouched in the farthest corner of the room beside a motionless form. Without awaiting Darris' confirmation or interference, Griff picked his way cautiously through the confusion.

Focused on Ra-khir, Griff scarcely noticed the others around him. Occasional moans cut over the shouted needs of the healers. The elves' silence seemed eerie in comparison, though they worked at least as fluently together. Even though Griff knew of their mental communication, he found the difference disquieting. In contrast, the other humans in the room did not seem troubled at all. Moving out of the way of a page with a precariously balanced bowl, Griff stepped over a middle-aged man gasping the intermittent, deep breaths of the dying. Fear provoked a sudden rush of tears.

Kedrin shifted to allow space for Griff in the corner, out of the way of the healing staff. The heir wriggled into position carefully, gaze so riveted on Ra-khir's familiar, handsome features he could not even look away to ascertain his seat. The red-blond hair, so like his father's, fell neatly away from closed eyes, a finely set nose, and the sculpted jaw. Slightly parted, his lips revealed a straight row of white teeth. His chest rose and fell in a peaceful rhythm. Griff said nothing. Any question would sound inane, and the father would speak when he chose to do so. Darris stood apart from the vigil, his presence one too many to allow the healers free access.

The knight-captain did not delay. "Your Majesty, thank you for coming."

Griff had traveled with Ra-khir long enough to know better than to ridicule the formality. "Béarn's army couldn't keep me away. How is he?"

"The healers say they've done everything, Sire. If he wakes up, he'll be fine. If not. . . ." Kedrin trailed off, a choked sob the only sign of his grief.

Finally, Griff managed to pull his gaze from the son to look at the father. Red lines etched his eyes like lightning, and the proud features looked desperately sunken. Though in obvious pain, he did not burden his ruler by sharing.

Griff recognized unspoken need. Deference might hold others distant from him in times of trouble, but he would not allow the same fate to befall the awesome captain of Erythane's knights. The king's massive arms encircled Kedrin, the bearlike hands clasping each meaty shoulder.

Surprise tensed every muscle in Kedrin's body. Then, gradually, Griff felt the tension flow from him. His silks readily absorbed the tears, warm and wet against his chest. "He'll be fine," Griff assured, a promise he had no way to keep. Faith, however, made him certain. "The gods would never let you come so close, only to lose one another again."

Experience gave Kedrin the words to contradict without condemnation. "I wish my faith were as strong as yours, Majesty."

The "Sires" and "Majesties" wore on Griff, but he weathered them in silence. Asking Béarn's staff and citizenry to speak otherwise would make them at least as uncomfortable as he felt being addressed in that fashion. Foreign dignitaries would likewise suffer. It made more sense to change his attitude than millennia of convention. In time, he suspected, he would cease to notice what others chose to call him. "I've faith enough for both of us. There *is* justice in this world."

"There is now." Darris' voice floated over the rattle of pans and scattered bursts of conversation. Griff missed the reference to his return, not bothering to make other sense of the comment.

Kedrin eased free of Griff's embrace, no longer stressed to the point of breaking. His gaze slipped to Ra-khir, gentle breaths stirring his chest at regular intervals. A sparkle of hope softened the terror that glazed Kedrin's pale eyes. Griff turned his attention to Darris. The bard's expression told a different story, harsh and judgmental. He did not wholly approve of Griff's technique, raising expectations that might prove devastatingly false. He would not speak of it, however, a courtesy that stirred irritation. If Griff accomplished nothing else, he would see to it his wise bodyguard always freely spoke his mind. He hoped Darris' stony silence stemmed from the intention to discuss the matter in private rather than to ignore it completely.

Having gained Griff's attention, Darris spoke. "Majesty, there's nothing more you can do here, and we've other matters to attend. The healers have the situation under control."

Griff glanced at Kedrin once more. He had stirred hope. The rest lay in the gods' hands. Lingering would not assist the process, only reduce the space available to others who wished a turn at vigil and force Kedrin to attend king as well as son. The Béarnide nodded. "Captain, if you would like me here, at any time, let me know." He added emphatically, "You don't need a reason."

Kedrin tore his gaze from Ra-khir to execute the appropriate, if arcane, gestures to acknowledge the honor the heir bestowed upon him, respect, and a formal parting. His ability to remember the protocol while his son lay dying floored Griff and made him all the more certain he needed to leave. Kedrin would fare better concentrating on his own grief rather than worrying about offending his soon-to-be-crowned king. "Thank you."

Griff turned, trotting after Darris, careful to avoid the bustling jumble of healers, maids, and other servants who gave him a wide berth as well. *Lonely,* the scepter had said, and Griff knew now more than ever it had spoken truth. "Where are Kevral, Tae, and Matrinka?"

"Matrinka's working, Sire." Darris glanced among the injured and attendants, pointing out the princess among the healers. No one shied from her as they did from her cousin. Though as much an heir as he for the moment, she did not suffer the loneliness that would become his daily lot. "The others are in the temple." Darris steered Griff out of the makeshift infirmary and through the door. "What's left of it. They tarried long here but needed some time away."

Griff pursed his lips, understanding. "I know we have a lot to prepare and decisions to make, but I'd like some time alone, too."

"Of course, Majesty."

Rantire joined them in the hall, trailing in a sullen hush that revealed her dissatisfaction with the current arrangement. As Griff headed back to his personal chamber, he realized he needed to handle this problem before any others. "Darris, about the inner circle of guards."

"Yes, Majesty?"

"Do the rules specify how I pick them?"

"Not formally, Sire." Darris did not look at Griff, but his brow furrowed. "It's traditional for the king to select a guard captain he trusts and let him choose top soldiers from Béarn's troops."

Griff stiffened at the implication. "They killed the guard captain, too?"

"No, Sire." Rantire led the way up the staircase while Darris remained at Griff's side. A painted mural, carved into three dimensions, depicted mountain ledges and ascending wildlife. "Captain Seiryn's well. It seems as if the dark elves destroyed anyone whose job required physical proximity to the king, probably to keep them from seeing through the illusion."

Griff cringed, recalling that Darris' mother fell into that category.

"After that, their killing became more random."

Griff took Darris' hand and gave it a sympathetic squeeze.

The touch clearly startled the bard who tensed so suddenly he missed a step. He scrabbled awkwardly for balance, ripping his fingers free. Rantire whirled, prepared to rescue Griff from this unexpected danger should he teeter as well.

Darris regained his equilibrium, sheepishly staring at his feet. "I'm sorry, Sire."

"No." Griff refused to allow Darris to take the blame. "I'm sorry. About your mother and about nearly throwing you down the steps." He smiled at Darris, hoping the bard would take the joke and run with it, as Kevral and Tae always did.

But Darris remained stiffly serious. "Thank you, Sire."

Griff gave Darris the benefit of the doubt. *He has to keep his replies short. Or he has to sing them.* Yet that contradicted the detailed reports Darris had delivered to him, a moment ago and in the recent past. Curiosity fueled by the incongruity, Griff did not press now. The timing seemed wrong.

Reaching the fifth-floor landing, the three headed toward Griff's chambers. Brackets in the shapes of animals supported torches whose flames trailed their movement. Between, gilded tapestries depicted bear cubs wrestling, bears perched regally on rocks, and massive male bears engaged in battle. Occasionally, an edge of a painted wall scene peeked out from beneath the weavings. Rantire crouched at the door to the king's chamber, anticipating Griff's command.

Darris caught the latch, the heavy teak door emblazoned with the royal crest. The ruby eyes of the rearing bear seemed to glare with powerful anger, and sapphires surrounded the emblem. "You were asking about the inner guards, Majesty," he reminded.

"Quite right." Griff had forgotten. He inclined his head toward the door. "The two of us can finish our discussion inside." He deliberately excluded Rantire. She would expect nothing different.

Darris opened the panel, glanced casually inside, then ushered Griff through. The Béarnide trotted to the bed and sat on the edge, then motioned for the bard to use the desk chair.

Darris complied. "Captain Seiryn's an able warrior and a superior strategist."

Griff nodded carefully. "I would expect nothing less from my grandfather." The words raised a pang of sadness. He wished he could have met King Kohleran before his death. "I gladly place selection of the inner circle in the captain's hands."

Darris' chest rose and fell in a silent sigh of relief.

"Except one," Griff added.

Darris closed his eyes, clearly bracing for the worst. "One, Sire?"

Griff did not drag out his thought. That would only torture Darris. "Rantire."

Darris' lids rose, first to a neutral position, then further still. "Rantire?" He shook his head slightly. "She's Renshai, Sire."

"Yes." That hardly required mention. "Do inner circle guards have to be Béarnides?"

Darris opened his mouth, then closed it, brow furrowing. "I suppose not. They always have been, but nothing says they have to be." He added, as if in afterthought, "Sire." His head cocked to the left as he contemplated further. A smile eased onto his features. "It's a wonderful idea, Majesty, and it should appease Rantire. I don't know if she'd accept the job, but the fact that you asked will mean a lot." He seemed restless, as if he wanted to say more but chose silence instead.

The revelation floored Griff. "Why would she refuse?"

"Sire, she's Renshai," Darris repeated, as if that should make it obvious.

Griff shook his head.

"First, they're clannish. I've never heard of one leaving the Fields of Wrath, except while serving duty in Béarn. It has to do with their training. Second, regimentation, strategy, following orders—they're not things Renshai feel comfortable with."

Griff appreciated Darris' opinion. "So you think I shouldn't ask her."

"Sire, I think . . ." Darris started, then stopped. He glanced at Griff as if to judge him.

"*Please*, speak freely," Griff fairly begged.

"Well, Sire, I see merit in the idea. Especially if Rantire refuses. That would place her in the position of having willingly sacrificed her guardianship." Darris continued eyeballing Griff, reading his reaction. "But if she agrees, she may drive every one of us insane. She may ignore or belittle her commander. She might shackle herself to you again, making my job impossible and depriving you of any possibility for privacy."

Griff saw Darris' point. "You don't think it's a good idea."

Darris shrugged. "I see two sides, Majesty."

"And if you were me?"

Darris paled. "Sire, I wouldn't dishonor you by placing myself in such a position."

Griff sighed and sought different words. "What do you advise?"

"Sire, that wholly depends on what you're trying to accomplish."

It seemed obvious to Griff. "A place for Rantire that pleases everyone."

Darris lowered his chin into his hands as he considered.

Griff discovered an answer as the bard thought. "What about 'relief' bodyguard?"

Darris' brow furrowed, and he caught his chin between a thumb and forefinger. "Excuse me, Sire?"

"You once told me the bard has to travel, that you won't be with me all the time."

"Right."

"When you're gone, Rantire can be you."

Darris grinned, sitting straight in his chair and releasing his face. "Brilliant, Sire." He could not help muttering, "If you can stand it."

"Darris," Griff added.

"Yes, Sire."

"Don't be away too much."

For the first time, king and bard shared a good laugh.

CHAPTER 15

Law's Heir

Truth is less significant to a title than the effect it inspires. To the people of the West, you will become the Golden Prince of Demons. To the Wizards, Colbey, you always have been.
—The Last Eastern Wizard, Shadimar

Dh'arlo'mé scarcely noticed the gemlike eyes that studied him through gaps between trunks and foliage. His followers watched him with emotions the staff's influence made tangible. Respect mingled inseparably with fear, curiosity, and an awe bordering on reverence. The staff guided him through magics his puny ability once rendered impossible and turned his thoughts toward functional spells the scattered chaos of elves once made unthinkable. With a pointed finger, he caused leaves to dance against the wind. Patterned breaths created breezes. He learned to fly, a feat new not to the elves but to himself. And the Staff of Law promised so much more.

Personal power overcame the need for vengeance. Dh'arlo'mé ceased to worry about destroying humanity; chaos and mankind's own frailty would see to that. The staff's presence became a reassuring constant: swaddling, teaching, molding. The need for sleep receded. His genius seemed to grow in daily leaps. Decisions that would once have required the combined wisdom of the Nine found easy answers. It never occurred to him to ponder how the Dh'arlo'mé of old would have responded to those same problems. He had grown into something vastly superior, bonded to the seemingly infinite knowledge of the Staff of Law.

It's nearly time, the staff interrupted a lesson to announce.
Time?
To face your fear, Dh'arlo'mé.
The comment rankled. *I have no fears.*
Very well, then. The staff did not argue, though it did not

accept the proclamation either. *You will now learn to summon and control.*

Summon? The boldness left Dh'arlo'mé, replaced by an icy sweat. *You mean . . . ?* He trailed off deliberately, letting the staff fill in the gap.

Demons, yes. Are you prepared?

Dh'arlo'mé tried to force an affirmation that would not leave his lips. His fingers trembled, beyond his control. *No,* he admitted. *I can't control them.*

I can. WE can.

No, Dh'arlo'mé repeated, though beyond his superficial thoughts, his mind clamored for the experience. Had he become the Northern Wizard he had apprenticed for, he might already have gained the knowledge and power to do so. His heart pounded. Images of the black mass of claws and teeth flashing down on him would not leave his mind, and panic scattered excitement into delay. *Not yet.*

Soon, my champion. Soon. First, I have bindings, wards, and banishments to teach you. It's not enough to bring it here. You must control it.

Yes. That having been exactly the problem, Dh'arlo'mé appreciated hearing the solution. Patience, once routine, then an annoyance, flourished again among a people whose lives spanned centuries or millennia. Dh'arlo'mé could wait while humans destroyed themselves with the help of chaos. He placed his trust, and so much more, firmly into the Staff of Law's grasp.

And the elves followed their leader.

Left alone again, Griff rested his arms on the window ledge and looked out over the city soon to be his. Massive men and women, so like himself, bustled through the streets, restoring order to a town destroyed as much by discontent as by the cruelty of its leadership. The attitudes of the people had changed vastly since the day Griff entered Béarn for the first time. They moved at a brisk pace, faces turned toward one another, eyes meeting as they chatted. Distant laughter touched his ears like music. Yet, though he loved the sound, Griff did not smile. Their joy sprang from the hopes they placed on him, the certainty that he would rule Béarn with the wisdom and competence of his ancestors.

Griff turned from the window, banishing the images of a joyous populace, of multicolored courtyard gardens, of flawlessly carved statues beckoning him to explore a world he could never before have imagined his. He reveled in the beauty, yet felt as if a shapeless lump of granite hung from his neck. So many lives had become dumped into hands accustomed only to play and the lightest of farm chores. His mother had never trusted him with the harvest; how could a country dare to risk so much on one so patently unworthy. "Why me? Why me?"

A presence brushed Griff's mind, too weak to answer but clamoring for attention. Certain of its source, Griff turned toward the scepter, but he did not bother to take it in hand. Its attitudes contrasted sharply with a logic and judgment too simple to consider discarding. He did not wish to argue with it now.

Griff never doubted his bloodline or his companions' certainty that he must rule, only his own ability to do so properly. He still felt like an awkward child, too clumsy even for farm work, too dull to grasp plowing let alone the intricacies of rulership. His massive frame had always made him feel out-of-place in Dunwoods, as ungainly as a bull attempting flight. The rare children he met edged away from him, put off by his size. The adults turned him knowing looks, their smiles sympathetic to the point of condescension. His lack of understanding of simple farm equipment, his unworldliness, and his girth made them believe him a dullard. Eventually, he had come to believe it himself.

Desperately alone, Griff buried his face in his hands. "Ravn, where are you?" His fingers smothered a plea he expected no one to hear. Tears streaked his palms, and the enormity of the task ahead drove him to wild sobbing. His presence alone had brought happiness to so many, yet he could never hope to maintain the joy, security, and needs of a city. He would do all he could not to fail them, yet it seemed inevitable. He had no means to contemplate the damage his ineptitude might inflict on so many innocents. "You said you'd always be with me when I needed you. One way or another, you said, you'd be here."

Ravn perched on Odin's High Seat, *Hlidskjalf*, knees tucked to his chest and a booted foot resting irreverently against the colorful array of inset gems in the arms. One hand lay on his knee, the other draped casually across the hilt of the scimitar at his left hip. The sheathed tip of his opposite sword dangled over the seat of the chair. Though relaxed to the floppy extreme only adolescents could manage, he could defend himself in an instant should the need arise. Yet his thoughts remained distant from combat, and his heart thudded a slow, sad cadence as he shared the agony of his human friend.

Ravn remembered his promise in Béarn's gutted temple, though he had made it under duress. The sorrow of the innocent child turned king had burned through him, then as now; and the words had seemed natural and necessary. He had not meant them literally, though he realized he should have expected Griff to assume so. The Béarnide's simple caring and forthright honesty left little room for allusion; it was not enough to remain with Griff in spirit. *He needs me*.

Springing from the chair, Ravn headed from Odin's Hall. He respected his father, and his mighty ability to punish, too much to attempt contact without permission again. He had also come to understand the precariousness of the balance Colbey protected and the damage the influence of a single god could inflict on his work and on the world. The image of Griff, head bowed, agony almost tangible knifed through Ravn's conscience; yet soothing one could not take precedence over the stability of the universe. Sighing at the anticipated cost, he shuffled through Asgard's blue-green grasslands toward the open field where his father usually practiced.

Smooth, perfect trees, their slender branches crowded with leaves, blew in gentle patterns until the path seemed lined with dancers. Ravn cherished their grace and beauty, eyes drawn to them from unbreakable habit. His father's appreciation for his mortal years had left a lasting impression. Colbey delighted in luxuries and the natural radiance the gods took for granted, and he pitied their loss. Ravn had long ago vowed to share his father's never-ending excitement for details the gods disregarded as petty. Though the others dismissed Colbey as a gawking, inferior outsider, it also added a precious dimension to his life.

Ravn wandered past a stream, enjoying its ceaseless, high-pitched music and studying the jewellike highlights the sun etched in its surface. He broke from the cover of the forest and discovered the gold-and-silver blur of his father's practice. Ravn choked. For all he had attuned himself to treasure Asgard's wonders, the image of Colbey engaged in *svergelse* always captured his attention fully. The swords whipped around him, their flight swift and sure. Ravn's eyes could not follow the movement, and often the blades blurred to invisibility. No matter how much he envied and emulated, he seemed incapable of matching a skill won fully by practice.

Ravn loosened one scimitar, then the other in its sheath. Excitement plied him, tainted by dread. The idea of assaulting the deadly figure in the field seemed a madness beyond contemplation. Colbey had trained warriors for longer than half a century, and Ravn for all of his sixteen years. He used only live steel, shunning sparring weapons as farm implements and clubs unfit for barbarians. In all those years, no session had ever resulted in spilled blood, except one. A smile eased onto Ravn's lips as he recalled that battle. Then, elves had captured Griff, and Ravn would let nothing stand in the way of comforting his mortal friend. The wavering of the world's balance had stolen the stability of the Sword of Balance as well. Even Colbey's inhuman skill fell prey to the jerky shifts in equilibrium. A defense had fallen short just enough to allow Ravn to inflict a scratch that won him the match and his time with Griff.

Griff needs me. The realization lent Ravn courage. *I hope you appreciate the pain I suffer for you.* Without further consideration, he charged Colbey Calistinsson in a bold frontal attack befitting a Renshai. "Have at me, old man!" His swords rasped free as he ran.

Colbey seemed to take no notice of the attack, continuing his *svergelse.* Yet as Ravn's right-hand scimitar swept for his head, he parried deftly, in time to rescue his chest from his son's second strike. Even as he defended, he sheathed Harval, fielding two blades with only one.

Ravn bore in, his only defense a frenzied web of attack, as Colbey taught. He swept in with a high arc while his second sword tore low, seizing the advantage of his extra weapon. Colbey dodged both easily, returning an attack Ravn jerked in both blades to defend against and then, only barely. Colbey's blade rang musically against his block, immediately withdrawn and rethrust before Ravn could muster another offense.

Self-directed rage flared, even as Ravn deflected the assault and managed a stiff riposte. Colbey redirected, feinted low, then high. The maneuver drew both Ravn's scimitars in defense and left him nothing when the elder Renshai bore in for a gut slash. *Damn!* Ravn leaped backward. The long sword followed him, and only a frantic sideways dive saved him from a deadly strike to the head. He flung up both swords as he rose. Luck as much as skill hammered Colbey's onslaught aside, and Ravn managed to regain his feet. Realigning left him no time for anything but defense. He missed three openings, but the delay placed him firmly back into the battle. Only then, he wove a savage offense designed to exhaust his father's single sword arm.

Colbey met every attack with a casual defense that never seemed to tax him. *I might as well batter a brick wall!* Frustration fueled Ravn's already raging battle madness.

"A brick wall doesn't hit back!" Colbey violated his own rule about conversation in battle. He allowed this fault when it properly demoralized an enemy.

This time, it only served to further enrage Ravn. "Damn it, Father!" His looping cut gained power. "Get out of my thoughts."

"I can't help it." Colbey diverted the scimitar with a dexterous flip. "You're radiating them to me."

"Read this thought . . ." *. . . you irritating bastard.* Ravn knew better than to swear at his father aloud, though Colbey's invasion of mental privacy allowed it. The elder stuck solidly by his vow never to violate the mind of one he respected, yet intense emotion and thought wafted to him without intention. Momentarily, Ravn wondered how much of his desperation touched his father's senses as well.

The longsword swept under Ravn's guard. The tip slid between his crosspiece and index finger, hammering steel. Swearing, Ravn winched his hand closed, too late. The scimitar tumbled from his fingers.

Ravn sprang for the errant weapon, aware courtesy would force Colbey to do the same. Ravn's hand closed over his father's fingers, already around the hilt. He shouldered in, using his superior size and strength to attempt to off-balance his father. His second sword thrashed for Colbey's head.

The elder Renshai ducked, still clutching the scimitar's hilt. Ravn's second sword tangled, then severed strands of yellow hair. *Got him.* Ravn savored rising triumph only a moment before Colbey's longsword slammed against his groin.

Agony lanced through Ravn's body. Losing control of his legs, he plummeted, instinctively clutching one scimitar as he released the other to his father's care. Unable to escape incapacitating pain, he rolled erratically on the grass, feeling nothing less substantial than the deep, dull ache in his gut.

After an eternity, Ravn managed to wrench his eyes open. The sun flashed rainbows from streaks of tears clinging to his lashes, and Colbey stood over him. Ravn tensed for a lecture. As one type of suffering faded, another would surely begin.

But Colbey did not scold his son. He simply sheathed his sword, held the scimitar nonchalantly in one hand, and reached to assist Ravn with the other. "Are you all right?" He sounded genuinely concerned.

Ravn accepted the assistance, still sore. "As long as you and Mother don't expect any grandchildren."

Colbey stifled a smile, badly. He handed back the second scimitar.

Ravn inspected it routinely before returning it to its scabbard. He sighed, disappointment a heavy ache across his shoulders.

Colbey examined his son with evident curiosity and an unmistakable fondness. Ravn believed he read some pride in his father's icy blue-gray eyes as well, but he attributed that to hope and his own imagination. "To what do I owe the honor of a spar?" Colbey's grin emerged freely now. "And a haircut." He shook back his locks, and they fell into well-cut feathers around the familiar, ruthless features.

Ravn lowered his head, unruly bangs the same straw-yellow as his father's falling into his blue eyes. Though wiry, he had also inherited some of the musculature of his god ancestors. He had outgrown his father, in height and breadth, a year earlier. "Griff needs me."

"And?"

Ravn met his father's gaze, surprised by the need for clarification. "You let me comfort him the last time I bested you in spar. I thought that offer might still stand."

Colbey made a thoughtful noise that neither confirmed nor denied the assumption. "Go ahead."

Ravn drew in a deep breath and held it, knowing his father too well. "You mean 'go ahead' and try to best you?"

"You may," Colbey said, his tone implying the possibility of other actions. "I'd like that. Or, you can go comfort Griff."

Ravn blinked wordlessly, scarcely daring to believe he had heard his father correctly. "I can go?"

"Yes."

The urge seized Ravn to charge for Midgard before Colbey changed his mind, but suspicion held him in place. "There are conditions, right?"

"Of course."

Ravn nodded, indicating that his father should continue.

Colbey shook his head, clearly baffled by Ravn's need for clarification. "Nothing new. Don't harm any humans or elves. Use subtlety. Try not to interfere more than necessary. Don't tip the balance so we all topple irrevocably into oblivion." He stated the last as matter-of-factly as the others, his facetiousness obvious. He added more seriously, "I thought you'd learned all of that. If I believed otherwise, I would never have agreed."

Ravn rushed to assure Colbey. "Of course I've learned all that. I guess I'm just stunned by the ease with which you agreed to let me do this after forbidding me before."

"You hadn't learned before." Colbey placed an arm on Ravn's shoulders and led him across the field. Despite the obvious significance of the topic, the eyes of father and son swept the glory of Asgard's aqua sky, shared joy in the blue-green beauty of the grasslands, and reveled in the emerald bounty of leaves on flawless trees. At the edge of a pond that had become as much a sanctuary to father and son as the Grove had once been for Griff, they sat. "Ravn, the balance is in grave danger."

Ravn nodded his understanding. The gods had twice met to discuss the situation, and many disapproved of Odin's choice for Keeper of the Balance.

"I may not save it."

Ravn's trust in his father was unwavering. "If you don't, we will all die secure it could not be saved by anyone."

Ravn believed he saw a smile crease Colbey's face before he turned his head to hide it. "Most do not share your faith."

A shrug demonstrated Ravn's contempt for those Colbey indicated.

Colbey paused, displaying more patience than most gods believed him capable of, presumably to regain his composure. When he looked upon his son again, the smile had fully disappeared. "If I do, there will come a time when I hand the charge of balance to you. If you take some responsibility in handling this matter now, you'll have the experience to do so on your own."

Ravn met his father's hard gaze, trying to find some logic to a dictum that made no sense. Finally, he laughed, an action that deepened Colbey's sobriety to a frown. "You're thinking like a human again. You're immortal, remember? You don't have to pass on anything you don't want to."

"Maybe," Colbey said carefully, "I want to."

Icy terror prickled through Ravn, and he felt as if someone had hurled him into Northern waters. "Are you talking about suicide?"

Colbey shook his head, then finally allowed a smile. "No more than usual. If you believe the people of my day, I was—"

"The Deathseeker," Ravn interrupted.

Colbey stiffened, and Ravn took pleasure in the motion. Rarely did he have the opportunity to startle his stoic father.

"Captain, the elf, got me started. I've done a lot of research since then." Ravn tried to embarrass Colbey. "You never told me you were a hero. Sixteen years, and I have to find out from strangers."

"A hero, huh?" Colbey laughed. "Three hundred twenty-odd years is a long time to rewrite history. Hero." He laughed again. "Maybe to Renshai. Even most of the gods and prophecies called me the Golden Prince of Demons. Not exactly a term of endearment."

That name Ravn had not heard. "Why Golden Prince of Demons?"

Colbey rolled his eyes to regard the sky as he remembered facts long buried. "Renshai were pretty universally hated in those days, especially in the West. Some towns and villages put people to death merely for saying the word. So most Westerners called us 'the golden-haired devils from the North.' Though never an official leader, I was probably the best known Renshai, so I became the Golden Prince of Demons."

"Shouldn't it have been the Golden Prince of Devils?"

Colbey shrugged. "I didn't make it up. I didn't care much for it. And, by the way, I didn't answer to it." He paused a moment as another recollection came to mind. "In fact, if I remember correctly, the name originally came from a prophecy written by a Western Wizard millennia before my birth." He tapped his fingers on Ravn's shoulder, thinking. "In an Age of Change/When chaos shatters Odin's ward/A Renshai shall come forth . . ." He paused, the rest eluding him for several moments. ". . . Hero of the Great War/He will hold legend and destiny in his hands/And wield them like a sword./Too late shall he become known to you:/The Golden Prince of Demons." Colbey removed his arm and turned to face Ravn. "That's close."

"*Hero* of the Great War," Ravn repeated.

"Well, all right." Colbey shrugged, never one for false modesty. "If you took a vote at that time, more people would have called me a lunatic than a hero. I'm not fond of the prophecy either. Both gods and Wizards used it as a reason to try to destroy me."

"Why?"

"They said it heralded the *Ragnarok,* and I'd have a hand in it."

Ravn recognized the irony. "It did. And you did."

"True," Colbey conceded but did not surrender the point. "But I was the one trying to keep balance. *I* didn't cause the *Ragnarok*, I only changed the course of it. For the better in my opinion."

"Everyone's opinion."

"Not everyone's. Remember the meeting?"

Ravn did. Many of the gods appreciated Colbey rescuing Frey and, subsequently, mankind from annihilation; but a large group believed he should have assisted Odin at the *Ragnarok*, as the AllFather had planned.

"All of which," continued Colbey, "has absolutely nothing to do with my point. I expect you to take over for me because, eventually, I'm going to get too far removed from my mortality to influence affairs on Midgard without disrupting the balance myself."

Finally the pieces fell together. "And you want me to take your place then."

"Right."

Ravn weighed his need to assist Griff against making a point that might influence eternity. Dutifully, he chose the latter. "Father?"

"Yes, Ravn?"

"I was born less mortal than you'll ever become."

Colbey's brow crinkled. "What do you mean?"

Ravn stared, certain his father made mockery of a concept so obvious it did not require speaking. "I mean I'm the son of a goddess and a half god, born and raised on Asgard. Everything in my life has been perfect, the best. My mother is the female ideal; my father's very name means skill. The trees, the air, the water." He made a broad sweep to indicate the entirety of his world. "You can and have taught me to appreciate it, but that doesn't mean I can imagine living with less."

Colbey stared. "You're sixteen. I'm damn near four hundred."

Ravn made a snorting noise of dismissal. "I've started taking Idunn's youth apples. In four hundred years, I'll be about." He calculated swiftly. "Maybe sixteen and a *half!*"

"Your point?" Colbey pressed.

Ravn rose. "Four hundred years is nothing for a god. Father, you still think like a mortal. You're thinking like one now. But I've never been mortal." Recollection crowded in of the one serious conversation he had carried on with a mortal. "I did spend some time talking to Rantire. A Renshai."

"What did you think?"

"Her philosophies?"

Colbey nodded.

"Nonsense. Totally insane. Like you, most of the time."

Colbey managed another smile, though it seemed strained. "Now you're talking like an adolescent."

"I am an adolescent," Ravn reminded him.

Colbey loosed a noise that sounded like a muted chuckle. A moment later he started laughing in earnest.

Ravn could not help joining his father's mirth, though he had no idea of its source. He regained composure first and waited for Colbey to do the same. At length, he asked, "What was that all about?"

"You think I'm insane now? Just wait until I've survived three thousand years with a son in his teens."

The humor was lost on Ravn. "See, that's what I mean. A mortal joke. I don't get it."

"Neither would Freya," Colbey said, but that did not keep him from another round of uproarious laughter.

Eager to comfort Griff, Ravn found the lapse irritating. "Fine. You've had your fun with me. Twice now." His hand slid naturally to his gut, where the pain had turned to a nausea immediately behind his navel. Remembered agony made him cringe, and he accused, "You could have pulled that blow."

Colbey did not deny the allegation. "Then you wouldn't have learned the lesson."

"Which lesson is that?" Everything of value Ravn had learned, he had learned from his father. Full understanding and grudging appreciation usually came months after the event, if ever. "Castration? Not to interrupt a Renshai's practice."

"I hope that's not the lesson I taught." Colbey surely referred to the second possibility. "For a rousing battle, you may interrupt my *svergelse* any time. The lesson is: It is an honor to die delivering a killing blow, but don't drop your guard just because you believe you did."

Ravn conceded Colbey's point. He had believed his head strike fatal; in a different mood, his father would have given him the match as a win. Having been granted what he sought, he kept that thought to himself, along with the realization that he had not intentionally opened himself to counterattack. "I believe you could have made that same point more delicately."

"True." Colbey acquiesced again. "But would you remember it as long?"

Ravn had to admit he wouldn't.

Ravn found Griff sprawled across his massive, decorative bed, his arms thrown wide and his snores saturating the king's chamber. Despite the noise and his size, he looked innocent, like a sacrifice staked out for some monster's repast. Ravn could not help smiling at the image. He took one meaty hand in his, and the fingers curled naturally around his own. He smoothed back coarse, black hair from youthful features a year older than his own. Fuzzy stubble coated Griff's chin and cheeks as he worked at growing the standard, Béarnian beard.

Something disembodied brushed Ravn's mind, and he stiffened. The strangeness of the touch sent chills jangling through him. "Father?" he tried, hoping Colbey had not contacted him to keep him from awakening Griff. If his father expected him to learn the ways of mortals, he would need to do more than observe one sleeping. The sensation continued, as if a distant or weak presence attempted to judge him beyond the range of its ability. Ravn concentrated on it, unwilling to dismiss it as harmless so long as it remained in his mind.

Eventually, the presence faded into oblivion. Ravn waited a few more moments to assure himself of its disappearance. Then, with no more idea of its source, he returned his attention to Béarn's soon to be crowned king.

Whatever had touched Ravn had not disturbed Griff. He remained asleep, raucous breaths stirring the covers and rattling the windows.

"Griff," Ravn hissed, immediately feeling stupid. If those snores did not awaken his friend, a whisper would accomplish nothing. "Griff," he said louder, directly into the Béarnide's ear. He shook the huge hand in his grasp.

The snores broke into a series of snorts. Griff curled onto his side but did not awaken.

Oh, for . . . Ravn threw up his hands in surrender, then committed himself fully to the job. "Griff!" He shook the king violently. "Griff, wake up."

Griff stretched, sucking in a deep lungful of air. As he settled into a new position, Ravn growled in frustration. Only then, he found deep brown eyes regarding him from a web of red vessels. "Ravn?" A smile split Griff's face, and he launched himself suddenly at the young deity. "Ravn! You're here."

Scooped into mammoth arms, Ravn allowed himself to get

squashed for several moments, his cheeks scratched by Griff's wild hair.

"You're here. You came." Griff finally released Ravn enough to allow a peek at the gentle features.

"Of course I came," Ravn said. "You needed me."

"I needed you an hour ago." The heir's expression melted from excitement to a curiosity tinged ever so slightly with accusation. He withdrew from the embrace. "What took you so long?"

Ravn laughed, aware Griff intended no malice. "I had to get permission from my father. I'm here, but it may have cost me my manhood."

"Your manhood?" Griff asked innocently.

Ravn smiled. "You don't know my father." He added under his breath, "Consider yourself blessed."

"Or my father," Griff said with a soft sadness that made Ravn wish he had never spoken of the matter. "And I miss my stepfather."

At the moment, Ravn believed, he would have traded his father for either one; but it seemed cruel to voice the thought aloud. "I know, Griff. When this all gets settled, you can send for your mother and stepfather."

"I know." Griff sighed, casting aside the sorrow that had haunted him since leaving Dunwoods. Lamenting would not change that situation, and time would bring solutions.

"Is that what's bothering you?"

"It makes me sad," Griff admitted, "but other things worry me more now."

"The responsibilities of rulership," Ravn guessed.

"Yes."

Ravn made dents in the coverlet with his fist. "Does it help to know that anyone in your position would have doubts?"

"Not much." Pained wrinkles crossed Griff's features. "What if I make the wrong decision and people suffer?"

"Griff?"

"Yes."

"You could make the right decision, and people would still suffer."

Griff sat in silence, blinking a few times as if to clear his mind. "Are you trying to soothe me, or cripple me?"

"Neither. Just trying to infuse a bit of reality." Ravn added more furrows to the blankets with his balled hand. "My point is that people suffered long before your birth and will continue to do so long after you're dead. All you can do is make the best decisions possible while you're on the throne."

Ravn had clearly hit the problem squarely on the head. "But how do I *do* that?"

"Use your heart, Griff. Perfect neutrality is programmed into you. It's a part of you."

Griff rose, drawing in a deep breath and loosing it in a long exhale. "Ravn, I think I'm the wrong one. I don't have all the answers. I don't feel like I have any at all."

"Don't question my judgment." Ravn tried to sound deeply offended. "Trust me. You're the one."

Griff stared at his feet and shook his head.

"Griff!"

Apparently struck by his friend's tone, Griff looked up swiftly.

"I'm a god, remember? Don't question me. You *are* the proper heir to Béarn's throne. Everyone knows it, except you."

Griff just stared.

"You'll make the right decisions. You'll also make mistakes. And, sometimes, the right judgments will cause suffering."

"Oh," Griff finally managed.

Ravn was not finished. "It's normal to have doubts. Every king has had doubts. You know what your biggest problem is?"

"I'm not very smart?" Griff tried.

Ravn could not help teasing. "That's your *second* biggest problem." He winked to show he did not mean it. "Your biggest problem is that you never saw a king at work, never got the experience of watching a father or grandfather rule. Had Kohleran groomed you as his successor, he would have confessed his doubts to you. And you could see how normal they are."

"Oh," Griff said again. His manner revealed what his words did not. Many of his muscles uncoiled, and his face returned to the unlined innocence Ravn recalled from the Grove. "I just feel so alone. I don't know who to trust."

Ravn tapped his chest, reminding Griff to make decisions from his heart. "Who do you think you should trust?"

"Darris."

"The bard?" Ravn approved. "Good choice."

"For competence more than ideas, I also trust Rantire, Kevral, and my grandfather's guard captain."

"Good."

"Knight-Captain Kedrin."

"An all around good man, if irritatingly rigid."

The exercise opened floodgates. "Matrinka, Ra-khir, Captain
. . . should I keep going?"

Ravn grinned. "Only for yourself. I'm not the one who needs
convincing."

"What about the scepter?"

The question caught Ravn off guard. "The what?"

"The scepter." Griff pointed to the gem-tipped staff braced
against a post of the bed. "It's supposed to guide kings, yet we
don't seem to agree on much."

Curious, Ravn reached for the scepter.

As his fingers closed around the smoothed haft, the presence
that had touched him earlier returned, much stronger now. *Finally, you've come.* It seemed to glide into his head, searching,
probing, and testing before he could think to release it. A vast
sensation of approval flashed through him before the object
contacted him directly again. *Perfect.* It seemed to purr. *You
are the one. The king is nothing in comparison.*

The one what? Ravn returned, confused. Never before had
he communicated with his mind, despite his father's intensive
training.

*My champion. The one fit to wield me. Between us, we have
more power than all humans together could embody. Join with
me, and no being, no army of beings, could stand against us.*
It added concepts far stronger than its words, promising Ravn
abilities even the gods must envy. It drew him inexorably, fascinating nearly beyond the power to resist.

Ravn set the scepter carefully on the bed and reluctantly released it. "Where did you get this?"

"A peace offering from the dark elves when they left. It belonged to the elfin kings."

"Elfin kings?" Ravn had never heard of such a thing.

"I don't want to insult the dark elves, but I don't like that
scepter. I don't want it. What do you think I should do?"

A sense of possession seemed to seize Ravn in a stranglehold. He fought greed aside. "What do your advisers think?"

"Darris seems convinced it's best for me. Kevral and Kedrin
believe the same."

Ravn glanced at the scepter, surprised to find his fingers
creeping toward it. Deliberately, he placed his hands in his lap.
"And you?"

"I don't want it."

As Ravn recognized his own inexplicable interest in the
scepter, Griff's words surprised him. "Why not?"

"It bothers me. Not dangerous or anything." Griff sought the proper explanation. "If it was a person, we'd have nothing in common."

The description made sense to Ravn. "What do you want me to do?"

"Will you take it? I mean, if I said I gave it to a god, who could take offense at that?"

Ravn had never wanted anything more, yet that realization alone troubled him. One thing seemed certain, the scepter clearly represented the very danger Griff denied. "I . . ." he started, then stopped. He would not allow desire to cloud his judgment. He had vowed to do nothing that might upset the balance of the universe. If he took the scepter, he would only do so for the proper reasons. Every instinct screamed for him to remove it from Griff's responsibility, yet he worried whether wisdom or rationalization truly guided him. "I . . ." he began again but still could not finish. Irony struck him, and he laughed. "A lesson, Griff. Even gods don't always know if they make the right decisions."

Ravn expected at least a smile from Griff, so the horrified look that stole over his friend's face surprised him. Immediately, he berated his stupidity. Finally, he discovered the power of words spoken by gods, even those that seemed so simple and obvious. *Father is right.* "I'm sorry, Griff. I'm kidding. I didn't mean to damage your faith."

Griff gnawed at the side of his fist, still clearly distressed.

Ravn knew Griff well enough to understand his clarification had become too general. Only something straightforward could bother the naive heir so much. "What's wrong?"

Griff swallowed hard, letting his hand glide down from his face. "It's just that I told Knight-Captain Kedrin the gods wouldn't let Ra-khir die now. But if gods make mistakes, then I'm wrong. And poor Kedrin . . ." He let the thought trail off, more, Ravn guessed, because he did not have the words to finish it than because he felt the effect would prove stronger.

I should have known Griff would worry more for harming someone else's faith than his own. Ravn kept his smile internal. He had the facts to soothe Griff this time. His view from *Hlidskjalf* gave him answers. "Don't worry. Ra-khir awakened, and he'll be fine. A servant came to inform you, but you were asleep. No one—except me, of course—was cruel enough to wake you."

A burst of released tension passed through Griff visibly, and a grin seemed to encompass his whole face. "Thank you," he said.

Ravn resisted the urge to deny his involvement. One brush with destroying a man's religion seemed enough. "I have to go." Ravn believed his work finished here, and he worried for the damage his presence alone might have caused. He might have created a mess for his father, and his final action could compound the difficulty. "And I will take the scepter." His hand closed around the haft, and the presence joined him immediately. He only hoped he had made the right decision.

CHAPTER 16

Toward Balance

Armor is for those too lazy to dodge.
It takes away the need to learn defense.

—Colbey Calistinsson

Balmy temperatures and intermittent breezes made the constant, golden beaming of Asgard's sun a pleasure. Sitting beside Ravn, Colbey studied the pond's glassy waters and the lazy paddling of its multicolored ducks. Weeds broke the surface, perfect triangles surrounded by circles of water; the bugs skimmed the surface at intervals. He smiled. More than three centuries had not stolen his appreciation for the natural beauty of plants and animals. "How did it go?" he asked softly, the question unnecessary. The nervousness radiating from his son told much of the story.

"Fine," Ravn replied with the same inane timbre as a man questioned about his health during a greeting both parties intended to keep brief. "I think I'm really beginning to understand the need for subtlety, though I haven't mastered it yet."

Colbey tore his eyes from the ducks to regard his son and the emerald-tipped staff he clutched with an intensity that left his hand white-knuckled. "Did you harm someone?"

"Not to my knowledge." Ravn managed a tense smile. "But I did take something." He tapped the base of the scepter on the ground. "I probably overstepped my boundaries, and I'm prepared to face the consequences." The grimace that followed the grin suggested otherwise. "But I do believe, whatever else, it doesn't belong with Griff." The pain seemed to intensify as he spoke the next words. "Nor with me."

Colbey's brows arched tautly over blue-gray eyes. "Why's that?"

Ravn weighed every word, as if expecting his father's wrath. "I'm not yet skilled enough to control it." He tapped his head to indicate mental rather than physical powers. "If I tried to wield it, I believe that, eventually, it would wield me."

Colbey made a thoughtful noise, bothered by his son's limitations yet pleased by his recognition of them. Sudden alarm jangled through him. "Did it harm Griff?"

Ravn's smile seemed misplaced. "If I am to believe it, Griff is too simpleminded to influence."

Colbey nodded. His knowledge and experience told him more. "Naive. Innocent and, therefore, incorruptible. That's why Odin placed it into his care in the first place."

Ravn's smile disappeared instantly. "*Odin* placed it there? I made a giant mistake, didn't I?"

"No." Colbey glanced at what he now felt certain was the Staff of Chaos. It seemed impossible that the staff had not already contacted him from Ravn's hands, though whether to manipulate or threaten, he did not anticipate. Seeking logic and regularity to chaos was a feat doomed to failure. "It was never meant to go to the King of Béarn alone."

Ravn blinked, head cocked back and eyes enveloped in creases. "He was to share it?"

"No." Colbey smiled at Ravn's misunderstanding. "The staves were supposed to remain together." He shook his head, not wishing to detail the entire event to Ravn. So much had happened the day the Wizards took their lives, most of which he preferred to forget. "Give me the staff."

Ravn hesitated an instant that most immortals would never have noticed. He passed the Staff of Chaos to his father.

Still warm from Ravn's grip, the wood nestled against Colbey's calluses as if crafted to fit them. Instantly, a presence touched his mind, far weaker than he anticipated. Colbey allowed it to search for a moment, not bothering to expend the energy necessary to expel it. So long as it did not manipulate, it could not harm. A moment later, it withdrew, and a voice filled his senses. *You're the one.* Raw excitement accompanied the assessment. *We were meant to work together. To meld. To become a force more powerful than any other.*

Colbey sent it amusement. *You don't recognize me, do you?*

I recognize you as the one meant to wield me.

We've met before.

Impossible. I would remember you.

Colbey's memory ground back centuries to an incident long gone from his surface thoughts. He had undertaken the Seven

Tasks of Wizardry, tests designed to judge the worth of Cardinal Wizards. Failing at any one meant death. The other Wizards had warned him away from the optional eighth task, informing him that no one who attempted it had lived. He had planned to follow their advice; yet, when the time came, curiosity drove him to understand what had destroyed so many considered the best Midgard had to offer. He discovered it required those who attempted it to survive all that they feared. In every case prior to Colbey, that list had included death; but the eldest Renshai had spent too long chasing his demise to fear it. He had overcome other fears, fears too terrifying to consider now. And surviving the eighth task had won him a prize he had never wanted: choice of either the Staff of Law or of Chaos.

Odin's words came back to him now, clear despite the passing centuries: "With this Staff, I control all but have no rule. With this one, I control none but my rule is sure and long. Which will you have? Make your choice well, Kyndig."

Then, Colbey's tie with the Balance had consisted purely of instinct. The Wizards had spoken of the ultimate power that would result from completing the eighth task, but Colbey cared nothing for it. Renshai honor came from within. They shunned armor as cowards' protections, relying only upon their own skill in battle. Always, he had refused ornamentation, concerned it might accidentally field an enemy's blow and steal the valiant death in combat, the place in Valhalla he had worked toward since birth. He had refused his own sword after the Eastern Wizard had placed magic upon it, at great risk to himself and to the world, until Shadimar assured him that it would neither assist nor interfere with Colbey's personal skill. The sword would remain the tool, Shadimar had promised. The sorcery would only allow him the ability to strike creatures of magic: those of chaos, called demons and those of law, the Wizards themselves. In the end, Shadimar had taken his own life with the sword he had created: Harval.

Colbey had refused either staff, but that had not satisfied Odin. Finally, Colbey had agreed to take both, giving Chaos to Shadimar and keeping Law for himself. The Staff of Chaos should know him. *We met centuries ago.*

Centuries? The essence in the staff dismissed the significance, though their meeting had ultimately resulted in the *Ragnarok.* *I was an infant then, a tiny, disorganized seed of what I would become.*

The description seemed madness. Colbey recalled the oppressive reality of the Staff of Law, and its insistence that the Staff of Chaos equaled it in power. This puny entity could not compare to the ravaging torrent that had once occupied this plain piece of wood. Colbey pried loose the wooden setting of the emerald. It did not belong there, as gaudy as a blond mop of hair vandalized onto an Easterner's portrait. Only one explanation fit. Odin had drawn the essence from the Staves of Law and Chaos, yet he had left a spark in each. Presumably, he had done so to allow the staves the job of together judging the worth of heirs. Something, Colbey knew too little of magic to speculate what, had fanned that flame into a bonfire. Few could understand the danger the staves' return represented. *Ragnarok* had destroyed the extremes, including most of the gods, because the world no longer needed them. Now they had returned. The effect on the balance could prove devastating, but surely less so than allowing one force to act unopposed. Once, he had accepted the responsibility of carrying a staff and maintaining balance. Another's turn had come. *How long have you existed?* he sent halfheartedly, uncertain the answer truly mattered.

The primordial chaos has existed forever. Long before law arrived with its tedium and symmetry. Once, the world consisted only of genius.

Colbey refused to be sidetracked. Genius without structure lacked purpose. *How long have you occupied that container?*

Fleeting irritation and a panic akin to claustrophobia touched Colbey so briefly he scarcely identified it. *I've been aware less than a century but believe I existed long before that.* The blank that had followed the flash of emotion turned sullen. *I may not seem powerful enough to you, but I tap the primordial chaos. Over time, nothing can exceed my power.* It added carefully, *Except for one thing.*

Colbey took the bait, continuing to work the decoration free. *And that is?*

You and I together. Nothing in the universe could compare.

Except the Staff of Law and its champion.

The Staff of Chaos did not attempt bluff, as Colbey expected. *Perhaps,* it admitted grudgingly. *But I believe you and I together can surpass even them.*

Colbey accepted the grandiose display without dispute. Arguing details or semantics served no one. Under the circumstances, the staff seemed correct. Law and Chaos should prove equals, and Colbey surely held more power than Dh'arlo'mé.

Yet he knew otherwise from experience. The staves' vitality so overshadowed their champions' that differences in the latter's relative strengths became immaterial. Any human could assume the roll of chaos' master.

Colbey believed that the case, though tiny details niggled at his mind, not quite fitting the straightforward, simple scenario he had constructed. When he observed the interaction between Dh'arlo'mé and the Staff of Law, the elf's essence had seemed nearly nonexistent in comparison to the force he chose to champion. In comparison, the Staff of Chaos seemed weak. Midgard naturally regressed toward balance, and nature alone seemed incapable of allowing the staves to mature at such noticeably different rates. But the changes in Harval supported the observation. The worlds tipped dangerously toward order. Colbey could only guess that attachment to a champion had spurred the growth of law far out of proportion. If so, he needed to link chaos fast.

Madness! Colbey scarcely dared to believe this strategy otherwise. To support the growth of chaos' power might result in the destruction of everything. Yet to allow law free rein would eventually accomplish the same end. This way, he could maintain the balance until the extremes clashed and destroyed one another. Then it would fall to Colbey to prevent the world from exploding with them. *If I can.* He only hoped, and doubted, the gods would keep their vows not to interfere. Their intrusion would add astronomically to a task already nearing impossibility.

The emerald and its setting fell to the ground at Colbey's feet. Ravn ended his patient silence by pointedly clearing his throat.

Bind with me, the Staff of Chaos insisted, its single conveyance growing into a chant. *Bind with me.* It surged for his inner core.

Colbey held it at bay with a simple barrier and chose to address his son instead. "Ravn, you did right bringing this to me."

"You're going to wield it?" Concern radiated from what otherwise seemed a simple question. Clearly, Ravn wondered if the staff had corrupted his once-mortal father.

"No." Colbey thumped the base of the staff on the ground, maintaining his barricade without need for energy or concentration. "Another will, but only with understanding of the consequences." He met Ravn's blue gaze. "Let's go to *Hlidskjalf.* There's someone I need to find."

Leaving the gemstone in the dirt, Colbey and Ravn headed for Odin's Hall.

Charred, shattered timbers lay in awkward piles or clung to damaged walls and ceilings like dark, eerie growths. Ash coated the floor, jumbled with unidentifiable hunks of rubble that tripped the unwary. The acrid stench of old smoke pinched Kevral's nostrils as she sparred with Ra-khir amid the wreckage of what had once served as Béarn's castle temple. Tae watched in attentive silence.

Kevral had chosen the site as much for the uneven terrain as for privacy. No one would have reason to visit the gutted ruin, and it gave her a practice ground different from the usual clearings, rooms, and woodlands. Her *torke* had taught her to seize such opportunities where she found them. It was not enough to understand her sword and her abilities. A battle could occur anywhere, and the more places a warrior practiced or sparred, the better prepared for any situation.

The temple had seemed ideal to Kevral. Debris could shift beneath her feet, hidden by a dusky layer of ash. Dust billowed with every movement, hiding feet and sometimes even the all-important hands. Dangling beams posed a hazard for swordsmen too intent on opponents to watch positioning. But Ra-khir's strategy stole all advantage from the terrain. He chose only defense against Kevral's blistering attacks, fielding her blade with his or with an enormous shield he kept always in front of him. Simple pivot steps kept him safe from Kevral's strikes.

Kevral hammered at Ra-khir's defense, sword clanging against shield in a musical cadence. Repeatedly, she struck for minuscule openings that proved too tiny even for Renshai twists. The knight-in-training could never win the match without offense, but the length of the spar required a patience Kevral could not spare. Having won back the kingdom without a single blow, Kevral needed an outlet for her battle excitement. Ra-khir, it seemed, offered only tedium. Even as Kevral feinted for Ra-khir's side then cut for his head, she longed for the Renshai warriors, now headed back to the Fields of Wrath, who could at least give her a challenge. Ra-khir ducked behind his shield, and she lunged in for another attack.

As Kevral moved, she sensed the presence of another. She jerked aside, whirling to meet this new threat; and a golden-haired warrior appeared beside her. Though not large, his sinewy body revealed decades of training. Short, feathered locks swept back from scarred features most would consider unremarkable. To Kevral, they defined perfection. She recognized Colbey Calistinsson at once. He clutched a staff in his right hand. The sword in his left looped around Ra-khir's shield in a lightning spiral Kevral memorized. Steel severed the leather thong of its handle. The shield crashed to the floor with a deafening ring. The flat of Colbey's sword caught Ra-khir a blow to the chest that sent him sprawling. Ash splashed upward, obscuring the Erythanian in a gray cloud.

Colbey did not pursue his advantage, only stepped back and sheathed his sword. Kevral smiled, returning her blade to its scabbard as well.

Ra-khir rose, brushing dirt from his silks with brisk strokes. He executed a deep, formal bow to Colbey, then turned to Kevral. "I believe, m'lady, that you cheated."

Colbey smiled. "How pleasantly unusual. A Knight of Erythane with a sense of humor."

Ra-khir made an abbreviated bow, lacking the previous flourishes but still conveying respect. "Apprentice knight, Lord," he corrected.

Kevral feigned offense. "Oh, like there's a *rule* against having a god take my place."

"Apprentice god," Colbey could not help adding.

The three laughed, though Kevral felt nearly as strained as Ra-khir sounded. The idea of joking with one she had emulated all her life seemed disrespectful at the least, more likely a sacrilege. Colbey addressed Kevral, though he surely spoke as much for Ra-khir's benefit. "The thing to remember is that an enemy with a shield will always block his own vision. The moment he does, that's your opening. If Ra-khir hadn't stuck that sheet of metal over his eyes, he would have seen me coming and at least tried to guard against the attack."

Kevral doubted Ra-khir had the necessary speed to dodge Colbey's blitz, but the point remained the same.

"Give him a few repetitive maneuvers to draw him off guard, then feint to the head. Works almost every time. He blinds himself, and he's done your job for you. He might as well plunge his own sword into his chest."

"Thank you," Kevral said, awed more by receiving a lesson from Colbey than the content of the speech. Each word seemed to resonate in her head, and she doubted she could tear her eyes from him. Drawn with the fatal fascination of a moth to a flame, she wanted, more than anything in the world, to become a part of him. The intensity of the desire surprised her, though she had experienced it before in his presence. Since discovering he still existed and turning her intimacy toward mortal men, she had stopped constantly mimicking his dress, manner, and speech. She believed she had passed the phase of infatuation, but the fire that burned within her now spoke otherwise.

As if sensing her emotions, Colbey stiffened. He set the base of the staff on the floor and slanted the shaft toward Kevral. "I'd like you to do something, Kevral." He glanced at Tae, who watched quietly from a far wall, his dark clothes merging him with the shadows. Having acknowledged the Easterner's presence, Colbey paid him no further heed but returned his gaze to Kevral.

"Anything," Kevral said and meant it. She gazed into the blue-gray eyes, and even their coldness could not keep her from becoming lost in them.

Ra-khir moved up beside Kevral, his protectiveness surely more habit and instinct than intention. "With all respect to the divinity of our guest, shouldn't you hear his proposal first?"

The words seemed ludicrous to Kevral. "Would you refuse any request of a god?"

"Kevral . . ." Ra-khir placed a warm hand on Kevral's arm. ". . . if it went against my honor, I'd fight it to my last breath. I expected no less from you."

The interruption seemed inappropriately rude. "Ra-khir, Colbey isn't deaf."

"Of course not." Ra-khir nodded deferentially toward the elder Renshai. "At the risk of sounding presumptuous, I believe he would understand my concern."

Colbey nodded back politely. "And agree with your point." He looked around the room again, gaze pinning each of the other three occupants in turn and ending on Kevral. "The favor I ask is enormous, and you have the right to refuse it." He exhaled sharply, then drew in a great breath. "I want you to wield the Staff of Chaos." He spoke as if the task outweighed all others and as though they should understand the significance.

Recalling history and Captain's story on board the *Sea Seraph,* Kevral tried to put the pieces together. "The Staff of Chaos. As in the Staves of Law and Chaos?"

"Correct."

"The staff you turned over to the Wizards and they believed

they carried law and . . ." Kevral's eyes widened as her own words emerged. ". . . caused the *Ragnarok?*"

"Correct again," Colbey confirmed.

"You championed law . . ." Kevral started slowly, trying to elicit whether or not she would have to stand in opposition to her idol.

Colbey corrected, "Balance. I championed balance. I merely carried the Staff of Law."

"And had you carried chaos?"

"I still would have championed balance."

The greatness of the favor finally penetrated as myriad possibilities paraded through Kevral's mind. "Do you still have the Staff of Law?"

"Dh'arlo'mé has it."

The name alone sparked hatred. *Was that the staff we passed around the parley? It seemed so convincingly harmless.*

Colbey responded to the thought. "A masquerade. The staff's magic. When circumstances without definitive answer seem certain, that is when you should most doubt."

"Oh," Kevral merely said, feeling foolish. When nothing else followed, she questioned further. "Surely, you don't want me to cause another *Ragnarok?*"

Colbey resisted the urge to continue answering with as little information as possible. "I want you to use your own judgment."

Kevral stared.

Colbey added, "No one wants another *Ragnarok*. No one would survive it. But if law acts unopposed, we may get something just as bad. The world could stagnate into oblivion." Colbey's gaze went distant as he contemplated memories Kevral could not begin to guess. "By using your own judgment, I mean in general, not just in regard to the *Ragnarok*."

Kevral still did not understand. "So all I have to do is carry this thing?" She pointed at the staff.

"It's not that simple." Colbey straightened the staff so that it stood as tall as Ra-khir. "Chaos is an entity, bound inside the staff. It will offer you power that may well prove irresistible. Even if you chose to refuse it, chaos would give it to you insidiously. Likely, you will become a single entity."

"Likely?" Ra-khir prodded, with concern.

"Very likely," Colbey affirmed, which Kevral took to mean "definitely," tempered by his own experience. Law had not managed to assimilate with him. Apparently reading her thought, Colbey explained. "Law must keep promises. Chaos, never. There were times when the vows I made the staff take were all that kept it from binding. Also, my mind powers far exceed yours."

Ra-khir's face darkened, and his lids rose in increments. "If Kevral became random and lacking honor, she would no longer be Kevral."

"Yes," Colbey said, returning to minimal answers and letting Ra-khir speak the obvious consequence.

"This task will destroy Kevral."

"Almost certainly."

Dense silence followed Colbey's words. Ra-khir and Tae stared anxiously at Kevral, both surely knowing that to advise her one way would almost guarantee the opposite decision. No matter how awful, the choice belonged to Kevral. She had sat in this same position once before, when the laws of Pudar allowed her to imprison herself in Tae's place after his jailbreak, bound by his order of execution. Then the choice had proved none at all. She had believed Matrinka would volunteer if she did not, and Ra-khir surely would have done so had he guessed the intentions of either woman. Then, too, she had trusted Tae to return rather than allow her to die for his crime. In the end, the only thing that mattered was that she had not faltered in her decision. The king had chosen to bargain: Kevral would train his soldiers for a year in exchange for her freedom and, ultimately, Tae's.

Ra-khir sought a loophole. "But, Lord, if you're seeking balance and an elf carries the Staff of Law, shouldn't an elf also champion chaos?"

Colbey shook his head, his expression tolerant. "The nature of elves does not allow them to oppose their own. No one would stand against Dh'arlo'mé."

"Captain did," Tae inserted. "Have you asked him?"

Kevral jerked her head toward Colbey, worried for Tae's insolence and implication that the ultimate Renshai had made a mistake.

Colbey took the verbal challenge in stride. "Captain pledged himself to the balance millennia ago, even while serving the Northern Sorceress, the last champion of goodness. He could never accept charge of chaos." Colbey sighed deeply, dredging patience for details he had, apparently, already considered and discarded. He did not have to explain himself to Tae, yet he did so without complaint. "Captain and his few followers are vital to other aspects of the balance. If one of them wielded chaos, elves and mankind would lose any chance for peace. Even were none of that the case, I do not command elves. The one who does would never agree to place one in a situation of sure destruction."

Kevral looked at Colbey, the harsh sentence he passed over her never dulling the perfect grace of his slightest movement. Desperately, she yearned for his skill, had done so since infancy. She would do anything for the Renshai turned immortal, but she would not abandon a vow without at least asking about options. "Can this wait a year? Once Griff is coronated, I'm pledged to Pudar's service that long."

Colbey continued to look directly at Kevral, as if loath to weather the glares of her companions. "No, Kevral. Pudar will have to be happy with the sacrifice you make for all: gods, men, even elves. If you wish, once you start carrying the staff, you may go to Pudar. It's unlikely, however, that your vow will mean much to you then."

Kevral asked the most important question. "And when I die? It will be in battle?"

The soft sough of breath drawn in and held followed Kevral's words that sounded so much like a commitment. She did not try to guess whether it came from Tae or Ra-khir. Both would despise her cooperation with the task Colbey offered.

Colbey shrugged, strong shoulders rising and falling symmetrically. "No one can know that. It seems likely you'll die locked in battle with law's champion, but once you're chaoslinked, you're unlikely to fight your battles physically."

Alarm seized Kevral in a grip so tight, it took several seconds just to manage breathing.

"Magic is chaos," Colbey reminded. He did not bother adding the obvious: Kevral would be chaos, too.

The world narrowed to a single need, the reply to a question Kevral could not gather the air to ask yet.

Tae broke in with one that should have seemed obvious; yet it, like anything besides Valhalla, seemed insignificant to Kevral now. Her goal since birth was fading, and she clung desperately to all that mattered. "So Dh'arlo'mé will have no magic?"

Colbey glanced at the Easterner. "Dh'arlo'mé already knows magic. Law is control, and it will greatly enhance his existing power. Conversely, Kevral would add the control to chaos needed to channel magic. Should she take the assignment . . ."

Colbey left the option clearly open. ". . . her magical power would exceed Dh'arlo'mé's, yet her spells would have many more unintended consequences. Dh'arlo'mé's power would stem from his control." An upward pitch at the end of his speech left the understanding that he was guessing.

Finally, Kevral's pinched throat admitted sound. "Then it's unlikely I'll reach Valhalla."

"Not impossible," Colbey started, obviously trying to be reassuring. He glanced away, too committed to the Renshai not to specify. "But highly unlikely."

Kevral read the latter as nearly impossible. The burden ached through her, a desperate decision that one of her age should never have to make. Dying never frightened her, only the means of that end and her final resting place. She had tried to mold herself in Colbey's image, only recently realizing she could never become what he had been. Now he offered her that opportunity. She could not resist it, though it required paying the ultimate cost. "All right," she finally said, ignoring Ra-khir's stricken look. "I'll do as you ask, with a condition." She met Colbey's blue-gray eyes with a directness that evoked a slight smile. She never doubted her boldness, rather than her concession, was the thing that pleased him. The coldness of his eyes stung, yet Kevral refused to glance away. "You let me look upon Valhalla once before I take up this cause."

Colbey recoiled, visibly startled. He broke the eye contact, a contest he seemed unused to losing.

The reaction surprised Kevral at least as much as her request seemed to bother Colbey. He should certainly have anticipated it. Renshai had dedicated themselves to dying in glorious combat, to taking their place among Valhalla's heroes, the *Einherjar,* since millennia before his birth. He had given his all to the same goal.

Unable to comprehend the change in Colbey, Kevral pressed. "Surely, you could grant that request."

"I imagine I could." Colbey's voice seemed vacant, inappropriately dispassionate for the topic of conversation. He tipped his head, as if battling confusion within himself. "Of course. You deserve nothing less."

"Please, Lord. I want to go, too," Ra-khir said, more demand than request.

"And me," Tae added.

"All right," Colbey said finally. "I have no magic to get us there, but I'll make the arrangements. Wait here for me." A moment later, Colbey and the staff faded into the dappled destruction of Béarn's temple, leaving Kevral to sort the confusion into which her life had collapsed. She never bothered to identify the arms that held her.

CHAPTER 17

Valhalla

Damned is right. One of Hel's own children.
                    — *Valr Kirin, about Colbey*

Colbey Calistinsson paced the bank of his favorite pond while
Freya perched on a hillock, calmly watching her husband's agitation with a patience of which only gods and elves seemed capable. Always before, Colbey had noticed how the faultless
colors of Asgard seemed to imitate Freya: the sky the same
shade as her depthless eyes, the sun the perfect gold of her cascading tresses, the clouds emulating the alabaster hue of her
skin. The fluid circles of the ducks lost their fascination, this
once. The widening rings that accompanied their paddling still
sparkled like bracelets, yet Colbey noticed none of it. His attention was riveted inward, searching for an answer he believed
should have seemed obvious.

Freya's gaze followed Colbey without judgment. A simple
green dress fanned around her bent legs, and flat-soled slippers
peeked out beneath the fabric. Despite its looseness, it could not
hide the firm but gentle curves of a figure human women could
only envy. Only the sword strapped around her waist ruined the
image. On any other, the combination would have appeared ludicrous, like a princess attending a ball blithely wearing shackles in place of jewelry. Even had the irony touched Colbey, he
did not have the concentration to appreciate it.

Colbey shifted his track so that he walked back toward
Freya rather than in a line in front of her. The sword at either
hip bumped against his side, the uneven listing of Harval like
dead weight. The Staff of Chaos seemed out of place in his fist,
and its length hampered his otherwise gliding steps. Colbey
stopped several paces before he reached Freya, planted the
base of the wood on the ground, and dropped to a crouch. He
ended the pacing to commit himself to conversation, but restlessness still drove him to movement. He quelled the need, in-

stead explaining the situation regarding the Staves of Law and Chaos. He told the story directly, devoid of opinion or prognostication. She needed to understand the situation to be of assistance.

Freya listened in interested silence while Colbey detailed his story. He stopped just before Kevral's request and looked askance at the goddess.

Freya assumed a cross-legged position, then smoothed wrinkles from her dress. Soft blue eyes met Colbey's. "You are the Keeper of the Balance. I trusted your judgment when the other gods turned against you. I still do."

Colbey nodded, appreciating Freya's support, though he would have had no choice but to proceed without it. They both knew many of the gods would oppose his new decision, so neither bothered to speak the concern. Colbey had not yet reached the true dilemma, the one still missing an answer. Freya seemed to sense that lack.

Finally, Colbey said, "Kevral agreed to take the staff. She asked to look upon Valhalla before doing so."

"A reasonable request under the circumstances."

"Indeed," Colbey agreed. They had reached the crux of the matter, and he admitted weakness to Freya as he would never have done to any other. "So why does it bother me?"

Freya had a ready answer. "For the same reason you haven't looked upon Valhalla in the three hundred twenty-seven years you've been here."

Freya had an undeniable point, Colbey knew, but he still could not explain his lapse.

"Last time we discussed this, you told me the time wasn't right yet. Is it now?"

"I don't know," Colbey admitted. "I haven't figured out what's been wrong."

Freya blinked deliberately. She shifted into a more defensible position, from which she could rise and draw a weapon should the need arise. "Colbey Calistinsson/Thorsson, you're afraid."

Colbey stiffened, the insult worth the attack she obviously expected. No crueler words existed in the Renshai language than those for cowards. "What!" He was on his feet before he realized he had moved. "How dare you! I'm not afraid, I'm just . . ." No explanation followed, as if his mind shut off the part of his brain that did the thinking, leaving him incapable of further speech. "I'm just . . ." he repeated. "I'm just . . . !" Enraged by his inability to continue, Colbey fell silent. Images filled his mind, of Odin's enormous, mocking form. Everything the gray god said whipped him into frenzied irritation. Odin had bought the knowledge of the universe with an eye, tortures beyond human endurance, and a hanging for nine days and nights that should have killed even him. Though knowledge of the future still eluded him, it never seemed that way. Every prediction he made came maddeningly to fruition, no matter how hard the gods tried to resist.

I thwarted him. Colbey reminded himself of the betrayal at the *Ragnarok*. Yet memories crowded in on him, pounding on his sensibilities. Odin had decreed he would fight in the Great War. The AllFather had known, before Colbey's birth, that he would choose to undergo the Eighth Task of Wizardry, even that he would take both staves. Odin had insisted Colbey would take the cause of balance upon himself and accept the immortality he despised. All of those things, Colbey had done. That he had taken them all on willingly did not matter. He had acted according to Odin's wishes, as had every creature through eternity. *But I thwarted him once.*

Again, Colbey recalled his first meeting with the AllFather, as the Keeper of the Eighth Task of Wizardry: "You do still fear one thing. And although you wouldn't have any way to know it yet, that fear has been recognized. You will never reach Valhalla." *Never reach Valhalla.* Realization outraged Colbey, and his hands closed around his sword hilts, not to battle Freya but himself. "You're right," he said, the words the most difficult of his life. "I've been afraid." The self-loathing he expected did not come. The fear had remained beneath the level of his understanding. He could forgive even himself for acting upon an emotion unrecognized. Now that he had identified it, however, he would fight it with the same savagery he displayed in war. He would confront his fear with the same ruthless courage as the most powerful enemy in the universe . . . which it was.

Freya did not gloat over her triumph. Not even a hint of a smile eased onto her face. She shared Colbey's concern, loving him too much to enjoy being right at his expense. "What are you going to do?" she asked softly.

"I'm going to Valhalla, of course." Colbey could not conceive of any other course. He would prove Odin wrong again, or perish in the attempt. "If you will indulge me by performing the magic necessary to bring Kevral and her companions here."

"They can't walk?" Even those gods capable of magic avoided it as much as possible, especially spells that might affect Midgard's balance.

"It would take too long. The matter is urgent, and the risk less than delay. Every moment Dh'arlo'mé goes unchallenged raises the danger."

"Very well." Freya rose, taking Colbey's callused hand into her own. "I'll work on the spell. You get yourself ready." She did not specify whether she meant emotionally or physically, avoiding insult.

Colbey settled into the patterned calm that always preceded battle, yet a hint of wild excitement sneaked through his composure. If all went as planned, he would soon look upon Valhalla.

The flawless golden circle of Asgard's sun beamed down upon the emerald grassland, and a cyclical cool breeze fluttered each spear in a delicate wave. Weather never disrupted the perfect days of the gods' haven. The ponds remained full without rain, and the fluffy white clouds served no purpose but decoration. Twining puffs of wind kept the temperature steady, attuned to the gods' comfort. Colbey had always found it a trifle colder than his ideal, yet that better suited his many sword practices. Over time, he had grown accustomed to it.

Kevral, Ra-khir, and Tae did not seem to notice the chill. They stared, gazes glued to one of Asgard's many wonders before jumping restlessly to find another. Colbey did not interrupt, allowing them to orient themselves, sharing their thrill not wholly vicariously. He still enjoyed the highlights Asgard's sun sparked from the grasses and the arching sky that seemed to define the color blue.

At length, Colbey followed the route he had avoided, without considering the reason, since arriving on the world of gods. Evergreens composed of symmetrical triangles alternated with towering deciduous trees not found on man's world. Seed pods spiraled to the ground, myriad shapes, each with its own aerodynamics. These Colbey studied with the same intensity as his companions. He had never seen this type of tree before, and its rain of pods promised years of entertainment.

Forest soon gave way once more to Asgard's vast stretches of meadow. Clover and wildflowers grew among straight grasses never taller than his ankles. A wrought iron gate became visible in the distance, and Colbey headed toward it, swords tapping

his hips reassuringly and the Staff of Chaos clamped tightly in
his fist. His human companions scurried at his heels, too preoccupied with location and future to bother with anything more
complicated than whispered exchanges about the scenery.

Yet despite their silence, their emotions gave them away.
Concern wafted clearly to Colbey, Ra-khir's and Tae's desperate while Kevral's seemed more sad and curious. Excitement
waged a furious battle against Kevral's worries. Anticipation of
visiting Valhalla filled her with unabashed desire that he should
have shared without misgivings. Once, Colbey would have attributed his distress to the concern that Valhalla might not live
up to expectations built on several lifetimes of anticipation.
Now he knew the truth. His thoughts returned to the *Ragnarok*
and the ghastly war he had waged against Odin at a time when
the gods needed them both. Centuries later, Colbey could still
revive the feeling of the AllFather's presence in his skull, assuring him he had been born and lived only for the honor and
pleasure of rescuing Odin from his fate. Colbey had fought off
Thought and Memory, Odin's crows, as they drove him toward
the combat between Odin and the Fenris Wolf. Later, Odin's co-
ercion had turned to threat, manipulation, and finally pleading.
No strategy could work, nor did it. Colbey had already dedicated himself to mankind's cause.

Colbey steeled himself for inevitable combat. Though long
dead, Odin had surely left some barrier to Colbey entering Valhalla. Had the battle involved an obvious opponent to pit
weapons and skill against, he would have approached it with
the zealous passion of every war rather than the trepidation that
haunted him as strongly as the anguish Tae and Ra-khir suffered
for Kevral.

Movement flashed between the wrought iron bars, and the
clang of steel floated like savage music on the breeze. Battle
madness stirred within Colbey. A long time had passed since he
had wielded his swords in anything but spar. Not since the *Ragnarok* had his skill claimed lives; and even forcing his wife and
son to use sharpened blades against him did not stir his blood to
fire as war once had. His heart rate quickened, and his palm
went slick around the staff. A smile jerked onto his features.
Valhalla. His thoughts soared as the scents of blood, heat, and
sweat perfumed the air. *Valhalla*.

Kevral charged the gates, hands grasping the black, square-
shaped rods that enclosed the battlegrounds, face shoved
against the rectangular opening between them. Ra-khir and Tae

drew up beside their companion, also looking through the gate, though they did not touch it.

Colbey leaned the Staff of Chaos against the bars and took his first look at *Valhalla*. The *Einherjar* fought in couples and groups, dressed in everything from Renshai tunics to encasing armor. Swords, axes, and polearms cut gleaming arcs through air or slammed against shields with thumps that added percussion to the lighter chime of parried blades. Every man fought with a dedication Colbey understood with every modicum of his being. Only the bravest warriors wound up here, chosen on the battlefield by the Valkyries or by Freya for glorious deaths in the wild, courageous flurry of combat. Now they spent their days in the warfare they loved, the euphoria of blood lust a constant. Those who died rose at night to feast among the winners and fight more battles on the morrow.

Colbey circled *Valhalla*, seeking an entrance. Beyond the myriad battles, a common house sat in the middle. Otherwise, it consisted only of a vast grassland sprinkled with the blood of warriors slain for the day. His gaze clung to the violence, and he found his own blood warming in response. Nothing could please him more than charging into the fray, battling until every muscle in his body screamed for mercy, then thrilling to the pain itself while still waging the war. His wife and son remained the only things more sacred than this place, the only deterrent to remaining permanently among the *Einherjar*. Here, at last, Colbey had found his place, exactly where he had always known it was.

Colbey found himself back at his starting point too soon, recognizing it only by the presence of Ra-khir and the Staff of Chaos. He had found no entrance or exit, realizing only then that *Valhalla* needed neither. Those who earned it came by magic and could never leave, even should the desire ever touch them. And only those chosen could enter. "Where's Kevral?" Colbey did not look at Ra-khir as he spoke, unable to tear his gaze from the combat.

Suddenly, Colbey recognized the agitation radiating clearly from Ra-khir.

"There," Tae's voice floated down from on high.

Grudgingly, Colbey tore his attention from the battles to find Tae clinging to the wrought iron, near the top of the gate. He followed Tae's pointing finger back into the compound. Only then, Colbey bothered to dig individuals from the mass of combatants, not just by strokes but by appearance. Kevral capered like a warrior possessed, exchanging Renshai maneuvers with a blond in war braids whom Colbey recognized as Modrey. Terror accompanied irony. In Colbey's final days as a mortal, the Renshai tribe had grown to three couples from which all members of the tribe currently descended. Kevral fought her own ancestor who, if killed, would only rise in the evening to share ale, boar, and roots with the other *Einherjar*. If mortal Kevral lost, she would simply die.

Seizing a bar in each fist, Colbey shinnied up gates that towered to three times his height. Not meant for climbing, the cold metal left him little purchase and no ledges for his feet. He braced against the sides, relying on quickness as much as friction. Kevral could only have entered in this manner, and he never doubted his ability to do the same. He kept his attention riveted on the battle below. Modrey had improved considerably, though the same lack of natural dexterity that had made him the least competent of Colbey's students then still hampered him now. Kevral gave her all to every stroke and defense. Colbey expected nothing less; yet her ability to hold her own this long against a Renshai centuries more practiced impressed him.

Colbey struggled to the top, using a horizontal support to brace his feet while he clambered over the upper spikes. Once on the opposite side, he scrambled down like a spider, leaping the last several feet into the compound. The instant his feet touched the ground, he galloped for Kevral and Modrey.

A light sheen of sweat bathed Kevral's radiant features as she slammed in a low stab that Modrey scarcely dodged and raised her second sword to parry his return. Her sword looped around a feint instead, and Modrey's blade screamed toward her head. She jerked up her attacking sword, but Colbey could see it would arrive too late.

There was no time for finesse. Colbey barreled in low, hurling himself at Modrey. His shoulder struck the man's legs, bowling him to the ground. Colbey spiraled to his feet, drawing, anticipating Kevral's riposte. He blocked easily, redirecting her hand toward him. Catching the hilt of her sword, he pirouetted under the second, using the tip of his blade to cut it from her grip. His spine slammed her abdomen. Impact staggered her a backward step, but she managed to save her balance as Modrey had not. He caught her falling sword in the same fist as his own, neither tearing free nor releasing her other hand. "What in Hel are you doing?"

Modrey clambered to his feet, studying the newcomer first in confusion, then disbelief.

Kevral loosed a snorting laugh, and only the esteem in which she held Colbey kept it from becoming derisive. Excitement emanated from her in waves that seemed to crash against Colbey's sensibilities and even to usurp his own. "What am *I* doing? I'm not the one who dove like a maniac into someone else's battle."

"Colbey," Modrey said softly.

Colbey had eyes and ears only for Kevral. He sheathed her sword properly, then released her other hilt, seizing her forearms. "You're not an *Einherjar*. If you die, you're dead."

Kevral smiled, shaking her head at the absurdity of Colbey's words. "If I die fighting bravely, I *am* an *Einherjar*."

She's right. Colbey froze, a flush creeping over his cheeks. "That's not the point." He hid his discomfort from Kevral; she would never know how foolish he felt. "Right now, I need you alive."

"Colbey!" Modrey shouted. "It's Colbey!"

The sounds of battle became irregular, slackening and interspersed with whispers.

Kevral stared back, saying nothing, expression hidden behind a taut and painful mask. Colbey read her thoughts, though whether because they slipped to him unbidden or because they so matched his own, he did not know. Kevral needed that battle, and she had nothing to lose. If she accepted the task that Colbey offered, no reason remained for her to live. No feat could compare to the chance to pit her skill against *Einherjar*. She embodied a perfect paradox, the rare win/win situation. If she lost the battle, she won the fight and a place among them. If she won the battle, she had bested the best. That victory might hold her even through the desperate task Colbey gave her. Regardless of the outcome, the chance to fight *Einherjar* was irresistible.

"I'm sorry," Colbey said, inflicting a pain beyond that he had already caused her. "I didn't bring you here for war. I forbid this. Return to your friends and your purpose."

Kevral tensed, as if she might challenge Colbey. But respect and awe won out over desire. Kevral slammed her other sword into its scabbard and stormed toward the gates.

With a deep sigh and a painful pang of guilt, Colbey watched her go and tensed to follow. The burden of eyes on his back became too heavy, and he turned to find the *Einherjar* massed behind him. They studied him, expressions somber, eyes tracking up and down his person with an attentive scrutiny that made him feel like a chicken in a market square. He recognized several even as they struggled to do the same: students, rivals, and enemies. Knowledge he had not used for centuries eased back into his mind. First, he recalled their pet maneuvers, their strengths and weaknesses, the strokes and weapons most suited to their strengths, sizes, and muscular development. Their names returned to him only then:

Ashavir, Kesave, and Bohlseti, ancient students who died when the Northmen annihilated the Renshai with a surprise night attack. He found Rache Kallmirsson, the only survivor of that attack, tossed as an infant into the sea. Once crippled by a gladiator, he now stood solidly, sword dripping blood on the grassy plain. Colbey saw several of the enemies who gave him the greatest battles of his mortal years, and he smiled. He would celebrate, never begrudge, a valiant enemy his time in Valhalla. He discovered others as well, competent warriors who had served as peers or who had impressed him in his youth: Santagithi, a brilliant strategist without whom the West would never have won the Great War; his daughter, Mitrian, the first person of non-Renshai blood accepted into the tribe and from whom those of the tribe of Tannin descended. The array of familiar faces stunned Colbey, and the bridging of time seemed incomprehensible. He wondered how many of his own distant ancestors he looked upon and discovered both of his mortal parents among the others.

For several moments, no one spoke, as if trying to determine who deserved that honor first. Colbey could tell Kevral had stopped moving behind him, watching the cluster of *Einherjar* examining Colbey. The din of battle died to the occasional pound of weapon against shield and the scratch of blade down blade. A few of Valhalla's heroes continued their fight, disinterested or unaware of the gathering near the fence.

Colbey expected the first words to come from his mother. Ranilda Battlemad had rushed into every challenge, not always bothering to assure need before antagonizing. But another stepped from the cluster to face Colbey directly. Gold hair bound into braids, hawklike nose appearing huge between hard blue eyes, Valr Kirin broke the hush. "Finally, Kyndig, we meet here." He spoke the name the gods had ascribed Colbey, one also used by the Northern Sorceress Kirin had championed.

This man had virtually symbolized goodness. "I've waited a long time." The words demanded an explanation that every gathered *Einherjar* strained to hear.

Colbey imagined it must have seemed strange for some to reunite with aged grandchildren before a man older than themselves came among them. Surely they must have believed age or illness claimed him, relegating him to Hel. Yet no one seemed surprised to see him. Valr Kirin clearly questioned only the timing.

"It's a very long story." Colbey glanced at his parents, Calistin the Bold and Ranilda. He would tell them first, in private, that they were not his biological parents. The Renshai woman who had coupled with Thor died shortly after in combat, and Sif had transferred him to Ranilda's womb. No one else needed to know; and, to Colbey, they would always be his only mother and father. "Someday, I'll tell it. For now, I have matters to attend." He looked at Valr Kirin's predatory face, at the somberness that seemed permanently affixed, and knew Kirin deserved more. He had earned his prefix "Valr," meaning "Slayer," as a hero in the war against Renshai. Their final battle had occurred under arranged circumstances, their agreements over single combat changing the course of history. Win or lose, Kirin promised that the Northmen would no longer hunt the last few Renshai. Both promised they would allow the loser to find Valhalla.

Agony accompanied memory of the battle. Kirin had proved a worthy opponent for a non-Renshai. Inevitably, Colbey had won; but, when the moment came to deal the mercy stroke that would end Kirin's life, the Slayer's son had interfered. Protecting himself from a dishonorable attack, Colbey had accidentally severed Valr Kirin's arm. Kirin never saw his son's betrayal, knowing only that Colbey had broken his vow. At that time, all Northmen believed that to die with parts missing barred a warrior from Valhalla. For centuries, Renshai had capitalized on this belief, dismembering Northern enemies for the purpose of destroying morale. And Valr Kirin had died cursing Colbey with his last breath.

Valr Kirin lowered his head. "My men told me of my son's actions." He sighed. "Olvaerr never made it here." He rolled his eyes upward, contemplating Colbey from the extreme edge of peripheral vision as if to read the old Renshai's reaction to his son's name. He wished for news of the boy, though Colbey had nothing positive to offer. That story would have to wait like so many others. "I'm sorry I doubted your honor. I saw you fight among the gods at the *Ragnarok,* and I know my mentor was wrong when she claimed you would betray mankind and your own to serve chaos. Had I known that, things would have gone differently."

Colbey knew Valr Kirin spoke truth. Under other circumstances, they would have become powerful allies. "Your death taught me much, too. I knew you found Valhalla, and I questioned every tenet of my faith when you did so missing a part." That reminded him of a question Kirin would expect him to ask. "Your brother?" Despite having lost a hand in battle, Kirin's brother had served as a general in the Great War, leading other than Northmen. The latter refused to follow one who could not lead them to Valhalla.

Kirin smiled, raising his head. "He was here. He died with most of the others at the *Ragnarok*." He added, with emphasis, "Bravely."

Colbey nodded stiffly, glad for an explanation for the absence of others he expected to see here. The conversation had come to a natural conclusion. Colbey knew he still had much to explain and discuss, with Kirin and others; but the balance had to take priority now. He started to turn.

Kirin would not let Colbey leave that easily. "Wait."

The other *Einherjar* pushed forward. They all deserved time and explanations as well.

"I never got that fair fight you promised me." Without awaiting a response from Colbey, Valr Kirin drew his sword and leaped toward the Renshai.

The air filled with emotions, ranging from euphoria to great envy. In the fractions of a second between Kirin's attack and his own need to defend, Colbey realized every *Einherjar* longed for a chance at him. He could not help laughing with wild abandon as he drew his sword and blocked in a single, fluid motion, the strength of Kirin's assault like a runaway cart against his forearm. He hissed in pain, riposting only once before Kirin lunged for his gut.

This time, Colbey dodged. Cutting beneath Kirin's sword, he slashed for an armpit that disappeared in an instant. His second attack gashed Kirin's shoulder, missing the neck by a whisper. A line of blood beaded the injury, but Kirin only laughed. His rabid battle joy seemed to merge with Colbey's. Frenzied excitement suffused Colbey, and he became giddy as a child at the discovery. He had finally found eternally eager partners for his sparring. Always before, he had had to pull his strokes, fearing to slaughter students. Now he could strike with abandon, without fear of causing injury. He could not harm men already dead. The bravest of the brave, the most committed of swordsmen, had become his to battle at will.

Colbey howled, his joy too strong to contain; and Kirin whipped in with a savage blur of attack that challenged Colbey's abilities for the first time in centuries. He fended every stroke, refusing to allow luck to handle even one, returning attacks at least one for one. Then a lightning Renshai maneuver caught Valr Kirin too slow to defend. Colbey's sword tore flesh, disemboweling the Northman. Colbey's follow-through opened Kirin's throat, killing him before he hit the ground. He would not leave a worthy opponent to the slow torture of an intestinal wound.

The world seemed to converge on Colbey at once, friends, family, and followers all eager to pit their new skills against his. Colbey back-stepped, war rage like a bonfire in his veins. He could have battled through days and never noticed the passage of time; yet pressing matters would not allow it. He had not forced Kevral from the fray just to join it himself.

Colbey made a brisk gesture behind him, indicating Kevral should climb if she had not done so already. He wanted the battles confronting him now to the point of rationalizing need. The *Einherjar*, too, hungered to test the skills they had honed over centuries against a man they considered the consummate warrior. Many sought information only Colbey could deliver. Misconceptions and misjudgments needed fixing, and mistakes required tallying. The idea of an endless parade of ultimate battles enticed, but the emotional baggage that accompanied facing every moment of his past seemed overwhelming. Colbey would handle all of that and see it as the ultimate reward, but he could not do so now—not because of weakness but because of time constraints.

Colbey retreated slowly as the *Einherjar* advanced, measuring the location of the fence by memory. He hoped Kevral had obeyed his gesture. For the moment, he could not spare the distraction of checking.

Several warriors charged Colbey suddenly. Forcing down the instinct to wade into battle, Colbey leaped for Valhalla's fence. Catching two of the wrought iron bars, he scampered beyond reach, then paused to explain an action that could pass for cowardice. "You'll all get your chance, I promise. I'll be back." He

singled Rache Kallmirsson from the group for a special nod and
wave. Dodging a prophecy that implied their meeting would
kill Rache, Colbey had avoided the young warrior. Rache had
internalized the evasion, pained by the belief that the *torke* he
admired despised him as a coward. Colbey had often wished for
the chance to explain his actions to Rache. "Nothing could keep
me away."

Those who had rushed Colbey glanced at one another, returning to their places. None had anticipated the others; each
had sought single combat. The longing radiating from them became a nearly collective anticipation. Several shouted good-
byes or challenges saved for future combat. Colbey gave them
a brisk salute before clambering over the upper spikes and shin-
nying back to the outside ground. Kevral had done as he bade,
and was again staring between bars at the combats that resumed
before Colbey's feet reached the ground. Only then did he
bother to wonder about the consequences of himself dying
locked in combat with *Einherjar*. He suspected Freya would
know the answer, yet he decided not to ask her. If he discovered
he could join them, that nothing lay at risk, it would take some
of the excitement from his battles.

That thought spurred others, and the simple truth behind
Odin's claim became obvious. *When he said I would never
reach Valhalla, he didn't mean that I would never come here.
He meant I would never come as a warrior plucked from a
battlefield.* In that new context, his previous fear seemed
childish. *Once again, concern for Odin's prediction caused
me to fulfill it.* He thought of Rache again, how his own concern for the young warrior's life had kept them apart until
Rache's death call in battle drew him. Rache had died at their
meeting, but not as a result of it. Colbey had lost the last
months of Rache's life, the time the only survivors of the Renshai massacre could have spent together, to meaningless
words. Three centuries without the best sparring partners the
gods created had resulted, once again, from trusting Odin.
Never again.

A gentle clearing of Ra-khir's throat redirected Colbey's attention. He glanced at the redheaded knight-in-training, already
grown into his warrior musculature.

Ra-khir moved nearer, keeping his words too soft for
Kevral to hear. "Lord." He made a formal gesture of respect,
as if to a prince in Béarn's court. "I would like to wield the
staff."

Colbey stared, struck dumb. The image of a Knight of Erythane championing chaos floored him. "You want to wield the
Staff of Chaos?"

"Yes, Lord." Ra-khir's eyes remained fixed on Colbey's face,
stalwart. His tone betrayed nothing of the discomfort and hesitation that Colbey's mental gift brought to him.

"A Knight of Erythane?"

"Apprentice knight," Ra-khir corrected doggedly.

Colbey shook his head. The knights pledged themselves to a
code of honor so rigid they could wield it as a weapon. Ra-khir
seemed unlikely to carry through on this task, and Colbey
doubted the world would appreciate the results. Ra-khir could
serve mankind better in his role as a knight. "No," Colbey said.
"I'm sorry."

Ra-khir turned his gaze to Kevral, but not before Colbey
caught a glimpse of welling tears. The Erythanian's love for
Kevral struck Colbey as a yearning wave of passion. He would
do anything for her, even destroy himself. "Please, Lord.
Please."

Tae seized the Staff of Chaos where it lay propped against the
solid fencing. "Of course you can't have it. It's mine!" He
danced beyond sword range, hovering over the staff with an animal glare of paranoia. "I'm going to wield it."

Only the strength of Tae's radiating concern revealed his
greed as a hoax. Though his reaction to the staff patterned those
of others in the past, altruism drove his actions. Like Ra-khir, he
sought to rescue Kevral from the task.

Touched despite himself, Colbey sucked in a deep breath.
He looked at Kevral, who studied the battling *Einherjar* with
unabashed awe. His glance strayed to Ra-khir, pleading desperately for her life, willing to sacrifice his own sanctity and
sanity for the woman he loved. Though he chose methods
more apparently selfish, Tae's intentions proved equally pure
and innocent. They were humans, mortals whose lives
spanned too little time to place their needs over those of the
timeless universe. Yet Colbey dismissed that concept as be-
longing in the mind of a god. A conversation returned to him,
and where he sought the solution to a situation without winners, he found solace in the least likely place—the words of
his own young son: *I was born less mortal than you'll ever become*. Grammatically, the claim made little sense now, but the
concept it embodied stuck with Colbey. *I tried to pass my*

charge to Ravn when even he realized I could wield it better. Why?

The answer appeared along with his final understanding of why he had avoided Valhalla. *To defy Odin who decreed it my destiny.* Loathing rose in Colbey, directed against himself. *What is this hold Odin has over me?* He amended, *Over all of us that it lasts centuries beyond the grave.* Infuriated by the realization, he studied logic that would have defied him days earlier: *Just because I choose to do something that Odin told me I would doesn't mean he caused it to happen.* Colbey shook his head at an understanding that seemed staggering. *Odin never forced anything on me. Every prophecy that came to fruition did so because of my actions, every mistake because I acted to avoid or defy his word.* He followed the understanding with a vow. *No more. I'll do as I believe right, whether it verifies or opposes Odin's presumption.*

"Give me the staff." Colbey gestured for Tae to come to him.

The Easterner remained crouched and still, clutching the Staff of Chaos like a lifeline. "It's mine."

Only Colbey understood the danger of Tae holding the staff too long. Either it would find him worthwhile and bind, or it would despise his intrusion. In the latter case, it might choose to destroy him.

"Give me the staff," Colbey repeated.

Tae raised a foot, as if to come, then drew the staff to his chest and stood defiantly.

Ra-khir watched in uncertain silence. Kevral finally tore her gaze from the *Einherjar* to watch the nearer proceedings. "Tae, do as he says."

"No. It's mine. You can't have it."

Colbey chose a course he should have long ago. "Tae, you're right. She can't have it. But I can."

Tae's eyes narrowed, and he back-stepped carefully. "You're playing with me."

"No," Colbey said. "You're right. Give me back the staff, and I'll wield it myself."

Tae shook back his tangled, black hair and regarded Colbey with dark eyes that seemed more like huge pupils than irises and pupils together. "Kevral's free to go?"

"Except for her mortal bindings. She did vow to work a year for the King of Pudar."

Relief seemed to flood from Ra-khir. Tae edged forward hesitantly, offering the staff to Colbey who closed his fingers around it. The Renshai exerted no physical pressure, but the staff tapped against his consciousness, demanding entry. Colbey blocked it out.

Finally, Tae released the staff.

"That's it?" Kevral asked uncertainly, hope raging beneath a necessary dampening.

"That's it," Colbey confirmed.

"I'm not going to wield it?"

"No."

Kevral swallowed, hiding the difficulty of her next words. "You know I will. The needs of the world come before even a promise made to a rash colleague." She gave Tae a warning look. His attempt to appear greed-driven had not fooled her either.

"I didn't change my mind because of Tae." Colbey spoke matter-of-factly, trying not to belittle the Easterner. "I heeded the words of a wise man whose genius I rarely appreciate." He gave Tae his direct attention now. "My son. So many believe in me, and I've gained so much self-confidence of my own, I sometimes forget that those I teach can teach me, too."

The necessary radiations did not come from Tae, so Colbey drove his point home.

"Do I sound like someone you know?"

Tae's brow furrowed as he considered, then the wave of understanding Colbey sought washed through him. "My father?" he guessed.

"Don't give up on him, Tae. You're not wrong. You know it, and I know it. You just have to convince him. And if you never see eye-to-eye, at least make your peace. If either of you dies without doing that, you'll never forgive yourself."

Tae closed his eyes, fighting a war inside himself that Colbey politely ignored. It did not last long. When his lids rose, a look of determination filled the dark eyes. He nodded to Kevral. "You're traveling northwest, right?"

"To Pudar," Kevral confirmed. "I have to go."

"May I accompany you?" The formality of the question seemed more suited to Ra-khir.

Kevral laughed. "Of course."

Ra-khir winced, but Colbey did not need to tell him his responsibilities lay in Erythane. He needed to finish his knight's training, help Kedrin, and serve Griff.

All four had destinies to face, and no one knew that better than Colbey Calistinsson/Thorsson, the Keeper of the World's Balance. The chosen of Odin.

CHAPTER 18

The Unwelcome

To the immortals, centuries pass like months;
but the shortest-lived see every moment's glory.
It is they who first notice the need for change.
And they who adapt most quickly to it.
                              —*Colbey Calistinsson*

Ravn discovered his father in his favorite practice area, a clearing carpeted with Asgard's emerald-colored grasses yet near enough to woodlands to provide the varied terrain Colbey preferred. Boulders, branches, and debris lay neatly piled at the boundary between meadow and woodlands, obstacles Colbey scattered randomly prior to his *svergelse*. Uncharacteristically sedate, Colbey perched upon one of those stones. The Staff of Chaos slanted in his right hand, its lower end buried in the dirt and its upper pointing at Asgard's ever-present sun. As always, he wore a sword at either hip. Blond feathers hid his expression.

Disturbing the elder Renshai's practice was insult worthy of death. Colbey did not guard his other activities so fiercely, not even his rare moments of quiet meditation. Nevertheless, Ravn approached with a quietness bordering on silence. His feet scarcely ruffled the grasses, and he kept his breathing controlled. The news he brought his father was bad.

Though intent, Colbey glanced in Ravn's direction the instant he entered the clearing. A chill traversed Ravn, and he paused in position. His own swords, the left a longsword and the right a scimitar, felt warm and reassuring at his sides. His yellow hair had grown just long enough to fall into his eyes during battle, and his mixed choice of swords always irritated his father. He suspected Colbey had mentally sensed his presence rather than heard anything to alert him to his son's approach.

Colbey rose, tunic stained by sweat and dirt. Everything else in Asgard always seemed pristine, from the grounds to the gods, and Colbey eternally jarred from this image. A smile split the familiar features, emphasizing the ancient scar across one cheek, left by a demon's claws. The blue-gray eyes lost their hard edge, replaced by a sparkle of delight. "Did you come for a spar?" The staff shifted to vertical, but Colbey leaned none of his weight upon it.

Though he had not, Ravn knew better than to decline the opportunity. "Later. There's a meeting."

Colbey sighed, as if Ravn had named the most painful part of his existence. And, perhaps, he had. For a warrior, sitting in council seemed grotesquely tedious. "So we'll be late."

"I'm already late." Ravn gauged his father's reaction. "You can't possibly be late."

Colbey hesitated less than a second before catching the underlying meaning. "I'm not invited?" he guessed.

Ravn lowered his head. "Vali made that very clear." He added for emphasis, "Very clear." He recalled the expression on the face of Odin's son: intense and harsh with eyes narrowed into slits that made him look as dangerous as live coals.

Colbey made a thoughtful noise but said nothing more.

Ravn shifted, uncomfortable. "I thought you should know."

"Vali wanted you to tell me."

Ravn could not tell if Colbey meant the words as statement or question. "He didn't say that."

"He didn't have to."

Ravn's eyes tracked naturally to the staff; its continued presence unnerved him. "Why would Vali want you to know he didn't invite you?"

The smile returned. "He wants me to come."

Ravn withdrew slightly, startled and confused by his father's assessment. "Then why did he exclude you?"

"He wants me to come uninvited."

"I see," Ravn said, but he didn't. His gaze fixed fanatically on the staff that should no longer grace his father's hand. "You still have the staff I brought."

Colbey nodded, apparently seeing no reason to respond verbally to a self-evident point.

"Weren't you going to give it to a mortal?"

"I was." Colbey hefted the Staff of Chaos, spun it from hand to hand, then returned it to its position. "I changed my mind."

"Oh." Ravn tried not to let too much worry seep into his tone. He recalled the yearning the staff had created in him. Had he held it too long, he might have attempted to wield it. He had understood the need to rid himself of it swiftly, but he never expected it to have such a profound effect on a being with his father's mental power and control. "*You're* going to wield it?" This time, incredulity leached into his voice.

Colbey responded to the thoughts rather than the words, a habit that never ceased to intimidate Ravn. "I haven't allowed more than superficial contact. It was my choice, fully, not the staff's influence."

Ravn wished for a way to ascertain his father's words but knew he would find none.

Again, Colbey read his concern without words. "I could let you hold the staff, but you can't trust it. It'll tell you whatever it believes will stir more chaos. Or, perhaps, what it thinks I want you to know. I can't prove what I say. You'll just have to trust me."

Ravn looked at his father, seeing a man who had weathered more than most of the gods in a far shorter span. Nature had endowed him with none of his biological father's size, strength, or temper. Though plain in size and features, he could never become lost in a crowd. Whether from stance or simply Ravn's knowledge of his prowess, he seemed to radiate a dangerous aura that created followers or enemies in an instant. Something about Colbey Calistinsson awed Ravn as none of the gods did. He did not attempt to differentiate how much of that respect grew from the natural bond between father and son, how much from the lightning swordplay, and how much from something undefinable. He might not understand why, nor ever explain it to others or to himself, but he trusted Colbey with a faith no one could shake. "So are you going? To the meeting, I mean."

Colbey shrugged. "I wouldn't want to disappoint Vali." Though not a direct answer, the words told Ravn that, as always, Colbey would do as he pleased.

"I could refuse to go." Ravn tried to show his support in the only way the situation allowed, though the token seemed hollow. Like his once-mortal father, Ravn despised the tedium of conferences.

"No." Colbey made a gesture that dismissed Ravn's sacrifice without belittling it. "Someone with common sense should be there. Besides your mother, of course."

Ravn grinned at the compliment, shaking his head simultaneously at blasphemy Colbey never would have suffered, from himself or any other, in his mortal years. "All right, then. I'll see you later." He did not specify when. His father would determine that.

Ravn trotted onward, Asgard's sun a pleasant warmth on his shoulders and the grasses tickling through his sandals. He did not attempt to anticipate the meeting. Only one topic could drive Vali to invite every inhabitant of Asgard except Colbey. Ravn could only guess the reason for Vali's concern, though it likely paralleled his own: The Staff of Chaos. Unlike Ravn, Vali did not trust the old Renshai. And he had made that quite clear at their last meeting, that one in Colbey's presence.

Though not as large as the gods', Ravn's rapid strides brought him swiftly to the gold-and-silver behemoth of the meeting hall. The sunlight sparked highlights from the chaotic arrangement of gemstones, and Ravn's movement brought different ones into focus in a wavelike pattern. The intermittent glimmers looked like stars winking into and out of existence, tiny lights on a background of silver. The appreciation Colbey had taught allowed Ravn to enjoy the display each and every time he entered or passed the building. Unlike his father, who considered the display gaudy and wasteful, Ravn found beauty in the meeting hall's wealth. Now he enjoyed it as much as he dared, rocking his head to bring different gemstones into the light as he reached for the door.

Ravn tripped the latch, and the panel swung silently open on a somber array of gods and goddesses at the iron-bound, oak table. Diamonds glittered from the frame, the last exhibition before followers' sacrifices gave way to the austere interior. Again, Vidar sat in Odin's seat, as if to remind the half brother who had called the meeting of his station. Vali took a position at Vidar's right hand, once Vidar's own seat in the days when Odin ruled the heavens. Odin had died long before Ravn's birth, so the positioning of the assembled held little significance to him. Balder the beloved, Vidar's once-dead brother sat to his left. Beside Balder sat his wife, Nanna, then Modi and Magni, the redheaded sons of Thor. As always, their father's hammer lay on the table near either's hand. Across the table from Nanna and Thor's sons sat the goddesses Sif, Sigyn, and Idunn. Hod and Frey sat opposite one another in the very next seats, Hod beside Magni and Frey beside Idunn. Freya took a place beside her brother. Ten chairs remained vacant. Ravn chose the one across from his mother, and only she so much as glanced at him as he entered. She granted him a smile and a nod, without chastising his lateness.

Ravn took only a moment to orient himself to the conversation, and tuned it out shortly thereafter. The gods discussed trivialities: Midgard's weather, the faith of followers, and the status of human systems of belief. Such details did not concern Ravn. He had no temples dedicated to him; only a rare human knew of his existence. The *Ragnarok* had brought an end to most of the gods' charges and concerns. Giants no longer existed, leaving Asgard without enemies. Loki no longer lived to stir trouble in their midst. Odin's terrible commands had died with him, leaving no prophecies to fulfill. Hel no longer prepared for war. Without the extremes, the world assumed a balance that scarcely teetered . . . usually. And, as Ravn knew it must, the conversation eventually turned to Colbey.

Vali claimed the floor. "As you know, I called you here." He added from duty, "With my brother's permission."

Vidar gave Vali a single nod that conveyed a request to continue. From their leader's expression, Ravn perceived that Vidar did not know Vali's intentions but chose to listen to them.

Vali cleared his throat, breaking the last few lingering conversations and drawing all eyes to himself. "I have serious concerns about the Keeper of the Balance."

A rumble swept through the gods. Ravn caught some mumbles of agreement interspersed with suggestions that Vali not bother to identify a topic they already anticipated.

Vidar sighed wearily. "We've already heard your concerns, Vali. At the last meeting."

Ravn guessed the young leader of the gods had listened to Vali's ramblings several times since then as well, on an informal basis.

"A new problem has come to light." Vali swung his head toward his brother, a war braid flipping over his shoulder with the movement. "I've been watching Colbey."

The words irritated Ravn more than he expected. "You've been spying on my father," he grumbled beneath his breath.

Apparently, Freya heard him. She shook her head, frowning. The gesture bespoke forbearance.

Vali took no verbal notice of the exchange, although his attention did swing to Colbey's wife and son. A half-smile played over his features. "Our Balance-Keeper will destroy us."

Vidar's frown matched his half brother's, but with different source. "The King of Béarn was restored. The balance must naturally follow."

"It hasn't," Sigyn blurted. "It's dangerously tipped."

"Toward law," Vali confirmed.

"Your point?" Vidar demanded.

Vali threw up his hands, as if it should seem obvious. "Colbey believed he could manage the feat without tipping the balance. Clearly, he overplayed his hand."

Freya's foot pressed against Ravn's. The time had not come yet for either of them to speak.

Sif shook her metallic gold tresses, and wavy highlights reflected on the wall. "Any of us would have done worse. Even Colbey admitted his hand might have become too heavy to meddle in Midgard's affairs. If he withdraws, the balance should correct itself."

"Exactly!" Vali glanced around the room, light eyes returning every stare. "But Colbey made the decision to wield the Staff of Chaos instead. He plans to correct an imbalance of his creation by leaping personally onto the other side." Vali paused without making the obvious point, leaving the gods to contemplate the results. Each could conjure the endpoint his or her own imagination found most horrible.

Even Ravn could not stop himself from considering the facts Vali presented, especially in light of what little he knew. He understood the danger of gods meddling. Although he had witnessed no catastrophes, Colbey, Freya, and the gods had described ones that horrified him enough. His own father had forbidden Ravn's associations with Griff when they affected the balance, for the very reason Vali detailed. Ravn stared at his hands, unable to deny Vali's assertion yet fiercely certain of his father's competence.

Freya's grip on Ravn's shoulder increased. He looked into his mother's pale eyes and ivory features, and she sought some confirmation or denial from him. Without the facts, she could not argue.

"He has the staff," Ravn whispered, careful to ascertain no one could overhear. "And he does plan to wield it."

Consideration narrowed Freya's eyes, bringing the long lashes together. No condemnation reached her expression. She wondered about, but never doubted the propriety of, Colbey's decision. Her allegiance to Colbey never wavered, adding fuel to Ravn's own.

Lines creased Vidar's face, and he looked at Vali around bangs that fringed his forehead. "Are you certain of this?"

"Quite certain." Vali's tone and expression left no doubt.

Ravn glanced around the room at the other gods, surprised to find many gazing at him. Most looked away as he met their stares. Without Colbey in the room, their condemnations fell naturally to him. Unlike humans, however, they realized the folly of blaming a father's insanity on his son. No one verbally tossed responsibility his way. Magni had reached naturally for Thor's hammer, his fist tensing and loosening on the short haft. Modi's brows beetled in anger. The other deities seemed as much confused and apprehensive as outraged.

There seemed no defense to the action, and no one spoke for a long time. Freya finally found her moment in the silence. "Colbey wielded a staff before amid condemnations far more vehement. Those who stood against him were wrong then . . ." She added carefully, ". . . too."

Sigyn dismissed the argument. "It's not the same, Freya. The mistake was believing he carried the Staff of Chaos, not Law. This time, he *has* chosen chaos."

"Colbey carried law, never sanctioned it," Freya reminded. "He always worked for balance. That's why Odin picked him."

Ravn listened to both sides carefully. That he had already chosen his loyalties did not matter. Until he heard all parts, he could not gather the logic to argue.

Vali shook back his errant braid. "But we're talking about chaos here. Kyndig could control law. It's predictable. It keeps vows scrupulously. Even Odin couldn't fully handle chaos."

"Colbey was Odin's choice," Balder reminded politely. "We have to trust Odin."

"A century after his death," Vali said. "Two centuries, maybe. But things change over time. Even Odin switched strategies. He traded the system of Wizards for a Keeper of Balance."

"True." Freya confirmed Vali's words, only to disparage them. "After *millennia*. Give Colbey some time. And, for once, some benefit of your doubts."

Vidar had remained unusually quiet during this time. He shifted in his seat like a human child trapped at a day-long ceremony. It seemed impossible that his habit of listening rather than speaking had earned him the title of the silent god prior to the *Ragnarok*, before circumstance forced him into Odin's place.

Vali placed Vidar further into his uncomfortable position. "So, are you with me?"

Vidar threw up his hands, clearly agitated. "What do you mean by 'with you'? We're all in this together."

Vali planted both palms on the table, leaning toward his half brother at the table's head. "Over time, the Staff of Chaos will corrupt Colbey. Do you want another Loki in our midst?"

Modi and Magni recoiled, hissing. Several others appeared agitated, by expression or movement. Only Freya remained in place, a wistful smile crossing her face so swiftly Ravn doubted he had seen it at all. History mentioned times when Freya and Loki had worked together grudgingly, as respectful rivals. The troublesome god of mischief and chaos had also seen through Colbey's switching of the staves, recognizing the need for the deception and for the *Ragnarok*.

Vali rose to deliver the coup de grace in a loud voice that assured the full attention he had already garnered. "We must stop Colbey's foolishness. We have two choices I can see: remove the Staff of Chaos from him or take his title as Balance-Keeper and his status among us."

Vidar's gaze strayed first from Vali to the door. Others followed in a line. Only then, Ravn felt the faint breeze of the opening at his back. He whirled, along with several others.

Colbey stood framed in the doorway, the Staff of Chaos gripped loosely in his hand. "And you, Vali? Are you volunteering to take the Staff of Chaos from me?"

"See!" Vali shrieked in a triumph that sounded rehearsed to Ravn. "Just as I warned. Who else interrupted a meeting of gods to which he was not invited?"

Ravn guessed from context that Vali referred to Loki. Sage nods swept the room, from those who recalled the incident. Freya rolled her eyes at the madness.

"The way I see it, Vali, your two choices are these: either trust me to handle the job Odin endorsed . . ."

Ravn noticed Colbey avoided saying that Odin assigned him the task. He had always claimed a willing hand in the decision.

". . . or you can face me in fair combat. If you kill me, you can take any items you wish. If I kill you . . ." Colbey shrugged. ". . . the gods lose a fool."

A fire blazed in Vali's eyes, but he did not accept Colbey's challenge. Instead, he gave Vidar a warning look, again placing the problem into his half brother's hands.

It no longer shocked Ravn to realize Colbey's sword skill surpassed most or all of the gods'. Vali would not face Colbey because he knew he would lose the battle.

Along with the remaining gods, Vidar studied Colbey.

Forced into the position of speaker again, Colbey remained in the doorway. The thought entered Ravn's mind that his father might taunt, forcing at least some of the gods into a hopeless battle. Whether they won or Colbey, the loss would prove a tragedy. But Colbey did not resort to name-calling. Instead, he opened the challenge. "Anyone? My sword arm is ready." His gaze swept every member of the gathered entourage. Modi's fist tightened around *Mjollnir's* haft, but even he did not accept Colbey's invitation.

Finally, Colbey's gaze found his son and rested there. The blue-gray eyes beckoned, and Ravn realized his father expected something from him. The inducement confused him. He supported his father and had no wish to wrest control of chaos from him. He had already willingly given up the Staff of Chaos. Still, Colbey's attention riveted on Ravn, so cold and focused it drove the youth to a restless fidgeting. He cleared his throat and asked the question plaguing him since he found Colbey with the staff in the clearing. "Why, Father? Why would you wield that thing?" He waved vaguely toward the Staff of Chaos.

The gods' regard remained fixed on Colbey in the ensuing pause. The Keeper of the Balance smiled. "Ah. So I will get a chance to explain my actions, thanks to my son. The rest of you would condemn me based only on presumption."

"The facts," Magni said, "speak volumes."

"The facts, *brother,* are not all present," Colbey supplied, emphasizing their blood relationship as if the word were insult. "Even among humans, the accused usually has the opportunity to speak."

Vidar waved a hand. "Speak then, Kyndig. We're listening."

If you were listening, you'd know his name is Colbey. Ravn could not fathom why some of the gods still used their name for him when Colbey walked among them and could bluntly state his preference.

Colbey avoided the petty for matters more significant. "I've always believed that, left undisturbed by immortals, the world balances its own forces. But the Staff of Law's power vastly exceeds Chaos'. At first, I thought it came of a particularly strong bond between it and its champion. Dh'arlo'mé's thoughts tell me otherwise. The Staff of Law regained its sentience long before Chaos, and it has grown beyond expectation. I can't explain it with logic—yet. I do know one thing. No mortal could stand against it. I may not have the strength to do so either, but I'm not afraid to try. Stand with me or against me." He shrugged, denying the significance of Asgard's deities with the motion. "Your opposition will make an already difficult task harder. Perhaps, you will ruin me and assure the destruction of our world. I didn't make an easy choice, just a moral one. Anyone who stands against me will die."

The words settled over the gathering, and Ravn could only imagine the thoughts racing through every god's head. His own considerations fell to concern over the fate of the balance. He never doubted that his father must champion chaos, nor that Colbey found the job as distasteful as his peers. He just could not conceive of Colbey binding with chaos and remaining Keeper of the Balance.

Vidar broke the hush. "The force in the Staff of Law has become so powerful that it requires the combined forces of an immortal and the Staff of Chaos to balance it?"

"To challenge it," Colbey corrected. "The balance, I believe, would still tip into its favor. And remember, law is bound also, to a near-immortal."

"Perhaps someone more powerful should bind with the Staff of Chaos then," Frey suggested.

Colbey confronted the god of weather and elves, his brother-in-law. "Are you volunteering?"

Frey shrugged. "I doubt I'm the best choice. What would it entail?"

"Joining with chaos. Essentially, 'becoming Loki' as Vali might put it."

Ravn felt a sensation of aversion, as if the whole room had recoiled from the suggestion at once.

Colbey continued. "A constant struggle against law. Eventually, a cosmic battle with, hopefully, the total destruction of both."

"'Both' meaning?" Vidar prodded.

"The Staff of Law and its champion. The Staff of Chaos and its champion."

Dread crept up Ravn, paralyzing, beginning at his toes. He looked to his mother for support, but she stared at her husband, her features ashen.

Frey stated the obvious. "You're talking about suicide."

"I'm talking about the total annihilation of the bearer of the Staff of Chaos." Colbey displayed a grin more like a rictus. "Now, who's my first volunteer? Vali?"

Vali sat. No one took the challenge.

Setting his jaw, Ravn rose. "Father," he started.

Freya closed her eyes. Colbey frowned. "Ravn, I appreciate the sacrifice, but I won't waste your life. Even should you kill me, I don't believe you're strong enough to face this threat. Someday, certainly. Not yet."

Ravn shook his head. "I won't try to take chaos from you. It's the balance I'm after."

Colbey nodded. "Come here, Ravn."

Clambering down from his seat, Ravn approached his father with trepidation. As the reality of Colbey's sacrifice became more clear, Ravn's steps grew more difficult. His feet felt leaden. Tears stung his eyes, and he kept his head low to hide them.

Harval rattled from Colbey's sheath with a suddenness that sent Ravn skittering into a defensive crouch, his scimitar half-freed before he realized his father offered the hilt.

Colbey brought his voice so low the others could not hear. "The balance is yours, Raska Colbeysson. Guard it well."

Ravn reached for the sword, hesitated, then caught Colbey into an embrace instead. "I'm going to miss you," he whispered as tears coursed down his cheeks. "I love you, Father."

"I love you, too," Colbey gave back as softly. "But don't give up on me yet. I've never been good at dying."

Ravn clung, never wanting to let go. Colbey's warm, living presence, the pleasant clean odor of perspiration, the soft tickle of hair against his ear became a pleasure Ravn would cling to for eternity. Understanding of Colbey's words came only several moments after their speaking. *The Deathseeker.* Colbey had hurled himself into every lethal conflict since birth, had weathered even the *Ragnarok,* yet he often lamented that death eluded him. For all his reckless courage, he had never died in the many wild flurries of battle that should have claimed him. Maybe this time, too, he could survive the downfall he willfully embraced.

Ravn pulled free, taking Harval in exchange for his longsword. Both men sheathed their new swords. "Meet me on the practice field after the gathering," Colbey said. "I've got a lot to teach you before I go." He raised the Staff of Chaos in a gesture of salute. "From that moment on, temper your trust with understanding." Turning, Colbey headed from the meeting hall.

Ravn watched his father's retreating back, the light step that never faltered, the careless toss of short golden locks by the wind. The hopes and dreams of an endless lifetime might die in the ensuing practice. He would cherish those final moments with his father, knowing that the other deities would cease to allow Colbey's presence once the transformation began.

Colbey's form blurred into the surrounding foliage as moisture destroyed Ravn's vision. He let the tears fall where they would.

CHAPTER 19

Send-offs

Competence is infinite.

—*Colbey Calistinsson*

Though not particularly large for Béarn's castle, Kevral's temporary room seemed massive to Ra-khir. Painted an off-white that bordered on pink, the walls stood in plain contrast to the murals and tapestries in the hallways. Tunics lay strewn across the bed as Kevral sorted through them, folding most into her pack. She had left all six of the bureau drawers open, and wind streaming through the window had carried the lightest of her belongings to the floor. Ignoring the chair pulled away from the desk, he scrambled after a comb and a scarf blown from the top of the dresser.

Ra-khir placed the items on the desk, away from the draft and beside a scattering of writing implements, rags, and sword oil. He struggled for control of his emotions, driven to plead with Kevral to break her vow to King Cymion of Pudar and stay with him in Béarn. The dishonor inherent in such an action kept him silent. She had made a vow, and he could never allow—worse, suggest—that she break it. He found his mouth open, and the need to speak became a torment. He searched for better words than those that begged speaking. "I'm going to miss you terribly," he finally managed.

Kevral looked up from her packing, flashing Ra-khir a smile that spoke volumes more than words. "I'm going to miss you, too." She paused just long enough not to cheapen the sentiment. "Could you hand me whatever's still in the left top drawer, please."

Ra-khir walked to the indicated drawer, pulling out a simple headband made for keeping sweat and hair from Kevral's eyes rather than for decoration. He passed it to Kevral, then pulled out the only other item in the drawer, a flimsy undergarment. Before he could think to squelch it, his mind conjured an image of Kevral wearing it and nothing else. Warmth burned through him, and his groin twitched instantly to life. Embarrassed, he covered his lower regions with the garment and reluctantly forced the picture from his thoughts, replacing it with scenes of the Renshai in battle.

Kevral took no notice of an excitement Ra-khir felt certain he had broadcast to the world. She accepted the undergarment without comment, tucking it amidst her other clothing.

The savagery disappeared from Ra-khir's memory. He saw only Kevral's lithe form, leaping, twisting, and turning, the swords steel extensions of her arms. Battles once grotesque and bloody transformed to dances of such grace and beauty he could only stare, spellbound.

Kevral's sudden touch brought Ra-khir back to reality. Her fingers skimmed his forearms lightly, and her striking, blue eyes held a note of concern. "Are you all right?"

Ra-khir could only nod stupidly. Instead of attempting speech, he seized Kevral's arms, drew her to a stand, and kissed her. The taste of her lips, her breath in his mouth, brought back the euphoria of their night together in the elves' prison. Excitement had turned imminent death into a forgettable backdrop. Nothing had mattered but the two of them, their embrace, the loving interlock of their bodies. The warmth in Ra-khir's loins became a bonfire, and he had no choice but to gently end the kiss.

Ra-khir tried to make his withdrawal appear casual, but Kevral had not finished with him yet. She caught his head even as it retreated and pressed her mouth against his again. Her breasts smashed against his chest, and he could feel the impressions of her nipples. Her thigh brushed his groin, and need became an agony. Ra-khir returned the kiss as long as he dared, wishing for more himself but worrying for his self-control. Again, he pulled free, this time walking briskly to the door before Kevral could stop him. Remaining inside, he closed it, cutting off the draft drawing from the window.

Returning to Kevral, Ra-khir knelt at her feet, pressing her callused hand between his own. "Kevral, I love you. I asked you this once before and now again. When you return from Pudar, will you marry me?"

Kevral's gaze went directly to Ra-khir's green eyes and held there. A parade of emotions seemed to flicker through her glance. A slight smile twitched at the corners of her lips but never formed. She sat on the bed.

Ra-khir took a seat beside Kevral and placed a strong arm around her. Every moment of hesitation dragged like six eternities.

"I love you, Ra-khir," Kevral finally said.

Hope trickled through Ra-khir, staunched by the second pause that followed her words.

"If I was going to marry someone today, it would be you. I just need time."

"Time?" Ra-khir repeated carefully.

"I'm not quite sixteen."

Ra-khir did not understand the connection. "Women in my culture come of age at fourteen. And you've been an adult by Renshai standards for longer."

"Were you ready to marry at fifteen?"

The question seemed irrelevant. "I didn't know you when I was fifteen." Despite his need, Ra-khir refused to press too hard. "You're telling me you're not ready for marriage. Or is this a polite way of telling me you don't want to marry *me*."

Kevral snorted. "Have I ever bowed to politeness before?"

Answering seemed rude, so Ra-khir remained silent.

"But you may be right that it's not really age that's bothering me." Kevral sighed. "I do love you. If I was staying in Béarn, I'd almost certainly marry you. But I'm going away for a year. A lot can happen in a year."

"And hopefully will." Ra-khir anticipated completing his training and winning his knighthood during Kevral's time in Pudar. He could not, however, shake the image of Kevral traveling for weeks with Tae. The adversity they would surely face along the way would likely draw them closer.

"If our love is as strong as I believe, it'll weather a year apart. If we both feel the same way when I return, we'll marry."

Ra-khir clung to those words. "Promise?"

"Promise," Kevral agreed. "If a year away can't shake what I feel for you, I couldn't suffer another parting."

"I'll count the days till your return." Ra-khir cradled Kevral to his chest, the closeness instantly reawakening desire.

"No," Kevral said softly. "No, please. If it's to be a true test, you have to see other women."

"What?" Ra-khir let go of Kevral, not daring to believe what he had heard.

"How many women have you been with?"

"That depends." Ra-khir scooted around to face Kevral. "What do you mean by been with?"

"Romantically."

Ra-khir started to ask for further qualification, then realized it was unnecessary. Whether Kevral meant sexually or platonically did not matter. The answer was the same. "One. The only one I need."

"How do you know that?"

The question seemed patently ludicrous. "I counted?" Ra-khir tried.

Kevral laughed, the sweetness of the sound breaking the tension. Ra-khir could not help smiling. Kevral clarified, "I meant how do you know I'm the only woman you need."

Ra-khir shrugged. "How do I know the sun will rise? I love you. Once I marry you, no other woman matters."

"That's exactly it!" Kevral made a grand gesture, as if Ra-khir had just said something profound. "Think of this as your year of freedom, your time to make certain you're making the right decision. If you don't see other women, you'll always wonder."

Ra-khir thought the point moot. He would never cheat on nor abandon his wife, even if she could not cut his heart out for doing so. Kevral had a point he had to consider. He would never have suggested that they separate for a year just to assure their love. But, since circumstances required them to part, it only made sense for them to use the time wisely. "All right," he finally agreed, doubting he really ever had a choice. "I'll see others, and I know you will, too. But I don't have to like it."

Kevral nodded her agreement. "I can only bind your person to agreements, not your heart. Never doubt that I love you and I'll miss you every moment of every day. Now, let's seal our vows with something stronger than a kiss."

Ra-khir's heart rate seemed to double in that instant. He struggled with his honor. Sleeping with a woman before marriage still seemed wrong, yet the damage had already been done. They had discussed the survival of their love but not yet the survival of their persons. Kevral would soon blithely head onto roads filled with Easterners trained and paid to slaughter travelers. She would fling herself into battle joyfully and face death with all of the excitement she had revealed in Valhalla. The urge to accompany Kevral, to protect her, welled up in Ra-khir; but he had vows of his own to follow. Honor bound him to the Knights of Erythane.

Kevral wrapped her arms around Ra-khir, and he willingly surrendered to love.

* * *

Oa'si stood among the gathered elves on Nualfheim's shore, glancing through golden eyes at the sea of legs that blocked his view of Dh'arlo'mé. A vast blanketing awe settled over the assemblage, unsettling him. Seized suddenly with the urge to run and hide, Oa'si caught the nearest hand without bothering to identify its owner. The adults all served as mothers and fathers, and the specifics of who had given birth to him held no significance to the others or to himself. The unfettered sexuality of elves meant any male could have conceived him. At thirty, he was the youngest of the elves, the only child.

Warm fingers closed reassuringly over Oa'si's pudgy hand, soothing. Dh'arlo'mé continued speaking of matters Oa'si scarcely grasped. He called those gathered the *dwar'freytii*, Frey's chosen ones, and condemned the traitor elves, the *lav'rintii*. The knowledge of the old elf seemed to have grown endless, his magic stronger, his confidence enormous, even as it appeared his physical health declined. Oa'si based his judgment on the staff Dh'arlo'mé had taken to carrying, leaning more heavily upon it with each passing day. For all his apparent frailty, Dh'arlo'mé's voice remained vibrant, piercing the crowd at a booming volume and without hesitation.

The elves remained in place while Dh'arlo'mé spoke of human destruction and the hellion, chaos, that would sweep them to their dooms. He lauded these elves who had followed the ancient honor placed into their race by Frey at the time of creation. Oa'si listened with little understanding, his patience vast but not nearly so long-lived as that of his elders. After hours of silent concentration, his mind wandered to other matters. A story returned to his thoughts, one told to him by the human the elves had kept prisoner. She had spoken of so many things unknown to him and foreign to his culture: heroism, individuality, competition. Those things had seemed nonsensical, negative concepts at first; and it had taken many discussions and stories to intrigue him.

Oa'si smiled at the memory, missing the evenings of conversation with Brenna. He tried to construct his own story in the pattern of hers, most of which featured the swordmaster, Colbey Calistinsson. Oa'si pictured the old Renshai as Brenna described him: a wild swirl of golden hair and clothing, his swords silver blurs around a torso never still.

Oa'si Brahirinth Yozwaran Tril'frawn Ren-whar! The *khohlar* slapped his mind with a suddenness and strength that sent him lurching backward with a gasp. *Pay attention to your leader.* The final word seemed steeped in concept, suggesting divinity rather than simple command.

The elf who had held Oa'si's hand looked down to attend to the youngster.

Oa'si felt tears sting his eyes, and shame settled over him like a suffocating blanket. He knelt, unable to comprehend the terror that blossomed inside him, one that simultaneously drove him to run from and to Dh'arlo'mé. He could not help recalling Brenna's descriptions of human worship, strange blendings of unconditional love and respect with the panic of facing the gods' colossal might. He believed he finally understood, and he hurled himself to the ground to escape the discomfort, torn between curling into a groveling ball and crawling to Dh'arlo'mé to pledge himself to the leader's every cause.

Another voice touched Oa'si's mind, this one soft and gentle in the wake of the previous power. *Are you all right, little one?*

Oa'si nodded, trusting neither his voice nor his *khohlar*. As the initial impact of the previous encounter faded, he dared to wonder how Dh'arlo'mé had known his thoughts were wandering. Elfin mental contact allowed only communication, never probing, yet he now believed he understood another human concept. He felt deeply violated and terribly afraid.

The elf's violet eyes remained trained on Oa'si, expressing concern.

I'm all right. Oa'si finally managed. He rose, bowed his head until the dark, regular bangs fell into his moist eyes, and concentrated on Dh'arlo'mé's words.

Kevral set out the following day, euphoria from the previous night dampened by her parting from Ra-khir. Maneuvers kept the knight-in-training from seeing her off, but the image of his red-blond hair, aristocratic features, and gentle green eyes remained locked in her memory long after trees, brush, and the dark mane of her mount replaced the vision. The warm, human smell of him became lost beneath the all too real dampness and the sweet, musky odor of her horse.

Tae proved poor company, constantly riding or running ahead, then returning to lead Kevral quietly in another direction. They broke trail, avoiding not only the open road but the deer paths and temporary trails created by camping humans. Branches whipped, until her face felt like a mass of scratches

and bruises. Even tucked tightly to the horse's neck, Kevral
could not fully escape some of the massive limbs blocking their
route. These abraded her back as she passed beneath them.
More than once, she found herself trapped between trunks too
close to allow her horse passage or felled trees with branches
too dense for the gelding to jump. Turning, she would retrace
her steps, swear words burning her lips.

Still, Tae returned at irregular intervals, to point out a new direction. His dark eyes seemed eternally restless, and his black
hair lay in a hopeless tangle speckled with twigs and leaves.
The paths he chose became an irritation that wholly banished
the joy of Kevral's night with Ra-khir. Tae held them to the
darkest, unexplored regions of the forest. Time disappeared beneath the interweave of branches that blocked the sun, and only
the growling and gnawing of her stomach confirmed the hours
spent wrestling foliage.

Evening also brought the cold, and Kevral drew a cloak from
her pack that initially sufficed, then grew less comforting over
time. Boxed into another stand of crowded trees, she kicked her
horse through a dangerously small opening. The gelding slid
through obediently, smashing Kevral's left knee against a trunk.
Pain screamed through her leg as tree, flesh, and horse all refused to yield. Bark shredded her britches. She jerked the horse
into a careful backward motion, and her knee came free. Agony
died to a dull throb, and anger flared to replace it. Drawing both
legs up to the horse's neck, she urged it forward again, this time
managing to squeeze through the hole.

Tae met her on the opposite side, taking no notice of the ordeal. He pointed right, a direction that Kevral worried would
complete a circle.

"I'm sick to death of this infernal zigzagging," Kevral announced, meeting his soft, dark gaze with her glaring blue. She
read exhaustion in his stance, but pain disrupted any chance for
sympathy. "Where's the road?"

Tae resisted playing coy and went right to the intention behind the question. "We're not taking it."

"I am. Whether you come with me or not."

"I get it." Tae's expression turned hard. He was in no mood
for games. "When you said we'd travel together, you meant
we'd go the same general way until you tired of my company."

"Company?" The words seemed nonsensical. "Do you consider the six seconds you spent with me traveling together?"

Tae slumped on his black's withers. "Would you rather confront the eighty-two Easterners I managed to sneak us around?" He groaned at his own question, anticipating the answer.

Kevral did not disappoint him. The image of hacking through an endless tide of enemies usurped pain, and even irritation. Her hand fell to one hilt. "Yes. I would. Death in—"

"—glory. A place in Valhalla," Tae finished for Kevral. "I've heard it. A thousand times was enough."

A hot flush of anger swept Kevral. Her eyes narrowed, and her fist tightened on her hilt. "Are you ridiculing Renshai honor?"

"No," Tae returned with the enunciation of an adult calming a screaming child. "Quoting it." He added carefully, "I understand your need to die in battle, so much more so since looking upon Valhalla. I just don't see the purpose in wasting your life on a gang of low-life, mustered criminals."

Kevral shrugged, seeing the point yet unwilling to admit it. "Battle is battle." She slid naturally into citation, "The glory comes of clinging to one's own honor even as the enemy abandons his. So long as a Renshai dies giving his all to the battle, the name and face of the enemy bears no significance."

"Still borrowing Colbey's words?"

Kevral took no offense. "He's the greatest swordsman who ever lived, and the hero of my people. He also happens to be right."

Tae smiled. "No longer will Renshai fight just for the joy of combat. We will remain the fiercest of warriors, savage swordsmen who shun fear, but only when the cause is right. For now, the Renshai need allies more than battles."

Kevral stared, brow slowly crinkling. "Who said that?"

Tae's grin broadened. "Colbey."

The surprise of Tae knowing a Colbey quotation she did not erased Kevral's anger. "How do you know that?"

Tae plucked a familiar book from his pocket, one he had given to Kevral as a gift, along with a figurine of Colbey. It chronicled Colbey's days as the general of Pudar's army during the Great War centuries past. That Tae had it after she had packed it into her belongings only two days earlier surprised her only half as much as his decision to read it. "What are you doing with that?"

"Preparing myself for this precise moment." Tae looked away, revealing another motive that the need for strong appearances would not allow him to confess.

Kevral guessed at the answer Tae would never speak. He

wanted to understand her in detail, even the philosophies that
had shaped her life since birth. Recognition of his dedication
dispelled the last of her clinging annoyance. Rather than apologize for her mood and behavior, a gesture that would surely
embarrass them both, she resorted to humor. "Now I've got you
figured out, Tae. If you keep stealing back presents, you can
keep giving the same one to all your friends."

"I'm sorry." Tae's chuckle ruined his apology. "You know I
always planned to return it."

Kevral checked her pockets, ascertaining that the gemstone
eye Tae had given her, and the figurine, remained in place. She
took the book from him, sliding it back into her pack. "All right,
point made. We'll keep avoiding the scum, so long as we're still
headed toward Pudar."

"We are," Tae assured unnecessarily.

The darkness thickened around them, and Kevral's vision
disappeared as the sun fell below the horizon. Until that moment, she had not realized just how much light muddled
through the forest canopy. She shivered beneath inadequate
clothing. "I might have difficulty with eighty-two soldiers.
They'd crush you. If you're going to keep wandering ahead,
we'll have to work out some signals in case you blunder into
trouble."

Blackness swallowed Tae's responding nod. "Let's make
camp. I'm half-starved, and it's getting late."

No suggestion could have pleased Kevral more. She lost control of her jaw to the fluttering need for warmth, and her teeth
made rapid clicking sounds. Nevertheless, she sacrificed desire
for need. "Isn't it safer to travel at night?"

"Not this tired." Tae's voice came from below. Apparently,
he had dismounted. "Nor against this crowd. They're more accustomed to working during the night. Better to find a secure
spot and hole up now."

Kevral clambered from her bay gelding, mourning the fire
they dared not kindle.

"You practice." Tae knew, as did all Kevral's companions,
that nothing could keep her from her evening *svergelse*. "I'll
make camp."

Kevral surrendered her horse to Tae's care, then practiced
sword forms in the close, dark clearing. Exertion chased away
night's chill, and the excitement of a new situation in which to
practice warmed her insides as well. For more than an hour she
capered and slashed among the trunks and vines, while Tae pa-

tiently moved from preparing camp to quietly securing the area from prying eyes and ears. When Kevral finally quit, limbs bathed in a sweat that swiftly grew icy, Tae offered her food and drink. Hunger drove her to bolt it, so it took several moments to realize the randomness of the fare. In the dark, Tae had pulled out whatever fell into easy reach, not bothering to sort a logical and balanced combination. Cold and famished, Kevral did not complain. Exhaustion caught her as the last bit of food passed her lips. She curled up on the ground, huddled into herself, and fell asleep before she thought to close her eyes.

Kevral awakened to the soft warmth of a blanket being drawn into place around her. She snuggled into it, then opened her eyes at the oddity. Moonlight fought through the leaves and branches, managing only a thin glaze barely differentiable from the surrounding darkness. A shadow lay etched against the contrast, barely discernible as human. She grabbed for the other, opposite hand straying naturally to the sword at her side.

Tae instinctively scurried out of reach. "I'm sorry," he whispered. "I didn't mean to wake you."

Kevral smiled, appreciation for the cover's warmth folding into guilt at the realization that Tae had sacrificed his own comfort for hers. She had traveled only in the late spring and summer, and her lighter blanket had served her well. Against autumn night, it proved insubstantial. "No reason you should suffer for my poor packing."

"It's my fault," Tae returned. "I'm the only one with travel experience. I should have helped you pack. I just didn't want to interrupt . . ." He trailed off. His swarthy skin and dark cloak blended into the background, but Kevral still thought she detected a blush. "Ra-khir was helping, and it was the last time he'd see you in a long time."

Kevral nodded, raking short locks back into place with her fingers, then cringing at the massive snarl Tae could never comb out of his own hair. Fatigue still weighted her, but the realization that she had left security fully to Tae niggled at her conscience. Sensing his need for conversation, she sat up and raised a corner of the blanket. "We can share. Two blankets and combined body heat ought to handle the chill." She hooked her pack with a finger and drew it closer. As Tae settled in beside her, she rummaged through her belongings, withdrawing the comb and brush. "If you don't get those knots out, you'll have to cut it all off."

Tae shrugged, drawing his corner of the blankets around him. "Short hair doesn't seem to bother you any."

"But I like yours long." Kevral knelt behind Tae, reorganizing the blankets around them both. She set to work with the comb on a task that seemed hopeless but would keep her busy while they talked. She started at the top where the hair remained silky, enjoying the feel of it through her fingers. A sudden rush of emotion caught her unexpectedly, and all of the love she had shoved aside returned in an instant. Its presence surprised her, leaving a wake of frustration mingled inseparably with relief. She wavered between mourning lost certainty and blessing the moment with Tae that might have saved her from a lifelong mistake.

"It is still you and Ra-khir." Tae spoke casually, but hope tinged his tone.

Kevral avoided a statement rightfully intended as a question. "He asked me to marry him."

"Of course," Tae said, voice still cautiously monotonic. "He'd have to."

Though true, the suggestion seemed unfair. Ra-khir would have proposed regardless of the act that, to his honor-driven mind, made her unweddable by anyone else. She tugged at the tangle, drawing several strands free and working on those until the comb passed easily through them. She pried loose another bunch.

"And you accepted?" Tae guessed.

"No."

"No?" Excitement touched Tae's voice despite his best efforts. "Because of . . . me?" he tried, somehow managing to keep the query modest.

"Because of me." Kevral worked on the newest handful of hair, debris tumbling to the ground behind Tae. Though it needed washing, she liked the satiny softness of his hair and the dusty odor of his scalp. "I know I promised to make a decision when we finished our job, but I've still got Pudar hanging over me. We're going to be separated for a year. That gives us all a chance to work through our feelings, set priorities, grow a little." Kevral bullied through a knot. "Ra-khir needs more experience before he settles on one woman."

Tae loosed a sharp breath, the only sign that he noticed the punishment Kevral inflicted with her comb. "So I'm still a possibility?" He sounded more surprised than hopeful.

Kevral realized now that, in the back of her mind, her indecision had proved the deciding factor in choosing to put off Ra-khir's proposal. All that she had spoken was true. She and Ra-khir, perhaps even Tae, needed more age and experience before making such a commitment. The idea of losing either man rankled, yet she had never expected either to put up with her inability to choose for this long. Time might make the decision for her. She felt unworthy of either man.

Like Ra-khir, Tae did not seem to share her feelings of unfairness and inadequacy. He spun around before the tangle had become halfway handled and caught Kevral into an embrace. He kissed her, dragging her closer, his boldness an invigorating contrast to Ra-khir's strong uncertainty.

This time, Kevral resisted. "Tae, this isn't the time or place." Even she detected the hesitation in her voice. Propriety demanded that she wait until marriage to sleep with either man, yet circumstance had already driven her to both. She had given Ra-khir two chances, and it seemed only fair to allow Tae the same. Besides, his exploring hands excited her wildly. After this time, she would bow to decorum before she started to feel as dirty as proper women would name her. She briefly wondered what Matrinka would think of her lapse and doubted the kindhearted princess would judge.

A moment later, desire consumed Kevral, and she gave herself to Tae in a savage frenzy of ecstasy that left no room for guilt. Then, still warm from lovemaking as exciting as battle, they slept together beneath the blankets.

CHAPTER 20

Lord of Chaos

Law is only the structure.
Chaos is what lives, grows, and evolves.
— Colbey Calistinsson

Darris hunched over his desk in his quarters adjacent to those of Béarn's king, pressed far past exhaustion yet unable to sleep. Griff had insisted on inviting the entire populace to the celebration, on meeting each of his thousands of citizens and listening raptly to their desires and concerns. Darris had advised against the timeless nightmare, suggesting many alternatives that fell by the wayside. The compromise had landed far into the king's favor, as it always must. A court ceremony formalized to tedium by the Knights of Erythane resulted in the naming of King Griff's new ministers, inner guards, and staff. This was followed by an open coronation that stretched Darris' security to its limit and lasted far into the night.

Darris rose, working kinks from his legs, and walked to the room's only window. His feet left indentations in the thick, soft rug. The desk, low bureau with mirror and chair, and the bed remained in the locations he had found them. Rearranging them would leave holes and slashes in the plush carpet where their legs had sat since before his mother's marriage. By convention, the bard lived in these quarters until family needs drove him or her to a cottage on the grounds.

Binding half the curtain aside, Darris leaned against the sill and looked out over Béarn's courtyard. Moonlight glimmered from a pond three stories beneath him. Statues surrounded it, so lifelike he could almost see them moving and hear the splashes of their play. Stone turtles and frogs perched upon granite lily pads. A family of ducks stood, frozen in time, on the bank. The ever-present bear slashed a carved fish from real water. As Darris stared, the image blurred. At first, only the sharp edges of the masons' craft eluded him. Gradually, as he passed from misting to frank tears, the whole became a gray smudge lost in night's darkness. Reuniting with his father, the head pastry chef, had given him a companion to share the depths of grief into which losing his mother had plunged him. Though it still plagued him, time had smoothed the raw edges of his sorrow. Another sadness haunted him now.

With a heavy sigh, Darris left the window. The scene had failed to soothe him, only driving restlessness through him. He paced quietly through the lane between bed and desk, worried about interrupting the king's sleep. This concern, at least, seemed ludicrous. Griff's snores shook the wall, fully audible from the next room, and the clink of mail wafted to him at irregular intervals. If the patrolling guards did not awaken the king, it seemed unlikely that Darris' barefoot ambling could do so. Nevertheless, he kept his step light in contrast to the heavy thoughts that seemed bent on dragging him down.

Béarn's peasants had spoken their minds on many matters, yet the one theme that recurred was the need for Griff to marry swiftly and create as many heirs as possible. Darris understood and even agreed with them, in concept. It was the specifics that rankled. More than one had raised the same idea as several members of the new council, including Prime Minister Davian and Internal Minister Aerean. The populace wanted to assure that future heirs carried enough of the royal bloodline to guarantee their suitability as rulers. They pressed for at least one queen who carried King Kohleran's blood. *They want Matrinka.*

Darris' tears quickened, and a sob racked his body. He had long known this moment would come. The differences in their stations would have forbade them marrying whether or not she ever found another. Years of accustoming himself to it, however, did not make it any easier. His heart felt crushed to powder in his chest, and his head pounded with the enormity of a reality that distant anticipation could never match. When he detached himself from the situation, forcing himself to look upon it as an outsider, he realized Matrinka would make the ideal first queen for Griff. Properly mannered, beautiful, and only a year younger than the king, she suited him admirably. Her knowledge of kingdom functions would serve Griff well.

That logic did little to dispel Darris' discomfort. Sharp agony lanced through him, due either to the depths of sorrow or overwhelming fatigue. Unable to walk another step, he collapsed onto the bed and let the weeping overtake him. Several moments of frenzied tears only intensified the pains in chest and head. He calmed himself with the many positives that would come of such a union: Matrinka would have the best of all possible men, one Darris knew would never harm her. Her offspring would likely sit upon Béarn's throne, her line forever immortalized. And, as the appointed bodyguard to the king, Darris would always remain close to the queens as well.

That last thought managed to soothe where all else had failed. The instant of comfort tore a hole that admitted the tiredness he had, so far, held at bay. Still curled in a fetal position on his bed, Darris fell asleep.

As the first rays of sunlight filtered through his windows, King Griff started awake. Morning confusion left him empty of memory, and he sat up, surveying the room. The familiar furniture of the royal suite filled his vision, and remembrance of the coronation came flooding back in a rush. His crown lay on the bureau nearest his left hand, tossed casually over the fur-trimmed robe he had worn the previous night. He rubbed a hand through his coarse, black curls, scratched at the growing beard that still seemed out of place, and yawned.

For the first time since his arrival in Béarn, the idea of fulfilling the duties of kingship excited Griff. The populace and the new council had given him so many ideas, he could scarcely wait to get started reversing laws and moratoriums placed by the dark elves. Myriad ideas battled for attention at once. Regular walks around Béarn would expose him to the citizenry and their needs. He would create a popular council to inform him of necessities outside the castle. And, of course, his daily court would remain open for anyone to meet with him.

Griff dressed swiftly, excitement driving him like a hot brand. Soon, servants would gather to anticipate his awakening and tend his every desire. He could not wait for them. The hallways of the castle beckoned. He wanted to scurry through them, unhampered and unattended, even by his personal bodyguard. He wanted one chance to negotiate the many hallways, to study the tapestries and murals without the historical detail and understanding Darris' knowledge would add. Like a child of visiting royalty, he wanted to scamper among the animal-shaped torch holders and the strings of hanging jewels without a cautioning parent stumbling after to take the fun from banisters and balconies with warnings about their danger.

The new king bounded into the corridor, full of childish exuberance and knowing his spree would last only until the first guard or servant spotted him and restored the necessary dignity and decorum. He studied the familiar crest that graced his teak door: a rearing golden bear with ruby eyes, hemmed by sapphires. Servants had removed covering tapestries of bears in action to reveal long murals depicting past kings and queens, their most significant actions or decisions permanently captured in paint. Flat, gray rectangles interrupted the intricate artwork, space for future rulers to become immortalized. A half-finished work displayed King Kohleran in his courtroom, the pre-painting etchings suggesting a mass of cheering townsfolk.

Though driven to study the details of the pictures, Griff dashed through the hallway, determined to see as much as possible while he still maintained his short-lived freedom. He laughed at the irony. Scant days ago, he had mourned the loneliness his station created. So much had changed since that time, beginning with Ravn's removal of the dark elves' gift. That action alone had relieved Griff of a magnificent burden. The ardor of the populace seemed delightfully contagious, and he came to recognize how much he could do to assist them. The decisions Darris and the ministers had so far brought him had proved as easily handled as Ravn had promised. Most importantly, the citizens' clamoring for heirs promised him a life with loved ones and, he hoped, several score of children to nurture.

Tapestries and doors whizzed past Griff. He gave them only a passing glance and a promise of future study. He imagined himself dancing with his daughters, their lacy dresses throwing glitters from the torchlight and their laughter belling through the hallways. He twirled and leaped through the corridor, reveling in the future giggles, not caring who witnessed their stout king spinning like a ballerina amid ornate furnishings and flawless artwork.

Griff noticed the elf in the hallway in the instant before he crashed into her. His bulk sent her sprawling. The cup she carried rang against the stonework, and its contents splashed the king's face and tunic. Attempting to decrease the impact, too late, Griff lost his balance, too. He thudded to the ground onto the slender elfin legs, then stared directly into sapphirine eyes that went from startled to frightened in an instant.

Shock held both in silent stillness for far longer than decorum demanded. Fine, gold curls with a touch of elfin red outlined an oval face with high-set cheekbones and heart-shaped lips, then fell to delicate shoulders. Her beauty touched Griff. He felt his heart rate quicken before rationality intervened and forced him to question his sanity. The idea of looking upon an elf as he would a woman seemed madness beyond contemplation, no more logical than considering marriage to a horse or a bear. Only then he realized one more thing. *I must be crushing her!*

Griff lurched to his feet, several apologies rushing to his lips at once and the whole emerging as an incomprehensible series of grunts.

The elf gathered her cup as she executed a mass of disorganized bows and curtsies. "I'm sorry, Sire. I didn't know, Sire. I was just going to . . ." She looked at the liquid splattered across the floor, then followed the cascading droplets to Griff's clothing and face. She drew in a sharp breath. "Oh, my!"

Laughter burst from Griff. He could not possibly have held it back.

The elf looked further dismayed by his reaction. Her eyes swiveled to his, and she must have read a gentleness there. She calmed visibly, her glazed eyes reflecting blue highlights from the torchlight. A high-pitched snort slipped from her lips then, suddenly, she joined his laughter.

The two laughed for an inappropriately long time that seemed perfectly natural to Griff. The liquid from the cup tasted bitter on his lips.

Finally, Griff gained enough control to speak. He drew a handkerchief from his pocket, mopping at the mess now mostly drawn into his beard. "What's your name?"

The elf curtsied again, to Griff's enormous pleasure. He enjoyed watching the fluid, animal grace of her movements. "Tem'aree'ay Donnev'ra Amal-yah Krish-anda Mal-satorian." She flushed, apparently realizing she had given her full name, one too long for most humans to remember. "I'm called Temmy by the humans."

"Temmy," Griff repeated with a frown. It did no justice to the musical syllables she had first uttered. "Would you mind if I called you Tem'aree'ay?" He gave it the same emphasis as she had, pronouncing it Teh-MARR-ee-ay.

Tem'aree'ay curtsied again, this one bringing a smile to Griff's lips. "Majesty, you may call me whatever you wish."

Again, Griff cursed the title that placed obstacles between him and the others of Béarn's keep. "True. But you can still mind."

She smiled. "I don't mind at all. In fact, I prefer it." The elf studied the king, and Griff thought he read pleasure in her strange eyes.

Insanity. Griff shook the assessment away, attributing it to a mood too upbeat to last. Dogs and cats never coupled. Creatures of different species could not find one another attractive. *But they can become friends*. Griff could not explain his attraction to Tem'aree'ay, but he knew he wanted to spend more time with her. "Where were you going so early?"

"Sire, I'm a healer." Tem'aree'ay amended, "Well, I'm trying. I'm not the best yet. I was taking this to a noble with indigestion and . . ."

". . . and . . ." Griff finished, ". . . now we know *I* won't have any difficulty with breakfast."

Tem'aree'ay smiled prettily. "I—I guess I'd better go get more, Sire. I'm terribly sorry."

"Please," Griff returned. "It was entirely my fault."

"True," Tem'aree'ay returned, only a faint smile revealing her sarcasm. "But I'm not allowed to blame the king."

A grin split Griff's face, and his heart seemed to leap in his chest. *Finally, someone willing to treat me as a human rather than a glass ornament—or, maybe, she's treating me like an elf.* He never wanted the playful give-and-take to end.

With a final curtsy, Tem'aree'ay turned and headed back the way she had come.

"Wait!" Griff called.

Tem'aree'ay stopped in her tracks, turning to face him again. Having no idea what to say next, Griff hesitated.

Tem'aree'ay waited patiently, not seeming to notice the inappropriate length of his lapse.

"Maybe we could take a stroll through the gardens later? And talk some more."

"I'd like that, Sire."

Griff wanted to set a time but had no idea when he would be free. Already, he heard approaching footsteps. Their laughter had not gone unnoticed. "I'll send for you when I can."

"I'll look forward to it, Sire." Tem'aree'ay stood in place for a lengthy period, apparently waiting for more words or a dismissal. When none came, she said, "I'll see you then, Sire." Whirling, she headed down the corridor.

Griff watched after her until her slight frame disappeared down the hall. At last, it seemed, he had found a friend.

It took longer than a week for Colbey to find a quiet corner on Asgard and to build himself a comfortable cottage that little resembled the great halls of the gods. He took food, a few articles of clothing, and a blanket in addition to two swords and the Staff of Chaos. His good-byes to Freya and Ravn had proved every bit as difficult as the knowledge that he courted his own destruction. Likely, he would see them again, but he did not trust his own disposition once bound, even minimally, to the Staff of Chaos. For three days, Colbey had spent his excitement amid the *Einherjar*, battling all comers and often two or three at once. Through war, he made his peace with many. During that time, he allowed himself to forget the task that plagued him, promising to take it up again, in earnest, on the fourth day.

That time had come. For hours, Colbey sat beside his cottage on a hill that overlooked much of Asgard. The beauty of the changeless sky thrilled through him. Evergreens bobbed in the gentle breezes, as if bowing to the Lord of Chaos on the hill. Clouds sat like pillows amidst the perfect blue of the sky. As always, he saw his wife's eyes in its color, her hair in the gold of the sun. His life paraded across his thoughts in vivid detail. Every battle against a worthy opponent, he remembered. He recalled the names and weapon competence of his mortality as if no time had passed, though many of the faces blurred. Amid the *Einherjar*, he had reunited with his own *torke*, whose skill he had surpassed even in his mortal years. He found his namesake, the Colbey ahead of him, whom Renshai tenets claimed watched him from Valhalla. Now, the name seemed certain to die with him. As Odin had said, he would never find Valhalla, at least not in the true sense of becoming *Einherjar*.

Colbey took the staff in hand and lowered his head. No presence touched him. Using the meditation techniques strengthened by his previous exercise, he forced down the barriers. Therein lay his greatest power, his chance to forestall the doom carrying the Staff of Chaos would guarantee any other. The Eastern Wizard had never believed Colbey's claim that he did not deliberately place barriers in his mind. For Colbey it took energy to draw his natural shields down while, for others, the difficulty came with the crafting. The discrepancy had arisen from a combination of Renshai mind techniques and millennia of Western Wizards whom he had battled and unwittingly slain. The title had been thrust upon Colbey, without his understanding or consent by a desperate, dying forebear. Colbey had no way to know that becoming a Wizard meant incorporating the thoughts and talents of each of his predecessors. Believing himself mad, he had battled them for years until he had destroyed them.

Colbey deliberately dragged down a barrier, admitting the whisper of chaos that occupied the staff. *Finally, we can become one.*

No, Colbey said. *If you do not content yourself with a partnership, then I will have no choice but to destroy you.*

Anger and disappointment radiated from the staff. It thrust for deeper parts of his mind, foiled by the walls. *You would leave law unopposed.*

Which is the only reason I've agreed to work with you at all. I am your champion, not your slave or a body for you to manipulate. Colbey appreciated that the staff-presence remained too weak to penetrate his defenses, but he did not allow complacence. Already, he could feel its power growing. As it gained might, it could shatter his barriers. These thoughts, however, he did not allow it to share. He turned it only an aura of competence and a mental stance of deadly warning.

We will work better together than at odds.

I agree, Colbey returned. *Respect my boundaries, and I will accept your gifts.*

Frustration plied Colbey, and he could almost follow the staff's direct intentions. It fluttered through an array of tricks, finally settling once more on the truth. *You cannot hold me to promises or details.*

I could. Colbey continued to hide his weaknesses, most of which stemmed from inexperience and ignorance. *But it would cripple you beyond use. I can use your power, but without a wielder, you cannot function at all. Your might may seem to overshadow mine—eventually. But never forget that, without me, you become nothing.*

The frustration remained, now tinted with grudging pleasure.

Believing anticipating the staff's reply might rattle it enough to make it behave, Colbey sent, *You were about to say something similar, weren't you? That I am puny without your power.*

No! it denied, too vehemently. It had no choice but to deny predictability. *Certainly not. I am saying only that for us to function together, you must open your barriers and let me share my power. There is no other way.*

Genius sprang from chaos, never law. Therefore, it surprised Colbey when he found the answer chaos denied. *You're wrong.*

The staff displayed mocking interest.

Open yourself, Colbey suggested. *And let me come to you.*

The Staff of Chaos made no attempt to hide its surprise. *It can't be . . .* The staff paused, rejecting its own statement of impossibility. *It's not done . . .* Shock melted into wild excitement. *No being of law has ever entered chaos' world.*

Colbey shrugged, outwardly trivializing an event that sent his thoughts spinning in crazed spirals and his heart pounding his ribs. *Nothing of law?*

No being of law, The staff amended its terminology. *Small bits of law have penetrated. These become the seeds that spawn demons.*

The revelation caught Colbey off guard, though he hid his amazement behind unbreachable mind walls. Wizard lore had taught him that all creatures of chaos were known as demons. The stuff of disorder could hold no form, so it only made sense that touches of law gave demons their form, however transient and malleable. Colbey returned his attention to the matter at hand. Contemplation would serve little purpose here. He could never predict the primordial chaos. *Open yourself,* he repeated. *And let me come to you.*

As you wish. Guarded curiosity slipped from the staff. It seemed uncertain whether to mourn the proper and conventional binding or to revel in the unconventionality of its new champion. *And, Master?*

Yes, Colbey returned, relieved by the lull in the struggle for control.

You are definitely the one.

Colbey brushed off the compliment. He had chosen a route so unpredictable even chaos had not anticipated him. Therein might lie his only chance to survive the coming holocaust, yet he worried about the price. *Have I already fallen to chaos' influence?* He did the world no good destroying the overwhelming forces of law and chaos if he remained alive to continue inflicting chaos on them. *But my cause is balance.* Colbey shook his head, concerned for the choices he had already contemplated. If chaos bound him too tightly, he could never rescue himself from the clash—nor should he. *Let's go,* he sent to the staff.

Cling tightly, the Staff of Chaos warned. A vortex rose, swirling the air around Colbey in a gray blur that eclipsed his view of Asgard. *This will probably destroy you.*

The winds quickened, their crescendoing roar wiping out even Colbey's ability to mindspeak. Unable to question, he shoved aside the Staff of Chaos' threat. He had spent a lifetime surviving battles even he believed would kill him. Always he gave his all to the war, and always he had triumphed. He had already committed himself to personal destruction. The prospect did not frighten him, nor would he ever prove a willing victim.

The whirlwind grew erratic. The air became alternately cold and tepid, icy and fiery, never at one temperature long enough to do more than register. Flotsam wove through the currents, its flight capricious and lacking logic. Blurry shapes whipped through Colbey's vision in an instant, unidentifiable and replaced, unpredictable moments later, with others. Darkness descended on him, colors knifing patternlessly through the chaos-stuff. Colbey's reason upended. Directions disappeared, and he could not have guessed his position. He lost track of his own limbs, and he seemed to float without form amid thought-provoking emptiness.

A sudden surge of panic stabbed Colbey as his being fragmented toward nothingness. He clung to his thoughts as shards snapped free, drifting. He recognized the stray floating bits now: pieces of himself breaking away from the whole that should not exist in such a place. He concentrated, attempting to draw images of self in his mind, even as memory dispersed and he struggled with an understanding that had once seemed too deeply rooted to dispel. *I am—* The rest would not come. Colbey hurled all that remained toward the central dot that still remained of his focus. *I am . . .* he started again, struggling frantically for comprehension. Other ideas came, celestial concepts of stars as bodies instead of lights, worlds beyond the nine, and diseases controlled by creatures too small for human vision. Fascination gripped him, and the urge to follow revelations once beyond his barest inkling loomed strong. He fought the need with understanding. If he lost self amid the chaos, he would cease to exist.

I am Colbey. Managing the name added enormous power to his efforts. Colbey threw what remained of himself into the task, ignoring all else in chaos' soup. He had lost form, clinging to a last bastion of thought that seemed impossibly small and weak. *Colbey . . . Calistinsson . . . Thorsson.* He clawed frantically for his dispersing parts, dragging back memory of the body. He knew every muscle, every vein, and every tendon in intimate detail; becoming the most competent swordsman he could had depended upon that understanding. Even the clarity to which he had learned himself scarcely proved enough. By the tiniest fragments, his person drew back toward itself, re-forming the familiar body and soul. The effort exhausted him, yet intensity and need drove him beyond fatigue, as it had so many times in the past. He could not afford to lose any battle, this one least of all. He ignored all around him. No danger could surpass the urgency of self-destruction.

Colbey drew more of himself together, and the process grew simpler as he became more practiced. At length, he became whole again, adding only the last, necessary piece: the Staff of Chaos. Finally, he allowed tiredness to touch him, his mind gliding naturally to the vision of a blade. The staff appeared in his hand, though he knew it only by the touch of its contact. To his eyes, it resembled his longsword. Colbey smiled at an irony that did not seem to bother the staff at all.

Once having undergone the reconstruction, Colbey found clinging to his substance simple, no longer requiring the fully-focused attention. More cautiously now, he examined his surroundings. They remained shapeless, formless, and ever-changing. Light and darkness tumbled through one another, like kittens playing. Though oriented to self, Colbey found no similar grounding for anything of chaos. Direction lost meaning, even concepts as basic as up and down. He assigned them randomly, the artificial constructs meaningless yet assisting his bearings.

Demon, the staff sent.

Colbey's vision carved slightly more distinct shadow from a patch of darkness, even as the creature descended upon him. An undefined appendage lashed out, and he met it with a deft stroke of the staff-sword. The blade cleaved the member, and it dispersed into chaos' soup. A stab for the central core met resistance, and the creature dissolved. *Doesn't it know we're on the same side?*

Side? The staff conveyed with a word the absence of the law-based concept of loyalty. It explained further, *Demons evolve from scraps of law that leak into our world. Form is unnatural for chaos, and it resents the intrusion. Always angry and uncomfortable, demons kill anything they find. Unless they're called to law's world, that usually consists only of one another.*

You're a demon, Colbey reminded.

The staff radiated a nonphysical concept strangely similar to a human shrug. *I'm contained chaos with purpose. Call me as* *you will. Demon is a word and words, by definition, are law-constructs.** It broke off to warn, *More demons.**

Colbey's eyes carved three of the creatures from the twinkling, ceaseless background. He charged in with bold exuberance, his war cry shattered to alternately echoing and muffled noise. The staff-sword slashed through semi-substances scarcely differentiable from background. He shattered the first at the farthest extent of sword range. Another impaled itself on Colbey's stop-thrust. The third plowed through, slamming into Colbey with the power of a galloping horse. Colbey collapsed, tumbling through the soup, barely gaining his feet in time to face twenty appendages gouging for him. He hacked at these, severing four in a stroke, then looping back to tear through sixteen more. A final jab dispersed the creature. Shoulder bruised by the impact, Colbey crouched, surveying the area for more. *How many of these are there?**

The Staff of Chaos sent a concept of potential infinity. *The ones deeper have larger amounts of law. Would you like to meet them?**

Nothing could hold Colbey from a challenge. *Yes. But not this time. I'll work my way up, thank you.**

*Strategy.** The staff mumbled the word like a curse. *Logic.**

*I am a creature of law,** Colbey reminded.

*For now.**

Colbey did not argue. The staff had a point. Colbey would need to lead chaos against law, yet he saw no means to organize that which held no loyalty or predictability. The task seemed beyond impossible.

*Demon,** the staff sent again.

Colbey battled the fifth only mindlessly, the ease of the attack not requiring concentration. He definitely faced the weakest of chaos creatures. He recalled his battles with demons on man's world, and much of what he knew found focus. Even the weakest of demons had given him a desperate battle there, strengthened by the very law they claimed to despise. It gave them more intense form, allowed for them to haul their genius into tactic. He remembered, too, stories about the worst of demons, the *kraell* who terrorized their own kind. He had killed one once and nearly lost the war himself, his facial scar a reminder of that conflict. If he faced them in their own world, he might find them easier to beat. And while his sense of fairness and his joy of battle drove him to fight them at their strongest, the situation called for the opposite. He had not yet bonded with chaos enough to place all of lawkind into danger for his own pleasure.

Let's take a walk, Colbey suggested.

A walk?

An amble. Whatever you do here. I need to survey my kingdom.

Your kingdom? A liberal dose of mockery suffused the staff's words, though Colbey meant nothing funny.

He kept the last thought to himself, *Who would have believed an ancient prophecy so literal? Perhaps I must truly become the Golden Prince of Demons*. For once, the title did not seem insult.

CHAPTER 21

Love's Hold

If you strive for personal skill, you do not need praise.
You can rely on self and sword alone.

—Colbey Calistinsson

The odor of mulching leaves, the splash of air against Ra-khir's hot face, and the powerful surge of the horse beneath him brought fond memories flooding back. He crouched over his gray's neck, pike clutched in his fist, eyes locked on the ring dangling from the wooden stand. He sighted along the straight, heavy pole, the bobbing of its tip no longer a distraction. He had learned to anticipate, and naturally correct for, the bounce of the horse's hooves, to remain steady in the saddle, and to ignore the tickle of sweat beneath armor and padding. What had once seemed like too little time to properly aim had become comfortably workable. He drove the tip of the pike home. The ring jerked free, rattling down the blue- and gold-striped shaft.

"Yes," Ra-khir whispered his triumph only to himself, allowing no trace of pride to enter his demeanor. He listened for Armsman Edwin's reaction, having grown accustomed to his teacher's patterns. A smile conveyed approval, a single clap more, and a double clap revealed Edwin's delight. He slowed his mount to a trot, reined it in a half-circle, and headed back toward his peers.

Hearty applause filled Ra-khir's ears, and he suppressed a grin. He had heard Edwin give a series of claps for complicated maneuvers expertly performed, but he and his apprentice peers had never earned such enthusiasm before. He raised his head, only then realizing the sound came from his right, not ahead. He glanced to the rail to find half a dozen adolescent girls perched there, all cheering his success. Two young boys sat quietly nearby.

Neither sight seemed unusual. Erythanian boys often gathered to watch the knights work, emulating their honor and prancing about as if to copy their swordplay. Before Ra-khir had joined the search for Griff, he had grown accustomed to young women watching him work. The apprentices had practiced since first light, and he had not noticed spectators gathering, so intent was he on capturing the ring.

The sideways look proved Ra-khir's undoing. His horse shied from something in its path, and the sudden movement, though not broad, claimed his balance. Ra-khir tumbled from the saddle. He struck the ground an instant later, pain thudding through his hip and breath momentarily dashed from his lungs. He gasped once, then his diaphragm reexpanded and he normalized his breathing. The gray stood beside him, nuzzling his armor as if to ask how his rider got all the way down there.

Stupid. Ra-khir had remained seated through bucking and through simulated combat and could scarcely imagine how such a minor movement could have unhorsed him. He climbed back into the saddle, as gracefully as the armor allowed, and settled back into place. The second smattering of applause from his makeshift audience flushed his cheeks. Riding back to the armsman, he dismounted and executed as formal and respectful a bow as the armor allowed. Mud spattered his helm and face.

Armsman Edwin met Ra-khir with raised brows and a tolerant expression. The hard brown eyes studied the apprentice from beneath a perfectly straight fringe of sandy bangs. Pursed, his bountiful lips appeared enormous, and his cheekbones tightened to the point of gauntness. With slow deliberateness, he raised both hands, then placed the palms soundlessly together. "You would have earned a real one had you not paused to admire your audience."

Ra-khir lowered his head sheepishly and hoped the helmet kept his face in shadow. He felt as if his cheeks had caught fire. His classmates honored their teacher too much to laugh, but Ra-khir knew he would pay for his lapse with merciless teasing later.

Edwin let Ra-khir off the hook, turning his attention to the next student in line while the one after set another ring in reasonably proper position. Ra-khir handed his trophy to the fourth knight-in-training, meeting mischievous blue eyes that revealed pestering thoughts taking place behind them. The youngster winked, and Ra-khir managed a strained smile before retiring to the end of the line. The idea of his companions' good-natured ribbing did not bother him; their games had become tiresome. Before he had left on his mission, he had joined their boisterous fun. Though it skirted the ponderous lectures on honor, the knights overlooked the apprentices' horseplay and practical jokes, so long as they remained harmless and only among one another. Though two of Ra-khir's six peers were the same boys he had wrestled and taunted in his own time, he no longer felt comfortable among them. Their antics seemed childish, and only the lessons of the armsman and the other knights felt right.

The apprentices rode through the ring exercise three more times, and only Ra-khir skewered every one, managing to earn a double clap. As the morning practice drew to a close, Ra-khir held the day's record with seven successes and two misses, his closest competitor succeeding at only five and two never catching a ring. Though pleased, Ra-khir said nothing, refusing to gloat. His honor would not allow it, even in playful jest.

"That's all for the day," Edwin announced as the last apprentice returned to the group. "Tomorrow: free-form sword." He gave Ra-khir a humbling look, a reminder that, for all his accomplishment with pike, sword was his weakest skill.

Ra-khir said nothing. Though bound from teaching Renshai maneuvers, Kevral had still given him many lessons, intentionally and otherwise. Some might go against the knight's regular training, but that would not matter. So long as he did not violate the honor, free-form competition left him leeway.

Sir Edwin mounted his muscled, white charger, the blue and gold ribbons spotless in its mane. "Until tomorrow, knights-in-training."

"Until tomorrow, Armsman," the seven called back in unison.

Sir Edwin rode from the practice grounds, and Ra-khir watched the haughty stallion and his tall rider until they disappeared over the crest of a hill.

By the time Ra-khir turned back, the youngest of the group, a quiet boy of sixteen, had headed to gather his gear. The way the others hung back cued Ra-khir to a prank. With a deep sigh, he followed the youngest toward the piled pikes. The sixteen-year-old reached them first, pulling his own from amidst the others. The mound shifted. As his point came free, something moved. Anticipating a joke, Ra-khir only stiffened. The boy caught a corner of the eye glimpse of the dead rooster one of the others had slipped over the tip of his weapon. Startled, he gasped, prancing backward, and tripped over the shaft of his pike. He tumbled to the ground, rolling and glancing behind him simultaneously.

The other apprentices burst into laughter, and even some of the girls watching snickered.

The sixteen-year-old recovered control, shaking the chicken from his pike. "Oh, real funny."

The others continued laughing as they finished the practice field cleanup, packing away personal and shared gear. Ra-khir worked methodically, intentionally slow. As the others departed, in singles and groups, he remained behind to practice. With his father in Béarn and his mother unwilling to see him, he felt in no particular hurry to return to Kedrin's empty cottage. Danger had kept him close to Kevral, Tae, Darris, and Matrinka day and night for months. Now he suffered a hollow feeling far beyond the hunger pangs that came of a small, hurried breakfast and skipping lunch.

Ra-khir stripped to his padding, wiping sweat and mud from the pieces of his armor before placing them carefully in his pack. After an especially grueling workout, the apprentices would sometimes disrobe to undergarments or nakedness on their practice field, but spectators removed this option. Instead, he took his time, hoping the tedium of watching a man clean and arrange pieces of leather and metal would bore any remaining outsiders into leaving. Under other circumstances, he might have given the young boys the thrill of learning a few moves from a real apprentice knight. But tonight he had neither the emotional nor physical energy to do so.

Only after Ra-khir had packed all of his equipment and freed his sword from the bundle did he bother to glance around again. His horse grazed the field, white mane trickling down its gray neck. The sun sank toward the western horizon, trailing multicolored arches that merged into a solid pink above him. Three girls remained near the wooden rail that surrounded the knight's practice field. They studied him, exchanging whispers. One tossed back a cascade of dark hair and struck a seductive pose: back arched and one leg raised.

Ra-khir acknowledged them with a patient nod, then launched into a sword practice with the dedication of Kevral to nightly *svergelse*. He lost himself in the breeze of the sword passing around him, letting the advice of armsman, father, and Renshai fill his mind. The field seemed to disappear, leaving only himself, his sword, and the grass beneath his feet. As he repeated a sequence Edwin had taught, his thoughts slipped to golden images of Kevral. He could never match her grace, but he could not help picturing her mired in a deadly dance with her blades skipping around her. For several moments, the image brought him peace. Hunger and fatigue finally caught up with him, and he reluctantly ended the session.

Panting and sweating, he longed for the clean clothes still snug in his pack. He looked up. The sun had slid far enough to dull the sky to pewter. The three young women had drawn nearer, still watching him. Ra-khir closed his eyes, bracing himself for the politeness the situation demanded yet wishing they would leave him alone.

They nudged one another. The one he had noticed previously approached, again tossing back waist-length hair. Pursing her lips as if to kiss the air, she looked at him sidelong and shook her hair again. "Hello, Ra-khir," she said.

Ra-khir removed a lightly-oiled rag from his pocket and cleaned his sword, though the dryness of the day and lack of a target made the job mostly unnecessary. A bead of sweat from his hand had dribbled past the crossguard. "Hello," he replied properly. He continued working, turning her enough attention to fulfill propriety without demonstrating false interest.

"Don't you remember me, Ra-khir?"

Ra-khir did not, but the question forced him to examine her a bit more closely. She sported the plump curves that denoted beauty in the West and breasts large beyond proportion. The green-brown eyes and features did not spark more than superficial memory. He believed he had seen her before, but her name escaped him. "I'm sorry. I don't," he admitted.

She tossed back her hair again, shaking her head so that the silky strands slid across one another. "Asha. We've met once or twice here before."

Ra-khir nodded to acknowledge her explanation. He rarely recalled spectators, never paid them much attention. Kevral had proved a remarkable exception, though he had, at first, mistaken her for a boy. She had not come to watch him, rather to belittle him. Their relationship had, thankfully, come a long way since that time.

"Do you like what you see?"

The question confused Ra-khir. "Excuse me?"

"Do you like what you see?" Asha repeated, this time outlining herself with a gesture.

"You mean *you?*"

Asha giggled. "Yes."

Ra-khir froze, trapped by his honor. "I don't know you well enough to know. I don't *dis*like you." Ra-khir had the distinct feeling he had not answered the proper question, but this seemed like a strange situation for riddles.

One of the other girls cleared her throat. Asha glanced at them, then turned with obvious reluctance. She headed back over, walking with a pronounced wiggle that Ra-khir noticed only from a momentary glance. As soon as she seemed finished conversing, he stuffed his sword into his pack with the intention of making a graceful retreat. But even as he hefted the pack and headed for his horse, another of the girls approached him. Black hair, with just a hint of curl fell to her shoulders, and large brown eyes peered out from a round face. A bit thinner and less endowed than her companion, she approached him with obvious hesitation. "Hello," she said.

This time, Ra-khir just nodded a polite greeting, wondering if he would have to carry on trivial conversations with each in turn.

"My name is Carlynn. You were great out there." She gestured vaguely toward the field.

"Great?" Ra-khir repeated carefully, uncertain of the topic.

"Spearing those rings." Carlynn stabbed at the air with a simulated pike. "You did great. Best one out there."

"Thank you," Ra-khir returned, trying to keep his reply simple so as neither to disparage nor display too much pride in his accomplishment or her compliment.

Carlynn scratched at her shoulder, a gesture that seemed nervous. "I noticed you didn't leave for the midday meal like the others."

Ra-khir had no wish to detail his social situation. "I wasn't hungry."

"You must be starved now." Carlynn sounded genuinely worried for him. "A big man like you missing a meal and waiting so long for the next one." She touched the padding on his forearm. "Do you have someone to make you supper?"

Ra-khir shrugged. "I'll just head down to the Knight's Rest and get something there." Talking about food reminded him of his empty stomach, and it rumbled audibly.

"That sounds good," Carlynn said.

Ra-khir whistled for his mount. The gray head rose, and it paused momentarily, as if deciding whether it wanted grass or to obey its master more. Resignedly, it walked toward him, stopping only once for another mouthful. Ra-khir cursed himself for not bringing a carrot. Treats reminded the animal why it enjoyed coming to his call.

"Well," Carlynn said glancing toward her companions. "I guess I should head home."

Relieved for his solitude, Ra-khir finally fully joined the conversation. It was not so much that he enjoyed being alone as that he wanted loved ones, not strangers, with him. "That seems prudent. Your mother's probably got your supper on the table and is wondering about you."

"No." Carlynn lowered and shook her head. "My mother serves at the Knight's Rest. She won't get home till late, and she brings supper then. Her share of what's left. Most times it's enough to feed me and my brothers and sisters all right."

Ra-khir stifled a wince, knowing what had to come next. He had planned to eat alone, nursing his food and his thoughts, concentrating on his training to alleviate the pain in his heart. Yet he would not allow this woman to go hungry. She seemed far more pleasant company than her friend. An evening of conversation might distract him from brooding, and he had promised Kevral to see other women. "Why don't you eat with me? Your mother will be there to see you're not lost, and it'll save her a mouth to feed."

Carlynn smiled, pretty in the twilight, though Ra-khir felt no particular attraction to her. "I'd like that very much. Thank you."

"If you and your friends could just give me a moment of privacy to change, you won't have to endure the stench of my sweaty body all through the meal."

Carlynn laughed, the sound a bit throatier than her companion's giggle, yet still coquettish.

Ra-khir worried for his manhood that he found the sound silly rather than alluring. That concern, and his previous memory raised other doubts. He had never considered the significance of falling in love with a woman he had once mistaken for a boy. *Am I crazy?* His two nights with Kevral told him otherwise. Her femininity excited him wildly. It was Kevral he loved, not her appearance; and he found other village girls shallow because he could not help but compare them to her.

Carlynn dashed back to the others with unbridled excitement, and Ra-khir pulled fresh clothing from his pack. Hiding behind the horse, he peeled off clinging padding, replacing it with a clean tunic and breeks. He longed for a bath, too; but that would have to wait. By the time he finished, Carlynn waited alone.

"Ready?" Ra-khir steered his horse around Carlynn, taking a position between it and her.

Carlynn placed a small hand on his arm. "Ready."

They headed for the Knight's Rest Tavern, Carlynn clinging to Ra-khir. Feeling like the object of a contest, Carlynn's living trophy, Ra-khir walked quietly in the moonlight and wished he was with Kevral.

The Knight's Rest Tavern had existed for centuries, its location, size, and proprietorship changing nearly every generation. The name and reputation, however, never seemed to change. It catered to the knights, its higher prices discouraging the usual lot of revelers and brawlers. Locals worried for their purses or persons tended to come here, willing to pay extra for the security; and visitors from other parts of the West chose it to catch a glimpse of or conversation with the legendary Knights of Erythane.

Carlynn ate with a dainty slowness. In contrast, Ra-khir seemed to bolt his food, though he made every effort to painstakingly chew and swallow. With each careful portion, he fought the hunger goading him; and, gradually, his stomach calmed enough to relieve him of the burden of concentrating on eating. Manners came naturally, from years of training. Sluggishness did not.

Shallow small talk and the need to watch the speed of eating did distract Ra-khir from his loneliness, though it did not draw him closer to his dinner companion. Carlynn's mother had clucked and cooed over him like a farmer acquiring a prize bull, and she slipped them special extras and the finest portions. The treatment made Ra-khir uncomfortable. He did not have enough money to cover what she gave him, but chivalry obligated him to pay. He saw no choice but to give her all the silver his father had left him and spend the next two days until Kedrin's return scrounging what he could from their meager larder.

The night wore on, the inn windows blackening as if painted. Restlessness assailed Ra-khir, but politeness kept him still in his seat, nursing his third mug of watered fruit juice. The splash of ale that purified the water added a bitter aftertaste he had scarcely noticed after the first two helpings. Now it kept him drinking at Carlynn's snail's pace. He had exhausted every strategy for keeping his attention on the woman and her superficial conversation. He wanted nothing more than to return to his father's empty cottage and sleep.

At irregular intervals, the door to the Knight's Rest opened, flashing bars of moonlight across the interior. Most of the patrons glanced at every newcomer, but Ra-khir properly kept his gaze on his own companion. He sensed a presence at his back only a moment before his father's familiar voice boomed out a welcome. "Ah. Here you are, Ra-khir."

Ra-khir stiffened, then whirled, an enormous grin appearing suddenly on his face. Kedrin stood beside his son's chair, the red-blond hair meticulous, the green eyes shining, and every fold of his clothing in perfect order. He sported a blue and black shirt with orange at the cuffs and a pair of tan britches, a jaunty combination of the Erythanian and Béarnian colors that knights always wore. "Papa!" In his excitement, Ra-khir used the child's term rather than his usual respectful "Father." Leaping from his seat, he hastily executed the proper gesture of regard before enveloping Kedrin in an excited embrace.

The greeting lasted only moments, as politeness demanded introductions. "Carlynn Diega's daughter, my father Knight-Captain Kedrin Ramytan's son."

"Pleased to meet you," Carlynn said.

"My pleasure completely." Kedrin bowed, as if to nobility, and Carlynn averted her eyes with a flirtatious smile. As the woman looked away, Kedrin immediately turned his attention to his son. "We'll talk when you're finished here."

Ra-khir found the notion of waiting even a moment a torture. His father's early return might herald a tragedy in Béarn, but that worry scarcely diminished the excitement of Kedrin's arrival. "We're finishing now." He inclined his head toward the woman. "Carlynn, would you like anything more?"

Decorum decreed Carlynn decline. Coyly, she peeped around her black hair, then gradually restored her gaze to Ra-khir. She studied him fondly, with the shining attentiveness of a lover. "Another fruit juice would be nice. And I hoped you would walk me home."

Ra-khir felt horse-kicked. He nodded once, revealing nothing of his disappointment. "As you wish." He turned Kedrin an apologetic look. "I'll meet you at home?"

Kedrin returned a stiff confirmation. "I'll wait for you there."

Ra-khir wrestled impatience as Carlynn drank her juice, conversation a burden as his thoughts slipped repeatedly back to his father. Carlynn's words drifted past him mostly unheard, despite his best attempts to concentrate. Always, he caught enough of her words to reply, though he raised no topics of his own. The drink seemed to take an eternity to disappear, and the hovering of Carlynn's mother grew from interested concern to a bother. Still, Ra-khir held his tongue and clung to his mannered upbringing.

At last, Carlynn finished and grinned at Ra-khir as if they shared some deep and special secret. "I'm ready to go home now."

Ra-khir scrambled to his feet before he could think to try to make the gesture appear less joyful. Carlynn did not seem to notice or, perhaps, she interpreted his swiftness more to the anticipation of walking together in the dark, quiet streets. She slipped past him, toward the central portion of the inn leaving Ra-khir to empty his pockets of coinage on the table.

Ra-khir caught up with Carlynn and ushered her from the common room into the cool night air. She shivered at his touch, though he had placed his hand on her back only to hasten her. She leaned against him, snuggling into his armpit, and it seemed rude to move away. With a deep sigh that he hid from Carlynn, Ra-khir left his arm around her, using it to propel them a bit more swiftly than Carlynn's ambling gait would otherwise allow. To his relief, she remained mostly silent now, although she glanced repeatedly at him; and, when he looked back, he caught the edges of moon-eyed stares before she glanced away.

The walk seemed unbearably long to Ra-khir, and he felt like an only child trapped for hours at an adults' feast. Though he responded to Carlynn's occasional comment, the words seemed not to relate to him, as if another controlled his mouth and Carlynn chatted with this stranger. At length, he reached her family's cottage. Red light glowed in the largest window, a reflection of the fire beyond where father and siblings gathered. Born and raised in Erythane, Ra-khir realized she had taken him far out of his way to reach this place. A more direct route would have sufficed.

Ra-khir removed his arm and stepped back. "Good night."

Carlynn batted her eyes and gave him a look as innocent as a newborn foal's. "Surely, you'll come in and meet my family."

Ra-khir fought annoyance, worried that Carlynn might find a way to keep him indefinitely. Chivalry tore him in two directions: he should accept her invitation because she wished him to do so, yet remaining with her too long might imply that he wanted them to become a couple. Raising an expectation he had no intention of fulfilling seemed at least as bad as refusing. He considered his wording several moments so as not to offend. "Thank you, Carlynn, but no. I haven't seen my father in more than a week, and I really should get home."

"It won't take long," Carlynn promised.

So far, everything with Carlynn had consumed far too much time. "I'm sorry." Ra-khir remained polite but adamant. "Thank you, but I have to get home."

Carlynn shifted toward Ra-khir, near enough for him to smell the mixture of perfume, dinner, and her own defining scent. "I'll see you again?"

His social area violated, Ra-khir retreated slightly, shifting as if by accident. "You know where to find me," he said, hoping it would do. He had no intention of wasting another evening on tiresome, meaningless conversation and kittenish games.

Carlynn took another step toward him, which more than regained her the closeness his movement had lost. "You may kiss me."

The words, and Carlynn's closeness, brought a hot flash of animal desire that Ra-khir would never have known to feel before his night with Kevral. Humiliated by his body's betrayal, he recoiled with more abruptness than proper. "Carlynn, no. That wouldn't be a good thing."

"Oh," Carlynn said, disappointment clearly etched on cheeks just starting to tinge red. "I'm sorry. I didn't mean to push. I'm really sorry. I really am. I just didn't think . . ." She broke off, clearly stammering, and her discomfort sent a jolt of guilt through Ra-khir. He had not intended to embarrass her. "Please don't hate me."

"Of course I don't hate you," Ra-khir soothed, wishing for more to say yet afraid to stir false hope. He now knew for certain that she wanted him to love her, and he also felt sure he never could. An image of Kevral came instantly to mind, her childlike blue eyes filled with all the wonder of the universe, her short locks so unlike what he had once considered beauty now defining it, and her curveless muscled figure now the odd epitome of femininity. Most men would find Carlynn by far the prettier of the two, but he had fallen desperately in love with Kevral's wit and strength. Once, he had disliked the Renshai, too, and he had learned that his feelings could change. Yet he still could not imagine the explosion of passion and dedication he knew for Kevral roused by any other. "Please, go inside, and don't worry about it any more."

"Thank you." Carlynn managed a thin smile. "Thank you for everything, Ra-khir." She trotted toward the cottage, the curls at the ends of her hair bouncing with every movement.

"You're welcome," Ra-khir returned automatically, watching Carlynn only until the door yielded to her touch. He caught a glimpse of her whirling, kissing her palm, then waving before his own natural turn took woman and cottage from his sight.

Ra-khir loosed a pent-up breath. As he negotiated the shortest distance back to his father's home, a gentle chuckle escaped him. What most men considered a treat had become a tedious chore to him, and the thought seemed utter madness. *I'm relieved because I'm done spending the evening with a beautiful young woman who cares about me.* He did not dare to contemplate the implications too long. The answer came to him in a word: Kevral. No other woman could measure up to the one he loved.

The stroll through cobbled streets on a crisp, moonlit night now seemed the pleasure he had denied moments ago. He enjoyed the time with his thoughts and the thrill that rolled through him in waves at the anticipation of seeing his father. He felt like a homesick child, too old to pine for a parent. He had missed this excitement in childhood. His mother had always seemed angry, her beautiful features pinched by bitterness and her figure becoming more drawn with time. Though calmer, his stepfather, Khirwith, had always seemed trivial, his interests juvenile even to the child he was raising. Ra-khir recalled finding pleasure in the walk rather than the destination back then, and only after he discovered Kedrin three years ago had the source of joy changed.

These thoughts brought Ra-khir to the inn for his horse and gear, then home. He recognized the rosy glow of a fire through every window, and his father's shadow filled his vision at intervals. The pattern of movement suggested cleaning, but Ra-khir now knew his father well enough to recognize restlessness. Ra-khir had kept things in their places, leaving little to straighten. The motions allowed his father's hands and legs to work in more constructive ways than pacing.

Ra-khir stripped pack, saddle, and bridle from his horse and set them on the ground. Seizing a currycomb, brush, and hoof pick from hooks on the side of the cottage, he gave the animal a thorough grooming before loosing it into the paddock with his father's white stallion. Hefting his things, and the horse's, he opened the door to reveal the familiar main room of the cottage.

A wooden bench spanned the area in front of a roaring fire, and a mantle over it supported assorted bric-a-brac that ranged from a dented buckler that had saved Kedrin's life in battle to a mis-shapen wooden hawk he had carved for Ra-khir's mother that she had later hurled at him in rage. Kedrin stood near the pantry entrance, straightening a portrait of Ra-khir as a child. He spun toward the door as it creaked open and smiled a warm greeting.

"I'm sorry I took so long," Ra-khir said, closing the door with his foot, then arranging the tack on one end of the bench. He hauled his pack into his bedroom and left it on the floor near his mattress. He would need it for practice in the morning.

"No need to apologize," Kedrin's voice wafted from the main room, growing louder as he approached. "I didn't mean to interrupt. When I didn't find you here and it got late, I worried that—" He broke off suddenly, amending, "I worried."

Ra-khir finished the thought with ease. *Worried that I went back to Mother.* He did not voice his understanding. It would slam Kedrin's honor to point out his mistake, fretting for a situation he had given Ra-khir his blessing to return to. His mother had spoken the ultimatum that Ra-khir could associate with her or Kedrin, never both. Unless and until she lifted that demand, even loneliness could never drive Ra-khir back to her. Kedrin's love, he knew, bore no conditions. Ra-khir looked up to find his father watching him from the doorway. He headed toward the opening.

Kedrin stepped back to allow Ra-khir into the main room again. "Did you enjoy your evening with Carlynn?"

"No," Ra-khir admitted, returning to the bench. "I mostly found it boring. And I spent months with Béarn's bard."

Kedrin pulled leather soap, oil of cloves, and rags from beneath the bench, then sat. He left space for Ra-khir between himself and the tack. "I'm sorry to hear that."

Ra-khir shrugged. "One more life experience." He forced a smile. "If I don't suffer boredom, how can I appreciate fun?"

Kedrin nodded, passing a rag to Ra-khir and placing the cleaners between them. "Very profound for a seventeen-year-old." He gestured for Ra-khir to pass him some tack.

Ra-khir took the rag and gave over the bridle, keeping the saddle for himself. He appreciated his father's assistance but would never think to take advantage of it. "Thank you." He did not direct the gratitude toward words or deed. He appreciated both. "I didn't expect you for two more days." He probed for information without forcing the issue with a question. Realizing he needed to say one thing more, he added. "I'm glad you're back, of course. I just wondered why. I hope there's nothing wrong in Béarn."

"Wrong?" Kedrin grinned, coating his rag with soap and rubbing the bridle straps vigorously. "King Griff has handled court affairs as if born to rule Béarn."

"Which he was," Ra-khir could not help adding.

Kedrin's laugh sounded richly deep, and Ra-khir knew a moment of pleasure at eliciting mirth from his usually stoic father. "True enough. He's frighteningly naive, but that's always been the case for Béarn's kings. His judgments are sound, and the people love him already."

Ra-khir grinned with such raw joy he could not speak for several moments. He scooped a dollop of soap onto his rag and dragged the saddle into his lap.

Kedrin continued, "Things are well under control in Béarn. I thought you needed me more." He added, "Not that I didn't trust you by yourself."

Ra-khir sought phrases to tell his father how much he missed him without sounding desperately needy. "I lost a childhood with my father. I want as much time together as I can get, but I understand your responsibilities. In fact, I've taken them on myself."

"How *is* your training going?" Kedrin asked casually, though Ra-khir knew the answer meant nearly as much to him as the proper rulership of Béarn.

"Reasonably well, I believe." Modestly, Ra-khir did not mention his successes at the ring joust. "Sir Edwin would be a better judge."

"And you know I'll ask him."

"Of course." Ra-khir smiled, but he did not look up from his work on the saddle. Thoughts of his days on the field wilted the grin, and he asked a question plaguing him almost since his return to Erythane. "Father, when you did your training, did your fellows play tricks on one another?"

"Oh, yes." Kedrin let the soap soak into the leather and switched to the other end of his rag to work on the buckles and fittings. "Especially Edwin."

Ra-khir jerked, startled to incredulity. "*Armsman* Edwin?" He could imagine no one more sober and straightlaced than his teacher.

"*Now* Armsman Edwin," Kedrin confirmed.

"You?"

Kedrin shrugged, though the hint of smile escaping his pursed lips told more. "Me, too. I had my moments."

Ra-khir sat in silence, managing nothing more significant than blinking for several moments. Finally, he returned to his work.

Kedrin did not allow the matter to drop. "Are you asking because you've gotten into trouble for pranks or because you're the butt of them?"

"Neither," Ra-khir said. "I just don't find them funny anymore."

"That's because you've gone to war."

Ra-khir assumed Kedrin referred to the battles he had fought restoring Griff to his throne, but understanding proved insufficient. "What do you mean?"

"Once a boy has placed his life, and those of his friends, at risk, he becomes a man whether or not he's come of age." Kedrin swiped at a decoration on the bridle. "We consider barbaric the ancient Renshai custom of calling a man or woman adult immediately after his first kill, whether at two or fifty. Yet that feels much more natural to me than choosing an arbitrary age. No question, once a warrior participates in war, the day-to-day annoyances become impossibly petty."

Ra-khir looked to his father with a warm pride nothing could dispel. He had captured the feeling exactly. "That's it. That's how I feel."

"You're not alone, Ra-khir."

"I am among my peers." Ra-khir glanced at his father, busily cleaning the bridle, then back at his own handiwork.

Kedrin made a wordless noise of concession, and Ra-khir appreciated that he did not make suggestions for how to cope with or change the situation. Ra-khir would have to discover the strategies that worked best for him.

They worked in quiet for several moments, the warmth of the fire and its changing pattern of intensity and color a welcome contrast to the streets. The night could have lasted an eternity with little complaint from Ra-khir. At length, however, he broke the silence. "How did you and Mother come together?"

Kedrin winced so slightly Ra-khir wondered if he imagined it. The knight-captain set aside the horse's bridle, hanging it from the edge of the bench before addressing the question. "She used to come and watch me practice."

Now Ra-khir flinched, struck by the similarity between

Kedrin's description and his evening with Carlynn. "Then what happened?"

Kedrin wiped soap and oil from his hands with the cloth. "The usual. We started doing things together. Fell in love. Married." He turned Ra-khir a sidelong look clearly intended to remind his son that he did not feel comfortable with the topic.

Ra-khir stuck with the early details, before the separation that ruined three lives. "Why her? Was she the only one who watched you practice?"

Kedrin rocked back, eyes rolling upward as if to capture the memory directly. "Ra-khir, people waste a lot of time wishing they looked handsome or chasing those who do." He drew in a breath and loosed it slowly, weighing words to make a point without vanity or false modesty. "I was as guilty of it as anyone. Your mother was a beautiful woman. Still is." He returned to the point. "Looks are nice, if you have them, but they cause no end of trouble, too. An attractive man, like one with power or money, never knows people's motives toward him. If he has more than one . . ." Kedrin shook his head, trailing off, mouth twisted into a grimace of frustration. "I'm not putting this well."

Ra-khir understood. Like himself, his father had always been a handsome man. Their appearances would always draw more than their share of attention, and this could prove bad or good. "I understand."

Kedrin seemed relieved by the chance to abandon a subject that made him uncomfortable. He had never spoken of his comeliness, or Ra-khir's. "Getting back to your question, your mother was only one of many women who came to the practices. But she was the most persistent and, gods take me for caring, the most beautiful. We married too young and for the wrong reasons."

Ra-khir nodded, pensive.

"Don't let my mistake stop you from getting married," Kedrin chimed back in swiftly. "Just be more careful. And wait till you're ready."

Ra-khir closed his eyes, preparing for the explanation that had to follow.

Kedrin picked up immediately on his son's dismay. "What's wrong?"

"When Kevral and I were prisoners of the elves and believed we would soon die . . ."

"Yes."

"We didn't want to die without . . ." Ra-khir flushed, cursing the stammering that suddenly plagued him. "Without . . . you know. Knowing what it was like. To do . . . what men and women do."

"Oh," Kedrin said.

Ra-khir dared to peek at his father, unable to gauge reaction from tone alone. "I have to marry her now."

Kedrin's features revealed nothing more than his voice had.

"Right?" Ra-khir needed a response.

"Of course." Kedrin's features creased with worry, and he set aside the cleaning supplies to move closer on the bench. "I'm sorry, Ra-khir. You made a mistake. We'll have to make the best of it."

Ra-khir felt it essential to correct the misconception. "Immoral, perhaps, Father, but no mistake. I proposed months before. I *want* to marry Kevral. I've never wanted anything more."

Kedrin blinked, saying nothing. His brow furrowed. "Kevral?"

Ra-khir nodded vigorously.

"The Renshai?"

Another nod.

"The one who insulted your honor, who you believed deliberately and repeatedly undermined you in front of your friends?"

Ra-khir grinned. It seemed so long ago. "Who could have foreseen that?"

"You love her?"

Ra-khir did not hesitate. "Absolutely."

"You want to spend your entire life with her? To share all that either of you are or will be?"

"Without reservation."

Kedrin fell silent, rocking slightly in place. "You want to raise children together?"

Ra-khir's cheeks warmed. "Eventually."

"Eventually?"

"I'm seventeen," Ra-khir reminded. "I'm not ready for fatherhood yet." His own childhood flashed before him in an instant, wound through with the bitterness of his mother's lies. When the time came, he would work at parenting with the same dedication as his honor. He would first master his father's gentle patience, experience, and knowledge.

Kedrin placed an arm across his son's shoulders. "Ra-khir,

either Khirwith or I was remiss. Surely you know that if you do 'the thing men and women do together,' you will become a father."

Ra-khir stiffened, shocked to discover he had never considered such a possibility. Denial, not stupidity or ignorance, had separated sex and conception in his mind. He had known the truth of Kedrin's statement, yet his mind rejected the association until that moment. Terror formed a lump in his throat and his voice emerged thinly. "The first time?"

Kedrin shrugged. "Not likely, but it happens. And the chances increase the more times you get together. Healers pronounce families who couple for four months without creating a child unlikely to ever do so."

Thoughts swirled through Ra-khir's mind, all centered on the certainty that no infant would grow from their two unions. So many things made it unlikely: stress, their youth, Kevral's physical immaturity. Kevral's wild practices seemed hostile to a tiny, fragile life. A part of him felt certain that coupling without the intention of conceiving would prevent it from happening, magical thinking contradicted by fact. Tae and Matrinka had read the sage's notes as they pertained to Griff's parents. His father, Petrostan, Kohleran's youngest, had impregnated a cousin before either turned fourteen. At an age when they understood nothing of making babies, they had done so and gotten themselves banished for the error.

Apparently reading his son's agitation, Kedrin eased away from the topic. "If you love her and want to marry her, the only problem I see is Carlynn."

Panic shattered Ra-khir's composure. He found himself taking wild, gulping lungfuls of air and slowed his breathing to a deep, regular cycle. Gradually, he gained enough control to explain Kevral's year away and his promise to see others in her absence.

Kedrin listened without comment throughout his son's description, his attention rapt despite his silence.

Ra-khir finished and looked to his father for advice. "Carlynn bored me beyond belief. No one else is Kevral."

Kedrin tousled Ra-khir's hair, his touch sympathetic. "A bad situation, Ra-khir. You *do* have to marry her, but not against her will. You can't force her to spend the rest of her life with you."

Ra-khir looked at his feet and watched them blur to puddles as tears welled in his eyes. "I know that," he whispered. "But she does love me. And I love her. Nothing else should matter."

Kedrin said nothing. There was nothing to say.

"What if there *is* a baby?"

"It's unlikely, Ra-khir."

Twice as likely as you think. Ra-khir kept the thought to himself. When they believed themselves moments from execution, it had not mattered. He should not have allowed the second time.

"I'm sorry I mentioned it. I just want you to consider the consequences before you act. If you did such a thing with another woman, you would dishonor her, yourself, and your family."

"I would never do that!" Ra-khir burst out, desperate for Kedrin's understanding. "If not for imminent death, I would never have done it with Kevral before marriage. I swear on the honor of self and kingdom." Guilt pounded at his skull. He could not explain away the second time so easily.

"I believe you," Kedrin said with sincerity. "I'm not angry at you, just concerned. Whatever happens, I'll weather it with you. You're my son."

"I don't want to see other women." Ra-khir wished nothing to do with the giggling lot of female children who came to ogle the knights-in-training. If Kevral refused his proposal, he would have to find another woman with her strength and self-confidence, an equal, not a trophy. "It's torture."

"Your word is your law," Kedrin reminded.

Ra-khir groaned, dreading his forced social life far more than the grueling practices and tests Armsman Edwin inflicted on his students. "Why did I ever agree to such a thing?"

To this, Kedrin had no answer.

CHAPTER 22

The Price of Loyalty

Lessons from brutal teachers are learned fast and well.
— Weile Kahn

Dark, frigid, forest nights yielded regularly to balmy days, warm for autumn. As Kevral and her mount grew more accustomed to breaking trail, trapping themselves against copses, close-spaced trees, and deadfalls become less common. Twining branches with their interwoven leaves formed a mantle that protected them from the rain, and she noticed only its patter and gentle roll of droplets through irregular gaps. The damp, close odor of molding leaves and the sweeter scents of sap and seedlings became too familiar to register. An occasional whiff of musk or the stench of an ancient carcass broke the pattern at rare intervals.

Irritability no longer plagued Kevral, replaced by cautious anticipation. Though far different than training Renshai, her experiences in Pudar might grant her the basis for becoming a *torke*, the profession most respected by her people and one Colbey had considered the pinnacle of his life. She had grown to rely on Tae's skill, believing he could steer silent armies past Weile's men without their knowledge. His nightly fatigue bespoke an effort his successfulness belied. His warmth against her each night awakened a depth of love in a heart she had truly believed, less than two weeks earlier, belonged only to Ra-khir.

Kevral sighed. Reading her mood, the horse snorted, tossing its head up and down until she loosened her grip on the reins. *This is too cruel.* Kevral blamed herself for the hurt she inflicted on both men. She wished the situation easier on them all. For her indecision, she deserved to suffer, but the men remained innocent. *It's all my fault, yet I'm the only one who can't lose.* Whether she chose Ra-khir or Tae, she would spend her life happy; yet only one of them could have his heart's desire. *I must choose*. The idea of doing so now rankled. Tae held the advantage of the last eleven days. Experience taught her that the one she was with seemed always the only one. *A year without either, a year of distance and responsibility, should make things fair.* Still, Kevral could not shake the guilty wish that chance would rescue her from the agony of selecting. One or the other, maybe both, would find another love. The idea of forfeiting either stabbed her chest like a sharp, hot brand. *I deserve to lose both, and they deserve happiness.*

Tae's signal interrupted Kevral's self-deprecating line of thought. *He's in danger!* Battle rage slammed her, boiling her blood. She reined the horse in a wild circle, kicking it viciously into a canter.

The horse responded sluggishly, hampered by sticks, narrow openings, and detritus. Kevral directed it toward the open road. Already discovered, she saw no reason to hide from enemies. Speed had to take precedence. The gelding scrambled through the brush, branches stinging Kevral's cheeks and eyes. She thundered through the underbrush and onto the pathway, swinging the animal's head toward Pudar.

Tae whistled again, the sound piercing brush as no voice-cry ever could. Accustomed to woodland acoustics, she followed it without difficulty, charging straight until the third call touched her ears, slightly behind and to the left. She hauled on the left rein, jerking her horse suddenly sideways.

The bay whipped around, stumbling into the too-sharp turn, then plunging obediently into the underbrush. The blood wrath buzzed through Kevral like an illness. Fire seemed to burn through her veins, and her heart hammered the slow cadence that always preceded war. The gelding dropped to a dancing trot, foam sprouting from its chest and nostrils. This time, Tae's whistle came from just ahead. The horse wound between a cluster of packed trunks that required Kevral to hunch and lift her feet into the saddle.

Eight Eastern men ranged beneath craggy, tall-limbed evergreens, their feet tearing slashes in drifted brown-and-green needles. Two held bows, both nocked, one drawn and aimed upward. Four others clutched swords, while the remaining men had not yet readied weapons. Several glanced toward Kevral as her horse rattled through the brush.

Kevral did not bother to identify the Easterners' target; Tae surely perched in the tree. Driving her heels into the horse's flanks, she leaned forward in the saddle. Her swords left their sheaths as her war cry echoed through the forest.

As one, the men faced her. A sword slashed for her leg and the horse's side. Her boot crashed into its wielder's face, driving him under the unshod hooves. The horse rocked, floundering for solid ground. Kevral executed a frenzied loop that slashed a deadly line across another's neck. Blood jetted, bright red, and its warmth on her face only spurred the riot of war lust within her. Unwilling to waste the seconds the horse needed to regain its balance, she sprang from its back, directly onto a bowman.

The man collapsed beneath Kevral's momentum, flailing wildly with the bow. Kevral drove between the crazed defense, swords stabbing deeply into flesh three times before the Easterner beneath her went still. She rolled to her feet, blood stinging her eyes and salty on her lips. The last five surrounded her, their movements cautious, their eyes trained directly on her. She shook her head, splattering herself and them with their companions' blood. Crouched, she growled like an animal, goaded to attack in blind fury yet trained to control her every movement.

Tae's voice wafted down from on high, using the guttural Eastern language that Kevral did not know. An enemy took his eyes from the Renshai for an instant. Kevral dove for the opening, slashing beneath his sword and pounding his neck with a deep-biting cut. She did not possess the strength to sever bone, but the wellspring of blood proved enough. She whirled, cutting separate arcs in front of her with the swords, hoping to send the others scuttling backward while she prepared to battle four at once.

One Easterner bolted. As if it were a signal, the others followed, kicking up a wake of needles.

Kevral cursed, blood fever still high. She ran back toward her horse, halted by Tae's soft but authoritative call in the Northern tongue. "Let them go."

Fury exploded through Kevral, aimed toward the one who dared to interfere with a Renshai's battle. She whipped a hostile glance at Tae, seeing the familiar form high in a tree, her examination disrupted by the irregular slash of branches. The sun sheened from a wet, scarlet stain soaking the left side of his tattered tunic, and occasional droplets of blood pattered to the needles. *Tae's hurt.* The realization suffocated the desperate need to kill, and concern rose to replace it. She lowered her swords. "Are you all right?"

"Fine," Tae returned, skittering from the trees with the uncharacteristic clumsiness of a newborn calf. Boughs shattered beneath him, showering Kevral with splinters and needles.

Kevral stepped back, instinctively raising a bloodstained hand to brush bark from her face, then catching herself in midmovement. She contented herself with a brisk head shake that dislodged some of the pieces, then set to a cursory cleaning of swords and hands with the promise of a complete job after she assisted her companion.

At length, Tae half-climbed, half-fell to the ground. He clenched his left arm to his side, and his breaths came in quick, shallow puffs.

Kevral sheathed her swords and went to tend Tae. "Graceful dismount." Blood discolored his left sleeve from wrist to shoulder, ran down his hand in trickles, and gradually spread across his chest. Dread raised the hairs at the nape of her neck. "You're hurt bad, aren't you?"

"I'm fine," Tae repeated, though he remained sitting on the needles without attempting to rise.

Kevral knelt at Tae's side, reached for the tunic, and tore. "I've seen your idea of 'fine.' That scar on your chest—this much deeper . . ." She held up a needle, ". . . and you'd have been as heartless as Ra-khir named you."

"You're ruining my best shirt," Tae lamented facetiously. "It's just an arm wound. Arrow went through it."

"Arrow?" Kevral's search uncovered the source of the bleeding, a hole through the flesh a hand's-breadth above Tae's elbow. "What idiot shoots for the arm?" She wrapped the rent tunic around the wound and tightened it to staunch the bleeding with pressure.

Tae demonstrated by cringing behind his uninjured arm. "They didn't aim for the arm, I deflected it."

Kevral teased, "Hmmm, block an attack with a body part. How clever. Why haven't I ever tried that?" She looked pointedly at the bloody tunic. "Oh, yes. That's why."

"Yeah, well." Tae's tone suggested he realized Kevral had chosen good-natured ribbing more to keep his mind from the pain than to antagonize. "Only Renshai can block retroactively. I had a choice between letting the arrow hit my arm or my face, and I'm not displeased with my decision." He paused a moment, brow furrowing. "Ra-khir called me 'heartless?'"

Kevral laughed at Tae's delayed reaction, alert to sight or sound of the Easterners' return. Even tending a companion would not allow her to drop her guard. "Long ago. Before he learned to tolerate, let alone like you."

Tae nodded, accepting. No blood seeped through the layers of makeshift bandage.

Kevral kept the cloth in place, knowing from experience that removing it too soon would allow the bleeding to restart and require her to begin from scratch. "What did you say to those road dogs that sent them running with their tails between their legs?"

"You're not going to like it."

"I already don't like that you didn't let me kill them. I'll deal with it."

Tae kept his eyes on Kevral as he spoke, judging. His face had gone pale, presumably from blood loss. "I told them I would make certain the whole of the Eastlands knew a woman killed them."

Kevral waited for more, the words too inoffensive for such a reaction.

"It's a major insult in the East."

Kevral made a vague, meaningless noise. Until that moment, she had never considered the significance of Tae's upbringing. She knew men treated women like property in the Eastlands. Tradition no longer required wives to suicide on their husband's pyre, but most still did so. Those who did not dishonored their families and were shunned. Eastern law contained no provisions for crimes against women, and females who disobeyed law or husbands received punishments far beyond those of males. Since the first day they met, Tae had always treated Kevral and Matrinka with respect, yet she finally bothered to wonder whether, if they married, Tae might eventually revert to the attitude of his culture.

Although Kevral said nothing of her thoughts aloud, her features must have betrayed her. Tae launched into a defense. "Hey! Just because I use someone's warped, stupid ideas against them doesn't mean I believe them. I learned my attitude toward women from my father. He idolized my mother. Still does. He always believed she was smarter, handsomer, wittier, more clever—you name it. She never told him to quit doing what he did, because if she did, he would have. But she understood his passion, and he helped fulfill any desire she had as well. They were a team." Tae blinked several times, as if remaining awake had, in itself, become an effort. "It's the men . . ." He paused thoughtfully, "the women, too, for that matter. The people without self-confidence who need to prove themselves superior by denigrating others. If my father ever re-marries, it won't be an Eastern woman. They don't have the spark and spirit to replace my mother. Even if I wasn't wholly in love with you, I wouldn't consider an Eastern woman either. The idea of my beloved scurrying like a slave to provide my every comfort makes me vomit."

"You definitely wouldn't get that from me," Kevral felt ob-ligated to supply.

"That's for certain," Tae muttered. He finished at his normal volume. "The thing that fully convinced me the world had no natural justice is that my mother is dead while Ra-khir's miser-able excuse for a female parent still stinks up the world with her presence."

Kevral smiled as she carefully unwound the cloth to replace it with a neater pressure dressing. "Don't downplay your emo-tions; tell me how you really feel."

Tae grinned at the sarcasm.

Kevral continued working. "All right. You've finally admit-ted your mother's dead." Part of Ra-khir's distrust had stemmed from Tae's secretiveness about his past. "Tell me about her. How did she die?"

Tae stiffened suddenly, clearly in pain. Instinctively, Kevral halted her ministrations, believing herself at fault.

Tae closed his eyes and lowered his head, his agony certainly internal.

Kevral returned to tending the injury, waiting in silence for Tae to either explain or reject her request. The long delay spoke volumes. Their relationship had reached a point of crucial im-portance, and his willingness or refusal to share the pain he had kept to himself for nearly half his life would determine whether or not he truly loved and trusted Kevral.

Gradually, Tae's eyes came open, soft and moist. He met Kevral's gaze levelly as he began his story.

Weile Kahn sat stiffly upright, his favorite, cushioned chair no more comfortable than the floor. Crouched at his right hand, Alsrusett waited in silence, gaze playing over the simple room he already knew by heart. A desk and wooden chair occupied most of one wall, crammed full of supplies and topped by a chessboard. Crude shelves cut directly into the earthen wall held an assortment of foodstuffs, mostly dried fruits, salted or jerked meats, and hard breads. One doorway led to the privy, a hole and bucket arrangement that the bodyguards kept regularly emptied. The other led to a bedroom where Daxan currently slept and, farther, to his own sleeping quarters.

"A game?" Alsrusett suggested, nodding toward the chessboard.

Though he knew the focus of Alsrusett's attention, Weile looked to it from politeness. Discovering his bodyguard's competence at the game of strategy had helped wile away those boring hours induced by a life of continual hiding. But Kinya's news from earlier that morning kept Weile's thoughts embroiled and his muscles tense to the point of pain. *A young, male Easterner traveling with a single Renshai.* Weile shook his head. Distance and a hood had kept the Easterner unrecognizable, but he could not lose the image of Tae Kahn introducing the blonde woman and the red-haired man at the edge of the chasm. *Could it be my son?*

Weile closed his eyes, picturing an encasing wall of stone around his heart. *I can't let the past unman me. I ordered him killed, and I could do nothing else under the circumstances.* Still, he could not chase away the image of Kinya, goading his commander for a mercy he dared not speak, the elder's hard eyes demanding a reprieve that Weile could not grant. *My son betrayed me.* Another thought came to him, in the voice of his wife. *But he is still your son.* Weile bunched his lids tighter, determinedly concentrating on the image of granite he had conjured.

The first knock rang through the room so suddenly, Weile jumped to his feet, eyes snapping open and heart pounding. Alsrusett rose, too, as much in response to his charge's reaction as the sound. Kinya's familiar pattern followed, the same he had used earlier that morning.

Weile remained in place but did not sit. Alsrusett climbed the rungs to the top of the shaft, disappearing into the darkness. A moment later, his single answering knock sounded. Weile heard the scrape of the door opening, followed by a stifled grunt and a quick series of thumps. Silence followed. Weile strained for the sound of Alsrusett's heavy tread on the upper rung. It did not come, and the bodyguard called down no explanation for the strangeness.

Weile recognized danger instantly. Swift and quiet, he dashed into the sleeping rooms where Daxan had already awakened. As he hurtled off the bed, the compact guard looked askance at his leader.

"No response. No return," Weile explained minimally in a hoarse whisper. Likely, he knew, Alsrusett had stepped out to assist Kinya and had forgotten to mention this to Weile; but protocol demanded they escape first and find explanations later. Daxan darted ahead of Weile Kahn, into the other bedroom. Squeezing beneath the bed, he wriggled through the bolt-hole designed for just such an occasion. Weile dove through after his bodyguard.

The cold soil felt like water brushing against Weile's skin, an image foiled by the moist, dirt aroma surrounding him. Daxan scrabbled through the hole, then paused to pound aside the boulder blocking the opening.

Daxan hammered and huffed far longer than seemed appropriate or necessary, but Weile remained quiet, attributing the delay to his own distorted sense of time. Earth pattered down the tunnel in a fine shower of clumps filled with detritus. After an interval that felt like an hour, Daxan finally grunted in wordless frustration. "It won't budge."

The words set off alarms in Weile's mind. "What?" he asked carefully.

"The exit's blocked. We're stuck."

Weile refused to verbalize the dread chilling through his chest. Whoever had wedged the opening had probably already come through the entrance. If they'd managed to cut off the tunnel opening beneath the bed, they had effectively trapped Weile and Daxan in a tomb of their own making. The walls seemed to crush in on Weile before he managed to force aside the image of slow suffocation. Without a word to Daxan, he whirled and charged for the tunnel entrance, the bodyguard scrambling at his heels.

The glaze of light seeping into the hole restored Weile's composure. His hand slipped to his hilt as he emerged, shoving the bed aside rather than compromising security by crawling into danger hunched and half-blinded by positioning. The metal legs of his cot scratched grooves across the dirt floor with a hiss. As he leaped free, Weile drew his sword, leaving space for Daxan to spring between him and any threat. The bodyguard sped gracefully into a defensive position, sword also readied.

Aside from the new position of the cot, the room remained as they had left it. A wooden chest held his gear, a brass candle holder and striker resting atop the closed lid. A metal bowl beside it held dozens of candles. A matched ceramic pitcher and bowl sat in a corner near the entrance, undisturbed. Gesturing Weile back, Daxan crept into his own quarters, then through the opening to the main room. "Intruders!" he shouted abruptly. His footfalls pounded echoes through the chamber.

Though trained to escape while his bodyguard fought, Weile had no place to run. Steel rang against steel in the common room. Daxan would sacrifice his life for his charge's freedom, but Weile's only escape lay at the opposite side of the battle. Sword still bared, Weile pressed his back to the wall and cautiously approached the thump and thrash of combat. Crouched, he whipped into the main room's entryway to find Tae Kahn physically blocking the exit, his left sleeve empty and his expression unreadable. Daxan's sword dangled from his hand. A blonde woman, little more than a child, pinned Daxan to the wall, two swords crossed at his throat. Weile recognized her as the one Tae had called Kevral.

"Run!" Daxan hissed, eyes measuring his smaller opponent for the barest breach. If he believed suicide would gain Weile an opening for escape, he would gladly hurl himself upon the blonde's weapons. But the high positioning of Kevral's swords would grant him nothing more than a slit throat and too little time for Weile.

Weile resigned himself to the inevitable. He had always known he would die violently. He turned his gaze directly on Tae, seeking some tiny flicker of mercy in eyes so like his own. The dark orbs revealed nothing. He used the common trading tongue, "Did you come to kill me?"

Tae gave no reply but that inscrutable stare. The silence stretched far beyond politeness or even effective threat. As the captive whose home was violated, Weile had already overstepped his boundaries by speaking first.

At length, Kevral spoke, imitating Tae's voice admirably. "No, Father. I didn't come to kill you. I love you."

The woman's voice mobilized Tae as Weile's had not. He nodded once, then swallowed hard. "She speaks well for me."

Weile would have preferred to hear the words directly from his son, but this would have to suffice. His gaze drifted to the empty sleeve, and he believed he could see the bulge of an arm against the fabric of Tae's tunic. *Injured not amputated.* The thought brought back memories of his own father's accident of birth and the agony that deformed limb had become. A cold sweat prickled his back.

When Weile paused too long, Kevral took over again, this time copying Weile's harsh Eastern accent. "And I love you, too, my son."

Weile smiled carefully, wanting a reconciliation more than anything but uncertain how to achieve it. "You're right. She does speak well."

The two men continued to stare at one another.

Kevral cleared her throat. "This is the part where you call off your thug." She inclined her head toward Daxan, removing the swords as if Weile rather than she had made the suggestion.

"Thank you, Daxan," Weile said. "Your caution is no longer necessary."

Daxan returned a look clearly intended to test Weile's command and how much the threat of Kevral's presence influenced his leader's decision.

Weile gave his bodyguard a strong nod that conveyed his seriousness. "Tae Kahn, your arm . . . ?"

Tae raised and lowered his shoulders slightly, the gesture clearly intended to convey contempt for a minimal affliction.

Irregular footsteps clomped around the entrance to the hideaway. *More company?* Weile glanced toward the sound, keeping Tae in his peripheral vision in order to gauge his son's reaction. *Is it one of theirs, one of mine, or enemies?* A boot slammed unsteadily onto the upper rung, followed by a verbal curse. Then, Alsrusett plummeted through the opening. Tae dodged clear as the bodyguard crashed to the ground, enormous body quaking the room. Alsrusett attempted to scramble to his feet, his movements strangely awkward. His head swiveled toward Weile, his relief at finding his charge alive evident. Gaining a crouch, he tensed to lunge at Kevral.

"Alsrusett, be still." Without waiting to see if the man obeyed, Weile turned his attention to his other guard. "Daxan, uncover the escape route and secure the entrance, please."

Daxan glanced from Alsrusett to Kevral to Tae and back to Weile, his concern obvious. In no condition to protect anyone, Alsrusett could not keep Weile safe during Daxan's brief absence. Weile understood the worry, but it seemed ludicrous to him. Daxan had already proved he could not handle Kevral either, especially weaponless.

After a hesitation based on protest, Daxan crossed the room and climbed the rungs. The patter of dirt sounded dully beneath Alsrusett's groan.

"What happened?" Weile did not care who answered.

"She hit me over the head," Alsrusett glared at Kevral, jabbing a thick finger toward her.

"Three times," Kevral asserted. "Hard skull."

"I tried to fight her. She outmaneuvered me." Alsrusett frowned at his own words, as if he had not intended to speak them. "Where does a woman learn to fight like that?"

Kevral looked bemused, and Weile deigned to answer in her place. "In this case, probably the Fields of Wrath. Like all Renshai."

"Daimo." Alsrusett spat the Eastern slang term for Renshai like a curse. Weile glanced at Kevral, who did not seem to take offense, though Tae's features bunched into a scowl.

Weile attempted to fully defuse the situation. "Why don't we bury all the steel and sit?"

Nods greeted the suggestion. Kevral sheathed her swords, drew a third one from her belt, and offered it to Alsrusett.

The massive bodyguard reached for the weapon, a spark in his eyes and a coil in his movement warning of imminent danger. Weile back-stepped, surprised to see his son do the same. Only Kevral seemed fully unconcerned. Though the top of her head scarcely reached Alsrusett's shoulder, she met his dark stare with eyes like blue fire. Alsrusett accepted the weapon with a growl that barely resembled gratitude, then returned the weapon to its sheath.

Weile and Tae breathed identical sighs of relief. To encourage the others, Weile sank into his favorite chair, Alsrusett lounged into a corner beside him. Kevral and Tae accepted the other two seats, the Renshai's casual position mocking the bodyguard's stiff pose. Weile remained unfooled. Though she appeared comfortable, Kevral kept her legs curled under her, and her hands rested not-quite carelessly near her hilts.

"It's me," Daxan called from above. His boot sole clicked against the upper rung, followed by the thump of a boulder rolling into place. He trotted down the makeshift ladder with all the grace his companion had lacked. Once down, he took up a stance at Weile's other hand.

"Here." Tae tossed Daxan's sword to the floor at his feet.

Daxan bent to retrieve it, never taking his eyes from Kevral. Rising, he resheathed it.

Silence returned to the room. Weile glanced at his son. Tae sat with one knee bent and the other straight, a habit he had assumed from his mother. The straight hair, combed to a sheen, belonged to her as well; and he recognized his own influence on his son's features. Memory showed Weile the infant snuggled into his beloved's arm, the innocently helpless features, and the tiny arm that escaped the blanket's covering. The first moment he looked upon his son, he had felt a wellspring of emotion too strong to contain. It had changed him, he had believed, forever. Now the urge seized him to cradle Tae like the baby he had once been, to hold the child in his lap, rock him, and whisper vows for a better future. *I promised him so much and delivered so little.* Yet Weile found his mouth too dry for words, and the presence of Daxan, Alsrusett, and Kevral constrained any words worth speaking. "Tae Kahn," he finally managed. "We need some time alone. Will you stay?" He added carefully, "Voluntarily, of course."

Tae sat quietly for several moments, as if considering a proposition for which he surely held a position long before his arrival. "I can come and go as I wish?"

Weile caught himself shifting restlessly and turned it into deliberate-appearing motion. "Even I don't come and go as I wish. It requires too much work for Kinya and others to keep making places like this."

Tae settled deeper into his chair, turning his head but not quickly enough to hide a grimace of pain. The arm hurt worse than he would admit.

"How about this for a compromise?" Weile tried. "You may stay as long as you choose and leave freely when you wish to do so."

"Reasonable," Tae admitted.

"Good." Glad to have one small part of the problem solved, Weile started to turn his sights on another when he recognized the flaw in his own bargaining. Love and stress had confounded logic. He sighed, feeling like a madman who changes personality in mid-sentence. "Tae Kahn, you know there has to be more to that agreement."

To Weile's surprise, Tae replied, "I know."

"Security."

"I know too much," Tae supplied.

Weile considered a statement that could have come from his own lips but had not. "Or not enough, depending on your viewpoint. You know I'd like you to take my place. There's still much I can teach you."

"And much I've learned on my own."

Weile managed a half-smile, despite the sobriety of the discussion that had to follow. "Obviously." He heaved a deeper sigh. "We're father and son. If we can't agree, at least we should be able find a peaceful way to disagree."

"One would think so." Tae turned his father a pointed look, the black bangs falling into eyes nearly as dark. "But one of us tried to kill the other. And the other could have but didn't."

Weile pursed his lips, filled with regret. He could not argue Tae's point, but he wanted the opportunity to discuss it privately. He glanced at Kevral. "Would it be possible for my son and me to talk alone?"

Kevral made a throwaway gesture. "It's your . . ." She paused, the proper term clearly eluding her. ". . . home?" She raised no questions about remaining with two warriors who despised her, a strategy Weile applauded. Her obvious lack of fear gave her the upper hand, and he suspected she felt as unconcerned as she appeared. Confidence, not stupidity, kept her silent on this matter.

Nevertheless, Weile felt obligated to discuss it. "Daxan, Alsrusett. Treat Kevral like a welcome guest. This may take a while."

Alsrusett grumbled something incoherent, but neither man gainsaid their leader aloud. Rising, Weile ushered Tae toward the bedrooms. The young man came to his feet with a grace that portrayed his slowness as blasé unhurriedness. Gang habits died hard.

As Tae slipped past his father, Weile turned to follow. Hesitating, the elder Kahn closed his eyes, feeling like a packhorse laboring under a heavy load. Likely, this would prove his last chance to rescue his relationship with the son born of a love he would never know again. So much was at stake, he believed the right words should flow into his head like a golden tide. If the world held any justice, it would guide him. Yet never in his life had he felt so alone.

The discussion between Tae and Weile lasted well into the night, interrupted briefly to assign sleeping places and to eat. Lit only by artificial light, the hideaway left Kevral nothing but her own fatigue by which to measure the passage of time. At length, Tae settled down on Weile's bed while his father used one of the bodyguards' mattresses and Alsrusett the other. Daxan remained awake through the night. Kevral curled onto one of the plushly cushioned chairs in the main room, covered by her own blanket. Though Tae and Weile had both offered her the bedroom, she refused it, preferring Tae to have the rapid means of escape should such become necessary. He did not re-quire guarding. He slept even more lightly than she did.

As the night deepened, Kevral grew restless. In the morning, she planned to leave for Pudar, certain Tae had negotiated her safe passage. In a logical world, a father would never kill his son, but she held little more faith in divine fairness than Tae and his father did. Once she left his side, Tae's safety, and her own, were no longer assured.

Colbey sent him to reconcile with his father. That thought brought some comfort where every other had failed. If her hero believed this course best, Kevral would never refute its value; but it did not reassure her enough to sleep. For hours, Kevral lay, staring at the ceiling and attentive to every tiny sound or movement of light. Only one event would satisfy her concerns: a clear-cut warning to Tae's father about the consequences of mistreating his son again. Though it seemed unwise as well as unnecessary, Kevral saw no other means to relieve her discom-fort and worried that it would follow her to Pudar and remain until she reunited with a healthy, uninjured Tae.

Kevral shoved aside the blanket and sat up in the chair. Crickets sang discordant notes that gained an echo quality in the hideaway's confines. Otherwise, she heard no sound. She turned her head toward the entry into the bodyguards' room. Her hand crept naturally to the swords that never left her side, one strapped in its usual place and the other on the arm where the blankets would not hamper her reach. Her eyes swept the cavelike walls to settle on the bedroom opening where Daxan stood, eyes fixed on her, mouth scowling, position so set and still someone could have replaced him with a statue and he would have looked no different.

Casually, Kevral tugged the second sword into her lap, be-yond Daxan's sight. She met his cold gaze directly. "I need to talk to Tae's father."

Daxan did not bother to glance toward his leader. "Weile Kahn is sleeping. I won't disturb him for you."

"Daxan." The soft voice wafted from farther in the room, and warning tinged its tone.

Kevral could not stop the smile that curled onto her face, though it clearly magnified Daxan's irritation. His glower deep-ened, and his eyes narrowed to angry slits.

Kevral heard nothing to indicate Weile had chosen to move, but a moment later he appeared beside Daxan in the doorway. Draped in a loose cloak and britches clearly intended for sleeping, he wore no evident weaponry. Kevral dismissed him as a threat; no matter the number of secreted daggers he carried, nor the swiftness of his attacks, he did not have the skill to best a Renshai.

"I'll speak with her alone," Weile announced softly.

Daxan stiffened, and his expression grew harder, if possible. He grumbled something in the Eastern tongue that Weile dismissed with a wave.

Stepping past his bodyguard without any visible wariness, Weile turned Kevral a pleasant smile. "You wished to speak with me, Kevral?" He gestured at her chair, then sat in the one across from her with his back to the bedrooms.

Kevral glanced at Daxan, who remained in position at the entry.

Without bothering to confirm the focus of her attention, Weile made a crisp, dismissing motion over his head.

Daxan jerked a hand in a gesture of warning that only Kevral could see, then he disappeared into the other room.

Kevral drew her legs onto the chair and studied Weile Kahn. Curly black hair swept back from a stubby forehead, and he shared Tae's mysterious eyes. Emotion hid, unreadable, behind a mantle of dark assurance. Kevral had broken through Tae's facade, but she had neither the time nor inclination to do so with his father. She would have appreciated more privacy, but this arrangement seemed the best she could hope for under the circumstances. If their voices remained low, even the annoyingly alert bodyguard could hear nothing of their conversation. Now that she had the attention she sought, Kevral had no idea how to put her intentions into words. She started simply. "I'm leaving in the morning."

Weile nodded. "Tae Kahn said you probably would. You'd like me to assure you safe passage to Pudar?"

Kevral shrugged. "Oh, I'll get there. Your assistance only determines whether or not I have to kill a bunch of Easterners on the way."

Weile's brows rose slightly, and a hint of a grin played at the corners of his mouth. "My men mean nearly as much to me as my son."

"Nearly as much as nothing." Kevral snorted. "That's not reassuring."

Weile tensed for a moment before his mantle of casual confidence returned. "I love my son. You said so yourself."

"I said what I hoped was true. What should be true. Your actions speak otherwise."

"Now?"

"No." Kevral slid her legs back onto the floor, instinctively assuming a more defensible position as conversation drifted toward verbal attack. "When you blackmailed your son into staying with you. When your men shot him . . . surely at your command?" Kevral gazed deliberately into Weile's eyes, trying to force the honest answer he clearly found unnecessary.

"I've made mistakes," Weile admitted.

"The problem isn't that you've made mistakes," Kevral pressed. "Every parent has. The problem is that you've made *catastrophic* mistakes, and you're still making the same ones."

Weile sat in silence for several moments. When he spoke, the words emerged with a steady, controlled caution. "People without children believe parenting is an innate skill. The child is born and, like animals, we know exactly what to do and how. It just doesn't work that way." He paused, shaking his head as if to insinuate Kevral could not possibly follow his point. "When you have children, you'll understand."

"If I do have children," Kevral returned, still pushing, "I'll make mistakes, too. But they won't be *fatal* ones."

Weile shifted, as if no longer certain of his security. "Given who and what you are, you're almost assuredly wrong."

Rage pulsed through Kevral, but she maintained control. Words, however, did not come as easily.

Weile continued, obviating the need for Kevral to speak. "I've already admitted I made mistakes. Fixing them is between Tae and myself." He regained his inhuman composure, though his tolerance had clearly waned. "We've already discussed it; and, quite frankly, I don't have to answer to you."

Weile's words sounded a challenge that tightened Kevral's grips around her swords. From experience beyond Renshai training, most of which she had gained from Tae, she managed to keep her response verbal. Weile Kahn had a definite point. "You're absolutely right. On the matter of parenting, you don't have to answer to me." Kevral released her grip on her right-hand sword, finger tracing a groove in the knurling. "Tae's safety is a separate issue." Unable to rely on size or appearance for intimidation, Kevral hoped Weile read her gesture. "If anything untoward happens to Tae, it won't be enough for you to have an alibi. Your reach is long, Weile Kahn, and I don't care for your methods. You hide well, too, but . . ." Kevral paused for emphasis, grinding her sapphire gaze into Weile's as if it were a physical entity. Though pale, large, and childlike, those eyes could sustain an icy glare. ". . . I will find you. And not a trace of you, or what you created, will remain."

"Well." Weile managed a thin smile, and he softened the mood without belittling. "I guess I don't have to ask if that's a threat." He sobered. "You've made it impossible for me to say anything that sounds sincere, but I'm still going to try." He leaned forward, and he returned a look at least as hard as Kevral's own. "I do love my son, and I will do everything I can to keep him safe and to solidify our relationship. I don't know if it's possible, but I'll try my best. As for you, young lady . . ."

Kevral prepared for a lecture on manners.

". . . my son is lucky to have you as a friend. People spend lifetimes searching for such loyalty and never finding it. Without you, he would already be dead, and me as well. I could never have forgiven my mistake." He shook his head. "If you ever tell anyone I said that—" He broke off with a laugh. "Like I'm going to threaten you." He continued on a serious note, "Anyway, as much as I dread permanent close contact with you, I can't think of any woman more suited to Tae Kahn. I hope I'm not misinterpreting the affection you seem to share."

The last response Kevral expected was a welcome to the family speech. Men like Weile valued the strength and confidence that irritated or threatened those less self-secure. Those who remained in power so long, without delegating or resigning, usually did so because they faced, even relished, challenges. He had turned the tables, neatly regaining the upper hand and reminding her how leaders maintain peace. At times, they found it worth losing battles to win wars.

The only reaction Kevral gave Weile was a blank-eyed stare.

CHAPTER 23

Changes

Every sword stroke and its result changes the style of my combat. Every competent maneuver used against me remains vivid in my memory.

—Colbey Calistinsson

Kevral took the main road to Pudar, the easy terrain and lack of Eastern ambushes a comfortable change from trail-breaking. Branches shaded the path, their autumn colors fading and their edges curling to herald the coming winter. At intervals, young branches groped out over the trail, requiring her to swerve or duck beneath them. Merchants and travelers would have seen to these annoyances, hacking them down for the convenience of others or for their own return trips. The Easterners had no cause for such fastidiousness.

The gates of Pudar hove into sight in late afternoon, sooner than Kevral expected. The city looked ominously different. Though she could see figures pacing on and in front of the walls, it felt empty and ghostlike. For several moments, the reason eluded her, until her mind finally conjured details of memory. The crowd thronging the gates had disappeared, and their cheerful harangues and appeals no longer seasoned the air. Once, the faithful of odd religions, panaceas, and magic had flocked to foist their beliefs upon those entering the city. The children of farmers and craftsmen too poor to maintain stands in the city sold their wares in disorganized huddles that added a charm to the great market city.

Now weeds had sprung up where once the constant pound of feet had kept them at bay. An ice-grained breeze stirred them into quiet dances that mocked the bustling masses that remained only in memory. The clink of mail and the rattle of stems seemed strangely loud in contrast. Kevral reined toward the gates. Experience taught her they remained open until after sundown, warded only enough to separate overeager zealots from visiting dignitaries and merchant caravans. Months ago, Pudar denied entrance to no one.

"Prepare arms!" a voice commanded from the city, and the click of cocking crossbows resounded and echoed from the walls.

Kevral stiffened on her horse, a wash of excitement at the thought of coming battle tainted by the knowledge that she could not win this time. Legend claimed Colbey could cut arrows from the air, but even he could not defend against so many. She hoped that her direct approach would gain her the benefit of explanation. Dragging her horse to a stop, she dismounted and waited. Fatigue weighed on her more than she expected. Though she had remained awake most of the previous night, she had slept well into the morning.

The voice that had readied the crossbows boomed again. "Stranger, state your business and your name."

Too far to pick out individual figures, Kevral could not locate the speaker. "I'm no stranger!" Kevral returned, but she could not generate the volume of the commander.

"Louder! I can't hear you!"

"I SAID I AM NO STRANGER!" Kevral belted out, but her voice did not raise the echoes the other managed.

"What!"

"I'M . . . NOT A STRANGER!"

"You're a what? Speak up!"

"I'M NOT A . . ." Kevral started again, then gave up. "Oh, for heaven's sake, I'm coming closer so you can hear me." Grabbing the reins, she led the horse farther down the road.

"HALT!" the man shouted. "Don't come any closer."

Kevral weighed her alternatives and chose to stop. Patience waning, she watched as a single form separated from the others and headed toward her down the path. At length, she identified the standard mail of the Pudarian castle guard, covered by a brown tabard sporting a silver wolf. He stopped at twice the polite speaking distance and examined her intently.

Kevral returned the scrutiny. Wisps of sandy hair poked from beneath an unadorned helmet, and he gazed at her through hazel eyes much like Darris'. A mustache sprouted from beneath a broad, scarred nose, and a neatly trimmed beard hid his chin. He carried a poleax, and a sword hung at his left hip. "The captain wishes to know what you claimed to be."

Kevral blinked once and ran the first verse of a lullaby through her head. The calming technique managed to keep her physically inactive, but it scarcely dulled her tone. "I'm an angry, tired, irritated Renshai. If you don't allow me to come close enough to talk like a normal person, you'll leave me no choice but to plow through all of you like I did the Easterners who tried to keep me from traveling."

The man's mouth opened, but no sound emerged for several moments. "Oh," he finally said. "I'll relay that to the captain." Turning on his heel, he headed back the way he had come.

Kevral watched him go, shaking her head, gaining some solace and satisfaction from the realization he would probably deliver her words verbatim. She watched as the soldier returned to Pudar's gate and waited several moments for the ensuing discussion. Shortly, the commander called back. "Disarm yourself and approach."

Kevral cleared her throat, forcing herself to maintain the calm dignity she had, so far, shown. If she was to train these men, she would have to retain their respect. "Renshai!" she reminded at the top of her lungs.

A quiet pause followed during which the men surely discussed the implications of requesting a Renshai to remove her swords. They might just as well have asked her to literally sever her arms.

At length, the captain amended his demand, "Approach!"

Having gotten exactly what she requested in the first place, Kevral seized her horse's bridle and hauled the beast toward the gates. As she moved nearer, details became clear. She counted approximately two dozen bowmen on the wall, all with weapons readied. The closed gates looked uncharacteristically formidable and, for a moment, she actually doubted she approached Pudar. Half a dozen men, including the sandy-haired one who had communicated her message, stood in front of the gates. These wore swords or axes and carried polearms. At least a dozen more watched her from beyond the gate. She spotted the captain by the reverse colors of his tunic. He perched on the wall in a wide-based stance, a longbow slung across one shoulder and a broad-bladed sword on his belt. He stared at her, features at first a study in stony strength, then warping to obvious surprise. Stunned by her appearance, he missed his cue to stop her, and Kevral drew near enough to make the ground guards fidget.

"Halt!" the captain shouted belatedly. "You're a child."

The insult stung, but Kevral held her tongue until she felt she could reply with the pride of a *torke*. "Certainly not. Adult three years by Renshai law."

Apparently Kevral's voice revealed a second shock. "You're a girl."

"Woman," Kevral corrected. "Now, if you could please stop stating your personal observations aloud, we could proceed with our business."

"Which is?" the captain prodded.

"First, command your men to stop treating me like a bulls-eye. Then, I have business with King Cymion."

"You do, do you?"

"I do, do I." Kevral gestured at the parapets. "Please."

The captain glanced from bowmen to Kevral. "At ease, men."

The arrows bobbed downward, no longer aimed at Kevral. The captain continued to study her. "I haven't figured out your game yet, but I have a pretty good idea." He spoke to the nearby guardsmen, too softly for Kevral to hear. Soon, those on the outer edges dispersed around the wall, leaving only the captain and three others on the parapets. Some of the courtyard soldiers disappeared as well. "You're a distraction, aren't you?"

"A distraction?" Kevral repeated.

"You keep the guards busy while your father and his companions attempt to assault the opposite gate or climb over the walls."

Kevral stared. "You're paranoid."

"Paranoid?" the captain repeated. "For months, no one has penetrated these roads. No one. Not even heavily armed caravans. Then, a single girl-child comes to the gates alone, not even bloodied. Not even cowed."

"I'm Renshai," Kevral reminded.

"Even Renshai are mortal."

Kevral sighed. The only way to prove her claim would leave corpses, perhaps even her own, and enrage the king she had come to serve. "Look. I made a vow to King Cymion. Only he can release me from that vow. If he says he doesn't want me in Pudar, I'll go peacefully. Otherwise, you leave me no choice but to demonstrate how I cut my way through the Eastern hordes." She added pointedly, "They had crossbows, too."

The captain drew breath for a reply, but a winded voice from below cut him short.

"Captain Larrin!" Bootfalls hammered against stone as a man climbed the parapets, hidden from Kevral by the wall. At length, he drew himself to the top, dressed in the same mail and tabard as the others. He exchanged several short phrases with the captain, both glancing at Kevral at intervals.

As the soldier clambered back down the steps, Larrin addressed Kevral again. "What's your name?"

"Kevral."

Larrin nodded. "It seems the king does wish to see you." Even as he spoke, several of the courtyard guards worked the latches and drew open the heavy gates.

That's what I've been trying to tell you! Kevral kept her irritation hidden, duplicating Weile Kahn's careful expressions. She could not blame Pudar for its caution. They had reason to mistrust, and cause to protect their city. The current problem handled, she turned her attention to watching them move. Most lacked the natural grace that helped to shape soldiers into warriors, and she saw little of the excited spark kindled in Renshai from birth. The way they carried themselves, how they moved, even how they wore their swords, polearms, and axes told her much about them. And she found them wanting. The task to which she had bonded herself seemed like a hovering tedium rather than the challenge teaching Renshai would have evoked. It might well prove a very long year.

The instant Kevral stepped through the gates, the attitude of Pudar's guardsmen underwent a staggering change. Appending "ma'am" or "lady" onto their every utterance, they swept her through the city streets to the castle. Though surrounded by men, Kevral noticed the quiet solemnity of a market once gaily thronged by locals and travelers. More than half the stands lay closed, despite the early hour; and the open ones held foodstuffs and necessities. Gone were the silver-tongued salesmen hawking glittering gemstones and clothes wound with silk and filigree. The few patrons strode directly for their purchases without the milling and gaping that had always seemed a permanent part of the city.

Ushered to a guest room as fancy as any in Béarn, Kevral had no time to do more than glance at the furnishings before female servants flocked to measure every part of her. Only after she rejected seventeen dresses on their hangers did they finally accept her plea for a simple tan tunic and breeks, much like the clothing Renshai wore when in service to Béarn's king. The servants left in the same flurry they'd entered with, clucking at the strangeness of the king's new guest.

Nearing exhaustion, Kevral collapsed on the bed, only to be interrupted, seconds later, by a new whirlwind of servants ushering her to a feast in her honor. Hungry and certain refusal would prove useless, she accompanied them to the dining hall. After a brief argument over whether or not she could bring weapons to a royal function, she arrived with both swords in place and her clothing scarcely ruffled. Introduced to too many guests to recall any, Kevral examined the few who mattered: General Markanyin, a graying, robust man with a beefy face and callused hands and his three lieutenants, Darian, Chethid, and Nellkoris. The names of civilian nobles flowed past her, mostly unheard, soon replaced by a series of scribes and ministers who seemed bent on questioning her at exactly the moment she placed a morsel in her mouth.

Gradually, Kevral fell into a pattern of eating and speaking as messengers scurried between her and King Cymion, working out the specifics of what her teaching would entail, the timing, and the anticipated results. Stuffed with salads and soups, she scarcely had room for the main course, which seemed to consist of every meat, vegetable, and bread in existence. The warm room, the constant hum of conversation, and the long day following a mostly sleepless night drowned her in a dizzy exhaustion that grew unbearable. As servants collected the dinner dishes, preparing for dessert, Kevral excused herself for the night.

But it did not end there. The scribes and ministers trailed her to her room, still hashing out details. The rich, heavy food sat poorly in Kevral's belly, and she added nausea to the expanding list of discomforts. Three times, she vomited into the pillow-surrounded hole that served as her connection to Pudar's deep sewer while servants waited in the main bedroom to attend to the king's business. By the time the main scribe brought a thick sheaf of papers for her signature, stars dotted the dark view through her window and she huddled, knees tucked to her abdomen, on the bed.

"No more," Kevral groaned.

"This should be the last, Lady. Sign and you're finished."

Kevral opened bleary eyes, rolling her gaze to the sharply dressed man she had seen too many times that night. "I'll sign tomorrow."

"I'm sorry, Lady," the man said without any true trace of regret. "The king wants this settled tonight. He believes it best for you."

"The king," Kevral returned, "is wrong."

The minister looked taken aback. "Lady Kevral, the king is never wrong."

"Of course." Kevral raked the sheaf of papers to her, wincing at the size of it. A glance showed her most of the details she had discussed and the compromise reached. The idea of reading the entire pile seemed a torture far beyond her current reserves. She glanced at the papers, at the minister, and back at the papers. Her head buzzed and spun, foiling concentration. Logic dictated that signing without reading could prove dangerous, yet the king's childlike excitement at her return seemed anything but feigned. The questions she had fielded suggested he believed she could train his men to recapture the roads. With or without Tae's and Weile's help, she might just manage to do so. Only one thing seemed important. Renshai law forbade her teaching any of the Renshai's special maneuvers outside of the tribe, a pledge kept inviolate for centuries. Her loyalty to her people would always take precedence over any piece of paper, but it seemed prudent to forestall any possible misunderstanding about this matter. Any lesser error, she could handle or correct. "Where's the part where it says I can't teach the Renshai maneuvers?"

The minister took back the papers and studied the first page. "Here." He poked a finger at the third paragraph of hundreds.

Taking back the papers, Kevral read. The eloquent, repetitive language, and her own tiredness, forced her to reread seven times before she felt satisfied that it protected her substantially. "Is this really necessary?" She grasped the entire stack and shook. The parchment rattled, and some pieces slipped out of configuration.

The minister stuffed the edges back into place. "I'm afraid so. You need to sign each and every page."

Kevral sighed. "Tonight?"

"Tonight."

Stomach lurching, head pounding, lids drooping, Kevral set to work.

On his seventeenth trip to the primordial chaos, Colbey finally learned to focus on the differences rather than seeking sameness in the ever-changing soup. With the revelation came knowledge, formless genius, and a means to navigate the instability that defined a world without true definition. With practice, he learned to keep himself whole with a bare thought and turn

his concentration alternately to ideas once far beyond his reckoning and to attacking demons. Anticipating that the demons
would assail him every trip, learning nothing from the one before, Colbey was pleasantly surprised to find them quick learn-
ers. Chaos gave them no basis for loyalty. They did not obey or
follow, but they did come to fear him.

On each descending level, the demons grew more powerful,
a new challenge for chaos' champion. Had they learned to work
together, Colbey suspected they could defeat him. But pattern
and strategy did not fit the primordial derangement that comprised chaos' world. Individually, he fought them and, one by
one, defeated them into keeping a terrified distance. And, each
time, fewer dared to challenge the Prince of Demons at all.

As the world of chaos grew more familiar, Asgard became
ever less scrutable. The gods' devices, sand clocks and water
clocks, became vehicles of madness. Their patterned sounds
made him restless. Night and day lost meaning; and the solid,
regularity of objects became a troubling tedium. Colbey found
himself clinging to self, even on a world that once seemed natural and peerless. He turned rarely to the Staff of Chaos' guidance. It grew stronger with the passing days, but it still seemed
incapable of violating his mental barriers.

On either world, loneliness became a haven.

The youngest of the elves, Oa'si, flew to his perch on the
lowest branch of a *doranga*, while the others took their usual
places as well. The coldness of the wood seeped through the
seat of Oa'si's britches, a chilly contrast to the stagnant, salty
damp of Nualfheim's island air. He studied the trunk's jutting
rings of bark, watching elves shift into position. Experience
told him exactly when the door would open and Dh'arlo'mé
would make his usual morning appearance from the common
house.

The elves all found their places. Exactly on cue, the door
swung open, and Dh'arlo'mé exited to the regular cadence of
his followers' chanting. Oa'si joined in, as he must, head bowed
and mouth repeating "Dh'arlo'mé" without any need to consider the action. It had long ago become meaningless sound, a
shortened form of a proper elfin name.

Over time, Dh'arlo'mé looked different to Oa'si, his tread
more solid, his speech patterns more human, his bearing frighteningly confident. His face had turned ashen, almost gray.
When his eye found Oa'si, it seemed to pin him in place, filled

with terrible knowledge that no elf should ever bear. In Dh'arlo'mé's presence, Oa'si always teetered between awe and horror, strangely attracted and, at the same time, repelled to the verge of panic.

Dh'arlo'mé raised his arms, the staff clutched in his right hand. "Elfin faithful!"

The chant died to a silence so sudden and absolute it seemed as if the entire world had ceased to function. Dread stole over Oa'si, as if the natural forces of the world also hung on the words of their leader. Then, gradually, the pounding of surf on the shore and the rattling of leaves in the wind returned to Oa'si's hearing, their irregularity soothing.

Dh'arlo'mé spoke over the silence, his voice booming and colored with simultaneous, universal *khohlar*. "It seems the disasters that should have befallen mankind have not wholly come to pass and need our assistance. For the good of elves, the world, and all its natural wonders, we need to use the skills the gods have given us." The *khohlar* added concept the words lacked, and Oa'si received the idea that Dh'arlo'mé counted himself among the divine rather than the elves. "What we cannot directly conquer, we can spur into ruination." The rest came only as *khohlar*, Dh'arlo'mé's plans to choose leaders from among them and place them in charge of their greatest skills. Thinkers would find a niche as strategists, organizers and commanders, and those magically adept as warriors. Dh'arlo'mé's sending whipped them into controlled excitement: a moment of change for a lifetime of stronger and better order.

Memories of freedom rushed through Oa'si's mind, remembrances from the recycled soul that occupied his body. He had never lived on Alfheim, but he saw the bubble-fruited trees and felt the swish of rushing air. Giggles filled his head, ghostly echoes of a time when elves did only what they pleased . . . and when. It felt so right to him, the natural state of elfinkind. Yet the loyalty, the oneness, of elves went at least as far back as these ancient recollections. He was an elf, first and foremost; and whatever elfinkind chose to do could not be wrong.

And though the last thought felt more alien than its predecessors, Oa'si had little choice but to follow it.

An icy breeze glided through Béarn's courtyard, sweeping down King Griff's hood and spilling his black hair into fine tangles. Hardy perennials had replaced the annual flowers, their colors duller and rangeless and their aromas nearly nonexistent.

Clever gardeners had replaced some of the living gardens with arrangements of amber, scarlet, and orange leaves. Now, these, too, faded to lifeless brown, curling like the fingers of an arthritic ancient. The statues remained, spotless and artistically displayed.

Not wishing to lose a moment of his break, Griff hurried toward the ceilinged bench garden where he knew Tem'aree'ay awaited him. His long legs carried him swiftly through the courtyard, and he did not notice that his pace forced Darris into an undignified trot. His thoughts remained on the elf and the gentle friendship she had extended to him since their chance meeting in the hallway. Somehow she managed to break through the barrier that held all others at bay. She spoke directly to his heart, without need for words; and her gentle *khohlar* had become an obsession. He had found many he liked among Béarn's staff and nobility, but only this one seemed to define friendship.

Griff did not realize he had broken into a run until he hurtled into the garden and skidded to an awkward stop. Tem'aree'ay started from a marble bench to her feet. Darris caught Griff's arm in a steadying grip, preventing a fall. The familiar square of benches surrounded an exquisitely carved, rearing bear that spat a constant stream of water into an obsidian bowl. Blinded to these familiar details, Griff rushed to comfort Tem'aree'ay, bashing his shin on the edge of the fountain in his haste. "I'm sorry I frightened you," he said, voice high-pitched from pain.

"Sire." Tem'aree'ay wrapped her warm, small hands around his massive arm. "Are you all right?"

Griff ignored the agony still shooting through his leg. "I'm fine, my lady," he said, knowing the inappropriate title discomforted her. He caught her into an affectionate welcoming hug before sitting on the bench at right angles to hers. Darris took a seat beside him, and Tem'aree'ay returned to her spot.

Griff stared, never tiring of the red-gold ringlets that framed her outworld face and the steady, blue eyes, so like the sapphires in his treasury. Like all elves she seemed genderless yet, at the same time, irresistibly feminine. Her heart-shaped lips bowed upward, more subtle yet infinitely more beautiful than a human smile; and her gaze shifted to Darris. "Please, play us a song," she begged. "Please, sir."

The king glanced at his bodyguard, reading none of the reluctance such requests usually raised. Darris could scarcely walk a hallway without at least one noble soliciting music. "I would be honored." He ducked through the strap that secured his favorite lute to his back and floated it into his lap like a mistress."

"Something pretty," Griff added. "A song of love." Having spoken without thinking, he cringed at his own words. It would not do for the king to seem taken with one outside his species. Uncomfortable with his own words, he missed the pained look that crossed Darris' features.

Then, music burst from the lute strings with a sudden radiance that held Griff spellbound. After an introduction that seemed beyond human creation, Darris' voice added a second melody to chords that blended perfect harmonies with a tune that grew into the very definition of romance. The song conjured images of a love so raw and innocent nothing in the universe could match its purity. Yet through the whole ran a pattern of bitter sorrow, a convention of law that held those lovers at bay. Tears sprang to Griff's eyes, and the world became a blur suddenly pierced by a sight every bit as beautiful as Darris' composition.

Tem'aree'ay had risen from the bench and begun to dance.

Tem'aree'ay's slender body swayed and spiraled, like the solid personification of the music. Her clothes swirled around her, red and yellow contrast to her every movement, as if she danced amid a roaring fire. The golden curls bobbed like separate tiny dancers. Her feet never stilled on the earth, and her long-fingered hands seemed to beckon Griff to ecstasies yet unknown. Only this could have pulled his attention from Darris' god-granted talent. He found himself unable even to blink. His heart heaved in his chest, and the guilty flashes of desire he had suppressed so often in her presence washed into a frenzied tidal wave of passion. Darris' song robbed him of shame. He lived the words to the roots of his soul: the ultimate love and the impossible union. All of his wealth and power could not change the fact that a human and an elf could never interbreed.

Song and dance ended much too soon, leaving Griff awash in bitter yearning and desperate sorrow. Yet the approach of Prime Minister Davian assured him that more time than he believed had passed. Tem'aree'ay sat, once again the fragile elf he had come to know well. Darris restored the lute and, this once, his music seemed to have affected him as well. A tear floated down his cheek, and he surreptitiously wiped it away.

Davian executed a handsome bow. "Majesty, I'm sorry to bother you. You're late for the supper meeting, and I must brief you on the topic." His hands looped repeatedly through one another, as if he were washing them.

Darris and Tem'aree'ay rose. Each returned a proper bow or curtsy. Griff also stood, granting the renegade turned minister a nod of acknowledgment. "You handled an entire coup. I think we can survive a meal." Walking to Davian, he placed a hand on the new prime minister's shoulder. "Whatever the topic, things always seem to work out fine. Trust me."

Davian positioned himself to propel Griff in the proper direction, expertly making the motion appear unintentional. "Oh, I trust you, Sire. In an affair of politics and despite your . . . um . . . well . . ." Impatient with minor diplomacy, Davian used the proper rather than the most careful word, ". . . inexperience. But this is a personal matter, Sire."

Griff swiveled his head to address Tem'aree'ay before he walked too far for good-byes. "Can you meet me here prior to supper?"

Tem'aree'ay hesitated a moment that raised a scowl of impatience on Davian's face. "I'll do my best, Sire."

Davian quickened his pace as Darris drew up beside the king. Memories of the dance still filled Griff's head, and a rough rendition of the lute-song cycled through his hearing. Only dignity kept him from skipping down the garden paths. The chances that Tem'aree'ay would come to the garden seemed even: anything from her healing duties to elfin irregularity and carelessness with time might keep her away. Whether that night or on another day, they would come together again.

Davian walked faster, forcing Griff and Darris to do the same. "Sire, the regular citizens and the nobles worry for Béarn's heirs."

"I'm seventeen," Griff reminded.

"Yes, Sire. And I've yet to meet a man your age who didn't believe himself immortal." Davian gritted his teeth and continued with a speech obviously intended to bludgeon sense into their adolescent king. "If I knew the gods would grant me one wish, any wish, Majesty, it would be that you were the exception. But you're not, Sire. And the people want heirs, Sire. And the people deserve them."

"But," Griff protested as the gardeners' desperate attempts at preserving the courtyard's spring beauty disappeared behind them. "I haven't found a woman I love yet."

Davian turned his gaze skyward momentarily, then stopped unexpectedly. Griff swept two steps beyond before noticing, then whirled to face his prime minister. Darris remained quiet at Griff's side, gaining sudden and intense interest in the positioning of his sword and lute.

"Your Majesty," Davian said carefully. "Love is not a requirement for marriage. Or for the creation of heirs."

Stunned, Griff stood speechless.

Though Davian winced as if it might kill him, he seized on the king's silence. "A single marriage, Sire. A child. Maybe two or three. That will appease the populace." He took a step to close the gap between them, as if revealing a great secret. "As the king, you're not limited to one wife. Sire, you can marry for love the second time. Or the third. Without the staff-test, we have no choice but to fall back on prior conventions. Sire, that means you can assign any successor to the throne. Your queen by love. A child of that union. The captain of your guards, if you so choose. Your Majesty, your options are endless."

Griff stroked his beard, finally accustomed to its presence. "A marriage will please Béarn?"

Davian started them walking again. "Not just *any* marriage, of course, Your Majesty. Your choices are limited by lineage, and there's no debate about who would best suit you, Your Majesty."

Griff remembered. "Matrinka."

Davian glanced over, seeming more friend than minister for the moment. "You like her?"

"I like her," Griff admitted. "Very much."

The decision seemed sound, yet a painful tension hung in the air. Stalwart beside his liege, also his charge, Darris hid his tears.

CHAPTER 24

The Off-Duty Tavern

A skilled warrior needs no weapons or protections but uses those of his enemy against him.

—Colbey Calistinsson

Kevral rolled in her sleep, blankets and sheets sliding silkenly across flesh. Warmth washed over her, and light bathed her closed lids, waking her instantly. She lurched to a sitting position, blinking in the intensity of the sunbeam slanting through the single window. Her gaze played over the strange, fine furnishings: delicate curtains drawn back from an oval window taller than herself, a bed canopied with feminine frills, a cedar wardrobe with edges carved into flowery spirals, a chest of drawers that supported a mirror and toiletries on its surface, and the door into her personal privacy room. Reality returned with a hot jolt of anger. She had requested an awakening at daybreak.

Seizing her swords, Kevral glided from beneath the covers and sprang gracefully from the bed. The sudden movement shocked nausea through her, an unexpected leftover from the previous night. A dash for the sewer opening scarcely brought her there in time, and she vomited into the opening for the fourth time since her arrival in Pudar. *Damn royalty's food.* The purging brought some peace to her swaying gut, leaving only a residual nausea that she would not allow to interfere with her work. Returning from the alcove, she dressed in one of the twenty drab brown tunic and britches combinations the servants had folded into her drawers. Adding her sword belt, she placed the blades in their proper positions at her hips, then strode through the teak door and into an empty hallway.

Irritation returned as Kevral strode through grand corridors filled with tapestries, weavings, and framed paintings. Regularly spaced shelves held lanterns and knickknacks of a variety Kevral would not have believed possible had she not viewed them the previous day. Though costlier than Béarn's carvings, they lacked the precision and the continuity. The masterful artwork of Pudar changed scene and style with every panel.

A servant exited a room into the hallway, shuffling backward as she dragged out a pail filled with cleaners and a broom. "What can I do for you, Lady?"

To start, you can stop calling me "lady." Kevral drove right to the point instead. "Where can I find the minister?"

The servant closed the room's door and straightened, smoothing rumpled skirts over thick legs and an ample abdomen. Wisps of brown hair, liberally mixed with gray, escaped from a knot at the nape of her neck. "Which minister are you seeking, my lady?"

Kevral drew breath before she realized she could not recall the man's name. She had met so many the previous night and clung only to those highest in Pudar's military hierarchy. "The one who talked to me last night."

The maid shook her head.

Kevral gave a brief description of the minister of visiting dignitaries, watching the woman's expression turn from confusion to consideration to guarded hope.

"I believe you mean Minister Daizar."

The name sounded familiar. "Right."

"He's holding court, Lady."

"A minister?" Kevral knew little of royal affairs, but she had learned that the king handled such matter, at least in Béarn.

"He takes care of the grievances of important visitors, Lady." The servant leaned toward Kevral conspiratorially, though her gaze locked on the swords as she did so. "Getting trapped here for months has made a lot of them surly. Wouldn't want his job. No, hoy."

"No, hoy." Kevral repeated the strange expression, rage still coiled in her chest. "Where would I find this court?"

"I'll take you there." Before Kevral could protest the need, the woman abandoned her supplies and whisked down the hallway.

Kevral trailed the plump form and her wake of flying skirts and balled hair bobbing at her collar. They wove through several wide hallways and descended two flights of stairs, arriving at a broad door sporting a silver insignia of a wolf. The walls around it held an odd mixture of foreign objects: tiny statues from Béarn, the coarse weavings of the Westland towns farther east, and gem-encrusted pottery from the distant Eastlands. Barbarian flint-tipped spears leaned against the edging of the doorway, and a shelf across from the entry supported two vials of amber kelp-wine and the broad-bladed swords of the North.

A pair of guards drifted from a smaller room next door. Dressed in sharply tailored tunics sporting Pudar's symbol over leather armor, each wore a sword at his left hip. One executed a bow, while the other accorded only a slow nod. "Did you wish to see Minister Daizar?" the first asked.

Kevral did not bother to answer. "He's in there?" She jerked her thumb toward the door.

The guards edged nervously between her and the entrance. "Yes," the first admitted. "But you can't just barge in."

The servant inched away from the conflict but did not retreat far, watching.

Kevral took a deliberate step toward the door, though this brought her threateningly near the soldiers. "Why not?"

"He could be busy with someone."

"Is he?" Kevral demanded, warmth flushing her face. Delay would fan her anger into a bonfire.

"He could be," the second said, dark mustache twitching.

More attuned to Kevral's mood, the first said, "We have to announce you." Taller and broader than his companion, he sported a shock of sandy hair that could fall into his eyes in combat.

Kevral spoke through gritted teeth. "Do it quickly."

The dark-haired guard's brows knitted, but the other opened the door before he could speak again. It swung wide to reveal the minister who had kept Kevral awake to sign the papers. His tunic flared into baggy breeches that nearly reached his knees, and high boots covered his legs. A sash at his waist, stiff lace collar, and leather gloves completed his attire. He lounged on the edge of a dais, an entourage of four guards chattering with and around him. Garbed exactly as the two at Kevral's side, they otherwise looked nothing alike. They ranged from a little taller than Kevral to the height of Béarnian nobility, though none carried the southern kingdom's breadth. All four were clean-shaven, three brown-haired and the last as blond as Kevral. His ivory skin and pale eyes identified him as a Northern descendant or transfer.

"Armsman . . . er . . . woman . . . uh . . . Armswoman Kevral to see you, sir," the larger of Kevral's escort announced.

Kevral ignored the stammering over her title as she had the addition of "lady" to her name. Aside from *torke,* which meant "teacher," the Renshai language and culture worried not at all for titles and rank. She fixed her glare directly on Daizar. "You were supposed to have me awakened at sunrise and the guards all gathered on a central practice ground."

The guards shuffled into position around Daizar, too slow for Kevral's liking.

The minister shrugged a shoulder, insolently dismissive. "King Cymion said not to wake you. He heard about your sickness last night and thought it best that you sleep."

The minister's words irritated nearly as much as his gesture. Kevral's eyes narrowed, and the urge to strike his tongue from his mouth sparked to life. "Stomach pain is not enough. When my guts lie open on the battlefield, we'll talk about missing lessons and practice." She lowered her head like a snake preparing to strike. "Maybe."

The guards stared. Even Daizar jerked backward slightly, surely taken aback. He remained seated on the edge of the dais, hands in his lap. "I answer to King Cymion, may his reign outlast the sun. He wants you in your best condition to instruct his men."

"My health," Kevral said, her flat tone betraying her rage, "will never affect my teaching."

Daizar made a fluttering motion with his fingers to indicate that the matter did not rest in his hands. "The king doesn't think you're ready."

"The king is wrong."

"The king," Daizar corrected for the second time, "is never wrong."

Kevral refused to concede. Cymion had imprisoned her under threat of execution in place of the man he believed had murdered his eldest son. If the king found more value in her instruction than assuaging his rage with her death, he would surely forgive her impudence. "This time, he is."

The guards tensed. Several appeared nervous. The blond studied her through slitted lids, his hatred evident and misplaced. Centuries ago, Northmen and Renshai had despised one another; yet history claimed they had made peace in Colbey's era. Ensconced in the southwest corner of the Westlands, Renshai rarely found opportunity to consort with Northlanders.

Kevral wondered briefly if some Northmen still harbored the ancient grudge.

Daizar drew a sharp breath, loosing it gradually. "Lady, when the king decides you're ready, the teaching will commence."

Kevral had heard enough. "I'll show you ready." She eyed the guards, gauging strengths and weaknesses in a glance. She believed she could kill them all, yet the training would proceed more competently and smoothly if she earned their respect without humiliation. The hostility boiling inside her needed a target, and she could feel her control slipping.

The blond huffed out a derisive laugh. "What are you going to do? Draw your sword and kill us all?"

Kevral took three deliberate steps toward him, accompanied by her escort. She met eyes like sea foam in a face beyond youth but not yet coarsened by middle age. "No," she said carefully. Without warning, she lunged toward him. The blond reached for his hilt, too late. Kevral's palm closed around it first. As it rasped free, he caught a sharpened edge, swiftly releasing it before it sliced open his hand. "I wouldn't dishonor my blade by spilling *your* blood on it."

The blond retreated, growling vulgarities. The others drew their weapons, as Kevral executed a broad sweep with the guard's sword that kept them at bay. The maneuver gained her the moment she needed to reorient. As the guards formed a semicircle between her and the minister, she slammed the blade down a finger's breadth beyond another's hand. His fingers jerked back. His sword plummeted from his grip.

Kevral caught the hilt as much from habit as homage, and spun. The swords cut the air around her, clearing a blade-length ring. The four armed guards charged as one. Admiring their strategy but disdaining their competence, she ducked one, chopped two hilts from their wielder's grips, and dodged the fourth. She managed to catch one of the airborne weapons. The other crashed, ringing, to the tiles where she stomped on the blade, pinning it. She assumed a defensive position as the armed guards cautiously realigned and the others scurried beyond range.

"Halt!" Daizar shouted. He remained in place on the dais, not even driven to stand by the violence. Only a flush to his gaunt cheeks and a pursing of his lips to lines betrayed the fear he hid so well. "Men, at ease. Kevral . . ." He lifted his gaze to her.

Kevral turned her attention to him, but she kept track of all six of the guards with peripheral vision. Only the blond seemed in any danger of violating the minister's command. The others wore clear expressions of relief, their stances wholly defensive. She doubted even the Northman would charge her weaponless.

". . . I'm convinced. I believe I can talk the king into allowing your dawn awakening and guard assemblage in the morning."

Kevral tossed the swords back to their proper owners, saving the blond's for last. She flipped them gently, so that the hilts came easily to their hands. All but one, the tallest, managed to snatch his grip from the air. That man tried, nails scraping the leather, then the sword clattered to the floor. He scooped it up and restored it to its sheath. Though she remained alert for attack, Kevral maintained an aura of quiet composure. If necessary, she could disarm them all again. "There're twenty-five hundred soldiers?"

"Approximately," the minister of foreign dignitaries said.

During negotiations, Kevral had suggested she train twenty-four each morning and the same in the afternoon. They would, in turn, use their off-time to train their fellows. She had tried to reserve the right to rotate her company to ensure every Pudarian guard received proper teaching. The king had resisted this, preferring forty-eight elite guardsmen to 2500 equal but lesser soldiers. Though uncertain of the exact terms that had finally appeared in the written document, Kevral assumed she needed to gather the original forty-eight. Further details would become clear when she found time to read the papers. "Divide them into groups of about 250 and find a field where they can practice. I'll select my students today."

"Today?" Daizar repeated, tone incredulous.

Kevral nodded.

"But we haven't got a field big enough to stack 250 men at once."

"I'll find one." Kevral took her eyes from Daizar to scan the guardsmen. The blond glared, a scowl etched deeply onto his features. The others watched silently, their expressions more benign. The sandy-haired one who had served as an escort, and been disarmed, bobbed his head, reliving the mastery of Kevral's attack in detail. His quiet trip into assessment pleased the woman who would soon become his teacher. Analyzing swordplay befit a warrior. "I'll make one if I have to. And I'll spend some time at the barracks. We'll need to make some definite changes." She glanced at the one deep in thought. "Starting with hair ties and cuts." With that, she pirouetted, not worrying for the back she turned to Minister Daizar's guards. And left the room.

Voices seeped through the crack as the door swung closed. "It's going to be a long year," one said. The blond uttered a Northern vulgarity for Renshai.

The sandy-haired guard spoke last. "I, for one, am going to pray I'm chosen."

The closing click of the door cut the rest into silence.

He was chosen. And the sullen blond whose name, Kevral discovered, was Tyrion. This once, the latter replaced his stony glare with a wrinkled mask of confusion.

With the help of two off-duty guardsmen, Kevral had staked out a rectangle in the market square, taking up a block that had once held bustling crowds and now only abandoned stalls and stands. The few remaining merchants required little coaxing to move to an area not roped off for combat. The soldiers swung and sparred, while Kevral meandered through them, selecting her forty-eight students from the ranks. Spectators crammed along the ropes, eager to catch glimpses of the king's new swordmistress or to watch the guardsmen hammer at one another with practice weapons. Even the king had come, perched upon a spotted and gaily beribboned stallion. He held his head high, the gray and auburn curls meticulously arranged and his blue eyes intensely watchful. Clearly, he sought the subtle differences in technique that motivated Kevral to sort his men.

Kevral suspected her system baffled him. She placed potential over talent, judging natural dexterity and strength from the arrangement and use of muscle groups and from movements that had little to do with winning spars. As often as not, she chose the losers of such contests. Other details caught her eye. She collected men with few natural abilities but a determination that would allow them to learn the skills with which the gods never blessed them at birth. The sandy-haired one fell into this category. Tyrion, she chose for other reasons. Though able and strong, his attitude attracted her more. He would prove an offensive fighter, a necessity to Kevral's Renshai mind. He would prove a challenge, one she preferred within grasp and sight rather than lurking in the shadows.

"Finished," Kevral announced as twilight stole color vision and the last batch of soldiers returned to their dinners or posts.

Only then, King Cymion approached her. "Are you aware you only accepted one of my three lieutenants and three of my ten captains?"

Kevral had paid no attention to these distinctions, but she found a sure answer better than placing her observational skills in doubt. "Yes, Sire." She bowed, though a curtsy seemed more appropriate.

Apparently awaiting an explanation, the king sat in silence. When none was forthcoming, he shrugged. "Very well, then." He reined his horse toward the castle, guardsmen surrounding him from every side. Apparently, his contract gave her free decision on this matter.

General Markanyin remained behind while the king and his entourage disappeared.

Kevral paid him no heed, instead dividing her troop in half. She addressed Tyrion's group first. "Daybreak on the south practice field. Bring swords, nothing else. Every moment you're late is an extra hour you stay into the next class. See you tomorrow." Giving a similar speech to the others, she dismissed them as well. After all of the guardsmen headed off, she finally turned her attention to the general.

Stubble perched on a rectangular head, gray spreading from the temples. His thick neck and torso held more muscle than fat, and he kept his enormous hands at his sides. "Good evening, Armsman."

"Good evening, General," Kevral returned, eager for her own practice. Like an addict too long without his drug, she yearned to commune with her gods through the all-consuming violence of swordplay.

"I wondered if you would be willing to add one more student to your afternoon session."

Despite her distraction, Kevral made the obvious connection. "You?"

Markanyin shrugged. "I can't have my men outmaneuvering me."

Kevral nodded in agreement. "All right. It'll unbalance the group, though. When we get to sparring, you may have to face off with me."

"You won't embarrass me, will you?"

Kevral made no promises, quoting Colbey as answer. "Nobody can embarrass a man; he can only embarrass himself."

She did not intend to humiliate anyone who did not deserve the disgrace.

Markanyin laughed, a surprisingly jovial sound for a man of war. "I guess I take my chances, then."

Kevral had no answer. The conversation drifted into polite silence, during which Kevral's thoughts turned back to her *svergelse* and which moves most needed practice.

Markanyin's voice startled Kevral. "The men are concerned that you're going to take away their pleasures." He dodged her gaze, obviously uncomfortable with the turn of the conversation.

The words made little sense to Kevral. "Their pleasures?"

"The card room. Their off-duty time. Women. Ale."

Kevral grunted her understanding.

Another hush fell, again broken by Markanyin. "Are you?"

"Going to take away their pleasures?"

"Yes."

Kevral threw up her hands in a noncommittal gesture. She would never have guessed she had such an option, and she suspected she still might not. Markanyin seemed to be working around to explaining the limits of her authority, a lecture she wished to avoid. As long as she did, the possibilities remained open. Again, she looked to Colbey for answers. "I care about three things: that my students come on time, that they give every practice their all, and that they respect me and one another. What they choose to do when not in my class does not interest or concern me." She lowered her head and raised her brows, a clear warning. "Any activity that decreases their ability in class, they will surely voluntarily surrender." She would not tolerate sloth. Sickness, whether due to chance or excess, was no excuse for slacking.

"A reasonable compromise." Markanyin made a courtesy movement of his trunk, more good-bye than bow. "I'll see you tomorrow afternoon, then."

"Tomorrow afternoon," Kevral confirmed. Without waiting to see whether or not the general left, she turned on her heel and headed for the courtyard. There, she believed, she could find a place to practice that would not strike worry into Pudar's citizenry. Unused to drawn steel on their streets, especially in the hands of women, they might not take well to her swordplay.

Kevral took dinner in her room that night, but it still sparked the nausea she had suffered the previous day. She managed to struggle into bed without vomiting, cursing the food of the affluent and promising herself a simple meal tomorrow from whatever tavern or inn the citizens preferred. She could not do it every night, as she had brought minimal coinage with her and all of that of Béarnian mint. Though Pudar accepted money from every country, they tended to favor their own currency when it came to bargaining and purchases. She curled into a fetal position, suffering waves of discomfort. Turning her thoughts to her *svergelse*, she analyzed every movement, drawing her mind from the discomfort that had not existed while ensconced in swordplay. In a flurry of movement, now wholly mental, she drifted off to sleep.

The sickness followed Kevral into morning, lasting only until she purged it. Skipping breakfast, she bounded out to the practice field beside the guard's barracks precisely at daybreak. All twenty-four students chattered and milled on the grassy field that, had they practiced as they should, would consist only of trampled mud. Soon, Kevral assured herself, it would.

Taking a position at the front of the group, Kevral cleared her throat, a sound lost beneath the tumult. Most of the guards went politely quiet and directed their attention to her. Others continued speaking, a disrespect Colbey Calistinsson never would have tolerated. Kevral frowned, giving them several moments longer than she believed they deserved. Without warning, she drew and lunged. Startled guards skittered out of her way. Her sword licked a finger's breadth from a talker's throat, and he choked back his words. Bindings cut cleanly, his cloak slid to the ground behind him.

An alarmed silence followed.

Kevral sheathed her sword in the same movement. Calmly, she stepped back into place. Having seized everyone's notice, she no longer dwelled on the plight of the white-faced brunet who clutched at his throat, seeking blood. "My name is Kevral, and I'm going to teach you how to wield a sword."

Kevral drew breath, waiting for someone to shout or mutter that they already knew; but the abrupt violence a moment earlier seemed to hold even Tyrion to a respectful hush. At least, for the moment.

"Some of it may seem simple, at first. But you have to relearn the basics, properly this time, to gain any competence with the complicated . . ." Proper wording failed her this time, and Kevral ended lamely with, ". . . stuff." This time, she thought she caught a mumbled indecipherable comment. She ignored it. "Do everything I tell you with confidence, aggression, and your best effort. Fall short of that, and you'll come to hate me."

"I loathe you already," Tryion could not help informing Kevral.

The reactions ranged from horrified stares to suppressed smiles. No one dared to laugh aloud. Kevral nodded good-naturedly, "Good. Chances are, I'll give you plenty of reason." She glanced around at the others, all of whom had recovered from their initial reactions and now stood in stony-faced silence. "Any questions?"

The smallest of the group, a spry brunet with a close-cropped beard spoke. "Only sword?" On the selecting field, he had used a staff, and she chose him because his style suggested he knew no other weapons and would benefit greatly from her teachings.

"Only sword," Kevral confirmed, suspecting his basic question demanded a "why" as well as a "yes or no." "Sword is superior to any other weapon."

A few skeptical noises ran through the crowd, none of them fully verbalized.

"It has greater versatility, allowing you to slash, stab, or bludgeon as the circumstance fits. It has the best reach to balance; its weight does not cluster at the tip. Warriors of every size, weight, and strength can learn to wield it competently. Its double edge makes it two weapons in one." Kevral glanced around, her reverence for her blades drawing her to an awe the others might not share. "As in chess, the sword is the queen of the battlefield."

"Any more questions?" Kevral glared pointedly at Tyrion, expecting something snide; but the Northman only met her gaze with a quiet smirk. Mischief danced in his pale eyes.

"All right, then." Kevral began her first lesson.

It was after sunset before Kevral finished teaching and a long *svergelse*, the latter needed as much to forget the ineptitude of her students as to luxuriate in the natural rush of body chemicals exertion always inspired. She sought good in bad, pacifying herself with the realization that she could not help but improve Pudar's soldiers. The sickness that had assailed her since that first night in Pudar still haunted her, but concentration on sword work kept it at bay. Just as she would not accept such weakness from her students, she would not tolerate it in herself.

Enemies on the battlefield would not make allowances for illness, and neither would circumstance.

Remembering her internal promise the previous night, Kevral headed from the practice field, through the castle gates, and out into the city. Darkness cloaked the tarp-covered stands into shapeless masses, and cottages huddled against a twining autumn wind. Lanterns lit many of the windows, the light warped through thick, flawed glass. She padded away from the market area and farther toward the older living areas. The taverns nearer the stores would cater to foreigners, and she sought a bland meal that would not upset a stomach that had never before proven so unforgiving.

Mud-chinked stone homes, most with thatched roofs, soon lined the roadways Kevral chose. She avoided alleys, seeing no reason to invite conflict, though she never feared it. An inn or tavern would likely sit on one of the wider, more well-traveled streets. Occasional people passed her, but few bothered to exchange greetings or even to glance up from beneath their hoods. The few who did shied from her evident weaponry, and Kevral did not corner anyone for directions.

Kevral's stomach growled, empty since dinner the previous night. Driven by its protests, Kevral searched for a patrolling guard who would not feel so discomforted by her presence. Before she could find one, however, the creak of a suspended sign reached her hearing. She followed it around the corner to an old but comfortable-looking tavern. A metal pole dangling a chain from each end supported a weathered sign reading: "Off-duty Tavern." Lanterns under the eaves gave the outside a cheery glow, and smoke twined from the chimney.

Kevral loosed a chuckle, suspecting the place catered to guardsmen. Too hungry to seek another establishment, she headed toward it.

Before Kevral trotted halfway down the street, the door banged open, admitting a stronger beam of torchlight into the street. Two men exited, one staggering and the other clutching an arm to steady him. Laughter funneled out into the street, along with mandolin music that, though adequate, sounded hideously discordant after Darris' talent. A few patrons milled around a porch with a hitching post that currently held no horses. Kevral quickened her pace as the door swung shut, smacking the lintel with a crash that surely irritated the neighbors. She imagined it occurring at irregular intervals into the night and cringed. *Surely any early or light sleepers would have moved away by now.*

As Kevral approached the "Off-duty Tavern," she recognized three of the five men on the porch as guards she had not selected from the mass. She could not memorize all the faces in a day, and she suspected the others might be guards as well. Exchanging nods with them, she caught the door latch, its brass icy from the night air. Tripping it, she shoved the door open.

Torches hung in simple brackets that consisted of little more than twisted pieces of discarded metal. A fire blazed in the hearth, and some of the smoke trailed backward, dimming the interior despite its many lights. Several of the tables held patrons, all male and many familiar. The aroma of freshly baked bread mingled with the acrid odor of the fire, beer smell, and a crisper scent of meat. Kevral's stomach grumbled another protest. She discovered several off-duty guards, including Tyrion who sat with three others from her morning class. A few of her afternoon pupils had come as well.

Kevral considered joining them momentarily, then decided against it. The general had expressed the concern that she might interfere with their pleasure time activities, and her presence could do so every bit as much as directly forbidding them. Realizing her decision now could set the stage for all future relationships during her time in Pudar, she still chose solitude. Finding a small table near a relatively dark corner, she sat alone and tried to watch the others without staring.

A boy of about twelve years wound through the crowd and stopped in front of her table. "What can I get for you, sir?"

Kevral did not bother to correct the misconception. "What's dinner?"

"Roasted chicken, starch root, and carrots."

Kevral heaved a relieved sigh. Her guts would surely appreciate the plainness of the fare, lacking the castle's gravies, sauces and spices. "A plate of that, please. And some water."

The boy smiled, grin broad beneath a large nose. Sandy bangs hung into his eyes, rendering them nearly invisible. "You don't need to settle for water. That man over there said he'd buy your first ale." He jabbed a finger toward Tyrion.

The mere thought of alcohol reawakened Kevral's nausea. The water would contain a hint of wine to counteract whatever human waste tainted the supply, but she had grown used to that. "Thank him for me, but please bring me water."

Brown eyes appeared from beneath the fringe of hair. "Very well. Thank you." He bustled from the table in obvious confusion. Surely no one had refused ale before.

Kevral studied the fire while she waited, watching flames of yellow, orange, and red caper along the logs. In the heat of battle, with her reserves flagging, she had often conjured images of a great conflagration devouring everything in its path. Often, she had emulated that picture, hewing through enemies with the same fearless unstoppability. The serving boy's mistake about her gender turned her thoughts to Ra-khir and the day of their meeting. His red-blond hair seemed to match the more subdued portions of the fire, and she missed the solemn green eyes and handsome features. She could still sketch him into her mind's eye, but the edges of memory blurred. The year had scarcely begun, yet it seemed so long since she had seen him. And she missed him terribly.

A deliberate movement nearby gained Kevral's attention before her thoughts could turn to Tae. She glanced up to see Tyrion approaching her table. Bracing for trouble, she eased her chair slightly back from the table and let her hands fall to her lap. She waited only until he came within earshot, knowing that to speak first when he expected to do so would gain her the upper hand. "Thank you for your generosity."

Tyrion continued toward Kevral. "I understand you refused it."

"Yes," Kevral admitted. "But that doesn't make the offer any less generous."

Tyrion did not stop until he stood at the opposite side of the round table. He rested his fingertips on the surface and glared down at Kevral, emphasizing the size difference between them. "In Pudar, refusing a gift is an insult."

That had not been Kevral's experience during the months she lived in Pudar, but she did not quibble. "I wasn't aware of that. I apologize for insulting you. You can buy my water if you wish."

Tyrion did not blink. Nearly colorless eyes continued to study her beneath lashes so blond they all but disappeared. "If you wanted to fit in, if you wanted to become one of us—"

Kevral interrupted, not seeing the purpose of such an argument. "What I want is some water."

"Oh, so we're not good enough for you?"

"I'm teaching you, aren't I?"

Tyrion removed his hands from the table and straightened,

switching to another tactic. "Now I understand. You won't drink the ale because you're a coward."

Tyrion had used the worst insult Renshai knew. Rage flashed, then immediately died. The accusation had no basis to sting. "What does cowardice have to do with ale?"

Tyrion made a dismissing gesture, as if it should seem obvious. "You're afraid to drink the ale."

Kevral snorted, the conversation nonsensical. "First, my decision not to drink ale has nothing to do with fear. Second, there is no cowardice in choosing not to dump liquor into my body. More often, there is cowardice in facing life with its support." Kevral met the blue eyes squarely. "If you challenged me to battle and I refused, then you might have reason to criticize. Baiting a Renshai warrior is rarely considered wise."

"Why's that?" Tyrion asked, though he surely knew the answer.

"Because I could choose to kill you."

Tyrion nodded. "With your sword, probably."

Kevral believed she understood Tyrion's game. If he goaded her into attacking him, he could claim self-defense if the matter came to trial. His only chance for victory lay in a contest that pitted only strength against strength. Likely, he had hoped to ply her with alcohol first, believing it would lower her violence threshold as well as impair competence and judgment. She leaned forward with a cautious smile. "Tyrion," she said. "I could kill you with *your* sword." As she had already proved that once, Kevral saw no reason to enforce her statement. "Go back to your friends and your ale. Show me this kind of exuberance at practice tomorrow. Now that I've seen what you're capable of, I won't accept less."

Tyrion lowered his voice, assuring that only the two of them could hear, though Kevral doubted anyone could have previously sorted their conversation from the hubbub. "This isn't over, Renshai."

Kevral smiled. "I'd be disappointed if it was." She waved him away.

Tyrion hesitated a moment, hostility still smoldering in his eyes. Then he turned and walked back to his companions.

On his heels, the serving boy appeared with Kevral's food. She ate slowly, savoring the plainness of the food. Mediocre, even for common fare, it served her purposes well enough. She guessed the ale was of higher quality and accounted for the popularity of the tavern.

By the time Kevral finished, Tyrion and his companions had departed. She had not noticed them leaving, though she had heard the door slam closed on several occasions. The comings and goings of the Off-duty Tavern did not interest her. Her own thoughts made better company, focusing mostly on coming lessons, anticipating Tyrion's next move, which would likely come at the next morning's practice, and consideration of her friends back in Béarn. She wondered how Griff was faring as king and whether or not directing and protecting him had worn Darris to a frazzle. She hoped Tae and his father had fully reconciled.

At length, Kevral stood, stretched, and paid her tab. Unless the king accorded her a monetary allowance of some sort, she could not afford many more of these meals. Offers such as Tyrion's might seem like godsends. She smiled at the idea and headed from the tavern.

Kevral yawned as she pushed open the door. Recalling her assessment of the bother to the neighbors, she eased the spring-loaded panel closed so that it made only a quiet click. A new group of patrons relaxed on the porch, including General Markanyin.

"Hello, Armsman!" He boomed a friendly welcome.

"Good evening, General," Kevral returned with warm sincerity. Over the past few hours, she had come to appreciate his attitude. He could have felt threatened by a respected newcomer working with his men, but he chose to see her in terms of her value to Pudar's soldiers. Kevral made a mental note to compliment the king on his choice of war leader.

"Don't worry," Markanyin said, winking to indicate he was not chastising or implying she had come to spy on them. "I'm headed back in a moment. I'll be fresh, rested, and ready to learn at midday."

"Good," Kevral returned in the same spirit. "Maybe you'll get through it with a minimum of bruises."

"My aching muscles from today are enough, thank you."

"You're welcome." Kevral laughed as she bounded down the steps and into the street. General Markanyin's humor would go a long way toward allowing the men to look at their training, however brutal, as a positive experience.

Buoyed by the simple exchange, Kevral managed to set aside the irritation created by Tyrion's animosity. She padded through the streets with a new feeling of hopefulness. Teaching a bunch of *ganim* to use swords might not prove nearly as tedious as she expected. She could hear voices and footfalls echoing through the streets behind her and hoped it meant General Markanyin had meant the words he had spoken mostly in jest.

Tyrion's familiar voice wafted from a crossroad. "So sword's the best weapon, is it?"

Kevral resisted the natural urge to stiffen. She would never reveal that he had caught her off guard. Instead, she turned with a confident air intended to imply she still held the upper hand. "It is."

Tyrion stood halfway down the alley, a drawn longbow aimed at Kevral. "So, Swordmistress, tell me how you'd use a sword against this." He let the arrow fly.

Kevral could tell by the trajectory that it would miss her. The shaft flew past her waist, its movement a cool breeze that stirred her tunic. It embedded into a knothole in a rain barrel, clearly its target.

Rage kindled fire in Kevral's veins. She sprang and drew simultaneously, reaching Tyrion before he could nock a second arrow. Her left-hand sword severed the bow, and her right caught him a clouting blow across the skull. "I don't need to use a sword against an incompetent who chooses a coward's weapon."

Tyrion crashed to the ground with a bellow of anger. An edge of his broken bow slashed his sleeve and arm, and scarlet stained the fabric in a spreading circle.

The urge to slaughter Tyrion and leave his body on the cobbles seized Kevral, but she resisted. She doubted Colbey would murder a student, no matter how irritating.

"I missed you on purpose," Tyrion muttered, clamping his good hand over his bleeding wrist. "If I'd have aimed for you, you'd be dead."

Several men rushed to the scene. Kevral recognized most of the guards she had watched on the practice field, though only one other was a student of hers. General Markanyin shoved his way through the others.

Kevral ignored them for the more important purpose of teaching. She sheathed her weapons, glaring down at her wayward student. "Never ever shoot, stab, or swing to miss."

"I saw the whole thing," General Markanyin announced. He looked at Kevral. "He attacked you."

Tyrion groaned, clapping his face into his palms. Clearly, he had chosen the wrong place and time for challenges.

The general finished. "Shall I clap him in irons?"

The entire alleyway awaited Kevral's pronouncement. Despite all the men present, the wind whistling through the narrow threadway made more noise.

Finally, Kevral said, "As long as he's out in time for class at daybreak."

General Markanyin smiled. "It would be my pleasure."

CHAPTER 25

Knight-Testing

*There's no honor in allowing steel to fend an enemy's blows
instead of skill. In personal skill only there is honor.*
— Colbey Calistinsson

Ra-khir sat on the floor of his father's cottage, knees drawn to
his chest and arms clasped around his legs. Six knights, including Kedrin, sat on the bench and on chairs near the hearth. Ra-
khir kept his fingers laced to control their nervous shaking, and
his eyes fixed on whichever of his mentors chose to speak.
Soon, he hoped, he would sit as an equal among them. Today's
trials and testing would decide whether he became a Knight of
Erythane or ended his training forever.

Armsman Edwin explained the details, his dark eyes fixed on
his student and his round head bobbing at the most important
words. "Once the testing begins, nothing may interrupt it, Ra-
khir. We're assessing stamina and patience as well as courage
and competence, knowledge, intelligence, and honor. Few have
the qualities necessary to become a Knight of Erythane, and
failure at this is no judgment of your value. You represent the
best Erythane has to offer, or we would never have accepted
you for training. Knighthood does not suit many good men."

Ra-khir listened raptly, trying to internalize Edwin's words.
His lips felt cracked, yet he resisted the urge to lick them. His
mouth seemed equally parched. In the past, he had never found
looking at another human being difficult. Now, staring directly
into Edwin's eyes too long seemed aggressive but avoiding
them made him feel shifty. In the end, he compromised by politely studying the armsman's face. Every expression, each look
required a concentration they never had in the past, and he
found himself reading the knights just as carefully. For the first
time since his training started, he could not imagine himself on
a white charger, its mane flowing with gold and blue ribbons,

his tabard displaying the colors of Erythane and Béarn, his place between two of the knights he so admired.

Only after a lengthy pause did Ra-khir realize they probably intended for him to speak. Sudden terror struck him at the possible rudeness of his silence, and he sought words in a mind that seemed to have turned to liquid. "Thank all of you, sirs," he managed, "for the opportunity to achieve the world's . . ." Words failed him, and he allowed a soundless prayer for what he had accomplished. ". . . highest honor."

The knights nodded their acceptance of his appreciation in a line, as if they had rehearsed it. Edwin continued, "Gather your practice weapons, armor, and horse and meet me on the practice field as swiftly as you can."

Ra-khir waited only until the others rose before rushing to his room to fetch his weapons. He had prepared his possessions the previous night and had only to snatch up his heavy pack, haul it to the paddock, and lash it securely to the gray's back. He saddled the horse and tied the bridle carefully atop his gear. Taking the gelding's lead rope and a pike, he led the animal up the hill by its halter. As he hurried to the practice ground, he heard his father's soft call behind him, "Good luck, Ra-khir."

Ra-khir gave Kedrin a stiff gesture to indicate he would make his father proud. He turned to look, but Kedrin had already withdrawn, and only the cold face of the cottage remained to encourage him. Ra-khir quickened his pace.

Though eager to become a Knight of Erythane, Ra-khir savored his last moments of childhood as he rushed toward the Bellenet Field that had served as the knights' training area since long before the birth of the oldest ancestor he could trace. He sucked cold air through his nostrils, a chill, refreshing contrast to the nervous sweat forming beneath his tunic. The hopes and dreams of a lifetime rested upon this day, and he felt suddenly wholly unprepared.

As Ra-khir topped the rise, the familiar wood and wire fence came into view and, beyond it, the scaffolding held a ready ring. Whatever else the knights would test, he would, apparently, be given the opportunity to display his skill with pike. This did not surprise Ra-khir; charging had been the favored fighting method for as long as the Knights of Erythane existed. Simply thinking about his preferred maneuver, and that at which he held the most skill helped control the wild beating of his heart.

The armsman met Ra-khir as he drew his horse to its usual grazing spot. Two other knights held a position near the fence, standing gravely at attention as if attending a feast in Béarn Castle. Dressed in formal silks with tabards, they stood motionless, their postures a perfect match. Three young women perched on the upper rung of the fence. None but the knights and Erythane's king knew when a testing occurred, so these must have come to watch the morning practice, canceled for Ra-khir's trials. A man leaned against the fence as well. Ra-khir had to glance at him twice to realize he was another of the knights. His slouching, easy position, casual clothing, and uncombed hair rendered him almost unrecognizable. He wore a narrow-bladed sword at his hip, and Ra-khir caught a glimpse of a shield in the grass beside him. A fifth knight, in appropriate dress, stood near the scaffolding.

Armsman Edwin cleared his throat, instantly gaining Ra-khir's attention. "Prepare for ring joust."

Ra-khir responded instantly, hauling down his pack. Drawing out his armor and underpadding, he donned them in proper form and sequence, keeping the horse between self and spectators. Although covered at all times, strangers' eyes watching him dress sent uncomfortable chills coursing through him. He buckled the bridle over the horse's head. Edwin hefted the pike while Ra-khir prepared, then helped him into the saddle.

"Thank you, sir," Ra-khir said, taking the weapon from his teacher.

Edwin acknowledged the appreciation with a barely noticeable movement of his head. "You may make your first pass when ready."

Ra-khir rode into position, the hand on his pike growing slick before he reached it, and with a desperate tremor seizing him. *This is not good.* Ra-khir cursed his nerves. *Surely they'll take the situation into account.* He doubted the thought as soon as it arose. *Battle is frightening, too; and there's no reprieve there.* Lowering his head, he quieted his nerves by visualizing his own wild ride through Eastern ambushes. Then he had left his friends to find the antidote to a poison killing Kevral. The information he gained, though not a cure, had been too important to lose. Perched on Colbey's charger, he had rammed through enemies with a makeshift spear, need too great to tolerate delay. He tried to recapture the mind-set of that moment. The trembling left his fingers, and his grip on the pike steadied. He concentrated on the tiny ring held in place by the scaffolding and placed at the level of a mounted enemy's chest. Smiling at the new measure of control, Ra-khir raised his head and charged the ring.

Ground disappeared under the gray's hooves, and the ring became a minuscule target dangling amid a world of air. The point of Ra-khir's pike seemed a mile away, bouncing with every movement of self or horse. Then, suddenly, the scaffolding came upon him. Ra-khir's steadiness did not betray him. The point of the pike skewered the ring, and it clattered down the pole. He bit back a grin as he overran the scaffolding, and the knight placed another ring into position.

Ra-khir caught a glimpse of Edwin raising his hands, then lowering them back to his sides. Under other circumstances, Ra-khir would have received at least one clap. Now, however, the armsman had turned from teacher to tester and, soon, Ra-khir hoped, to peer. Success on the first pass allayed most of his fear, and he lost all doubt that he would handle at least the ring jousting portion of his examination admirably. For now, he let the realization that he did nothing else as well as this disappear. Confidence would serve him better than self-doubt. Perhaps catching the first ring would prove his ability in this regard well enough. Riding to his teacher, Ra-khir handed over the ring.

Edwin accepted it. "Again," he said.

Or not. Ra-khir rode back into charging position as the knight near the scaffolding finished preparing the second ring and Edwin returned him the first. Waiting until both had moved safely out of the way, Ra-khir kicked his mount into a gallop.

By the twenty-fifth pass, foam speckled Ra-khir's gray, and it snorted its protests in loud, sudden bursts. Ra-khir had managed to catch fifteen rings, including the last two. He did not know how that compared to King Humfreet's and Griff's knights, but he knew none of his fellow apprentices could come close to matching it. He forced himself to savor no pride in that achievement, refusing to belittle respected peers as the source for his competence. Despite winter's biting chill, and the icy wind that swept exposed flesh, sweat trickled from every part and he felt suffocated beneath his helmet. His arms felt as weak as twigs, cramped and aching from the need to elevate the heavy pike so many times and for so long.

Edwin accepted the latest ring from Ra-khir. "You may pack your armor now."

Though relieved, Ra-khir resisted a bubbling show of gratitude. He returned only a formal nod before dismounting and setting carefully to work. No matter his fatigue, he would treat his armor properly. The knights on the field judged his every gesture and word. He would show them even fatigue and anxiety would not make him careless. Each piece of armor found its place in his pack: wiped, oiled, and wrapped. He had just started on his padding when Sir Jakrusan, the knight in civilian attire, approached him.

"A skilled display." Jakrusan shook back unruly, brown hair and pinned Ra-khir with muddy eyes that held just a hint of green. Though large for his age, Ra-khir stood two fingers' breadths shorter and not quite as broad as the knight. A hawk-like nose gave him a hard, predatory look, magnified by his lack of colors.

"Thank you, sir," Ra-khir said with clear appreciation.

"Don't get too swell-headed." The knight used a gruff tone and slang that did not suit his station. "I was lauding your horse, not you." He studied the gray, pacing a semicircle that left the animal watching him warily. "If I had a beast like this one, I could do better'n you."

The words made little sense. Like all of the knights of Erythane, Sir Jakrusan rode a white charger that put the apprentices' grays to shame. Clearly, the role-playing was a part of Ra-khir's testing, and he understood he should treat the knight like any citizen. Ra-khir returned a polite nod. "Very good, sir. You must be a ring jouster of considerable skill." Ra-khir hoped the underlying pride inherent in the statement did not meet with disapproval. Indirectly, he had complimented his own ability as well.

From the corner of Ra-khir's eye, he saw a grin touch Edwin's lips and disappear. Self-confidence violated no tenets when spoken in such a humble, indirect fashion.

Jakrusan continued to examine the gray. "I want this horse. How much?"

The question confused Ra-khir. "How much what, sir?"

Jakrusan turned his stare to Ra-khir. The dark eyes held a hint of contempt. "How much to buy him?"

"Oh." Ra-khir shook his head. "He's not for sale, sir."

"Nonsense," Jakrusan boomed. "Everything is for sale at the right price."

Ra-khir chose to explain rather than disagree. "This horse doesn't belong to me, sir. I'm an apprentice Knight of Erythane. This horse belongs to King Humfreet. Even should I wish to sell him, I couldn't."

Jakrusan's eyes narrowed. "I could kill you and take the horse."

Ra-khir's brows shot up, and he resisted the natural urge to speak Kevral's words: *You could try*. He kept his response true to a knight's honor. "If you're challenging me, I have no choice but to accept. However, killing me would not change the fact that the horse belongs to King Humfreet."

"A battle, then," Jakrusan shouted. "But not to the death. We'll spar until one of us deals the equivalent of a killing blow."

Ra-khir acknowledged the choice with a benign gesture. "You called the challenge; that is your decision. You also have the right to choose weapon, location, and timing."

Jakrusan glanced about them.

Ra-khir looked around also. The knights had not moved from their positions, still judging him. Edwin said nothing. The women watched intently, one white-faced and another clutching her hands to her lips. They did not have the benefit of knowing Jakrusan tested him.

The challenging knight drew his sword. "Here and now suits me fine."

Ra-khir did not allow face or voice to reveal his disappointment. Though the most common, sword had always proved his worst weapon. Kevral's instructions, however, stole some of the discomfort from Jakrusan's choice. His skill had come a long way in a short time; it might even surprise his armsman. "Very well." Ra-khir returned to his pack for his sword, turning his back on his opponent as a gesture of trust. An honorable opponent would never stab him in the back, and to mistrust the other's honor would prove grave insult. A smile touched his lips as he recognized the cultural differences even between neighboring people who served the same kingdom. On the Renshai's Fields of Wrath, turning one's back on a warrior was a sign of disdain, indicating skill so far beneath one's own that defense was unnecessary. Retrieving his practice sword from his pack, Ra-khir faced off with the knight.

Ra-khir assumed a defensive position as Jakrusan did the same. True to Kevral's teachings, he did not remain there long, but lashed a controlled stroke toward Jakrusan's head. Apparently startled by the swift bravado, Jakrusan scarcely parried. The need for sudden defense gave the next strike to Ra-khir. This time, he cut low. Jakrusan leaped backward, then lunged back in with a gut stroke that Ra-khir battered aside before delivering a slashing riposte. Momentum carried him to Jakrusan's side, but he did not bother to align before dodging and boring back in.

The exchange of thrust and parry continued, Ra-khir dedicating his all to the battle. Neither knights nor kings could afford one among them who lacked courage as well as skill. That Jakrusan had selected Ra-khir's least competent weapon would prove no consolation should he fail this test. Once, Kevral's back to basics approach had irritated him. Now he understood the need. He had forgotten the early necessities as more complex maneuvers engrossed him. Constant repetition had branded them into his thoughts and motions. He executed them now without the need for memory, leaving concentration for the more difficult procedures required to triumph.

Jakrusan broke character to speak. "You've been practicing." His blade swept for Ra-khir's throat.

Ra-khir jerked away, not bothering with a reply. Kevral had taught him not to talk while fighting with a vehemence that reawakened bruises now long healed.

The spar lasted longer than even Ra-khir expected, and he found himself battling the fatigue and aches of his ring jousting session. His breath came in ragged gasps, and his eyes stung from sweat and the dryness that came from following Jakrusan's sword. Finally, Jakrusan scored a touch across Ra-khir's thigh. Apparently oblivious to his win, the knight lunged in for another attack.

Ra-khir retreated, signaling Edwin to end the match.

"Call!" Edwin shouted.

Ra-khir lowered his sword.

Jakrusan pulled his strike, brows furrowing in confusion. "Why are we stopping?"

Edwin looked at Ra-khir for an explanation.

"You won, sir," Ra-khir said.

"He did?" Edwin returned.

"I did?" Jakrusan said, almost simultaneously, then shook his head. "I didn't deliver a killing stroke equivalent."

Ra-khir did not hesitate. He was not mistaken. "Here, sir." He traced the line of the sword across his leg. "In a real fight, you would have cut the artery. Death in moments."

A murmur startled Ra-khir. The intensity of the battle had allowed him to forget the spectators.

"Well, then," Jakrusan sheathed his sword. "I get the horse."

Ra-khir remained calm, though the repetition and his exhaustion wore on him. "No, sir. The horse belongs to King Humfreet, mine to use until he reclaims it."

Jakrusan glared, hands falling to his hips and dangerously close to his hilt again. "I bested a knight in fair combat. Isn't there a law that says I get the horse?"

"I'm only a knight-in-training, sir," Ra-khir reminded him. He shook back strawberry-blond hair matted by drying sweat and crushed by the helmet he no longer wore. "The law states that if you *kill* a Knight of Erythane in witnessed fair combat, you can replace him *if* the king of Erythane or Béarn deems you worthy of the honor *and* you take the proper vows." He resisted the urge to add something sarcastic about the lack of rewards slaughtering an apprentice knight would gain him. In his case, ultimately, the man would battle a full-fledged knight. He doubted his father would let his murder go unchallenged.

Jakrusan made a noise deep in his throat. "You stupid knights, and your weird, rigid, stupid rules."

Ra-khir recoiled, more taken aback by the source than the words. He knew what had to follow, though the idea made him wince. He wanted nothing more than a quiet nap. "You've insulted my honor, and the honor of my peers. I have no choice but to call you out."

"Very well," Jakrusan said. "I've beaten your sorry hide once, and I can do it again."

Ra-khir ignored the snideness. "One hour. Here. Poleax." He deliberately chose an obscure weapon.

Jakrusan looked stricken. "But I don't have one of those."

"I'll lend you one," Ra-khir promised, certain his father would let him borrow his for the cause.

Jakrusan stomped his foot like a child, the acting overdone. "But that's not fair! I've never used one in my life."

Ra-khir glanced at Edwin, hoping for a clue as to how to properly handle the situation. By the law, the other's competence did not affect Ra-khir's choice of weapons, yet his personal honor allowed him to sympathize with the character Jakrusan played. Edwin's stony face gave him no answer, so Ra-khir followed his own integrity. "All right, sir. What weapons do you know?"

"Sword," Jakrusan said swiftly. "And shield."

Ra-khir awaited a longer list, but received nothing. Torn between his need to display competence and fairness, Ra-khir clung to the latter. "Very well, then. Sword and shield."

"Could we please do it here and now?" Jakrusan added. "We both have things to do later."

Ra-khir suspected he had little choice in this matter. The knights intended to test his endurance, and they would not allow the hour of rest he craved. "Fine. Could I, at least, select the endpoint?"

Jakrusan smiled. "It's your challenge." He trotted off to retrieve his shield from the grass, and Ra-khir hauled his from his pack. The gray grazed placidly, untroubled by the shouting or the waving steel. Shortly, he returned. "Now, about that endpoint?"

Ra-khir adjusted the shield strap on his arm, for once agreeing with Kevral. With his arms hammered by sword blows and muscles screaming from hefting the pike, the shield seemed more burden than help. "Disarming," he said.

Jakrusan's face fell into an alarmed mask. Edwin shook his head disapprovingly and intervened. "Ra-khir, I know Sir Jakrusan has been an excellent actor, not to mention incredibly irritating, but bloodletting and amputation is taking the game too far."

Ra-khir bowed to his teacher. "With all respect, armsman, I did not demand either to end the duel." He gave Edwin a look intended to convey he had not taken leave of his senses and he had control of the situation. Inhaling deeply, he held his breath, awaiting the answer. If he could not earn his teacher's trust, he did not belong among the Knights of Erythane. He understood he had placed a burden on the armsman as well. Disarming techniques were tricky, difficult to direct, and dangerous. Even his practice sword held enough edge to mangle, if not sever, a finger.

Renshai armsmen needed to master myriad disarming techniques, and Kevral had modeled her life after the greatest *torke* in her people's history. Whether used to restrain a student taunted to murderous rage or teach a desperate lesson, disarming guaranteed an end to the conflict without the need to land a blow. As per the laws of her people, Kevral had taught him none of the Renshai maneuvers, but she had taken his sword often enough to reveal more standard methods. Jakrusan was right about one thing, Ra-khir had practiced.

"Very well," Edwin finally said, the worried creases still lining his middle-aged features. "Ra-khir." He nodded at the apprentice. "Stranger." He managed a faint smile as he indicated Jakrusan.

The knight returned a miffed stare, though whether at Edwin's humor or judgment, Ra-khir could not guess.

"Begin," Edwin said.

This time, Jakrusan made the first attack, a looping cut that Ra-khir took on his shield. Though he hated the time wasted on realigning, Ra-khir did so. Accuracy mattered here more than strength. His sword licked for Jakrusan's hilt but met his shield instead.

Colbey's words in the temple came into Ra-khir's head: *The thing to remember is that an enemy with a shield will always block his own vision. The moment he does, that's your opening.* He parried another strike, then feigned a riposte for the knight's face. Jakrusan raised his shield to block. The instant he did, Ra-khir hammered the shield with his own and redirected his attack. His sword licked through Jakrusan's blind spot and carefully sliced the hilt from his hand. The sword plummeted as Jakrusan made a wild grab for it.

Despite Kevral's teachings, Ra-khir did not attempt to catch the hilt. Renshai, not knights, considered it disrespectful for an honored enemy's sword to touch the ground, and he would as likely cut his hand as retrieve it. The awkwardness of his attempt would not please his armsman.

Jakrusan smoothly caught his handguard before it landed in the dirt, but the match had ended. Ra-khir executed a bow to Edwin, then Jakrusan. Each returned him a formal gesture of esteem. So far, he believed, he had done well.

"Come with me." Edwin pointed toward the pathway from the hill. "Sir Jakrusan will tend your horse and gear."

Ra-khir hesitated. As his father taught, he preferred handling his own belongings and mount. The idea of a knight serving an apprentice unbalanced him.

"Please," Edwin insisted. "You would insult Sir Jakrusan to refuse. You still have much to do."

Ra-khir glanced at the knight he had twice battled. Jakrusan's attitude had changed, his knight's manner and posture returned. He nodded to indicate Edwin spoke for him.

"Thank you, sir." Ra-khir bowed again. "You honor me." He followed Edwin down the hill, ignoring the whispering women who had lost their show. The two knights who had remained in place throughout jousting and dueling turned stiffly and marched after Edwin and his charge. The man at the scaffolding walked toward Jakrusan, presumably to assist.

They headed into town, Edwin's silence painful. Ra-khir

tried not to fidget, wrapping his nervousness in the calm realization that he had done his best in every situation. If he failed the test, he would at least do so honestly, knowing he had given his all. Knighthood would suit him, and he could not imagine himself doing anything else. He did not allow his mind to pursue that course, however. Matrinka had seemed deserving of Béarn's throne, yet she had failed the staff-test and learned to live with the devastating consequences of the gods' judgment. Once that lapse had seemed tragic. Now he and Matrinka could see that Griff fit more properly into kingship, and she contributed far more to Béarn as a healer. If the Knights of Erythane would not have Ra-khir Kedrin's son, he would turn to her for a solace she had the experience to share. He would find another way to serve the kingdom.

Tears burned at Ra-khir's eyes as he trailed Edwin through Erythane's streets. He steered his thoughts along the brave path from necessity, yet the idea of failing these proceedings ached far deeper. He could scarcely remember a time in his life when he did not want, with all of his soul, to become one of Erythane's knights. He wrestled with the realization that failure might well destroy him, and Matrinka could do little to salvage what remained. It did not fit his honor to think this way, yet he could not help the emotion that pounded him at the idea of accepting defeat with dignity and grace. His self-esteem would simply shatter, and he wondered if he could bear to continue living.

At length, Edwin and Ra-khir reached a modest cottage at the edge of town nearest the practice field. The armsman opened the door onto a sparse room that held a table surrounded by hard, wooden chairs. He waved toward one of these. Ra-khir entered, and the other two knights followed him inside. He waited until all of the others sat before joining them at the table. They deliberately left him the head position, directly across from Armsman Edwin, and Ra-khir felt like a rabbit surrounded by eager hounds.

Edwin ran a hand through his sandy stubble, and his brown eyes pinned Ra-khir. "What did you think of your performance in the ring joust?"

What did I think? Ra-khir blinked in abashed silence, uncertain of the answer Edwin sought. *It only matters what you think.* He kept these thoughts to himself, giving an honest answer. "I did my best, Armsman. I only hope it was good enough."

"Are you capable of better?"

"I—I don't know, Armsman," Ra-khir admitted honestly. "If you mean do I believe I could have done better today, I don't think I could have. I intend to keep practicing, though. There will surely come a time when I improve on this performance." He could feel his heart hammering his ribs, and it felt too low in his chest.

Edwin accepted the answer. "When Sir Jakrusan challenged you, how did you feel?"

Feel? Ra-khir swallowed hard, placing himself back in that moment. "He had challenged me, sir. I felt nothing other than the need to meet that challenge bravely and with honor."

"How about when he chose the endpoint?"

Ra-khir glanced toward the others at the table, wishing one would reveal something, anything, to indicate what they wanted from him. "Armsman, I was glad he chose a spar rather than the battle to the death he originally suggested. I truly believe my sword arm could serve Béarn well." He copied Colbey's tone, stating compliment with a blandness that sapped it of pride. "If he could best me, Erythane or Béarn could use him, too. It seemed a shame for either of us to die in vain."

Edwin started a nod, then caught himself. "When your opponent scored a killing blow but did not notice, did it ever occur to you to continue the fight?"

Ra-khir did not pause to consider. "Never, sir."

"Not for a moment?"

The question was an insult. "No, sir."

"Not even for a bare second?"

This once, Ra-khir allowed his irritation through. "Armsman, you are coming dangerously close to besmirching my honor. If you persist in this line, you will force me to call you out as well."

The two knights thus far silent, widened their eyes. A twitch at the corners of one's lips gave away his approval. Edwin returned to stony unreadability, looking to either hand to encourage the others to question.

The knight to Ra-khir's right, Sir Garvin, spoke next. "Why did you give up your right to choose weapon and time after you called the second challenge?"

Finally, the intention of the inquisition became clear to Ra-khir. Actions spoke loud, but only he could reveal the intention and thought behind them. Doing the right thing by accident would not suit a knight. "I judged, sir, that the only thing at risk was my own life. Turning to personal honor, I found myself uncomfortable with knowingly forcing the contest into my favor."

Edwin turned then from scrutinizing Ra-khir's motivations on the field to endless questions about kingdom procedure and formality. Hours stretched into a painful tedium that pushed Ra-khir's exhausted mind to its limit. Never did he allow his answers to grow sloppy or disrespectful. Too much depended upon his responses to let them sour or allow incaution to taint them. One by one, the knights dragged him through scenarios determined to test his honor to its limit. Ethical dilemmas that defied the ages were fired at Ra-khir, demanding answers in the moments such situations would leave him. Superficial replies did not prove enough. The three delved to the core of his decisions, the reasons behind his choices bared to a scrutiny that left him feeling naked and vulnerable.

Day stretched into hungry night. Ra-khir had managed to stomach little for breakfast, and the knights' testing had left him not a moment since for eating. Nausea fluttered through his gut, churned by excitement and terror; and he doubted he could handle food even if they offered it. Finally, the barrage of questions stopped, followed by a session of memorization. Edwin and the others kept him standing attentively while they fed him the words to the knight's oath. The gist came easily: he would pledge his service to the kingdom of Béarn first, then to Erythane, and always to his honor. These things he had known since his training began. Yet flowery wording stretched the whole into pages that he seemed incapable of jamming into a mind so tired it no longer registered emotion.

The pound of a fist against the door startled a gasp from Ra-khir. Somehow, he managed to maintain a blank mask and his rigid posture despite the interruption. An angry frown cut across Edwin's features. "Come back later," he shouted. "I can't permit interruptions now."

Despite his command, the door winched open slightly, and Knight-Captain Kedrin stuck his head through the crack. The handsome features looked as tired as his son's, and the blue-white eyes radiated pain. He turned Ra-khir an apologetic look before addressing the armsman. "Sir Edwin, you know I wouldn't interrupt this unless it was of the utmost importance."

The anger seeped from Edwin's face, replaced by worried creases. "I'm sorry, Captain. Come in." He looked at Ra-khir. "Stand at ease."

Ra-khir barely moved. He had never seen his father this rattled, not even when Baltraine had pronounced his execution in the courtroom.

Kedrin cleared his throat. "I don't have any way to soften this." He glanced at Ra-khir. "Son, your mother threatened to kill herself if you complete your testing."

Ra-khir's heart seemed to stop, and the sensation of imminent death washed over him. "What?" he squeaked out.

"Your mother," Kedrin repeated dutifully, though they all had clearly heard him. "I don't know how she found out the testing was today . . ."

Ra-khir believed they would find the answer among the spectators at his ring joust and sparring.

". . . but she's locked herself in her cottage and threatened to kill herself if you don't come talk to her now."

Ra-khir remained locked in place, not even capable of leaving the alert position that had seemed too painful moments before. "Armsman." He scarcely managed to turn his eyes to Edwin. "May I go?"

Edwin flinched, and Kedrin turned away. "I'm sorry, Ra-khir. I don't have the authority to change protocol. As I told you this morning, your testing cannot be interrupted. If you leave, you can no longer become a Knight of Erythane."

All of the ethical tests the knights had thrown at Ra-khir had not prepared him for this moment. Myriad ideas flashed through his head at once. *My mother's life against everything that matters.* The far-reaching consequences finally struck him. *My mother's life, or my own.* He thought of the mother he had not seen in months, not since the day she laid down her ultimatum. The more of her deceit he uncovered, the more he had come to despise her. Yet he had never gone so far as to wish her dead. Tears sprang to his eyes, and he studied his father through the blur they created. "Can't you . . . reason with her?"

Kedrin crossed the room and gripped Ra-khir in a strong embrace. "I did everything I could, Ra-khir. I've never been good enough for her; you know that. She wants you."

She wants me. She still thinks I'm a child. She still wants to control me. Ra-khir wondered where it would end. Would she threaten suicide every time he tried to do anything of which she disapproved? His father's arms closed tighter around him. Just as when he recovered from the elves' poison, Kedrin shared his agony.

Ra-khir closed his eyes, peace settling over him as he made a decision he would rather forgo. "I have to go," he said simply, reopening his lids. And headed for the door.

The world seemed to explode around Ra-khir. As he pushed open the panel, winter air slammed his face, cold agony against the tears. Disconnected from his body, he felt himself stride out into windy dampness, shuffling in the right direction from instinct rather than intent. *It's over.* All the work, all the learning, all of the pain had gone for nothing. Years of hopes and dreams lay crushed beneath his mother's threat. He would rescue her because his honor would not allow anything less, yet his disdain and hatred could only grow stronger.

A figure appeared suddenly in Ra-khir's path. He tried to step around, but the other moved with him. Slowly, he raised his head and met Kedrin's pale eyes and worried features. Again, the father enfolded his son into a warm hug. His breath hissed into Ra-khir's ears in words that took longer than necessary to decipher. "Ra-khir, come back. Your mother is in no danger. It was part of the test."

Ra-khir jerked backward. "What?"

"I'm sorry," Kedrin said, and suddenly the origin of his pain became clear, role-playing that felt more like cruel lying. "Come back, and we'll explain."

Bewildered, Ra-khir returned, his breath huffing in clouds against the frigid air. He let Kedrin lead him back into Edwin's house and return him to his chair at the head of the table. The others sat in their regular places, and Kedrin remained standing at Ra-khir's right hand.

"A test," Ra-khir finally managed.

Edwin nodded.

"A cruel test." Ra-khir could not help judging. His heart still felt as if it hung in tatters, and little thought had moved in to replace the emptiness that had followed his decision.

The armsman lowered his head. "Can you explain your decision?"

Ra-khir blinked, scarcely daring to believe it had not ended even yet. "Why I chose my mother's life over becoming a Knight of Erythane?"

"Yes," Sir Garvin said. "Why?"

Beneath the table, Kedrin caught Ra-khir's wrist and gave it an encouraging squeeze. The apprentice suspected the others would not approve of this gesture; at the moment, he did not care. "My honor required it." Ra-khir's fogged mind left few words. He sought a long, solid explanation, but it evaded him.

Edwin reminded gently, "Your pledge is first to Béarn."

Ra-khir completed the detail, "And *always* to my honor."

Sir Garvin pressed, "Could you not best serve Béarn as a Knight of Erythane? Is that not worth the life of a single citizen, even that of your own mother?"

Ra-khir saw the point. He drew a deep breath, hoping the bitterness that followed would not outrage his father's peers. "If I was so shallow as to place different values on human lives, my mother's would register less, not more, than that of others." He glanced at his father and hoped Kedrin could read the apology in his expression. The knight-captain had always taught his son to see the good in everyone. "Knighthood means everything to me, but I could not accept a life, any life, as the price for fulfilling my dreams. The vow stands, but I had not taken it yet. I could serve Béarn in other guise, as a common soldier, perhaps."

"Very well, Ra-khir," Edwin said. "Retire through that door." He pointed to an entryway into another room. "When we have finished deliberating, we will call you back."

Ra-khir did as Edwin bade, heading into a small neat room that Edwin clearly used as sleeping quarters. Finding no chairs, and thinking it rude to sit on another's bed, Ra-khir flopped to the floor in a quiet corner. The murmurs of the knights in the other room made the walls seem to hum, but he deliberately avoided picking out individual words. Excitement still hounded him, risen from the ashes of despair; but now rest seemed nearly as welcome. He let his eyes fall closed.

Even then, Ra-khir received no reprieve. Sir Garvin poked his head through the doorway before sleep found the exhausted knight-in-training. "Ra-khir?"

Ra-khir opened his eyes and rose to his feet. He bowed politely.

Garvin's face gave him nothing. "Return, please."

Ra-khir followed in silence, the jarring of each step necessary to keep his mind from lapsing into the rest stolen from him by combat, questions, and now the decision of his life. Each of the four knights kept his face frozen in an unrevealing mask. Ra-khir studied his father's features. The set of mouth and cheeks told him nothing, but a light dancing in the familiar milk-blue eyes gave him away.

Armsman Edwin spoke the words Ra-khir anticipated. "Congratulations, Sir Ra-khir. Report to King Humfreet's court tomorrow to recite your vows and to claim your steed and your assignment."

Once again, father and son embraced, but this time they wept tears of joy.

CHAPTER 26

Betrayals

I know my swords better than most men know their children.
—Colbey Calistinsson

Colbey Calistinsson blinked in Asgard's brightness, the constant light a torment to eyes accustomed to the dark flurry of chaos' world. The solidity of trees rooted in place, the riffle of the pond in wind, the lazy paddle of ducks, once right and proper, now seemed a slow and monotonous torture. Looping patternlessly and exploring lesser known tracts of land suited him far better now. His senses remained sharply tuned, as they once had for the flash of a demon through the chaos ether. Now the shapeless dwellers of chaos' world ran from him or delivered strange gestures of obeisance to their prince. As individuals, they followed and feared him, unable to bond in a cause. The loneliness that once haunted Colbey became a treasured sanctuary. He had no interest in the demons' fealty. Their terror pleased him more.

Colbey traipsed toward home with only a glance at the scenery that had once held him daily spellbound. He left the Staff of Chaos in the sword-form his mind bent it into on chaos' world. It hung on his left hip, his lesser weapon looking no different at his other side. This constant companion tapped at the barriers to Colbey's mind, its strength tangibly increased over the months he had wielded it. Cautiously, alert to tricks, Colbey opened his superficial thoughts to its opinion.

You don't belong here anymore.

Colbey frowned, the warning unnecessary. *I go where I please.*

The staff in sword-form accepted the answer with a faint tingle of pleasure. *True enough, but there's still work to be done down below. You have yet to defeat the kraell.*

Colbey dismissed the words with an internal shrug. The largest, most powerful demons could wait. *The kraell will*

have their battle. I have matters to attend here.* Without awaiting a reply, he shut off the contact. The staff-sword told him
nothing he did not already know. He continued toward home
until the faint chime of steel touched his ears. He raised his head
and stopped, listening.

The music of swordplay filled his head with a gladness even
months among demons could not disperse. For a moment, he
felt right amid Asgard's changeless tedium, and the urge to
charge into battle with Modi's name on his lips became an obsession he could scarcely deny. The sounds came from the field
on which he had once daily practiced before a new world gave
him constant battles and unfamiliar places to perfect his sword-
arm. He rushed toward it.

Topping a slight rise, Colbey discovered two figures engaged
in spar. Both moved with impressive speed and a grace that held
his attention as nothing but his own identity had since taking on
the Staff of Chaos. Silver flickered around slender arms and tor-
sos, and the sun glinted from golden tresses. Then, almost as
soon as he noticed it, the swordplay ceased. Blades drifted
downward, and the two moved closer, one clutching the other
from behind to demonstrate a maneuver. Colbey stared, missing
the symphony of steel striking steel and caught up in the perfect
vision on the field. He scarcely noticed the staff-sword's clamoring for an attention he did not accord it. Time receded, and he
saw himself as a child again, caught up in learning, his *torke*'s
touch an honor he scarcely deserved.

Colbey drifted toward the figures on the field, recognizing
them within a dozen steps: Freya and Ravn. The goddess held
an offensive stance that trebled beauty already beyond peer.
The slim sword in her small, callused hand added what no cos-
metic ever could. Ravn crouched in thoughtful silence. The disheveled yellow hair and adolescent proportions stole nothing
from his long-trained dexterity. A moment after Colbey's obser-
vance, both of their heads swung in his direction. He stopped,
still the length of six horses from them.

When Colbey did not move toward Freya and Ravn, they
sheathed their swords and approached him. He watched them
come, measuring every step, each swing of arm or body. He
braced for a flood of emotion that, strangely, escaped him. His
mind read the situation, and experience told him how he should
feel. His thoughts registered Freya's beauty, knew Ravn as his
son, realized that a meeting should overwhelm him with affec-

tion that made thought impossible. Yet, beyond this logic, he felt nothing.

"Colbey," Freya said, her tone sounding more confused than excited. She studied him, stiffening as if to do something, but remaining in place. Ravn said nothing, but his expression revealed the excitement wafting from him.

Colbey delved further. Reading revealed the boy's desires as well as his hesitation. He wanted to run to his father's arms, yet something in Colbey's manner held him back. Turning his attention to Freya's thoughts, he found much the same, with a taint of bitterness that Ravn had not manifested. Emotions beyond her control held Colbey to blame for choosing to champion chaos over his own family. Or, perhaps, she damned circumstance. Seeking subtleties would have drained Colbey more than he would allow. Though the staff could lend him additional strength, he discarded that possibility. He had relied on himself too long, had disdained protections and magic too severely, to accept its assistance now.

Colbey tried to break the tension. "Ravn, how about a spar?"

Excitement danced through the adolescent's eyes. His hands shifted naturally to his hilts, Harval at his left hand and a scimitar at his right. In contrast, his head rolled slowly back and forth in denial. "No, Father."

The words caught Colbey by surprise, and he sought the core of Ravn's intentions. He read mistrust there. Ravn doubted his father would still pull his deadly strokes.

The discovery enraged Colbey. His eyes narrowed, and he glared at a boy he no longer felt certain deserved to be his son. "You don't trust me."

Ravn would not deny what his father already knew as truth. "You're right." The words emerged strong, yet Colbey read the pain beneath them.

Though recently accustomed to ruling through intimidation, without loyalty, Colbey quivered from the pain of his son's betrayal. "How can you treat your own father this way?"

Ravn pulled himself to his full height; he had outgrown Colbey by half a hand's breadth. "You've linked yourself to chaos and disappeared for four months. Have you forgotten I now champion balance?"

Having given Ravn that charge, Colbey could not argue the point, other than to deny Ravn's need to fear. "I am your father. Have I not earned your respect?"

"Many times over," Ravn admitted. "But . . ." He glanced

at Freya, who returned a warning nod but allowed him to finish his speech without interruption. ". . . you once vowed never to read the thoughts of one you respect. If you do not respect me, how can I trust you?"

The words took Colbey momentarily aback, draining some of his anger. He was guilty of the crime Ravn described. Worse, he had violated his own honor without a modicum of guilt. Rage turned instantly to terror. *What am I turning into?* The realization that chaos had penetrated deeper than he expected unbalanced him. Nevertheless, he found himself unable to abandon the fight. Whether or not he mistrusted his father, Ravn should never retreat from a challenge. "I did not raise my son to be a coward."

"Nor a fool," Ravn returned as swiftly. "When chaos drives you beyond salvation, you will likely come and kill me. Until then, I hope enough of the father I loved remains in you to delay the inevitable."

Colbey glanced at Freya. She stood stalwart, holding her expression to a taut mask. Yet moisture blurred her eyes, and her hands balled into bloodless fists. Her voice emerged in a flat but deadly tone. "If you try to harm our son, you will have to fight through me as well."

Rage slashed Colbey, and he turned away, uncertain whether he hated them, circumstance, or himself more. He had not realized how much time had passed since he saw his family, nor how completely chaos had taken hold of him. *I was an idiot to believe I could maintain neutrality in the midst of chaos.*

Grass rustled behind Colbey. For a moment, he considered remaining in position and allowing whichever of his family attacked to slaughter him without a fight. Instinct won out, and he whirled to face Ravn. The young man's swords remained sheathed, and a boil of emotions radiated from him, so strongly Colbey did not need to violate confidence to become enmeshed in them. This time, Ravn did catch his father into an embrace. Strong arms enfolded Colbey's shoulders, and his son's breath brushed warmly against his cheek. "Papa, I love you," he whispered. "I always will. I need you, and the balance needs you, too."

The world narrowed to kinship and commitment; law and chaos, the balance between them, ceased to exist. Nothing mattered but the desperate constant that was his love for his son. "I love you, too," he returned. "And I'll try to return. But not until the extremes have been destroyed and the balance rescued."

More than ever, Colbey suspected that moment would herald his own doom. "Carry on, Raska Colbeysson."

Ravn retreated enough for Colbey to pull free. Without another word, Colbey headed back the way he had come. He did not turn again until he reached the place where he had heard their spar. Then, he looked, only to find Freya and Ravn still watching him. Lowering his head, he continued onward.

The Staff of Chaos tapped at Colbey's barriers, unanswered.

The songs of a hundred musicians still resounded in Matrinka's ears as she retreated to the king's quarters. By the time the door closed, however, she remembered only Darris' last song. Hauntingly beautiful, it was filled with imagery that only she and he could understand, the secret symbols of love that belonged only to their shared experiences. The gathered nobles and servants had heard only a radiant wedding hymn, yet she had scarcely managed to maintain her composure. Ra-khir's presence among the knights had held her attention enough to allow her to enjoy their litany, and their crisply attentive display. Without him, it, too, would have become an unnoticed part of the wild celebration that passed, for her, in a desperate blur.

Flopping down on the massive bed, Matrinka paid no heed to the rumpled pile of lacy skirts that comprised her wedding dress. Mior wound through the folds, claws entangling in the tatting. Yowling and spitting at the pattern and textures that hindered her progress, she finally reached Matrinka's face. Lying so close she all but suffocated Béarn's queen, she purred loudly.

Halfheartedly, Matrinka worked free a hand and placed it on the furry back. She did not bother to move or even to glance at the calico.

I love you, Mior sent.

Matrinka sighed deeply. The word caused more pain than comfort now.

Are you crying?

So far, Matrinka had maintained her composure. Mior's question opened the floodgates, and she sobbed once in response.

Don't cry now. Griff's coming. I hear his step in the hall.

Matrinka heard nothing but trusted Mior's senses more than her own. She jerked to a sitting position so swiftly that Mior tumbled across the coverlet. Wiping her eyes with the back of her hand, Matrinka rearranged her skirts. The rustling of the fabric drowned the sound of the knob, and the door opened before she anticipated it. Griff entered, closing the door behind him. He looked uncharacteristically handsome in his tailored wedding silks and furs. He removed his hat and hung it on the bedpost, revealing black hair combed to a sheen and slicked back with perfumed oils. His soft, cowlike eyes met Matrinka's, and it startled her to realize how much he now reminded her of the grandfather she had loved.

Mior shook herself, then walked a dainty path back across the bed. She settled into Matrinka's lap, dignity too ruffled to purr.

Without a word to Matrinka, Griff crossed the room to the central window. Shoving aside gauzy curtains with Béarn's crest, he gazed out into the darkness. Though he surely saw nothing through the blackness, he continued to stare long after the silence grew uncomfortable.

Matrinka petted Mior and tried not to cry. She would do her duty for Béarn; she had no other choice. Griff, she knew, would treat her with kindness and dignity. She could not possibly have married better and stayed within the laws of the kingdom. She studied the strong, young back, the large Béarnian frame, and the childlike stance. Over time, she would grow accustomed to these. She would learn to love her husband and to embrace the responsibilities, and the privileges, of queenship.

Finally, Griff turned toward Matrinka once more. Again, her dark eyes found his. She read pain there, surely a reflection of her own.

He deserves to know the truth. As usual, Mior struck to the heart of the matter.

Matrinka cringed. *What truth is that?*

Mior's tail writhed, and she sent a sensation of irritability prior to giving Matrinka words. *Don't play games with me and him. Tell him how you feel.*

I feel lucky. And I feel frightened.

And sad, Mior added. *Don't forget sad.*

Matrinka tore her gaze from Griff to turn it on the cat. *That would only hurt him.*

He deserves to know the truth.

Griff walked toward Matrinka, eyes still locked on hers. Neither of them noticed the footstool in his path until his shin slammed against it and he toppled over it to the floor. He thumped to the ground with enough force to shake the boards beneath the carpet.

"Oh!" Mior sprang to the floor a split second before Matrinka jumped up and dashed to Griff's side. Seizing his hands, she helped him stand.

"Oh," Griff repeated, wrapping his fingers around hers. Though large, her hands seemed to disappear into his massive grip. "That was astoundingly graceful, wasn't it?"

Matrinka tried to hide her smile. She led him to the bed, and he sat in her former position. "Are you all right?"

Griff rubbed his right cheek and shook back the hair that had fallen from its carefully oiled position into his eyes. Once again, he looked like the simple, innocent companion who had accompanied them from the elves' island and through so much. "I'm fine." He hesitated, mouth bowing into a frown. "At least about the fall. Matrinka . . ." He looked up at her, seeming more guileless for his lower position. "I'm afraid I don't . . ." His gaze flickered downward, to his feet. ". . . love you."

Matrinka froze in place. "You don't?"

"Well," Griff admitted. "I do. You're my cousin, and my friend. But . . ." He shook his head, unable to continue.

Hope touched Matrinka, but it refused to blossom. She could not fathom the use of such information. It only seemed to deepen the tragedy. "You don't love me like a wife?" she guessed.

Apparently, the ease with which Matrinka took the news comforted Griff. "I don't really know, I guess. I've never been married before."

Matrinka restrained a laugh. *That's usually the way it works.* "You don't love me like a lover?"

Griff's huge shoulders rose and fell with a sigh. "I don't really know that either. I've never had a lover."

"Neither have I," Matrinka assured him.

Griff looked up hopefully, as if he wished for her to dismiss his concerns as normal for the situation.

Matrinka could not supply the reassurance he wanted. "But I know what it feels like to love someone *like* a lover."

"This isn't it?" Griff supplied.

"This isn't it."

Griff opened his mouth as if to say something, but no words emerged. Only a glow that flickered across his features briefly suggested that he wanted to claim he understood the feeling, had even experienced it. Matrinka could only guess that some woman in his past inspired it. "So what do we do?" he finally asked.

Matrinka felt Mior's touch against her mind, but the cat

shared no words. She understood the delicateness of the situation and would insert neither animal-simple logic nor humor. Matrinka cleared her throat. What she wanted and what would prove best for Griff or Béarn clashed, and she had little choice but to consider the latter two first. "It's not necessary for a husband and wife to love one another to perform their . . . duties."

"Duties," Griff repeated, without the cautious emphasis Matrinka had given the word. "I will continue as king and you as first queen."

"Right," Matrinka said, surprised naive Griff would place himself in the position of separating personal responsibilities from sexual ones. She had lumped all together to spare him.

"I," Griff started, then stopped. His jaw set, and he forced out a full sentence. "The queen's quarters are next door. I think you should stay there." His eyes rolled up to meet hers again, though only briefly. "I still value your friendship, of course. I thought I could go through with this, but I've known all day that I can't."

Matrinka did not request clarification. Griff's words had come with too much difficulty to challenge. Apparently, he did not want her in his bed, and for the moment that decision was a relief.

Griff drew a deep breath and continued. "I'll call Rantire back. For now, I'd like the bard to protect you, instead. When he's not attending court or to your safety, I'll have him remain as your personal steward."

Matrinka swallowed, seeking words and finding only diffuse concepts. The populace would surely read the switch as a token of the king's love for his new queen. The better warrior would still guard him, but he would assign his bodyguard to the woman for whom he had pledged lifelong responsibility. She knew better. In his own sweet, unworldly manner, Griff had just sanctioned her relationship with Darris. When words continued to fail her, Matrinka hurled herself into Griff's arms and held him. Her respect and her affection for him grew from a spark to a bonfire in an instant, yet it still transcended physical attraction.

Griff held her, too, sadness apparent in his smile. He led her through the door and into a hallway where they caught Darris pacing frantically. Clearly shocked, he scurried to bow respectfully to his liege and to the queen of Béarn. Griff did not wait for his bard to assume the proper position. He herded Matrinka to her next door quarters, then gestured for Darris to join them.

The bard broke from the half-finished gesture of courtesy and trotted to them without hesitation, his face lined by confusion. "What can I do for you, Majesties?"

Matrinka entered her room and turned to shut the door. The conversation between king and bodyguard did not involve her, and her eavesdropping would only discomfort them both. Mior followed, rubbing against the door frame as she entered and delaying Matrinka's action long enough for her to catch the first of Griff's commands.

"First, please ask Tem'aree'ay to my chambers. Then . . ."

Matrinka closed the door, tears burning her eyes, though they seemed as much from joy as sorrow.

Sad, isn't it? Mior said.

Matrinka nodded. The observation could apply to many aspects of the current situation, but the cat's focus seeped through with her words. *Love works in strange and horrible ways. I'm glad Griff has a confidante.*

But he's falling for her.

What? Matrinka shook her head, smoothing down her many skirts. *That's nonsense.* She shook her head again. *Crazy, Mior. She's an elf. It would be like him falling for you.*

Mior sat, raising a back leg skyward and grooming it from thigh to claws. *Not so crazy. You'll see.*

Matrinka snorted. *I'll see what? What will I see?*

You'll see him mooning around the castle like you used to do for Darris.

Matrinka could not imagine the childlike king morose. *Impossible.*

Love unfulfilled does strange things to people. Mior lowered her leg. *You could take some lessons from cats.*

Matrinka gathered the animal into her arms. *We call women who act like cats "harlots."*

Mior settled into the crook of Matrinka's arm. *And what do you call women who mate with men who aren't their husband?*

Struck by Mior's harsh words, Matrinka dropped to the bed without bothering to survey the plush furnishings of her new quarters. For now, they all merged into an insignificant blur. *I haven't slept with Darris.*

Yet.

Tears welled from Matrinka's eyes. She flopped backward, drawing the furry form to her chest. *Oh, Mior. I'm wrong to want him, aren't I? Am I a horrible person?*

Mior's words remained devoid of the judgment Matrinka supplied. *I don't know. But you're a damn good cat.*

Matrinka's crying quickened.

Mior continued, feigning offense. *I meant that as a good thing.*

Matrinka wept, fighting guilt.

Matrinka, if your husband sanctions, even arranges it, how can it be wrong? Doesn't a good wife fulfill the wishes of her man? Doesn't a good woman follow the orders of her king?

Do you really think this is what Griff wants? I mean, really wants. He didn't actually say it.

It's what he meant, Mior assured. *I can't promise it's really what he wants, but I do know it's what you want. And Darris. You've been fighting love a long time, and now you've been given the chance to have it. The king freed you from the constraints of the law. He gave you the best of all possible wedding gifts. Are you going to let strangers' ideas of what's right destroy your dream?*

A knock sounded on Matrinka's door before she could answer. Startled, she jerked to her feet, this time managing to keep hold of Mior. "Come in."

The door slid soundlessly open, and Darris stood in the doorway. The hazel eyes still held the bewilderment his face had finally liberated. As she admired the curl of brown hair that had settled over his thin brows, the large straight nose, and the broad lips, she lost all ability to compare him to other men. His features had become too familiar, too special to consider as one among many.

The answer to Mior's question became a foregone conclusion.

Kevral sat on the pillow of her bed, knees tucked to her chest, eyes shut, visions of the day's training session parading across her closed lids. As the lessons, *svergelse*, and entertainment settled into a pattern, life became pleasant and easy. During her four months in Pudar, she had added personal touches to the plush furnishings of her room, and the upper left drawer of the desk held presents she had collected for her companions. Through his ministers and servants, the king not only granted her a stipend, but, so far, had delivered anything she had requested. Mostly, this had consisted of freshly forged swords for self and students; her harsh specifications had sent the royal blacksmith into blustering fits of rage.

The king had also honored her appeals for blander foods prepared in the style of the southwest. Initially, this had done little to appease the nausea that churned through her gut on occasion, then disappeared for hours at a time. The vomiting had resolved during the second month of her stay, and the queasiness disappeared a few weeks later. She had not realized how much the sickness affected her until its resolution. Then, her appetite soared. For the first time in her life, her stomach developed the bulge so favored by the men of Erythane, Pudar and, especially, Béarn.

Kevral held her focus to the vision of those she taught, refining her techniques to suit individuals. Since the incident in the alleyway, neither Tyrion, nor any other, showed the faintest hint of disrespect. At times, they cursed her; but she had expected nothing less. All of the *torke* she had known strove to create hatred tempered by admiration. Learning required pain and the anger that accompanied it. As long as they treated her with respect, they could despise her to the ends of the world.

A knock on the door dispelled Kevral's train of thought. She opened her eyes. "Who is it?"

The voice of a young woman wafted through the panel. "A healer. May I come in, Mistress Kevral?"

Kevral sighed. The king's ceaseless concern about her health, while understandable, irritated her. He had not sent a healer to her room since she dismissed one during her first weeks. Annoyance prickled at her manners, but she saw no need to harass what was probably a frightened young woman for the king's indiscretion. "Briefly," she returned.

The latch clicked, and the door edged open. A woman in her early twenties poked her head through the opening. She carried a calico cat in her arms.

The similarity to Matrinka jarred Kevral, and she sat in stunned silence longer than decorum demanded.

The healer closed the door and looked at Kevral. Apparently trying to understand her expression, she shifted from foot to foot nervously. "Is it the cat, my lady? I can leave her outside."

"Not necessary." Kevral scurried to the edge of the bed, then waved the healer toward the desk chair. "Sit, please." Her thoughts turned from the means of chasing the newcomer swiftly away to listening. Only at this moment did she realize how much she missed having friends who treated her as something other than an object of fear or awe. "What can I do for you?"

"For me?" The woman fairly squeaked. "No, my lady, no. I'm here to help you. They tell me you've been sick pretty much since you got here."

Kevral hoped "they" had not turned her gastrointestinal problems into common knowledge or gossip. "Thank you for your concern, but I'm feeling fine now. I just had a little difficulty adjusting to the differences in food."

Finally, the healer sat, perching on the edge of the chair as if to flee at any moment. "My name is Charra. May I ask some personal questions?"

Kevral considered carefully.

"In confidence, of course."

"You mean you're not going to tell the king or his ministers?"

The healer met Kevral's gaze with sweet yellow-brown eyes. "Certainly not. It would violate my healer's oath." The cat leaped from her arms and sniffed along the edge of the rug. Aside from its color, it little resembled Mior in figure or action.

"Then you may ask."

"You've been vomiting, my lady?"

"Was vomiting," Kevral corrected. "I told you that went away."

Charra nodded her understanding. "Have you noticed anything else abnormal?"

Kevral shook her head.

Charra pressed. "Fatigue?"

Kevral considered. "Tireder than usual, yes. I suppose. Been working harder, too. Explains that well enough." She deliberately minimized the discomfort in case word returned to the king. She had not let the fog that pressed her over the last several months interfere with her lessons.

"How about your courses?"

"My what?"

"Your courses, my lady." Apparently realizing it was the term, not her volume, Charra rephrased the question. "Your monthly bleeding."

Kevral shook her head. "Monthly?"

Charra stared, her expression mingling confusion with surprise. "How old are you, my lady?"

"Sixteen."

"And you've never had a bleeding time?"

"Once or twice," Kevral admitted. "Not monthly."

Charra turned her gaze to the ceiling. Several moments passed in consideration.

Kevral supplied Matrinka's theory. "A friend of mine, who's also a healer, thinks it has something to do with Renshai developing slowly. And with the harshness of our training."

"Oh," Charra said. "Well." She fidgeted more.

Kevral watched the cat slither under her bed. With the animal out of sight, the woman in front of her seemed more like one of the flouncy adolescents that bored her than a potential partial replacement for the Béarnide she missed.

"Lady Kevral, I don't know how to say this, except to just say it."

Kevral listened to the arrhythmic thumping of the calico chasing dust beneath her.

"I think you're pregnant."

The words drifted past Kevral, mostly unheard.

"Like me."

Gradually, the ensuing silence seeped into Kevral's consciousness as the words had not. "What?" she finally said.

"Like me," the healer supplied.

Kevral shook her head, uncertain whether she wished to restir the waters. "Before that."

"Oh." Charra fidgeted more than the first time. The cat shot out from under the bed, paws thumping against the floorboards, then darted back beneath her again. "You're . . . we're . . . pregnant?"

This time, the words seemed to overregister, echoing through Kevral's head, the meaning all too clear. Her eyes narrowed, and fear clutched at her chest. "That's impossible."

"It is?"

"I'm not married."

"Neither am I, my lady."

"Are you sure?"

Charra turned Kevral a strange look. "Lady Kevral, I'd know if I was married."

Kevral gripped her knees tightly. Matrinka would have properly intuited the meaning of her question. "I mean are you sure about. . . ." She lowered her eyes to her abdomen.

Charra followed Kevral's gaze. "Pretty sure. I can examine you and know for certain, my lady. You're big enough to have felt something moving in there by now."

Kevral shook her head, hope fluttering to life. "I haven't. Does that mean I'm not?"

Charra shook her head, without a verbal reply. "Lady Kevral, I apologize if I'm insulting you. But if no one ever told you how things like this happen—"

Kevral cut her off. "I know." And she did, although certain aspects did not fit the situation. She had believed that creating a baby required intention on the part of both parties. Even then, it did not always happen. Colbey himself had lost a marriage to infertility.

"All right, my lady." Charra accepted Kevral's claim without asking for a recitation. "So it's impossible because you've never been with a man?"

Kevral needed time to think. She hoped, but doubted, Charra would leave if she answered the question affirmatively. Ultimately, lying would catch up to her, and it seemed ludicrous to alienate the one person in Pudar who might share her predicament. She had never met an unmarried pregnant woman before and doubted she could easily find another. She opened her mouth to admit the truth, but the words seemed to stick to her tongue. Her mind could not accept what her heart had already admitted. When the proper words did not escape, she finally managed others. "Do your exam."

Charra motioned for Kevral to lay down on the bed, and she complied. Removing her hands from her knees left blanched prints against the flesh. The healer looked and prodded, the scrutiny feeling strangely intrusive, even before it moved from abdomen to breasts. She had allowed her companions to investigate every part of her after taking wounds, and once poison, in battle. Those examinations had never bothered her; oddly, this one did.

At length, Charra stepped back and motioned for Kevral to cover herself fully. Complying, Kevral sat up.

"My lady, where did you get those scars?"

"In battle," Kevral replied impatiently. "Am I . . . you know . . . pregnant?" She finally squeezed out the word.

The drawing of breath for reply seemed to take an eternity. "Lady Kevral, you are."

"I am?" Understanding still eluded Kevral.

"Undeniably. Five months, at least. Maybe six."

Kevral counted back to when the elves imprisoned her and Ra-khir, then shook her head vigorously. "Now that really is impossible. Five months ago at most."

Charra took the news in stride. "Big baby, then."

Baby? Gods, there's going to be a baby. My baby. The implications of the pregnancy only now went beyond the immediate. *I'm too young. I'm not ready for this.*

"Is the father a big man? Big men make for bigger babies, I believe."

"He's—" Kevral started, then choked on realization. *Ra-khir or Tae? I don't even know who the father is!* "—big," she managed to finish. *Ra-khir is anyway.* All of the bravado she showed in matters of warfare and sword work disappeared. She felt like a frightened child in desperate need of a mother.

"Is he one of ours, my lady?"

"You mean a Pudarian?"

Charra nodded.

"No." Even at her most vulnerable, Kevral would not admit that she had slept with two men. She might lose the only support she might ever have. For now, she hedged. "Tell me about your man."

Charra sat beside Kevral, a wistful smile touching her features. "A visiting merchant from Hopewell. Handsome, rugged, intelligent. I spent the most blissful month of my life with him." She lowered her head, and a curtain of mouse-brown hair fell over her face, hiding her eyes. "I loved him, and he said he loved me. He promised to marry me, which is the only reason I lay with him. But when he found out about this . . ." She placed a hand across her own abdomen with its small but definite bulge. ". . . he refused to see me again." She quivered, probably crying.

Taking her cues from her time with Matrinka, Kevral placed an arm around Charra's shoulders. The healer grasped Kevral in return, face lost beneath hair and against Kevral's sleeping gown. Her muffled voice barely reached the Renshai's ears. "Men will say anything—promise ANYTHING—to get a woman to lie with them."

"I'm sorry you found a bad one." Kevral placed her other arm around the healer. "You're probably better off without him."

Charra jerked up suddenly, wiping her eyes so thoroughly, they scarcely appeared reddened. "You don't understand, Lady Kevral. All men do that."

Kevral shook her head, feeling odd in the role of comforter, yet glad for the distraction from her own maelstrom of emotion. She could feel pain and uncertainty, huddled and raw. The moment Charra left, she would have to confront affairs of the heart. She would rather have faced two dozen enemies weaponless. "Don't let one bad man color your attitude toward all of them."

Charra's features went deadly serious. "You still don't understand, my lady. I've talked to a lot of women since then, and a lot of men. They tell things to healers they would never admit to anyone else. Nearly every woman has had at least one man profess undying love and marriage for the chance to lie with her. The smart ones forced the issue. Some of the men wanted it enough to marry them, but most did not." Charra's desperate gaze held Kevral's. "My lady, this is the part that frightens me. Every man admitted he had or wanted to go into his marriage with experience. And not a single one was willing to marry a woman he knew was not a virgin. None would go near an unwed mother, unless she was the beloved widow of a brother."

Kevral shrugged, a tiny part of her considering what the rest dismissed as impossible. "Maybe Pudarian men are like that."

Charra would not let the matter rest. "My lady, I tend foreign dignitaries, diplomats, and their families. Men everywhere are the same." She leaned toward Kevral conspiratorially. "If I were you, I would find a man swiftly, before your condition becomes too obvious, and marry him."

Kevral blinked. The possibility had never occurred to her. "Why haven't you done that?"

Charra shook back her hair. "Don't you think I've tried? I spent too long chasing after the baby's father. He seemed so sincere, I just couldn't believe he would abandon me. Lady, we were soul mates. He loved me. I was positive. Now, I'm looking, but it's too late for me." She placed her hands over her abdomen. "Men get frightened off when they hug you and feel something move inside you." She pointed at Kevral's gut. "That, my lady, is a baby. It's also a symbol of shame. It tells the entire world what you did."

Warmth came to Kevral's cheeks unexpectedly. "I don't care what others think."

A knowing nod from Charra followed the words. "I didn't think I did either. But when your family disowns you and people call you whore, you may find feelings you didn't know you had. You need to at least think about your future. That baby needs a father."

"The baby will have a father. When I get back to Béarn, Rakhir will marry me."

Charra's glance was patronizing.

Kevral smiled. "He's a Knight of Erythane. His honor

wouldn't have allowed him to lie to me about his feelings. And it won't let him abandon his child."

The cat slunk out from beneath the bed, dust clinging to its spotted fur. Charra stared at Kevral, the condescending creases smoothing and eyes widening. "The father of your baby is a knight?"

Kevral confirmed the half-truth with a nod. *Probably.*

Charra paused, silent for longer than politeness allowed, seeming torn between congratulations and other thought. Finally, she cleared her throat. "That's good news, Lady Kevral. But you had best hope that baby looks exactly like him."

"What do you mean?" Kevral watched the cat bathe itself with its raspy, pink tongue.

"Because a man's best defense is that a woman who would lie with him before marriage would lie with others. If he can convince himself the baby isn't his, he has no responsibility toward it. A knight's honor would never allow him to marry a woman carrying another man's baby."

Alarm trickled through the facade of assurance Kevral built. Behind her bland expression, her thoughts boiled, begging consideration. "I need some time to myself."

"I understand." Charra rose and hefted the calico. "If you need me, you need only ask for me." She headed toward the door but stopped with her hand on the latch. "Don't wait too long, though. When my pregnancy becomes obvious, they'll throw me out of the castle for certain. You may not be able to find me." She whirled quickly, as if to hide tears. The latch clicked, and the door swung open.

"You can always find me," Kevral returned, uncertain whether Charra heard as she exited and pushed the panel closed. The click of the closing door released the tidal wave of thought Kevral had, so far, held at bay. She blew out the candle, darkness turning the furniture into familiar shadows. Moonlight filtered through thin curtains, providing enough illumination for Kevral to see the patterns in the coverlet but too little to show colors. Crawling beneath them, she sought the sleep she needed. Tomorrow would place the problem at a distance; and she would make better decisions when, through sword practice, she could pray to the gods for guidance.

But thought hounded Kevral. She considered Charra's words, though she would have found them nonsense just a day before. Tae's love seemed too sincere to deny, yet the healer had said the same about her own lover. Logic fought memory, of moments he surely could not have feigned, details better kept to himself that he had chosen to share only with her. *Was it really only with me?* Kevral knew she was not the first woman to lie with Tae. Perhaps he had perfected the words to talk women into his bed. She would never have doubted her skill in warfare. He or she who bested her would kill an opponent eager to die for Valhalla. But affairs of the heart befuddled her. Meager experience and knowledge made for terrible uncertainty. She wished for Matrinka's expertise and knew she had little choice but to settle for Charra's.

Kevral's thoughts turned to Ra-khir. He would marry her, she felt certain. Nothing would allow him to abandon his honor. Yet doubts pecked at her assurance again. Tae and Ra-khir looked so completely different, there would be no mistaking the baby of one for the other. Eventually, she had planned to tell Ra-khir about her nights with Tae; but she did not know if the knights would allow him to marry a woman with another man's baby.

A baby. What am I going to do? Kevral rolled, now all too aware of the bulge. A million questions and concerns pounded her in a wild and painful avalanche that went far beyond thoughts of marriage. *Maybe Charra's wrong. Maybe I'm not pregnant at all.* The idea quelled some of the worries, and Kevral tried to convince herself of the truth of the words, but her thoughts would not release reality. A retreat into self-delusion would not work for Kevral. Her mind would not allow it.

I have to sleep. Kevral flipped to her other side, using Renshai mind techniques to empty her head of thought. Sleep slid gradually within her grasp. *A baby.* The thought slipped through the walls she had built, widening a gap that admitted all. Again, she found herself assailed. Worry mingled with fear. She alternated between sorrow and rage, feeling fire and icy terror at once. Eventually burning hatred swallowed all, directed at the unwanted thing growing inside her. *Maybe it'll die. Maybe if I double my practices, I'll miscarry it. Maybe if I stop eating, I'll starve it.*

Words Colbey had spoken burst through the muddle, as if directed by another's intent. "Each month I hoped with a desperation that tore holes as painful as any weapon. Each month, I mourned the death of the baby that could have been but wasn't." *A child is a blessing that the ill-fated never experience and others never learn to appreciate. A baby is a gift from the gods.* The thought seemed distressingly foreign, yet Kevral could not help but contemplate it. *I'm too young. I'm not competent to raise this baby. The best, the most loving, thing I could ever do for him or her is to find a mother and father whose failure to conceive has taught them the value of the treasure that is a child—someone who will love and care for this baby as I cannot.*

Though Kevral knew finding such a couple would prove difficult, she trusted Colbey to assist the search. His pain ran deep, even centuries later and sixteen years after the birth of his own son. Yet something more stayed her. When she considered only the baby and herself, the plan seemed perfectly sound. The child would find a proper home and she could return to Béarn without obvious change. No one there had to know about the baby.

Words Ra-khir had spoken came next to haunt Kevral, based on the bitterness he harbored against the mother who had tried to replace the father he loved, and who loved him, with another man: "If and when I have a child, no man or woman could take him from me." Ra-khir might excuse her lying with Tae, but he would never forgive her stealing his child. *He has the right to know about the baby, and so does Tae.* For so long, Kevral had hoped circumstance would make the decision between the men for her. Now it had, and she felt no better. If he would still have her, she would marry whoever turned out to be the baby's father. If he refused her and the baby, she would then do whatever she felt in the best interests of the child.

The moment of decision and resolve broke down a moment later. Thoughts raced through her head, none sensible. She saw a life of whispering, banishment from the Renshai, and a baby hated by all for being the offspring of a whore. Terror battered at self-worth, fueled by the quiet desperation of Charra's concerns. In this irrational world that Kevral created, Tae and Ra-khir despised her along with other friends, family, and strangers. For hours, snippets of idea assailed her, and the moments she managed to doze brought dreams as absurd as her waking thoughts.

At length, Kevral sat up, throwing the covers aside. Rage became an inferno, directed at the men, herself, the baby, and circumstance in turn. It became a wheel, rolling eternally. Even the Renshai mind techniques could not rescue her, and Kevral sought other distraction. Not wishing to disturb Charra's sleep, she glanced around the room for something on which to focus.

As her gaze swept her desk, the answer came. In the top central drawer, Minister Daizar had placed the agreement she had signed for the king. Several times, she had attempted to read it, the flowery language so dull her thoughts had always slipped off in other directions. Now, she hoped, she could force herself to read it.

Rising, Kevral jerked open the drawer. She found the papers on top of an assortment of inks and styluses and a pile of parchment. Taking the sheaf of pages, she returned to sit on the pillow, legs splayed out in front of her. She reread the first two pages as an exercise at directing her attention. Here, the Renshai mind techniques helped, funneling strength from body to thought, a weird phenomenon she had never believed practical. Always before, she had needed to channel in the opposite direction. Where they had failed her earlier, now her practices paid off. The passages that had once seemed discouragingly unreadable gained comprehension after two or three readings.

As Kevral continued, the focus of the contract changed from the details she and the king had discussed to matters she had never considered. Soon she no longer needed the intentional restructuring of thought in order to maintain her interest. As the strangeness of the wording became familiar, the intention behind each paragraph became more swiftly clear. At length, one stopped her cold. The first reading suggested that she had to make up missed days of work with two days at the end of her year. The king's and minister's early attempts to force her to wait until she felt better to teach gained a new and sinister meaning. Subsequent readings confirmed her original impression. Anger sparked anew, and she resolved to confront Minister Daizar about the problem in the morning.

Other points came to light, the minor details the minister had assured her held no importance. The contract decreed that every day she directly taught fewer than fifty students, she owed the kingdom another day and a half. Yet, the king had said nothing about her morning class containing twenty-four students. She daily taught forty-nine instead of forty-eight only because the general had added himself to the afternoon session. Kevral calculated quickly. By this gross reckoning, after four months of intensively training the guards, she now owed fourteen months of a one year commitment.

Kevral seized the sword beneath her pillow and added it to the scabbard and sword at her waist. The urge to slice her way through the help to Minister Daizar's bedroom became an obsession. She turned the mental techniques toward control. Slaughtering innocents would only compound the problem. She would not discount violence, only add some finesse and direction. First, however, she needed to complete her arsenal. Carefully, she lay on her stomach, contract pinned beneath her hands, devouring every paragraph. Most of the rest outlined the test the guardsmen would have to take to prove her training had gained them skill. Despite intensive discussion, the terms seemed reasonably vague, allowing loopholes for the king to trap and hold her. If the guardsmen failed the testing, she owed the king another two years. If, after that, they still did not pass, she owed four more. Ultimately, her time in Pudar could spiral into infinity.

An animal growl of outrage slipped from Kevral's throat, and she found herself halfway to the door before she realized she had moved. Nothing could stay her now. Bunching the contract into her belt, she stormed from her quarters. A night maid shied from the fuming Renshai, cringing as the door banged shut loud enough to awaken her neighbors. Kevral did not care. The whole of Pudar could plummet into a swamp, and she would consider it a just punishment for supporting such a vile creature as king. She tromped down the hallway, ignoring tapestries, trinkets, and the jeweled lanterns that lit her way.

A male servant scampered toward her from ahead. "Swordmistress, may I . . ." His voice disappeared as Kevral swept past without pausing. The chill funneling through the corridor did not bother her; the fires of anger warmed her well enough.

Kevral passed a patrolling guardsman and recognized him as one of her afternoon students. Without acknowledging his presence, she continued toward the stairs. The clomp of his boots and rattle of mail chased her down the hallway, then he drew up and paced her. "Armsman, what's the problem?"

Kevral kept her eyes ahead and did not slacken her stride. "Octaro, you're a good student; and I'd hate to lose you. Stay out of this one."

"But . . . ," he started. "Can you just explain . . . ?"

Kevral turned him a searing glare as she reached the base of the staircase.

Without another word, Octaro stopped, and Kevral hurried up two flights without him. The paper rattled with every movement, and the left-side sword banged painfully against her thigh. Only as she topped the landing did it occur to her she should probably have put on daytime clothing and some shoes. She chose not to correct the mistake. Her power never stemmed from appearances; and if she returned to her room, some of the rage that drove her might slip away unvented. She found Minister Daizar's bedroom easily and the pair of guards crouched in conversation in front of it.

Before either could move, Kevral drew her sword and pounded the pommel against the door. The hollow thunk of her striking echoed through the corridor.

Both guards leaped to their feet at once. "What in Hel are you doing?" one demanded. He grabbed for her arm.

Kevral whirled, slamming the flat of the blade against his head. The guardsman plummeted. The tip came to rest at the other's throat. "Get your hand off your hilt. I'm not in the mood."

He glanced at his grounded companion, then carefully held up both hands. "What are you going to do?"

"I'm going in," Kevral informed him.

"I can't let you do that!"

"Then stop me." Removing the threat, Kevral grabbed the knob and twisted.

The sound of rasping steel at her back sent her spinning to a crouch. Her eyes found the target as she moved, sword flat crashing against his fist. He dropped his hilt with a howl of pain. Kevral bore in, slapping him across the cheek with her free hand. "I'm your teacher, damn you. Learn some respect." She jabbed the sword back into its sheath, leaving a fuming, red-faced guardsman at her back. This time, he did not attack, only shouted a warning as she kicked the door open.

The two sentries inside came to attention more quickly, surely cued by the noise outside. They blocked the entry, swords springing into Kevral's path. *At least,* she noted with satisfaction, *they're all using swords now.* Beyond them, she could see a room half again as large as hers with assorted pieces of furniture carved from fine teak. A bed against the far wall held the minister's seated form. Like Kevral, he wore a sleeping gown, the blankets clutched to his chest.

Kevral studied the two men in front of her. "Move," she commanded.

Both tried to conceal nervousness, though Kevral read fear in one's white-knuckled grip. The other chewed his upper lip. Daizar looked around them without leaving the bed. "What are your intentions, Swordmistress?"

"My intentions," Kevral said carefully, "are to have these two gentlemen move. If I have to move them, piece by piece, I'll be that much hotter by the time I get to you!"

Daizar looked from Kevral to his sentries, and back. By now, they had her surrounded, two in front and one behind. Kevral could hear the awkward scuffle of the fourth man scrambling to his feet, and it pleased her. Any head wound hard enough to drive a man to unconsciousness could also kill him. The quicker he awakened, the less likely she had inflicted permanent damage. The guard had done nothing worse than his duty.

Despite odds that appeared in his favor, Daizar read the truth in the situation. It would take more than four Pudarian guards to control an infuriated Renshai. "Stand aside," he commanded his men without taking his gaze from Kevral. "Lady Kevral, can't this wait until morning?"

Kevral moved at the same time as the sentries, and they scarcely stepped aside swiftly enough to avoid a collision. Ignoring Daizar's question, Kevral strode to the bed, dug the parchment from her belt, and slapped it down on the blankets covering the minister's lap. "What in coldest Hel is this?"

Daizar's head dropped. Dark hair fell onto his cheek, crusted with old oil and smelling of sweat as much as perfume. He glanced at the papers only a moment before returning his attention to the Renshai. "Why, it looks like the contract you signed and agreed to about four months ago." The minister sounded matter-of-fact, but the need to remind Kevral of details she already knew suggested he anticipated her argument.

Kevral flipped to the offending page. "Look at this!" She jabbed a finger at the first paragraph of four that added time to her stay.

Daizar did as she bid, saying nothing.

"And this." She poked at the second with enough force to bend the paper and jam the tip of her finger into Daizar's leg.

Daizar stated the obvious. "Are you displeased with certain aspects of your contract?"

Kevral resisted the urge to slap him. "Yes." Her tone conveyed irritation more fully than her answer, laced with threat.

"Then," Daizar said with careful calm. "You should not have signed it."

Kevral closed her eyes, dredging forth composure through savage, boiling rage. Daizar's quiet fearlessness undermined her authority and gave him the upper hand. If she did not change her tactics, she would become forced to kill him just to maintain dignity. "As you know, I signed it in a state of exhaustion. And illness."

Daizar gave her a respectful nod. "Which, by Pudar's law, gave you three days to retract your signature. It's been four months, Swordmistress." Only a slight movement of the covers gave away his nervously twisting hands. He worried for his life as well, but he would let his guards see nothing but cool-headed determination.

Kevral glared. She did not know Pudarian law, but the minister did have a point. The sheer volume of work heaped upon her, servants' interruptions, and her own need for prayers, sleep, and practice had stolen time; and the tedium of the contract itself had made reading all but impossible. She had trusted the king and his scribes. "Your contract, and your methods, were deceptive."

"Not deceptive," Daizar corrected. "Clever."

Kevral did not argue semantics. "We destroy this agreement and start again."

"I'm afraid that's impossible." Daizar shrank ever so slightly away from Kevral.

"Then I destroy you *and* the contract."

The guards shifted toward them with resigned boldness, awaiting a command Daizar did not give. "I can't stop you from killing me or from ruining this copy of the contract. But murdering me would not release you from it. My death would only guarantee your execution."

Kevral clamped a hand to her hilt. "Execution might be worth the satisfaction."

Daizar shied but still did not call for help. He spoke swiftly, words slurring together in his haste. "Numbers and arrows can kill even Renshai. If you escaped Pudar, and the assassins on the roads, no kingdom would shelter you. They're all allies."

The blathering suited Kevral well enough. Regaining the guards' respect required breaking his irritating composure, not necessarily killing him. As the wild, uncontrollable phase of anger ebbed, a plan slipped to the fore. "Very well, I'll stick to the terms of the contract. Tomorrow morning, dismiss my current students. Gather every one- to five-year-old in the city on the choosing field."

"One to five . . ." Daizar's features screwed into a confused knot. "You mean children?"

Kevral shrugged. "Renshai don't differentiate children by age. Call them what you will. One- to five-year-olds. I'll need fifty, at least."

The minister no longer tried to hide his discomfort. "What are you up to, Kevral?" The titles of respect disappeared from his side of the conversation as well.

"Just following the contract. Here." Kevral paged to the front. "Paragraph seven." She read aloud, "Whereverfore not restricted by the legalities and lawful limitations placed upon her by Renshai injunction, the party of part one . . ." Kevral looked up, clarifying, "That's me."

Daizar made a crisp, waving gesture to indicate he did not need her to define terms for him.

Kevral cleared her throat and continued, ". . . shall henceforth implement techniques of education that embody the methodology of Renshai." She smiled, only now realizing the king, scribe, and ministers had probably assumed her illiterate. Most subscribed to the common belief that warrior skill and intelligence rarely meshed. In peaceful cultures, that often proved the case, as brainy men chose occupations that did not place their lives in danger. Those who could not rely on their mind skill developed their bodies and reflexes instead. However, all Renshai learned warfare, and Kevral had always striven for perfection in every aspect of her life. Her need to learn the Western tongue with proper accent had led her to visit Erythane. Without that trip, she might never have met Ra-khir.

"Your point?" Daizar prodded.

Kevral smiled. Now she truly held the edge. "Renshai technique involves beginning training as soon as a toddler's hand can grip a sword. In order to 'implement the methodology' of Renshai, I have to teach only younglings. I allowed up to age five because I'm also bound to fifty students, and the dullest Renshai could, theoretically, take that long to really begin learning sword." She deliberately chose complicated words to drive home the point that she was not only literate, but smart as well.

Daizar drew his hands from beneath the blankets, knotting them. "How do you get around the terms 'guards' and 'men'?" The question seemed pointless to Kevral. "In the Renshai culture, age has no bearing on terminology. If I train them to guard your city, then they are guards."

Daizar sat in miserable silence, hands clinging to the covers and eyes to the writings on the page. No words could counter Kevral's argument. Without violence, she had bested the minister at his own game. "You're a sneaky woman, Renshai."

Kevral smiled at the insult. "I prefer to think of myself as clever."

CHAPTER 27

Honors Challenged

So long as a Renshai dies giving his all to the battle, the name and face of the enemy bears no significance.
—*Colbey Calistinsson*

Perched upon a root in Westland forest, Tae Kahn watched his father settle into a position of aloof composure on the chair his bodyguards had carried and placed for him. At Weile's side, Alsrusett held a crouched stance that defined threat, a crossbow balanced near his left hand. Daxan paced wary ovals around the meeting site. A ring of low bushes, laced with thorny vines, surrounded the clearing. Tae appreciated its privacy at the same time he cursed the obscuring of his own view. Soon, he would meet the elves who had convinced his father to serve on their side and observe the business Weile had rarely conducted in his childhood presence.

A breeze meandered through the clearing, bobbing branches. The supple leaves of early spring made scant sound as they swept against one another. The wind ruffled Weile's curls straight backward, opening his dark eyes to a strange innocence that did not fit him. Tae looked away. Four months of reconciliation had brought him much peace but little progress. They had settled family matters. On many of the details of Weile's business, however, they had only agreed to accept disagreement. Someday, Weile stated, Tae would understand. Bewildered by many of his father's choices, Tae hoped the reverse would prove true.

Footfalls beyond the hedge seized Tae's attention. He glanced toward Daxan to assure himself the guard had heard them also. The squat Easterner clearly had. His head jerked toward the sound, and he moved into a position to intercept. Tae could discern only one set of footsteps, surely Kinya's. The elves' light, delicate maneuvers would keep them silent in the familiarity of woodlands. A moment later, Kinya's current whistle code blared above the songbirds, a three beat pattern: one long and medium-pitched, the second lower and shorter, and the third a high momentary shrill. Daxan met him at the opening, ushering Kinya and three elves through the shrubbery.

In the company of an aging human and a broad, muscular guard, the elves appeared every bit the slender, delicate fairies Tae's Béarnian nursemaid had described in stories. A male with white hair stepped through first, canted green eyes sweeping the clearing. If he worried for the discrepancy in numbers, he showed none of his concern. In fact, he demonstrated no emotion Tae could read, the subtlety of his body language and face definingly elfin. The female who followed also sported white hair, the sun striking reddish highlights that made it look on fire. High cheekbones set nearly at the level of her eyes gave her an animal appearance that matched the narrow angles of her body. Tae knew from experience that the apparent fragility hid a constitution stronger than any man's. The last was also male, with hair as dark as the others were pale. His heart-shaped lips seemed better suited to a woman, yet Tae had no more difficulty divining his gender than if he had worn a beard. Even after a capture and a battle, he could not comprehend the clues that distinguished elfin males from females. This last carried a coffer.

Alsrusett gestured the elves to a long root in front of Weile. They obligingly moved into position but chose not to sit. Kinya exchanged a glance with Weile and made a gesture Tae could not read. The underworld leader gave back a movement of his fingers at his side that Tae almost missed. Kinya nodded. After so many years together, the two understood one another without need for words with an eerie accuracy that nearly matched elfin *khohlar*.

"Welcome," Weile said, also rising. He did not attempt any of the usual signs of greeting that human populations exchanged, nor did he return to his seat. Tae attributed that to the emotional advantage of the higher position. Taller than the elves, he forced them to look up to read his eyes or expression. Though not large or particularly tall for a human, Tae's father struck an imposing, powerful figure he had rarely noticed as a child. He had only feared Weile when red anger tinged his soft, dark eyes and pursed his lips into pale lines. It occurred to Tae now that it had made little sense to worry about his father's intentions even then. Weile had never struck him or his mother. Tae supposed that working with the most frustrating, obnoxious, and irritating humans in the world probably had much to do with his impressive self-control. He had seen the way other Eastern men treated their women and children, sons as well as daughters.

Alsrusett drew nearer and just ahead of his charge. Daxan stepped back to his opposite side.

Tae envied Weile's ability to intimidate without resorting to threat. Different in gesture and from a culture once devoid of violence, the elves would take little notice of Weile's posturing. Still, Tae took careful note of stance and expression for his own future dealings with humans. Weile was right about having much to teach his son.

The white-haired male spoke after a pause unpleasant to Tae's human-cultured ways. "Dh'arlo'mé'aftris'ter Te'meer Braylth'ryn Amareth Fel-Krin is pleased." His voice held a reverence Tae had heard only from the most devout priests and from warriors so devoted to their religion they chose to die for it. Tae's brow crinkled before he could think to hide expression. Captain had led him to believe the elves saw gods more as allies than objects of worship.

Weile tipped his head in acknowledgment of the compliment. He met the catlike eyes directly. The black-haired male glanced at each human in the clearing, Tae last. He looked back to the conversation, stiffened suddenly, and studied Tae more carefully. Apparently, he communicated with the woman using *khohlar* because, a moment later, she examined him as well.

Tae allowed a slight smile to touch his features. *Recognize me, don't you, you ugly bastards. Try and figure this one out.*

Oblivious to his companions' focus, the white-haired male continued. "He has a new project for you." Without turning, he made an arching gesture toward his back.

The other male jerked his gaze from Tae to carry forward the coffer. The speaker opened it, only then glancing in Tae's direction, surely in response to a silent communication. His attention did not linger, however. He frowned minimally and returned his gaze to Weile and the coffer.

Tae rose casually, straightening his tunic and surreptitiously rearranging breeks that clung uncomfortably to his buttocks. He wanted a look in that coffer, but his position allowed only sideways scrutiny. Even then, he identified glimmering coins and gemstones.

The sun sparked blue and gold accents onto Weile's cheeks,

and the crime lord's expression told Tae more than his own eyes. His father could not fully hide his appreciation. Apparently, the box held a fortune.

Tae returned to his seat, ignoring the female's persistent scrutiny. In a moment, he would discover the extent of his father's morality, and he suspected he would despise what he learned. No one would offer so much for anything less than evil. He closed his eyes and loosed a quiet sigh. Likely, the time had come to part company.

The speaker seemed unconcerned with Weile's silence. "Dh'arlo'mé'aftris'ter Te'meer Braylth'ryn Amareth Fel-Krin asks that your men join us in assaulting Pudar."

Tae's eyes flew open. His head jerked to his father. All three of the elves turned their gazes there as well. The speaker set the coffer onto Weile's arms. A pearl necklace crowned with an emerald slithered from the pile to the ground at Weile's feet.

Apparently accepting Weile's quiet thoughtfulness as acquiescence, the elf explained. "We'll meet—"

Weile cocked a wrist around the coffer, a gentle plea for the elf to stop speaking.

The white-haired male complied.

"You want us to help you attack the city of Pudar?"

"Yes."

"Why?"

The elf did not move. His gemlike eyes never seemed to blink. "You've not needed reasons before."

Weile casually shook a curl from his forehead. "And I don't need one now."

Tae felt his heart sink into his gut. He lowered his head, though this sent a shaggy curtain of black hair into his eyes.

"The answer is no."

Tae could not hold back a massive grin and appreciated the unruly mane that hid it from the elves. He forced his lips back to their normal configuration before raising his head and raking the hair back behind his ears.

"You wouldn't refuse us." The lead elf's tone contained just a hint of disbelief, enough to make it clear he did not threaten.

"Oh, I would," Weile assured him in a voice that left no room for argument. "And I did." He held out the coffer, but the elves made no move to take it back.

"You want more money," the speaker guessed. "Have we not been generous enough?"

Again, Weile attempted to return the coffer, and the elves ignored the gesture. The attempt required him to stand unnaturally close to the white-haired male. "Tell Dh'arlo'mé'aftris'ter Te'meer Braylth'ryn Amareth Fel-Krin . . ." He did not stumble over a syllable of the protracted name. Memorizing details was part of his job. ". . . that our dealings are ended." When the elf still did not accept the payment back, Weile overturned the coffer. Gold and silver, copper and precious stones, gem-studded trinkets and jewelry spilled out in a rainbow wash of color. Coins clinked and clattered. Gemstones bounced, rolling across the dirt and the feet of men and elves.

In the moment when every eye was drawn inexorably to the money, the lead elf clapped a hand to Weile's face. All else seemed to happen at once. Weile recoiled, dropping the coffer with a pained curse. The elves ran. Alsrusett snatched up the crossbow. Daxan drew his sword and charged. Tae surged to his feet, hand springing to his own weapon. Kinya brandished an ax, physically blocking retreat. The elves sprinted toward the exit, Daxan at their heels. A moment later, the elves bounded into the air and flew over the hedges. A quarrel speared the space the speaker once filled.

"Let them go," Weile said, voice coarsened by pain that went beyond a simple slap. He removed the hand he had clamped to his left cheek, studying it for blood.

Tae reached his father's side first, seeing the angry, red burn in the shape of a small, long-fingered hand. "What is that?"

Weile stepped back farther from the coffer and its scattered contents. "He was trying to brand me an elf-enemy."

Tae jerked a rag from his pocket. "How do you know that?"

"He told me."

Mentally, Tae guessed. Spitting on the cloth, he dabbed at the wound.

Weile pulled away. "Ow! Sheriva's demons, what are you doing?"

Tae lowered the cloth. "You got a better way to wash off any residue? If he left something caustic there, it'll eat deep enough to scar."

"Scar, who cares," Weile grumbled. "Let the whole world know I'm a damned elf-enemy. It's better than having someone grind filth into an open wound."

"Hey!" Tae protested the insult to his oral hygiene. "I'm trying to wash off the dirt."

Weile shoved his son aside with a garbled response as Alsrusett and Daxan returned to tend him. Both wore stricken looks.

"My fault, sir," Alsrusett said, sounding near to tears. "I should have cut off his hand before he touched you."

Weile waved off his bodyguard as well. "It's my own damned fault. I let him burden my hands, then stepped into harm's way. I deserved what I got." He mumbled, "Dropped that stupid coffer on my own foot, too."

Tae could not help smiling. He was pleased when his father dropped pretenses, a thing he only did in the singular presence of himself, the personal guards, and Kinya. "I'm proud of you, Father."

Weile whirled on his son. "Great. I finally figured out how to earn your respect, and it requires me to break my toes."

Tae snorted. "No, that part just amuses me. I'm proud of the way you put morality over money."

"Survival over money," Weile corrected. "Before, I could reconcile the elves' jobs to self-defense. I won't get involved in their war against humanity. You and I know they're not going to stop at slaughtering Pudarians. Given the chance, they'd use us till we destroyed the rest of mankind, then turn on us as well." He placed a hand on Tae's shoulder, and the expression he showed his son revealed pride. "You were right, Tae. I only wish I'd believed you sooner."

Tae felt a cozy glow kindle inside of him. It was a feeling with which he had little familiarity, but he liked it.

Daxan interrupted the moment. "Sir, what would you have me do with the payment?" He made a broad gesture to indicate the coins and jewelry.

Tae met his father's dark gaze. The idea of taking tainted money rankled, yet he could understand its allure. Weile had already refused the elves' demands. They had chosen to leave it.

Weile approached the biggest pile. Hands on his hips, he examined the sparkling treasures, more than even most nobles saw in a lifetime. He touched a hand to the livid, scarlet mark on his cheek. It would surely blister, but Tae doubted it would leave the brand the elves had sought. Burns that scarred were ominously painless.

"This." Weile kicked the stack. Ornaments and coins sailed toward the hedges, and others plowed beneath leaf mold and dirt. He whirled suddenly, placing an arm across Tae's shoulders and leading his son from the clearing.

Tae had never loved his father more.

* * *

King Cymion of Pudar sat on a hard wooden chair in one of the castle's many meeting rooms, his adviser, Javonzir, seated beside him and seven guards attentively around him. The overseer of the east wing staff stood nearby, leaning against the table now pushed up against the wall, fingers lacing nervously through his beard. Though distracting, Cymion preferred that to the wild pacing that had preceded it. The room contained no other furnishings, and the door on the far right-hand side of the room remained closed.

Though three quarters of a year had passed since Cymion's eldest son's death, sorrow still haunted him, a grim specter that perched eternally upon bowed shoulders. Life in the castle had returned to its routine long ago, yet it would never seem the same. He still found himself turning to elicit Crown Prince Severin's opinion or to teach him a finer point of law, only to stare at an empty chair or worse, a startled guard or courtier squirming beneath the king's sudden scrutiny.

Cymion ran a hand through auburn hair flecked with gray. As his fingers twined through, they straightened curls that sprang immediately back into place. *Time for a haircut,* he decided mechanically, the thought a throwback to his warrior training when sweat would plaster those locks to his forehead and unbind them enough that they slid into his eyes. He smiled slightly at the ancient instinct, mind gliding back to the days before his father chose him over his brothers as the heir to Pudar's throne. He and his cousin Javonzir had trained for war together, filled with dreams of a life of service to his elder brother, competing for the position as general. Even after so many years, he recalled their wrestling matches, their chases through the palace hallways that often sent them careening past glowering nobles, and their spars with crude wooden weapons that usually ended in bruised limbs or smashed fingers. Though he kept his arm honed and his frame robustly muscled through practice, more so than Javonzir, the life of king and adviser suited them better.

"She'll be here, Majesty," the overseer said reassuringly for the fourteenth time. "I'm sure of it."

King Cymion gave no reply. He did not doubt his retainer, only wished the man would not worry so much. He had delayed his court to come to this meeting, believing the words of the young healer more significant than standard affairs. The woman performed a great service for the kingdom, and he saw no need to rush the process or her awakening.

Just as the overseer opened his mouth again, the latch clicked. The door eased open, and Charra slipped inside. Without glancing to the far end of the room, she carefully closed the door. "Well, I spoke with the violent little slut—" She turned, raising her head. Only then, her eyes fell on King Cymion and widened as if to encompass her entire face. With a high-pitched gasp of shock and terror, she hurled herself, prostrate, to the floor.

Cymion glanced at the overseer, who cringed and shook his head carefully. Apparently, he had not found the time to warn Charra of the king's appearance. Not wanting to leave her worrying too long, Cymion addressed Charra. "Rise, please, Healer. Approach."

Charra climbed to her feet and headed hesitantly toward the assemblage. She stumbled a bit, as if reeds had replaced her legs. As she drew near enough to politely speak, she curtsied deeply. "Your Majesty, my humblest apologies. I–I didn't . . . know . . . I . . . you . . ."

Cymion spared her the need for explanations. "Is the Renshai with child?"

"Yes, Sire," Charra returned. "About five months along."

The math bothered the king, though he suppressed a frown. Charra might worry that she had displeased him, and it would make her even more nervous and more afraid to recount details. "What more did you learn?"

Charra curtsied again, yellow-brown eyes dodging Cymion's harder blue ones. The gesture seemed more nervous habit than courtesy. "Sire, the father is a Knight of Erythane."

King Cymion stiffened, unable to hide his startlement. "A knight. Really," he muttered. The naming of his own kin as father could not have surprised him more. "How odd."

"I don't believe she was lying, Your Majesty." Again, she glanced at the overseer for direction.

The king did not bother to watch the man's reaction. He would encourage her to speak openly.

Charra carefully cleared her throat, hiding behind a curtain of mousy hair. "Sire, for all her strength on the battlefield, the Renshai's a regular, naive adolescent when it comes to 'woman things.' I don't think she knew she could get pregnant doing what she did. She seems scared and confused."

Now, the king allowed himself a smile. "Good. And you enhanced that worry, I hope?" He avoided looking at Javonzir. He could almost feel his adviser's unspoken disapproval.

A shaky grin touched Charra's lips as well. "Of course, Your Majesty. I've started the process, but there's still much that needs doing."

"Consider this your only necessary responsibility for at least the next half year."

"Sire, I'll likely have to get ousted from the castle."

Cymion stroked his beard. "I understand. Even as you pretend to live alone on the streets, you'll have our support. I only regret you'll have to suffer some real humiliation. If we tell too many the truth, it'll jeopardize your hard work."

Charra nodded. "I'll suffer it gladly in the service of the kingdom, Your Majesty. I only hope my husband will be well taken care of in my absence."

"Of course," Cymion reassured. "And promoted. One way or another, we'll find a way to properly reunite and reward you. Your baby will not suffer for your service."

"All the gods bless you and your generosity, Your Majesty." Charra curtsied again. "I'll do my best." She hesitated just long enough to suggest she had something else to say.

Cymion did not dismiss her yet. "Is there more?"

Charra kept her head bowed. "Sire, I was just wondering about the necessity of the cat."

"Kevral used to travel with a healer who had a calico cat. I think it best that you keep it with you. Has that been a problem?"

"Only a bit, Sire. She tends to wander." Charra answered the direct question before moving to compliments. "A masterful touch, Your Majesty."

King Cymion focused on the problem rather than the praise. "It's been suggested that the best way to keep a cat a companion is to carry treats and feed them often." The cook had told a minister that just the previous day.

"Thank you, Your Majesty. I'll do that."

"Anything more?"

"Not yet, Sire."

"Dismissed, then."

Charra whirled and hurried to the door without a backward glance. Opening it, she slipped through, pushing it gently closed behind her.

Cymion sensed Javonzir's need to speak, but he continued to

ignore his cousin. He would weather his adviser's words only in private. "You're dismissed, too, Overseer."

"Thank you, Majesty."

The overseer rushed from the room looking every bit as uncomfortable as Charra had.

Cymion sighed. "Guards, wait for me outside."

The men broke ranks with quiet precision and filed from the room without comment or backward glance. Cymion closed his eyes as the door clicked closed behind the last of them and waited for Javonzir to speak.

The silence stretched interminably. Cymion opened his eyes and studied his cousin.

Dutifully, Javonzir lowered his head, a spare gesture of deference and respect. Dark brown hair scarcely slid with the movement, and the hazel eyes studied Cymion evenly.

After the long hush, Cymion's voice sounded booming. "You think I'm handling this wrong."

Javonzir blinked but said nothing.

As the silence once again became uncomfortable, King Cymion pressed. "Well? Do I no longer deserve an answer?"

"You always deserve answers, Majesty. I was simply awaiting a question."

The formality irritated. Javonzir only became this stuffy when he wished to contradict but knew his advice would meet severe resistance. Cymion savored a deep breath. As he did so, he reminded himself of his adviser's magnificent insight and wisdom. He trusted Javonzir's counsel, even when it clashed with his desires. "Speak your mind, Javon. I want to hear it."

Javonzir blinked once, with far more deliberation than such a natural action required. "Majesty, a man makes stronger alliances through kindness than trickery."

"Yes." Cymion understood the concept. "But this ally would not stay without both."

"Perhaps if you gave her a chance, Majesty."

Cymion shook his head. He had seen the closeness between Kevral and her companions. Once, when his own words had threatened Matrinka's freedom, Kevral had prepared to battle his inner guard force and himself. She had surrendered herself to him for execution in Tae's place. Thoughts of his son's murder narrowed Cymion's eyes, and deadly rage darkened his features. He shook the thought from his mind, concerned Javonzir might believe the anger directed at him. Pudar could never sever such ties, yet Cymion saw no way to buy Kevral's tremendous loyalty for himself and his kingdom. Keeping her expertise in Pudar, preferably along with her family, had long ago passed from desperate desire to urgent necessity. His vision of Renshai serving him and his heirs as soldiers, armsmen, and higher officers had become as tangible as reality. To sacrifice that dream now meant weakening Pudar. "Do you have any ideas about how to do that?"

"Yes, Sire. I do."

Cymion stiffened, turning sideways in his chair to look directly at Javonzir. "You didn't before." The statement was not wholly true. The adviser had made a few suggestions, none strong enough to carry the situation, however.

"Your Majesty, circumstances have changed. I've had more time to consider."

"And?" Cymion pressed eagerly. Perhaps Javonzir would even find a way to lure the knight into his service.

"Crown Prince Leondis, Sire."

The title jabbed through Cymion like a spear, raising tears he banished too slowly. Leondis displayed few of the qualities that had made his brother so suited for rulership. Cymion had deliberately not considered his heir since Severin's murder. "What about my younger son?"

"Sire, perhaps it's time for him to settle down and become a proper heir."

"Yes." Cymion could not deny the assertion, though he saw no connection to earning the Renshai's permanent allegiance to Pudar. In his grief, he had neglected the new crown prince's education.

Javonzir studied the king's face as he spoke, measuring the moment that his advice crossed dangerous lines. "Leondis is no Severin, of course, Majesty."

Cymion nodded vigorously.

"But he's not a bad young man, and I think he'll eventually make a pretty good king."

Cymion did not agree. He had mostly hoped to use his youngest son as a tool to create more heirs. Though approaching fifty, Cymion remained strong and healthy. He planned to rule at least long enough for Leondis' sons to grow up, so that he could train one to take his place. "The only things he takes seriously are his parties and his women. At least on a night-to-night basis."

A hint of a smile strayed to Javonzir's thin lips. "Sire, a family might settle Leondis."

A snort escaped Cymion. "It would simply turn his carousing into affairs."

Javonzir's smile grew. "Not if his wife could kill him for the indiscretion."

Cymion inhaled a mouthful of saliva and broke into paroxysms of coughing. For a moment, he feared he had swallowed his tongue as well.

Javonzir waited patiently while his king choked and hacked.

Finally, Cymion managed to speak again, his eyes moist and his voice hoarse. "You mean marry Leondis and Kevral?" His raw windpipe forced him into another bout of coughing.

"Why not?"

"The crown prince of Pudar married to a Renshai?"

The smile remained, and Javonzir's brows rose in question.

"The crown prince of Pudar married to a foreigner pregnant with another man's baby?" Cymion glared at his cousin. "Have you gone mad? That bare suggestion is treason!" The declaration lost its vehemence as coughs racked Cymion again.

"Majesty, it ceases to be treason when the king requests the speaker speak his mind."

Cymion nodded resignedly, still coughing. He would never prosecute Javonzir for anything, and they both knew it.

"Hear me out, Sire." Javonzir surely realized the cough assured that anyway. "You have a Renshai who has already improved your army two hundred percent and an elite group ten times that. Understandably, you want to keep her in Pudar as long as possible. She desperately needs a husband and a father for a baby whose blood father is a Knight of Erythane, of all things. Sire, you have a crown prince who needs to learn responsibility and discipline. And seems incapable of siring children of his own."

The last words hit Cymion nearly as hard as the understanding of Javonzir's intentions. "Incapable of siring children?" The guttural quality of his voice came not wholly from the irritation in his windpipe. "Javon, why would you say such a thing?"

"Sire," Javonzir said cautiously. "If Leondis is only half as . . . um . . . experienced as rumored, we should have bastards running all over the castle."

"There's Leosina." Cymion named the three-year-old daughter of a west wing maid, claimed as Leondis' illegitimate child.

Javonzir folded his fingers together. "Sire, perhaps this is the time to mention the striking resemblance between that girl and the young man who serves dinner to the west wing nobles."

Cymion knew the deception should enrage him; yet, for now, it took a back seat to the more significant matter. "No grandchildren?"

"Majesty." Javonzir placed a hand on the back of Cymion's chair. "I don't know that for certain. And your sister has several sons who could sit upon the throne, if you so chose. Your line would not be lost if Leondis cannot sire offspring."

The urge to slam his arm across the chair until he pounded it to rubble seized the king, but he controlled it from long practice. It did not do for the king to show too much emotion, even in private and with the one person who made him feel wholly safe. *Severin should have succeeded me. Severin's children should carry on our blood.* The line of thought served no constructive purpose. He never doubted Javonzir's idea could come to pass. No commoner could refuse a prince's proposal. If Charra did her job well, Kevral would agree to marry a servant, let alone a prince, of Pudar. For all his faults, Leondis was an eye-pleasing, charming man of manners, well liked by the ladies. If he could not entrance the young Renshai, no man in the city could do so. Yet the idea of a Pudarian prince marrying a low-born, a Renshai, or a woman carrying another's child rankled, beyond consideration, at least for the moment.

Javonzir cleared his throat, indicating Cymion had remained in hushed contemplation too long. "Sire, another matter. Minister Daizar quite suddenly requested a place on the court docket this morning."

The strangeness of Javonzir's announcement pulled Cymion, finally, from his thoughts. "Why?"

"I don't know, Majesty. Rumor among the guards is the Renshai attacked him last night."

"She did?" Guarded curiosity awakened, Cymion sought Javonzir's opinion.

Javonzir shook his head. "I don't believe it, Majesty."

"You don't?" Cymion gestured for his adviser to continue.

"Majesty, if a Renshai had attacked him last night, he would not be alive to request audience this morning. The news beyond the rumors is that she refused to see her students this morning and plans to replace them with young children."

Cymion groaned, certain he would learn the details in the courtroom. Things did not look good; and, ultimately, he could blame no one but himself.

CHAPTER 28

A Demon and a Sword of Chaos

Every time you draw that sword, it's a real fight.
                                        —Colbey Calistinsson

In the main room of the elfin common house, Dh'arlo'mé sat straight-backed upon a jeweled chair stolen from Béarn's castle, his position regal without lapsing into rigidity. He clutched the staff in his left hand, its base on the floor and its end towering over his head. His right hand lay still upon the arm of the chair, occasionally rising in a subtle gesture to counterpoint his words or *khohlar*.

One by one, his lead scouts paraded into his presence and struggled to avoid the pinning scrutiny of his single green eye. Their fear had become a tangible commodity on which he thrived. It kept them desperately loyal, to him and to his every cause; and their awe grew as powerful as that of a true believer for his god. The staff had granted him knowledge and so much more: the bearing that turned his elves from companions to worshipers, the ability to read thoughts and emotions, the competence to summon and control demons. And, gradually, it won him the confidence to use all those things in the cause of elves and law.

The first lead scout reported the racial wars of the North that raged without stopping for months. Already, one of the ten tribes had been obliterated, its lands incorporated by its neighbors. Dh'arlo'mé had read so much beyond the words: the violence elves could scarcely understand, the unfathomable ability to find honor and glory in slaughtering others of one's ilk, and the desperate vengeance that forever propelled and reincited the wars. Chaos had taken its toll also in the East, where a scramble for the throne had resulted in a conniving and brutal king, one more interested in his own power and entertainment than in the future of his country. It had proved simple for the elves to stir paranoia and jealousy. Soon enough, the East would fall.

Even the vast majority of the Westland towns had crumbled into riot. Scores of humans died from violence and starvation caused by the inability to transport supplies. Farmers watched their crops fall into decay, unable to deliver, while those a day's travel from plenty fell victim to hunger and disease. Dh'arlo'mé learned the horrors beyond the straightforward reports of his lead scouts, and they filled him with fierce elation. Finally, his revenge would succeed. Chaos and humans had become a single entity in his mind, and they would die together.

Three human strongholds still held fast against the hysteria that tore apart all others. That Béarn could remain so cohesive with the Staff of Chaos in its midst once floored Dh'arlo'mé before law, and its knowledge, became so much a part of him. Now he understood that the king of Béarn was the central focus of neutrality. His influence over his territory existed only in pockets, but a god-mediated tradition did not easily die. Cut off by mountains, the city of Santagithi never relied heavily on trade and even now maintained order. Eventually, Dh'arlo'mé intended to steer the warring Northmen toward the wealth and necessities there, after the battles claimed most of their own. Dh'arlo'mé awaited the lead scout's report on the third holdout.

A vast sense of restless anxiety accompanied Mith'ranir Orian T'laris El-neerith Wherinta through the doorway. His every discreet gesture demonstrated a respect that bordered on worship. Dh'arlo'mé demanded none of the cumbersome formality of human rulers, as much to avoid the conventions of enemies as because it seemed wholly unnecessary. The quiet awe of his followers, and their willingness to obey his every command, served him well enough.

Green eyes glanced at Dh'arlo'mé around white bangs, then skittered away. Mith'ranir sent *khohlar: *The Easterners refused our offer.**

A surge of surprise, then anger jolted through Dh'arlo'mé, easily controlled. He sat impassively, revealing nothing.

Mith'ranir continued, gemlike eyes returning to Dh'arlo'mé's face, seeking clues to his disposition. *They will not work for us any longer . . .**

Dh'arlo'mé savored the lead scout's reverent confusion. The king of the elves had perfected stoicism. His eye fixed on the scout, and even it gave away nothing of Dh'arlo'mé's temper.

Mith'ranir continued to explain the situation while Dh'arlo'mé gleaned details that obviated words or even *khohlar.* Mith'ranir's memories gave him more than he needed, even the shock and rage on Weile's face when the elf had marked him. The man who had assisted the escape of King Griff and the captured Renshai from the elves' dungeon had influenced the Eastern criminal's decision. And, as Mith'ranir concluded his story in the moments *khohlar* took, Dh'arlo'mé brushed an older thought lost amidst the turmoil of Mith'ranir's mind. It involved the heir to Pudar's throne.

Mith'ranir ended with a question. *What would you have us do now? Should we assault Pudar without them?*

No, Dh'arlo'mé returned swiftly, without need for consideration. *We cannot spare even one elfin life.* He forced realization of Mith'ranir's incaution at the meeting with Weile Kahn. Getting self and companions safely away should have taken precedence over attempting to brand an enemy. He fought the smile that naturally followed realization. *If the humans will not do the job for us, then we must resort to another.* His mind went immediately to demons, and the few remaining threads of his original personality recoiled from the idea. Memory of the slaughter near the shore had become tattered and distant, yet it remained. It seemed unremittingly wrong to draw forth chaos into the service of law.

The staff battered back doubts it read as weakness. It hammered at that small piece of Dh'arlo'mé not yet bonded to its will. *What could be more lawful than tying chaos to law's service? It will claim its blood from Pudar, and together we can control and destroy it. A blow to humans and chaos at once.*

Dh'arlo'mé accepted the explanation easily, but frustration plied him for other reasons. It seemed unfair that elves required natural death to reproduce while humans could spill out their violent, squalling brats at will. In the reverse situation, destroying the human race would prove so much simpler. The closest the gods had come to balancing that natural flaw was the fleeting length of human existence. Dh'arlo'mé latched onto that thought. If humans could use elfin reproduction against him, surely he could find a way to use their short life spans against them. The answer, he realized, lay in Mith'ranir's memory. He confronted his lead scout. *Do I recall you did something to Pudar's crown prince?*

Mith'ranir looked at his leader strangely. *We had him murdered, remember? The humans arranged with us so that the blame fell on an enemy of theirs.*

Dh'arlo'mé remembered the incident well enough. *I mean

*the current crown prince of Pudar. Did you do something to him?**

Mith'ranir brightened. He sent the concept of sterilization, created through magic.

Excitement took form behind Dh'arlo'mé's uncompromising mask. He berated himself for the foolishness of not previously thinking of such an obvious strategy. *Humans unable to reproduce will last only so long as their babies grow to old age.* Experience told him eighty years or less, a pittance to an elf. **Can you do that again?**

I shouldn't need to. I believe it's permanent, Mith'ranir sent, a modicum of pride touching the sentiment, a relatively new emotion to the elfin repertoire.

Dh'arlo'mé broadened the concept, to indicate the human race en masse.

Clearly daunted, Mith'ranir made a gesture of uncertainty to accompany his *khohlar*. **It took me all night to handle him, and much difficulty.**

Perhaps a jovinay arythanik?**

Mith'ranir sent a vigorous agreement. **It would still take time, and I don't know how much distance I could cover.** The *khohlar* degenerated into bits of thought. *Perhaps with others also casting. And a long distraction. And a big* jovinay arythanik. *An area at a time.* He returned to communication mode, though Dh'arlo'mé had heard everything between. **Possible, I think. If we work together.**

We always do, Dh'arlo'mé reminded. **We ALWAYS do.**

Formal affairs of court, personal training, and drills left Rakhir little occasion for anything more, yet he still found himself with more free time than he could manage. The life of a Knight of Erythane included dinners with family, and he had no one with whom to spend his evenings. Kedrin was needed in Béarn, and Ra-khir counted the days until his shift would take him there as well. He missed Darris, Matrinka, and Griff, perhaps even Rantire. And, most of all, Kevral.

Ra-khir wandered the streets of Erythane, his course taking him naturally up the hill to the Bellenet Fields. Spring breezes tugged at his hat, freeing strands of red-gold hair, and ruffled at his tabard. Lowering sunlight sheened from Béarn's gold and blue on the front, shifting with every movement. His clothes fit him without wrinkle, perfectly tailored and properly colored. The icy edge to the winds did not bother him. The southern lands rarely saw snow or temperatures low enough to warrant anything heavier than a woolen cloak, and winter now lay behind them.

Ra-khir leaned carefully against the wooden fence, tracking the sun's downward progress in the sky. The joy of earning his knighthood still thrilled through him most times, liberally accompanied by disbelief. Often, he worried he would awaken and find the whole a pleasant dream. Yet the stiff soreness of his muscles was real enough, and loneliness managed to taint his usual excitement. It seemed impossible that only five months had passed since Kevral's and Tae's departure. It seemed like a previous lifetime. He wondered how they fared, forcing himself, as always, to believe they had arrived safely. But, tonight, doubt gnawed achingly at his thoughts. Caravans could not penetrate the blockade to Western travel. Even his faith in Kevral's skill could not always overcome knowledge.

The sun tipped over the horizon, leaving a rainbow wake that paraded colors across the sky. He watched them layer, the purple expanse fading to blue, sweeping into an emerald line before melting into yellow. This gave way, in turn, to a brilliant scarlet that made earth and sun seem on fire. The radiance stole away his concerns for a moment, and he caught his breath with a soft gasp of pleasure.

A gentle voice wafted from beneath Ra-khir's left arm. "Beautiful, isn't it?"

Ra-khir stiffened, jerking away from the fence. A young woman sat in the brown, brittle grass, several arm's lengths to his left. Straight, brown hair fell to her waist, and blue-green eyes studied him from beneath long lashes.

"I'm sorry," she said, stifling laughter but not a smile. "Did I startle you?"

Ra-khir would not lie, not even to save face. "Yes, Lady." He grinned back sheepishly, politely removing his hat. "I was so caught up in my thoughts I didn't see you there."

The smile spread across her face. "You don't recognize me, do you, Ra-khir?"

Guarded curiosity rose in Ra-khir. Women seemed to follow him everywhere, especially since his promotion. He had politely staved off advances so many times, he had lost track of the numbers, names, and faces. Many seemed eager to forget the terrible stigma of unmarried pregnancy if a knight sired the child. They knew honor would force him to marry them afterward if they could not woo him before. Ra-khir realized his face and build won him more than his share of female admirers. He found himself disliking the rigid need to keep self, horse, and clothing meticulously groomed or wishing he had inherited less of his parents' beauty. He did not attempt to commiserate. Few would believe comeliness more curse than blessing. At least, Kevral's attraction to Tae proved she loved him for something other than his status and appearance. He shook his head gently. "I'm afraid I don't recognize you, fair lady. I am sorry for the rudeness."

"I'm Mariell. Sushara's sister."

The name penetrated memory slowly. Gradually, Ra-khir recalled the playmates of his childhood, including a neighbor girl named Sushara. A bit more thought brought images of a gawky younger sister with enormous front teeth. This vision scarcely resembled the woman who sat on the Bellenet Fields. "You're Mariell?"

She nodded, still smiling. Highlights shimmered through the cascade of hair, and her ample lips broadened to reveal teeth much whiter and smaller than he remembered. Apparently, her second set fit her mouth better.

"You've changed, my lady. And all for the better."

"You too, Ra-khir. You look nothing like your father." Mariell clearly blurted the words before she had time to consider them. She covered her mouth with a hand. "I meant that as a compliment. Khirwith was *not* a handsome man."

"He also isn't my father," Ra-khir felt obligated to explain. He dangled his hat over the upper rail.

Mariell stared. "You're going to have to tell me about that."

"And I will," Ra-khir promised, shocked at how comfortable he felt. The sunset formed the perfect background, and the conversation felt right. The other women seemed only interested in discussing his knighthood and in pressing up close to him as swiftly as possible. "But first, I'd like you to tell me what you're doing here."

Mariell drew her long legs to her chest and looked up at Ra-khir. "I like to watch the sunset. My father and I used to come up here a lot at night. "He's dead now, you know; but I always feel connected to him when the sun goes down. The colors . . ." She trailed off, her embarrassment evident in the way she buried her face against her hands. "I'm sorry, Ra-khir. You don't want to hear all this."

"I do," Ra-khir insisted. And he really did, to his own surprise. He walked over and sat carefully next to her. "Please go on."

Mariell obliged, explaining how the colors reminded her of different moods of her father and how his spirit seemed to touch her in the moments they hovered in the sky. The two discussed Ra-khir's situation next, then the conversation shifted to memories of childhood. Loneliness and sorrow disappeared into a camaraderie Ra-khir desperately missed. Dusk slipped quietly into a darkness speckled with stars and only a sliver of moon, a gorgeous night to follow a gorgeous sunset.

The first lull came only after hours of talk that made it seem as if no time had passed since their days of childhood play. Their eyes met, and Ra-khir wondered idly if he had ever known a woman more beautiful. He could not have stopped himself from kissing her if he tried, and she did not resist him when he did. At first, she only yielded, then she clumsily returned it. Warmth suffused Ra-khir, and he realized how natural it would seem to lever Mariell down on the grass and make love beneath the stars.

Ra-khir retreated from the thought as well as the kiss. "I'm sorry," he said.

Mariell granted him a shy smile before turning away. "I'm not. But thanks for stopping. I was so caught up in the moment, I would have let you go as far as you wanted. It wouldn't be right."

"No, it wouldn't," Ra-khir agreed, though he could not wholly escape the surge of masculine need that told him otherwise.

"Virginity is a gift the gods grant each human only once. Losing it should be the most special moment in a person's life." Mariell gazed up into the vast array of stars. "Only after a man and a woman have joined their souls for eternity should they complete the union of body as well."

Ra-khir's gaze followed Mariell's, though a tear glazed the sky to a black plain broken by golden zigzags of light. His thoughts went back to his own first time, locked in a prison with death hovering moments away. His love for Kevral would never allow him to complete the act with Mariell that his body craved, even had his honor not already rescued him from the mistake. Given the opportunity to relive his life, he would wait, even against Kevral's protests. Regret formed a vivid picture of their wedding night, the proper time for the innocent exploration they had already savored. "You're right, Mariell." Ra-khir could think of nothing better to say. "And I shouldn't have kissed you."

Mariell rose, giving Ra-khir a quick peck on the cheek. "I really should go home now. My mother will worry."

Ra-khir scrambled to his feet, rescuing his hat from the dirt. "It's not safe. I'll walk you back." He offered from politeness, not from desire. The moment of passion embarrassed him, and it had fully passed, leaving nothing but fear in its place.

"No." Mariell glanced toward town. "I walk this way alone all the time."

"I can't let you go by yourself."

"No," Mariell repeated. "I want some time by myself to think."

Ra-khir stepped back. He shared her need.

"I'll see you again, won't I?" Mariell's gentle question revealed much unspoken. Although she worried for the speed of their relationship, she did not want to lose it entirely. From that one line, he realized she wanted to turn a moment of desire into a slow courtship.

Under other circumstances, Ra-khir might have wished for the same. Now he could not allow it. Despite his promise to Kevral, he would not let himself become trapped the same way she had. His honor drove him to settle one affair before opening another. He loved Kevral. He could come to love Mariell, if he allowed it; but he did not have the freedom to do so now. "Mariell, you're wonderful. But if there is a time for us, it isn't now."

Mariell headed away, her reply floating to Ra-khir at a low volume he scarcely heard. "I understand." He had expected any other answer.

Ra-khir replaced his hat and returned to his position against the fence, watching the horizon where the sunset had once flaunted its magnificent palate. West and north, he looked, toward Pudar, his thoughts and heart on Kevral alone. More tears escaped his eyes. *Kevral, I hope I've seen enough, because I can't do this anymore.* His vows to the knighthood, once the essence of his universe, now bound him like a trap. His duties prevented him from joining her in Pudar. *I have to know where you are. I have to know if you're all right.* Ra-khir listened to the wind, hoping for some consolation he did not receive. Somehow, some way, they would come together again.

Kevral would never let King Cymion know how much she despised the life her defiance had bought her. Pudar's children knew nothing of swords or dedication; and their mothers hovered, encouraging tears and tantrums with their suffocating overprotectiveness. Her days among the guards, once a chore, now seemed a distant reprieve. But pride kept her from admitting Minister Daizar to her chambers for discussion and from answering any summons to his court. If she had to suffer another fifteen months in Pudar, she would see to it the king received no benefit, except the confidence of his youngest subjects.

Clouds shot in suddenly, graying an otherwise bright, cold day. The wind picked up, flinging road dust across the practice field hard enough to sting exposed flesh. A recalcitrant three-year-old threw down her practice sword, screaming for her mother.

Kevral rushed in for swift intervention, but the girl preferred kicking and shrieking to gripping the hilt of a sword. Gentle discussion changed nothing, and Kevral turned to harsher tactics. "You'll stay here until you get this, if it means you stay here through the night."

The admonishment did nothing to slacken the little girl's howls. "I don't WANT that!" she shouted. "No! Noo-ooo!"

Kevral reached for her arm, just as General Markanyin rode up on a wildly snorting bay. He pulled the horse to a sudden stop, and it skidded into a half turn, kicking up clods of grass. "Armsman, we need you!"

Kevral scowled, not wishing for word of her difficulties to reach the king yet glad for any interruption. With young children, time often made the difference between fits and reason. Unwilling to let the general know she appreciated his arrival, Kevral whirled on him. "You'd better have a very good reason for interrupting a Renshai's teaching!"

"Armsman, we're under attack."

Alarm rang through Kevral. Only dire necessity would drive the king to send his general to her rather than leading his troops into battle. Exhilaration exploded through her, scattering the warm ecstasy of coming battle. She stifled the urge to charge with reckless abandon. Doing so would lose any advantage she had gained against the king and his minister. "Why is this my concern?" she managed calmly, hoping Markanyin could not read the desperate war she fought inside herself in her flushed cheeks and quivering hands. More than anything, she wanted to fight. "My contract spells out my responsibilities clearly, and defending Pudar is not among them."

Markanyin drew a deep breath, as if to bellow a command.

Clearly, he struggled against long-ingrained habit as well, accustomed to soldiers' unconditional obedience. "We need you, Kevral. It's not an army. It's a thing—indescribable. It mangled a patrol, and it's headed toward the walls."

The sky darkened even in the moments Kevral listened to the description, and a familiar sulfurous odor carried on the wind. *Demon!*

"The king shredded your contract when he sent me. He's been trying to apologize. He's even authorized me to offer his son's hand in marriage."

The words swirled by Kevral, mostly unheard. Her heart hammered in her chest, battle rage a sheer ecstasy she could no longer control. She would have fought the demon without a single concession. "Get these young warriors to safety!" she shouted to their desperately hovering parents. "General!"

Guessing her need, Markanyin lowered a hand. Catching it, Kevral scrambled up behind him, even as the horse broke into a run toward the castle.

"Darkness, claws and teeth," Markanyin explained over the thump of the horse's hooves and the diminishing shouts of parents and children. "And it's enormous. Headed toward the west gate."

Kevral could scarcely hear the general over the roar of blood in her ears. As they plunged through the city streets, ordered shouts and commands from ahead replaced the chaos into which her young students had degenerated. As they rounded the castle, amassed soldiers hove into view, and the ramparts teemed with bowmen. Clouds swallowed the sun, casting Pudar's warriors dull silver against the massive black shapelessness that flashed toward them.

"Fire!" the bowmen's captain screamed.

Kevral leaped from the slowing horse as shafts arched and sped toward the demon. Rolling, she did not see them strike, noted only that the creature still blustered toward them, unslowed. Blood lust burned like acid through her veins, and she could do nothing else but run for the barred gates.

"Armsman!" General Markanyin shouted, the sound swallowed in the din of cocking crossbows and the windlike howl of the demon.

Deafened except to her own need, Kevral skittered up the gate. Fists the size of her torso hammered the wall suddenly. Stone rumbled, shifting; and men plummeted, screaming, from the ramparts. Others loosed shafts in ragged disarray. Kevral reached the top just as the giant hands slammed the wall again. Sound thundered against her ears, deafening. Mortar shattered, and rock flew in all directions, soldiers tumbling and scattering beneath it. The gate trembled and leaned, only partially affixed. Drawing her swords, Kevral dove for the demon.

Memory struck Kevral as she flew toward it. *My weapons can't hurt it. I'll glide right through it.* In midair, she changed her expectations, planning a wild roll that might save her from breaking limbs. Plunging both swords into the bulk of the beast met no resistance. She tucked, preparing for the transition from nothingness to solid ground. Too soon, she struck something fleshy, the demon, with bruising force. Momentum broken, she slid to the ground, unhurt. Instinct and training kept both weapons in her hands.

Kevral sprang to her feet. The demon braced itself on four legs, and two clawed hands tore down hunks of Pudar's wall. It seemed to take no notice of her. Her attack had inflicted nothing more than the myriad arrows and bolts scattered on the muddy ground. She swung at it anyway, swords cutting repeatedly through a darkness that now seemed no more substantial than air. Clearly, this demon had a solidity the other lacked, yet it still did not admit her weapons. She could affect nothing.

The screams of the dying mangled the commanders' cries for order, and chaos ruled briefly among Pudar's soldiers as well as its enemy. Hopeless frustration washed over Kevral. Courage meant nothing in such a war. She did Pudar and herself little good jabbing useless weapons into a formless creature. Her mind raced, seeking a solution that, this time, did not exist. No magic here, nothing that could harm the demon. A spear flew gracefully through the creature, without pausing. Arrows and bolts toppled in an awkward rain, one tearing a furrow above Kevral's left ear. Pain shot through her head, and warm blood trickled down her cheek.

Kevral staggered, swearing. "Modi!" she gasped, the pain call instantly rousing her to a battle she had no hope of winning. Her swords could not cut; but, miraculously, something else did. As if from nowhere, a sword slashed the demon's side, spilling thick, tarry blood. Kevral's blurry gaze followed the hilt to a steady hand and a wiry blond warrior she guessed was Tyrion.

The demon roared, whirling toward the wound. Its shoulder struck the wall, sending more rubble pounding to the ground. Even as it turned, the warrior seemed to disappear. Kevral followed the blur that had once represented a man and now seemed merely a part of the demon itself. She back-stepped, blinking, trying to regain the senses the injury had stolen from her.

Abruptly, the man appeared at Kevral's side, not Tyrion, but Colbey. "Here," he said, tossing her the sword.

Kevral snatched the hilt from the air, more shocked by the gesture than by his sudden appearance. A Renshai never surrendered a sword, and the fact that two more graced his sword belt did nothing to lessen the honor. Kevral did not question, consumed with the realization that the massacre had now become a battle she could fight. Howling like a wolf, she dove for the sable bulk of the demon, new sword carving a line that leaked sticky blood. Even as the sword performed, it vaporized in her hand.

The demon lashed out, limbs sucking back into the soup and appearing in places nearer to Kevral. Red eyes glared from a narrow head on a stalklike neck, and it struck, snakelike. Kevral scrambled backward. Its teeth clicked closed, barely missing her face. A dribble of saliva burned her arm.

"Be still!" Colbey commanded. It, she hoped, not her.

The demon reared up, head towering over Pudar's wall. A voice rolled from its nostrils, accompanied by dense smoke. "I am bound by Odin's wretched law. Even you cannot unbind me! Prince of demons, your influence is nothing here."

Colbey spoke beneath the rumble of its words. "There is much chaos here, not all of it from the demon. Elfin crafting. The sword is composed of chaos. My belief and yours give it form." Raising a hand, he clutched it around nothing, and another sword took shape in his fist. He tossed it toward Kevral.

Again, Kevral snatched the hilt from the air. Finished talking, the demon slashed for Kevral even as she lunged in for a strike. The claws overreached her, but the demon's wrist slammed against her shoulder, driving her sideways and to one knee. Her sword opened a cut in its chest, and a stench more like feces than blood accompanied the gooey black liquid that seeped from the wound. The sword faded in Kevral's hand.

Kevral could no longer see Colbey, but his mind joined hers. *Concentrate! Use the mental training your torke taught you!* He steered her muddled thoughts toward the scraps of magic in her hand, reshaping them to sword form.

Kevral focused her mind, and the blade straightened in her fist.

Good! Colbey encouraged, then slipped away.

Regaining her balance, Kevral charged. The demon mutated again, this time growing half a dozen arms like branches. She dodged beneath all of them, suddenly barraged by an uncoordinated hail of arrows and bolts again. Pain scored her shoulder, unnoticed. She drew all attention to maintaining the sword in her fist and dodging the demon's deadly strikes. The power in one of those appendages could kill her instantly. And the claws . . . memory managed to seep past the intensity of her concentration, Captain hurling himself like a living shield to spare her the scratches of a demon. "Ten years each," he had gasped. "I can afford it. You can't." Kevral did not dare to wonder what would happen to her if the baby aged instantly inside her. The sword grew ephemeral, a ghostly impression of its former reality.

"Fools! No more shooting!" someone shouted.

Kevral never noticed whether anyone obeyed. *Sword!* She reassured herself of its presence, forcing certainty of its reality. She hammered doubt with the same wild strength as her enemy. The weapon wavered, then returned as steady as it had been in Colbey's hand. She hacked and sliced at the ever-changing creature, jabbing for the center of its being and evading its ceaseless attacks. Skepticism died as need became a frantic boil of answered certainty. Doubt had no place in a mind fired with war lust. Soon, she no longer had to concentrate on the sword. It simply was.

The demon warped shape again, this time a horse's head on the body of an enormous cat, hawklike talons jutting from its chest. Kevral bore in, her thoughts scrambled by pain and excitement. Her sword lopped off a claw, showering her with foul-smelling tar. The demon screamed, snapping as much from pain as attack. The flat teeth crushed the hollow between Kevral's neck and left shoulder. Agony speared her arm, then it went limp. Raw, hot rage sputtered through her. "MODI!" she screamed again, and power seemed to accompany the call. She hurled herself at the demon, her sword as evanescent as the creature she challenged. The realization scarcely penetrated her consciousness that Pudarian soldiers now battled beside her, their weapons useless but their courage spurred by her own.

Now no worry for aging or death could stop Kevral. She had written off her own life, and nothing mattered but taking the enemy with her. The endless glory of Valhalla awaited if she died audaciously enough, and the world itself might depend upon her success. If the demon survived, no one on man's world, except Rantire, might have the weapons necessary to halt its spree of destruction.

The demon scrambled backward, needing distance for its massive limbs to gain momentum. Kevral moved with it, driving ever toward the center. She cut under a graceful tentacle, corkscrewed through two others, and jabbed the blade deeply home.

A scream echoed across the Westlands, discordant to the level of pain. Kevral felt as if her eardrums had shattered, and the wail set every bone to aching. The demon thrashed, curling over onto itself like a dying snake. A frenzied tentacle slammed Kevral, bowling her backward. The demon's savage death throes stamped bruises across her flesh. She rolled, scrambling as best as her weakened arm allowed. Then, something heavy thumped against her brow, and she knew nothing more.

CHAPTER 29

Chaos-Threatened

I've yet to meet a creature nastier than me.
                                   —Colbey Calistinsson

A flat plain of blackness stretched in front of Kevral, and she stood in a world empty of sight or sound, other than her own breathing. Devoid of thought or memory, she stood in silent anticipation of an event she did not bother to characterize. When it happened, she would know.

A voice wafted to her then, quiet yet filled with godlike authority. "Mankind shall never again suffer the minions of chaos charged into the control of law." The promise seemed to echo through Kevral's thoughts, and relief flooded her. Pain trickled into her senses, though she did not bother to contemplate its source. The wounds were old.

Colbey appeared in front of her, his sinewy form defining competence. Though scarred, his face would always remain the criteria for male perfection in Kevral's mind. The short golden locks lay in peaceful feathers above blue-gray eyes radiating less warmth than sapphire chips. Two long swords lay thrust through his sword belt. "A second *Ragnarok* is coming, Kevral. One with far fewer players yet so much more at stake. I will strive to keep the devastation from enveloping man's world, as before; yet I do not know if I have that ability anymore. The more power I accept, the more certain the destruction."

Kevral did not understand the words, but concept came more easily. She sensed a great war: Law versus Chaos. These would clash and, hopefully, obliterate one another, leaving the world fragile. Colbey hoped the human race, anchored by King Griff, could rebuild the proper balance. He fretted for his own role, whether the forces would match closely enough to assure mutual destruction, whether balance required small amounts of both, whether his assistance would truly help or hinder. So much lay at stake, more than her mortal mind could comprehend. So she tried to understand and discarded that which went beyond her ken.

Kevral listened in silence as Colbey continued. "If law overpowers me, if demons stalk mankind again, I will not leave you weaponless." He unclipped one of his swords, still sheathed, from his belt, and it hovered in the air beside him. "In four hundred years, I never gave away a single weapon. And now two in the space of months." A grim, sobering smile touched his lips. Satisfaction seemed to leach from him, too, yet it had an alien quality. It felt to Kevral as if Colbey's remaining sword took satisfaction in becoming his only weapon. Normally, she would have passed the sensation off as ridiculous. Now, ensconced in a dream world somewhere between life and death, it seemed perfectly natural for a sword to radiate envy.

Kevral opened her eyes, and the world popped into strange focus. Human forms moved around her, their conversations rumbling indecipherably. Pain seized her suddenly, starting low and general, shifting to the side of her head and both shoulders, and crescendoing into a sharp agony. She stiffened, inciting several more, though lesser, aches. Her mind waded through a thick soup that made thought and action difficult. "What's going on?" she asked, her tongue feeling enormous and her words sounding dampened.

"She's awake," someone said in a hollow voice.

A face appeared directly over Kevral's, and she recognized Charra's gentle features and soft, dark eyes. "Lady Kevral?"

An answer seemed unnecessary, but Kevral nodded. "Where am I?"

A middle-aged man replied before Charra could. Kevral caught a sideways glimpse of bearded features and a face with wide pores. "You're in your bed. You'll be fine. We're healers."

Kevral attempted to sit, but dizziness drove her back to the bed. Her hands slid naturally to her hips. The left did not obey. The right found no sword belt or hilt. The shock of rage and worry was too diluted to drive her. "My arm."

Charra patted Kevral's hand comfortingly as the man spoke. The conversations disappeared around them. "Can you move it?"

"No." Watered down panic touched Kevral, barely.

"Shoulder's badly swollen," he explained. "Nothing seems broken. Likely, the use will return as the swelling subsides."

Kevral latched onto the uncertainty, wishing her mind and emotions would function fully. "Likely?"

"Likely," the healer repeated. "Time will tell."

The terror remained, too weak to drive Kevral, yet punishing with its constancy. "I have to know now."

The healer rolled his eyes. "Then pray. Only the gods know the future."

A stifled twitter followed from the other side of the room. Kevral did not bother to see who voiced it. Better she never knew. "My head's not working right either."

"That's the pain medication," Charra said before the man could say anything sarcastic about the previous sanity of one who would leap into battle with a demon.

Kevral licked parched lips, despising the inability to concentrate. "No more. Please."

The male healer snorted. "You'll change your words when this wears off."

"I doubt it." Kevral attempted to emulate Colbey's icy stare. She did not think the pain could worsen much, and she wanted her thoughts clear. "Where are my swords? Is the demon dead?"

"The creature is gone." The male healer gestured to others Kevral could not see. The door opened, and she heard their footsteps filing into the hallway. "Your weapons." He pointed to a heap on the chair that represented her sword belt and weapons, then to the desk where a lone sword lay in a battered but well-oiled sheath. Kevral studied it in the glaze of twilight that her partially open curtains admitted. Though nothing about it appeared special, its foreignness alone explained its origin. *Colbey's sword.* The urge to leap out of bed and test the weapon became an obsession she could not currently satisfy. Tripling her current level of pain seemed well worth the opportunity to savor her gift from the greatest of all Renshai, the one after whom she had built her entire life.

"I'd like to be alone," Kevral said.

The healer nodded, heading after his entourage. Charra hesitantly shuffled after him, then stopped, turning Kevral an imploring look.

Even through the fog, Kevral could tell the pregnant healer needed to talk. Doing so might pass some time until the painkiller wore off enough to allow her to fully appreciate Colbey's sword. "Stay behind, Charra, if you would, please."

A lopsided grin split the woman's face, and she hurried back to Kevral's bedside. The door clicked closed behind the healers.

Kevral shifted into a sitting position again, back braced against the headboard. Vertigo struck like a hammer blow, and she fought through it without following her own movements. Gradually, the whirling spots receded, and she met Charra's glance.

Tears dripped from the doelike eyes, and Charra clutched her bulging abdomen. "They found out about the baby."

For a moment, Kevral worried over her secret. Then logic intervened. Charra referred to her own. "What happened?"

"Ridicule." The tears quickened. "They made me feel worthless. Stupid. Maybe I am."

"You're neither," Kevral assured.

Charra would not accept the support. She heaved a deep sigh, the tears slackening slightly. "I shouldn't have done what I did, my lady."

"You did it for love."

"Can't you see, Lady Kevral, it doesn't matter?" Charra sat on the edge of Kevral's bed. "If I was a moral person, I wouldn't have done it anyway. And if he really loved me, he would have married me first. I shouldn't have let this happen." She rubbed her abdomen. "I *am* wanton and sinful."

"Stop saying that," Kevral insisted, fighting the fog that made finding the right words an impossible chore. The differences from her own situation seemed obvious: Ra-khir had requested her hand, and she believed Tae would also if he thought she would accept. Yet shame still welled within her. The fact remained that she had slept with a man before marriage. She had slept with two different men, and she had done so four times. She could justify the first as desperation in the face of death, but the others could not be rationalized so innocently. A new thought struck her, raising an icy wave of guilt. *I talked Ra-khir into abandoning his honor. If I come home with his baby, will he lose his knighthood?* The idea struck as hard as any blow of the demon. Becoming a Knight of Erythane had meant as much to him as her Renshai coming of age did to her.

"I lost my position as healer, my lady." Charra spoke so softly, Kevral had to strain to hear. "And my welcome in Pudar's castle."

"What?" Kevral tried not to move too swiftly, wishing Charra had sat nearer her right hand. The need to comfort made her all too aware of the arm that did not function and might never again. "They can't do that."

Kevral's obviously false statement did not elicit a response.

"Let me talk to them. The king owes me a meeting at least. I believe he'll let you stay on if I intervene."

"No." Charra lowered her head almost to her lap. "Please don't do that, Lady Kevral. Please. I want to go."

"You do?"

"I can't stand the accusations of those I once trusted. I don't know them anymore, and it hurts too much to remember how they once were. How I once was." Charra covered her face. "I don't know how to explain it, my lady. I can bear, even dismiss, the taunts of strangers. But that look in Tanna's eyes—I've lost his respect, and I'll never truly have it again. It just hurts too much." She shook her head. "Lady, when your condition becomes apparent, they'll know why you helped me. And you'll pay for the kindness."

Kevral smiled. "I can handle them. No one will say anything disparaging to me. Not if he expects to ever speak again."

Charra sighed again, raising her face to reveal smeared tears. "Lady Kevral, I don't know how to make you understand. I know you believe violence can handle anything, but killing the speaker isn't going to make the truth hurt less."

How do you know? Kevral kept the thought to herself. She would not add to Charra's burden. "Where will you go?"

Charra shook her head wordlessly.

Taking that response as hopeless uncertainty, Kevral volunteered, "Family?"

"Like this, my lady?" Charra winced. "No. No family."

Kevral did not request elaboration. Whether Charra had no one at all or simply no one who would take her in under the circumstances did not matter. "I can give you *some* money. Not a lot, but enough to rent a room in the visitors' quarter."

Charra peeked at Kevral through the fingers in front of her face. "Lady Kevral, your kindness is appreciated, though I can't accept it. I would feel better . . . well . . . finding my own way."

Kevral tried to interpret the words as the veil gradually lifted from her thoughts. It seemed as if Charra wished to undergo the hardships thrust upon her, and Kevral guessed it had to do with shame. Either Charra believed she deserved the punishments heaped upon her, or pride would not allow her to accept Kevral's charity.

Charra explained. "Lady, I made a mistake. If I don't suffer for it, I might repeat it. Or worse ones."

Kevral did not believe that to be the case, but she did not have the strength, or the words, to argue. "So you'll live on the streets?"

"Until I find a job."

Tae had detailed some of the trials of street orphans, and Kevral doubted Charra truly realized to what she had committed herself and, eventually, her child. She sought a compromise. "How about if I treat you to dinners? That way, I still get to see you, and I know you and the baby are getting one good meal a day." *And I'll know if anyone bothered you so I can keep it from happening again.* Kevral kept the thought to herself, certain Charra would not appreciate it. "You'll have news of the castle and also know how to contact me if you change your mind."

Charra hesitated.

"It's not just you I'm worried about. The baby is innocent."

"I'd like that, Lady Kevral." Charra managed a smile. "The dinners, I mean."

"Meet me after practices."

Charra nodded. She wiped away the tears and turned, one leg tucked under her, to face Kevral directly. "My lady, there's an innocent inside you, too. You should be more careful."

Kevral did not see the pregnancy as an issue here. "Had I not fought that demon, many innocents would have died." She pointed at her belly. "Including this one."

"I just think you should slow down a bit."

Kevral dismissed the possibility. "Renshai women have been fighting wars *and* having babies for centuries."

Charra made a throwaway gesture. She might disagree, but she would not argue the point. "My lady, if you had not called out for me where you lay in the dirt, I would already have been driven from the castle. They tolerated me helping you because you asked for me. And, Lady Kevral, because I was there, I could direct which herbs they used. If you're injured again, who will choose the ones that won't harm your baby?" Suddenly, she laughed, the sound strained and unnatural after so many tears. "Not that that will be a problem much longer. Soon, my lady, everyone will know." She clasped her arms in front of her to indicate a grossly swollen womb.

Kevral gave no reply. She had much thinking to do once the effects of the drug dissipated.

"Please, Lady Kevral. If not for yourself, think of your baby. Find a man, any man, and marry him before that child's birth. If you don't, it won't matter how wise or powerful he or she becomes, people will see him always as 'that bastard child.' Even among royalty, this is so. In Béarn, illegitimate children of the king do not exist for ascension purposes. In Pudar, they do, but the result has always been disastrous. The kindest king cannot get past the circumstances of his birth."

Too tired to argue, Kevral only listened. She could feel doubts hovering, clamoring for an attention she could not afford them now. Regaining the use of the arm, Colbey's sword, and her job took precedence. Worries about the baby and its future would have to wait a few days longer.

Colbey wandered the worlds of chaos freely, creating scenery with deft flickers of thought that now required only the barest concentration. The random swirls of light and color had always seemed boundless, yet Colbey knew otherwise. If other worlds existed, this one had to end. Choosing a level at random, he walked onward, seeking edges he could not find. For hours that passed like days, he sought walls that seemed not to exist in scenery that changed as swiftly as he focused on it. Sanity no longer required order, and the ceaseless tide of chaos soup did not hinder his search. But the lack of finality did.

Colbey stopped, needing a practice. More from habit than need, he dedicated his sword work to his goddess, Sif, strengthening mind as well as body. The Staff of Chaos sang around him, slicing curled chips from the jumbled nothingness that replaced substance on chaos' world. He remained whole because he pictured himself that way. The staff held sword shape because his thoughts maintained it. Demons could not exist without a seed of law to hold them into a form, no matter how malleable. The answer came a moment later. The framework of the world existed wherever he placed it. Without the assistance of law, it held no solidarity.

Colbey threw himself into a frenzied session of slash, parry, and cut, wholly devoid of pattern. Law had selected a magical champion and so much of its power came of constraining chaos. Now, Colbey realized, he needed to become the opposite. He had to learn to use his physical presence as a weapon for chaos. *A touch of law inflicted on chaos.* The idea pleased and worried him at once. If law could use chaos for its magic, the reverse should also prove true.

Colbey ended his practice, scarcely winded, the air ceaselessly changing density and temperature. Once, that strangeness had made his lungs ache. Now it seemed natural and normal. He lowered his head, squaring off lines in his mind's eye. For a moment, nothing happened. Then, gradually, chaos conformed, like water, to the shape of his container.

At first, Colbey noticed only that he had finally discovered/crafted the periphery. He studied the new walls, finding the gaps that allowed chaos to leak inexorably onto man's world, the same through which those of law could summon demons. Colbey set his sights on these, weaving tight patches over the openings with a focus he had never dedicated to anything but his swords. Honed as a needle, his thoughts punched through the dense fabric he had created to repair holes not of his making.

The Staff of Chaos tapped at Colbey's barriers. The intensity of his concentration did not allow him to notice until he mended forty of the sixty-three flaws. By then, the staff was flinging itself against his mind with a force that made his shields quiver and threaten to shatter. Pain hammered and howled through his skull, but he showed no physical sign of the torment. He would not give the staff the satisfaction, nor reason to attempt something more violent. Reluctantly, he shoved aside his project and opened a pinhole into his psyche.

The Staff of Chaos arrowed through the hole, its sudden presence filling Colbey's head like a shout: *WHAT IN COLDEST HEL ARE YOU DOING?*

Isn't it obvious? Colbey returned with a calmness that made the Staff of Chaos seem like a frantic civilian caught in war.

You're sealing in chaos. Its manner changed from accusatory to nasty. *Trying to. It won't work. Even Odin couldn't wholly contain chaos.*

Colbey tossed the mental equivalent of a shrug. *I'm not trying to contain chaos. I'm protecting demons from summoning.*

Fool! The staff granted no quarter. *The result will be the same. The holes that grant magical creatures access to chaos also provide a means for chaos to leak out.*

Yes. Colbey saw no reason to argue. He had once watched a healer blend the ground, acid seed of *wertel* with vinegar in a corked phial. Showered with glass shards and liquid, Colbey had politely told the healer he would rather let his wounds fester. Yet that same mixture in an open bowl had resulted in a quiet poultice that burned fiercely yet cured infection.

Is it your design to utterly destroy chaos? The Staff of Chaos did not await an answer. *Because that won't work. What you propose will ruin all the worlds—and law as well as chaos.*

Colbey waited for his companion to relax enough to listen.

He had enough information to argue the point. Until Colbey, no being of law had survived on the plains of chaos. Even Odin, who had crafted the world to which he had banished the primordial chaos, had deliberately left the openings Colbey now worked to plug, leaving a means for tiny amounts of chaos to affect man's world. To do otherwise would have resulted in total stagnation, law wholly unopposed.

Desist at once!

The command irritated Colbey. *Are you finished attempting to order me?*

If you do not cease, you leave chaos no choice but to destroy you.

I'll take that as a 'no.' It seemed Colbey's true intention, to leave a single opening that he could monitor, would never get explained. *When you're ready to stop assuming my motives and hear my reasons, let me know.* With that, he slammed shut the barriers to his head, ignoring the wild tapping from the staff that followed.

Colbey returned his attention to the task at hand, plugging more of the gaps that connected the plains of chaos to Midgard. The staff's entreaties became faint, drumming background. Finally, it disappeared completely, leaving Colbey wholly at peace.

Colbey worked long past exhaustion, through the night and into another day of patternless mutation. As he worked on the fifty-ninth hole, warning prickled through him. His senses screamed of a danger so absolute it radiated no color at all. It hovered, its malevolence tangible, yet without substance. Colbey's hand slid naturally to the hilt of the sword embodied by the Staff of Chaos.

The thing spoke to Colbey in ten thousand voices, all conveying the same message with different words or concepts. It led him to understand that he faced chaos in total, a personification of the primordial soup. Where the demons could not organize against him, they had found a way to face him in unison. By becoming a joined entity, contained by his boundaries, it could enforce the combined will of all. *Join us,* it/they directed him. The patience of chaos had run its course. *You are chaos. Bind and become a part of the whole.* It glided toward him, a maw emerging from the shadow to swallow him.

No, Colbey did not retreat. The sword rasped from his sheath . . .

. . . and melted in his hands. A second creature appeared beside the first. It took the form of a man, pose displaying admirable grace and features handsome even beyond youth. Blond hair framed chiseled features, and blue eyes filled with mischief studied him triumphantly. *There is no need to fight, Colbey. You and I are one.*

Colbey watched the figure in front of him, feeling naked without a weapon. The being did bear a striking resemblance, not only to himself but to the dead god, Loki. Once, Colbey could not have seen the similarities. Now, they held him spellbound. The creature that came from the Staff of Chaos could as easily pass for either. He reached out a gentle hand. *It's your destiny, Colbey.*

The words broke the spell. Colbey had heard the same from Odin when the gray leader of the pantheon had insisted Colbey's birth, life, and ascension existed only for the moment of rescuing Odin from his fate at the *Ragnarok*. Colbey gave the same answer as he had then. *I don't believe in destiny.*

Loki/Colbey smiled. *Semantics, only. You chose this course. You knew this moment would come, and it has. You cannot win against Dh'arlo'mé unless you become one with me.*

Colbey crouched. The primordial chaos continued to drift closer. He could see that its many appendages enwrapped something which was struggling. *I don't believe that to be the case.* He sent the truth, yet it lacked the backing of certainty. When he had championed balance, he had never doubted his motives or his many courses of action. Now he felt as if he had lived his whole life safely strapped into a cart that naturally made the right turns. He felt vulnerable, devoid of the sureness necessary to act in the best interests of gods and mankind.

Colbey battled self-doubt, delaying. *What happens to me if I bind?*

When you bind, the creature returned, emphasizing the first word, *you cease to be the Prince of Demons. You instead become chaos' extension into the other worlds. You'll have all the power of chaos behind you, to tap at your will.*

Still Colbey hesitated, as he never had in war. Renshai through the ages had quoted him: "Warriors make their decisions on the battlefield, faster than an eye blink. They cannot afford to be wrong." He had known this moment would come, had known resistance might prove even beyond his skill, had even known that resistance might not prove the best course. Yet even after chaos had become so much a part of him, he still clung to self and balance. *I'd become Loki,* he realized aloud.

The human representation of the Staff of Chaos laughed. *If you wish. Is that such a bad fate?*

Colbey recalled his first conversation with the shape-changing mischief-maker of the gods, the first father of lies. Loki's explanation came to him, verbatim, assisted by the staff: "Chaos is necessary. Even some of the men and gods who realize it refuse to be the ones who champion it. What we truly need is balance. But I'm one god working alone against many. If I just stood behind symmetry, I would accomplish nothing. When so many back law, the only chance for balance is to embrace chaos." With Colbey's help, the gods had come to recognize the need for balance. Yet, now, a massive force of law threatened the world as surely as if every god still stood against it. Someone had to champion chaos, and that someone was Colbey Calistinsson. He recalled all the sessions in the temple, his mother's horrible stories about the gods' champion of chaos. *Loki, I take back all the hatred I harbored against you as a child. I understand everything you did.*

You are forgiven, the staff returned.

Colbey stiffened. He had not sent the thought from his mind, and the Staff of Chaos should not have been able to read it. Clearly, he had left a gap in his defenses. He banished reservation, strengthening his barriers. *I understand what you did,* Colbey repeated. *But I will not duplicate your mistakes.*

The demon began its forward progress again. This time, Colbey retreated a step. With a sword, he could at least battle to his death. Without one, he had no chance at all to find *Valhalla*, only a hideous and dishonorable death.

Mistakes? the creature said.

I will work with chaos, but I will not bind with it.

Resentment covered Colbey like a blanket. *That, my partner, is a mistake beyond any Loki ever made.*

Loki had known, as Colbey did now, that the clash between law and chaos would destroy those bonded to it. He had clung to the understanding that he would personify the fires that razed and cleansed the worlds, that a new order would spring entirely from his destruction. The personification of death did not draw Colbey as it had his predecessor. He still clung to the hope that the extremes of law and chaos could demolish one another without affecting humans, elves, and gods. *Be that as it may, I will not bind.*

The staff-creature's face twisted, though it could not shake the beauty Loki's features granted. *I thought you might prove reticent. That's why I brought some reassurance.*

Several of the demon's arms opened to reveal the struggling figure it still gripped by the shoulders, thighs, and mouth. Ravn heaved against the black tentacles, tattered tunic revealing slashes and bruises the length of his body. He had not proved an easy hostage.

Colbey froze. Even his heart seemed to stop beating in his chest.

Bind now?

Colbey latched his gaze on his son. Ravn's blue eyes held pain and rage, but no fear. *Would you want me this way?*

I'll take you any way I can get you. Brutal honesty from a force that championed lies.

Colbey had already known the answer. He had asked more for procrastination. He licked his lips, faced with a true choice. Bowing to such a ghastly ploy bothered him; yet, if he did so, it would have no bearing on future dealings. From that moment forth, he would become merely an organ of chaos. He could buy his son's life with his own, a more than fair trade. Whether or not he completely bonded, he would still likely die in the end. If he phrased the exchange well enough, he might still rescue Ravn from the same fate.

Well? Chaos pressed. The subtext came through clearly. It would not allow inordinate delay.

Chaos believed it could not lose, Colbey realized suddenly. Whether he came to it willingly, or it invaded his mind during the weakness that would follow watching his son slaughtered, it would have him. A whisper of outrage joined the desperate concern. A sword in his hand would make all the difference. Suddenly, he understood why the Staff of Chaos had reveled in his decision to pass his other weapon to Kevral. It had feigned envy to hide long-planned deceit. "Let the boy speak for himself."

The Loki/Colbey being nodded. The demon's arm retreated from Ravn's face, leaving a purple bruise in its wake.

Ravn took a moment to compose himself before speaking, which Colbey appreciated. The responsibilities he had placed on the adolescent shoulders had aged his son. "Don't do it, Father. I'd rather die horribly."

And you will, the staff being hissed. The demon's grips on arms and legs tightened, and the flesh blanched, blood driven from it. Soon, the bands would constrict enough to damage the tissue beyond salvation. Ravn would lose his arms and legs.

The pain evident in Ravn's pale eyes struck through Colbey as well. The urge to promise anything welled up in his throat, but the words did not emerge. He wanted to hurl himself at the demon, to unleash his deadly skill against it. Helpless as a toddler, he stood before it. His bare flesh could not harm it. Without a weapon of law-confined chaos, he could only look the fool, a child swinging furiously in a hopeless tantrum. Colbey closed his eyes. The answer could only come from within. *STOP!* he shouted. The flat, black plain of his eye-closed world seemed a new blank slate for the story of the universe. For the moment, truth existed only as he saw it. He kept his mind barriers wholly in place. Even the drone of the Staff of Chaos could not penetrate it. There was only Nothingness.

Nothingness. Primordial chaos. The world before creation. In his own mind, Colbey finally felt godlike, the author of a world that existed only because he forced all else away. That it existed only because he had blocked out reality did not matter for the moment. Its existence was all there was.

Gradually, a thought sifted in, wrecking the virgin quiet of Colbey's world. *Running from truth is as much cowardice as fleeing battle.* The idea was his own, yet the cruelest of Renshai insults did not affect him. *Why not?* The answer shocked him, and Colbey felt a grin stretch his face. *Because chaos is my realm. The world I created is not an escape. It is reality!* A rumbling laugh escaped his throat, and his lids sprang open. All remained as he had left it. The Loki/Colbey figure glared at him. The demon clutched Ravn, while the young man gritted his teeth against agony.

"This isn't real," Colbey said.

Nonsense, Chaos shot back. No weakness there.

Colbey stared at the demon grasping his son, seeing instead a million weaker representations of chaos, a vast flat of ever-changing nothingness without substance or pattern. The struggling adolescent shimmered.

Bind, the staff creature said. *Bind, damn you. You're deluding only yourself. Your child will die for your foolish denial. You cannot dismantle reality with thought.*

Doubt battered at Colbey's intentions. He forced it away, clinging to the mind control that battling Wizards had gained him. *I am the Prince of Demons. Chaos is whatever I make it. If you resist, I will destroy you, too.*

Delusion! The staff fought with the weapons of skepticism

and self-doubt. It sent concepts instead of words, a bold certainty that dream and want could not affect actuality.

Colbey did not waver. *My dream is your reality. My want is your truth. My creation is your world.* Ravn dissolved to a dark mass of mutable chaos goo, a demon too meek to bother its prince. *And you are my weapon, never my master.* His mind nudged the creature that had once resembled self. Again, it took the form of a sword, honed edges readied for the battles of its wielder.

This war was over. And Colbey Calistinsson had won.

The Keeper of the Balance

No mortal war has given me what I've searched for all my life—death in glory.

—*Colbey Calistinsson*

Ravn kept his hands clasped in his lap to hide their telltale shaking. The same quaking apprehension that brought him first to Asgard's meeting hall also goaded him to flee before the others arrived. Perhaps he could pretend that he had not received the summons or that he remained coolly aloof from the proceedings. The latter would not surprise the other gods; they would attribute it to his father. And, at least for the moment, the comparison bothered him nearly as much as the anticipation.

Ravn looked around the room, but even this third inspection failed to reveal details. His eyes sent images his mind evaded, tortured by more significant matters than vision. He forced another, slower scrutiny, this time managing to register the domed ceiling, the plain gold walls that contrasted strangely with an exterior studded with jewels, and the table and chairs that constituted the room's only furniture. Far above his head, a massive chandelier with a dozen tiers held hundreds of candles. Magically lit, they never sputtered or burned out. Their myriad flames reflected yellow highlights from tabletop and floor.

The heavy teak door opened, revealing a delicate lace of diamonds embedded in the jamb. Light scattered, cut into colors by the facets. Ravn could not stop himself from cringing. The stares of Asgard's finest, so often blasted on his father, would now pin him. He had long dreaded this moment.

Freya entered the portal, closing the door quietly behind her. Hair cascaded past her shoulders, a golden waterfall outshining the diamonds. Her pale eyes steadied him with gentleness from features so perfect they defied his description. The simple tunic and sword belt could not hide her well-muscled curves.

Ravn loosed a pent-up breath, though he knew the reprieve short-lived.

"I thought I might find you here." Freya turned her son an encouraging smile that revealed symmetrical teeth in two straight rows. "Nervousness dissipates patience."

"I'm not nervous," Ravn said, in jest. He knew his mother would easily see through the lie.

The grin remained, though Freya did not laugh. "Sit here." She gestured to a seat on the left-hand side, with only one seat between it and the head position.

Ravn shook his head in short, sharp movements that revealed his trepidation.

The corners of Freya's lips slid downward, past neutrality to a slight frown. "Ravn, your father's life, the whole of mankind, and the gods' themselves may depend upon you convincing staid old goats who never believe themselves wrong. The more confident you appear, the better chance you have. Colbey always understood the significance of good positioning."

The words struck Ravn at many levels. First, he feared his suggestions the wrong ones. It seemed more as if he might lead the gods to their doom than rescue them from it. With restless guilt, he wondered whether Colbey's destruction might ultimately become the better course. His father dealt with every matter as if it were a battle, and his wars of words with the gods proved no exception. Ravn still recalled his very first meeting, when Colbey had sat in the sacred seat, once Odin's. That maneuver had won him as much rancor as respect, yet it had paved the way for Vidar to later claim that chair as his own. Without a word Ravn rose from his seat near the door and moved to the indicated spot. His anxiety level rose near to panic the farther he moved from the exit, and he desperately wondered whether his mother had made the right decision. She claimed the chair to his right, even as the door opened again.

In singles and pairs and sixes, the deities selected places around the huge, rectangular table. Thor's sons, Modi and Magni, took the seats directly across from Freya and Ravn, their father's hammer wedged between their chairs. Vidar claimed the head seat, his half brother Vali the one at his right hand. The goddesses Sif, Nanna, Idunn, and Sigyn clustered beyond Freya and Magni. The once-dead Balder and his blind brother, Hod, sat on either side of the women, the nearest ones to the door. Ravn's uncle, Frey, arrived last. Left the choice of the empty chair between Ravn and Vidar or sitting beside either

Hod or Balder, he chose the latter. Quietly hooking the chair on Balder's end, he sat and studied his hands on the table. Ravn saw the decision as a positive one. For most of Asgard's denizens, the farther they chose from the head of the table, the less confrontational they felt. Ravn did not want any trouble, least of all from the elves' creator.

The instant Frey chose his spot, Vidar opened the meeting. "As those of you who do not know have already guessed, I gathered you here to discuss the current state of the balance."

Ravn stiffened, gasping in a bit of floating debris. He held his breath, fighting the natural urge to cough and choke. Nothing short of bolting in terror could make him look less in control now. He had anticipated more discussion of other matters, perhaps some dull routine business, before Vidar cut directly to him.

Every head shifted to allow every eye to fall directly on Ravn. He won the battle against hacking, loosing only a composed cough. He hoped his cheeks had not become too flushed or his eyes too teary.

Vidar continued, though it seemed unnecessary. "Keeper of the Balance, Ravn, please enlighten us."

Ravn cleared his throat, and it sounded funny. His voice would surely rasp. He did not glance toward his mother or his uncle for assistance, verbal or supportive. It would make him look childish and weak. For the moment, he felt both. "It's . . . well . . . it's balanced."

A startled murmur swept the room. Vali fairly beamed, a state that seemed wholly uncharacteristic after the snapping rages he had displayed against Colbey and his every idea. "I knew the balance would thrive once it sat in divine hands. We should have wrestled its control from that galling human long ago."

Vidar frowned to indicate his displeasure, but he made no verbal reminder that the god Vali praised was "that galling human's" very son. He gave the table a thoughtful tap and turned his attention as glaringly on Ravn as the others. "Is it not true, then, that humans slaughter one another in furious wars and jealous executions? That greed and selfish power have become the driving force of most of the civilizations of mankind?"

Ravn forced himself still, wooden, gaze on Vidar's eyes to avoid the others' withering stares. He wished himself anywhere else. "That appears to be true."

Vidar's eyes widened in question, but he did not give Ravn the chance to elaborate before asking another. "Is it also true that a power-mad elf has uprooted the fabric of elfin society and works toward destroying humankind?"

"That is untrue," Frey returned, his voice nearly a growl.

The words startled Ravn as much as anyone, especially since he had planned to answer in the affirmative. His gaze, along with every other, jerked to the god of weather, fortune, and elves.

Frey did not languish under the scrutiny, as Ravn believed he personally had. "Dh'arlo'mé is no longer an elf. He is *svartalf*, and I disown him."

Nods swept the table. No one bothered to point out that *svartalf* literally meant "dark elf." The compound word seemed to take on a meaning wholly its own.

Vidar refused to allow semantics to ruin his point. "Fine, then. A power-mad *svartalf*."

Ravn hesitated before taking his eyes from Frey, giving his uncle another chance to interrupt if he felt it necessary. Ravn appreciated anything that took the gods' attention from him. "True also."

Vidar's brows joined his upper eyelids, arching into definitive challenge. "The Sword of Balance should be bucking in your hands like an unbroken stallion."

Freya placed an unobtrusive, comforting hand on Ravn's leg. If she could, she would have shared her strength.

"It should be," Ravn agreed, "but it isn't. Harval is rock stable. The worlds sit in perfect balance."

Murmurs arose from the gods and goddesses then, whispered speculation that seemed unlikely to graze the truth Ravn believed he knew. Impulsive Modi phrased the query on every tongue. "How can that be?"

Ravn swallowed hard. The moment had come. "Colbey." His father's name sounded strange on his tongue, but "Father" or "Papa" seemed embarrassing.

Silence beckoned Ravn's explanation.

Ravn deliberately avoided indefinite word choices, such as "I believe" or "I think." "Human chaos is partially balancing Dh'arlo'mé's binding to the Staff of Law."

Vidar made a bold dismissive gesture. "If that were the answer, the Sword of Balance would feel unstable, teetering with each large sway toward law or chaos."

Ravn nodded. Colbey's descriptions of Harval suggested that Vidar had assessed it accurately. Ravn could see how his untrained hands might miss minor fluctuations in the balance, but the massive shifts that seemed to be occurring should yield clearly to his touch. "I believe . . ." Catching himself about to equivocate, Ravn smiled and changed his tack. ". . . you're correct." He continued, "Colbey is assuredly the answer. Dh'arlo'mé seems to be gaining power far more swiftly than the human devastation could possibly manage to match. Colbey's taking up chaos as needed to keep pace and maintain equilibrium."

A deeper hush lingered after Ravn's suggestion than before it. Every deity considered the possibility, and the implications, of such a revelation.

A fist crashed suddenly to the table, and every eye jerked to Modi. Usually, his temper resulted in such an action; this time, his slower intellect required more thought before the rage he was named for could arise. The noise had come from Vali, who used the sudden attention it gained him to speak his piece. "His method is understandable, taking as little chaos as the moment necessitates to rescue the balance."

Heads turned more slowly to Vali, including Ravn's. Though not particularly kind, those were the least negative words Vali had ever spoken about Colbey. Ravn waited for the other shoe to fall, his mother's hand tightening on his leg.

"He gained us a lull, but it's a false one. The more chaos he binds, the less of himself remains. Eventually, it will control him, resulting in the same desperate rush for total power that law has made."

No one denied the assertion. Vidar spoke gently, "Colbey understood that when he accepted the Staff of Chaos as his charge. He knew it would destroy him, and it surely will."

"The problem," Sigyn asserted, "is that he based everything on the assumption that the Staff of Law's champion and the Staff of Chaos' champion would destroy one another, paving the way for balance."

Vali continued, war braids flying as he punctuated verbal points with solid movements. "He based that on several assumptions: First, that he could steer chaos against law even after he became its automaton."

Ravn drew a hissing breath but did not contradict. He tried to focus on Vali's point rather than on his callous references to the certain death of the father Ravn loved.

"Second, that the aftermath of that battle would leave balance or only a minor, correctable shift. The shambles human civilization has become suggests otherwise."

Abruptly, the teak door slammed open, and a breeze stirred the war braids of the assembled. Colbey stood in the doorway. He looked none the worse for his time embroiled in chaos, his golden hair still clipped into short feathers, the same smattering of gray, and the familiar scars manifest. He stood in a battle stance, his usual grace clearly evident. The blue eyes had gained a glimmer of mischief, softened by the gray that now seemed to contain the ancient wisdom of the ages. He wore only one sword, currently at his left hip.

Freya's nails gouged Ravn's flesh. Someone gasped, though Ravn did not bother to identify the source.

"I would have been here sooner," Colbey said with mocking calm. "But once again my invitation to the meeting was never delivered."

Vali glanced sternly at Vidar. The new leader of the gods remained silent, contemplating every angle of the situation. As Colbey stepped across the entry, pulling the panel closed behind him, Vidar finally spoke. "Kyndig, you're not welcome here any longer."

The door clicked closed, the sound loud in the quiet room. Colbey waited until he secured it before addressing the speaker. "Ah, then. That would explain it." He glanced at Ravn and Freya, smiling.

Ravn froze in place, attempting to shield his thoughts, though he knew it a hopeless effort. If Colbey wished to violate him, Ravn could not stop the process, nor even know whether or not it occurred.

Vidar followed the direction of Colbey's gaze, a gesture that sent Ravn into uncontrollable fidgeting. "Are you going to invoke family privilege, as Loki once did? Or will you leave peacefully?"

Colbey placed his hands on the far end of the table, leaning over the last chair, though he did not sit. "Those two choices are not mutually exclusive. I intend the second. Whether or not I invoke privilege depends on you." He could not help adding, "*Uncle* Vidar." The relationship, though honest, had never before been mentioned. As Thor's half-brother, another son of Odin, Vidar did bear a blood relationship with Colbey.

"That answers that," Vali muttered, earning a glare from Vidar. Another son of Odin, he was just as much technically Colbey's uncle.

"What do you want?" Idunn asked with evident hostility. "Are you going to taunt us the way Loki did?"

Balder grew as restless as Colbey's son. Loki's session of directed malice had resulted in Balder's death and a tedious wait in Hel for the *Ragnarok* and his return.

Magni shifted the mighty hammer from floor to tabletop, flaunting his aversion.

"I'm not Loki," Colbey said.

Sif disagreed. "You might as well be."

"I am *not* Loki," Colbey repeated, his voice resonant but in no way defensive. "I have more important matters to attend than bandying insults with you."

Ravn studied his father curiously. Something about him had changed, definitely for the better. Weeks ago, when Colbey returned, he carried a definitive air of chaos. Now, that seemed to have disappeared or, perhaps, only become more internal.

"Then why did you come?" Modi asked, fiery beard bristling.

"Because I have as much need as you to know how my actions—"

"—antics," Vali substituted.

Colbey shrugged. "—how my *antics* have affected the balance and reality." He looked directly at Ravn now.

Caught staring at his father, Ravn flicked his eyes abruptly away, immediately wishing he had not. It made him appear culpable for a natural curiosity.

Ravn cleared his throat, delaying. Though he did not share Colbey's talent, he could feel the hostility radiating from the gods. It had to be burning Colbey, yet he showed no notice of it. Vidar's eyes jumped to Ravn, and his hands discreetly gestured caution. He would not tell Ravn what to report, only warn him to consider before doing so.

"Almost since you turned over the sword, the balance has remained intact." Ravn would not lie. Even if his father did not deserve his respect, Colbey could read his mind and had shown that he was at a time when chaos had a lesser hold over him.

"Thank you," Colbey said, with genuine appreciation. "And now I leave in peace."

A collective sigh ensued, broken by Colbey's next words. "Except for one thing."

Vali glared, his look conveying what his voice did not. He knew Colbey would not leave without causing some measure of trouble.

"After the meeting, Ravn. A spar?" Colbey's head tipped slightly, and his brows rose.

Only now, Ravn realized his mother's fingers no longer dug into his leg. She patted his breeks, the implication much like Vidar's a moment ago. She would not feed him an answer, only a plea for caution. Torn between appreciation for others acknowledging his burgeoning adulthood and wishing his mother would make a difficult decision for him, Ravn studied Colbey. He gained little from features or stance, but the eyes revealed much. He saw the love and respect that had disappeared from them on his previous visit. Yet Ravn could not lose the worry that what had changed in Colbey was the ability to lie better, not only with words but with his eyes. "What are the stakes?"

Colbey turned his head slightly, once in each direction. "No stakes, Ravn."

"To the death," Ravn guessed, still trying to elicit a motive. With the Keeper of the Balance dead, no one could warn the gods if chaos overtook law.

"No," Colbey said. "To whatever endpoint you choose."

The room seemed to hang on Ravn's answer. His hands itched, needing the chance to test his skill again against the greatest swordsman in existence. It seemed the mortal teachings of his father might betray him in the most ironic of situations. His thoughts kept shifting back to their final spar, the one before Colbey left to champion chaos. That moment seemed frozen in time, a symbol of the bond the Staff of Chaos had torn asunder. He remembered it as much as a time of love as of teaching, of understanding as of parting. *Will another spar now ruin or underscore that session.* The answer, Ravn realized, did not matter. By asking for a spar, Colbey tested his son's trust and loyalty. Once before, each had found the other wanting. This time, Ravn wanted to believe. Whether that came of truth, his own longing, or Colbey's new ability to influence, he did not know.

When Ravn did not answer, Vidar finally spoke. "This is between the two of you." He addressed the father first. "Colbey, I can't make you leave, but I can suggest it and warn you that we won't tolerate any trouble." He turned to the son. "Ravn, do what you feel best, but don't let anyone goad you into an action you regret." He gave his attention to the whole assemblage next. "This meeting is adjourned."

Colbey, Ravn, and Freya remained in place while the others filed out around them. Chaos' champion seemed to take no notice of the spiteful glances the others gave him, but his slight smile revealed otherwise. He knew they hated him, and it amused him.

Ravn's gaze followed the exiting gods, not from any specific interest in their movements, but to avoid the need to return his father's penetrating stare. As the door clicked closed behind the last, Ravn reluctantly faced his decision, only to find his mother already locked in a silent, studied war with Colbey.

Freya broke the silence first, though Colbey's mortal impatience made him the more likely candidate. "I told you I would not allow you to harm our son."

"I have no intention of harming Ravn." Colbey turned his attention directly on his son.

Unprepared for the sudden scrutiny, Ravn squirmed, hating himself for the lapse. He forced himself still, returning his father's stare.

"I only wish a spar," Colbey continued. "It may well be my last chance to do something special with my son."

Memories of their last spar together surfaced again, only shallowly buried. Ravn recalled the affection that had filled his father's eyes and every movement, even as he hammered and pounded at Ravn's defenses. They had discovered a closeness Ravn never knew could exist, the barriers that even sons and fathers place between themselves lifted for the realization that Colbey would likely die. The fondness remained, instantly sparked by consideration of what was supposed to have been his last remembrance of his father, a gift more valuable than any symbolic trinket. "Why did you have to come back?"

Colbey's head drew back, offense and surprise clear on his features. "Would you rather I died?"

Colbey's question startled Ravn nearly as much. He had not realized he had spoken aloud, and a trickle of irritation suffused him at the thought that his father had invaded his mind once again. But his mother's quiet nodding told him otherwise. She had heard him, too. "No," Ravn said swiftly. "I want you to live and return, but not until after the battle." He gathered words to justify his cruelty, but Colbey found them first.

"I'm sorry I ruined your memories." Colbey's hard blue-gray eyes found Ravn and Freya alternately. "When I came back before, I didn't have full control of my realm. Now I do, and I want to fix that mistake." He turned fully to Ravn again. "And, no, I'm not reading your mind. I'm reading your expression."

Ravn shook back blond locks, as always a bit longer than his father preferred. "Am I that obvious?"

Colbey did not bother to reply. Instead, he headed for the door. "As Vidar said, the decision to trust or not is yours. I'll be waiting."

"Don't wait," Ravn returned.

Colbey stopped with his hand on the knob, head low and feathered locks hanging.

"I'm coming with you."

"Ravn." Freya's tone held warning, but she said nothing more.

Colbey's head rose, but he did not turn to display features that, right now, might reveal much. Father and son exited the gods' hall together, into the glittering array of colors sparked from the gem-studded outer walls. Most of the gods had remained nearby, their conversational groups appearing not-quite casual. Freya slipped out after her family, joining Frey's group near a stately, bubble-fruited tree.

Ravn tried to commit himself to the trust he had placed in his father, but doubt remained unbanished. Colbey had seemed so changed at their last meeting, and so much the same now. Perhaps he had overcome the chaos that had seeped into his soul or, more likely, he had become a master of deception. Ravn knew agreeing to the spar was madness. He only hoped he had gained enough skill to counter his father's strokes should they become murderous.

Ignoring the divine audience, Colbey chose an area not far from the meeting hall. Ravn approved of the choice. Even before chaos had claimed Colbey, he occasionally reveled in irritating the denizens of Asgard. He could have led them for miles across the countryside, eventually even returning to where he started. The gods, they both knew, would nonchalantly follow them anywhere, privacy an airy hope. Colbey had chosen not to make an issue of the gods' mistrust. It amused rather than irritated him.

"Ready?" Colbey asked, drawing a sword that seemed to blur and buzz at the edges. It was not the one he had so long carried as Harval's partner.

Ravn's gaze fell to Colbey's sword belt, where no other weapon hung. His brow creased, even as his own fists wrapped around his hilts. "What sword is this?"

Colbey studied his own blade. "You don't recognize it?"

Ravn shook his head. "It's not the one you carried when you left."

"I gave that one to a mortal so that mankind was not helpless against the demons that law called against them."

Ravn considered those words. It seemed more likely for chaos to consort with demons, but he did not question. From Odin's high seat, he had watched Dh'arlo'mé conjure up the creatures of chaos.

"Have you ever battled a demon?" The question seemed casual, yet a catch in Colbey's voice suggested a significance his tone otherwise hid.

Ravn grew cautious. "That depends. Are you a demon?"

"No," Colbey said. "Definitely not."

"Then I've never battled one," Ravn admitted honestly.

"One has never dragged you down to the world of chaos? Or attempted to do so?"

Ravn shook his head. His skin felt as if bugs swarmed over it, but he resisted the need to fidget. "Why?"

"Good. Very good." Despite his words, and a slight smile, Colbey seemed concerned. "Ready?"

"No," Ravn returned. "I'm not ready. What's bothering you? Is a demon coming to get me?"

Colbey shook his head. "One had me believing it already had, but it *won't* bother you again." He said the words emphatically, as if instructing it not to happen as much as informing Ravn. He laughed then, the sudden change in demeanor strange. "Drop the 'again.' I suppose I should just say it won't bother you. My worry is for the extent of my own power, the influence I seem to have gained in more than one world. If I survive this ordeal, I won't miss the mastery chaos gives me. Ravn, savor those skills that come only of hard work and dedication. The ones handed to you, unearned, don't matter. A curse, not a blessing."

The words took Ravn back to the carefree days of his earliest lessons with his father. However else chaos had changed Colbey, he remained wholly Renshai. Ravn drew Harval. "I'm ready."

"You've left a weapon sheathed," Colbey reminded.

Ravn shrugged. "One apiece. A fair fight."

Colbey pointed to his own chest with his free hand. "More experience. An unfair fight." He winked. "You'll need the other."

Only a fool would argue, and Ravn did not believe himself one. Seizing the second hilt, he drew and charged at once. In his right hand, Harval danced toward Colbey's neck, while the extra jabbed toward his abdomen. Colbey's sword wove over Harval, then under the other, faster than Ravn's eyes could follow. Driven centrally, Ravn's blades clanged together as Colbey also managed a split second riposte.

Ravn jerked, slamming both of his blades against Colbey's, a clumsy but effective parry. Irritated and exhilarated at once, Ravn bore in again. War joy surged into his veins, the first since his father's leaving. His mother could still best him, but only Colbey could consistently spur him to knowledge born of desperation.

Colbey grinned at his son's boldness, meeting the double attack with a dodge that foiled both. His sword slashed for Ravn's head. Ravn ducked, sacrificing attack for defense. The blade whistled over his brow, the wind of its passage cold against his scalp. *Too close*. Terror joined the battle lust, and he worried that his trust had become a fatal mistake. He wove a wild web of attack, hoping the movement would foil Colbey's strikes, if not his shielding. Usually, the crazed randomness of the maneuver kept an opponent solely on his guard. But Colbey met each lightning slice with a block of his own. Steel chimed at a reckless pace, simulating song. Ravn's arms ached with the effort, and he knew he would have to change his strategy or tire beyond any hope of besting Colbey.

Ravn hesitated a moment so brief it scarcely existed, yet Colbey found the opening. Boring in, he cut Harval from Ravn's hand with the tip of his sword, without inflicting so much as a scratch. The Gray Blade flew in a patterned spiral, as if consciously rushing to Colbey's hand. The elder Renshai caught the hilt without any gesture of triumph. Sheathing his own sword, Colbey wrapped both hands around Harval and lowered his head, lids drooping closed as he concentrated on the sword once his.

Ravn froze, uncertain of the significance. As the Gray Blade remained in Colbey's hands several seconds, the sound of rasping swords filled the clearing, like echoes. Colbey's eyes snapped open, but he paid no other heed to the sudden menace of gods' swords that surrounded him. Clearly, they now believed he had come to steal the Sword of Balance, and they made it clear they would not allow it. Ravn held his breath, uncertain whether or not they were right. Concern fluttered at the edges of his mind, seeking entrance. Whether or not Colbey Calistinsson had come for the sword, the threat might drive him to battle the gods who challenged him. The massacre that would surely follow would force Ravn to choose between his father and his peers, perhaps even his own mother. Battle lust trickled away, leaving him desperately chilled and lonely.

The scene seemed to freeze into eternity, and Ravn understood Colbey's hatred for the gods' infernal patience. Then, as if the others did not exist, Colbey tossed Harval back to Ravn.

Ravn caught the hilt, shoving that sword, and the other, back into their sheaths. He looked at his father and smiled. "Welcome back," he whispered.

Colbey smiled, too. A warm promise of incorruptible love brushed the edges of Ravn's thoughts. Without invading, Colbey made his feelings known.

Ravn concentrated on his own devotion, hoping Colbey could read it without the need to delve.

"I have much to do," Colbey said. "It's still more likely than not I'll not survive. But, at least now, I have a chance."

"*When* you return . . ." Ravn attempted to radiate the certainty he felt. His father could accomplish anything. ". . . I'll be here."

Colbey turned, but not before Ravn caught a hint of moisture in the icy blue-gray eyes. Colbey strode off across the vast plains of Asgard.

And every god but Ravn heaved a windlike sigh of relief.

CHAPTER 31

A Suitable Heir

To love someone only because he shares your blood is as hollow and meaningless as loving someone only because he's young and beautiful.

—*Colbey Calistinsson*

Twilight bathed Kevral's room in a dull grayness disrupted by the candle on her desk. The whetstone rasped repeatedly against the edge of her sword blade, its progress in her left hand irritatingly slow and graceless. Only two days had passed since her run-in with Dh'arlo'mé's demon. Against the healers' protests, she had returned to teaching her classes, again composed solely of adult guardsmen. She noted the conspicuous absence of three from her morning group and five from the afternoon. Four recuperated from injuries, and two had died beneath the shattered ramparts. One had turned coarse-featured, hair graying and thinning, the aftereffects of two of the demon's claws. A promising young student had aged two decades, but Kevral would see to it that he returned to class. The last, she learned, had died fighting at her side.

Kevral hailed the final man as a hero, his earned place in Valhalla a reward to cheer instead of mourn. The use of her hand was returning in frustrating increments, and her handicap and personal concern stole much of her control over men grieving for the lives of friends and hiding secret guilt for their own survival. Their skills had slipped. How much came from their time off while she trained children and how much from the consequences of the demon's attack, she did not try to guess. Either way, it disappointed, and she had more work ahead than she had guessed.

There had followed a frustrating spar, her timing horrible and her left hand flopping like a dead fish. For once, she did not dedicate her practice to the god and goddess of Renshai. It humiliated her to think they might have observed it, and she would not call attention to anything so inadequately executed. Then had come her first dinner with Charra, a depressing affair during which the healer detailed the cold horror of life on the street. The first kick of Kevral's own child had come then, with the worries and desperate burdens of another expectant mother loud in her ears and thoughts.

Now, safe in her own room, Kevral threw her concentration into the sword Colbey had given her, tending it perfectly to make up for the poor performance she had forced it to attend. A dark fog of sorrow hovered over her, driving her nearly to tears. All that had once seemed obvious, proper, and right melted into a terrifying reality. Childhood lay behind, and the adulthood ahead seemed terrifying in a way she had never considered in the past. All the things in her life that mattered, all the people she once loved, lost significance. She sat at the desk in a morose, dull-eyed silence, complete except for the repetitive scrape of flint against blade.

A pounding knock broke the quiet. Kevral stiffened, wishing whoever had come to see her would disappear. She wanted to be alone. "Who is it?" she asked tiredly.

"Leondis Cymion's son, Crown Prince of Pudar," a voice shouted through the door, surely that of a servant.

Kevral groaned, lowered the sword to the desktop, and placed the whetstone beside it. "See him in."

The door opened a crack, and a middle-aged man in servant's livery appeared at the entryway. "Announcing Leondis Cymion's son—"

"You said that already." A handsome youth in his mid-twenties cut off the repetition, much to Kevral's relief. She had been a breath away from interrupting herself. "Thank you, Boshkin. I'd like to speak with the swordmistress alone, if you please."

"Very well, Sire." The servant gestured the younger man, apparently the prince, through the door, then bowed and closed it behind him.

Kevral gave the prince a halfhearted scrutiny. Dark brown hair, with just a hint of curl, fell nearly to his shoulders. The king's blue eyes stared out from between long lashes. The slender form beneath tailored linens sported enough muscle to suggest some weapons' training. Though not as classically handsome as Ra-khir, he was pleasant to look upon. She gave him a shallow curtsy and hoped that would prove enough. "What can I do for you, Sire?"

"May I sit?"

Kevral made a vague gesture to indicate that he should do as he pleased.

Leondis glanced about the room. Finding only the edge of the bed unoccupied, he sat carefully. "I'm sorry to bother you, Swordmistress."

Kevral had tired of the titles that lengthened every speech interminably. "Kevral will do, Sire."

The prince smiled, which lit up his entire face. "And Le for me."

Too listless to explain that Northerners and Renshai rarely shortened names, Kevral let it stand unchallenged. Though she did not like it known, her given name, which she hated, was actually Kevralyn. Worried for the possibility of a tedious and awkward conversation, she cut to the significant. "Look, I know your father made some desperate promises when he needed me to fight that demon. I'm going to let you off. You don't have to marry me. I'll finish out my year here beginning the day I arrived and adding any days I've missed or will miss but not the extra time in the contract. And I'll continue training the guards, replacing any who died or have become incapacitated."

Prince Leondis laughed. "You're as blunt off the practice grounds as on."

Kevral managed a slight smile. "Damn right."

"I was going to make pretty much the same offer, except for one thing." The prince's fair gaze played over Kevral with unexpected interest. "We leave the marriage thing as an open possibility."

Few words could have shocked Kevral more. "What are you saying, Sire? You *want* to marry me?"

"Le." The prince shrugged. "Not today. I'm just saying I'd like to get to know you before I discount it completely."

"Why?"

"Why not?"

"Let's start with 'we don't love each other' and work from there."

Leondis clearly did not see that as a problem. "Aside from new parents and infants, no one loves anyone else immediately. Plenty of families arrange marriages, and they grow to love one another."

Kevral doubted she could love a passive man. "Doesn't it bother you that the king just up and gave away your freedom as payment for a debt?"

Leondis drew a silk-shod foot to the bed but did not wrap his arms around his bent leg, as most civilians did. Despite the casualness of his position, he had left room to defend himself if the need arose. Such a posture could only come from war training. "Did it ever occur to you, Swordmistress Kevral, that it was *my* idea?"

Kevral blinked. It had not.

Leondis continued, "Why don't we get to know each other and see what happens?"

Kevral traced the edge of Colbey's sword, appreciating that the prince had drawn her from depression, at least temporarily. "You won't like what you learn."

The prince shrugged. "I like what I've learned so far." He rose and stretched, the movement emphasizing his fine physique. His gaze fell to the weapon on the desktop. "First, I know never to ask to borrow a Renshai's sword." Instead of a "second," he executed a kata with a pretend blade that combined the lessons of the past week with reasonable skill.

Kevral stared. "How did you learn that?"

Leondis laughed, a solid happy sound that did not ridicule. "Remember? Your students teach the rest of us during their times off. I'm in General Markanyin's class and learning a lot."

Kevral noticed the discrepancy at once. "But you put today's lesson in that sequence. The general's in my afternoon class. You shouldn't learn that until tomorrow."

Prince Leondis reclaimed his seat. "All right. You caught me. I often peek in on you. Patience isn't one of my strong points." He added conspiratorially, "I think it comes from being a prince and getting about everything I want."

Shocked by the dedication, Kevral blurted before thinking out her words. "You're a warrior? I thought princes just hung around court and entertained nobles."

Leondis cleared his throat and said good-naturedly, "Usually, it's a good idea to prefix a statement like that with 'no offense, but . . .'"

Kevral's cheeks warmed. "I'm sorry. I'm not usually quite that blunt." Her own words triggered a realization. *I'm not usually depressed either. Or moody. Or in turmoil and doubt. I've been all of those over the last few months.*

"It depends on the prince. And the kingdom. My brother was the crown prince, you know. That left me with a few choices at inheritance time. I could leave, or I could make myself useful. I'm not stupid, but I'm more a man of action than of thought. So I've been working my way toward becoming a military officer."

"Now that you're the crown prince, you don't have to anymore."

"But you're playing with me now." Leondis gave Kevral a gentle scolding look. "You know as well as I that, done right, warrior training becomes an obsession. I couldn't quit if I wanted to, and I don't."

Many thoughts flitted through Kevral's head, seeming alien. At a time when she struggled to choose between two men she loved, it seemed madness to take a chance on adding a third. Yet much about Prince Leondis intrigued her, most of all his ability to understand the warrior way in a manner she believed only Renshai did. Neither Tae nor Ra-khir had ever spoken of the euphoria that accompanied swordplay, and the knight had never quite comprehended her need for daily practice. Finally, it seemed, she had discovered one who did. She thought of the Renshai, knowing she should find a husband from among her own yet certain she never would. Her own people had never cared for her endless quests for perfection, her attempts not just to emulate but to practically become Colbey Calistinsson, and an attitude her mother described as imperious. The *ganim* males, however, seemed not to share the Renshai dislike for her, perhaps because they did not see her as competition.

Kevral's cheeks flamed hotter as she realized the immodesty of her own thoughts. She knew she could not compete for appearance with the curvaceous, long-legged beauties that most men found attractive. She kept her blonde locks hacked short, and calluses scarred her palms. Her harsh, sarcastic manner and disdain for anyone not sword-competent should have turned away any man not already repulsed by her looks. Kevral could not conceive of how two men, and now a third, became interested in her. An answer nagged at her, chilling for its logic. People thrown into desperate situations often grew close. Within the first few weeks, she had grown to care more for Matrinka, Ra-khir, Darris, and Tae than anyone except her parents. Surely the two men had gravitated toward her because Darris and Matrinka were already an obvious couple and the princess unattainable, even to the one she loved. Surely, given longer than a year apart from Kevral, they would discover women more attractive than her.

Unaware of Kevral's contemplation, Leondis continued, "Prince Severin was kindhearted and friendly. The type who walks among his people to understand the effects of his polices on them. I'm wilder than my brother, and that worries my father. Who is also a warrior, by the way. And was a lot like me in his youth." Leondis winked at Kevral even as his description of Severin conjured images of Griff. "What my father doesn't realize is that I'm just like him. He's forgotten what it's like to be a warrior prince in his twenties."

Kevral's contemplation raised one certainty. Despite Charra's advice, she would not begin a relationship with deception. If Prince Leondis truly wished to court her, she would not keep him ignorant. "There's something I have to tell you." Her hand slid naturally to the bulge in her abdomen.

"You are with child," Leondis finished.

Stunned, Kevral stared. "How did you know that?"

"I'm . . . not blind," he tried carefully.

Kevral studied her lower regions and the swelling hidden beneath her leathers. "Is it that obvious already?"

"People are starting to talk."

"So you knew."

"I guessed."

Kevral began to shake some of her surprise. "And it doesn't bother you?"

Leondis shrugged. "I'm not a virgin either," he admitted.

"Men don't have to be."

The prince sat up straighter. "Look, Kevral. I'm going to be as honest as possible here. Do you mind?"

"I wouldn't have it any other way."

The prince gave his head one acknowledging bob. "Very well, then. No one's going to blatantly mistreat you, because they're all afraid of you. But they'll discriminate against you in more subtle ways that hurt more. Unlike you, the child will suffer openly."

Kevral had heard enough of this from Charra. "I can protect it."

"You can't be with it always. And violence can't guard against everything."

"What's your point?"

"Simply this." Leondis became even more forthright, his blue eyes pinning Kevral's. "Marriage benefits us both. It not only rescues your baby from illegitimacy, it turns him or her into a prince or princess. You know you'll always get the utmost respect here. You can teach without restriction and practice freely. I get the chance to become the best warrior I can and a wife who challenges me daily. My father gets two competent officers and a crown prince he can respect."

And the baby's father, whoever he is, never knows about his child. Confusion and doubt settled over Kevral, and she found the suggestion difficult to judge. It seemed wrong and a kindness at the same time.

"So," Leondis finished. "Will you at least agree to let me woo you?"

"All right," Kevral said, not at all certain she had made the right decision.

The baby kicked vigorously in the womb.

Darris paced a hundred and thirty-seven courses in front of King Griff's door, yet that did not expend one iota of tension. His collar seemed to choke him, an unrelenting vise that did not lessen even after he adjusted, then pocketed the upper clip. His skin felt tingly, and every touch of the fabric against his body sent his nerves jangling near to breaking. *I could stomp a rut into the hallway, and it isn't going to help. Delay won't change reality.*

The truth of those words had already come home to him as a month, then a second drifted past and the gods did not free him from the dilemma. Denial had served him well for several weeks, but it broke down in the face of logic. Each day that ticked by had become an agony heralding this moment. Further postponement would only heighten the ghastly anxiety that already tortured him. *He's a good king, a gentle man. He'll understand.* Yet in Griff's position, Darris doubted he would prove merciful though he considered himself good and gentle, too.

Darris made three more passes in front of the door while these thoughts ran through his head. Finally, he forced himself to stop, the abrupt change from movement to stillness sending a flash of vertigo through his head. In that moment of dizziness, before coherent thought returned, he managed to knock.

Griff's deep bass wafted through the iron-bordered teak, as if issuing from the ruby-eyed bear that graced the door. "Come in."

The abrupt urge to run seized Darris. Until the king saw him, he could still delay. His hand seemed to trip the latch of its own accord, and the door opened quietly on well-oiled hinges to reveal Griff perched in the window seat. "Your Majesty, how many times have I told you that, when I'm not with you, you need to identify callers before inviting them into your chambers?" The words came out from habit, and Darris cringed. *Great. Irritate him before you deliver bad news.*

The king reluctantly took his gaze from the tended gardens, where the nobles' children played a noisy game of "take." He smiled. "But it's always you. Or a servant. Anyone who wants to hurt me isn't going to knock."

He had a point Darris could not deny, even if his mind allowed him to focus on it. He bowed deeply and with highest respect.

King Griff frowned. "What's wrong, Darris?"

"Wrong?" Darris found himself repeating stupidly. He had expected a friendly conversation before needing to launch into his report. His own skittishness upset him. Usually, he handled all affairs with assurance.

"That." King Griff made a loop with his finger to indicate Darris' grand homage. "Worthy of Ra-khir, perhaps. Not like you at all."

"I'm sorry, Sire."

"Sorry for bowing?" Griff's eyes narrowed with concern. He rose, and Darris immediately wished he had not. His Béarnian size, worthy of his lineage, left him towering over his bodyguard. Taking Darris' arm, he led the bard to the bed and gently helped him sit. The king seized a padded chair covered in plush fabric, with a hunt scene painted on back and seat. Sliding it to Darris' side, he sat.

Darris' gut lurched, and he worried suddenly that he might throw up on his king. *I can't believe this. I should be supporting him.*

"What's wrong, Darris?" Griff repeated, his voice gaining the same command he used during the gravest court matters.

For the first time ever, Darris feared the lovable king of Béarn. "Sire, I . . . I mean Matrinka . . ."

"Matrinka?" The dark eyes widened in alarm. "Sick? Hurt?"

Darris' lids sank closed. "Your Majesty, she's pregnant." Through the self-imposed darkness, he felt movement and anticipated well-deserved violence. "I swear we were careful. Herbs, timing . . ."

Darris' words disappeared beneath a wild whoop of joy. He opened his eyes to find the potbellied king of Béarn flitting and spinning like a dancer.

"Sire?"

Griff leaped back onto his chair but did not sit. He seemed as full of nervous energy as Darris had in front of the door. "A baby! This is wonderful."

"It is?"

"Of course, it is! The queen is having a princeling. Or a princessling." Griff laughed at the word he invented. "Darris." He clasped the bard's fingers between his own massive hands. "I'm going to be a father."

Now Darris understood why Griff responded with excitement instead of fury. *He doesn't understand.* "Sire, *I'm* the one going to be a father," he said, scarcely above a whisper.

Griff laughed, as if Darris had told a particularly funny joke. "Matrinka is *my* wife, remember. *I'm* going to be a father."

Darris groaned. The idea of explaining reproduction to a grown king seemed tricky enough without having to do so in song.

Unable to sit long, Griff returned to prancing around the room, his body jiggling and swaying.

Darris sought a shorthand clarification that might not require accompaniment. "Sire, to make a baby, a man and a woman—"

Griff interrupted. "I know where babies come from, Darris. I'm almost eighteen, and I grew up on a farm."

Darris stopped, his mouth still open.

Griff smiled, all innocent sweetness, as always.

"Sire, are you saying you wanted Matrinka and me to . . ." Darris trailed off, the thought virtually unthinkable. "Why?"

Griff sat again, one leg tucked beneath him as if to resume his frolic at any moment. "The populace wants an heir with lots of King Kohleran's blood, but they don't understand. Matrinka and I are first cousins."

Darris nodded his understanding, though incomplete.

"Our neighbors had a favorite sheep that threw twins, male and female. They kept the male as their breeder and had high hopes for the female as well. But every baby she delivered was malformed or dead. He was going to butcher that sheep, but my father offered to buy her. Once in our herd, she had beautiful, healthy babies."

Again Darris nodded, not wholly certain how the story related to Matrinka. "They were deformed because the sheep were brother and sister, not because the ewe could only produce bad offspring."

Griff nodded. "Animals too closely related make weak babies."

"But, Sire, you and Matrinka are cousins, not siblings. Cousins marry all the time."

Griff did not deny the assertion. "But Béarn's ruler is limited to marrying nobility. Béarn's nobles all descend from Sterrane, some more distantly than others. My parents were first cousins. So, for me, marrying a second cousin is like marrying a first cousin. Marrying a first cousin is like marrying a sister."

Darris stared, wordless as much from the unexpected, instantaneous resolution of a problem he had fretted over for weeks as from the king's deduction that went even beyond his own. Griff had always seemed so simpleminded.

"One of the farmers in Dunwoods married his first cousin. They had only one child, a strange-looking dullard too dim-witted to ever leave their protection. I didn't want to inflict that on my people, and certainly not on my wife." Griff looked directly at Darris, his eyes as soft and brown as a puppy's. "Matrinka loves you in a way she could never love anyone else. Why shouldn't you sire her children?"

"Why shouldn't I?" Darris sputtered, forgetting titles in his haste. "Because the heir to Béarn's throne is supposed to carry royal blood, not mine."

Griff dismissed the concern. "Matrinka carries exactly as much of the royal blood as I do. What's the difference whether her blood or mine runs through our children?"

Darris gathered breath, but no words accompanied it. The whole conversation seemed an impossible dream, so far from the million scenarios he had envisioned that he had no idea where to take it. Flooded by too many emotions, he felt none of them, just a cold, empty void. Excitement warred with grief. Kindness battled selfish need. And certainty of his execution or imprisonment slowly faded.

"I know other things about babies that you might not. For example, animals that have litters can bear babies from more than one sire. I had a cat once . . ."

Darris let the words flow past unheard. Until now, he had considered the pregnancy only for its danger to himself and Matrinka. The king's acceptance forced him to consider the result: the coming baby. *I'm going to be a father?* Even his own thought could not sink deeply. Griff's words kept returning to haunt him. *Matrinka is my wife, remember? I'm going to be a father.* The realization seemed as terrifying as bearing the news once did before. *Griff's right. I sired it, but the baby is his.* He managed joy and excitement for the king of Béarn, but sadness stifled it to a trickle. He spoke, not even realizing he rudely interrupted his liege. "Congratulations, Your Majesty." He tried to sound happy, but his tone did not even fool Griff.

"Darris, this is a good thing."

"I know." Darris hoped he sounded convincing.

"The child will be raised as a prince or princess. It'll want for nothing."

"I know," Darris repeated. He tried to meet Griff's eyes, but barely managed to roll them toward the king. "I'll get to spend some time with the baby. Won't I?"

Griff placed a pawlike hand on either side of Darris' face and turned it toward him. Finally, Darris met his eyes. "When you're not with me . . ." Griff said very slowly and distinctly, as if attempting to communicate with someone just learning the language, ". . . you're with Matrinka. You'll surely spend more time with the baby than I will." The last words emerged wistfully. Given the chance, Griff would spend his entire day playing with Béarn's children.

"Majesty, but what if I slip? What if I accidentally tell him . . . or her . . . that . . . I . . ."

"Sired him?" Griff released Darris' face.

Darris nodded.

"What do you mean accidentally? He or she has a right to know something as basic as bloodline."

The words sent Darris into startled consideration. "Really?"

"Of course."

"And if he or she tells someone? And the whole kingdom knows?"

Griff's huge shoulders rose and fell. "That's the child's right. To tell or not tell. It's his bloodline, and he has the right to share it or hide it as he wishes. Or she, of course."

"But, Sire, he wouldn't be a real heir." Darris fell into the same convention of using "he" to define the unborn. "You're not really his father."

Griff's broad mouth bent into a frown, uncharacteristically severe. "Oh, I *am* really his father. Béarnian law defines legitimacy by marriage, not bloodline. The child is mine. And a very real heir to the throne. Currently, the only one."

Darris knew the truth of Griff's words. Mostly, the convention had worked in the reverse, bastard offspring of heirs who could not inherit if their parents later married. He sat, stunned, not knowing whether to feel blessed or cheated. "You'll marry again, won't you, Sire? And have more children. I mean, I just can't imagine my mixed bloodline on the high king's throne."

Griff's expression softened back to his usual smile, and a strange wistfulness filled his eyes as well. "I hope so. And I expect more from you and Matrinka, too. Béarn's corridors should always be filled with children." He returned to the more serious matter at hand, though his features did not change. "If we find the staves, they can decide if the child inherits, or even if I remain king. If not, I choose. And, if one of your bloodline is best suited, he will succeed me."

All of the irritation fled Darris. It did not matter who the populace named the child's father. He or she could only benefit from living as a prince or princess, from the love of King Griff, of Matrinka, and of Béarn's bard equally. In the end, Griff would take nothing from him, only grant the baby more opportunities than Darris could ever offer. *Opportunities.* Realization hammered Darris then, the last pack on a burden already nearly too heavy to bear. *My firstborn carries Jahiran's curse. The bard of Béarn may serve himself as bodyguard.*

The whole proved too much for Darris to contemplate. He hoped for the child's sake, and that of Béarn, that Griff sired a more appropriate heir.

CHAPTER 32

The Long Arm of Weile Kahn

It's so easy to blame the unknown on demons, so much simpler to explain skill by magic than by superior effort and dedication.

—*Colbey Calistinsson*

Captain's fist thumped hollowly against the thick oak door. At his side, Khy'barreth jumped, overreacting to the sudden sound, and Captain heaved a sad sigh. The dark elves had left Khy'barreth behind, locked in Béarn's prison, surely as a means to control him. Since his discovery, Captain had kept the moronic elf by his side, taking care of his needs as he might a baby's. *Khohlar* seemed not to penetrate what remained of his mind, and he responded only to the most basic of commands. Though he could still walk, communication of any kind remained beyond him. Captain wondered, as he had so many times before, what might have caused the ruination of Khy'barreth's brain. The idea that the *svartalf* might have a spell to inflict similar injury on others haunted his nights and many waking hours as well. Magic of that magnitude could destroy the *lysalf,* turning them into milling dimwits locked into cages until old age claimed them and malleable infants took their places. He worried how such a plan might backfire, the damaged soul permanently clinging to the spell such that babies without brain function resulted. Sometimes he wondered if Khy'barreth suffered and if death might not prove kinder than life. Yet they needed him to succumb to age, if not for the soul it might free for a newborn, then to see if the havoc bred true.

When Tem'aree'ay did not respond to the first knock, Captain repeated it. He glanced at Khy'barreth. This time, the elf stiffened visibly but did not startle. Captain accepted that as a good sign; at some level, he could learn.

The door swung open, and Captain stepped inside. "Good evening, Temmy." He shortened her name to Béarnian convention. "I'm gathering—" Looking past her and finding King Griff seated on the floor, he broke off abruptly and bowed. "I'm sorry, Sire. I didn't know you were here." Though curious, he did not question the king's presence. Convention did not allow it, even of an elf who would be assumed mostly ignorant of protocol. He guessed Griff probably had a healing matter to discuss.

Griff made a friendly gesture of dismissal, indicating Captain should continue with his business.

Tem'aree'ay moved aside. Captain led Khy'barreth inside the room and closed the door behind them. "Actually, Sire, this concerns you as well." Without awaiting a confirmation, Captain continued. "There're a lot of people out there . . ." He made a broad, looping gesture to indicate the entire Westlands. ". . . unable to get food, clothing, and other necessities because of assassins on the roads. Now that things are settled here, I'd like to take whichever elves would like to come with me and do what I can to help those in need."

"Thank you," Griff said. "But I'm not sure it'll prove any easier for you. Remember the elves who arrived with Ra-khir and Kevral? The assassins had orders to single them out."

"True." Familiar enough with human conventions to feel uncomfortable staring down at the king, Captain knelt. "I've given that a lot of thought, Sire. Handed a detailed description and a time to expect them, the humans could tell *lysalf* from *svartalf*. Without that assistance, I doubt they could."

Tem'aree'ay remained silently in place. Griff again responded. "But they might have orders to kill any elf coming from Béarn. Or have worked out a code word to identify *svartalf*."

Captain accepted the possibility. "It's unlikely Dh'arlo'mé gave orders to kill elves. It would harm them as much as us."

"Why's that?"

Captain studied Griff, knowing that the fewer humans who understood elfin reproduction, the safer they remained. However, he could think of no one more trustworthy than the neutral king of Béarn. He would act always in the best interests of the West, including those of the elves who now dwelled in his domain and beneath his protection. "Sire, to my knowledge, only one other human knows what I'm about to tell you."

Griff lowered his head once, a silent promise to keep Captain's confidence.

"Elfin sexuality isn't like humans."

A strange sadness accompanied Griff's nod of understanding.

"Sire, the souls of baby elves come from elders who die of age. Without that ready soul, no pregnancy results from intercourse."

Tem'aree'ay found humor where Captain could not. "Which is good considering the frequency of elfin mating. We'd overflow the world."

Captain saw a flush creeping over the king's face. The open discussion of sex embarrassed him, as it did most humans. He would have expected the king's farm background and pending fatherhood to make him a bit more worldly, especially when discussing the reproduction of another species. It should seem no different to him than discussing the antics of the family bull. "Those who die of violence do not result in offspring."

"Ahh." Griff pursed his lips. "That explains why they left him." He inclined his head toward Khy'barreth.

"They knew we'd keep him safe at all cost, Sire, and now they don't have to deal with him." Captain looked up at Khy'barreth who swayed behind him, mouthing soft nonsense. "My point, Sire, being that Dh'arlo'mé would instruct his assassins not to harm us." He did not express his greater fear, that the *svartalf* would have them captured and work a similar affliction to Khy'barreth's on them.

Griff accepted that happily. "The kingdom would appreciate anything you could do to assist. Thank you."

Captain rose and bowed. "Sire, I only apologize for not suggesting it sooner. I still tend to forget how much more a few months means to humans than to elves." He glanced at Tem'aree'ay. "Which brings me to why I came here. I'm giving every elf the option of accompanying me or staying."

A tangible tension entered the room. "Do you need me?" Tem'aree'ay asked.

"No." Captain sensed Griff's desire to keep her in Béarn, though he did not wholly understand it. "Béarn can surely use your healing skills, too. I just didn't want to leave anyone out who might want to come."

Griff stood, clearly intending to speak yet waiting for Tem'aree'ay to give her answer first.

"I'll stay, then."

"Very well." Captain looked to the king before leaving.

"You might want to take some humans with you."

Captain shook his head. "Not necessary, Sire. Most of us

look enough like humans to pass among those without experience with Outworlders." He only hoped he judged correctly that the *svartalf* had not revealed themselves to others. He saw no reason to insult Griff by revealing that most of the elves who chose to go along had done so because of the opportunity to interact with their own kind. While none of them disliked humans, the strangeness of their ways had become a daily burden.

"Do you think you might travel near Santagithi?"

"Need might bring us there, Sire." Captain had not planned a particular course. "Why?"

"I'd like you to deliver a message."

"Of course, Sire."

Griff glanced to Tem'aree'ay, then Captain before a faraway look replaced the directness of his stare. Sorrow and hope tinged his tone. "Could you tell my mother I'm all right? And, maybe, if it's possible, bring her and my stepfather here. I mean, if they want to come."

"Sire, it would be an honor." Captain turned to hide his grin and herded Khy'barreth from the room.

As winter gave way to spring, the journey of Weile Kahn's men across the Westlands became a pleasure. Relieved of the scouting role he had assumed with his friends, Tae enjoyed the wind ruffling through his hair, carrying the clean odors of damp and aging greenery. Every evening, as they camped, Weile pored over a pile of information carried on a vast chain from the East. Through it, they learned the sorry state of the kingdom they once called home, the succession of power-mad kings who gained the throne through murder and violence, a citizenry plundered of talents or forced into various services for leaders they despised, and women squashed back into the freedomless objects they had been in centuries past. Crime abounded openly, no longer the realm of the underground.

Each morning, Weile reacted to the information he had considered through the night, sending back strategies for his men to execute. At first, these made little sense to Tae. Meager suggestions to improve the lot of those living under a despot seemed, at the least, uncharacteristic for a crime lord of his father's stature. Time, and the occasional explanation, brought understanding. Weile had prepared the citizenry for his return, had planted his own to spread a seed of hope and organized dissent among them. Consolidation had always proved his father's strength, the ability to draw even those most chaotic and unlikely together in a cause.

Finally, as the closest followers of Weile Kahn, those most loyal, accompanied him through the mountain passes that led to the Western Plains, Tae dared to guess his father's intentions. He rode his dark bay close enough to Weile to earn a watchful glare from Daxan that he ignored. Weile trusted his son, and he seldom made mistakes.

"Father, you have your eye on Stalmize's throne." Tae took care not to phrase it as a question. He would not leave the topic open for denial.

Weile did not turn to look at his son, but a smile eased onto his face. "A wise man once said it was my duty to reunite the Eastlands and become its king."

The wise man Weile quoted was Tae. It seemed years, not months, ago. "And you said you didn't want a kingdom."

"I didn't." Finally Weile turned his head. The swarthy features and dark eyes made a fine contrast against the craggy grayness of the Southern Weathered Range. "You argued well. I changed my mind."

An idea right in theory now seemed only madness. Tae tightened his grip on the reins. "Insanity, Father. And you know it."

Weile dismissed the insult. "Apparently, you changed your mind, too."

"Father, your men. Your son. Yourself. Criminals. Have you forgotten that?"

Weile tossed his head, and his curls scarcely moved. The gesture reminded Tae of his own wild snarl, which he had never gotten around to cutting. It had not become this tangled since Kevral combed it out, and the memory of her ministrations warmed him. "I have not forgotten what I am or where I come from. Tae Kahn, there are some things only one who has endured hardship can understand. I've done that, and so have you. And so have those who follow me. Reprieve has not come from nobility. It's time for such as us to try."

Tae considered his father's undeniable point. Weile had more than demonstrated his ability to unify, and it seemed the Eastlands needed that more than anything. Beneath a cruel exterior still dwelt the softhearted man who had slipped into Tae's bedroom to tuck him in at night. The same who had tossed his son out on the streets, then secretly paid informants to watch over the boy. Over the last few months, Tae had discovered that nearly everything he had ascribed to luck growing up had his father's hand behind it. The detail with which Weile described incidents he could not otherwise have known convinced Tae they had happened as his father claimed.

"Tae, believe me. I could eat a man for breakfast each morning and still prove fairer than the warring princes who have preceded me."

Once out in the open, Weile's intentions became more logical to Tae. He mulled them over in quiet judgment, as much to force himself to believe as to understand the chain of logic that had brought them to this stage.

The remainder of their journey eastward brought them through barren sand flats and dunes, swamps choked with forests of water weeds, and the dull roar of the ocean always in their ears. Weile deliberately brought them past the flagstone quarry in which an ancient Eastern general secreted his men and, ultimately, assured their deaths. Cued by spies—or as legend claimed, by Wizards—the combined Westland armies had swarmed the upper ledges and nearly turned the war into a slaughter. Despite the somberness around him, Tae smiled at his memories of Darris. When they had sailed to the elves' island, the bard had pined for a glimpse of this place to help satiate his birth-cursed quest for knowledge.

They camped only a few hours' ride from the passes through the Great Frenum Mountains that would take them into the Eastlands, though they could have reached civilization before nightfall. Tae slept fitfully, every wakening finding his father ensconced in conversation with another group of men. The exchange of information became a barrage that would not allow Weile Kahn to sleep, even should he not have matters to attend directly. Halfway between full darkness and first light, he finally rested, too. For hours after twilight, the men performed their duties nearly in silence, allowing their leader the sleep he needed. Though he had long known his father's occupation, Tae was astounded by the deadly respect his father commanded. He had never seen so many of Weile's men gathered in one place.

In late morning, they continued toward the Eastlands. Men came and went, some boldly and others slinking from behind crags to whisper furtively at the fringe of followers before disappearing once again. The constitution of those who rode with Weile and Tae gradually changed. Wrestling with his own memories, Tae scarcely noticed. The familiar lands of his childhood beckoned, but the desperate struggle to flee his father's enemies would not leave him. His heart pounded rapid strokes that he could not calm back to normal. Left to its own devices, his horse floundered and struggled along the rock-strewn pathway that served as the single passable route between Eastlands and Westlands. Only as the thoroughfare widened to admit glimpses of jagged buildings squeezed into a city too small to contain them did he notice that the thirty men surrounding his father consisted almost exclusively of loyal, clever talkers.

Terror struck through Tae. *Assailed by enemies, plotting to steal the kingdom of Stalmize, and he let all the warriors but Daxan and Alsrusett go.* The strategy made no sense to Tae, but he did not question. Weile would only smile and declare the answers part of Tae's learning experience. No games or theories to Weile's lessons; the first leader of the Eastlands' criminals played only with reality and stakes of life and death.

The city of LaZar seemed to burst open like a dam too small to hold its waters. People streamed out, surrounding Weile's entourage amid a tide of questions that reached Tae as an indecipherable rumble. Con artists, swindlers, and snake oil salesmen set to the task of explaining Weile's policies as they rode toward Stalmize. Hand slipping to his sword despite his best efforts, Tae veered near enough at times to sort individual conversations from the din. They all proceeded nearly the same way; hopeful LaZarians begging knowledge were answered with the phrases they most wished to hear. Yet, Tae noticed, Weile's speakers maintained an air of reasonableness, using words such as "strive toward" and "try" instead of promises. As they reached Rozmath and wove through half a dozen smaller towns, Weile's objectives, at least according to his supporters, became clear. He would restore order to a war-torn kingdom, return freedom and wealth to its citizenry, and work toward a new prosperity that hinged upon the opinions and ideals of its people.

Everywhere they rode, Eastlanders gathered in droves to cheer Weile Kahn as a savior. Driven away by awe and strangeness, Tae's memories became a secondary matter on which he could no longer focus. It required his full attention first to take in, then to wonder about the popularity Weile had managed to gain, mostly in his absence. Onward they traveled, through dusty streets with broken cobbles, hailed by a tattered, dirty citizenry. The sparkle of life in every eye belied their gaunt forms and battered-appearing faces. In a world of misery, they had placed their hopes on the least likely prospect. A man who had once prized his anonymity had, overnight it seemed, become the last hope for so many. Tae's heart went out to people once hearty and strong, now pale shadows of their former selves. And prayed his father would not betray their desperate faith.

Days and nights became filled with the ceaseless press of citizenry. Weile's men handled them all, from probing, hostile questions to pledges of undying loyalty with a patience that Tae could only envy. At length, the whole became a numb wash of repetitive sound, and exhaustion pressed heavily upon his thoughts and soul. At last, they arrived in Stalmize, their procession winding through main streets and avoiding the alleyways that Tae knew better than the creases on his own palms. Believing they would attack only after a full night's rest and gathering an army of more vicious and massive followers, Tae found himself swept to the castle, unready. Beyond the dark mass of teeming people, he saw the familiar gray-and-white structure stretching toward the sun. Six towers rose from polished stone block walls, their roofs peaked into sturdy triangles. Sunlight glazed the granite, emphasizing its smoothness. Even with tools, he would find the walls difficult to climb. Square windows and balconies interrupted the upper levels at regular intervals.

Shouts preceded Weile's party, and the drawbridge winched open with a grinding creak of welcome. Weile dismounted, and the others swiftly followed, including Tae. Poised for battle, Tae was astonished as a cluster of servants rushed in to tend the animals. Struggling against the instinct to scurry into a dark corner, he was swept through the castle hallways, at first by the sheer mass of his father's chosen, then, as these departed in singles or groups, only by inertia. He followed Weile, Daxan, Alsrusett, and Kinya in a dreamlike fog of disbelief that left no eye for simple observation. Bewilderment replaced his normal wariness, and he could not have found his way back through the maze of corridors with any more assurance than random guessing.

At length, they came to a study. Leaving Daxan outside, Weile, Tae, Kinya, and Alsrusett entered. Only then, did Weile's somber mask dissolve. He glanced at Kinya, exchanging a look usually reserved for furtive lovers, then they both broke into laughter. Even Alsrusett loosed a smile, the first Tae had ever seen cross his lips.

Tae just stared. He could manage nothing more.

Kinya clapped a wrinkled hand to the younger Kahn's shoulder. "What's wrong, Tae Kahn. You look stunned."

Tae cleared his throat. "I am," he admitted.

"Didn't think we could do it?" Weile guessed.

Tae shook his head, the hopeless tangle of hair scratching his neck. "I just didn't expect it to be so easy."

"Easy?" Weile's brows shot up. "Kinya, my son believes this was easy."

Kinya blinked, all mirth leaving his coarsening features. "May I, sir?"

Weile lowered his head and made a gesture to indicate Kinya should proceed.

Kinya tightened his grip on Tae's shoulder. "Come with me, please, Tae Kahn. There are things you should see."

Tae nodded, struggling against the shock that held him nearly paralyzed. He headed toward the door, and Kinya shifted his hand to Tae's back, encouraging him forward. Together, they left the study, nodding to Daxan. The bodyguard closed the door at their heels.

"Easy," Kinya repeated, head shaking. "Easy, he says." He escorted Tae down the main corridor to an oak door near its end. It opened suddenly. A servant scurried out, clutching metal tongs and revealing a huge room filled with rows of plain caskets topped with blocks of ice in various stages of melting. As the man rushed past him, muttering something that sounded like hurried respect, Tae estimated the number of boxes between fifty and a hundred.

Kinya ushered Tae inside, and he followed. The elder talked as he led Tae sedately down the columns. "These are the men who died bravely winning this castle for your father."

"Oh," Tae said, trying to remain appropriately deferential while shivering. The chill of the room seemed to seep through his skin. Realization dawned instantly. It had seemed easy to him because he had missed the battles. He could not guess for how many months Weile had sent messages directing those who fought for him, but Tae had to assume the whole had gone on at least since his suggestion, perhaps far longer.

"Weile Kahn's reach is long. His power extends far beyond his person."

Tae nodded. He already knew this. He just had not realized quite how far.

"While the princes warred for their share of gold and power, using the citizenry as their personal pawns, our men spread rumors, kindnesses, and promises through every level of Eastern life, from places royalty never imagined to directly within their gaze." Kinya bowed his head before several of the coffins, bobbing through the lanes with slow sobriety as he explained. "We prepared them for Weile Kahn's coming, and his lack of ties to the king's family only made him more attractive as an alternative. Resistance . . . um . . . had a tendency to disappear—not always our doing, and the hearsay regarding your father grew beyond anything his followers ever spread." Kinya's mouth twitched, as if he wished to smile, but the bleak rows of coffins prohibited displays of amusement. "By the final battle, even those guards who seemed faithful to the kings turned against them, tired of dying for selfish, brawling, royal brats."

Tae smothered a tired grin. So much had slipped past him in his attempts to reconcile with his father.

Kinya led Tae to a corner of the room as a servant returned hauling a cart of ice. The groan of the wood and the rattle of ice covered Kinya well enough, but he still chose to converse in a whisper. "Tae Kahn, in different circumstances, your father could have served as a king's strategist. He has a knack for bringing out the best in the worst and in composing plans that work even when the details fail or those involved have eyes for no one and nothing but themselves. I've worked closely with him since long before your birth, and I still don't understand how he does what he does. It's a gift and a well-practiced talent."

Tae listened in silence, hoping his expression conveyed his interest. He could think of no reply.

"Your mother, too, was a special woman."

Tae lowered his head. Surrounded by the dead, the mention of his mother sorrowed him even more swiftly than usual. He fought the memories that threatened to swoop down upon him again, forcing himself to focus only on Kinya's words.

"Always, she used to take me aside and make me promise to keep your father safe."

"Ironic," Tae managed, voice as frosty as the room.

"Yes," Kinya returned quickly, though he continued to consider the words, a light touching the dark eyes as he realized the truth of Tae's words. "At first, she tolerated your father's work because she knew he could do nothing else." His brow furrowed.

"Obsession," Tae filled in, to demonstrate that he knew passion, not incompetence or cruelty, steered Weile to his career. "I know. My father told me."

Kinya ran a hand through his thinning hair. "But, after a

while, she ceased to just tolerate and started to sanction." He looked at Tae, as if to assure he followed.

Tae was not at all sure he did. "What's your point?"

"My point is that your mother was not wholly the innocent bystander you believe."

"I don't want to hear this." Menace tainted Tae's tone. He would not allow Kinya to suggest his mother brought her own death upon herself and, nearly, upon her son.

Kinya raised a hand, a plea for tolerance and a promise to tread lightly. "I'm only trying to say that your mother supported your father's business not only because she loved him, but because she believed in it and in him. Perhaps one day, you will dedicate yourself to it, too."

Tae offered a noncommittal signal. "I've come to terms with him and what he does. I've even come to respect it, today more than ever. But I'm still not sure it's right for me."

Kinya drew in a deep breath. "You won't succeed him?"

Tae wondered if he was missing something. "I think you would serve that purpose better."

"Me?" Kinya seemed genuinely startled, loosing the air he had gathered in an undignified burst rather than the sigh he had surely intended. "No. I'm quite happy with my current position, thank you very much."

"My father has plenty of good years left in him."

"A normal life span is not a guarantee in this business."

That's right, Kinya. Try to sell me on the glamour. "But the business has changed, remember? He's like a king now."

Kinya still chose deference over smiling, but his eyes revealed sardonic humor. "It's not as different as it might seem, Tae. The most humane king in the best of circumstances still has enemies. Some people will cry around mouthfuls of cream and honey. The battle doesn't end when the new king takes his throne."

Tae considered information he had never had the upbringing to wonder about previously. The more he learned, the less he envied the lifestyles of royalty. "I'm sure there's some young punk as feisty as me eager to take my father's place."

"Many," Kinya admitted. "Their desire alone makes them fools. Your father believes in you. That, by itself, proves your worth. He thinks you inherited his talent for handling people. I do, too."

You're both wrong. Tae's thoughts slipped to Kevral and the losing war he waged against a Knight of Erythane. Eventually, he had won Ra-khir's trust, but he believed that more a matter of the knight's forgiveness than his own ability to win friends.

Kinya must have read incredulity on Tae's face. "Tae Kahn, the ability to lead, and to influence, does not come to anyone without work and practice. What I meant was that we see potential."

For the first time since his father had driven him from the East, Tae opened his mind to the possibility. And it frightened him.

Eleven elves joined Captain's mission, frolicking through the spring sunshine with a natural joy he had not witnessed since Alfheim's destruction. They laughed and capered, cloaks swirling around their delicate forms like wraiths. As woodlands filled more of the gap between the high king's city and themselves, they bandied bits of magic into colorful games and shared themselves with one another in a delightful abandon that Captain never joined. The light elfin language floated like birdsong on a day so like the pleasant weatherlessness he had known as a youth. Only Khy'barreth stood woodenly apart, rarely blinking.

Two weeks of travel had brought them farther into Westland territory, without a glimpse of a single human along the way. Their signs remained strong: broken branches hanging limply, sticks crushed to powder beneath heavy footfalls, and plants mashed into crooked array. Clearly, the Easterners had gone, taking quiet leave of the territory they had once paid for with the lives of countless innocents. Originally, Captain had planned to head directly to Santagithi, to relieve the suffering of the king's own parents, though he worried for the lives of many more cut off from supplies for months. Now, he saw no reason not to head first to Pudar's great city. It seemed likely their own networks of scouts had already identified the Easterners' departure, but the aggressiveness of the marauders might have prevented even the stealthiest spies from performing their duties. Eventually, Pudar would discover its new freedom, but not soon enough to save those on the brink of starvation or withering for the need of studied healers. A quick visit and exchange of information might shorten the time those most desperate needed to wait.

Captain passed this decision to his followers, and they shared the news with those too absorbed by their games to listen. The gentle chaos of the elves pleased him, and he only then realized how much he had missed it. He let them play, wandering alone among the brush and leaves, seeking the lonely solace of a bygone age. He had lived millennia on the open sea, his only companion the *Sea Seraph,* now wayward flotsam on the sea. Despite the bustle of Béarn and its many changes, he had spent much of his time alone, brooding the second loss of this one true love.

Captain glided between trunks, leaving the giggles of his companions behind. Suddenly, a figure appeared in front of him, tan and yellow tunic a bright contrast to the duller greens and browns of the forest. Limbs more sinewy than muscular complemented a torso that seemed too narrow for a warrior. The wind fluttered feathery locks around a face marked with scars, and blue-gray eyes glared out from familiar features. Captain found his eyes drawn to the belt supporting a single sword. Though one of the newcomer's hands rested against a trunk and the other hung casually at his side, nowhere near the hilt, Captain could not help fearing for his safety. "Colbey," he gasped.

Colbey studied the elf a moment, as if trying to read the emotion behind that shocked identification. "Are you sorry to see me, too?"

Captain grinned, the expression more natural on his face. "Not at all. I'm always glad to see an old friend. You just startled me."

Colbey nodded his understanding.

Captain had lived among humans long enough to guess that most would take Colbey's "too" as meaning he wished he had not run into the elf. Captain knew better. "Are you still causing trouble so that some would rather avoid your presence?"

"Yes," Colbey admitted, almost sheepishly. "Apparently, I'm not welcome in Asgard any longer."

"I'm sorry."

Colbey shrugged, as if he found it no big loss. "I never really tried to fit in."

"With all due respect to those I'm *blaspheming* . . ." Captain subtly reminded Colbey of the danger to himself. ". . . I don't suppose anyone really tries to fit in there. Understandably strong personalities."

Colbey finally smiled. "I can always count on you to see the big picture. You were the only one on Midgard who believed in me."

Captain knew Colbey referred to his time carrying the Staff

of Law. Nevertheless, he teased. "Spoken like a true immortal. Referring to events hundreds of years past without bothering with preamble." He meant the words as a joke, yet Colbey cringed, as if wounded. Not wishing to hurt anyone, especially a friend, Captain changed the direction of the conversation. "I was selected and trained to be nonjudgmental. Remember, I served goodness yet ferried Wizards who represented the extremes of neutrality and evil as well."

"I remember," Colbey said.

Captain suspected Colbey had come for more reason than a chance to chat, but elfin patience kept him from pressing. In time, Colbey would get to his point. Captain said, "The gods tolerate a lot from one another. As far as I know, they've only banished one other."

"Loki," Colbey supplied.

"Of course. What did you do?"

Colbey mulled the words a moment before saying, "Much the same, actually."

Captain recoiled a full step backward without realizing he had moved. "Oh. That surprises me about as much as their casting you out no longer does. You killed the most beloved of Odin's sons?"

Colbey shifted position slightly, still balanced for movement in any direction. Captain felt certain that the caution was habit and had nothing to do with himself. "I killed no one. My crime is wielding this." He drew his sword in a single motion, slow for Colbey yet still terrifyingly fast.

Abruptly menaced, Captain retreated several more steps. As his gaze trained fanatically on the sword, he watched it mutate, elongating and thinning until it held the shape of a sanded pole. "The Staff of Chaos, I presume?" He intended a casual delivery but detected a squeak that revealed his trepidation.

"Not my first choice, I admit, but someone had to wield it."

Captain offered proper suggestion, forcing himself not to judge. "A mortal, perhaps?"

"My original idea, too," Colbey admitted. "Yet an elf has law and, for reasons I still can't figure out, law far outpowers chaos in staff-form."

"Dh'arlo'mé?" Discomfort swelled nearly to panic. The damage Dh'arlo'mé could do, to elves and mankind alike, with near infinite power went beyond Captain's imagining. He had contemplated the world's annihilation once, before the first

Ragnarok. To do so again might plunge him permanently into madness.

"Who else?"

"Oh, no." Though clean and simple, the expletive expressed all of Captain's worries. "I have to warn him—"

"It's too late for that, Captain. He's bonded."

Captain fought hopelessness. "Why didn't you—" He broke off. "Why didn't Frey—" He stopped questioning the ways of gods.

"It wouldn't have mattered." Colbey looked beyond Captain. "Dh'arlo'mé wouldn't have listened, and you know the danger of immortals affecting events on Midgard."

Captain had served the Northern Sorceress too long not to understand. The gentle touch of a god's hand could send the worlds spinning out of control.

"If it makes you feel better, Frey appears to favor the *lysalf.* He disowned Dh'arlo'mé."

The words meant little to Captain, only confirming what he already assumed. "It'll make my followers happy."

"A start."

The conversation lapsed into silence, with Captain still certain Colbey had not broached the purpose of his coming. He doubted the Renshai would answer, but he asked the burning question anyway. "Have you bonded with chaos?"

"I began the process."

"Oh," Captain said, hoping his disappointment did not leak through his tone.

"Then I withdrew."

"Oh?" Captain repeated. "Is that possible?"

Colbey made a vague gesture. "Apparently." He sighed deeply. "I'm not sure I made the right decision."

Captain nodded encouragement. He trusted Colbey's judgment on such a matter more than his own.

"Law and I will battle. No avoiding that. And chaos will fall, with law or with me."

Captain continued nodding, not quite seeing the problem yet. The Cardinal Wizards had often addressed him riddles that he mulled during his long, lonely times upon the sea. Those he solved had brought tremendous self-satisfaction, but nearly as often the meaning remained obscure.

"Either way, extreme chaos is destroyed, but one guarantees my destruction as well. Only one assures the ruin of extreme law."

Captain believed he understood. "Unless both extremes die, we lose the world."

Now it was Colbey's turn to nod.

"If you bond, the forces defeat one another. You and Dh'arlo'mé die. If you don't bond, you have a chance to survive."

"Possibly at the cost of leaving extreme law. And stagnating the world into oblivion."

The problem became crystal clear to Captain, the solution less so. He did not know whether Colbey solicited his advice, but he would not give any. In the past, Colbey had not always followed the path of the wise, but when it came to matters of the balance, his intuition seemed as solid as any logic.

Colbey condensed the whole into a sentence. "My selfishness may doom the worlds."

"I do not think," Captain said carefully, "that wishing to save oneself is selfish."

Colbey laughed. "Isn't that the very definition?"

"No," Captain refused to concede. "It's easy enough for anyone moral to see the reason in sacrificing one for many, such as when an overburdened ship will sink if one onboard is not drowned. But—"

The icy blue-gray eyes met Captain's amber ones.

"But," Captain repeated. "The world doesn't work in perfect theoreticals. We never know for certain that a ship will sink, only that it might. I, for one, would rather risk all aboard than chance murdering one without cause."

"You've always done things differently, Captain."

The Captain's grin encompassed his entire face and felt at home there. "And so, Colbey Calistinsson, have you."

"Touché."

Captain beamed at his victory, yet worried over it as well. "Don't listen to the ramblings of an ancient elf. You've never wavered in your convictions before. The decision, Colbey, is rightly your own."

"Yes," Colbey returned thoughtfully. "Of course. My doubts were born of terrifying reality, when I realized an action of mine on one world influenced another."

"Welcome to Asgard."

The staff in Colbey's hand warped again, returning, swordlike, to its scabbard without any obvious attention from its champion. "It's different, though. Without binding, I have no control at all over the aftereffects of my actions."

Nothing remained for Captain to say. "What can I do to help?"

"Only this." Colbey's hard eyes seemed to pin the elf in place. "Whatever the outcome of the battle, believe I took the course I thought right. And did my best."

"Colbey." Captain kept his voice rock steady, hoping Colbey could read the sincerity behind the words. "With or without this visit, I would never have believed otherwise."

CHAPTER 33

A Mother's Love

Renshai violence is swift and merciless, but never without cause.

—*Arak'bar Tulamii Dhor*

Over the ensuing weeks, affairs of state kept Tae too preoccupied for anything more than a casual stroll around the inner corridors of Stalmize's castle. His father did not find even that much freedom, days filled with urgent messages and pleas and nights pounded into a deep slumber that left little time for personal brooding. Tae watched as the castle's hallway fineries disappeared, leaving rectangular, or more decorative, discolorations on the walls where they once perched. Neither Kahn missed the luxuries, and the favors these trinkets bought for individuals or masses seemed worth turning the castle corridors from garish to a simple elegance. Though Tae felt it unnecessary, his father assured him they had more than enough to spare.

Tae had sensed the unspoken proposition beneath Weile's reassurance. Anything they gave away, their thieves could reobtain. Yet later, Tae wondered whether Weile had meant any such thing. The truth of the original statement was driven home the day he saw the treasure room their predecessor, King Midonner, had acquired. Opening the door had sent mounds of gold, gems, and jewelry collapsing toward the corridor in a glittering, multicolored wave. The clatter of coins had seemed deafening, and the casual bounce and roll of diamonds, rubies, and sapphires seemed near to sacrilege.

Now Weile and his bodyguards, Tae, Kinya, and two others most trusted sat in a large but simply furnished room receiving the many spies and messengers in an endless chain. They had chosen this room for its shape, a shallow rectangle with two exits on the same side and a window on the other. Tae supposed it had once served as a library. It contained a table near the window that held bowls of fruit and carafes of water for the moments they managed to eat. Their six chairs formed a semicircle, facing the wall between the doors and an empty chair set there. Weile sat at the center, Alsrusett and Daxan standing and attentive nearby. Kinya and Tae occupied the chairs at Weile's either hand, and the last two sat on either end.

The right-hand door opened for the seventh time that morning, and a wiry, nondescript man stepped across the threshold. He strode straight for the only unoccupied chair, the one between the doors, and took his seat. Only then, he glanced furtively about, clearly unnerved by the audience. "I've got information about the interloper."

Weile leaned forward with obvious interest. They all knew he referred to the stranger who had come to Stalmize two days earlier, alarming the populace with claims that a curse had struck their women barren. "What do you know, Jeffrin?"

"He's about my height."

Tae estimated average, like everything about Jeffrin.

"Stooped. Skinny. He wore a cowl over his head, but his eyes sort of floated in the darkness. Green, like a cat's. Couple people saw long fingers usually hidden by the sleeves. Notably long."

Weile sat back, nodding slightly. They had already heard most of the description. Tae suspected they could trust Jeffrin's details more than earlier reports. Time would allow him to sort reliable witnesses from flustered townsfolk. The more people who separately claimed to have seen a certain feature, the more likely it truly existed.

"Gentle voice," Jeffrin continued. "Soft and high. Northern in pitch and caliber."

"Northern?" The possibility of finally tracing the origins of the stranger piqued Weile's interest again. "Are you sure?"

Jeffrin made a throwaway gesture to indicate that nothing was ever certain. "Leightar said to tell you he thinks it might have been one of . . ." His gaze measured Weile's face. ". . . them?"

Them? Tae looked to his father for clarification. He had his own theory, that the new description suggested an elf.

Weile shrugged. "Is that all, Jeffrin?"

Jeffrin nodded, dark hair slipping into standard, Eastern-brown eyes. "That's all, sir."

"Thank you." Weile turned his attention back to the door through which Jeffrin had entered.

Taking his cue from the con man at the end of the semicircle, the informant rose and trotted to the exit. There, Tae knew, a man outside would reward him and assign him another task.

The door had scarcely shut behind Jeffrin when the next man entered. Lean and lanky, he shuffled toward the seat. Once in place, he turned a scarred face toward his leader. He did not await acknowledgment to speak. "Satisfaction among the masses has slipped. We're squashing rumors that the sterility plague is Sheriva's punishment for a non-noble on Stalmize's throne."

A light flashed through Weile's eyes, and he glanced at Kinya before speaking. "Has it been nipped?"

The man smiled cruelly. "Mostly handled. Not expecting any real problems there."

"Thank you," Weile said. "And the . . . situation?"

The man shook his head. Even Tae could tell something bothered him. "Unsanctioned theft's way down. Murder almost nonexistent. There's been a sudden, definite surge in kidnapping."

Weile groaned. "Let me guess. Pregnant women, children, and women who have borne many babies."

"Yeah," the other confirmed without questioning Weile's intuition. He wiped his nose with the back of a grimy hand. "And rape's getting daring. Right in the middle of the street sometimes."

Tae cringed. They had only started working on reconstructing rights for women, and now a single, unidentified prophet had undermined every effort.

The informant did not await a dismissal, simply rose and headed for the door.

Tae twisted in his chair toward Weile. "Father, do you think—"

As the entry door glided open again, Weile waved Tae silent. Reluctantly, Tae abandoned his point, sitting forward in his chair. Usually, these sessions had allowed at least a few minutes between reports for discussion.

Tae recognized the informant who entered next, a tiny mouse of a man who had often brought Kinya information during their time in the West. Knowing the routine well, he skittered to his seat, seeming almost to melt against it. "Census completed, sir. As far as we can tell, there's not an Eastern woman less than three to four months along with child. Not even on the streets."

Tae held his breath. Given the time for discussion, he would have suggested that the stranger, who he now felt certain was an elf, had made up the sterility plague to create more panic and chaos in the East. Now, it seemed, he might have spoken the truth, and quelling gossip would not prove nearly enough.

"There's a farmer woman in Gihabortch with ten children, barren now despite five months of trying. I believe, sir, the plague is very real."

"Thank you, Shavoor," Weile said with cautious thoughtfulness. "The Net has done well. We need as much information as we can gather in this light."

"I'll handle it, sir," Shavoor promised.

Tae stole a moment from his thoughts to marvel at how, despite seeming distance and dense protection, his father managed to know and remember everyone's name. He saw the wisdom in the strategy, especially when working with the worst the East fostered. Men and women who had never received the positive attention of family thrived under even such simple signs of caring and self-worth.

Weile made a sign to the thief at the end of the row, and the man slipped out the entry. He returned shortly, announcing. "There's no one waiting just now. They'll hold any others until we tell them otherwise."

Tae sucked in a deep breath and released it in a relieved sigh. He needed some quiet time. "Father, how do you do that?"

Weile swiveled his head to his son. Despite the long days, his features revealed no fatigue. Dark eyes, nearly black, expressed interest in Tae's words. "Do what?"

"Remember hundreds of names without a mistake. I could never do that."

Weile laughed, the first release in many days. "Tae, you speak what? Forty *million* languages?"

Tae smiled at the exaggeration, getting the point. "About that."

"You obviously have the skill. If your life depended on remembering such details, you would." Weile winked. "It's hard but not impossible. I'll teach you a few tricks."

Kinya rose and stretched, immediately gaining the attention of Daxan and Alsrusett. "Sir," he said tiredly. "I think the elves have found their revenge." Heading back to the table, he poured himself a mug of water.

Tae nodded vigorously, his assumption seconded.

Weile accepted the supposition as fact. "The problem is trying to second-guess magic. Who does it affect? How long does it last?"

The con man ventured an opinion. He spoke rarely, only when he had something significant to add. Presumably to assist his scams, he had adopted an upper class accent and speech pattern that always sounded out of place. "The decision to announce the problem suggests a short duration. Otherwise, why bother?"

It took Tae a moment to follow the con man's point. As he did, realization struck a hammer blow. *If it's long lasting, they could just sit back quietly and watch us die, without children to continue humanity.*

"A good point," Weile said.

Kinya held up an apple and inclined his head toward Tae.

Tae nodded, and Kinya tossed the apple in a gentle arc. Snagging it from the air, Tae lowered his hand and spoke, "Not to complicate this, but remember we're talking about elves. They think and act differently than we do. Their logic defies at least my understanding."

"Another good point." Kinya pitched a *dero* fruit to Weile, apparently in response to a silent request.

"So what do we do, sir?" The thief who had not yet spoken pressed.

Tae looked to his father. He had no answers of his own. He took a bite of his apple, dry and wrinkled from winter storage.

Weile rolled the *dero* between his palms, loosening the skin. "We'll have to inform the populace in a way that calms them, but without lying. We'll lose them for sure if we claim the stranger's warning a hoax and it proves truth."

Kinya heaved fruit to Daxan, the con man, and the thief in turn. Alsrusett, Tae guessed, would eat after Daxan finished. The elder added his piece, "We need to work on explaining the reason for the sterility that has nothing to do with rumor."

The answer came to Tae with a mouth full of fruit. He chewed swiftly, wanting to speak the idea before someone else discovered it. "A new form of the clap. The worry over spreading it ought to decrease the rapes as well."

Weile beamed at his son, though the monotone of his response belied the pride his expression revealed. "Good. In the meantime, we need to gather more information. If someone manages a new pregnancy, we need to know the details. We'll send messages west. We need to find out if this involves just the Eastlands or other parts of the world as well."

The thief snorted. "Oh, yeah. They'll be glad to work with us."

"I think they will." Weile ignored the disrespect, his informality a study in contrast to the suffocating decorum Darris and Matrinka had described, and Tae had witnessed, in Pudar. "They have no way of connecting Eastern royalty with the assault against travel. And I think months without contact should soften them for messages from anyone. The matter is significant enough to want to coordinate efforts."

Nods circled the room.

"All right," Weile said, looking at the con man. "Tisharo, you work on the messages, please. Find Kinya when you think you have them right."

Tisharo responded with a single nod.

The thief did not wait to be addressed. "I'll work on getting the information we still need."

"Good," Weile returned. "Kinya, think on some details. Everyone grab food, and we'll reconvene here."

Tae remained behind while the others headed for the exits. As the doors closed, leaving only Weile, his bodyguards, and his son, the new king of the Eastlands tousled Tae's hair. The gesture spoke volumes of praise. Apparently jabbed by a lodged burr, Weile jerked his hand away so suddenly he tore out a few hairs. He rolled Tae a look that demonstrated waning patience. "Tae," he started. "This may be a stereotypical father thing to say, but . . ."

"I'll handle it immediately," Tae interrupted, only now realizing why he had not done it sooner. Both Kevral and his mother had preferred his hair long, and the memories of the gentle combing followed by passion would not leave him. "*And* grab food *and* work out details."

Weile replied with a mild bow. "My multitalented son at work."

Tae exited with a laugh, mood high despite the many problems facing the kingdom of Stalmize. He had to admit, albeit grudgingly, that he and his father made a solid, well-balanced team.

Light streamed through the glassless window of Dh'arlo'mé's study in the elfin common house, and dust motes danced through the slanting beams. He rose from scrutiny of one of the Northern Sorceress' most ancient tomes, no longer struck by the torrent of knowledge that entered his brain, far beyond the content of the pages. As he turned the last leaf, he paused to rub an eye too long focused on weathered print. Delicately, he flipped the thick back cover into place, closing it. He reached to heft it, an after-impression touching his senses, a prickling trace of chaos on the inner side that seemed more imagination than reality.

Dh'arlo'mé opened the back cover, finding nothing out of place. He closed it, this time suffering none of the strange tingling. He sat a moment in thought, drawn toward dismissing the whole as a consequence of prolonged concentration on pages nearing disintegration. Yet paranoia rose. Chaos did not belong here, except when expressly summoned to a task. Once more, Dh'arlo'mé opened the book, winding detection magics over the smooth surface of cloth-covered wood. The spell that held it intact beyond its time shifted into vivid focus. An ancient Northern Wizard had crafted the cover, the binding and pages replaced over time. With the amplification that magic added, Dh'arlo'mé again experienced the twinge. Apparently, there was something bound and hidden by magic beneath the cloth.

Dh'arlo'mé fumbled a utility knife from his pocket, slicing beneath the linen. Fabric parted against the blade, and a howl of pain slammed Dh'arlo'mé's senses as the magic shattered and died. The wood lay exposed in front of him, elfin *kathkral* sanded smooth. He studied it, seeking the evanescent magic that had brought him to this place and finding no traces of it. Frustrated, he called more detections. Power flared in his soul like fire, then quivering lines of chaos appeared in a square across the wood. He traced them with his finger: once, twice, three times. The secret magics collapsed with an ancient groan. A compartment snapped open, and a single sheet of vellum spilled to the table.

For several moments, Dh'arlo'mé only stared, fearing the air itself might raze the parchment to dust. Again, he called forth magic, gentling his touch as near to nothingness as he could manage. He seized it, unfolding, and a corner tore free between his fingers. Jerking back, he dropped the scrap, reduced to a pinch of dust that trickled to the table. He rose, twisting his head to read rather than risking another contact with the paper. He did not wonder how he recognized the writing as that of the first Northern Sorceress, Tertrilla. The magic had kept the paper alive for more than ten millennia.

The world disappeared around Dh'arlo'mé, and he caught his breath. An army could have burst into his room at that moment, and he would have died never acknowledging their existence. He understood, without need to question, that he had discovered something even the gods did not know existed. Desperately, he tried to read, but his eye refused to focus. The more he willed it to clear, the worse the blurring became.

Dh'arlo'mé loosed a visceral growl of frustration. He blinked once. When this seemed to help, he repeated the action fifty times in succession. His vision cleared enough to reveal the faint lines of Tertrilla's message:

Lyke untoo thee other Wyzards, mye fyrst profesy konserns thee Ragnarok. *Yettoo, eye kan not reelees thee ymage of a chyldhood dreem:*

Stunned beyond other action, Dh'arlo'mé fastened his gaze to the page. His eye seemed incapable of moving, the significance of what lay in the next paragraphs beyond that of life itself. When Odin, the grim gray father of the gods, divided law from chaos and crafted the many worlds, he had also created the system of the four Cardinal Wizards to safeguard the balance. To one, he gave charge of good, another evil, and the others neutrality. He designed a test for the day when the latter became powerful enough to champion law and chaos.

The first Wizards knew nothing of magic, creating only prophecies for their successors to fulfill. When they had accomplished their purposes, each passed his or her knowledge and understanding to a successor, charged with carrying out the earliest and simplest of their forefather's forecasts. So it had passed for millennia, the Wizards growing stronger as their collective consciousnesses grew until, the last prophecy fulfilled and law and chaos distributed, the system lost its objective. Odin had destroyed it in favor of a Keeper of the Balance, sparing only one Wizard and a single apprentice. And now, it seemed, one prophecy remained—that of a Northern Wizard. As the apprentice of the last Northern Sorceress, it had become Dh'arlo'mé's task to see the words that followed to fruition. The simple paragraphs held the fate of every being in the universe.

Dh'arlo'mé steeled himself to read:

Thee Father shal avert hys fate.
Then thee worlds shud celebrate.
But far ynto dystrukshon hurled

Law's vast plan ys then unfurled:
A new world to create.

All must dye to pave thee way.
A syngle god to rule thee day.
Thee only enemy wyll make
One small lapse; a fatal mystake
Leave thee world at thee mercy of Gray.

Dh'arlo'mé held his breath, reading and rereading until every word became a part of him. Understanding accompanied the first time through, yet he still found himself running over each line, turning it into a steady mantra. It was his responsibility, his very destiny, to destroy not only mankind but every living being on the two remaining worlds. From there, he would craft a whole new world, with himself as its only god. Dh'arlo'mé the Father. Dh'arlo'mé the Gray. Dh'arlo'mé the one true god.

The first grin in months tugged at the corners of Dh'arlo'mé's mouth. And though the form was elfin, the light that looked out from that single eye was the very essence of all things lawful.

The aroma of fresh bread and mutton wound through the common room of the Red Horse Inn, entwined with the warm odor of beer. Though past the popular dinner hour, patrons occupied most of the dozen tables, their conversations a dull buzz punctuated by occasional laughter. Seated at her usual small table near the farthest corner, Kevral suffered the grumbling, painful protests of her empty stomach and wished Charra would hurry.

Awakened by Kevral's long and grueling spar, and apparently also hungry, the baby kicked a wild dance inside her. Her abdomen touched the edge of the table, growing almost visibly over the last month. The additional weight threw off her timing, even as her injured shoulders healed and ceased to contribute to the problem. Gradually, she adjusted to the changes, but her *svergelse* lengthened to accommodate the variations in technique that allowed her to maintain her deadly quickness and accuracy despite the awkwardness of her condition. Her moods rose and plummeted strangely, and her judgment seemed uncharacteristically clouded. She found herself screaming at or bruising students for minor infractions or frailties, at times fighting or enduring tears over matters scarcely worth her attention. She continued to see Pudar's prince, comfortable with his warrior knowledge and charm, yet she dared not make a decision about the baby's future with her emotions in such turmoil.

A serving girl of about twelve, with large brown eyes and straight blonde hair approached her table. "Are you the swordmistress?" Her gaze fell naturally to the bulge. Everyone's did.

"Yes." Kevral kept her attention on the girl's face, a practiced technique.

Like most people, the girl looked guiltily away, gaze now higher, though she still dodged Kevral's eyes. Her tone added a sobriety to words otherwise neutral. "Sabilar's stable girl came by. Said you should meet your friend in the barn."

In the barn? Alarm replaced Kevral's steady composure. "Is something wrong?"

"She didn't say, but her face looked pasty. I think you should go quickly."

Kevral did not wait for the girl to finish the sentence. Rising awkwardly, she rushed from the common room, out into the gentle chill of spring evening. Though she had only been past it once, the route to the blacksmith's barn lay indelibly etched into memory. She followed the route mechanically, her thoughts stuck on vague concerns she had no way to identify. If anyone had hurt Charra, he would pay with his life. Sparing no perception for her grumbling stomach, passersby, or the flailing baby, she sprinted through darkening streets.

Kevral found the barn in dragging moments that stretched reality interminably. She tore open the first door she found. The panel banged against the wall, echoing dully and eliciting two wild whinnies and the tap of nervous hooves. "Charra!" she shouted.

A moan touched her hearing, followed by an unfamiliar young voice. "She's over here."

Dashing inside, Kevral trailed the words toward a corner filled with piled straw. A lantern opened the darkness in a circle, revealing red staining and clots. A mass of tissue Kevral could not identify lay in a dark pile. *An organ?* The quantity of blood worried her. "Charra? Charra!"

"I'm all right, my lady. Thank you for coming."

Kevral whirled, straw slippery beneath her feet. A girl not even into her teens knelt beside Charra, who lay in a pile of the golden silage, her face moist and pale. The Renshai scurried to her side and knelt. "Are you all right?" Realizing Charra had already answered that question, she scrambled for another. "What happened?"

"The baby."

"The baby?" Kevral looked down, only now realizing Charra wore no clothes below the waist. Straw matted to her thighs and privates, glued with clotted blood. Her abdomen had settled to a protrusion no larger than it had appeared months ago. She looked into Charra's face, streaked with tears and sweat. "Where is it?"

Charra sank to the straw, sobbing.

"Where is it?" Kevral asked again.

"I buried it," the girl whispered.

Kevral's heart seemed to somersault. Clutched by the horror of those words, she did not notice the deadpan delivery of a child paid well to lie. "Buried it? Why?" the obvious answer refused to register.

Charra covered her eyes. The stable girl shuffled, deliberately evading Kevral's questioning stare. "Get buckets of warm water, scrubbing sand, and a clean washrag."

The girl rushed to obey. Kevral knelt, cradling Charra's head. She stroked the damp, brown locks. "What happened? Was it abnormal? Did someone hurt you? Did someone do something to the baby?"

"A girl," Charra said softly, eyes closed, answering none of the questions. "A tiny, beautiful girl." A strangeness about Charra's voice bothered Kevral nearly as much as the catastrophe whose details she still did not understand.

"Did you deliver it here?" Kevral looked around at the blood.

"Yes. Safe. Reasonably clean." Charra opened her lids and peered at Kevral. She stiffened, as if to confess a desperate secret.

"What happened to the baby?" Kevral demanded, fearing what she might hear yet needing a truth she would never learn. Kevral could not know that Charra had birthed her daughter in the warm comfort of King Cymion's castle, nor that her husband happily cuddled the child while his wife lay splattered with pig's blood in a blacksmith's barn.

"Lady Kevral," Charra said tiredly. "I killed it."

Kevral recoiled with a suddenness that dropped Charra's head to the floor with a dull thunk. "What?"

Charra closed her eyes again, speaking between sobs. "It was best for both of us. I couldn't stand any more of this, and she would have suffered terribly. Better to spare us both the agony.

A future of stealing and selling her body on the streets." Her hands winched into fists of impotent rage. "My daughter deserved better."

Kevral's hands felt ice cold, and she went dumb, incapable of speech.

Charra continued, her voice gradually becoming the epitome of evil. "Now they might take me back at the castle. As a servant, of course. In time, maybe they'll forgive me enough to let me heal again. Some man might marry me, and I'll have another daughter. One I can keep."

The stable girl returned, setting the buckets beside Charra.

"Clean her up," Kevral said woodenly. Without another word, she turned and headed for the exit.

"My lady?" Charra called.

Kevral did not turn.

"Lady, please. You have to understand."

Kevral did not. Could not. She quickened her pace.

Charra's voice chased her through the exit. "When your baby is born, you'll understand. You might even do the same."

Outside, the air seemed to have turned frigid. Kevral ran toward the castle, tears freezing in her eyes, her legs pumping a rhythm she could not feel. "You might even do the same." *Never, Charra. Never!* Yet, even the day before, she would not have believed the healer capable of such an act. Guilt descended upon her for the many times she wished her own baby might die in the womb and release her from the choices and terrors its simple presence created. *Never!* She forced herself to focus on this moment, to eternalize it into a directive not even the worst of emotional swings would allow her to violate. One way or another, her baby would have a life . . . and a loving father.

CHAPTER 34

Garnet Eyes and *Khohlar*

For now, the Renshai need allies more than battles.
—Colbey Calistinsson

The bard of Béarn had often dreamed of the chance to visit the sage's tower, crammed full of books and texts chronicling history since the creation of the high kingdom. But now that he stood just outside the door, desperate worry assailed him. Beside him, King Griff stood in uncharacteristic silence, clearly touched by his bodyguard's concerns. The sage, like all his predecessors, never left his high tower. Alone, save for his apprentice, among archives both ancient and penned that day, the sage sent servants to report and to gather information. Never before had he requested the personal presence of King Griff at his quarters. To Darris' considerable knowledge, this sage had never solicited any king in his more than forty years of historically chronicling Béarn. Only matters of grave importance could spur him to do so now.

The page who had accompanied Griff and Darris bowed for the forty-second time, then drew open a thick oak door sporting a deep carving of a life-sized bear. The odor of parchment and ink filled Darris' nostrils, accompanied by only a trace of mildew. A pudgy-faced, grizzled man perched upon a stool, quill poised over a flat scrap of vellum. He turned his head as the door creaked open, revealing Béarnian eyes, a well-tended gray beard and mustache, and a frame unusually narrow for one of his race. Though hovering, his hand remained rock steady. As he recognized his visitors, he clambered from his seat and executed a bow archaic in its formality, nearly befitting a Knight of Erythane.

Darris' eyes darted around the room, coveting the information contained on every page. The sage guarded his notes with the ferocity of a wolf protecting cubs, and even the ranking nobles rarely managed to read the least confidential writings.

King's decree could override the sage's refusal, but Darris knew of no historical precedent. Usually, the sage's pleadings or threats of violence against himself sent the kindhearted line of kings searching for other means of information, such as the bard.

The page bowed, slipped out, and closed the door.

As customary, Griff spoke first. "What can I do for you, Sage?"

"Welcome, Your Majesty. And thank you for coming."

"The pleasure is all—" Griff smiled. "Darris'."

The sage chuckled. "He would not be the first bard of Béarn to hunger for the wisdom of the ages." His expression abruptly sobered. "Sit, please. I have two matters to raise, and neither will please Your Majesty." He indicated his stool.

Darris glanced around the room, forcing himself not to dawdle too long over the many books and scrolls. He could have read titles all day and never noticed his lapse. At length, he discovered another stool, surely the apprentice's, at another table. He trotted over, then hauled it back, replacing the sage's seat that Griff politely claimed. At least, Darris had managed to break the king of the habit of refusing chairs by demonstrating the discomfort this caused to the one left sitting while his liege hovered.

The sage glanced at Darris, silently offering to let the bard sit on the stool he had brought over.

Darris shook his head. "You sit. I can guard better standing." He hoped the sage would accept the hospitality without worrying about the insult. The king had nothing to fear in the sage's singular presence.

The sage did not question Darris' gallantry, only did as he bade.

Griff waited patiently through the exchange of seats, then questioned. "What's wrong?" His tone suggested an eagerness to solve, no matter the difficulty of the problem.

Darris did not feel as secure as Griff sounded. A dilemma raised by the sage would surely require brains rather than brawn to settle. One that bothered the sage enough to involve the king personally might prove far beyond their ability to handle.

The sage cleared his throat. His gaze slipped past his visitors. "The first, Sire, involves a secret that even my apprentice does not know. Before I impart it to you, I must know you listen willingly."

Darris leaned nearer, without realizing he had done so. The

idea of learning something even his predecessors had not drew him with the fatal fascination of a moth for a flame. King Griff nodded simply. "Tell me."

"Sire, you are aware that I gather much information through my pages."

Again, Griff nodded. The sage's servants were given freer run of the palace than any noble; no business, major or minor, was ever kept from them. The sage even knew the details of the anxiously awaited royal heir. Trained to observe without judgment and to deliver minutia accurately, the pages were chosen by the sage for positions that usually spanned a lifetime.

"When I moved from apprentice to sage upon the death of my mentor, I discovered something unexpected. Sire, the very walls of Béarn Castle deliver information to the sage's mind. Prior to the elves' coming, it seemed the only magic remaining on man's world."

Griff accepted the news in silence. Darris could not stop his thoughts from running with the realization. He savored the idea of the walls revealing information for which the sage did not even need to search. Privy to such, Darris would spend his days listening in desperate fascination, and the king would go unguarded, except by Rantire.

"Sire, the walls corrected misconceptions and deliberate lies. It informed me of events even the pages could not uncover. My private readings have revealed that the process began with the sage named Fevrin, in the reign of Xanranis Sterrane's son. Then, it gave only whispers of truth, supplementing the information he gathered in more standard ways."

Darris listened to every detail with a raptness that stole concentration from anything else. An assassin could have sneaked into the tower and slaughtered King Griff without his knowledge.

"Over time, Sire, the extent of its power grew until, by my time, it spoke with a command that often made me quail. Not all about it seemed good or pure, but every detail proved truthful."

"Something's happened to it?" Griff guessed.

The sage threw up withered hands. "Sire, it disappeared. Shortly before you ousted the *svartalf,* the day after Baltraine's death. It did not fade slowly away, as it had come. Simply, one day it was there and the next it ceased to be. I have not felt its presence in the half year since."

Silence fell. It took Darris inordinately long to realize the king looked to him for advice. "It would seem," Darris finally started, "that the dark elves discovered and stole it." He did not add the obvious, knowing it might distress the sage. Dh'arlo'mé might just as likely have destroyed it.

The sage toyed with the quill on his desk. "Sire, I can work without it. Sages have done so before me, and I trust my pages." He looked up. "I just worry about the effect its loss might have on Béarn. Or how the elves might use it against us."

"*Dark* elves," Griff corrected.

"Dark elves, of course, Majesty."

Darris said softly, "All of which is hard to surmise because we don't know what 'it' really is." He turned a hard gaze on the sage, ascertaining that the man did not know more than he would admit. The sages guarded their knowledge with the same zeal with which the bards sought it.

An understanding, partial smile touched the sage's thin lips. "I know only that it called itself the voice of Béarn Castle."

Darris could not keep his eyes from straying to the shelves neatly stacked with parchment and books. "So we don't know for certain it's the walls."

The sage nodded carefully. "In fact, it would now seem highly unlikely. It used to come directly into my head, from no particular source. I, and sages before me, just assumed the walls, that the castle itself provided the knowledge."

"What disappeared about the same time as the dark elves?" Darris studied the facts, then spoke before receiving an answer. "Are you thinking what I'm thinking?"

Griff shrugged helplessly. "Not likely."

"I believe I am," the sage supplied. "But I'd like to hear someone else say it."

"Mankind's only magic." Darris made a dismissing gesture. "The staff-test. It seems . . ." He stopped himself from saying "obvious." That would insult the king, who had not figured out the answer. ". . . likely."

Darris' brow creased. Surely the sage already knew they sought the staves. The populace had accepted Griff as their king unequivocally, but Darris and others in power still hunted for the staves that would demonstrate the gods' sanction. Now, more than ever, Darris wanted the staves to assure the proper heir succeeded Griff as well.

The sage explained. "Sire, I thought you should know the staves may contain more power than just determination of the proper king." He lowered and raised his head grandly. "A more than worthy feat in and of itself, of course, Sire. I don't know if it will inform the dark elves of the goings on in the castle, including those things only I should know." He made no exception, even for the high king. "Or worse."

"Rest assured, we'll do our best to retrieve it." Griff's promise did not hearten Darris. The *svartalf* would surely have enhanced their island security since he had journeyed there on the *Sea Seraph*. They had scarcely survived that raid. Besides, an attack seemed unjustified, even traitorous, after having promised peace. Dh'arlo'mé had promised fealty but systematically denied any knowledge of the staff-test. "You said you had a second matter?"

"Yes, Majesty." The sage ran a hand through his gray curls. "I thought you should know that the queen is the last woman in Béarn to become expectant."

Griff stared at the sage, clearly anticipating more. When nothing followed, his lids gradually lowered, creating creases in his otherwise youthful features. "That's only been two months."

The sage gave Darris a pointed stare.

"Four months, Sire," the bard corrected. He avoided Griff's eyes. "It took us a month and a half to suspect and another half to get up the nerve to tell you."

Griff accepted the news easily. "All right. Four months, then. Is it strange to go four months without a birth in Béarn?"

"Not . . . entirely . . . Sire." The sage slid the hand in his hair down to his lap and clasped them both there. "But, throughout history, a month has never elapsed after the announcement of a queen's pregnancy without at least three other conceptions."

"Why is that?" Darris had to know.

The sage had the answer, as always. "Some wish to share the joy of the populace, perhaps even secretly pretending the celebration is for their own child. Others hope for their offspring to become a playmate or even a suitor. Mostly, I believe the excitement that heralds the wait for the prince's or princess' birth creates a longing, even in those women who planned no more children."

King Griff shook his head, narrowed eyes still revealing puzzlement. "Strange, but hardly worth worrying about."

"I beg to differ, Sire," the sage jumped in. "And apologize for offending. I get the same feeling about this as I did about the so-called accidents and inexplicable illnesses that claimed most of your competition for the throne."

Darris made the connection. "Magic? You think elves are involved?"

The sage's thin shoulders rose and fell, and his expression opened fully. "I don't know for sure without the voice of the castle. The *lysalf* might glean more than I can. I only ask that you convey to me anything they discover."

"As always," King Griff replied.

Sterility. Darris' first thought, of his bloodline becoming the only one to carry on Béarn's royalty, floored him until reality dawned to a wider-reaching picture. Without offspring, Béarn, perhaps even mankind as a species, was doomed. "Gods," he whispered. "Gods." The worst he had anticipated had not reached the significance of one tiny announcement. The natural conclusion of his thoughts brought the same uncontrollable terror that kept him from contemplating death. That focus had driven more than one man mad.

King Griff rose, visibly unshaken. "Thank you, Sage." He spoke to Darris next. "To the *lysalf*."

"The *lysalf*," Darris repeated, reaching the door in a daze that left no memory of movement. He only hoped Frey's creatures would have happier answers.

Surrounded by the musky odor of horse and the sweeter aromas of hay, oats, and corn, Ra-khir curried his steed, Silver Warrior, with gentle swirling motions. The stallion stared out over the stall door, lines of dust outlining the patches of dried sweat in his coat. Ra-khir had walked the animal until the hair felt cool to his touch, yet he suspected he would have to bathe Silver Warrior to remove the grime brushes seemed unable to affect. White horses required three times the care to remain clean, and the immaculate standards of the Knights of Erythane made the task tenfold harder.

Silver Warrior whinnied, vibrations shaking through his muscled torso. Ra-khir glanced over the door to see a stable hand approaching. The Béarnide made a brisk gesture of respect before speaking. "Sir, your captain demands your presence."

Ra-khir glanced from his half-tended horse to his partial dress. He had doffed tabard, hat, and sword belt while he worked. Sweat slicked his limbs, and bits of straw clung to his tunic. Despite his relationship to the captain, he knew better than to delay. Kedrin would show him no special mercy.

The stable hand seemed to read his mind. "I'll take care of the horse, sir. Don't worry about him."

Ra-khir clasped his filthy hands so as not to dirty his clothes. Béarn's best handlers tended the knight's mounts, but Ra-khir still preferred to take care of Silver Warrior himself. It was not that he did not trust Béarn's grooms. Ra-khir was still bonding with the animal he had so long dreamed of owning, and tending to his mount had been an important part of his earliest training. "Thank you," he said, reluctantly leaving his mount to the other man's care.

Ra-khir headed directly to the trough and washed before donning his knight's garb. He spent several moments pressing wrinkles, adjusting his tabard to hide sweat and dirt, and combing his hair with his fingers. It would not do for a knight to appear disheveled, and he had already made enough mistakes that morning. Anticipating Kedrin's well-deserved reprimand, he saw no need to antagonize further by sullying the name and reputation of the knights with his appearance. He would need a bath, but that could wait until after his audience.

Ra-khir hurried from the stable, tensed for the inevitable delays. Since King Griff had announced his concerns about widespread infertility, the women of Béarn had become a daily burden. He understood their fears. While the light elves studied the extent of the plague and searched for exceptions and cures, each woman clamored for a chance at motherhood before the curse rendered her incapable. It only made sense for them to seek out knights, and the striking looks he had inherited from his father only made him more the target.

These thoughts engaged Ra-khir as he trod the short distance between the stables and his father's quarters, deliberately leaving by the servants' exit to avoid any who might await him out front. His mind forced him to relive a morning he would rather forget. He had failed inspection for a loop of tabard caught into his sword belt. During marching drill, he had mistaken right for left. Only Silver Warrior's training had rescued him from an unforgivable disruption. Twice, he had referred to the commanding knight, Cavalari, as Sir Kevral. And, worst of all, during an etiquette role-playing session, he had addressed the throne as King Griffy. During joust, he had not only missed an easy ring but had slammed into the scaffolding, bearing it to the ground.

As he walked, Ra-khir sighed, dismissing two young women who approached by making polite reference to his hurry. He quickened his pace, hiding his flustered need to rush. At all times, a Knight of Erythane must appear calm and controlled.

Three women milled at the entrance to the knights' quarters, one who appeared underage, the second in her twenties, and the third at least as old as his father. All moved toward him, eyeing one another like dogs claiming territory. That distraction held them long enough for Ra-khir to dash through the door. Once there, he let some of the tension drop from his shoulders. Only Knights of Erythane had permission to enter.

The hallways lay empty. Those knights not on duty either rested or ate, and Ra-khir passed no one before reaching his father's office. Only then, he paused, glancing toward the row of unadorned doors that led into each man's room. His own beckoned, a chance to wash the horse scent from him and change into fresh clothing. He weighed the crime of facing the captain while untidy versus leaving him waiting, and found the former the lesser of the two. Without further diversion, he knocked on the door.

"Who is it?" Kedrin sounded curt.

Ra-khir removed his hat. "It's Ra-khir."

"Come in, Sir Ra-khir."

Sir Ra-khir. The title still sounded strange to Ra-khir's ears. He opened the door.

Kedrin looked up from his desk, rolling a quill between his fingers. A wooden chair stood in front of the desk. Behind him lay neat stacks of books and extra gear. A window in the back displayed a view of the courtyard.

Ra-khir stepped inside and closed the door. He walked to the chair but did not sit. "You wished to see me, Captain?"

"Yes," Kedrin said. "Sit down."

Ra-khir obeyed, placing his hat in his lap. His father's expression revealed nothing, his regular formality too familiar to shed any light on his mood. "Captain, I apologize for my appearance. I was tending my horse, and I came directly."

Kedrin said nothing, waiting for Ra-khir to finish.

Ra-khir complied, "Captain, I apologize also for my many errors today. They were inexcusable." He lowered his head, feeling the sting of rising tears. Surprised, he banished them swiftly.

"Not inexcusable," Kedrin contradicted. "Merely puzzling." He dropped the quill and leaned forward, his tone once again that of a father. "What's bothering you, Ra-khir? Is it the women?"

Kedrin trod the edges of Ra-khir's concern. "In a way, Captain."

Kedrin sat back in his chair frowning. "It's difficult for everyone. I know you're getting more than your share, and some of them are quite . . ." He searched for a polite term for those few who dressed seductively or rubbed against the men to excite them beyond control. ". . . aggressive. And I remember eighteen well. It's difficult enough keeping your thoughts from such things."

Ra-khir awaited the "but."

Kedrin duly supplied the rest of the thought, "You can't allow it to interfere with your duties."

"Captain, that's not it." Ra-khir studied his hands, hoping his father did not notice the dirt that had managed to slip beneath his fingernails while working in the barn.

Kedrin came around the desk and crouched beside the chair. "The reprimand is over. 'Father' will do now."

Ra-khir appropriately amended, "Father, I'm certain the barrage of women has much to do with it, but it's Kevral who has stolen my concentration."

"Explain."

Ra-khir sighed deeply. Naming his concern brought it more strongly to the fore, and the tears threatened his composure again. "The dark elves gain little from sterilizing Béarn alone. Pudar is bigger. Assuming they track such things, even a few weeks without a new pregnancy should raise concerns." His hands began to tremble, shaking the hat in his lap. "Unlike us, they have no knowledge or experience with elves. They won't know the cause, and chaos might result." His voice dropped to a whisper. "Or something worse." He hoped he would not have to clarify. The idea of a kingdom organizing rape seemed an evil beyond contemplation.

Kedrin's soft voice pulled Ra-khir from the downward spiral his thoughts had become. "Ra-khir, if anyone could protect herself, it would be Kevral."

Ra-khir nodded agreement, though his words contradicted. "But Kevral's strength is also her greatest weakness."

"Meaning?"

"She believes herself capable of handling anything. She would stand when retreat would serve the world better, and any argument to the contrary would only assure she remained."

"And you want to marry this woman?"

Insulted, Ra-khir jerked his head up. He glared into the

white-blue eyes, finding a sparkle of mischief. A slight smile completed the picture. His father was joking. "I let her talk me into seeing other women in her absence, but I can't go on this way. If she's still alive, I have to see her. I thought I could wait for an answer, but I can't. I love her." Folding his hands between his legs, Ra-khir sank into the chair. "Is that bad? Is it against knight's honor to demand a yes or no?"

Kedrin ran a hand through Ra-khir's hair, so like his own. "Not the act itself. Only how you handle it."

"Not that it matters." Ra-khir shook his head, trying to clear his thoughts, though he knew the gesture futile. "I'm mortified about the errors."

"I know you are."

"I'll try not to let myself get distracted."

Kedrin stood, heading back around the desk.

The lack of reply bothered Ra-khir. He tracked his father's movements in silence.

"We both know it's going to get worse."

Ra-khir wished he could promise otherwise. "Am I on suspension?"

"No."

Ra-khir waited for the other boot to fall. When it did not, he dared to speculate. "I'm discharged?" He could not hide the distress.

"No."

A tiny smile of relief edged across Ra-khir's features. "I'll do the best I can."

"I know you will." Though the discussion seemed finished, Kedrin did not dismiss Ra-khir. "Elves have reported back that the Western roads may be safe to travel again. Béarnian scouts have confirmed that, at least in the near vicinity, no Easterners remain. It's probably a slow withdrawal, and we don't know how far. King Griff has urged caution. He doesn't want to lose anyone testing the limits."

Ra-khir waited, an excited tingling beginning in his chest.

"There's some sense in sending a small but strong force out to explore the roads. Make them safe, not only from Easterners but from the encroachment of the woods and damage of weather."

Ra-khir held his father's pale gaze.

Kedrin smiled. "I believe half a dozen Knights of Erythane should assist such a project. The council and the king agree."

He tented his fingers on the desktop and threw the floor open to Ra-khir.

"Captain, I'd like very much to volunteer for that duty."

"I'd counted on that, Sir Ra-khir. And so, apparently, did the queen. She requested that, if you accepted, you meet her in the covered garden at midday tomorrow."

"I'll do so," Ra-khir promised.

Kedrin pursed his lips, apparently loath to speak his next words. "Under ordinary circumstances, I wouldn't have to say this . . ."

Ra-khir lowered his eyes, certain something offensive would follow. Understanding the need born of his many errors that day, he steeled himself for the worst and held his pride in check.

"I know you have a long-standing friendship with Queen Matrinka, but the situation has changed. Please act and speak according to station."

Every beginning apprentice knew the proper approaches to royalty, yet repentance and growing excitement left no room for annoyance. "Of course, Captain."

"Dismissed."

All the anguish of the morning disappeared in an instant. *I'm going to Pudar. I'm going to Kevral.* Ra-khir practically catapulted from his chair and had to force himself not to run to the door. Finally, he caught the knob, only to have his father call him.

"Ra-khir?"

He turned.

"Bring yourself back alive, please." Kedrin stood behind the desk, his stance stiff and revealing. The decision to send his only son, the youngest of the knights, weighed heavily upon him.

"I'll do my best," Ra-khir vowed, opening the door. He headed to his room to wash and pack.

The road the elves traveled led, as most, to the walled trading city of Pudar. Although Captain had never come in person before, he recognized it at once from the many descriptions given to him by Wizards through the centuries. Rock walls towered to four times his height, sentries marching the parapets; and guards stood attentively inside a wrought iron gate. Some details did not jibe. Men toiled to reconstruct a smashed span of wall on the far side of the city. In daylight, as now, the gates should stand open. And the Wizards had described crowds of vendors who could not afford stands inside the city: children hawking misshapen vegetables, craftsmen with handmade creations, cults seeking converts, and an ever-changing host of others that seemed to rotate daily. Aside from the rubble, the Eastlanders' reign of terror explained the differences, and Captain did not question his destination. He approached the gates with calm confidence, his followers flitting after him like children hiding behind a mother's skirt.

The guards broke position suddenly, though their spear tips remained pointing skyward.

Taking this as a positive sign, Captain walked right up to the gate.

The leftward man, the taller of the two, spoke in the common trading tongue. "Who are you? And what is your business in Pudar?"

The nearest elves skittered behind their leader. Captain halted, knowing it best to show no fear or nervousness. He would more likely achieve his intentions by dropping Griff's name. "I am Captain. I'm in the employ of King Griff of Béarn, and I wish to meet with your king."

The speaker's fingers tightened on the haft of his spear. He studied the elf with overbearing intensity. "Which Captain shall I say has come?"

Captain tried not to consider the question beyond polite human convention. It seemed futile to attempt to explain that humans had called him by only this name for millennia and that he had forgotten any calling he might have had before that time. His elfin title, Arak'bar Tulamii Dhor, meant Elder Who Has Forgotten His Name; but Dh'arlo'mé had stripped even that from him in favor of Lav'rintir. Recalling Colbey's claim that Frey had disowned Dh'arlo'mé, Captain freely returned to his previous title. "You may call me Captain Arak." He wondered what the Pudarian would think if he knew the elf had addressed himself as "Captain Elder."

"Wait here please, Captain. I will relay your desire." The taller sentry motioned to the other, who trotted into the city. As they passed, the guards on the parapets slowed to study Captain and his party. They did not stop, however, which Captain took as a good sign. They did not see him as a threat.

Captain turned to attend to his followers, explaining the situation in terms they could understand. He placed Reehanthan in charge of the group in his absence, then selected out Hal and Dhyan. Reehanthan demonstrated organizational abilities, one of two who had approached the exiled Captain about assembling and leading the *lysalf*. Hal and Dhyan displayed an affinity for humans, having been the first to converse with the imprisoned Rantire and, later, with Ra-khir and Kevral. Captain gestured at Hal to raise his cloak hood, shadowing the huge, yellow-white eyes that would look strange to the Pudarians. Dhyan, like himself, could pass for human among people who had never met elves.

Shortly, the guard returned, accompanied by two others. They spoke briefly with the tall sentry. He nodded, then addressed Captain again. "Captain Arak, these men will accompany you to the castle."

"Thank you," Captain said, calling *khohlar* to Hal, then Dhyan, to join him.

The gate creaked open. Captain and his two companions slipped inside, and the other elves shied back toward the forest. "They'll wait outside," Captain explained.

The guards exchanged glances, then shrugged. Surely no human could understand travelers who preferred cold woodlands to the warmth and bustle of a city.

The guards led the three elves through the streets of Pudar, townsfolk staring unabashedly. The guards kept their weapons sheathed, but their manners remained rigid. They had spent too much time worrying about any who approached Pudar to fully lower their defenses, personal or citywide. Captain and his followers trailed in a silence that surely bothered the humans more. Elves could pass days without verbal or mental communication and never notice the lapse.

The marketplace seemed subdued compared to the competitive shouts and crammed walkways the Wizards had described. Tarps covered most of the stands, and the remainder housed dull-eyed merchants who let their wares, rather than voices, attract patrons. Foreigners trapped in the city had turned to local commodities, their drab displays no more interesting than the native Pudarians' any longer. A few displayed finely woven cloth or carvings that flaunted the talents of a Béarnide, yet the scattered buyers seemed more intent on necessities.

At length, marketplace gave way to cottages that gained complexity as they neared the colossal form of Pudar's castle. Towers and turrets cut jagged patterns against the expanse of cloudless blue. The courtyard gates opened without a command, and the guards walked Captain, Hal, and Dhyan along the main pathway. Captain nodded politely to each of the leather-clad warriors at the gate, and they stiffly ignored him, swords belted at their waists and polearms jutting skyward. The guards at the castle entry opened the door without a word. This time, Captain did not bother with a greeting.

A wiry man dressed in a puffy, single-piece outfit of gaudy gray-and-red stripes met them in the entry with a deep bow. "Welcome to Pudar's castle."

"Thank you," Captain said.

"Come with me." The man headed down the corridor with a grace worthy of an elf. Captain, Dhyan, and Hal trailed him, and the guards took up the rear. Traversing a corridor covered with artful tapestries that smelled faintly of mold, they arrived at an archway leading into a room. The greeter motioned them to enter. Captain and his companions complied. Two couches faced one another, and a table sandwiched between held a bowl of fruit. Captain sat on a central cushion, Hal and Dhyan taking seats on either side of him.

The greeter plunked himself down on the couch across from them. The guards took up positions at the door. "You must leave any weaponry with me."

"We have none."

"Ahh." The greeter glanced toward the guards in the doorway. "So, should I presume your title, Captain, is not a military one?"

Captain consciously forced the expressions elves rarely displayed, glancing at his companions as if the answer should seem obvious. "I pilot a ship. Hence, it's Captain."

The greeter nodded knowingly. "And you claim to be Béarnides?"

"No."

When Captain did not elaborate, the greeter pressed. " 'No,' you did not claim so? Or, 'no,' you're not Béarnides."

Captain followed the phraseology carefully. "No," he started carefully, "neither. I said we were in the employ of King Griff of Béarn." Elfin patience could have allowed the questioning to continue through the night, but Captain knew the formality would press a human to exasperation. "Do we see the king now?"

"No." The greeter waved a finger toward the guards. "But Lord Javonzir, the king's adviser, has agreed to see you. Will that suffice?"

Captain preferred the arrangement. It lessened his chances of violating proper decorum as well as assuring a wise audience. "Absolutely. We appreciate his time."

One of the guards left his post and disappeared into the hallway. Dhyan selected an apple from the bowl, passing it from hand to hand for several moments, then rolling it along his arms. He took another apple, then a third and a fourth. By the time the guard returned, with a medium-built, dark-haired man in tow, Dhyan was juggling the apples in lazy circles.

The greeter stood and bowed to the new man. "Announcing Lord Javonzir, adviser to King Cymion of Pudar."

Captain rose and bowed. Hal lurched up and did the same. Dhyan scurried after his companions, neatly catching the apples as he went, and executed a gesture of respect well-learned in Béarn.

Javonzir applauded the performance. "Well done, young man." He headed for the opposite couch, the greeter scurrying out of his path. The guards followed him inside, shoving aside the table to take positions between the elves and the king's adviser.

Dhyan bowed again, then tossed the apples in gentle arcs, back into their bowl.

Captain sat, calling singular *khohlar* to each of his companions to do the same. They obeyed in leisurely elfin fashion.

"So," Javonzir said, hazel eyes pinning Captain. "The guards tell me you're a sea captain in the employ of Béarn's king."

Even Captain had tired of the repetition. "Your guards speak truth, Lord."

"That would be King . . ." Javonzir prompted.

Finally, Captain realized the formality stemmed partially from the strangeness of the elves and their mission. Griff had arrived while Easterners still slaughtered messengers. "King Griff, Lord," he supplied. "Petrostan's son, Kohleran's grandson."

Javonzir absorbed that for several moments. "King Kohleran is dead?"

"I'm afraid so, Lord."

The news did not surprise Javonzir. Kohleran's illness had spanned years. "Well, then. What can we do for King Griff?"

Captain grinned. "Lord, I'm in King Griff's employ, and he sanctioned my mission. But he did not send me."

Javonzir glanced toward his greeter, who hunched sheepishly and left the room, apparently returning to his post. "All right, Captain. What can I do for you?"

Captain's gaze explored the guards, two dark-haired and the last Northern blond. He knew he did not need to ask about their loyalty. They would not have this assignment if Cymion did not trust them implicitly. "Lord, have you heard of Outworlders?"

"Outworlders?" Javonzir blinked. "You mean like elves?"

"I mean exactly elves."

"Only as mythology. Why?"

Captain knew relief that Dh'arlo'mé had not yet poisoned the kingdom of Pudar against them. Clearly, he still found secrecy the better weapon. "Because, Lord, you're speaking with some now. That 'young man' as you called him celebrated his four hundred seventh year last autumn."

Javonzir froze with his mouth still opened. "Uh huh," finally emerged, a thoughtful sound that was clearly patronizing. "Elves. Four hundred years. Is that right?" He stiffened as if to rise.

"Lord, look at us. Look closely." Captain sent *khohlar* to Hal. *Lower your hood.*

The cowl swept backward, revealing red-black hair in bangs and eyes like polished garnets in their canted sockets. Captain waited patiently while human gazes played intently over their high, sharp cheekbones, oval faces, and slender necks. He licked his lips to reveal the edge of a triangular tongue.

Javonzir flopped back into his seat, clearly not wholly convinced, yet at least no longer dismissing the claim as madness. "Elves, you say." He wanted more.

Captain considered magic, but his own repertoire included little more than healing minor lacerations and changing the weather. Lights could pass as parlor tricks, as impressive as Dhyan's juggling yet not convincing. Instead, he called a general *khohlar*: *We really are elves. And we mean no harm.*

Javonzir straightened dark locks with nervous gestures, though he need not have bothered. His thick, oiled hair remained in place even with the briskest movement. "Forgive my doubts. And my surprise."

"Both understandable, Lord." Captain filled the stunned silence that followed. "We came to try to assist those harmed by the halt in travel and trade. I would also inform you that the enemy appears to have departed, leaving the roads free once more."

Javonzir managed a careful nod. "Our scouts are ranging farther daily."

Captain considered how to broach the next subject, long

enough to leave a strained pause. "Lord, we come in peace, to foster healthy bonds between human and elfinkind."

"A worthy goal," Javonzir said. "One I'm certain King Cymion will sanction."

Captain smiled again, the gesture quickly disappearing as other concerns took the fore. "We are called *lysalf,* the light elves. There are others, the *svartalf* or dark elves. They mean to destroy humanity."

A light flickered through Javonzir's eyes. "These creatures, these dark elves. Are they huge, black beasts that change from one hideous shape to another?"

Captain recognized the description with alarm. "No. No, the dark elves resemble us in every way. Coloring has no bearing on disposition. Their darkness refers to intention. What you're describing is a demon." He swallowed hard. "Have you seen one?"

Javonzir hesitated, clearly weighing the newness of the association against the need to gather information. "One tore down part of our wall. Killed some men."

"Is it still loose?" Captain could barely keep his seat. The need to warn and assist jangled through him, a desperate alarm.

"It's dead, I believe. It collapsed, then disappeared."

Captain doubted Pudar could handle a demon. Even he and his entourage could offer little assistance. Only one human in Pudar possessed enough knowledge and skill to face such an abomination, though even she lacked the necessary magic to kill it. "Kevral assisted, didn't she?"

Javonzir's head jerked in surprise. "You know her?"

"We sailed together once." Captain downplayed the relationship, more concerned about the possibility that a demon still terrorized the Westlands. He left other details to Kevral; she would know better which information to impart to the Pudarians. The strategies humans employed to wield or withhold knowledge bewildered him. Elves shared everything. "Is she well?"

"Injured by the demon," Javonzir admitted. "But recovered nicely. Didn't stop her from teaching or practicing, of course. A great asset to Pudar."

"Irreplaceable . . ." Captain quoted a Béarnian guard who had served in the renegade band that restored King Griff. He kept the rest of the grumbled reference to himself: *. . . once you get past her pigheaded, Renshai arrogance.* "How long since the demon's attack?"

"About three months."

Captain released a breath he had not even realized he held. If the demon still lived, he would have seen or heard more by now. *The Staff of Law, no doubt. Dh'arlo'mé is a bigger fool than I believed.* "Surely, the dark elves called it against you." The information explained much about the traces of magic more sensitive elves had noticed growing stronger as they reached Pudar. "Lord, I'm afraid they inflicted something more on you at that time."

"More?" Javonzir repeated, shaking his head. "Was that not enough?"

Captain conferred mentally with his companions. He had detected nothing amiss, but several followers had delved into chaos left in the wake of a colossal spell. Surely the work of a *jovinay arythanik,* it must have required cooperation between every one of the *svartalf.* The Staff of Law, Captain now realized, probably also played a role. "The demon may have been more distraction than attempt to cause harm." Captain supposed Dh'arlo'mé had banished it once his followers had worked their magic. He hoped the leader of the *svartalf* retained enough sense to realize it posed as much hazard to elves as to humans, more so if he lost control. "While you battled the demon, it seems, the *svartalf* rendered your women sterile."

Javonzir flinched, but a knowing look in his eyes revealed that Captain's pronouncement did not wholly catch him by surprise.

Still ignorant of the power games humans played, Captain revealed his observation. "You knew, Lord?"

Apparently realizing Captain had read his expression, Javonzir schooled himself to look neutral. "A message arrived from the East a few days ago," he admitted. "Is there anything we can do?"

"I don't know, Lord," Captain admitted. He had already sent some of his followers back to assist those in Béarn at finding a solution, if one existed. It might take years to even find a lead. "We'll search, of course. In the meantime, I thought you might find use for the information we've gathered."

"Please." Javonzir tried to hide his thoughts, but Captain sensed desperation and some mistrust. The adviser surely wondered whether Captain intended to help or to worsen the problem.

"First, they seem to have targeted females." The strategy made sense to Captain, who understood that the dark elves would not have had the time to handle all humans, even if they managed to gain sufficient power. "And the magic is still functioning, which is how we detected it. Which means that as your girls reach sexual maturity, they will fall prey to the sterility as well."

"Can you lift the spell?"

Captain thought he had made that clear. "Not yet. Maybe not ever. As I said, we're looking for a way. But lifting it would only rescue those not yet affected. Once a woman is subjected to the spell, the sterility appears to be permanent. We'd have to find a way to reverse what's already done. That may prove impossible, perhaps even dangerous."

Javonzir closed his eyes, groaning. "It's hopeless, then?"

Captain shook his head. "You have some women currently with child?"

Javonzir opened his eyes to slits. "Yes. Always. Though we've had more early losses and stillbirths than usual."

"Those still pregnant are apparently still fertile," Captain supplied.

Javonzir's lids found the other extreme. "The magic won't affect those women?"

Captain hated to dash hopes, but humans needed the details to survive. "Eventually it will. If a cycle passes without another pregnancy."

"So." Javonzir thoughtfully put the pieces together, rubbing his chin with his thumb. "We need to focus on girls coming into their bleeding and women who have just given birth."

"If you're quick enough, you might find the window of opportunity before it closes." Captain believed the discovered loopholes would relieve Javonzir's anxiety, but it seemed to have the opposite effect.

Clearly agitated, Javonzir rose, then sat again. "Thank you for the information. Could we coax you into staying in Pudar? You'll have the best of everything, of course."

Captain started to refuse, then reconsidered. ★*Hal?*★

★*I'll stay,*★ the elf returned, intention filling the sending without specific words. He would assure that the Pudarians saw the positive side to elves and suppress the inevitable prejudice that might follow the understanding that other elves had summoned the demon and the plague. He could also help direct and protect if Dh'arlo'mé chose to attack again. Captain doubted the latter. Now that they had rendered human females sterile, the *svartalf* had no need of tactics other than buying time. Rescuing the humans, if such was possible, now lay in the hands of the *lysalf*. Hal seemed a particularly good choice because of his ability to speak the common tongue reasonably fluently, unlike Dhyan and many others of Captain's followers.

"Not myself, Lord," Captain said. "We still have much to do. But Hal . . ." He indicated the yellow-eyed elf. ". . . and maybe a few others will remain."

"Thank you," Javonzir repeated, still appearing distressed.

"Lord, I would appreciate it if you could inform the other kingdoms of our discoveries."

"I will," Javonzir promised, "though I'm afraid the news may doom some young women."

Captain did not contemplate Javonzir's words too long. The reproductive habits of humans still eluded his common sense. "Thank you for your time, Lord. I'll send Hal back with any others who volunteer." He rose, hating to add the necessary. "Please, guard their lives well. We cannot afford to spare any."

Javonzir also rose. "You have my word, Captain Arak. Your elves will receive the courtesies and defenses of highest born dignitaries. No harm will come to them."

Captain believed the adviser's sincerity. Accompanied by the same Pudarian guards, they headed from the castle. Retracing their steps brought them back outside the courtyard, into the streets of Pudar. There, one of the dark-haired sentries left them, and the blond pulled the other, who had helped guard the outside gate, aside. A moment later, the blond joined them, and the other sentry headed back toward the castle, grinning.

The blond explained. "Captain Arak." He bowed. "My name is Tyrion Farnarisson from the tribe of Asci. I traded an extra session of guard duty for the opportunity to walk and speak with you."

Captain returned the gesture of respect. "Unnecessary, sir. I will always find time for the most trusted of King Cymion."

Tyrion winced at the words. "Thank you for your consideration, though I don't deserve it. I got into trouble for an ancient prejudice I had no right or reason to act upon, and I'm lucky to come back into the king's favor. Lord Javonzir got me thinking." He stared directly into Captain's gemlike eyes. "Captain, do you have the ties to the North that lore and your accent suggest?"

Captain deliberately dropped into the Northern language, one all of his followers spoke, at least in a rudimentary form. "I suppose so. Why do you ask?"

Tyrion also switched to a smooth, comfortable delivery of his musical native tongue. "Are you aware of what's happening there?"

"In the North?"

"Yes."

"No," Captain admitted. "Is it different than here?"

Tyrion sighed deeply, gaze turning distant. "Constant war. It's gone far beyond the usual border skirmishes to a slaughter based solely on the tribe a man was born to. My bigotry, I believe, was born of that. I understand my mistake now and, fortunately, did not die for it. My brothers and sisters in the North are not so lucky."

"War?" Captain pressed, seeking the extent of Tyrion's description.

"Constant. Brutal and senseless. With no end in sight. Whole tribes have disappeared, and I would be afraid to learn how few of my own remain." Tyrion shook his head. "I heard you say you came to help. Is there anything you can do there?"

The urge to suggest mankind handle the problem passed swiftly. Captain guessed the *svartalf* had had a hand in this as well. "I don't know. We can try."

"Will you?" Tyrion fairly pleaded. "I fear the worst. Between the killing and the infertility, Northerners as a people may soon disappear."

Captain followed Tyrion's gaze, though he knew the Ascai warrior looked at nothing. Pudarians passed on the streets, pausing to stare at the three odd-looking strangers chatting in an unfamiliar tongue with a guard of the realm. "We came to assist the many people trapped into danger by the Easterners' tactics."

"But the Easterners have gone." Tyrion returned his steady, blue gaze to Captain. "And the new king in Stalmize has apologized and promised peace. We can attend those in need in the West." He clasped his hands, squeezing until the fingers blanched paler than his normal Northern coloring. "Even in the time we've spent talking, a dozen or more Northern warriors have died."

Moved by the words and touched by guilt for the damage Dh'arlo'mé inflicted, Captain nodded. "We will do our best. In exchange, I ask that you take over my mission in the West."

Tyrion nodded vigorously. "If the king does not give me leave, I'll quit. All my loyal years are more than worth a chance to save the North from annihilation."

Captain appreciated and worried about the Northman's faith.

"The first order of business is finding escort for King Griff's parents so they can join him in Béarn." Having informed Béarn of the reopened trade routes, he felt certain Griff would already have sent a messenger to Dunwoods.

Tyrion stared, then bowed deeply. "You've done me favor enough without bestowing this great honor as well."

"Just see it safely done," Captain said. "Please."

"I will," Tyrion promised with a sobriety that denied doubt. Captain felt certain the Ascai warrior would keep that vow.

CHAPTER 35

The King's Demands

Disrespect for a sword is the ultimate crime.
—Colbey Calistinsson

The aroma of *shucara* root and ginger wafted through an austere room on the second floor of Béarn's east wing, displacing the fouler odors of blood and vomit. Injured by a fall from a castle ledge, the laborer lay still and peacefully on his pallet. The same ale that had proven his downfall now wrested the pain from him and allowed the sleep he needed to recover.

Her work finished, Matrinka retreated toward the door, allowing lesser skilled healers and servants to take over the cleaning and her vigil. She had a meeting to attend with Ra-khir in the covered garden. It would not do to leave a Knight of Erythane waiting, though she knew he would never condemn, or even mention, her tardiness. No one ever did, a windfall that had rapidly become an irritation. Despite strangeness such as this, she usually delighted in her life since her wedding day. She relished the responsibilities of queenship, the excitement of the coming baby, her nearness to Darris, and Griff's gentle-hearted empathy. She had grown to love the cousin who had once seemed only a quiet and childlike enigma. The simplicity and ease with which he ruled his life and his kingdom hid a moral complexity beyond Matrinka's comprehension. In his easygoing manner, he had taught her to accept formality graciously; and only he truly understood the profound loneliness that accompanied power. The pregnancy-inspired intensity and changeability of her emotions was disconcerting to Darris and the servants, yet Griff took it as much in stride as everything else he encountered.

Matrinka seized the latch and drew the door open. It yielded too easily, propelled from the opposite side. In an instant, she stood nose to nose with Tem'aree'ay. The elf's canted, blue eyes glittered like perfect sapphires, friendly despite their hardness. Golden curls with a glint of crimson softened the high, sharp cheekbones, and the heart-shaped lips parted in a gasp of surprise. Tem'aree'ay's delicate figure poised, in elegant contrast to Matrinka's Béarnian bulk; and she dropped to one knee with a dancer's speed and grace. "Your Ladyship, I'm so sorry. I didn't know—"

Matrinka used her sweetest tone and offered a hand graciously. "Of course you didn't." So many times she had caught glimpses of Tem'aree'ay leaving Griff's quarters and had deliberately and politely pretended not to notice. "Please, no ceremony while we're working." She had instituted the rule shortly after the wedding, so as not to distract fellow healers and endanger lives. She only wished she could carry the directive into everyday dealings.

Mior slipped through the opening, meowing pitifully. *You left me out there so-oo long.*

Matrinka ignored the cat's whining, trying to smooth out a potentially awkward situation.

Tem'aree'ay accepted Matrinka's hand, though she sprang to her feet without applying any pressure. "Is it bad?" She gestured toward the stricken worker.

Mior arched her body against Matrinka, demanding attention. *Why couldn't I come in with you?*

"Broken arm. Several lacerations; three that needed sewing. Bruises." Matrinka paused to address Mior, *Because I don't believe the gentleman would appreciate fur in his open wounds.* She finished, "Could have been much worse." Overcome by sudden gratitude, she caught Tem'aree'ay into an embrace.

Mior scrambled backward, affronted by words as well as the need to dodge. *What's wrong with fur? It probably has healing properties you don't even know about.*

The elf weathered Matrinka's attention without stiffening, wrapping her own slight, long-fingered hands around Matrinka's broad torso. Elves always shared affection freely. "To what do I owe this honor?"

Matrinka chose to answer Tem'aree'ay and ignore Mior. "Thank you," she whispered. "For all you've done for King Griff. No one and nothing in his life has given him more joy."

People are staring! Mior exclaimed.

Matrinka herded Tem'aree'ay through the open door to the hallway, letting it swing shut behind them.

Mior squeezed through the crack as it disappeared.

"Thank *you,* Your Ladyship," Tem'aree'ay returned in a small voice. "But the pleasure is as much mine as his. I like spending time with His Majesty, but I didn't think you wanted me to."

Matrinka cringed, certain Tem'aree'ay got that impression from her deliberate avoidance. "Please, I appreciate your friendship. I even hope we can reach one of our own." Between their fondness for Griff and their shared profession, Matrinka suspected they could become fast friends. "I just worried I'd embarrass you if I drew attention to the time you spend with my husband."

Tem'aree'ay's fine features revealed the barest hint of confusion. Only months among *lysalf* allowed Matrinka to recognize it. "Ladyship, I don't understand. Why would that embarrass me?"

Matrinka thought it obvious. "Another woman. My husband."

Tem'aree'ay's expression did not change.

Matrinka broke the tension with a laugh. *Great, Matrinka. Create self-consciousness where it doesn't exist. Turn something innocent into an affair.* She had run into this problem before; because of their similarities, she could not help treating light elves as humans. Male or female, Tem'aree'ay belonged to a separate order. To imagine a physical attraction between her and Griff seemed ludicrous. *I'm going insane.*

I've been telling you that for years.

You're a great comfort, Mior.

I do my best.

"A human thing, Your Ladyship?" Tem'aree'ay guessed.

Matrinka smiled. "Exactly. I just want to make certain you know how much the king and I appreciate you." Despite the deliberate sincerity of her tone, Matrinka worried that Tem'aree'ay might misinterpret her goodwill as covert threat. *How do I tell her how much it means to me that Griff has someone so close, who can give him some of the things he needs and deserves but can't get from me?*

You can't. Mior sat in the corridor, cleaning her tail. *But you can show her. Over time.*

As usual, the cat's reply seemed profound in its simplicity. Matrinka promised herself to spend more time with Tem'aree'ay; anyone who could have such a positive effect on Griff would prove well worth knowing.

Tem'aree'ay grinned at the compliment. "I'm glad, Your Ladyship. You both deserve happiness." She motioned toward the door to remind Matrinka of her healing obligation.

Matrinka stepped aside, driven by duties of her own. "As do you, Tem'aree'ay." Briskly, she headed down the hallway toward the courtyard, the intensity of emotion subdued for the moment.

Mior trailed her. *So, what's your problem with fur?*

Matrinka stifled a chuckle but not a grin. *Nothing. I love fur—when it's still attached to you. When it's floating free, it's just dirt.*

And human hair is sterile?

Detached human hair's equally unpleasant. It just doesn't tend to leap from our essentially bald bodies. Matrinka whisked past bowing guardsmen with an amiable wave, and they held open the heavy doors for her. The sun beamed down on whitestone benches, blinding after the tunnellike corridors. *Are you still mad at me?*

Forever.

Leave it to a cat to hold a grudge. Flowers and pollen perfumed the air, and a happy childhood collecting bouquets for mother and grandfather returned to Matrinka in a wild rush. The gardeners' talent with arrangement and color floored her nearly as much as the craftsmen's realistic creations. *Could we talk about Tem'aree'ay a moment?*

Again?

Indulge me. Matrinka wound through the pathways, nodding to attendants and nobles in turn. The flower beds' vast array of hues claimed most of her attention, no matter how many times she traversed the same pathway. *I'm worried for Griff's future happiness. I don't begrudge their love, of course. Even if I didn't know most Béarnian kings have multiple wives, I have little right to complain about mistresses. But I'm afraid he's wasting his affection on one with whom he can't consummate.*

Mior jumped onto a bench, then to Matrinka's shoulders. Claws dug through linen as the calico balanced herself. *As opposed to you and Darris?*

Matrinka winced, as much at the parallel as physical pain. *That's exactly it. I know how horrible it feels.* A familiar vegetable garden came into view, outlined by two stone walls and a tarp stretched across them as a ceiling. The path disappeared beneath the cover, and she saw a distant figure dressed in spotless black breeks and a matching shirt with orange cuffs. A formal tabard stretched over his chest, emblazoned with Béarn's symbol and colors. A hat perched on his head, gold with a blue plume, and a sword hung at his left hip. Perfect posture, leather gloves, and oiled boots completed the picture of a Knight of Erythane. *Ra-khir.*

We can't consummate either. Is our love wasted?

Of course not. Again, Mior had cut to the significant buried beneath an avalance of chaff. *What a perfect question.*

Mior purred. *Cats are perfect animals. It's time you realized that.* She added, *You and Darris found a way. Don't be surprised if Tem'aree'ay and Griff do, too.*

Matrinka wanted more, but before she could question further, Ra-khir rose from a bench. Sweeping off his hat, he delivered a dramatic bow, ending on one knee with his head low. A curtain of red-gold hair obscured his face.

The formality grated. "Ra-khir, stop it. Get up before I kick you." They both knew she would never deliver on her threat, but she took a menacing step toward him.

"Your Ladyship." Ra-khir stood with a flourish equally grand. "You summoned me?"

"No. I summoned my old friend, Ra-khir. I don't know you, stranger."

"Ra-khir Kedrin's son, knight to the Erythanian and Béarnian kings: His Grace, King Humfreet, and His Majesty, King Griff." Ra-khir added, "At your service, Your Ladyship."

Matrinka's eyes stung. She hated the barriers station drove between her and those she cared for. "Sit, Ra-khir. Please."

Ra-khir obeyed, placing the hat on his knee.

Matrinka sat beside him, and Mior clambered down toward her lap. "You know I despise formality. Why are you doing this to me?"

"Your Ladyship, you're the queen."

Matrinka ignored the cat settling on her thighs. "I'm still Matrinka. Do I have to order you to treat me like a friend? Because it loses its special—" She surrendered control, tears dribbling over her bottom lids.

Ra-khir's stiffness vanished. He gathered Matrinka into strong arms. "Don't cry, Matrinka. Please. I'm sorry. I didn't mean to hurt you."

Matrinka clung, still weeping.

"My father insisted. He's my commander. He can hurt me a lot more than any kick from you."

Mior remained in place, glaring at the knight.

"I wouldn't . . ." Matrinka sniffled. ". . . really kick you. I couldn't hurt . . . anyone."

"I know." Ra-khir's grip tightened. "Now why are you really crying? A bow and a few 'your ladyships' can't hurt this much."

Until that moment, Matrinka had not considered a deeper rationale; but the answer to Ra-khir's question rushed to her lips without need for thought. "Tae and Kevral disappeared out here, with killers on the roads."

Ra-khir's embrace became nearly crushing. He did not lie or offer false consolation, which Matrinka appreciated. His presence was enough.

Matrinka sniffled, battling for composure that had grown impossible to maintain over the last few weeks. "It's silly to worry yet, I know. Kevral's year isn't up, and Tae never promised to return. But I can't help it. What if they're lying dead a stone's throw outside Béarn, and we just don't know it?" Self-delusion had carried her this far, the optimistic certainty that those two could survive anything; the illusion collapsed when a third friend chose to brave the roads.

"In that case," Ra-khir said softly, "we can do nothing. I'd rather believe Kevral's alive and I'll see her soon. I have to believe that. Otherwise . . ." He broke off, shaking his head, his hair soft against Matrinka's cheek. Pulling free, he studied Matrinka, his green eyes reflecting her sorrow. "Are you asking me to stay?"

Matrinka wanted to command it but knew she must not. The months until Kevral's return, if it happened, would destroy him. "No. Do what you must."

Relief flickered across strikingly handsome features. "Thank you. I'll do my best to bring us all back alive."

"I know you will." Matrinka's own words failed to comfort, and she confessed her concerns to Mior. *What if I lose all three?*

Then you'll still have Darris, Griff, me, and the baby.

Matrinka ran a hand across Mior's back, dislodging a handful of multicolored hairs that drifted and sparkled in the sunlight. The cat did not understand. *I could have a thousand Darrises, Griffs, and babies, yet I would still mourn not having a thousand of them, Kevral, Tae, and Ra-khir as well.*

Taking her hand, Ra-khir sat in silence. Nothing remained to say. Matrinka looked at him, attempting to memorize every detail. The enjoyment his appearance gave her brought a pang of guilt. Though it did not diminish the burning love she felt for

Darris, she found unexpected pleasure in the simple act of staring at the rugged beauty of his features.

Mior arched her back against Matrinka's hand. *Quit gawking and pet me.*

A thought followed the demand. "Ra-khir, would you take Mior with you?"

What?

"Excuse me?"

"Would you take Mior with you?" Matrinka repeated.

It's customary to ask the cat first, Mior grouched.

Ra-khir's eyes fell to the calico. "Are you sure you want to do that? It may be dangerous."

"All the more reason to take her."

Hey!

Matrinka ran alternate hands through the patchwork fur, her next words answering Mior's objection as well as Ra-khir's question. "At least I'll know what happened. Eastern assassins aren't likely to concern themselves with a cat, and she can let me know if you're in danger."

They all knew it unlikely that Mior could fetch help in time to save Ra-khir, but no one mentioned the flaw in Matrinka's suggestion.

You owe me big. Despite her verbalized disgruntlement, Mior delicately walked from Matrinka's lap to Ra-khir's. She lay across his legs, paws tucked beneath her chest.

"How does Mior feel about this?"

In response, Matrinka tilted her head to indicate the cat's new position. "Isn't it obvious?"

Ra-khir smiled, caressing the calico. The animal had always preferred the company of Matrinka or Tae. Clearly, the knight appreciated the attention and did not need to know about Mior's verbal reluctance, especially since Matrinka knew it for a sham. Mior's action and lack of argument spoke louder than the mental words. "If you don't mind, Matrinka, could you present the request to my father? He'll never believe the queen asked me to escort her cat to and from Pudar. You won't need a reason."

Matrinka understood Ra-khir's unspoken concern. To say that the cat could communicate with her would place her sanity in doubt. They had already agreed as a group not to mention the oddity to anyone.

Ra-khir watched fur fly at the end of every stroke. "There may be times when I can't take her with me. Like into the king's court. Will that be a problem?"

He thinks I'm a moron, doesn't he?

Matrinka frowned at Mior, then shook her head for Ra-khir. "Just tell her where to stay. She's brighter than a regular cat."

You're making me go with a man who thinks I'm a moron.

Matrinka called Mior's bluff. *Fine. I'll tell him I changed my mind.* She gathered breath.

You can't do that. He needs me.

"Done," Ra-khir said. "We're leaving at daybreak." He looked at Mior. "I'll meet you at the border." Turning his head, he winked at Matrinka.

He thinks I'm a moron, Mior repeated, skulking back onto Matrinka's shoulders.

"I'll have her there," Matrinka promised. "And arrangements handled. Your father may think me odd, but not crazy."

"My father," Ra-khir replied, "would never judge the queen."

Matrinka ignored the point and the worry tugging at her conscience. She had separated from the cat only twice and never for so long a period. "And, Ra-khir?"

He nodded.

"Please see that she makes it back."

Ra-khir rose, then executed another grandiose bow. "Your every desire is my command, Your Ladyship."

This once, Matrinka overcame her aversion. And kicked him.

The cramping started again before daybreak, as Kevral prepared for the arrival of her morning class. They had bothered her for days, undulating through the muscles of her uterus and stirring the baby into fitful bouts of punching and kicking. She ignored them, not allowing herself to miss a day of teaching until it became absolute necessity, refusing to prolong her time in Pudar. Counting back to the first night she and Ra-khir had spent together, the baby was not due for nearly another month.

The aching intensified throughout the day, grinding across Kevral's lower regions at short, regular intervals. Halfway through the morning session, discounting the pain became impossible. Instead, she channeled it into rage, as her Renshai training had prepared her, clinging to the wild battle madness it inspired. She had seen Renshai streaming blood and entrails, spurred beyond human ferocity and endurance into a war lust that left a wake of dying enemies. Kevralyn Balmirsdatter, her namesake in Valhalla, had died battling pirates with seventeen stab wounds and an arrow through her heart. If she could endure such agony and still fight, Kevral would do nothing less.

That attitude carried Kevral into the afternoon. The pains came even more frequently then, waves of agony followed by fleeting moments of normalcy that felt like nirvana in their wake. As she demonstrated a simple strike to General Markanyin, wetness gushed suddenly down her legs. For an instant, she lost her focus, and reality funneled through her defenses. Dizziness pounded her beyond thought. She staggered, losing the centralization that had carried her through hours of instruction despite heavy labor. The pain rose to an unbearable crescendo, and she lost control. Kevral collapsed to the ground. The world spun wildly, and a senseless roar filled her hearing. She clawed for the control that eluded her.

"Kevral!" The word scarcely pierced the buzzing that muffled sound into a sluggish bass. Hands seized her. Instinctively, she slashed for the grip, and it disappeared. More words rushed at her, unheard. The world disappeared behind a crackling curtain of spots and squiggles. The pain slammed her abdomen again.

Concentrate! Kevral scrambled for the mind command she had lost, but pain and vertigo clawed her back. Her other sword rasped from its sheath, not her doing. She flailed after it, cursing the blindness and ignoring the sharp sting of the pommel guard slipping past her reach. She managed a few desperate swings with the other weapon, hearing the satisfying snap of brush as footsteps retreated ahead of her.

"Kevral, calm down! We're trying to help." The words emerged as if through a tunnel, and it took her inordinately long to grasp their meaning. She caught her breath, rolling and searching frantically for the mental sanctuary she had too long hidden behind. A weight smashed her fingers, and they reflexively released the sword. A moment later, several figures rushed in. Hands gouged her wrists. She kicked wildly, hearing a sharp curse beneath the dull reassurances. Then, her legs, too, lay firmly pinned against the ground. Something hard forced her jaws open, and liquid sloshed into her mouth. She howled, choking and sputtering.

"Listen to me. Listen to me, Kevral." The familiar voice broke through where others had not. Kevral panted, lower muscles straining. She opened eyes that seemed useless, catching a bleary glimpse of Prince Leondis and General Markanyin against a background of gray sky. "Everything's all right. It's Le."

Kevral stared into handsome features with a look of worry. "If you stop struggling, I'll get you some help."

Kevral managed a nod, though it sapped her strength.

"Let her up."

Nothing happened for a moment. A lone voice questioned. 'Sire, are you certain that's a wise idea?"

"Let her up!" Leondis repeated with a growl that sent everyone into scrambling retreat.

Kevral remained still, catching sanity and breath. She realized now that, had she surrendered to the pain hours ago, she could have handled it. By holding it at bay for so long, she had forced it to a crescendo beyond bearing.

Leondis scooped Kevral into his arms and carried her toward the castle, shouting orders as he went.

"Push," Kevral breathed, uncertain if she spoke aloud. *Have to push.*

Apparently feeling the wetness of her breeks, Leondis looked at his fingers looped around her body. "Tell my father the baby's coming. And find that healer Kevral trusts. What's her name?"

"Charra," someone supplied.

Charra! No, not Charra! Kevral tried to protest, but only a dry croak emerged. She arched in Leondis' arms, forced into frenzied pushing.

"Not now, Armsman." Apparently more experienced with the process, Markanyin shoved her back into the crook of Leondis' arms. "Hold it! You have to hold it!"

Kevral closed her eyes, battling the instincts of her body and panting violently. She felt as if her insides would rupture. Attention turned fully inward, she managed to dull the pain as the rest of the world slipped by her unnoticed. She did not realize they had entered the castle, nor even that Leondis had set her down on piled blankets. She did not feel a lesser healer peel the sodden breeks from legs white with strain and speckled with gooseflesh. Then, just as she felt certain she would explode, Charra's soft voice reached her. "All right, Kevral. Push."

Kevral did not waste a moment. Her body gave a convulsive heave, and pain flashed through her lower regions. *Don't hurt my baby, Charra!*

Kneeling at her side, Leondis squeezed Kevral's hand. He

whispered, "Bad timing, I know; but you've got about an instant to make this baby legitimate. Kevral, will you marry me?"

Agony nearly wrenched a scream from Kevral. She fought for the breath to answer. Thoughts flashed through the fog in fleeting moments. Again, she heaved.

"Head's out," an unfamiliar voice said. Kevral wondered just how many people tended her.

"Kevral?" Leondis pressed.

Kevral opened her mouth to speak, but only a groan emerged.

"Careful," Charra shouted. "Careful."

Kevral felt something shift position. The pressure let up somewhat, but the cramps continued. She tightened her fingers around Leondis' hand. "No," she whispered, gasping. "I'm . . . sorry, Le. You're . . . wonderful . . . but . . ."

The presence in the birth canal disappeared.

"Don't . . . hurt . . . it," Kevral sobbed, feeling helpless for the first time in her life. Tears dribbled to mix with the sweat on her ashen face. Pain stabbed through her. "Still . . . need . . . to push."

A soft voice near her legs responded, the same who had declared the head free. "That's the afterbirth. Go ahead and push."

Kevral curled up, watching the red mass of the afterbirth slither free. A loud wail split the sounds of conversation. *The baby. It's all right.* Kevral lay back.

"Boy!" Charra declared over the noise. "A bit small but looks healthy. Lots of red hair."

Red. Excitement suffused Kevral. *Ra-khir's.* Calm satisfaction followed. She dropped back to the blankets, weak with strain. Suddenly, she realized she had never finished her response to Leondis. He remained in place, still clinging to her hand. She glanced around a gray, austere room. Two healers tended the baby and a third her. The only other person in the room was the prince. "I'm sorry. But if the baby's father will still have me, I—" Agony sledgehammered her low in the gut. This time, she could not bite back the scream.

Charra charged back, shoving aside the woman tending Kevral. "I knew she looked too damned big. Twins."

Kevral growled, enraged by her loss of control. Her grip tightened painfully around Leondis' hand, but he endured without complaint.

"Push, Lady. Push," Charra shouted.

Exhaustion overtook Kevral, and she slipped in and out of consciousness.

"What in Hel's wrong with her?" Charra's voice sounded distant. "She should be able to handle this. She's stronger than a damned phalanx."

"We fed her a sedative," Leondis explained.

Kevral vaguely remembered liquid flooding her mouth on the practice field. Now, she knew a tranquil joy, a quiet sensation of floating.

"Where did you get . . ." Charra started, then interrupted herself. "Never mind, Sire. I'm sorry." She shouted, "Lady Kevral, push!"

Kevral tried to obey. The instructions barely registered, and it took all her strength just to keep awake. She let her eyes sag closed, attending to need.

"Majesty, forgive the command, but, if you don't help her, that baby's going to die."

"Just tell me what to do," Leondis returned. He fought free of Kevral's death grip, shaking his hand. "And I'll use whatever isn't broken to assist."

"Shove here." Charra screamed directly into Kevral's ear, "Damn it, Lady. Push!" Then to another. "Grab on to the head and pull."

"I can't get a grip." Fingers pinched Kevral's privates, the pain minimal compared to the contractions. She strained, losing track of the reason as she did. She felt the head pop free, followed by a cry of triumph. Then, darkness descended over Kevral, and she drifted into quiet sleep.

Kevral awakened to a dull agony that throbbed from her abdomen into her lower regions. She lay on a clean pile of blankets, dressed in her training tunic and an enormous, lightweight pair of britches, without undergarments. Dark blood stained the crotch, surely that which had seeped out since the others had left her. She lurched to her feet too quickly. Dizziness hammered at her, driving her to a crouch to keep from tumbling. Gradually, her senses cleared, and she stood in increments. Bars filled her vision and, beyond those, stone walls tinged green. A faint odor of mildew reached her nostrils beneath the stronger scent of her own blood.

Where am I? Where's the baby? Memory returned in a bewildering rush. *Babies.* Terror ground through Kevral. *Charra had them. Baby-killing Charra.* She ran to the door and yanked so hard pain shot through her forearms. The iron gateway barely shifted. Kevral shoved at it, with no more success. Desperately, she jerked and thrust, the door budging fractionally in each direction and making tense clicking sounds with each slight movement. "Hey!" she shouted. "Hey! I can't get out!"

Only then, Kevral realized that her vision encompassed a row of cells along a dark corridor that trailed into nothingness beyond her vision. *A dungeon? Where? Why?* No answers followed. The whole situation went beyond any logic she could fathom. The need to pause and study her surroundings returned rationality. Charra had called for the prince's help to keep the baby from dying. That did not sound like the words of a woman who plotted murder. The fate of the babies still gnawed at Kevral, a desperate need, yet she no longer worried over their immediate safety. Her mind registered thirst.

A footfall thumped far down the hallway, beyond Kevral's vision. "Hey!" she shouted again. "Who's there? I need help."

No reply.

Kevral hammered at the door. It did not yield, so she turned her attention to the walls. Iron bars, with perpendicular braces at regular intervals, lay deeply embedded in the granite floor and rose to a stone ceiling. She had spent enough time in Pudar's prison to recognize her surroundings for certain. *I am in a dungeon. Why?* Only one possibility filled her mind. She recalled how tightly she had clutched Prince Leondis' hand when the agony grew unbearable. Training had taught her to respond to pain with violence. *I killed him. Gods, I killed the heir to Pudar's throne.* She could not help remembering the penalty leveled on Tae for the same crime; he was to have been drawn and quartered.

Only a mild trickle of fear accompanied the thought, though Kevral would have expected a torrent. Crazed by pain and battle wrath, she might have lost control; but she should have remembered such a desperate and horrible action. Weaponless and crippled by childbirth, she doubted she could have inflicted much damage before the healers overtook her. *I didn't kill Le.* Yet Kevral could imagine no other crime that might have condemned her to Pudar's dungeon.

Kevral inspected the cell for doors she might have missed, then the bars for weaknesses that could allow escape. Though time had pitted them into sharp irregularity, the thick metal remained stronger than any attempt of hers to budge it. Her stomach churned and rumbled, and her mouth felt full of dust. She had not eaten or drunk since a light breakfast, and she guessed she had slept at least partway through the night. Nearly a full day had passed, during which she had expended large amounts of energy and blood. Even the anxiety of finding herself here could not fully banish hunger and thirst.

More footsteps tripped down the corridor, this time definitely approaching. Wild echoes bounced from the walls, making a count impossible. Kevral retreated far enough from the door so a sudden spear thrust would not reach her. She did it from habit rather than any fear that such would happen or that she could not dodge if it did.

A feminine form appeared from the gloom. Gradually, the other became recognizable as Charra, more slender than Kevral remembered and clutching something to her chest beneath a shroud. The healer shook back dark hair and studied Kevral through the bars with soft, light brown eyes.

Kevral's gaze fell naturally to the object in Charra's grip. It moved beneath the cover, surely a feeding infant. The realization triggered her own letdown, and milk seeped into her undergarments. The lack of control embarrassed her, though Charra could not see through the thick leather of the tunic. "Is that my baby?" Kevral asked accusingly.

Charra shook her head. "Mine."

"Yours is dead," Kevral said flatly, tensing for a fight. If Charra intended to steal either of her infants, no iron bars could hold the Renshai back.

Charra's lips formed a nervous smile. "Lady, I was afraid. I thought she was dead. I told the stable girl to bury the body, but she gave the baby to her own mother instead. I found out and got her back."

The hostility wavered. Kevral did not know what to believe. "You said you killed her."

"I thought I did, Lady Kevral." Charra's voice assumed a breathy quality, but she did not cry. "I thought my decision to live on the streets had killed her."

The anger faded with a suddenness that left Kevral in an emotionless void. "I thought you meant—"

Charra interrupted. "I know you did, Lady. That's why you ran away when I needed you." The words stung. "That's why you thought I'd harm your babies. I wouldn't do that."

"I'm sorry," Kevral said, lowering her head. "I'm so glad you got her back."

Charra's smile was genuine. She hugged the baby closer beneath the wrappings.

Jealousy speared Kevral. "My babies?" she reminded.

"They're well, Lady." Charra gestured to someone lost in the darkness, and another woman sidled into view. Sandy hair hung to her shoulders in limp strands, and dull brown eyes swiveled toward Kevral's face then dodged back to a bundle wrapped in blankets. "Two boys."

Now, excitement claimed Kevral, the vast parade of emotions exhausting. "Let me see." She held out her arms, heart pounding. *My baby. A part of me. A part of Ra-khir.* Love seemed to howl through her like a gale, and the force and depth of the emotion would have frightened her had it not felt so pleasant. *My baby.*

The woman passed the baby she held to Charra who opened the wrappings to reveal a tiny, wrinkled face. Miniature lips pursed beneath a baby-flat nose. Dark eyes with just a hint of blue rolled beneath long-lashed lids. A gout of black hair clung to his scalp. A tight-fisted hand flopped free.

Still reaching for him, Kevral sighed. Realization sifted beneath the overwhelming rush of adoration. Eyes that color would gradually turn brown, and hair could not change overnight. "That's not my baby."

"Lady, it is," Charra insisted. "Mine is a girl and clearly several weeks older. Do you want to see?"

"You said he had red hair."

"The first one does. This is the second, my lady."

When it became clear Charra would not pass the baby to her, Kevral let her arms slip to her sides. Exhaustion pressed her, inside and out. She had run through her emotional repertoire, and the fatigue of a practice followed by an ordeal pressed her. *This is Tae's baby. This is* clearly *Tae's baby. How can that be?*

Charra startled Kevral with words that sounded like mindreading. "I've never seen twins less alike. It's as if they have different fathers."

"Impossible," Kevral forced out. If the king discovered that the man he believed had murdered his eldest son had sired one of the babies, he would surely kill it.

"Rare," Charra said. "But not impossible. I read about a whore who had one twin with an illness that ran in one father's family and a handicap from the other's."

"I meant impossible in my case." Kevral swallowed hard and hoped Charra did not notice her worry.

Charra chuckled, dismissing the observation. "Well, of course, Lady Kevral. I wasn't accusing you of such. Erythanians are as mix-blooded as Pudarians, even the knights. A dark-haired, dark-eyed man with redheads in his family could have sired both." She turned Kevral a measuring look.

Kevral wanted to ask whether a man of Ra-khir's coloring or an Easterner could have sired both, but closing the discussion seemed more prudent. In her heart, she knew the answer and tried not to suffer the decisions and consequences that had to follow. For now, understanding the current situation took precedence.

The baby's face screwed suddenly into a knot, and it let out a wail that stirred Kevral's milk a second time. Stepping forward, she reached for him through the bars.

Charra retreated, shifting her coverings. She slipped the second baby to her opposite breast.

Too stunned for outrage, Kevral could only ask, "What are you doing?"

"Lady, he's hungry." Charra explained the obvious.

"Then I'll feed him. He's my baby."

Charra licked her lips and back-stepped again. "King's orders, Lady. You are not to touch either baby until you agree to his demands."

Wrung out, Kevral would have believed herself incapable of emotion, but anger exploded through her. The details did not matter. Even if the king asked only for her dinner preference, the method forced her to defy him. "Where's my other baby?"

"With his wet nurse, Lady. Safe." Charra's face crinkled into bewilderment. "Don't you want to know the terms?"

"No," Kevral said, turning away. "My answer is 'no.' Give me my babies."

"I can't."

Kevral seethed, keeping her back to Charra. "Think how you felt when you thought your daughter dead and your arms were empty. Think about that, then give me my babies."

Charra's voice sounded distant. "Lady Kevral, I want you to have them. But there's more at stake here. The entirety of mankind depends on the cooperation of women like you and me."

"The entirety of mankind," Kevral repeated. Folding her arms across her chest, she swiveled her head toward Charra. The other woman had slipped back into the shadows. "Don't get melodramatic. Just let me hold my son."

"Kevral, be reasonable." For the first time, Charra used Kevral's name without the qualifying "lady." "You're asking me to risk my life and my daughter's future. If I give you your baby, you won't give him back."

Kevral refused to lie. "You're right."

"Then, Lady, I get punished and lose my daughter."

Kevral whirled. "Let me out. We'll fight him together."

"The King of Pudar?" Charra blurted the words, surprised. "Why not?"

Charra shifted the feeding babies, the question ludicrous beyond explanation. "Because, Lady, I've already listened to his demands and happen to agree with them. I'm doing as he bade and proudly. I love my king, and it's an honor to serve him."

Kevral cast up her hands. "Charra, grow a spine."

"Kevral," Charra snapped back. "Learn some tolerance. At least listen to the situation before you judge it."

Kevral glanced at the stained ceiling. Beneath the silence that followed Charra's shouting, she heard the faint sound of dripping water. Charra had a valid point. "All right." Kevral placed a hand on a bar brace. "Explain. Explain why I woke up in a dungeon. Explain why my babies were stolen. Explain why *your* king is breaking his word to me . . . again. Explain why I shouldn't chew my way out of this cell and through every citizen of Pudar."

Ignoring Kevral's angry questions, Charra detailed the fertility situation, including the specifics the elves had revealed. Her head made sweeping arcs to punctuate her points, and the dark hair that bobbed with every motion still reminded Kevral of Matrinka, even without the cat.

Kevral broke in when she believed she understood. "King Cymion wants me to lie with another man."

"He wants you to lie with the prince."

"What?" Clear anger accompanied the word. It was not that Kevral did not like the prince; she had even considered marrying him while the confusion that accompanied pregnancy kept her emotions high and muddled. She would not allow anyone to dictate what she did with her body.

"The king has chosen you to bear the royal heir. All kings and queens of Pudar will descend from your daughter."

"My daughter," Kevral repeated. "I haven't even agreed to this nonsense, and he already knows I'll bear a girl?"

Charra took a deep breath and moved even farther away. This

pressed her back against the musty wall. "If it's not a girl, Lady, you'll have to agree to lie with him again."

Rage overtook Kevral. Her hands clenched on the cage support, metal biting into her palms. "You're all insane. Every damned one of you."

"Lady, I don't like it either. I'm not ready for another baby. Hel, I wasn't ready for this one." Charra pulled a chubby, pink baby from beneath the shroud and passed it into the darkness, clearly to the waiting woman. She tucked Kevral's twin back into place. "But the fate of mankind rests on those of us who are still fertile. If your courses return before you get pregnant again, you can't have any more. Do you understand that?"

"Entirely," Kevral returned. "I'm a warrior, not a prize cow. I have two babies. How many more do I need?"

Charra turned Kevral a withering look. "Are you that selfish, Lady? You love your babies, don't you?"

"Yes." Kevral did not have to consider the answer. The idea of one nearly within reach drove her to distraction.

"Lady, put yourself in the place of the other women. The ones who weep nightly for the baby they can never bear. The breasts that never nourish. The arms that never know the sweet warmth of a child and never hear a soft voice calling, 'Mama.' "

Memory of Colbey's pain resurfaced, and Kevral hardened herself to it. "I didn't cause the plague."

Charra would not back down. "Warriors don't cause wars either, Lady Kevral, but you fight them eagerly enough. Think of this as a battle. You're one of an elite few with the weapon to fight it."

The analogy fell flat for Kevral. "Fertility is not a weapon."

"Lady, in this war, it is the only weapon that can win."

Kevral went silent, refusing to imagine her life as nothing more than a baby-making mechanism. Giving birth was risky; she had heard one in twenty resulted in the mother's death. If she became valuable, they would likely keep her imprisoned forever, to prevent her violent lifestyle from threatening the precious babies or herself.

Apparently, Charra interpreted the silence as Kevral's willingness to listen. "The king's new sages . . ." Charra referred to the elves in this manner, ". . . claim they can detect pregnancy at its earliest stages. You are to lie with the prince until either they detect one or your courses start. At that time, you are free to stay in or leave Pudar with the promise that, if a baby results, you return it here. If it's a healthy female, your obligation is finished. If sickly or a boy, it remains and you agree to lie with the prince under the same terms. In either event, the remainder of your teaching commitment to Pudar is waived. The twins stay as collateral until the new baby is delivered."

Kevral felt as if a fire had kindled in her chest and gradually washed over every part. "And if I don't agree?"

"Lady, you'll leave no choice but to force it upon you, unwilling."

Kevral exploded. "Get out of here, Charra!"

"Lady, the world needs you. If you see it as the honor it is instead of—"

"Get away!" Kevral howled like a war cry. "Leave me alone."

Frightened by the noise, the baby beneath the shroud screamed. Charra cradled it in her arms as she skittered away, and Kevral caught one last glimpse of her son.

Pacing like a caged lion, Kevral watched the shadows swallow up healer and baby, heard the howls fading down the corridor. Her chest ached, as if Charra had spirited away her very heart. The urge to kill seized her, to expend life and rage in a wild flurry of thrust and parry. Instead, she launched into a frenzied kata, imagining a sword with such intensity that it became more real than the bars and the memory of a situation too desperate to contemplate.

For hours, Kevral lunged, whirled, and dodged, until fatigue fully overcame rage. At length, she sat on the cold floor of the cell, trying not to contemplate what she could not change. The extinction of mankind lay in the hands of herself and others. *Let the others carry the burden.* Yet Kevral knew enough about pregnancy to realize that even the most persistent farm women did not produce offspring every cycle. Eventually, they would all fall prey to death or sterility. *One more baby. Two, maybe. Eventually a cycle will slip through, and my responsibility will end.* The idea that King Cymion intended to dictate who fathered the babies stirred the ashes of her anger. *I won't agree to that. He can find another woman to birth his royal bratlings.*

Again footsteps clomped down the hallway. Ire flared anew. Kevral did not want to talk to anyone, not while the burden of a species hung over her and a foolish king tried to dictate the future of her children and her body. She needed time to think out her next course of action, even her next words. Otherwise, she might condemn herself to a dishonorable death and her children to life as orphans. They deserved the right to come before the

Renshai chieftain, who would determine whether they could join the tribe. She would need to argue well to convince them that their fathers' bloodlines would serve, rather than dilute, the race. Only then could she give the boys the names of Renshai who had died in valiant combat who would then become their guardians in Valhalla.

Kevral grabbed the top blanket, hauling it into the center of the cell, then curling up on it. She feigned sleep. Only that night spare her from another round of unreasoning demands and whoever approached from violence.

The footsteps stopped at her cage. Metal clinked a random cadence. When the one who watched neither spoke nor left, Kevral opened one eye a crack.

A guard in a mail shirt knelt in front of her door, a steaming plate of food on the ground beside him, a key in one hand, and a mug of water in the other. A sword hung from a sheath at his left hip.

Kevral watched him with both eyes now as he inserted the key in the lock and twisted. A click snapped through the cell, and his gaze swung toward her. Kevral closed her eyes, remaining still, and the guard continued working. He set the mug down just beyond the door, so it would not spill when the gate pivoted shut. He turned and hefted the food.

Kevral rose and sprang. The guard dropped the plate and whirled, hand rushing to his hilt. Clay shattered against stone, flinging lumps of chicken and beans. Mashed roots splattered the floor and walls. Kevral darted for the opening as the guard shifted to fully fill it. The sword rasped from its sheath.

Unable to check her charge, Kevral nearly impaled herself. She ducked frantically under the hovering blade. Her foot mired in a blob of food, ruining the perfect *nalogtrad*, "needle and thread," Renshai maneuver she intended. The guard pivoted with her, sword speeding toward her again. Regaining her balance, Kevral spun. As the blade whipped for her, she dodged toward the guard, scooting beneath his arm. He followed the motion, and she reversed in an instant. Overshooting her location, he spun in a wild circle that lost him her position for a deadly moment. Kevral bore in, seizing his sword wrist by a well-learned pressure point. His own momentum twisted his wrist. He staggered, trying to rescue his grip on the sword. His foot slammed down on a shard of the plate. The scramble for balance stole attention from his hold. The sword plummeted,

and Kevral snatched it gracefully from the air. She finished with
a lightning head strike.

Terror filled the guard's eyes suddenly with the desperate
certainty of death. His frenzied evasion would not save him

At the last moment, Kevral pulled the strike, though it nearly
cost her her equilibrium as well. *Save your anger for the one
who deserves it.* She leaped backward and into a crouch, expecting the sentry to attempt to regain his sword.

He did not, nor did he run. "Thank you," he managed, gratitude, not fear, holding him in place.

Kevral made no reply, simply charged down the corridor
True to his appreciation, the guard did not announce her escape
with screams or warnings. The hilt in her fist felt heavenly and
as much a part of her as fingers and eyes. She thrilled to its presence, barely swallowing back a howl of fierce joy. Her bare feet
drummed silently against the stone, her step far lighter than the
guard's or Charra's. The two sentries farther up the hallway
scarcely managed to draw swords before she fell upon them
laughing with savage joy.

A single stroke battered both blades aside. She lunged in with
a low attack the larger one barely evaded. Her second offense
crashed against his knee, sprawling him. The hallway funneled
and amplified his screams to an ear-splitting cacophony. The
other swung for Kevral using the maneuver she had demonstrated the previous day. Instead of the leap backward she had
taught them to expect, she drove nearer, forcing him to retreat
When he did, she scurried past.

"Alarm! Alarm!" The sentry's footfalls and voice chased her
down the corridor.

Bastard. Kevral considered killing him to teach him a lesson
but the thought passed quickly. *And what lesson would I be
teaching him? How to bleed?* Instead, she quickened her pace
soon reaching a set of stone-cut stairs. She raced upward, taking
them two at a time. Halfway up, another figure blocked her exit
Tired of the game, the fires of anger growing with each encounter, she gave him a low growl of warning. "Out of my
way."

The guard did not budge. He, too, wielded a sword, true to
her teachings. As she rushed toward him, he executed a fluid
stop-thrust. Kevral cut beneath it with an angry jab he parried
wildly with more desperate luck than skill. The steps gave him
little chance for retreat. Behind her, Kevral could hear the other
sentry pounding toward her. "Move, you idiot."

To his credit, he answered only with another slice toward Kevral's chest. She evaded it with a swift sidestep. Her sword rove under his, trapping it. She scurried to his left, kicking the back of his knee. He staggered. She gave him a shove that sent him plummeting down the stairs. Ducking around a flailing arm, she sprinted up the final steps to a heavy oak door with a single barred window. Behind her, she heard the slam of bodies careening downward, the first guard sweeping the second with him.

Kevral seized the latch and tugged. The door did not move. *Damn!* Kevral yanked harder, then thrust against it. The panel still did not budge. Rage flared into a bonfire. "Let me out! Damn you all to the pits, let me out of here!" She hacked at the door, chopping splinters that scarcely marred the surface. A face appeared at the window, withdrawing in a wild scramble as her sword slammed the bars. "Open! This! Door!"

"Settle down," the man said with infuriating calm. Then, to a companion Kevral could not see, he instructed. "Inform the king."

"Yes," Kevral snarled. "Inform the king I'm going to cut his heart out." Footsteps tapped rapidly along the outer corridor. A thought slipped past the seething boil her thoughts had become. *The guards will have the key.* She spun, surprised the sentries in the prison had not already followed her up the stairs. Whirling, she clambered back to the bottom corridor. The guards were nowhere in sight. *Huh?* She stormed through the hallways, looking left and right for some sign of the men. She found them near the place where she had bruised one's knee. All four occupied the farthest wall of a cell, three standing and the last clutching his leg and moaning.

Kevral grabbed the door to their cell and pulled. It shifted minimally, metal clanking against metal. Kevral stared, surprise temporarily breaking through rage. "You locked yourselves in here?"

"Standard procedure," one explained. "Keeps out-of-control prisoners from killing anyone until reinforcements arrive."

"I'm not out of control," Kevral said through gritted teeth. "If I were, you'd all be dead."

The one Kevral fought on the stairs spoke next. "In control, huh? I guess I missed the moment we constrained you."

Kevral wished she had not started the semantics argument. "Just give me the keys." She held out a hand.

None of the guards moved. Except for the one on the ground they simply stared back.

Kevral shifted her gaze to the one who had thanked her.

He shook his head sadly. "I'd rather die on a Renshai's sword than be executed for treason. Either way, I die. One dishonors my loyalty and my family."

Kevral glared. "Slow and painful is in my repertoire."

King Cymion's voice snapped suddenly through the corridor. "Swordmistress!"

Every head swung toward the sound, including Kevral's.

"I understand you wish to speak with me."

No. What I wish to do is cut your fool head off. "My second choice. I'll take it." The voice had come from the staircase, and Kevral headed back that way. Soon she reached the bottom and started up the steps.

King Cymion's face swayed in the barred window. "Kevral?"

"I'm here," Kevral replied, deliberately leaving off the "Sire." She eased up the stairs, hoping the king's first view of her would be the deadly earnest promise of murder in her eyes.

Cymion eased back as she approached. "Swordmistress, return to your cell, and we'll discuss this rationally."

"There's nothing to discuss." Kevral resisted the urge to spit. The king's plans left a bitter taste in her parched mouth. "I heard your intentions. I'll suffer none of them."

"Kevral." Cymion used a commanding tone that usually quailed his guards. "Let me explain."

"Explain it to yourself. My answer is 'no.'"

Rage deepened Cymion's voice. A critical situation, and an unreasonable audience, drove him beyond the polite composure he always displayed in the courtroom. "I am the king."

"That doesn't give you the right to violate me, you bastard."

Cymion's eyes flashed with a fire as intense as Kevral's own. "It gives me the right to do as I please. And you *will* address me as 'Sire.'"

"Or what?" Kevral shot back.

The king gave the only answer he could. "Or I'll have you executed."

Kevral grinned and played her only card, "You won't do that. You need me."

"True." Cymion hesitated only a moment before returning Kevral's insolent smile, thoughts as ugly as her own taking shape behind it. She had underestimated his desperation. "But I don't need your sons. If you don't do as I say, I'll have them killed. Thirst will weaken you long before it will my guards down there, and I'll still get what I want. Your babies will die in vain."

"You wouldn't." Kevral swallowed hard, Cymion's words reminding her she needed a drink. She had lost a large amount of blood birthing two babies. "Sire."

"Return to your cell. When the guards have you locked in, they'll report back here. You'll get as much food and water as you want. Then, we'll talk some more."

Kevral remained rooted in place. She could either condemn her children to death or sacrifice her own freedom. The choice was none at all. Without another word, she turned and headed down the steps. Docilely, she walked back to her cage, tears of anger hot in her eyes. For now, the king had won. Somehow, eventually, she vowed to turn that victory against him. Head low, she dragged past the caged guards, mumbling as she did so, "Lock me in, damn it."

The sentries' gazes trailed her into her cell. Finally, one spoke. "Just pull your door shut. Hard."

Kevral wrapped her fingers around the door, hesitating. Once she slammed it, she would trap herself into a nearly intolerable situation. She felt certain the guards would use more caution when feeding her in the future. Her only hope lay with Prince Leondis. If she could get him into a compromising situation, with or without his cooperation, the king might bargain his own son for hers. She shoved the panel outward, and the lock clicked into place.

Only then, the guards freed themselves from the cage. One remained with the injured man while the others approached cautiously. "Hand out the sword."

"No." Kevral clung to her only comfort. She knew the king could wrest it from her with the same threat, but she would not surrender the weapon until he did so.

The speaker sighed, then turned to his companion. "Head up and ask whichever superior you find what we should do about the sword."

The guard rushed to obey, passing the third sentry who was assisting their limping associate toward the exit. Kevral recognized the Pudarian remaining near her as the one who had chased her up the stairs. Alone, he showed her a look of sympathy that bordered on pity. "Swordmistress, I don't know what you did, but I do appreciate all I've learned since you came here."

Too distracted for a thank you, Kevral only nodded.

Shortly, his companion returned. "His Majesty said to let her keep it." He glanced at Kevral as he shrugged. "We're to return to our posts, and they'll send another down to replace Brunar."

Kevral hefted the mug of water the guard had left and drank, licking the last few drops off the side. It barely moistened her mouth, sparking a thirst excitement had mostly kept at bay. She shoved the empty container through the bars, hoping the king intended to keep his promise. She wondered for the sanity of the king's decision to allow her to keep the weapon; but, for now, she did not scrutinize the windfall. Surely, he eventually planned to claim it from her. In the meantime, she would use it to the utmost.

Rising, Kevral pitched into another frenzied practice. Exhaustion weighted her limbs, and thirst disrupted concentration. She forced herself past physical discomforts, into a prayerful trance. The same Renshai mental techniques that had kept the agony of active labor at bay now did the same for the needs for sleep, food, and water. She dedicated herself to the religious experience that was combat, giving self and skill to the god and goddess of Renshai. Despite postpartum weakness, despite blood loss and the rabid boil of emotions that had swept through her since the birth of her children, she gave her all to the practice, seeking enlightenment in *svergelse* where she had found none in logic. The sword skipped around her, the very definition of dexterity. Her lithe body spiraled, capered, and reached. In a whirl as primal as flame, she explained her situation to the deities, seeking their assistance through faith and wisdom.

Kevral's head buzzed, and exhaustion skidded across her limbs as if turning her to stone. Her best practice ever crumpled gradually, battering through the mental defenses she had woven. She clung to those long after they failed her, plunging her world into darkness. The realization that the king had drugged her water flitted briefly across her thoughts before she collapsed and knew nothing more.

CHAPTER 36

Urgent Solutions

Urgent problems need urgent solutions.
                                        —*Colbey Calistinsson*

Kerval awakened to a pounding headache, and her tongue stuck
to the roof of her mouth. Her lashes peeled apart, stretching
tears that had dried nearly to glue. She worked her tongue free.
It seemed to rasp over her cracked lips. She reached to wipe her
eyes clear. Her right hand jarred, stopped after minimal movement, and pain flashed through her wrist. She scrabbled for her
sword with her left, only to find it similarly trapped above her
head. Her legs would not obey her either.

What now? Kevral rolled her eyes, taking in as much of her
cell as that allowed. She recognized the patchy discolorations of
the dungeon ceiling above her. Bars filled her vision. Straw
stabbed into her back, poking through the ticking that enclosed
it. A pillow beneath her head broadened her view but also stiffened her neck. Shackles encircled wrists and ankles. A blanket
covered her, protecting her skin from the draft that caressed her
face at intervals. She could feel the fabric's weave against her
otherwise naked flesh. *No.* Too weak to fight, she lay still. The
king's desperation went even beyond her own.

The clink of metal rings sounded just beyond her sight,
surely the movement of a mailed guard. Kevral did not bother
to look. She did not want to know who saw her at a time of ultimate humiliation. She berated herself for her surrender. *I
should have battled to my death.* Yet even now her heart longed
for the twins, the one she had not seen and the one she had. For
them, she would suffer in silence.

Booted footfalls retreated down the corridor. Clearly, he had
orders to inform someone when Kevral awakened. She closed
her eyes and waited, hoping Cymion would not come to gloat.
She had borne more than her share of shame for one day.

An eternity seemed to pass before steps again filled the hall.

The lock clicked, and the squeal of hinges followed. Opening her eyes, Kevral rolled her head toward the intruder.

As she turned, the other dropped politely to her level, acutely attuned to her discomfort. Towering over her would only have heightened the dishonor. She recognized the long dark hair and soft blue eyes at once. The prince of Pudar had come.

Kevral looked away. "Don't touch me." She added emphatically and with intense distaste, "Sire."

"Kevral." Pain tinged Leondis' voice. "I brought you some water."

Kevral closed her eyes, needing what he offered. If she died of thirst, she would damn herself to Hel. So long as she remained alive, she could find a way to die fighting and in honor. And exact revenge. Opening her eyes, she whipped her neck back toward him, immediately wishing she had not. The sudden movement crushed dizziness down upon her and ached through her head. "What kind of drug is in it this time? Something to make me your willing slave?"

Leondis accepted the hostility without comment. "It's just water. I filled it myself." Hefting a waterskin, he poured clear liquid into a mug.

The sight of it sparked need. Kevral's parched lips parted, and she cursed the mortal weakness.

Leondis raised the mug, then hesitated. "I'm going to have to support your head. May I?"

Like I could refuse. "Do as you please," Kevral said.

The prince placed a gentle arm around her head, lifting it to the mug. Kevral sucked down the contents in an instant. He repeated the maneuver three more times before Kevral finally felt satisfied.

"Enough," Kevral said. The word had many references.

Leondis placed mug and waterskin aside. "There's more if you need it. And I brought food as well." He skittered back to her side and sat.

Kevral returned a penetrating stare through eyes burned and bleary. "Do I get that before or after you rape me?"

Leondis cringed. "Kevral, please. Don't make this any harder."

"It's only hard for me."

Prince Leondis sighed. He reached up a hand, as if to brush a stray hair from Kevral's forehead. Catching himself in midgesture, he withdrew. "You're wrong. I don't like it either."

"Then don't do it."

"And let the best fertile woman in Pudar go sterile?"

Kevral had the perfect solution. "I didn't say I refused to have another baby. I can be talked into that. Let me free, and I'll choose a father."

Leondis ran a hand through his dark hair, then let it cascade back around his face. "You think my father trusted me with the key?"

"You're the crown prince."

Leondis replaced the canteen in a sack, then pulled out a loaf of brown bread and an apple. "And this is too important to my father." He drew out a jar containing a purple spread. "Kevral, you have to understand that whether or not mankind has a future depends on you and a handful of others."

"Charra made that point well enough."

"I'm sure you can think of worse men than me." With a utility knife taken from his belt, Leondis cut a slice of bread and spread it thickly with the purple substance.

"You mean, like your father," Kevral fairly hissed.

Leondis shrugged. His patience showed no sign of waning, despite having admitted he was accustomed to immediate satisfaction of his demands. "I won't convince you, but he really is a good man. The people uniformly like him, which is difficult enough for any king." Leondis shook his head, clearly frustrated by the need to detail what seemed obvious to him. "Historically, disruption of even a hated king's line results in chaos. People lose direction and faith. Wars over the crown ensue. Our line has done well for Pudar for centuries. It's only natural for the king to want to perpetuate it." He offered the bread.

Though starved, Kevral had to ask the question first, "Why at my expense?"

The bread hovered. "Because, as I said, you're the best fertile woman in Pudar. He can't settle for less. And I think he still hopes you'll decide to stay."

The suggestion seemed ridiculous. "After this?"

Leondis rolled his pale eyes. "You know you couldn't, and I know you won't. Just so it gets said, he promised that, if you stay until the baby's born, you'll get to raise the twins."

He'll let me mother my own children. How generous. Kevral kept the thought to herself this once. As Cymion had said, he could do as he pleased. The current arrangement assured she would not see her boys until they were at least nine months old. "He's not serious about keeping my babies." She glanced at Leondis, wishing she looked less vulnerable. "Is he?"

"Can you think of a better way to assure you bring his granddaughter back?" Leondis raised the bread to Kevral's mouth again.

"You taste it first."

Without hesitation, Leondis took a big bite. "Grape preserves. The best."

Kevral surrendered to the protests of her gut. The spread tasted sweet, a delicate contrast to the yeasty flavor of fresh bread. No food had ever tasted better. She spoke between bites. "So, there's nothing else I can say? You *are* going to rape me."

The prince waited until Kevral finished the entire piece. He rose from his hunkered position near her head and finally dragged away that errant hair from her forehead with a warm, easy touch. "Kevral, I won't hurt you. Whether it's lovemaking or rape depends wholly on you." He met her gaze with compassion, awaiting an answer Kevral did not feel ready to give. When she said nothing for several moments, he returned his attention to the bread, cutting her another piece and smearing on more of the preserves. "It's unfortunate but true, Kevral, that you've become as valuable to the world as you've been for Pudar's guards. We need you now, not as a teacher, but as mother to the world."

"Le," Kevral finally said.

A smile flickered across the prince's features, then disappeared. He looked up. "Yes?"

"Can I have one more night to think this over. To get used to the idea before we . . . start?"

Kevral read definite relief on Leondis' face. He did not want to inflict this on her any more than she wanted it. In a way, he was bound, too, though his chains were invisible. "I have no problem with that. Eat. Talk. Let me know how I can make this as easy on you as possible."

His words failed to soothe. Kevral spoke little, eating until her stomach felt queasy, then slipped into an anxious sleep.

Tae swept from the meeting room with an irritation that lengthened his stride. Momentum pushed back black hair now hacked short, and the cold touch of air at the base of his neck made him feel unprotected, vulnerable. Usually, Weile and Tae found compromise with minimal argument. Tae's compassion tempered his father's experience and wisdom, and Weile's eye for strategy turned Tae's wildest suggestions into viable alternatives. This time, discussion had become shouting, then lapsed into name-calling that, mercifully at least, could not include the usual jabs at mother and family. That realizaton had given Tae an idea; and he had ended the session with an insult, aimed at himself, that rebounded perfectly: "My father is an idiot!" He took some solace in the knowledge that he had left Weile Kahn laughing.

But the matter they had argued over would not leave Tae's mind so swiftly. The return message from Pudar revealed their new association with elves and the details of women spared by the infertility plague. Within days, every fruitful woman in the Eastlands became a ward of the king.

Those married were awarded housing for self and family near the castle, their babies raised either by themselves or by sterile women chosen by their husbands, depending partially on choice and partially on a formula Tae had not studied carefully enough to understand. Babies born of rape or single mothers were awarded to worthy couples. Men found opportunity to become fathers based on acts of loyalty to the kingdom.

The entire arrangement stabbed at Tae's conscience until it felt raw with guilt. He imagined the unwed women, their world narrowed to the third floor north wing of Stalmize Castle, their fate certain. Now the property of the king, they would carry infants until their wombs failed or childbirth killed them. He imagined himself as a young girl, not yet even of age, forced to lie with strangers and bear babies for others to raise. Tears stung his dark eyes, and he retreated deeper inside himself. For several moments, a frightened female child trod the corridors in Tae's place. Words, responsibility, and sensations he could barely comprehend bombarded him from all sides, a ceaseless attack of terror that drove him into a wild run for freedom. *Are a few extra generations of mankind worth the torture inflicted on innocents?*

Tae shook off this new role, eager to return to self and shocked that he had discovered sympathy so shallowly buried. The streets taught boys and girls to trust no one, to do nothing that did not directly benefit self. No matter their occupation, or fate, his parents had trained him better, instilling deeper lessons than he realized. He wondered if he had inherited the ability to place himself in others' places from his father and if the skill accounted for Weile's talent at organizing and rallying those whom most dismissed as hopeless.

Tae's thoughts brought him to the north staircase, and he climbed with trepidation. His father insisted that the arrangement pleased the vast majority of Eastlanders; near unanimity was a rarity he could not sacrifice for the Western values of an individual, even his only and much-trusted son. Tae intended to hear the women's viewpoint and to force it upon Weile as well. Perhaps, if the leader of the Eastlands heard their stories, it might trigger the same mercy that haunted Tae. Weile might come to realize the hardship he inflicted on them and find a better solution. *And what would that solution be?* Tae could hear his father's voice in his head, but his heart gave him no answers yet.

A pair of guards stood in the stairwell, in front of the third floor north wing door. Their rigid demeanors and unfamiliar faces revealed them as castle regulars trained by royalty and now happily in service to the man who'd brought the Eastlands peace. Apparently, they recognized Tae as he had not them. Each nodded, leather helmet shifting in acknowledgment, and they stepped quietly aside. Tae continued past them without comment, not knowing what to say. He wrenched open the door, hinges creaking, to reveal a festive hallway decorated with wildly unmatched pictures and amateur murals, most only partially finished. Doors on each side interrupted the corridor at regular intervals. A few women whirled toward the sound, then disappeared into openings like ants scrambling for burrows when a stone is overturned.

Tae closed the door behind him, then looked into a now-empty hallway. Eyes studied him from around doorway corners, and whispers spattered throughout the wing. He cleared his throat, the sound carving a loud echo, as if through a tunnel. Giggles followed, then a noisy shushing sound.

Tae suppressed an urge to tiptoe and headed carefully down the corridor. Women, many much younger than his own nineteen years, retreated into the darkness of rooms as he drew near. Even without looking back, he could tell by the shuffle of movement that most slipped right back to their doors as he passed. Soon, he realized the hallway would end in an enormous common room. Voices wafted from it in normal waves of conversation. The women there had, apparently, not yet noticed the intruder.

Soon the hallway filled with quiet footsteps behind Tae. He pretended not to notice as a host of women followed him toward their meeting place. His back prickled, long habit raising alarm. Though he knew they would not harm him, the idea of a horde behind him as he approached a dead end sent every nerve into jangling awareness. The need to glance at them became all-consuming; still, he resisted.

At length, Tae's long walk brought him to the entrance of the common room, and he looked over a disarray of stools, chests, and benches. Dark-haired women of myriad shapes and sizes had broken into comfortable groups. Most chatted. Others worked on the floor or at the few desks. A group of eight played cards at a rickety table. Tae counted nearly a hundred. As he turned to enter, finally letting his gaze play over those trailing him, he counted a like number in the hallway. All but a few sported the standard Eastern swarthy features and dark eyes. Many were round with child, though others carried only a subtle bulge or nothing at all to indicate pregnancy. They ranged in age from a child who seemed about twelve to a woman well into middle age. None looked particularly frightened or worried, their actions more curious than afraid.

The eldest looked up from a tiny sweater she knitted. "Hello, sir. Are you looking for someone specific?"

A group of young adolescents giggled, silenced by their companions' glares.

"No," Tae admitted. "I came to talk with all of you."

The speaker gave him a narrow-eyed look. "Are you favored by the king, sir?"

Even after four months, Tae could not get used to the title. Weile called himself a leader, never king. *Not at the moment.* "I'm his son. Tae—"

Whispers traversed the women, again swiftly silenced. Several dropped to their knees, then others followed in a disorganized wave. The speaker set aside her knitting, rising awkwardly. "Your pardon, Sire."

Tae suddenly wished he had not revealed himself. "Please, no." He gestured frantically. "Up! Up! Don't do this." For the first time, he understood why formality embarrassed Matrinka. "Act as you were, please."

Raggedly, the women obeyed. Their heads bobbed as they examined every part of him.

Beneath the intense scrutiny, Tae realized several things. First, by identifying himself, he had probably made it impossible to win their confidence. Second, they surely expected him to select a bride or, worse, just a breeder. And, third, he suddenly felt intensely edgy. Trying to salvage as much of the situation as he could, he selected an empty crate and sat. "My father didn't send me. I came to ask after your comfort."

Several women answered at once, everyone asserting joy and great honor.

Tae raised his hands, and they all quieted. "You don't understand. I want your honesty. Any complaints? I want to hear about them. No one will be punished in any fashion for candor."

Again, sundry voices alleged satisfaction. A ring tightened around him, a few touching him not-quite accidentally. Wedded to realism, Tae knew they were not attracted to his irresistible beauty. They loved his title, not himself, the honor of carrying the "prince's" baby.

Tae sighed, mentally kicking himself for his mistake. "No one is happy all the time. Please. Someone gripe about something."

Silence ensued, broken by a woman in her twenties who edged forward hesitantly. "I . . ." She glanced around for support. "Sire, I don't care for the way the cook prepares the peas. Too much *erenspice*."

A few nodded agreement.

Tae smiled. "Good." *A start, at least.* "But drop the 'sire.' Just call me Tae Kahn."

One of the youngest piped up in a squeaky voice. "Hate sharin' quarters with Zeldar. She acts like my mama."

A thirtyish woman, apparently Zeldar, glared at the speaker. Other complaints surfaced: "We need more red paint." "I gotta pee all the time." "Monika cheats at cards." "My legs are swollen, and the healers can't do nothing about it." "The man I picked gets rough sometimes."

The last earned the derision of her companions. Several sneered. One shouted, more child or doll than woman, abdomen enormous above legs like twigs. "You ain't knowin' rough. You ain't never been buggered by six bassards in a dirty alley."

Though Tae was no stranger to violence, the image the child's words conjured awakened outrage. "No, don't stop her. That's the sort of thing I want to know."

The knitting elder whose name, he discovered, was Niko, spoke, "The men we sleep with are interesting to you?"

"No." Tae watched the tide of women shift around him. The contacts continued, despite his obvious quest for something other than a wife. "I want to know if you feel like prisoners here. If it's freedom you wish, I'll do my best to see you get it."

Tae's words disappeared into a hush electric with tension. A child a year or two younger than Kevral started sobbing. Believing his words had touched her, Tae rose and walked to her side, women parting in front of him like water. The girl on the bench beside her moved away, and Tae sat, placing a comforting arm around her shoulders.

She flinched, head jerking suddenly upward and moist eyes dodging his gaze. "You can't send me back." She gasped for a breath, and her demands softened to desperate pleas. Sliding from the bench, she threw herself at his feet. "Sire, I beg you. Please don't make me leave."

Stunned, Tae found himself incapable of movement. He glanced at the nearest woman, who shrugged then indicated the pleader's belly. "Her own father's."

The cruelty inherent in such an act flashed anger through Tae again. He glanced around the room, seeing fear in many eyes that he had not noticed at the time of his arrival. "I'm not sending anyone away who wants to stay. Even if I wished to, I don't have the authority."

One of the women helped the crying girl back onto the bench. She calmed noticeably, though quiet tears still glided from dark eyes.

"Isn't there anyone who longs for freedom?"

The women spoke among themselves. Finally, Niko addressed Tae. "You don't understand what it's like out there." She made a sweeping gesture intended to include every Eastern street. "Rape. Murder. Both. Violence against women is no crime."

"We're working on that," Tae promised. Memories returned in a rush, suppressed from his own youth. During his time on the streets, survival had obsessed him. The idea of harming others had never entered his thoughts, though he knew many of those who served his father had started in exactly that fashion. He imagined how much worse matters might have become in recent weeks, frustrated men rationalizing rape and incest in the name of preserving their own perceived, unique qualities. In the West, he hoped, such a thing could never happen.

"It's safer here," someone piped up from the back. "And we're treated well. I'd carry eight babies at once if I thought it would keep me here longer."

Nods traversed the group.

Tae abandoned his preconceived ideas. He selected one woman at random, a thin adult who had apparently already delivered her baby and now worked toward another. "But what about your child?"

"I miss her terribly," she admitted, yet she smiled. "I've met her parents. Her father is gentle and loving. Her mother understands the precious gift a baby is because she'll never have one of her own. I've never seen people so happy, and I know *their* baby will be happy, too." The grin broadened. "No act in life so proves a woman's love as sacrificing her own joy for the welfare of the child she bears. Condemn her to my life?" She shook her head at the very thought. "Keeping that baby would have been the most selfish evil I could commit."

The woman's sincerity was undeniable. Tae believed he liked the change in attitude. When he lived among the gangs, most considered a baby a woman's punishment for sex, whether consenting or inflicted. No one considered the needs of the infant.

The sad stories continued, as well as the affirmations about the best interests of the children. Reacclimatization to the culture of the East saddened Tae to the reality at the same time bringing understanding. Several did describe happy childhoods and marriages that included gentle Eastern husbands and fathers who little resembled the predators who stalked the streets. Yet, Tae realized, he had deliberately chosen the wing of the unmarried. Widowed, raped, and/or orphaned, these women had become as desperate as those born to the streets. Few without a Renshai's strength and abilities would choose the life they once led over the luxuries and protection of Stalmize Castle.

And Tae was forced to suffer the bane of any nineteen-year-old's life: this time, at least, his father was right.

After a morning of discussing normal castle affairs into yawning detail, King Griff was happy to see the three elves entering Béarn's courtroom, even had he not recognized Tem-'aree'ay among them. The grin that filled the female's features made him giddy. The males fairly danced down the central carpetway, bounding like excited children. The guards shifted, discomforted by the oddness of their approach, but a smile pulled at the corners of Griff's enormous mouth. He had spent enough time with the *lysalf* to know that this was their natural state, the sedate shyness they adopted around most humans the peculiarity. It pleased him that they felt comfortable enough in his presence to slip into their normal demeanor.

At the foot of the dais, the two sentries who accompanied them waved to them to stop. Obeying, the males bowed and Tem'aree'ay curtsied.

At Griff's right, Darris remained still. To his left, Captain

eiryn watched the elves intently. Griff leaned forward, unable
to remove the silly grin. "What can I do for you?"

The elf to Tem'aree'ay's left, Eth'morand, turned sapphire-
colored eyes on the king. A blond mop of hair fell across his
eyes and in a shaggy mane to his back. "Majesty, our people
thought you should know that another *lysalf* will soon join us."

Griff recalled how the *lysalf* came among them, by abandoning Dh'arlo'mé's command. "Those who leave darkness for
light will always be welcome in Béarn. I will have servants prepare quarters for the new arrival."

The smiles on all three elfin faces broadened, though a moment before Griff would not have believed that possible. The
other male, as dark-haired as his companion was light, spoke
now, "Sire, thank you for your hospitality. But the new arrival
can share quarters with his mother." He indicated Tem'aree'ay.

The king's eyes zipped to those of his closest friend. He
scarcely dared to believe she had never mentioned she had children. His smile wilted, destroyed by the realization that they did
not know one another as well as he once believed. Surely, she
realized he adored the younglings. "I wasn't aware you were a
mother, Tem'aree'ay." He tried to hold sadness from his tone.
She might misinterpret it, believing that her offspring would
distance him.

"I'm not, Sire." Tem'aree'ay clearly did not take offense, the
smile still plastered on her angular features. "Yet."

Eth'morand sent *khohlar.* First came a concept of deep respect, followed by apology for the method of communication.
Lav'rintir said he explained elfin reproduction. Another impression followed, that of cautious joy, tainted by knowledge.
*We do not know which elf died of age. Lav'rintir is eldest, but
he has outlived scores. We worry for a competition with the
svartalf.* Understanding accompanied the words. Griff came to
realize the extent of that worry: whether the infant would turn
svartalf if his soul came from that pool. The male knew a desperate concern. If *lysalf* and *svartalf* competed for souls, they
might find it worth sacrificing a portion of the pool to keep the
lysalf from "stealing" the infants. Elfin war could result. He
fretted also over the possibility that Captain had died.

Oblivious to the *khohlar,* Darris nudged King Griff. "Sire, he
means she's having a baby," he whispered.

An elf baby. Yes, I knew that. A pang of jealousy speared
through Griff, though it felt as ludicrous as crying over a colt
born to a well-loved mare. He spoke aloud. "Congratulations,

lysalf. We'll have a feast, of course. The population will be ec
static, though a bit envious, I'm afraid." He did not mention tha
he spoke for himself as well.

All three elves shook their heads slightly. Resentment did no
exist in their culture, at least it had not before Dh'arlo'mé'
reign of terror.

Tem'aree'ay's mental voice touched Griff next. *Did Eth'
morand explain his concerns?*

Unable to return the *khohlar,* Griff returned a discreet nod
*They are immaterial. No one died for this baby. It can onl
be yours.*

Griff gasped, and all eyes shifted to him. As one, the guard
stiffened: Darris and Seiryn crouched, seeking a nonexisten
threat. Griff's mind went back to a night only a week ago
Tem'aree'ay's casually open sexuality had resulted in innocen
exploration. The anatomy proved enough like human's for cou
pling, yet it had never occurred to him that offspring could re
sult. Myriad questions clambered for attention at once. *Hov
could Tem'aree'ay know so soon? How does she know it'
mine? Is it human or elfin?* For the moment, his thoughts re
fused to run further.

Eth'morand bowed. "Thank you, Sire." He sent, *I only hop
our mourning will not disrupt the feasting. For us, death alway
precedes life.*

Not this time. Griff wished he could share their silent com
munication. More than air, he needed Tem'aree'ay's explana
tion.

The three elves turned, still grinning, and headed up the car
petway. Tem'aree'ay sent one last message, *Yes, I'm certain
Please, come to my quarters when you're free, and I'll explain
I hope you're not angry.*

Anything but, my love. Griff could scarcely wait for his mo
ments of freedom from the court. For now, he suffered mostl
desperate confusion.

CHAPTER 37

Compromise

I make my decisions as quickly as an eye blink, and the more important the decision, the faster I have to make it. I make my choices on the battlefield. Since I'm still alive, I've obviously never once made a mistake.

—Colbey Calistinsson

ontrolled by threat as well as chains, Kevral allowed Pudar's ison guards to move her to a cell at the far end of the dungeon. s odd system of pulleys and slots allowed her nearly full range movement, but whenever the door cranked open for feeding other visitation, the chains tightened, jerking her off her feet pin her helplessly against a granite wall. A square hole, too nall to admit her shoulders, vented the prison. Cool air fun-led through, chilling the shackles that pinched her wrists and ikles, the metallic coldness aching against bone and flesh.

Despite the indignity and discomfort, Kevral found her new iarters a relief. At least, most times, she could move freely. he guards who had accompanied her there promised that some f her personal belongings would follow, surely those things ie could not turn into weapons to use against prince, sentries, r self. She had never considered herself attached to objects, yet ie knew a flutter of emptiness at the loss of some. The missing vords pained the most, a suffering she could bear no more isily than the sacrifice of her own arms. She thought of the his-rical book about Colbey that Tae had gifted, stolen, and re-irned. She also missed his other presents: a carven figurine of ie most famous of Renshai riding into battle, and the strange, reen gem that was Dh'arlo'mé's missing eye. Visions of the rime lord's son drifted into her mind now: long, black hair a iagnet for twigs, leaves, and dirt; his eyes containing an evi-ent spark of wit; the dangerous features that concealed a gen-e caring few understood. She wondered, as she had so many

times before, whether he had ever made peace with his fathe
and, if so, what that peace had bought him.

Thoughts of others followed swiftly: Ra-khir's unsparin
face filled her mind's eye next, his green eyes holding a promis
of eternal love. She saw Matrinka and Mior, Darris and Grif
Captain and his many followers. She missed them all an
Kevral realized mournfully, she might never see them agai

The train of thought gained Kevral nothing, only added to th
sense of helplessness that had never before seemed within he
Renshai repertoire. She sought solace where she'd alway
found it in the past, springing into a wild flurry of *svergels*
Reasonably well fed and watered, now a night beyond chil
birth, she found more strength than at her previous practic
Again, she dedicated self and swordplay to the deities of Ren
shai, a frenzied whirlwind of prayer that begged direction. Sh
had seen waves bashing against Béarn's cliffs, had heard of
volcano that hurled tons of rock for miles. She patterned herse
after these, seeking the unbridled strength they represented.

Chain clattered against granite with every movement, an
the edges of the manacles carved skin from Kevral's wrists. A
before, her gaze etched a sword-form from the dank shadows o
Pudar's dungeon, tricking her mind into accepting its realit
The blade skipped through the air, weaving through imagine
defenses and cutting enemies who now all bore the likeness o
King Cymion. All except one. As Kevral pirouetted through
complicated Renshai maneuver, a lithe human figure appeare
amid the army of Cymions. Feathered blond hair barely move
though the sinewy muscles arched and thrust in a ceaseless mo
tion that stopped Kevral in mid-lunge and held her spellboun

Then, icy blue-gray eyes met hers, and the warrior who ex
actly resembled Colbey leaped toward her with an animal snar
of challenge. His sword jabbed toward her, trailing a multicol
ored wake of sparks. She jerked hers upward, a clumsy but ef
fective parry. Less than a heartbeat later, he jerked free an
sliced for her head. Kevral dodged, her foot slamming down o
a chain that bruised her instep. Pain incited anger. Changin
strategy in that instant, she rammed forward with a blazing as
sault on Colbey's neck. Suddenly defensive, he retreated with
laugh of fierce joy. A moment later, he had the upper han
again, but Kevral would never forget the bare instant she ha
dazzled Colbey Calistinsson.

Colbey waded back in with a brilliant in-and-out attack tha
left Kevral with an aching hip and no visual memory of th

ike. He disengaged only a moment before diving back in with
low feint, followed by a high feint, then a sweep that caught
r recovering too late. The side of his sword crashed against
r ear. Kevral staggered, tripped over a chain, and slammed to
e stone floor. She rolled, avoiding the blade intended to pin
r, though the maneuver stamped link-shaped wounds across
r spine. Colbey's tip cut the imaginary sword from her hand.
nce it left her grip, it disappeared, and he did not even bother
make a motion as if to catch it.

Kevral scrambled to her feet. "You're really here, aren't
u?" The realization made her sick. Embarrassed for the hu-
iliation her hero witnessed, she lowered her head and avoided
s eyes.

"I'm really here," Colbey admitted, sheathing his sword. He
anced around the cell.

"I shouldn't have let this happen," Kevral whispered. "A
enshai fights to his last ragged breath."

"A Renshai," Colbey corrected, "also knows when to fight
s battles and which ones to fight."

Kevral's brow furrowed, and she rolled her eyes upward to
atch him from peripheral vision. "Are you telling me there are
mes when Renshai may run from battle?" The words seemed
o impossible to speak aloud.

"I'm telling you that there are times when a Renshai may
void battle, when other solutions would serve better." Colbey
aused, apparently awaiting some confirmation or sign of un-
erstanding. When none followed, he continued. "Such as
hen an enraged student, friend, or family member attempts to
ill him. Such as when a worthy opponent would prove a better
ly than foe."

Kevral nodded, grasping his meaning but seeing no analogy
her own situation. "But Cymion is neither friend nor worthy."

Colbey walked to Kevral's side, kicked away loops of chain,
d guided her to the floor. He crouched beside her. "Kevral, let
e tell you a story about a Renshai warrior I knew named
ashi. One more dedicated to war and the tenets of our people,
u could not have found. One day, we opened a door to a semi-
rcle of enemy archers. Vashi threw herself on them without
inking. She died full of arrows, striking not a single blow of
r own. She was the only casualty on our side."

Kevral reveled in her hero's attention, though she did not be-
eve she fully understood his point. "She died bravely."

"Bravely, yes," Colbey concurred. "But without honor. Her

sword claimed no lives. She missed the savage joy of battle tha
the rest of us not only savored, but survived. It was not her ac
tions I condemn, but her timing. Our enemy had set up that si
uation to talk. Things might have turned out differently if w
had." A catch in his voice suggested that he wished they had
but he did not elaborate.

Kevral finally shed enough embarrassment to look at Colbe
"You're telling me to wait for the proper moment to fight Kin
Cymion."

Colbey shrugged, evasive.

"But, when I'm carrying his grandchild, it'll be too late."

"Will it?"

The question struck Kevral dumb. She had never considere
it otherwise.

"I'm not omnipotent, Kevral. If you want me to understan
the situation, you'll have to explain it."

Kevral complied, describing her problem, mostly in genera
terms while Colbey listened silently, his face displaying noth
ing judgmental.

He waited until she finished before speaking. "So the healer
want you to keep your fertility. The king wants you to produc
an heir . . ."

"A *female* heir," Kevral corrected. Sudden realization drov
a gasp from her. "Gods, I think I finally figured out why the
want a girl."

"Because, since the plague affects females, a boy woul
leave them with the same dilemma they have now."

"I'll bet they're planning to . . ." Kevral found herself unabl
to say the words. She made a noise of disgust. "No daughter o
mine is going to become a tool for incest."

Colbey did not need the thought spelled out. His mental pow
ers made such unnecessary, and Kevral's fear that they woul
marry or, at least, breed the girl back to Leondis seemed obvi
ous. "I understand what the healers want. And what the kin
wants. Kevral, what do *you* want?"

"I want my freedom. I want my sons." Kevral's eyes nar
rowed. "And I want Cymion's head tumbling off the end of m
sword."

Colbey sighed, the sound grim with impatience. "All righ
I'll rephrase that. Which of your current options do you want?

Kevral did not understand.

"It comes down to this: Do you want to keep your fertility o
sacrifice it?"

Kevral shook her head. "It's not that easy. If I keep my fertil-, I have to carry Cymion's grandchild. If I want my sons, ere's an even chance I'll have to carry another royal brat. If I se my fertility, I'm free. And my children, too." Even as she oke the words, Kevral wondered if she had the last part right. rely Cymion knew the danger loosing her would pose to his vn life and, perhaps, those of his guards and citizens. More :ely, if her courses started, he would condemn her to death.

"Let's keep this simple," Colbey said, ignoring everything e had just proclaimed . . . and thought. "Just answer my iestion."

Kevral tried to remember it.

"Do you want to keep your fertility or sacrifice it?" Colbey ompted.

"I don't know," she admitted.

"Exactly the problem." Colbey rose and pressed his back to e wall. "Kevral, you have to learn to make decisions."

Kevral rose, too. "I make decisions all the time!"

"Is that why you allow two good men to suffer while you find 'ery excuse to delay choosing between them?"

The barb struck a raw wound. Kevral hissed. "What's that it to do with the other?"

"Everything." Colbey crossed his arms across his chest.

Kevral stomped on growing rage, in favor of the bottomless spect in which she held this immortal. "I thought it best to arry the baby's father."

Colbey corrected, "You hoped the baby's biology would ake the decision for you."

Need to understand usurped defense. "Do those babies really ive different fathers?"

For all his lack of omnipotence, Colbey had, apparently, seen e boys. His tone lost its accusing edge. "It would seem so."

"Is that possible?"

"Happens all the time with animals. Rare among people, but ou wouldn't be the first." Harshness returned to Colbey's ice, "You're dodging the decision again."

"I told them to see others." Kevral turned away.

"In the vain hope one might fall in love with another woman id, once again, make the decision for you." No sounds of ovement came from Colbey's direction, but the breeze from e vent did cut off momentarily. "You've made them prisoners /ery bit as much as you are now."

"I'm sorry," Kevral whispered, guilt like a lash. She had

spent so much time caught up in her own problems, she ha
scarcely considered them.

"You're apologizing to the wrong person."

"I know." Kevral turned back to find Colbey staring directl
at her. Her cheeks flushed beneath his demanding scrutin
"I've weighed every option. I just can't make that final com
mitment. Having the babies changes everything."

"Under the circumstances, the babies don't affect which
the two you marry. Their effect is on other matters." Colbe
tossed her unusually direct advice. "My experience is this: I
after weighing all parts of a decision you still cannot make it,
is almost certain that the options are equal."

Kevral nodded vigorously. Colbey had identified the situa
tion accurately. "Then, what do you do?"

He smiled. "I pick one."

Kevral tossed her hands in frustration. "Circumstance ha
made the decision irrelevant."

"You're delaying again, Kevral. But the King of Pudar can
detain you forever. The next time you come upon Ra-khir c
Tae, you had best have an answer."

"I will," Kevral promised, the words hollow. She still had n
idea what she would do.

"And my question?"

"About the fertility?"

"Yes."

Kevral sighed, moved as much by Charra's pleas as Colbey'
own description, nearly a year ago, of the infertility that ha
plagued him until the birth of his son only sixteen years ago. "
want to keep it, but not—"

"Even though it means another pregnancy so soon?"

Kevral dropped her point to answer. "Yes."

"Even if it means carrying the king's grandchild?"

There Kevral drew the line. She liked Prince Leondis. Preg
nancy hormones had confused her enough to consider him
suitor, but she had never felt the deep intensity of love she knev
for Ra-khir and Tae. And he was Cymion's son. "No, nc
enough for that." She glanced at Colbey, at last driven to cu
riosity. "Why do you ask? It does me little good to make such
decision when I can't affect the outcome."

"You can't. Perhaps, I can."

Kevral stared. Colbey had made it clear on former occasion
that he would not play a role in the affairs of mortals, that suc

'ould, in fact, prove infinitely dangerous. "Can you release
ιe?" Hope became a tenuous quaver.

"No. Even if such an action would have no effect on
ʹidgard's balance, I don't have the keys. Killing guards to get
ιem goes beyond what I can safely perform."

Kevral waited, heart pounding, for details of Colbey's assis-
ιnce. Anything he did would prove better than nothing at all.

"My interference will become clear tonight. But it will leave
ou with another choice. This one, you must make swiftly."

"I will," Kevral promised. "But what . . . ?"

"You'll know." Colbey's presence faded nearly as swiftly as
ᵗ had come, leaving Kevral feeling more desperately alone than
·efore his coming.

Exhaustion still pressed Kevral, and she decided to savor the
ιst night before her responsibilities to Prince Leondis began.
·he curled up on the floor to eagerly await Colbey's interven-
ion. She would have believed sleep impossible; but it found
ιer, sprawled on the floor of Pudar's dungeon, and swept away
∍nsion and worry. Toward midnight, it also brought a dream of
young, golden-haired warrior who performed katas more
·eautiful than life. Kevral watched him in awed fascination, en-
ying every cut and strike, every graceful move. He seemed
lose to her own age, certainly Renshai by his skill, yet was no
·ne she had ever seen or met. The dream state kept her from
·onsidering the impossibility of such a thing. For hours he
vhirled, thrust, and parried, a vision her eyes could scarcely
·ollow yet could never abandon, even to blink.

At length, the warrior sheathed his sword and approached,
·owing as if to royalty. Kevral rose, chains clanking noisily,
ιnd curtsied in return. Neither required speech. She understood
vhy he had come and the decision Colbey had promised. Once
he elves proclaimed her pregnant, her obligation to Prince
∠eondis ended. *Retain fertility without carrying Cymion's
ʒrandchild.* That was the wish she had ultimately placed on
∶olbey and he had promised to fulfill. Now, she had only to
·hoose whether this Renshai warrior pleased her enough to
·arry his baby instead.

The choice was easy. Kevral beckoned him over, reveling in
he solution he offered. Though not ideal, it served better than
ιny other option. She worried only for one thing, that she
ηight, once again, carry twins of different fathers. Yet, with a
·urety about the future that can only come in dream, she knew
ᵗ would not happen twice. Strong arms enwrapped her, and

gentle lips found hers. The lovemaking that followed seemed more ephemeral, lacking the solid reality of her nights with Ra-khir and Tae. She awakened at peace, that serenity itself all that allowed her to believe in a liaison whose specifics had already faded, like smoke.

Kevral lay awake, sorting dream from reality and quietly plotting escape.

The journey through the Westlands proceeded at a crawl that twisted Ra-khir's nerves near to breaking. He rode in perfect formation with the other five knights, more from training than intention. At intervals, they dismounted to clear deadfalls and hack away brush intruding on the trails. Less often, they found the remains of travelers, stripped first by human predators, then scavengers. Some had lain by the roadside long enough to reek of decay, and Ra-khir fought his lurching gut to keep from vomiting. Each body found a decent burial and, gradually, the Knights of Erythane made their way to Pudar.

The guards at Pudar's gates gave the knights no challenge, eagerly ushering their white chargers through the city and to King Cymion's castle. There, they remained in rigid formation while servants tended their mounts and they awaited their turn in the king's courtroom. Ra-khir knew that, when Kevral and Matrinka came before the king, servants had briefed them on proper decorum in a lengthy blather that had driven the Renshai to distraction. No one bothered the Knights of Erythane with such formality. They simply stood at attention, their tabards immaculate, their demeanors perfect duplicates. Mior had gone with the horses.

After a short wait, a pair of guards beckoned the knights down a tapestry-lined corridor to a set of double doors. Two more guards swung open the heavy panels to reveal a courtroom half the size of Béarn's own. King Cymion perched upon a padded throne inset with gemstones in myriad colors. Lanterns set on rings sparked tiny rainbows on the high-arched ceiling. Auburn hair ringed the king's face, and crow's-feet massed at the corners of each blue eye. Broad musculature spoke of a warrior's background. A dozen guards fanned around him, their ranks jagged compared with the knights' obsessive precision. They wore mail over standard tan uniforms. Silver wolves graced their tabards, the background light brown.

Ra-khir noticed all of that in the instant before formality took over. Respectfully, he lowered his head to the proper angle to

match his companions. Removing his helm, he delivered a bow
of appropriate depth. All six returned to attention at the exact
same moment.

"Greetings, Knights of Erythane," King Cymion said. "Your
presence in Pudar is an honor."

The acting captain took a single step forward. He executed a
second bow while the others remained still. "Thank you, Your
Majesty. I am Shavasiay, son of Oridan, acting captain, Knight
to the Erythanian and Béarnian kings: His Grace, King Hum-
reet, and His Majesty, King Griff. The honor of your presence
is ours."

Cymion grinned. "Speak freely, Sir Shavasiay."

"Thank you, Your Majesty." Shavasiay bowed again. "We
are pleased to report that the route between Béarn and Pudar is,
once again, fully open to mercantile activities. Aside from the
encroachment of forest, we met no opposition during our journey and believe the murderous band of Eastern highwaymen
have finally been driven from our fair lands. Though we cannot,
at this time, rule out the possibility that they still lie in wait,
seeking less well-armed prey, they never before hesitated to assault envoys larger than our own, including other knights. As
far as the landscape, we have cleared the way for travelers and
tradesmen . . ."

As per his training, Ra-khir remained rigidly alert throughout
a long-winded speech that sent many of Cymion's soldiers into
restless twitching.

Shavasiay continued, "His Majesty, King Griff, sends his
best regards to Your Majesty, King Cymion. It is his sincerest
hope, as well as our own, that trade, communication, and visitation once again be restored between two countries so long and
happily allied."

The King of Pudar acknowledged the end of Shavasiay's
speech with an archaic gesture, clumsily executed. Clearly, he
rarely, if ever, used it, the movement relegated to the background corner of classes in diplomacy and manners. The
knights tended to bring nearly forgotten formality to the fore.
"King Griff's message preceded your arrival. We have rooms
made up for all of you in the east tower. Let any guard or servant know your needs, and they will be promptly attended."
Cymion pulled at his beard, a gesture that appeared almost nervous. It astounded Ra-khir that the legends of the Knights of
Erythane could make even a king uncomfortable in his own
court. "Is there anything more I can do for you, sirs?"

The acting captain glanced back at Ra-khir, who delivered a single nod. Shavasiay returned his attention to the king. "If it does not offend, Your Majesty, one of us has a personal matter he would like to bring before you."

"Permission granted." Cymion's gaze glided directly to Ra-khir, who suddenly found himself rooted in place.

As Shavasiay paced back into his original position among the knights, Ra-khir managed a deliberate step forward, though his feet seemed to move of their own accord. He bowed more deeply than Shavasiay had and forced himself to remain at stiff attention. "Your Majesty." His voice sounded squeaky after the self-assured knight who had preceded him. "My name is Ra-khir, son of Knight-Captain Kedrin." He shortened the title, as tradition demanded so soon after another knight's introduction "I wish to inquire after a Renshai warrior by the name of Kevralyn Tainharsdatter." Formality also dictated he use Kevral's full name, though he knew she despised it. "She left Béarn at a dangerous time, and I worried for her safe arrival."

A strange expression crossed Cymion's features. Ra-khir hoped he imagined the pain he read there, and in the faces of the many guards whose heads bobbed lower. The king cleared his throat; and the bright blue eyes, so like Kevral's, dodged Ra-khir's green. "Sir Knight, she arrived here safely. She trained many of my guards and did their skills justice."

The happy words could not assuage the fear building in Ra-khir's heart. They did not match the graveness of expression and attitude that otherwise filled the courtroom. He anticipated a "but."

"She also arrived unmarried and carrying some man's baby." The king's scrutiny intensified, the pale eyes no longer avoiding Ra-khir's.

Ra-khir lowered his gaze from the king's, as ritual demanded. The statement refused to register.

"I regret to inform you, Sir Knight, that Kevral died in childbirth. And the baby, too."

Died? That word penetrated where the others had not. Ra-khir gasped in a ragged breath but found himself incapable of loosing it. He stood, frozen in time and place, unable to move or even to speak. *Kevral is dead.* Despite her bravado, despite the many times Ra-khir had seen her dive into battles she had little hope of winning, despite having seen her once driven to the edge by poison, his mind balked at imagining her still and unbreathing form. The world could not possibly continue without er. Forever, it would remain, locked in this moment as he was. Then, gradually, understanding spread through him in a cold rash of self-recriminating terror. *She died in childbirth. In childbirth. A baby. My baby.* The logical conclusion of the thought turned chill into instantaneous conflagration. *I killed Kevral.* Flames hotter than the *Ragnarok* devoured his conscience. *Gods damn me to the deepest, darkest, coldest pit. I KILLED KEVRAL.*

Shavasiay called Ra-khir's name, first in gentle reminder then in irritated command. The syllables, when they finally pierced Ra-khir's consciousness, lacked meaning. Nothing seemed real but the words King Cymion had delivered and the elf-hatred they inspired. A fog closed over him. He remembered little of the moments between the news and when he found himself, huddled alone in a corner of the room the king had granted him. Vague scraps of remembrance remained, like ghosts of reality: Shavasiay's apology for his behavior, servants directing them to their quarters, and the sincere entreaties of peers who had tried to console.

When Ra-khir finally gained enough voluntary motion to stand, restlessness assailed him. He was alone. He walked to the window, shoving aside thick curtains to reveal a delicately paned window, with the thin glass only kings could afford. Beyond it, darkness huddled like a monster, broken only by rare stars, a crescent of moon, and the pale outline that completed its round figure. Strength refused to come, and he collapsed against the window, sobbing. The cold seeped into nose and cheek, and his breath fogged the glass, leaving impressions of his features against it. *Kevral. What have I done?*

Self-condemnation became the spear that prodded him from helplessness back into fretful need. Without knowing where to go, he left his room and drifted along the corridors like a sleepwalker. He noticed none of the guards and servants he passed, though several deferred with word and gesture and others requested his needs. His course took him to an exit, and the guards allowed him egress even when he ignored their questions. Polite conversation warped to gibberish, and humans became invisible casualties of his grief.

Kissed by the cool air of night, Ra-khir let the tears flow freely. He marched in circles around the castle, like a dutied sentry or a spirit returning to haunt the site of its slaying. Soon, the loneliness he originally sought became unbearable. Repeatedly, guilt stabbed his heart, his thoughts caught into the same uncompromising loop as his steps. He sought solace from one who could not judge, for he had inflicted more vilification than he could endure. Whether the other heaped more upon him or attempted to rationalize it away, he could not stand it, but he could no longer suffer the agony alone. Ra-khir headed for the stable where he would find Silver Warrior and Mior.

Ra-khir shuffled toward the dark shape of the stable, eyes burning and tears liquefying his vision. The shapeless blurs of castle, grass, and sky funneled past. The wind carried the faint sweet odor of horses. Ra-khir sucked in a lungful, understanding striking him with a clarity that superseded all other thought. He could atone for his evil in only one way. The penalty for murder was, and should be, death. He jerked to a sudden halt, suicide a balm to thoughts beyond suffering. He had heard of warriors falling upon their swords, guessed the process in a general sense, yet the details eluded him. Placing the blade sideways and into a slot between ribs made sense. He knew the location of the heart, yet finding the angle necessary to penetrate one's own seemed impossible. Any dagger of his would prove too short-bladed for a chest wound to do anything worse than bleed and sting. With a large enough rock bound to him, he might manage a drowning in Trader's Lake; but the energy required to find the supplies, figure out how to tie the knot so that the stone did not simply roll out, and seek directions to the lake foiled him. The simplest solution, slashing open thighs or forearms, seemed the best.

Yet even as the peace of a perfect decision settled over Ra-khir, reality shattered his newfound composure. The vows he had taken as a Knight of Erythane forbade suicide as a dishonor to self, peers, and kingdoms. Like all Renshai, Kevral claimed self-murder a coward's decision, and punishing himself in that manner would violate the very honor he died to preserve. *No*. Ra-khir choked back a frustrated howl of agony. The words rambled through his head in a ceaseless chant: *Kevral is dead. Kevral is dead. Kevral is dead.* "My fault," he sobbed aloud, his voice a spiritless croak. "My fault." He continued his shuffle toward the stable, feeling ancient and broken. Though no sword had pierced his heart, guilty sorrow had, leaving ruptured, bloody flesh where it had once beat in his chest.

The musky odor of horse grew stronger. The stable hands did not approach Ra-khir, apparently reading his mood from sidelong glances in his direction. He meandered between stalls, the white heads of the knights' steeds easily spotted amid the asorted browns, golds, and blacks of the king's beasts. Ra-khir eaded to the cluster of Erythanian horses, picking Silver Warrior from among them. His fingers refused to function properly, the regular latch a sudden mystery. The stallion whickered a greeting, swinging his head over the stall. Ra-khir patted the sleek neck and tickled behind one ear. The braided forelock slid over one deep brown eye.

Unable to open the door, Ra-khir gracefully clambered over and into Silver Warrior's stall. Startled, the stallion withdrew, throwing back his head as Ra-khir dropped to the straw. A moment later, he lipped at the red locks, slathering them with spit. With a vague memory of intricate drills about manners and formality, Ra-khir knew he should care—but did not. Turning, he wrapped his arms around the stallion's massive head. The tears became a desperate torrent, and he cried with a violence that made throat and eyes ache.

Silver Warrior remained stiffly in position, ignoring a grip that would have panicked lesser trained steeds and never once shifting a hoof. Ra-khir continued, sobbing in a frenzy that sapped his body of sensation other than the throbbing agony of his lungs. He vowed to any god who would listen that he would dedicate himself wholly to combat and knighthood, forsaking all women. No other could ever take Kevral's place.

Something brushed the back of Ra-khir's head. He remained still, irrationally hoping a god had come to end his misery. Softness swept across his neck, accompanied by a gentle weight on his shoulders. Then, it lifted, and he caught a glimpse of white fur through the hair that covered his eyes. *Mior.* Though he had instructed her to wait for him here, he had not noticed the cat when he first arrived. Her presence reminded him that he would have to tell Matrinka the fate of her friend, and a fresh round of tears assailed him. The pain he would inflict on the queen of Béarn was wholly his fault.

Mior mewed plaintively, pacing from Silver Warrior's back, to Ra-khir's, and returning to the horse again. She batted at the curtain of hair covering the knight's face.

Ra-khir ignored her, though his weeping diminished. He had cried himself empty.

Again, Mior swatted at Ra-khir's face, momentarily exposing an eye.

In no mood for games, Ra-khir growled. "Stop it, Mior."

She mewed again, the sound strangely muffled. Once more,

the paw whipped through the soft locks, this time, tapping hi cheek with sheathed claws.

"Mior!" Ra-khir jerked up his head to confront the calico o his mount's milky back. "Leave me—" The sight of a painte figure in the cat's mouth cut off his objection. "What's that?"

Mior stared back.

Ra-khir lifted a hand, and the cat released the item. It fell int the knight's palm, a carven rendition of Colbey Calistinsso during his mortal days as general of Pudar's army. He recog nized it instantly. *Tae gave this to Kevral.* He swallowed at th lump in his throat, barely budging it. "Where did you get this?"

Mior leaped from the horse's back to the top of the stall, the down into the lanes of the stable.

Ra-khir hefted the figure, studying it in the dim light. Achin eyes turned it into muddy shapelessness.

Mior fairly howled. She jumped, hooking her paws over th edge of the stall, clawing for purchase.

Ra-khir rescued the calico from struggle or fall, gathering he into his arms. Once settled, Mior sprang out of the stall again Understanding dawned slowly. *She wants me to follow. I aske where she got this, and she wants to show me.* Despite Ma trinka's explanations and Tae's claim that he had instructe Mior where to find the keys that rescued Griff from the elves Ra-khir still found it difficult to believe in an intelligent cat

This time, Ra-khir's fingers obeyed him. He tripped th stall's latch, pushed the door open, and escaped into the mair body of the stable. He gave Silver Warrior one last pat and con firmed that the horse had adequate hay. A bucket hanging nea his water held a few remaining kernels of corn and oats. Ra-khir shut the door. When he turned, Mior had disappeared.

Only then, Ra-khir dared to contemplate the significance o the figure in his hand. Likely, the Pudarians had buried it with Kevral or it had rolled from the flames of her pyre. He sucked in a worried breath. He would have to attend to the details o Kevral's funeral. Renshai had specific methods for celebrating death. *If the result of battle,* he reminded himself. For those who died otherwise, the means of disposing of the body did not mat ter. Kevral would not have wanted a hero's ceremony for the means of her demise. If Mior planned to lead him to the body or the site of burning, he would need to mentally prepare him self for what he might find.

"Meow."

The sound startled Ra-khir from his thoughts. He followed i

o the far side of a distant stall. The calico lashed her tail, impa-
ient for the knight to follow. "I'm coming," he promised.

The cat streaked off toward the exit, Ra-khir scrambling af-
er her. This time, he noticed the many stalls and their well-
groomed occupants: well-muscled mares and geldings with a
gleam of health in their eyes. The mingled perfumes of horse,
hay, and sweet mash wound through the open corridors. A few
boards bore the telltale signs of cribbing, mangled into ridges
by huge, flat teeth. Others held strips of lighter-colored wood,
replacement for damaged pieces, not yet weathered. He even
managed a fluttering greeting to a startled stable hand who scurried into a position of deference.

Moments later, cat and knight emerged into the false dawn.
Mior streaked across the grounds, a flash of white and patchy
shadow in the darkness. Ra-khir trailed, losing and finding the
cat at intervals. He made no attempt to hide from the sentries.
They watched him but, recognizing his knight's garb, did not
challenge.

At length, Mior led Ra-khir to an obscure corner of the castle. A grate stretched over a vent hole near the base of the
stonework. Mior butted an edge loose with her head, then
squeezed through the opening this created. The scratch of her
nails against stone echoed through the tunnel, then faded into
silence.

Ra-khir dropped to his haunches. Even if he tore the grating
off, he could not hope to fit his broad shoulders through the
opening. "Mior! Mior, get back here." He grumbled, "Who do
you think I am? Tae?"

The scrabble of nails recurred, more slow and distinct.
Clearly, the shaft led downward. Ra-khir placed his face against
the grate, staring through a single hole. He saw only darkness,
then, suddenly, a golden eye nearly touching his own.

Ra-khir jerked backward with a hiss of surprise.

Mior shouldered back through, this time dropping a gem at
his feet. He picked it up, instantly recognizing the green stone
Kevral had carried, another present from Tae. Guilt lanced him.
He gave her gifts, and I killed her.

Mior made a loud, hoarse cry, like the battle howl of a tom.

"Mior, is Kevral's body there?" Ra-khir hated to ask. He
could not remain here much longer without attracting guards.
They would allow him free passage, but loitering at a vent into
the castle would not go unchallenged.

Mior sat, enormous eyes fixed on Ra-khir's face, as if measuring him for attack. She meowed again.

A thin voice touched Ra-khir's ears, scarcely louder than the wind, "Mior?"

Ra-khir sprang to the grating. "Kevral?" he said, pitching his voice low to avoid attracting attention. *It can't be*.

No answer.

Ra-khir looked at Mior. "Is she down there?"

Mior mewed.

Ra-khir licked his lips, fighting desperate hope. For a moment, his sensibilities refused the possibility that the King of Pudar would lie. "If Kevral's alive, um . . ." He tried to think of a complicated enough command to assure the cat did not perform it accidentally. Recalling that Matrinka claimed Mior tended to count "one, two, many," he avoided instructions that required a tally. ". . . walk in a circle, then sit."

Mior tensed, then did as instructed. She flicked her head sideways, regarding Ra-khir, as if irritated by his denseness.

Ra-khir placed his face back against the grating. "Kevral!" he screamed, no longer caring who heard.

A trickle of sound returned. "Matrinka?"

Matrinka? Ra-khir hoped his voice did not resemble the queen of Béarn's. He guessed the one who answered could not hear him any better than he could her. Yet the decision to call out the name of Mior's usual companion fairly clinched the identity. "It's Ra-khir!"

More words returned, muddled mostly into incomprehensibility. He sifted a few from the mass, along with the thunk of a chain. "Guards. Prisoner. Help." From that, he made intuitive leaps. She risked the same discovery he did by shouting, and she was being held against her will.

Ra-khir drew breath to shout back a reassurance. Before he did, Mior laced against his legs, mewling a soft warning. Ra-khir glanced behind him at a pair of sentries definitely headed his way. *I have to go*. He weighed the need to comfort Kevral against detection and found the latter more pressing. If they moved Kevral, he might never find her again.

Reluctantly, Ra-khir clambered to his feet. "Come on, Kitty. By now that mouse is in his hole, brushing his whiskers and laughing at you." He hefted Mior, forced a smile for the sentries, and headed back toward the castle entrance. They watched him pass without challenge.

Dangling from Ra-khir's arm, Mior returned an alarmingly

uman glare, as if piqued by the indignity of being used as a
shallow excuse. She squirmed free of his grip but followed res-
olutely.

Ra-khir's mind awakened sluggishly to a situation growing
impossibly desperate. The urge to clamp his fingers around
Cymion's neck and squeeze until the blue eyes gaped and
glazed horrified him. As he walked, he forced rich, cleansing
breaths of night air. Its chilliness barely soothed the fire in his
gut, leaving a queasiness that merged horrible grief with blustering rage scarcely contained by the realization of a political issue that could spark war. He would have to find a way to handle
the matter with delicacy and still rescue Kevral from imprisonment. Exhaustion retreated, too insignificant to warrant attention. He would spend until sunup thinking. Somehow, he would
find a way. He would have to.

CHAPTER 38

Chaos Incarnate

[Colbey] is a Northman. To them, war is religion.
—*Santagithi*

Working as a unit, the *lysalf* managed to paint the Northern sky with images, raging above the heads of warring Ascai and Skrytila. With artistic magic, Chan'rék'ril drew haunting images while Captain's wind mastery granted the figures movement. The others chanted *jovinay arythanik* to add the power necessary to strengthen the works and convince.

Above the heads of battling mortals, familiar gods with angry visages demonstrated gruff displeasure at the display. Odin's single eye seemed to burn, backed by the boom of thunder and the background flash of lightning. Thor's red beard bristled in hot aversion, and Aegir glowered amidst an ocean of boiling clouds. The elves deliberately avoided images of *Ragnarok*'s survivors; Captain had warned against the sacrilege. In an age of change, when balance teetered and lesser deities ruled, tempers might flare at even a slight offense.

Gradually, the slamming chime of steel lessened. Human eyes flickered, then held, on the churning clouds and the unavoidable patterns they formed. Ascai warriors disengaged from Skrytila, and no one dared take advantage of the many distracted openings this gained them. A few fell to their knees in prayer, others following in a broad circle that finally included every man. Seizing the opening, Captain stepped onto the battleground. Reehanthan chose a more dramatic entrance, swooping down upon the men as if from the mural Chan'rék'ril painted. He landed beside Captain, inky hair flopping back into position and yellow eyes unlike anything the humans might have seen. Captain had chosen Reehanthan to accompany him mostly for the sharp features that, unlike his own, could never pass for human.

Warriors! Captain speared the area with *khohlar*, certain it would travel farther than his loudest voice. *Arise and look at me.*

Those nearest scrambled to obey. Whispers traversed the farther ranks, then those, too, stood in ragged rows. They drifted nearer to the elves.

From the corner of his eye, Captain noticed that, missing Reehanthan's voice in the *jovinay arythanik,* Chan'rék'ril struggled to maintain the pictures in the sky. The leader of the *lysalf* raised his hands and face, fingers spread. Slowly, he opened his arms, as if in silent communication with the deities. Taking his cue, Chan'rék'ril allowed a controlled fading of his magic, until nothing remained but brief flickers of lightning from the storm Captain had summoned. *My masters are displeased with their followers.*

The Northmen looked around nervously at their bloodstained blades and the littered corpses. A wounded man moaned loudly, beyond caring.

Captain lowered his arms and glared into the mass of warriors, deliberately seeking out gazes that refused to meet his own. *All Northmen are brothers, no matter their tribe. When you battle neighbors, you slaughter family. Odin has tired of your squabbles. The Valkyries have ceased taking those who died bravely in battle—they say Valhalla already holds its share of fools.*

Whispers and a dying man's screams broke the silence that followed Captain's words. *Where are the leaders among you?*

All the warriors' gazes swept the battlefield, settling on two disparate locations.

Captain gestured toward one site, then the other, hoping it appeared as if he plucked the generals' locations from the crowd himself. No one had directly pointed them out, and the warriors surely did not realize that every other man had done as he had. One gaze would have revealed nothing. "Approach me!" He watched as a burly redhead limped toward him, bearing a shield with the Ascai symbol, a sword through three wavy lines representing the sea. Skrytil's general rode a muscled bay stallion, weaving between his followers. Dents blemished his helm, and mail peeked through rents in his tunic. A nose more scar tissue than flesh jutted from beneath blond bangs. War braids swung over broad shoulders.

As the Ascai reached Captain, he attempted a bow, face

screwing into a pained knot. A bloody gash gaped in his thigh. "What are you?" he asked gruffly.

"Elves," Captain started honestly, then lapsed back into lie. "messengers of the gods." He gestured for Reehanthan to handle the Skrytila, then walked to the injured general and placed a hand against the wound.

The Ascai stiffened but did not pull away.

Captain called up magical remedies, as he had so many times during Rantire's captivity. Millennia alone on the sea had given him plenty of time to practice. The ability to heal had come naturally. His weather mastery had taken centuries of effort to craft and perfect. He watched peace settle over the Ascai's features as pain flowed from the injury. Then, gradually, the bleeding subsided and the flesh twitched minimally toward closing. Having reached the end of his ability, Captain withdrew, leaving a painless, partially healed gash in place of the vast gorge.

"Thank you, elf," the Ascai general said. He raised a stiff-fisted arm in the air, and cheers erupted from his assembled men. Captain glanced to Reehanthan. The elf chattered with the Skrytila general in the human Northern tongue.

Captain cleared his throat, then spoke in a resonant voice. "Generals, proclaim your blood brotherhood. Enemies no longer, Skrytil and Asci must bond as allies."

The generals eyed one another suspiciously.

"Do as I say!" Captain roared. "Or I will call the wrath of Thor down upon you both." He punctuated his words with an ear-shattering clap of thunder.

Startled, the Ascai stiffened. The Skrytila made the first move, holding out a massive arm swarmed with thick, blue veins. The Ascai glanced at Captain. Reading danger there, he clasped the Skrytila's hand. For several moments they held one another, at arm's length. "Brothers we are," the Ascai finally said. "And brothers will remain. So long as I live, you will have only allies among the tribe of Asci." The Skrytila returned the promise, then pulled the other general to him. They embraced, clapping one another on the back to seal the bargain.

Captain fought back a smile. Even after so much hardship, his face naturally assumed that expression, and now he had more reason than usual to grin. He could not imagine prejudice fully disappearing in a moment, but so long as they believed him a gods' herald, he felt he could at least maintain an uneasy accord.

The generals parted, lapsing into a low discussion that Captain could not hear. A moment later they both turned toward the battlefield. "Men," the Ascai called. "Sheathe your weapons. We are at peace."

"As are we," the Skrytila added.

The Ascai general bowed to Captain again. "We've agreed to abide by your division of borders. Whatever you decide will remain permanent, and you may assure the gods that we shall never again battle over who owns which piece of dirt."

"Very well, then," Captain said. "Perhaps the Valkyries will throw open the gates of Valhalla again, when you battle enemies as brothers." His piece spoken, he headed back toward the waiting *jovinay arythanik*. Much work still remained. As many as eight more tribes might require convincing, and he did not wholly trust even this tranquillity to last.

Nice work Reehanthan sent to Captain.

Captain acknowledged the praise with a tip of his head. It both pleased and worried him that magic subdued the world's most savage warriors. The *svartalf* also knew enchantment and *khohlar*. Surely, they had spurred the attacks and fed the intolerance, yet they must have done so in secret. Captain's boldness, not competence, had won the day. Soon, he hoped, it would end many more battles. And restore a brotherhood that had once made the Northlands strong.

Captain could no longer stifle a smile. Many problems remained, not the least of which was the infertility plague. But at least the process of peace had begun.

Once again, the Knights of Erythane formed a wedge in King Cymion's courtroom, but, this time, Ra-khir took the head position. The king's features displayed stoic interest, his curly hair and beard surrounding his face like a lion's mane. Pudarian guards remained in their semicircle around the throne, tiny imperfections in their formation grating on Ra-khir's sensibilities. Irritated by his focus on detail at a time when words mattered more, he cursed the obsession pounded into him by his knight's training.

Ra-khir bowed for the third time since entering the courtroom, waiting for King Cymion to speak.

Cymion turned his hard, blue gaze directly on Ra-khir. "What can I do for you, Sir Knight?"

Ra-khir licked his lips, forcing all judgment from his voice. "Your Majesty, I regret the need to bother you in this manner." He barely recognized his own voice, and the words seemed to issue from another. Syllables he had rehearsed tumbled forth, gaining meaning only after their speaking. "But it appears mistakes were made." He met the king's eyes momentarily. "Your Majesty, Lady Kevral is alive."

A light sparked in the king's eyes, then disappeared before Ra-khir could guess its meaning. The Pudarians' ranks became more crooked. "Alive?" Cymion sat back thoughtfully. "How can that be? I set her to the pyre myself." He added, "And the baby, too."

Ra-khir said nothing more, awaiting a less rhetorical question from the king.

The royal forehead wrinkled. "Did you see her?"

"No, Sire," Ra-khir admitted. "But I spoke with her."

"What did she say?"

"Your Majesty, I . . ." Ra-khir swallowed hard. "I couldn't understand much. It was garbled, and . . . she said she was a prisoner. Guarded."

The king ran his fingers through his beard. "Garbled, you say?"

"Yes, Sire."

Cymion nodded, studying Ra-khir with a new intensity. "You didn't see her, and her voice was garbled."

Ra-khir worried for the direction this seemed to be taking. He had not expected the king to crumble and, at least from the moment he claimed to have placed Kevral on her pyre, it seemed clear that he had a hand in her imprisonment. "Yes, Sire."

"Are you certain, young knight, it was Kevral you spoke to?"

"Yes, Sire."

Cymion leaned forward again, his look predatory. "How can this be so?"

"Your Majesty," Ra-khir started, without the necessary words to finish. Propriety did not allow him a back-step, though he could not help feeling as if the king might pounce at any moment. "I'm afraid I can't reveal that without violating Queen Matrinka's confidence." He had never actually promised Matrinka not to reveal the cat's intelligence, but he doubted describing it would accomplish anything more than raising concerns about his sanity.

The gaze of every Pudarian weighed heavily on Ra-khir, and he suspected the knights watched him as well.

"You didn't see her, and you didn't understand what she said. You're basing so grave a crime on that?" Cymion's scrutiny inensified, if possible. Then, suddenly, his expression opened, and he nodded. Some great truth had reached his mind. "I believe I understand now. You, sir, are the father of that baby. Aren't you?"

Ra-khir could feel his fellows stiffening behind him. Once he had discovered Kevral, he had believed the pregnancy fictitious, invented by the king to explain a healthy, young warrior's demise in peacetime. Decorum demanded he respond to the king's question, and its phrasing did not leave room for speculation. He sought a way to voice his doubts without offending the king. If such a baby did or had existed, it was certainly his. He answered the only way his honor allowed. "Sire, if the Lady Kevral bore a child, it could only be mine. Had I known of it, Sire, had I been contacted at the first knowledge of its existence, I would have stood by her side as her husband on the day of its birth."

No one dared to speak, but glances and gestures flew through the courtroom. Ra-khir felt hot tears building in his eyes again, more frustration than sorrow. He could say nothing now that would rescue Kevral. His request appeared to have gained him only public humiliation.

The king cleared his throat, nodding sagely. "That explains much. Sir Knight, I understand and forgive your need to believe the woman you love still lives. In the same situation, many men would let their hopes and dreams build the same scenario."

Ra-khir opened his mouth to assert his knowledge, but no words emerged.

The king spoke over him. "Do the Knights of Erythane have other business with the crown?"

Shavasiay's voice boomed at Ra-khir's back. "No, Your Majesty. Thank you for your accommodations and for your indulgence." A harshness in his tone was clearly directed at Ra-khir. "Had I full knowledge of the situation, Your Majesty, I would never have granted permission for him to waste the court's time." The knights bowed as a unit, even Ra-khir.

The king's lies fueled rage, but Shavasiay's mistrust ached more deeply. Though he hated the need, Ra-khir did as propriety demanded. "Your Majesty, I deeply apologize for any inconvenience or discomfort I may have caused." The words seemed to burn his lips, a poison he would sooner have swallowed than spoken. *Kevral, my hands are as chained as your own.*

Cymion crooked his head sideways, lips pursed and expres-

sion too sympathetic for Ra-khir's taste. "Apology accepted.
No harm done, and no offense taken. You may stay as long as
you wish and, always, Pudar will welcome the Knights of Erythane."

"Thank you, Your Majesty." Shavasiay glared at Ra-khir as
he stepped back into the ranks. "But I believe it best for us to be
on our way as soon as possible."

"As you wish." Cymion clapped his hands, summoning servants from the wings. "The stable hands will have your steeds
ready momentarily. Godspeed and best wishes to King Griff.
And you, young man, take care." He directed those last words
to Ra-khir.

Ra-khir detected a tinge of gloating in the king's otherwise
friendly demeanor.

"Dismissed," Cymion finished.

The knights gave one last formal bow, then turned and left
the courtroom.

The grounds of Pudar's courtyard rolled past beneath Silver
Warrior's steady hoof falls, and Ra-khir perched in the proper
position without need for visual clues. His mind, jumbled with
a million desperate thoughts, spiraled into helpless circles. He
rode without comment toward the castle gates. Once through,
he knew his head would begin to function again, yet the finality
of leaving would bring many horrible realities to bear. His
chance to rescue Kevral would disappear, dooming her to whatever dark purpose Pudar planned. Shavasiay's reprimands
would begin, and his own honor would hold him in abeyance.

No. That one thought broke through the tangled web. Nothing followed, and Ra-khir continued, swept along by training
that now translated into instinct. The courtyard gate loomed
ahead. Balanced on Silver Warrior's rump, Mior loosed a sad
howl. *No.* Sudden need gripped Ra-khir. His voice quavered
over the drum of hoofbeats. "Captain, sir, we have to stop."

Shavasiay barked a halt command that emerged like a curse.
The riders drew rein, and the horses obeyed instantly. Without
turning, the acting captain bade, "Ra-khir, come up here."

Ra-khir rode forward, despising the dry cotton that abruptly
filled his mouth. Silver Warrior drew up beside Shavasiay,
grinding to a halt without command from his master.

"Why," Shavasiay said, "do we have to stop?"

Ra-khir met the angry, brown eyes with a steady gaze. "Because, sir, we cannot leave Kevral behind."

Shavasiay's tone bore a flat quality, indicative of building rage. "She's dead, Ra-khir."

Ra-khir shook his head slightly.

"The king set her pyre himself."

"The king," Ra-khir said, gaze unwavering, "is lying."

Shavasiay's face whitened, and his hands clenched to blanched fists on his reins. "Ra-khir Kedrin's son. That's offensive, an unacceptable transgression."

Mior wound to Ra-khir's lap. He continued to return his commander's stare, hand falling to the cat's soft back. "Perhaps, sir. But it's also truth. My loyalty is to Béarn and Erythane, not Pudar. And always to honor."

Shavasiay lowered his head, the brim of his hat dropping his eyes into puddled shadow. His lips tightened, turning nearly as light as his features. "Your truth is not reality. It's a trick of your desire. I indulged your daydream once, not again."

Ra-khir did not give quarter, not even to defend himself. "The elves denied imprisoning the king, too. Had we accepted that answer, Béarn would still serve a crooked prime minister and a host of dark elves."

The acting captain sighed, "Ra-khir, we all know you and your friends acted bravely in the best interests of Béarn. But you're letting grief and guilt cloud your judgment."

"Kevral is here, sir. A prisoner in Pudar's dungeon."

"You sound certain."

"I am, sir."

Shavasiay glanced at the other knights, then back at Ra-khir. "Would it violate Queen Matrinka's confidence to tell me how you know?"

Ra-khir tapped a shoulder, and Mior clambered to his neck. "No, sir. But you wouldn't believe me."

About this, Shavasiay took Ra-khir at his word. "You are free to present your case to Captain Kedrin, or to the king, when you return."

Ra-khir nodded his understanding, the cat bobbing with him. "Understood, sir. And I'm certain King Griff would do whatever it took to free Kevral. She battled through the entire force of elves for him."

"That's a Renshai's job."

Ra-khir concurred. "It is, sir, but that doesn't make the king any less grateful. By the time we get back to Béarn, however, it'll be too late. Pudar will do as they please with Kevral and kill her or hide her where we'll never find her."

Shavasiay sighed. "So what would you have us do, Sir Ra-khir? I don't believe the king would weather another audience."

Hope blossomed with the caution of a rose in the moments before dawn. At least for the moment, the acting captain seemed willing to consider the possibility that Kevral lived. "We do whatever we need to."

"Storm Castle Pudar?"

"If necessary."

Shavasiay threw up his hands in abrupt and indignant frustration. "You're serious."

Ra-khir thought that obvious from the start. "Never more so."

"Ra-khir." Shavasiay's tone turned singsong, as if he confronted a child too young to grasp the intricacies of the situation. "I understand the shock of losing a loved one. I forgave your lapse in the king's court when you learned the news. Your behavior since that time, I cannot. You've embarrassed us in front of the king. You've uttered politically dangerous insults. And . . ." He loosed breath in a long sigh. "I'll let your father deal with what you did to that young woman."

Ra-khir locked his jaw. *He already knows, you bastard.*

"You're on report, Ra-khir. One more problem, and I'll recommend discharge."

Kedrin would have final decision in such a matter, yet Ra-khir knew his father would not rescue him. To do anything other than follow the acting captain's counsel would appear to be favoritism.

"Get back in ranks."

Silver Warrior tensed to move, but Ra-khir reined him back. Pudar's intentions for Kevral became suddenly clear. "No." His voice emerged soft but clear.

All empathy left Shavasiay's features. "Ra-khir, that's an order!"

Ra-khir went rigid. All of his life, he had envied the Knights of Erythane. For the last five years, desire for the position had consumed him. Only one other thing meant as much to him, the one he would lose if he followed Shavasiay's command. His mind cleared, and grim certainty filled him. He jerked off his hat, spilling red hair that whipped into his face. Mior leaped to the horse's flank as Ra-khir yanked his tabard over his head. Béarn's tan bear on blue flapped in the breeze, joined by Erythane's orange and black. He jammed both into Shavasiay's hand, then tossed over Silver Warrior's reins. He did not offer weapon and mail. Those belonged to him.

"What are you doing?" Shavasiay demanded.

Ra-khir sprang from the saddle, Mior leaping after him. "I have to follow my honor, Shavasiay, and it is clear about this." He clamped his hand to the hilt of his sword, eyes narrowing at the enormity of what came next. "I'm declaring war on Pudar."

The prophecy became a deep chant that cycled through Dh'arlo'mé's soul, a promise of a future wholly dedicated to him. He stood upon the island beach, sand warm beneath sandaled feet, ocean wind lashing his red-gold hair, and waves renting into monstrous mountains of water before battering the shore with bits of rock and shell. Spray splattered Dh'arlo'mé's face and hands, cold pinpoints that reeked of salt and dead things sucked deep beneath the waters. He noticed curious elves watching him from treetops and around the furrowed rings of the *doranga* trunks, but he paid them no heed. Creatures of Midgard withered; elves and men alike would breathe their last this day.

Dh'arlo'mé raised one arm. Once before, the elves had summoned a demon in this very place, in the control of a powerful young female named Baheth'rin. The madness in the demon's fiery eyes as it destroyed her had haunted Dh'arlo'mé long after the realization that it would never return to exact its revenge.

Where once it chilled, that remembrance now brought a smile to Dh'arlo'mé's lips. He had grown above such trivial matters. The denizens of Midgard had become less than trifles, and he stirred war among them for the joy of watching them tear one another apart. His true nature had finally matured to full reality, and it held an incomplete relationship to the law that had spawned it. The thoughts of an individual elf no longer mattered. The being, once Dh'arlo'mé, disappeared beneath the wild torrent of what he had become. And he did not have enough cognizance even to wonder for the past.

A new world! Dh'arlo'mé raised his other arm. *A new world wholly devoted to me.* A smile touched the broad lips, barely. The entity Dh'arlo'mé had become maintained a subtlety of expression that might discomfort even an elf. He delved for the proper words, imbuing them with timeless magic. It would not prove enough to summon any demon, as law/Dh'arlo'mé had done before. He sought chaos incarnate, the lord of all demons, the most powerful and hideous *kraell* to scour island and countryside free of life. Then, and only then, Dh'arlo'mé would banish the creature he had called, and the sudden tip to ultimate law would spur a second *Ragnarok* in Asgard. Once the gods slaughtered one another, nothing would remain but Dh'arlo'mé and the new world he built in deference to self.

> *Thee Father shal avert hys fate.*
> *Then thee worlds shud celebrate.*
> *But far ynto dystrukshon hurled*
> *Law's vast plan ys then unfurled:*
> *A new world to create.*

> *All must dye to pave thee way.*
> *A syngle god to rule thee day.*
> *Thee only enemy wyll make*
> *One small lapse; a fatal mystake*
> *Leave thee world at thee mercy of Gray.*

Dh'arlo'mé laughed, then commenced the evocation. The words of the spell rushed from mind to lips, torn away by wind that swelled with every syllable. He concentrated totally on calling. He did not bother with bindings; he fully intended the slaughter of all living things. He could almost hear the demon's malignant voice oozing into his ears: *Elf, you are either the bravest or most foolish creature in existence to call me here without protection.* It would not immediately attack him, he felt certain. It would know that only one of great power could bring forth its ilk, and no dullard could be so endowed. It would listen to his plans, then laughter would discharge in a thunderous rumble. Eventually, it would come for him, and he would banish it. If it turned on him immediately, it would lose the chance to shred elves and humans, sent back before it could feed. He would simply call another.

Playful ocean breezes howled into a gale. Waves bucked and slapped the waters, pummeling Dh'arlo'mé with spume. Hair stung his face. Clouds dropped from the sky to enwrap the world, darkening from white to dense gray. A figure black as a hole formed above ocean churned to frantic lather. The clouds dulled to shadows, and the shapeless thing absorbed them. It folded in upon itself, collapsing down to a density that defined a new color, darker than black. Wind blasted the trees, bowing them until their leaves touched the sands. Elves scrambled to earth, scattering away from a storm beyond any they had known

n their long existences. Dh'arlo'mé stood alone upon the
beach, eyes fixed on the creature he had summoned.

The demon appeared to collapse, its density shifting lower
and into a figure smaller than Dh'arlo'mé expected. It did not
worry him. When chaos became predictable, it ceased to be
chaos. Though bound to certain laws on this world, ones of his
own making, demons remained true to their own substance. He
had anticipated a ghastly monster, mountain-sized, all dagger-
clawed and poisoned fanged, hovering on formless wings. Yet
this creature dropped in the water with a muted splash. Legs
sprouted at the contact, and it took human shape, clutching a
sword that maintained the inky depthlessness, as if it, not the
entity, was demon.

The winds dropped in an instant. Color washed over the
summoned figure, settling into proper position as if placed by
an artist's brush. A light tunic of yellow-trimmed purple covered a sinewy frame. Blue-gray eyes filled sockets narrowed in
confusion. Golden feathers hung around a scarred but ageless
face.

Startled for the first time in his life, Dh'arlo'mé back-stepped
with a hiss. "You!" He pointed a threatening finger, scrambling
for different magics.

Colbey brandished the sword and charged.

CHAPTER 39

One Against A Kingdom

Sword work is based on quickness, not speed; on power, not strength.

—*Colbey Calistinsson*

A summer breeze wound through the turrets of Stalmize Castle, bringing the aromas of tar, smoke, and heated metal to Tae's nose. The irregular clang of a blacksmith's hammer rang through the streets, accompanied by the indecipherable rumble of myriad conversations. A child's giggle or shriek occasionally penetrated the monotone of adult voices. Tae tuned to more distant sensations, the occasional damp odor of freshly turned earth, the rare bleat that wafted dimly beneath other sound, and the rattle of wind sweeping leaves. Those latter perceptions brought his mind back to time spent riding or tramping through Westland forest. Although assassins had hunted him, and the party itself barely trusted him, those seemed like simpler, more carefree days.

Tae rested his arms on the stone rail outlining the fifth-floor balcony. Behind him, curtains fluttered in the breeze, gauzy fabric occasionally flapping against his tunic. Though Eastland affairs had not left much time to worry about his companions over the last few weeks, they never slipped far from his thoughts. He wondered whether Pudar had survived Kevral's brutal teachings and if Ra-khir pined for her love as much as he did. *Will becoming essentially a prince gain me any advantage in that contest?* Tae answered his own question with a vague shake of short, dark locks. If stature had mattered to Kevral, Ra-khir would have won before the contest started. He trusted her to base her decision on love.

As Weile and his men handled immediacies, luxuries shifted into position as well. Many entertainers had come to offer their services to the new king of the Eastlands, including several bards. Their music, though skillful, only raised longing for Darris. The healers awakened thoughts of Matrinka, and the slightest glimpse of a calico cat aroused painful waves of nostalgia. The thoughts that assailed Tae now dashed all belief in himself as a loner. A bizarre and oddly mixed cluster of companions had become as much a family to him as the father whose cause he now championed voluntarily.

Tae closed his eyes, savoring the breeze, as he recognized the decision his father would not allow him to ponder much longer. Weile Kahn had a right to know his son's intentions before he wasted more time grooming him as a replacement. And Tae harbored a growing suspicion that he would have to deliver an answer that would hurt his father more than the elder would ever reveal. He pondered how much of his leanings stemmed from his love for Kevral, how much from missing friends, and how much from the resentment he still harbored for Weile Kahn and his earlier methods. The answer arose from his heart, as yet untempered by logic. It seemed likely to fall apart if Kevral married Ra-khir and the others of the once close party separated to their various causes: Darris as the king's guardian and Matrinka as a healer. Perhaps they, too, would find a way to marry, leaving Tae the odd one out, an old acquaintance ignored for graver matters and left to slink back, like a whipped puppy, to the father he had abandoned.

Tae shoved that train of thought aside. No matter their couplings or stations, his friends would never discard him. And even if they did, his future did not lie here. Any of the fertile Eastern women would have him, yet the culture that spawned them had never suited him. Though Eastern born, he belonged in the Westlands. His thoughts turned in a new direction. With Weile's hand, and his own guidance, the Eastland culture would change for the better. The children of the East would shape their tomorrow. *What children?* Memory of the sterilization plague drove his thoughts back to grim reality. He chastised himself, *Tae, you've become a hopeless dreamer.*

A footfall behind sent him scrambling into a crouch, hand falling to the dagger in the folds of his cloak.

Weile Kahn stood at the entry to the balcony. "I didn't mean to startle you." A slight smile on his face displayed his approval. The hardships he had inflicted on his son had not gone for naught. Time spent safely in a castle had not softened his survival instincts.

Tae rose, turning to look out over the city of Stalmize. People flocked between huddled buildings, and women carried buckets from the central well. Weile moved up to stand beside him, and they spoke the same words simultaneously. "I've been thinking . . ."

Tae grinned but went silent, respecting his father enough to allow him to speak first.

Weile continued as if Tae had not spoken. "I never intended to take the title 'king,' nor to inherit the formality and trappings. But the people, here and abroad, insist on it."

Tae nodded. His father spoke truth.

"I have the hearts of the populace now, but not forever. Under me and . . ." He paused long enough for Tae to fill in "you," though he did not say the word himself. ". . . under me, it'll never really be a kingdom. Not like it was. Or how other kingdoms are."

Tae made a noise of clear agreement. "Is that bad?"

"No." Weile's gaze followed Tae's into the streets. "I think we have the best of both worlds, and we can maintain it. There'll always be those who rebel against the law. Those followers who seek respectability can have it, and those who prefer the dark way will still work for me in other guise." He placed an arm across Tae's shoulders, tenser than expected. For all his way with strangers of every ilk, Weile had failed with the one person who mattered most: his own son. "Those underground are unraveling organized enemies and recruiting young punks and gangs. Some of those don't even realize they work for the castle, which is probably just as well."

Again, Tae nodded, wondering why his father felt the need to talk about this now.

"That part's no trouble for me to direct. It's the open kingdom portion that's got me stumped."

Tae laughed. "Only my father would find it easier surviving starvation, the law, and assassins than to live as spoiled royalty."

Weile loosed a stiff chuckle as the irony reached him as well. He sobered suddenly and turned directly to Tae. "Son, I was thinking . . ." The conversation came full circle.

Tae turned his attention fully on his father, sensing the significant moment had finally arrived.

"Béarn has had a succession of well-loved kings, and Pudar has thrived beneath its own rulership. If we could learn the details of their successes, I believe we could use them to help the Eastlands become as strong."

Tae watched Weile's every gesture, still seeking clues to his intentions.

The shrewd, dark eyes continued to hold Tae's, shadowed by low-hanging curls. "I'm sure either would welcome an Eastern diplomat, especially one who speaks their language."

Tae blinked with slow thoughtfulness. Many Easterners, and nearly every Westlander, spoke the common trading tongue. Béarn would never demand a visiting dignitary know their city tongue, nor would Pudar expect one to speak the Western language. A dull thrum of alarm began inside him. "You want me to spy on my friends?"

"Not spy." Weile shook his head, the movement short and sharp but vigorous. "Openly observe. With their knowledge and consent."

Tae could feel his heart pounding in his chest. As usual, it seemed his father had read his mind, finding the perfect solution to his dilemma. He could visit his friends even as he gained knowledge for his father's kingdom and, eventually, for himself should he choose to succeed Weile. Then reality intruded, and he winced. "Observe Pudar? Have you forgotten that King Cymion believes I murdered his son? He'd as soon rip me into pieces bare-handed as let me through the gates of Pudar."

Again, Weile had the answer to a situation Tae had thought unsalvageable. "Not after I give him this." He pulled a neatly folded strip of vellum from his pocket."

"What is it?"

"A signed confession from the actual murderer." Weile brandished the paper like a weapon, then returned it to its place. "Now that Pudar knows about elves, I'm certain the king will believe your explanation. Besides, I understand the crime has already been punished, and Pudarian law doesn't allow two sentencings."

"True." Tae knew Kevral's year of service came of her promise to undergo execution in his place.

"After having lost his own son, I believe he'll hesitate to harm the East's crown prince."

"Me?" The word started from Tae's lips before he could stop it. *Of course, me. Who else?*

Weile shrugged. "Whether or not you choose to succeed me, King Cymion will see you that way. And, when I inform him the assassin found a proper end here, it should appease him, I believe."

Tae concurred.

"So, Tae Kahn, will you serve as Stalmize's diplomat?"

Tae studied his father, the familiar features so like his own, the curly locks that remained always in place, and the dark eyes that held a light he had never seen in them before. He thought of the last time his father had sent him West, at fourteen, pursued by killers and banished from returning unless and until he survived to the age of twenty. So much had changed in the years since that horrible moment. Hatred had flared and died, a new respect born from the ashes. Weile's look declared so much that pride would not allow him to speak. The desperate love for his only son that had driven him to find a compromise. The respect that had grown from the association between adults, still father and child.

It never occurred to Tae to refuse. "Of course, I will, Father. And relish the job."

A smile crawled onto Weile's face. "I'll keep in close contact. With messengers. I'll expect the same."

"I'd serve little use if I didn't."

Weile took a step toward his son, arms extended. "Tae Kahn, I expect that, eventually, you'll come home." The tone conveyed a pride and affection far beyond the words.

Tae wrapped his arms tightly around his father. Though he did not reply aloud, he knew the truth within him. He felt certain that, eventually, he would.

Ra-khir never looked back, leaving the Knights of Erythane for a mission his honor demanded, though he did not doubt it would kill him. Head high, gait sure, Mior trotting at his heels, he approached the entry to the castle of Pudar. A pair of guardsmen in tan tunics under belted mail shirts watched his approach. They remained at rigid attention, their halberds jutting skyward.

Ra-khir stopped directly in front of them, stiffly silent. For several moments, no one moved or spoke. Then, the leftmost guard, a sturdy brunet with a broad chin and lips so thin they scarcely existed, nodded his head in welcome. "Greetings, sir. What can we do for you?"

Ra-khir fastened green eyes on brown. "I wish to speak to your superior's superior's superior. The highest-ranking military officer of Pudar."

The sentry's stare did not even waver long enough for normal blinking. "Excuse me?"

"I sincerely believe," Ra-khir said steadily, "that you heard me."

The dark eyes rolled to his neighbor who shifted closer and took over the negotiations. "You want us to fetch the general?"

"Yes." The wind blew strands of red hair into Ra-khir's eyes. Though they bothered him, he did nothing to remove them. The motion might diminish his attempts to convey, with every word and action, the seriousness of his mission.

The first sentry found his tongue. "We'll need a reason."

Ra-khir made a crisp gesture without specific meaning. "When the general arrives, I will give him one."

Again the guards exchanged glances. The second made a motion nearly as vague as Ra-khir's. Their last orders surely bade them indulge the Knights of Erythane, and they recognized him even without the telltale tabard and hat. "Do as he said."

The thin-lipped guard trotted past Ra-khir, then around a corner of the castle and toward a stately barracks near the stable. Ra-khir turned his attention to the opposite sentry, a densely muscled, bull-necked warrior with mahogany hair clipped short. He wore a mustache without a beard, and a scar marred the skin between upper lip and right nostril. "He'll be back soon, sir," he said, returning to his post. He reverted to a statuelike state, obviously finding that more comfortable than trying to maintain a conversation with a decidedly nettled knight.

Shortly, the first man did return, a massive warrior in tow. Grizzled stubble covered General Markanyin's head, and the gray eyes radiated wisdom. He wore no armor, but the wolf symbol of Pudar graced his leather tunic. A heavy sword hung at his hip, the long hilt suggesting a two-handed grip.

Ra-khir stepped out to meet the general, as the sentry walked around him and resumed his position at the door.

Apparently guessing a need for Ra-khir to talk beyond earshot of the sentries, the general steered Ra-khir farther onto the lawn. He stood slightly taller than Ra-khir, a giant of a man. Though stern of features, his eyes revealed a gentleness his callused hands and size betrayed. "What can I do for you, Ra-khir?"

They had never met before, and Ra-khir appreciated two details the general revealed indirectly. First, he recognized Ra-khir from information, probably reported by his men. Second, he left off the title "sir," surmising the significance of the missing tabard and hat. Ra-khir could not help respecting the man's intuition, even as he measured his skill. "General, I'm calling you out."

Only a slight jerk of Markanyin's head revealed startlement. He met the news with quiet resignation. "Ah. And I suppose it would insult my honor and yours to refuse."

"Indeed." Ra-khir finally shook back the errant hair with a dignified toss of his head. "As soon as possible, and to the death."

The general ran a hand over a scalp nearly scraped to baldness. "Well, then. At least, might you be good enough to answer some questions before you kill me?"

It seemed a more than reasonable request. Ra-khir motioned to Markanyin to proceed.

"Did I do something to offend you?"

"No," Ra-khir admitted. "This is not personal, General."

The general's eyes strayed to the cat near Ra-khir's feet, then back to the former knight's face. "Is it not customary to inform a condemned man of his crime?"

"No crime." Ra-khir made a mental note of Mior's position. It would spoil the mood, and his self-respect, to trip over his own companion. He knew the general humored him by repeatedly following the assumption that he would lose the battle. The general's greater size and experience with warfare would certainly make up for their difference in age. "We're at war."

Now, Markanyin made no attempt to hide his surprise. "Béarn and Pudar?"

"No."

"The Knights of Erythane?"

"No." Ra-khir admitted what the general already knew. "I'm not among them. I am the one at war with Pudar."

"You. By yourself."

"Yes."

The general's head bobbed thoughtfully. "This has something to do with Kevral, doesn't it?"

"Everything," Ra-khir confirmed.

General Markanyin's expression turned sympathetic. "Ra-khir, I've met diplomats, dignitaries, and nobility of every stripe. Aside from my king, I've never respected anyone more than Kevral. Would you like to hear about her final day?"

Ra-khir refused to be patronized. "If it precedes mine, I hope to be there."

Markanyin sighed. "Ra-khir, I'm not sure from where the misconception stems, but I was with Kevral that day. We all were." He made a broad gesture to indicate the courtyard and, Ra-khir suspected, much of the guard force. "She would have done fine, except she fought the pain of labor like an enemy. She collapsed on the field, in front of us all. The crown prince himself carried her inside, and I'm sure the healers did all they could. For her and for the baby."

"You saw her die." Ra-khir found himself liking the general and hated to believe he was in on the deception.

"Not the final moments, no." Markanyin relaxed visibly as Ra-khir listened. Surely he believed he had at last broken through the delusions. "But Prince Leondis would not have left her side."

Undertones of that comment worried at Ra-khir's confidence.

"No one could have spirited her away without his knowledge."

"King Cymion could."

The general's eyes slitted, but he showed no other emotion. "You're speaking treason."

"I'm at war," Ra-khir reminded. "Now, our duel."

"You still insist?"

"More so than ever."

Still, the general hesitated. "May I ask a few more questions?"

Ra-khir scrutinized the motivation. "That depends. Are you truly doing so for information or for delay?" He could hear hoofbeats at his back, but he ignored them. Guards passing on watches posed him no danger yet.

"Information."

Ra-khir could not have condoned the cowardice inherent in the other reason. "Ask then."

Dark brows rose, creasing the general's high forehead. "After you kill me, what will you do next?"

Ra-khir had a ready answer. "Challenge the next highest officer. Then the next. As in any war, when enough men have died, the king must respond to my demands."

The general shook his head in obvious disbelief. He looked at something beyond Ra-khir, then back.

"You have one more question," Ra-khir reminded.

General Markanyin cleared his throat, gaze again straying. "If I happen to win this duel and kill you, what happens then?"

Ra-khir drew breath to give the only answer he could, one worthy of Kevral's unholy confidence. But, before he could speak, a voice boomed out behind him. "Then *I'll* call you out." Recognizing Shavasiay's voice, Ra-khir spun. The five Knights of Erythane perched on their horses, their formation broken only by Silver Warrior, empty-saddled behind them.

Sir Lakamorn spoke next. "Then me."

"Then me," Esatoric followed.

"And me," the last two added in turn.

Stunned beyond speech, Ra-khir awaited explanation.

The acting captain slid gracefully from his saddle, flourished his hat, and bowed to Ra-khir. "My deepest apologies, Ra-khir. If you can forgive me, I hope I can talk you into reclaiming the title you earned."

Ra-khir could think of only one thing he wanted more, and his response to the first depended upon the second. "What . . . ?" He licked his lips, mouth suddenly dry. He glanced at General Markanyin, who remained in place, bravely waiting for the knights to settle their differences while his own fate hung in the balance. "What, sir, changed your mind?"

Shavasiay offered Ra-khir's tabard and hat. "Elves met us at the gate. It seems the king requested they check a young woman in the dungeon for pregnancy. They recognized Lady Kevral." He bowed his head, removing his hat respectfully. "I regret to inform you. She is a week along."

I'll kill the bastard who did this. Ra-khir's hands balled to fists, and he whirled on Markanyin.

The general seemed not to notice the sudden threat of violence, his features crinkled in genuine confusion. "I swear I knew nothing of this." He back-stepped from Ra-khir, turning Shavasiay a look of guileless horror. "Captain, if you're all set on slaughtering me, I'll fight. But I'm sure there's a better way."

Ra-khir accepted the knight's trappings, flipping the tabard over his shoulders and arranging it into exact formation. He added the hat but did not move toward his horse.

Shavasiay remounted, executing a signal that passed command of this particular operation to Ra-khir. The grand show of trust, so close on the heels of threat, left Ra-khir in a slack-jawed silence that propriety demanded he break. He wanted, perhaps needed, something on which to vent his rage. But his honor would not allow him to use an innocent man as a target. "What do you propose, General?"

"Let me talk to the king. Or to his adviser, as reasonable a man as they come."

"I tried that," Ra-khir reminded impatiently.

Markanyin nodded. "But I'm his general. Short of allowing or causing harm to my king, I'll do everything within my power

) get Kevral released. Success or failure, I'll report back to ou." He clearly indicated all of the knights, not just Ra-khir. Will that suffice?"

Ra-khir knew better than to seek advice. The decision lay wholly in his hands, not as simple as it seemed. If Markanyin tumbled, the king would have ample opportunity to hide or slay Kevral. Yet Ra-khir doubted Cymion would do so. If he wanted Kevral for breeding purposes, it made sense that the child she carried held significance to the king. Murder seemed unlikely, at least over the next nine months. He would have that long to find her. "It will suffice," he said. He seized the general's hand in a solid grip. "Please. Do your best."

Markanyin clamped onto Ra-khir's hand. "Oh, did I forget to mention, young man? You're coming with me."

Ra-khir did not hesitate. He had tried once, but then without the support of peers and general. "Wouldn't want it any other way."

The ocean frothed around Colbey's legs, slowing his run toward the figure on the beach. He recognized the other immediately, and the familiar elfin features did not fool him. He read more from bearing than vision, and the movement as the other raced to meet him completed the picture. "Odin!" he shouted, leaping for the shore. Wet sand splashed beneath his landing. He executed a perfect slash/jab combination. Inches in front of his target, the blade slammed into something solid. The strike jolted pain through his arm, wrenching his shoulder to the bone. Through gritted teeth, he watched colors shoot outward from the point of impact, summoned chaos shaped into law. *I saw you die!* Colbey sent the message to test the permeability of the barrier, not waste strength conversing in battle.

A grin overcame Odin's new face. *Do you think I trusted my very existence to a cocksure Renshai with an agenda of his own? I had a contingency plan.*

It all made sense to Colbey suddenly. Somehow, Odin had preserved a tiny portion of self in the Staff of Law. At first, it had retained only a quiet spark. Over the centuries, it grew, gradually recognizing self. And, by way of balance, the Staff of Chaos had awakened also, though much later and more slowly.

An unexpected side effect. Odin responded to the thought, though Colbey had not intended the god to follow the path of his reasoning.

Colbey tensed. Odin had always managed to manipulate his

mind, as others never could. How could he hope to fight an entity of power beyond his comprehension?

Though it makes sense now. Where Odin exists, Loki must also.

That misconception revealed the vulnerability Colbey would not have believed existed a moment earlier. Unable to attack physically, he launched a mental assault. His consciousness flew outward, then crashed against a barrier with a force that sent him reeling. He funneled power for another attempt. Experience flashed a warning. His head pounded, the pain at two intensities. Not for the first time, Odin had twisted his perceptions. The mental wall he had battered so intently was his own. Had he persisted, he would have destroyed himself.

Odin laughed, the sound like the slam of wave against cliffs. Colbey rose to shaky legs. He felt the warmth of a mental attack an instant before it struck. Worried to take another strike at the barrier, he forced it down. Odin's thought-spear whistled through, toward another wall. Again, Colbey pulled it down. More slowly now, Odin's advance arrowed through. Colbey opened four more barriers, then trapped it neatly between two. Another thought-spear followed the first, again caged as its momentum dwindled. Odin seemed to take no notice.

Come on, Loki! Odin taunted. *It's you and me, Prince of Demons.*

This time, Colbey mounted a more cautious attack, though it went against everything Renshai. He would not fall prey to the same mistake again. This time, Odin admitted him to a vast chamber that promised wisdom beyond even the comprehension that so much knowledge existed in all the worlds. Words glowed upon a wall like stone, and Colbey knew without knowing how that it represented a prophecy:

> *Thee Father shal avert hys fate.*
> *Then thee worlds shud celebrate.*
> *But far ynto dystrukshon hurled*
> *Law's vast plan ys then unfurled:*
> *A new world to create.*

> *All must dye to pave thee way.*
> *A syngle god to rule thee day.*
> *Thee only enemy wyll make*
> *One small lapse; a fatal mystake*
> *Leave thee world at thee mercy of Gray.*

The message seemed clear, yet Colbey banished the words from his thoughts. As a Wizard, he had learned that these predictions did not occur without champions to deliberately fulfill them. Even then, deep interpretations remained hidden. He had suffered twice for mistakes in reading, the first when he had avoided Rache Kallmirsson. The second had sent all three of the Wizards hunting him. Ultimately, that mistake resulted in the *Ragnarok*.

Odin's laughter rang out again, this time directly on top of him, with all the fury of an avalanche. This close, the voice seemed a shout. *YOU'RE DOOMED, LOKI. WOULD YOU LIKE TO MAKE YOUR FATAL MISTAKE NOW, OR SURPRISE ME WITH IT LATER?*

Colbey kept his reply low and even. *Perhaps, Odin, my fatal mistake is not being Loki.*

Colbey! Recognition finally dawned, and the laughter broke off, as if choked. *Fool! Your mistake is clear. You didn't bind with the staff!* It seemed as much question as statement, suffused with shocked incredulity followed by triumph. *You played right into the prophecy.*

Colbey refused to let the grim gray father's confidence shake him. *I don't believe in prophecies.* Only then, he remembered that, while mental conversation did not cost him energy, time away from his body did. He jerked back to withdraw. And slammed himself against a solid barrier that had arisen as they talked.

The laughter rang out again. *Now what will you do, Colbey Thorsson? Your mistake has come to claim you. Your power can never outlast mine.*

Colbey did not grace the taunt with a reply. He gathered his energy for attack, only then realizing how weak he had already become. If he remained, his strength would slowly dwindle into nothingness. His only hope lay in battering at the walls that held him and trusting his power to shatter Odin's defenses.

Even as Colbey funneled his reserves to the task, he recognized his error. Odin need only twist him again. The desperate charge would slam against his own barriers, and he would waste the last of his strength destroying himself. *Will he use the tactic or not?* The life or death of the universe rested on Colbey's guess, and he made it in the instant between committing to the attack and striking. At the last moment, he jerked back his power. His mental being skidded against the wall with a gentle thud, and he looked back into a mind familiar and foreign at

once. The honor, the tenets of war, and the fading religion once
deeply ingrained sat in mirror image to his usual perspective
Gently, he flipped self around and looked back out of his own
eyes.

The moment he did so, a presence pressed him. *Bind now
It's our only hope.*

Colbey ignored the Staff of Chaos' entreaties to assess self
The mental sparring had tapped him even more than he real
ized. His legs felt rubbery, and the sword seemed like a lead
weight in his grip. His bleary gaze registered Odin as a gray
blur, like stone. Only one course of action remained, the one he
had trusted since infancy. He channeled his last desperate reserves and lunged for law. This time he met no obstacle.

Apparently also tired, Odin lurched backward with a hiss
The sword/staff slashed a line along his chest. It dragged
through strangely, accompanied by spits of lightning that spiraled through a rainbow array of colors. Colbey's vision disappeared. His world narrowed to the sensations in his arms. A
fragment of law winked from existence, accompanied by a like
amount of chaos from the sword. Then, something exploded
against him, searing flesh, pounding hearing, and hurling him
like a rag. Bright light slashed across his closed eyes. Agony invaded every part. He thumped to the ground with a force that
slammed the breath from his lungs, rolling from habit rather
than intention. He still clutched the hilt of his sword.

Scarcely daring to believe he still lived, Colbey opened his
eyes. He recognized the patternless swirl of the world that had
become his home. The blast had returned him to the plain of
chaos.

Ease up, the sword/staff demanded. *You're hurting me.*

Painfully, Colbey pried his fingers free. All his strength
seemed trapped in that one location. He lay still, waiting for the
return of the energy he had expended.

What happened? chaos demanded.

I don't know. Colbey gave the only answer he could,
though he believed he might have the right one. When the Staff
of Chaos met a being bound to the Staff of Law, they had canceled those parts of one another that had come into direct contact. Colbey had suffered the backlash, and it had blown him
back to the world from which Odin had summoned him.

Colbey let his thoughts run as strength gradually seeped back
into his mind and body. Remembering the mental attacks he had
walled away, he opened his barriers and released them. The tiny

anifestations of law met the randomness of chaos-stuff. parks shot from the contact with a high-pitched shriek, then zzled into nothingness. Colbey sagged to the ground, many nderstandings coming to him at once. He had weakened not lled the AllFather, foiled his plans for the moment, but more attles lay ahead. Colbey managed a weak smile at the thought. hree centuries of peace on Asgard had left him hungry for war, ut he did not relish facing off with Odin again.

The ancient, clichéd adage ran through his head: *Be careful hat you wish for. . . .*

After sending guards to fetch the king's adviser, General Markanyin led Ra-khir and Mior to a waiting room inside the astle. Two plush couches, piled with satin pillows faced one nother. A low table between held baskets decorated with rapevines dangling withering fruit. A few wrinkled winter ap- les lay in the bottom. When merchants once again traveled the nany roads leading to the world's largest trading city, Ra-khir uspected fruits of myriad shape and color would again cram ne king's baskets. A window at the far end of the room admit- ed the intermittent breezes, whipping the light curtains into un- ulating, fairy dances.

The general gestured at Ra-khir to sit. Though he would have referred pacing, Ra-khir remained true to the formal manners nighthood required. He was a knight all times, not only when : suited him. Markanyin also sat, directly across from Ra-khir n the opposite couch.

Mior walked lightly across the pillows, paws leaving inden- ations, then settled into Ra-khir's lap. He stroked her from eck to tail base, alternating hands in a steady pattern, appreci- ting her choice of resting place. It gave him a legitimate, repet- tive action on which to focus his nervous energy without iolating protocol. Dander skittered through sunlight beaming n the window, and Ra-khir carefully gathered up each shed hair hat settled on clothing or cushions.

At length, a middle-aged man appeared in the doorway, Iressed in formal silks. Rich brown hair fell in oiled ringlets to is shoulders. Though his expression revealed severe concern, is hazel eyes settled on Ra-khir without the guilty skittering he knight expected.

Markanyin tensed to rise. Ra-khir did so more quickly, lumping Mior to the floor to execute a flourishing bow that in- :luded the grand removal of his hat. The cat stalked beneath the table, flicking her tail to protest the assault upon her dignity. Markanyin and the man in the doorway also bowed. Stepping into the room, the newcomer claimed a seat beside the general. Ra-khir returned to his place, but Markanyin remained standing for introductions. He gestured at the man in silks. "Lor Javonzir, adviser to King Cymion." The general inclined his head toward Ra-khir. "Sir Ra-khir, a Knight of Erythane."

"Thank you, General," Javonzir said.

Markanyin sat.

Ra-khir leaned forward, fully on the offensive. This time, h would not cease the verbal attack until he won. He would temper his words with manners, but he would not allow them t cripple him. He had already once sacrificed his knighthood for Kevral. "My lord, Lady Kevral is alive." He made a statement of fact that he would not allow to fall into question again.

"Indeed," Javonzir said.

Hostility trickled from Ra-khir. After his bout in King Cymion's court, he had expected any other answer.

"The elves informed me not long ago." Javonzir hesitated, a if about to say more, then fell silent.

Ra-khir guessed at the words unspoken, realizing Javonzi had sent the elves to catch the knights before they left Pudar Likely, he had done so without the king's consent, which ac counted for his current secrecy.

"You're the babies' father?"

The query raised ire. Ra-khir had suffered enough for a claim that seemed as unlikely as Kevral's death had been. "My lord I'm not convinced that this dead baby, now four times mentioned, ever existed."

"Not baby," Javonzir clarified. "Babies. Twins. And they're very much alive."

Ra-khir gasped in a sudden breath. He choked, coughed, and sputtered while thoughts rushed through his mind. He had believed the baby a ruse created by the king to explain Kevral's falsified death. He had even considered the possibility that the king had spoken truth in this regard. He had never dared allow his mind to contemplate this last possibility. Guarded joy filled him. "Where are my children?" he managed, voice hoarse and weak. He could scarcely believe the words issued from him. *I have children. Children. Me. Precious, wonderful children.* He did not yet even know their gender, yet protecting them became an instant obsession.

"The boys are fine, Sir Knight." Javonzir looked toward the window, then back. "And their mother also."

Ra-khir found his normal voice. "Lord, thank you." Many questions sprang to mind, and it took all of his self-control not to demand all three be brought into his presence immediately. Knight training had taught him patience. Javonzir would surely explain the situation now that the reassurances had ended. Delicate negotiations had to follow such a serious admission of guilt.

"Ra-khir, errors were made, some of those grievous." Javonzir rose, decorum forcing Ra-khir to do the same. "Sadly, desperate situations sometimes result in such." He walked to Ra-khir. "Harm was inflicted on you and on Lady Kevral. You have my sincerest apologies, and the king's as well." He took Ra-khir's hands into each of his own, begging forbearance with gesture as well as words. His voice dropped to a whisper. "Had I only known sooner, I would have ended it before it began."

Ra-khir swallowed hard. The more he heard, the more certain he became that the fault lay wholly with King Cymion. "My lord, I understand." He mentioned nothing of forgiveness. The nature of the crime forbade it, and such could only come from Kevral. Memory resurfaced with a rush of pain. "Is it . . ." The question stuck in his throat. "Is it true that she is again . . . with . . . child?"

Javonzir winced but did not dodge Ra-khir's stare. "Yes."

Ra-khir wrestled his anger. "Whose?"

Javonzir politely tugged at his fingers. "The crown prince's."

Ra-khir finally realized that his grip had tightened painfully. He threw Javonzir's smaller hands free, and the adviser backstepped onto Mior's tail. The cat yowled, swiping a claw across his ankles. Startled, he stumbled aside, slamming a shin against the table and staggering to recapture balance.

Ra-khir hurried to the window, not trusting himself to speak. He looked out over a courtyard warmed by summer sunshine. Courtiers settled on benches, their shadows stretching across a green expanse of grass. In Béarn, he would have seen children giggling and ducking around statues, and their conspicuous absence forced him to contemplate a side that, moments ago, seemed only evil. He would always despise King Cymion, yet he could also understand the desperation that might drive a king, and a prince, to commit an act so loathsome. He could not excuse, but he would bargain as necessary. "My lord, just tell me what I have to do to release my lady and my children."

"Two promises," Javonzir said softly, "and all four of yc
may return to Béarn together."

Ra-khir appreciated that Javonzir did not add "against yo
honor." Such was unnecessary. No matter how much Ra-kh
despised the terms, he would never break his word. He whirle
Javonzir stood beside the couch he had once occupied. Gener
Markanyin had also risen, remaining as quiet as he had throug!
out the negotiations.

Javonzir fidgeted, finally displaying the discomfort he ha
hidden until that moment. "First, when the time comes, th
which belongs to Pudar is returned."

Ra-khir did not need explanation. Javonzir referred to th
baby forced upon Kevral. "And the other?" He refused to mak
concessions until he heard all parts of the agreement.

"Your word that the incident is kept between those who a
ready know, and that no retribution is carried out against Puda
for this unfortunate indiscretion."

Ra-khir disliked the terms, yet understood their necessity t
Pudar. They could have asked far more of him. "I can vow fc
myself. But I can't speak for Kevral."

The general said his first words of the meeting. "Ra-khir,
believe that is exactly what my lord seeks. Your promise tha
you will protect Pudar from the swordmistress' wrath."

I could easier contain a hurricane. Ra-khir sighed, hea
shaking. "I can promise only to do everything within my powe
To attack Pudar, she will have to kill me first. I don't think she'!
do that." *I hope not.*

"Then you agree to the terms?" Javonzir said softly.

Ra-khir could scarcely control his impatience. Every mo
ment he wasted cost Kevral another in the dungeon. His hear
ached for a glimpse of the babies. "Yes, lord, I do." Despit
their necessity, he hated the words. He fought to keep from
imagining prying Kevral's infant from her arms to bestow i
upon the man who had raped her. Yet, weighing Kevral's free
dom and the lives of her two other children, his own sons, h
could find no other answer.

Footsteps pounded echoes through Pudar's dungeon, thei
uncharacteristic speed jarring Kevral from another swordles
practice. She dropped to a pose of crouched defiance, watching
shadows shift between distant bars. A guard's voice rang
through the dank corridor. "She's in the cell on the end, sir." An

nal nails clicked against stone. Mior streaked suddenly into iew, squeezing through the bars to join Kevral.

"Thank you." Ra-khir's unmistakable tenor reached Kevral, nore pleasant music than Darris ever crafted.

Kevral's heart pounded wildly. She stared at the dark hallway utside her cage, following the single set of approaching boot-alls as it drew nearer. Ra-khir emerged from the shadows. Vorry creased features otherwise chiseled to sweet perfection. Ier gaze traveled over every part: the loving green eyes be-eath gently arched brows, the square chin, the well-muscled ody sculpted from years of heavy labor with sword and pike. Tears stung her eyes. She made no attempt to speak, knowing uch was momentarily impossible. She waited, breath gone till.

Ra-khir suffered none of Kevral's malady. "Kevral," he said, trong hands reaching for her through the bars.

Kevral hurled herself against the door between them. The chains yanked cruelly at wrists and ankles; she could not return his embrace. Ra-khir seemed not to notice. He wrapped his arms around her, oblivious to the solid columns of metal he clutched as well. He held her in silence, his relentless grip speaking the volumes his mouth did not. Words could never ex-press the intensity of the love his touch embodied.

Time ground past while Ra-khir clutched and Kevral sobbed against his ample chest. Then, with obvious reluctance, Ra-khir let go. He opened his hands to reveal the keys, fingers shaking as he placed one into the lock. Even as he turned it, tumblers dropping into proper position, Kevral recalled the pulley sys-tem that would drag her unceremoniously across stone and pin-ion her against the wall. Rushing into place, she managed to avoid pain and humiliation as the door rattled open. Mior dashed from her path, her run stiff-legged.

Clearly startled by Kevral's dash across the cell, Ra-khir stood slack-mouthed in the entrance. His gaze tracked the chains to the ceiling.

"Close the door," Kevral instructed, trapped against the wall.

Ra-khir obeyed swiftly, metal slamming into place. The ten-sion dropped from the shackles, and Kevral hurled herself back into Ra-khir's warm grip. Again, they embraced, this time adding a passionate kiss of welcome that left Kevral dizzy and weak-kneed. This time, she pulled away, seeking words to ex-plain the many details Ra-khir needed to know. She managed only three before they failed her again. "You're a father."

"I know." Ra-khir flipped through the key ring as he studie[d] manacles and shackles. "I had to barter the prince's baby fo[r] them." He selected the only key small enough to fit the lock[s.] "And your vengeance for your freedom." He finally met he[r] gaze. "I'm sorry. I need your vow against violence before I ca[n] free you."

Anger flared, then sputtered like a wet match. Later, Kevra[l] knew, she would despise the promise. For now, she could no[t] weather the desperate situation her belligerence would creat[e] for those she loved. The freedom of self and sons seemed wort[h] the price. "I promise I won't disembowel the worthless bastar[d] or his damned guards."

Ra-khir cracked a smile. "That's not exactly the wording [I] was hoping for." He did not press for more, however. It was th[e] best he could expect from a chained Renshai. One by one, th[e] shackles fell from her wrists, revealing chafed and filthy skin[.]

Kevral crouched again, seizing Ra-khir's hands and dragging him down with her. Though she would have preferred to leave the cell first, she needed to pack her few belongings and to tel[l] him news that should not wait.

"Ra-khir, there are things you have to know."

The knight nodded wordlessly, clearly struck by her obvious desperation.

"First, one of those twins isn't yours."

The skin behind Ra-khir's jaw tensed.

Kevral placed her hand against his lips to stop him from speaking a denial that did not matter. "It's Tae's."

Ra-khir shook off the restraining fingers. "That's impossible."

Kevral did not wish to argue. "Colbey confirmed it."

Ra-khir went quiet. He did not ask, but the pain in his eyes was clear.

"I'm sorry, Ra-khir."

He rose and turned away.

The gesture knifed pain through Kevral, but she continued. No matter the cost, Ra-khir deserved the truth. "And the baby I'm carrying might not be the prince's either. I may have dreamed it all, but I believe Colbey sent his own son to rescue me from that fate. If so, Pudar has no claim to it."

Mior trotted around Ra-khir to his front. A moment later, she appeared on his shoulders, her purrs a loud comfort even to Kevral's more distant ears.

Gradually, Ra-khir turned. He sank to one knee, his head low

s if the cat's weight proved too much for his neck. "Kevral, I
will love those babies the same, no matter their blood. I love
ou, and nothing else matters." He looked at her from around a
lump of red hair that had fallen across his forehead. "Kevral,
will you marry me?"

To Kevral's surprise, she had an answer. "Yes, my love. Definitely, yes."

Epilogue

For the second time in two weeks, elves stood before the throne of Béarn, Tem'aree'ay accompanied by Eth'morand and the black-haired male Griff now knew as Ke'taros. As before smiles decorated their faces, tempered by clear exhaustion. Sympathy stole any chance of sharing their obvious happiness. He wanted to hold Tem'aree'ay, as safe and warm in his arms as in his heart, thrilled to watching her flat little abdomen grow healthfully round with the consummation of their love. Even the childlike king did not miss the irony. The baby the populace hailed as the first prince carried only the biology he and Queen Matrinka coincidentally shared while the one he sired could never wear the crown. He could not have cared less. So long as the corridors rang with the laughter of children, their origins did not matter.

For several moments, Griff watched Tem'aree'ay in happy silence. Then Darris cleared his throat, reminding the king that no one else could speak until he broke the hush.

Griff glanced around the courtroom. Fourteen guards flanked the dais he shared with Darris and Captain Seiryn. No courtiers sat among the benches; the beauty of the day enticed them to the courtyard gardens. "Greetings, elves. Friends."

"Greetings, Your Majesty." As usual, Eth'morand spoke for them all. He had the best command of the trading tongue. "We bring good news."

Tem'aree'ay squirmed. Ke'taros grinned.

Eth'morand did not await encouragement to continue. "Sire, working together, we've managed to stop the plague's spread."

Griff nodded, uncertain he understood. "I thought all parts of the world were affected. Messages from East and West confirm it."

"Yes, Sire." Eyes as consistent and smooth as sapphires studied the king. "But we've magic to protect those females not yet rendered sterile. Those with child and immatures."

Now smiles decorated every countenance. Griff could not hold back a wild whoop of elation. Though not a perfect solution, it would pave the way for a future that, a moment ago, seemed hopeless to many. "Thank you," he said. It did not sound like enough. "Thank you," he repeated, "thank you." It still seemed inadequate. "Every human in the world thanks you. We just can't thank you enough."

Darris chuckled. "You've made a good start, Sire."

Laughter rang through the court, the first in a long time.

Eth'morand waited until it subsided to continue. "We'll keep working on fully reversing the spell, Sire. If a solution exists, it'll require a difficult process."

"Anything you need, just ask. If possible, we'll supply it."

"Thank you, Sire." Eth'morand bowed with a twirling gesture of his hand to indicate he had finished his piece.

Griff had spent time thinking as well. "Eth'morand, Tem'aree'ay, Ke'taros wait, please." He waved a hand over the guards. "Anyone not elfin or me, clear the court."

Seiryn sprang from the dais, barking commands to the guards. They formed a stiff rank, and he marched them around the elves in two single files. These joined on the carpetway behind Ke'taros. Two by two, they exited the courtroom, doors banging shut on the last pair's heels.

Griff swiveled his head to Darris, still hovering near his right hand. "Have you recently become *lysalf*? Or king?"

Darris stiffened, then bowed. "Your Majesty, surely you didn't intend for me to leave you."

"I meant," Griff said, "exactly what I said."

Darris did not move, straining even Griff's gentle patience. "Am I speaking some language you don't understand?"

"No, Sire." Darris' gaze went from the doors, to the elves, to his king. "I understand. I'm just weighing the worst you would do to what Rantire will inflict if she finds out I left you unguarded in the court."

Griff could not stop another smile. "I'll see to it she never knows. I'm sorry, Darris. I need to discuss a matter I promised never to speak of around any but elves." A moment later, Griff wished he had given no explanation. Bard curiosity would torment his bodyguard at the realization that a secret existed he did not know.

Tem'aree'ay's *khohlar* tickled Griff's mind. ⋆*Elfin soul cycling?*⋆

Griff nodded.

Lav'rintir won't mind the bard knowing.

Darris headed toward the edge of the dais, stopped by Griff's sudden touch. "The elves have approved your presence. I ask only that anything you learn remains between us." He spread his arms, encompassing the elves as well as himself.

"So promised, Sire."

The king clambered down from the dais to stand among the elves, Darris rushing along beside him. "Eth'morand, I've done some thinking of my own, and I believe I found a solution to your baby problems as well as ours."

As usual, Griff read no expression on the elfin faces, though he thought he detected a slight crinkle beneath Eth'morand's blond bangs.

"Have you discovered a death to explain Tem'aree'ay's pregnancy?"

Tem'aree'ay looked coyly away.

"No," Eth'morand admitted. "We've contacted Lav'rintir. He and those with him are fine. We managed enough spying among the *svartalf* to ascertain the eldest ten still live." He looked to Tem'aree'ay, alert to her sudden shyness.

"That's because the baby is mine," Griff announced suddenly.

Darris drew in a sharp breath.

"And wherever human souls come from, they don't require a prior death."

Minuscule nods rode through the group as Griff's idea became self-evident. Humans and elves populating the world together. An unlimited supply of half-breeds coupled with a pool of fertile females unaffected by the *svartalf's* magic. Once the two societies became inseparable, survival-linked to one another, no one would suggest the racial devastation that had led Dh'arlo'mé to advocate the slaughter of humankind.

"What an idea," Ke'taros said softly. "What a brilliant idea." His grin seemed to envelop his face. "Sire, you must be the wisest man alive."

The simple-hearted king of Béarn laughed at words he had never in his life expected to hear.

Appendices

WESTERNERS

Béarnides

Abran (AH-bran)—the aging minister of foreign affairs; killed in the elfin purge.

Aerean (AIR-ee-an)—a renegade leader.

Aranal (Ar-an-ALL)—a previous king.

Baltraine (BAL-trayn)—the prime minister.

Baran (BAYR-in)—an ancient guard captain; served Sterrane.

Baynard (BAY-nard)—an ex-soldier, turned renegade. Distant descendant of Baran.

Charletha (Shar-LEETH-a)—minister of livestock, gardens, and food; killed in the elfin purge.

Dalen (DAY-linn)—a cooper; a renegade.

Davian (DAY-vee-an)—leader of the renegades.

Denevier (Dih-NEV-ee-er)—minister assigned to relay Knight-Captain Kedrin's orders from prison.

Ethelyn (ETH-ell-in)—King Kohleran's daughter; killed during the second staff-test.

Fachlaine (FATCH-layne)—King Kohleran's granddaughter; deceased.

Fahrthran (FAR-thrin)—minister of internal affairs; descendant of Arduwyn; killed in the elfin purge.

Fevrin (FEV-rinn)—a past sage; served Xanranis.

Friago (Free-YAH-go)—a renegade.

Griff (GRIFF)—King Kohleran's grandson; heir to the throne.

Helana (Hell-AHN-a)—Petrostan's wife and Griff's mother.

Kohleran (KOLL-er-in)—king of Béarn.

Limrinial (Lim-RIN-ee-al)—minister of local affairs; killed in the elfin purge.

Matrinka (Ma-TRINK-a)—King Kohleran's granddaughter.

Mikalyn (MIK-a-linn)—the head healer; killed in the elfin purge.

Mildy (MILL-dee)—King Kohleran's late wife.

Morhane (MOOR-hayn)—an ancient king who usurped the throne from his brother.

Nylabrin (NILL-a-bran)—King Kohleran's granddaughter, deceased.

Petrostan (Peh-TROSS-tin)—King Kohleran's youngest son; Griff's father. Died in a plowing accident.

The Sage—the chronicler of Béarn's history.

Sefraine (SEE-frayn)—King Kohleran's grandson.

Seiryn (SAIR-in)—the captain of the guards.

Sterrane (Stir-RAIN)—a previous king of Béarn.

Talamaine (TAL-a-mayn)—King Kohleran's son; Matrinka's late father.

Ukrista (Yoo-KRIS-tah)—King Kohleran's granddaughter; deceased.

Weslin (WESS-lin)—minister of courtroom procedure and affairs.

Xanranis (Zan-RAN-iss)—Sterrane's son; an ancient king.

Xyxthris (ZIX-thris)—King Kohleran's grandson.

Yvalane (IV-a-layn)—King Kohleran's father; a previous king.

Erythanians

Arduwyn (AR-dwinn)—a legendary archer.

Asha (AH-shah)—an adolescent girl.

Braison (BRAY-son)—a young Knight of Erythane.

Carlynn (KAR-linn)—an adolescent girl.

Diega (Dee-AY-gah)—Carlynn's father.

Edwin (ED-winn)—a Knight of Erythane. The armsman.

Esatoric (EE-sah-tor-ik)—a Knight of Erythane.

Garvin (GAR-vinn)—a Knight of Erythane.

Humfreet (HUM-freet)—the king.

Jakrusan (Jah-KROO-sin)—a Knight of Erythane.

Kedrin (KEH-drinn)—a Knight of Erythane. The captain.

Khirwith (KEER-with)—Ra-khir's stepfather.

Lakamorn (LACK-a-morn)—a Knight of Erythane.

Mariell (Mah-ree-ELL)—an adolescent girl; Sushara's sister.

Oridan (OR-ih-den)—Shavasiay's father.

Ra-khir (Rah-KEER)—an apprentice knight. Kedrin's son.

Ramytan (RAM-ih-tin)—Kedrin's late father.

Shavasiay (Shah-VASS-ee-ay)—a Knight of Erythane; acting captain.

Sushara (Soo-SHAR-a)—an adolescent girl; Mariell's sister.

Pudarians

Boshkin (BAHSH-kinn)—a servant of Leondis.

Brunar (BREW-nar)—a dungeon guard.

Charra (CHAR-ah)—a healer.

Chethid (CHETH-id)—a lieutenant; one of three.

Cymion (KIGH-mee-on)—the king.

Daizar (DYE-zahr)—minister of visiting dignitaries.

Danamelio (Dan-a-MEEL-ee-oh)—a criminal; deceased.

Darian (DAYR-ee-an)—a lieutenant; one of three.

Darris (DAYR-iss)—the bard; Linndar's son.

DeShane (Dih-SHAYN)—a captain of the king's guard.

The Flea—a criminal; deceased.

Harlton (HAR-all-ton)—a captain of the king's guard.

Harrod (HA-rod)—a surgeon.

Jahiran (Jah-HEER-in)—the first bard.

Javonzir (Ja-VON-zeer)—the king's cousin and adviser.

Lador (LAH-door)—a locksmith.

Larrin (LARR-inn)—a captain of the guard.

Leondis (Lee-ON-diss)—the crown prince; Severin's younger brother.

Leosina (Lee-oh-SEE-nah)—young daughter of the west wing maid.

Linndar (LINN-dar)—the previous bard; Darris' mother; killed in the elfin purge.

Mar Lon (MAR-LONN)—a legendary bard; Linndar's ancestor.

Markanyin (Marr-KANN-yinn)—Pudarian general.

Nellkoris (Nell-KORR-iss)—a lieutenant; one of three.

Octaro (Ok-TAR-oh)—a guard.

Peter (PET-er)—a street urchin; deceased.

Sabilar (SAB-ill-ar)—a blacksmith.

Severin (SEV-rinn)—the late heir to Pudar's throne.

Stick—a criminal; deceased.

Tadda (TAH-dah)—a thief; deceased.

Tanna (TAWN-a)—a healer.

Renshai

Ashavir (AH-shah-veer)—a late student of Colbey.

Bohlseti (Bowl-SET-ee)—a late student of Colbey.

Brenna (BRENN-a)—false name used by Rantire while a prisoner of elves.

Calistin the Bold (Ka-LEES-tin)—Colbey's late father.

Colbey Calistinsson (KULL-bay)—the legendary Renshai now living among the gods a.k.a. The Deathseeker a.k.a. The Golden Prince of Demons a.k.a. Kyndig.

Episte Rachesson (Ep-PISS-teh)—an orphan raised by Colbey. Killed by Colbey after being driven mad by chaos.

Kesave (Kee-SAH-veh)—a late student of Colbey.

Kevralyn Balmirsdatter (KEV-ra-linn)—a late warrior; Kevralyn Tainharsdatter's namesake.

Kevralyn Tainharsdatter (KEV-ra-linn)—a young Renshai.

Kristel Garethsdatter (KRISS-tal)—first guardian of Matrinka, along with Nisse.

Kyndig (KAWN-dee)—Colbey Calistinsson. Lit: "Skilled One."

Mitrian Santagithisdatter (MIH-tree-an)—wife of Tannin.

Modrey (MOH-dray)—forefather of the tribe of Modrey.

Nisse Nelsdatter (NEE-sah)—first guardian of Matrinka, along with Kristel.

Rache Garnsson (RACK-ee)—forefather of the tribe of Rache.

Rache Kallmirsson (RACK-ee)—Rache Garnsson's namesake; Episte's father.

Randil (Ran-DEEL)—a member of Béarn's second envoy.

Ranilda Battlemad (Ran-HEEL-da)—Colbey's late mother.

Rantire Ulfinsdatter (Ran-TEER-ee)—a member of Béarn's first envoy.

Raska "Ravn" Colbeysson (RASS-ka; RAY-vinn)—Colbey's and Freya's son.

Sylva (SILL-va)—Rache Garnsson's wife. An Erythanian.

Tarah Randilsdatter (TAIR-a)—wife of Modrey and sister of Tannin.

Tannin Randilsson (TAN-in)—forefather of the tribe of Tannin. Tarah's brother and Mitrian's husband.

Thialnir (Thee-AHL-neer)—a chieftain.

Vashi (VASH-ee)—a late warrior.

Santagithians

Herwin (HER-winn)—Griff's stepfather.
Santagithi (San-TAG-ih-thigh)—long-dead general for whom the city was named.

EASTERNERS

Alsrusett (Al-RUSS-it)—one of Weile Kahn's bodyguards (see also Daxan).
Chayl (SHAYL)—a follower of Weile Kahn; commander of Nighthawk sector.
Curdeis (KER-tuss)—Weile Kahn's late brother.
Daxan (DIK-sunn)—one of Weile Kahn's bodyguards (see also Alsrusett).
Jeffrin (JEFF-rinn)—an informant working for Weile Kahn.
Kinya (KEN-yah)—a longtime member of Weile Kahn's organization.
Leightar (LAY-tar)—a follower of Weile Kahn.
Midonner (May-DONN-er)—king of Stalmize; high king of the Eastlands.
Monika (Moh-NEE-kah)—a fertile woman.
Nacoma (Nah-KAH-mah)—a follower of Weile Kahn.
Niko (NAY-koh)—a pregnant woman.
Shavoor (Shah-VOOR)—an informant working for Weile Kahn.
Shaxcharal (SHACKS-krawl)—the last king of LaZar.
Tae Kahn (TIGH KAHN)—Weile Kahn's son.
Tichhar (TICH-har)—a LaZarian emissary.
Tisharo (Ta-SHAR-oh)—a con man working for Weile Kahn.
Usyris (Yoo-SIGH-russ)—a follower of Weile Kahn; commander of Sparrowhawk sector.
Weile Kahn (WAY-lee KAHN)—a crime lord.
Zeldar (ZAYL-dah)—a pregnant woman.

NORTHERNERS

Olvaerr (OHL-eh-vair)—NORDMIRIAN. Valr Kirin's son.
Tyrion (TEER-ee-on)—ASCAI. an inner court guard of Pudar.
Valr Kirin (Vawl-KEER-in)—NORDMIRIAN. an ancient enemy of Colbey's, long dead.

OUTWORLDERS

Arak'bar Tulamii Dhor (ahr-OK-bar Too-LAHM-ee-igh ZHOOR)—the eldest of the elves; a.k.a. Captain a.k.a. Lav'rintir.

Ath-tiran Béonwith Bray'onet Ty'maranth Nh'aytemir (Ath-TEER-inn Bee-ON-with BRAY-on-et Tee-MAR-anth Nigh-A-teh-mayr)—a *lysalf*.

Baheth'rin Gh'leneth Wir-talos Dartarian Mithrillan (Ba-HETH-a-rinn Gah-LENN-eth Weer-TAY-lohs Dar-TAR-ee-an Mith-RILL-in)—a young elf.

Captain—the common name for Arak'bar Tulamii Dhor

Chan'rék'ril (Shawn-RAYK-rill)—an artistic *lysalf*.

Dess'man Damylith Char'kiroh Va-Naysin Jemarious (DESS-man Dah-MIGH-lith Shar-eh-KEER-oh Vah-NAY-sin Jem-AHR-ee-us)—a *svartalf*.

Dh'arlo'mé'aftris'ter Te'meer Braylth'ryn Amareth Fel-Krin (ZHAR-loh-may-aff-triss-ter Teh-MEER Brawl-THRINN Ah-MAR-eth Fell-krinn)—the elves' leader.

Dhyano Falkurian L'marithal Gasharyil Domm (ZHAN-oh Fal-KYOOR-ee-an Lah-mah-EETH-all Gah-SHAR-ee-ill DOHM)—a *lysalf*.

Eth'morand Kayhiral No'vahntor El-brinith Tahar (Eth-MOOR-and Kah-HEER-all Noh'VAHN-tor El-BRINN-ith Tah-HAR)—a *lysalf*.

Haleeyan Sh'borith Nimriel T'mori Na-kira (Hah-LEE-yan Sha-BOHR-ith NIM-ree-ell Tah-MOOR-ee Nah-KEER-ah)—a *lysalf*.

Hri'shan'taé Y'varos Fitanith Adh'taran (HREE-shan-tigh EE-vahr-ohs Figh-TAN-ith Ad-hah-TAYR-an)—a member of the council of Nine a.k.a. She of Slow Emotions.

Ke'taros (Key-TAR-ohs)—a *lysalf*.

Khy'barreth Y'vrintae Shabeerah El-borin Morbonos (Kigh-BAYR-eth Eev-RINN-tigh Shah-BEER-ah ELL-boor-in Moor-BOH-nohs)—a brain-damaged *svartalf*.

Mith'ranir Orian T'laris El'neerith Wherinta (Mith-RAN-eer OR-ee-an Tee-LAR-ihs Ell-ih-NEER-ith Whir-INN-tah)—a *svartalf*.

Oa'si Brahirinth Yozwaran Tril'frawn Ren-whar (WAY-see Brah-HEER-inth Yoz-WAHR-an Trill-FRAWN Ren-WAHR)—the youngest elf.

Petree'shan-ash Tilmir V'harin Korhinal Chareen (PEH-tree-

SHAN-ash Till-MEER VAY-har-inn KOR-in-all Shah-REEN)—a member of the council of Nine.

ree-hantis Kel'abirik Trill Barithos Nath'taros (PREE-hahntiss KELL-ah-beer-ik TRILL BAR-ih-thohs Nath-TAR-ohs)—a *svartalf* impersonating King Kohleran.

Reehanthan Tel'rik Oltanos Leehinith Mir-shanir (Ree-HAHN-than TELL-rik Ohl-TAN-ohs Lee-HIN-ith Meer-SHAN-eer)—a *lysalf.*

em'aree'ay Donnev'ra Amal-yah Krish-anda Mal-satorian (Teh-MAR-ee-ay Donn-EV-er-a Ah-MAL-yah Kreesh-AND-ah Mahl-sah-TOR-ee-an)—a *lysalf* healer.

The Torturer.

resh'iondra She'aric Airanisha Ni-kii Diah (Tresh-ee-ON-dra Shay-AHR-ik Air-ANN-ee-shah Nee-KEE-igh DIGH-a)—a *svartalf.*

Vincelina Sa'viannith Esah-tohrika Tar Kin'zoth (Vin-sell-LEE-na Sah-ha-vee-ANN-ith Ess-ah-toor-EE-kah TAR KEEN-zoth)—a *svartalf.*

Vrin-thal-ros Obtrinéos Pruthrandius Tel'Amorak (Vrin-THAHL-rohs Ob-trin-AY-os Proo-THRAND-ee-us Tel-am-OOR-ak)—a member of the elfin council of Nine.

Ysh'andra (Yah-SHAN-drah)—a member of the elfin council of Nine.

ANIMALS

Frost Reaver—Colbey's white stallion.

Mior—Matrinka's calico cat.

Silver Warrior—Ra-khir's white stallion.

GODS, WORLDS & LEGENDARY OBJECTS

Northern

Aegir (AHJ-eer)—Northern god of the sea; killed at the *Ragnarok.*

Alfheim (ALF-highm)—The world of elves; destroyed during the *Ragnarok.*

Asgard (AHSS-gard)—The world of the gods.

Balder (BALL-der)—Northern god of beauty and gentlenes. who rose from the dead after the *Ragnarok*.

Beyla (BAY-lah)—Frey's human servant. Wife of Byggvir.

The Bifrost Bridge (BEE-frost)—The bridge between Asgard and man's world.

Bragi (BRAH-gee)—Northern god of poetry; killed at the *Ragnarok*.

Byggvir (BEWGG-veer)—Frey's human servant. Husband of Beyla.

Colbey Calistinsson (KULL-bay)—legendary Renshai.

The Fenris Wolf (FEN-ris)—the Great Wolf. The evil son of Loki. Also called Fenrir (FEN-reer); killed at the *Ragnarok*.

Frey (FRAY)—Northern god of rain, sunshine, fortune, and elves.

Freya (FRAY-a)—Frey's sister. Northern goddess of battle.

Frigg (FRIGG)—Odin's wife. Northern goddess of fate.

Gladsheim (GLAD-shighm)—"Place of Joy." Sanctuary of the gods.

Hel (HEHL)—Northern goddess of the cold underrealm for those who do not die in valorous combat; killed at the *Ragnarok*.

Hel (HEHL)—The underrealm ruled by the goddess Hel.

Heimdall (HIGHM-dahl)—Northern god of vigilance and father of mankind; killed at the *Ragnarok*.

Hlidskjalf (HLID-skyalf)—Odin's high seat from which he can survey the worlds.

Hod (HODD)—Blind god, a son of Odin. Returned with Balder after the *Ragnarok*.

Honir (HON-eer)—An indecisive god who survived the *Ragnarok*.

Idunn (EE-dun)—Bragi's wife. Keeper of the golden apples of youth.

Kvasir (KWAH-seer)—A wise god, murdered by dwarves, whose blood was brewed into the mead of poetry.

Loki (LOH-kee)—Northern god of fire and guile. A traitor to the gods and a champion of chaos; killed at the *Ragnarok*.

Magni (MAG-nee)—Thor's and Sif's son. Northern god of might.

Mana-garmr (MAH-nah Garm)—Northern wolf destined to extinguish the sun with the blood of men at the *Ragnarok*.

The Midgard Serpent—A massive, poisonous serpent destined to kill and be killed by Thor at the *Ragnarok*. Loki's son; killed at the *Ragnarok*.

imir (MIM-eer)—Wise god who was killed by gods. Odin preserved his head and used it as an adviser.

Modi (MOE-dee)—Thor's and Sif's son. Northern god of blood wrath.

Njord (NYORR)—Frey's and Freya's father.

Norns—The keepers of past, present, and future.

Odin (OH-din)—Northern leader of the pantheon. Father of the gods a.k.a. The AllFather; killed at the *Ragnarok*.

Odrorir (OD-dror-eer)—The cauldron containing the mead of poetry brewed from Kvasir's blood.

Ran (RAHN)—Wife of Aegir.

Raska Colbeysson (RASS-ka)—son of Freya and Colbey a.k.a. Ravn (RAY-vinn).

Sif (SIFF)—Thor's wife. Northern goddess of fertility and fidelity.

Sigyn (SEE-gihn)—Loki's wife.

Skoll (SKOEWL)—Northern wolf who will swallow the sun at the *Ragnarok*.

Syn (SIN)—Northern goddess of justice and innocence.

Surtr (SURT)—The king of fire giants. Destined to kill Frey and destroy the worlds of elves and men with fire at the *Ragnarok;* killed at the *Ragnarok*.

Thor—Northern god of storms, farmers, and law; killed at the *Ragnarok*.

Tyr (TEER)—Northern one-handed god of war and faith; killed at the *Ragnarok*.

Valhalla (VAWL-holl-a)—The heaven for the souls of dead warriors killed in valiant combat. At the *Ragnarok*, these souls assisted the gods in battle.

Vali (VAHL-ee)—Odin's son. Destined to survive the *Ragnarok*.

The Valkyries (VAWL-ker-ees)—The Choosers of the Slain. Warrior women who choose which souls go to Valhalla on the battlefield.

Vidar (VEE-dar)—Son of Odin. He was destined to avenge his father's death at the *Ragnarok* by slaying the Fenris Wolf. Current leader of the gods.

The Wolf Age—The sequence of events immediately preceding the *Ragnarok* during which Skoll swallows the sun, Hati mangles the moon, and the Fenris Wolf runs free.

Western

(gods of this pantheon are rarely worshiped anymore)

Aphrikelle (Ah-fri-KELL)—Western goddess of spring.
Cathan (KAY-than)—Western goddess of war, specifically o
hand-to-hand combat. Twin to Kadrak.
Dakoi (Dah-KOY)—Western god of death.
The Faceless God—Western god of winter.
Firfan (FEER-fan)—Western god of archers and hunters.
Itu (EE-too)—Western goddess of knowledge and truth.
Kadrak (KAD-drak)—Western god of war. Twin to Cathan.
Ruaidhri (Roo-AY-dree)—Western leader of the pantheon.
Suman (SOO-mon)—Western god of farmers and peasants.
Weese (WEESSS)—Western god of winds.
Yvesen (IV-e-sen)—Western god of steel and women.
Zera'im (ZAIR-a-eem)—Western god of honor.

Eastern

Sheriva (Sha-REE-vah)—omnipotent, only god of the
Eastlands.

Outworld Gods

Ciacera (See-a-SAIR-a)—The goddess of life on the sea floo
who takes the form of an octopus.
Mahaj (Ma-HAJ)—The god of dolphins.
Morista (Moor-EES-tah)—The god of swimming creature:
who takes the form of a seahorse.

FOREIGN WORDS

A (AH)—EASTERN. "from."
ailar (IGH-LAR)—EASTERN. "to bring."
al (AIL)—EASTERN. the first person singular pronoun.
alfen (ALF-in)—BÉARNESE. "elves;" new term created by
elves to refer to themselves.
anem (ON-um)—BARBARIAN. "enemy;" usually used in reference to a specific race or tribe with whom the barbarian's
tribe is at war.

aristiri (ah-riss-TEER-ee)—TRADING. a breed of singing hawks.

aårvaåkir (AWR-van-keer)—NORTHERN. "vigilant one."

baronshei (ba-RON-shigh)—TRADING. "bald."

bein (bayn)—NORTHERN. "legs."

bha'fraktii (bhah-FROK-tee-igh)—ELFIN. "those who court their doom." A *lysalf* term for *svartalf*.

binyal (BIN-yall)—TRADING. type of spindly tree.

bleffy (BLEFF-ee)—WESTERN/TRADING. a child's euphemism for nauseating.

bolboda (bawl-BOE-da)—NORTHERN. "evilbringer."

brishigsa weed (brih-SHIG-sah)—WESTERN. a specific leafy weed with a translucent, red stem. A universal antidote to several common poisons.

brorin (BROAR-in)—RENSHAI. "brother."

brunstil (BRUNN-steel)—NORTHERN. a stealth maneuver learned from barbarians by the Renshai. Literally: "brown and still."

chroams (krohms)—WESTERN. specific coinage of copper, silver, or gold.

corpa (KOR-pa)—WESTERN. "brotherhood, town." Literally: "body."

cringers—EASTERN. gang slang for people who show fear.

daimo (DIGH-moh)—EASTERN. slang term for Renshai.

demon (DEE-mun)—ANCIENT TONGUE. a creature of magic.

dero (DAYR-oh)—EASTERN. a type of winter fruit.

djem (dee-YEM)—NORTHERN. demon.

doranga (door-ANG-a)—TRADING. a type of tropical tree with serrated leaves and jutting rings of bark.

drilstin (DRILL-stinn)—TRADING. an herb used by healers.

dwar'freytii (dwar-FRAY-tee-igh)—ELFIN. "the chosen ones of Frey;" *svartalf* name for themselves.

Einherjar (IGHN-herr-yar)—NORTHERN. "the dead warriors in Valhalla."

eksil (EHK-seel)—NORTHERN. "exile."

erenspice (EH-ren-spighs)—EASTERN. a type of hot spice used in cooking.

fafra (FAH-fra)—TRADING. "to eat."

feflin (FEF-linn)—TRADING. "to hunt."

formynder (for-MEWN-derr)—NORTHERN. "guardian," "teacher."

forrader (foh-RAY-der)—NORTHERN. "traitor."

forraderi (foh-reh-derr-EE)—NORTHERN. "treason."

Forsvarir (Fours-var-EER)—RENSHAI. a specific disarming maneuver.

frey (FRAY)—NORTHERN. "lord."

freya (FRAY-a)—NORTHERN. "lady."

frichen-karboh (FRATCH-inn kayr-BOH)—EASTERN. widow. Literally: "manless woman, past usefulness."

frilka (FRAIL-kah)—EASTERN. the most formal title for a woman, elevating her nearly to the level of a man.

fussling (FUSS-ling)—TRADING. slang for bothering.

galn (gahln)—NORTHERN. "ferociously crazy."

ganim (GAH-neem)—RENSHAI. "a non-Renshai."

garlet (GAR-let)—WESTERN. a type of wildflower believed to have healing properties.

garn (garn)—NORTHERN. "yarn."

Gerlinr (Gerr-LEEN)—RENSHAI. a specific aesthetic and difficult sword maneuver.

granshy (GRANN-shigh)—WESTERN. "plump."

gullin (GULL-in)—NORTHERN. "golden."

gynurith (ga-NAR-ayth)—EASTERN. "excrement."

hacantha (ha-CAN-thah)—TRADING. a type of cultivated flower that comes in various hues.

hadongo (hah-DONG-oh)—WESTERN. a twisted, hardwood tree.

Harval (Harr-VALL)—ANCIENT TONGUE. "the gray blade."

Hastivillr (Has-tih-VEEL)—RENSHAI. a sword maneuver.

jovinay arythanik (joh-VIN-ay ar-ih-THAN-ik)—ELFIN. "a joining of magic." A gathering of elves for the purpose of amplifying and casting spells.

jufinar (JOO-finn-ar)—TRADING. a type of bushlike tree that produces berries.

kadlach (KOD-lok; the ch has a guttural sound)—TRADING. a vulgar term for a disobedient child; akin to brat.

kathkral (KATH-krall)—ELFIN. a type of broad-leafed tree.

kenya (KEN-ya)—WESTERN. "bird."

khohlar (KOH-lar)—ELFIN. a mental magical concept that involves transmitting several words in an instantaneous concept.

kjaelnabnir (kyahl-NAHB-neer)—RENSHAI. temporary name for a child until a hero's name becomes available.

kinesthe (Kin-ESS-teh)—NORTHERN. "strength."

kolbladnir (kol-BLAW-neer)—NORTHERN. "the cold-bladed."

kraell (kray-ELL)—ANCIENT TONGUE. a type of demon dwelling in the deepest region of chaos' realm.

kyndig (KAWN-dee)—NORTHERN. "skilled one."

lav'rintir (lahv-rinn-TEER)—ELFIN. "destroyer of the peace."

lav'rintii (lahv-RINN-tee-igh)—ELFIN. "the followers of Lav'rintir."

lessakit (LAYS-eh-kight)—EASTERN. a message.

leuk (LUKE)—WESTERN. "white."

loki (LOH-kee)—NORTHERN. "fire."

lonriset (LON-ri-set)—WESTERN. a ten-stringed musical instrument.

Lynstreik (LEEN-strayk)—RENSHAI. A sword maneuver.

lysalf (LEES-alf)—ELFIN. "light elf."

magni (MAG-nee)—NORTHERN. "might."

meirtrin (MAYR-trinn)—TRADING. a specific breed of nocturnal rodent.

minkelik (min-KEL-ik)—ELFIN. "human."

mirack (merr-AK)—WESTERN. a specific type of hardwood tree with white bark.

missy beetle—TRADING. a type of harmless, black beetle.

mjollnar (MYOLL-neer)—NORTHERN. mullicrusher.

modi (MOE-dee)—NORTHERN. "wrath."

Morshoch (MORE-shock)—ANCIENT TONGUE. "sword of darkness."

mynten (MIN-tin)—NORTHERN. a specific type of coin.

naådenal (naw-deh-NAHL)—RENSHAI. Literally: "needle of mercy." A silver, guardless, needle-shaped dagger constructed during a meticulous religious ceremony and used to end the life of an honored, suffering ally or enemy, then melted in the victim's pyre.

nålogtråd (naw-LOG-trawd)—RENSHAI. "needle and thread;" a Renshai sword maneuver.

noca (NOE-ka)—BÉARNESE. "grandfather."

Odelhurtig (OD-ehl-HEWT-ih)—RENSHAI. A sword maneuver.

oopey (OO-pee)—WESTERN/TRADING. A child's euphemism for an injury.

orlorner (oor-LEERN-ar)—EASTERN. "to deliver to."

perfrans (PURR-franz)—a scarlet wildflower.

pike—NORTHERN. "mountain."

prins (PRINS)—NORTHERN. "prince."

ranweed—WESTERN. a specific type of wild plant.

raynshee (RAYN-shee)—TRADING. "elder."

rexin (RAYKS-inn)—EASTERN. "king."

rhinsheh (ran-SHAY)—EASTERN. "morning."

richi (REE-chee)—WESTERN. a specific breed of songbird.

rintsha (RINT-shah)—WESTERN. "cat."

Ristoril (RISS-tor-ril)—ANCIENT TONGUE. "sword of tranquillity."

sangrit (SAN-grit)—BARBARIAN. "to form a blood bond."

shucara (shoo-KAHR-a)—TRADING. a specific medicinal root.

skjald (SKYAWLD)—NORTHERN. musician chronicler.

svartalf (SWART-alf)—ELFIN. "dark elf."

svergelse (sverr-GELL-seh)—RENSHAI. "sword figures practiced alone; katas."

take—a game children play.

talvus (TAL-vus)—WESTERN. "midday."

thrudr (THRUDD)—NORTHERN. "power, might."

torke (TOR-keh)—RENSHAI. "teacher, sword instructor."

Tre-ved-en (TREH-ved-enn)—RENSHAI. "Loki's cross" a Renshai maneuver designed for battling three against one.

trithray (TRITH-ray)—TRADING. a purple wildflower.

Tvinfri (TWINN-free)—RENSHAI. a disarming maneuver.

Ulvstikk (EWLV-steek)—RENSHAI. a sword maneuver.

uvakt (oo-VAKT)—RENSHAI. "the unguarded." A term for children whose *kjaelnabnir* becomes a permanent name.

Valhalla (VAWL-holl-a)—NORTHERN. "Hall of the Slain." The walled "heaven" for brave warriors slain in battle.

Valkyrie (VAWL-kerr-ee)—NORTHERN. "Chooser of the Slain."

valr (VAWL)—NORTHERN. "slayer."

Vestan (VAYST-in)—EASTERN. "The Westlands."

waterroot—TRADING. an edible sea plant.

wertel—TRADING. a specific plant with an acid seed used for medicinal purposes.

wisule (WISS-ool)—TRADING. a foul-smelling, disease-carrying breed of rodents which has many offspring because the adults will abandon them when threatened.

yarshimyan (yar-SHIM-yan)—ELFIN. a type of tree with bubblelike fruit

PLACES

Northlands

The area north of the Weathered Mountains and west of the
Great Frenum Range. The Northmen live in ten tribes, each
with its own town surrounded by forest and farmland. The
boundaries change:

Asci (ASS-kee)—home of the Ascai; Patron god: Bragi.

Aerin (Ah-REEN)—home of the Aeri; Patron god: Aegir.

Blathe (BLAYTH-eh)—home of the Blathe; Patron god: Aegir.

Devil's Island—an island in the Amirannak. A home to the
Renshai after their exile. Currently part of Blathe.

Erd (URD)—home of the Erdai; Patron goddess: Freya.

Gelshnir (GEELSH-neer)—home of the Gelshni; Patron god:
Tyr.

Gjar (GYAR)—home of the Gjar; Patron god: Heimdall.

Nordmir (NORD-meer)—the Northlands high kingdom, home
of the Nordmirians; Patron god: Odin.

Shamir (Sha-MEER)—home of the Shamirins; Patron goddess:
Freya.

Skrytil (SKRY-teel)—home of the Skrytila; Patron god: Thor.

Talmir (TAHL-meer)—home of the Talmirians; Patron god:
Frey.

Westlands

The Westlands are bounded by the Great Frenum Mountains
to the east, the Weathered Mountains to the north, and the
sea to the west and south. In general, the cities become
larger and more civilized as the land sweeps westward.
The central area is packed with tiny farm towns dwarfed
by lush farm fields that, over time, have nearly coalesced.
This area is known as the Fertile Oval. The easternmost
portions of the Westlands are forested, with sparse towns
and rare barbarian tribes. To the south lies an uninhabited
tidal plain.

Almische (Ahl-mish-AY)—a small city.

Béarn (Bay-ARN)—the high kingdom; a mountain city.

Bellenet Fields (Bell-e-NAY)—a tourney field in Erythane.

Corpa Bickat (KORE-pa Bi-KAY)—a large city.

Corpa Schaull (KORE-pa Shawl)—a medium-sized city; one
of the "Twin Cities" (see Frist).

Erythane (AIR-eh-thane)—a large city closely allied with Béarn. Famous for its knights.

The Fields of Wrath—Plains near Erythane. Home to the Renshai.

Frist (FRIST)—a medium-sized city; one of the "Twin Cities" (see Corpa Schaull).

Granite Hills—a small, low range of mountains.

Great Frenum Mountains (FREN-um)—towering, impassable mountains that divide the Eastlands from the Westlands and Northlands.

Greentree—a small town.

Hopewell—a small town.

The Knight's Rest—a pricy tavern in Erythane.

New Lovén (Low-VENN)—a medium-sized city.

Nualfheim (Noo-ALF-highm)—the elves' name for their island.

The Off-duty Tavern—a Pudarian tavern frequented by guardsmen.

Oshtan (OSH-tan)—a small town.

Porvada (Poor-VAH-da)—a medium-sized city.

Pudar (Poo-DAR)—the largest city of the West; the great trade center.

The Red Horse Inn—an inn in Pudar.

The Road of Kings—the legendary route by which the Eastern Wizard is believed to have rescued the high king's heir after a bloody coup.

Santagithi—a medium-sized town.

The Western Plains—a barren salt flat.

Wynix (Why-NIX)—a medium-sized town.

Eastlands

The area east of the Great Frenum Mountains. It is a vast, overpopulated wasteland filled with crowded cities and eroded fields. Little forest remains:

Dunchart (DOON-shayrt)—a small city.

Ixaphant (IGHCKS-font)—a large city.

Gihabortch (GIGH-hah-bortch)—a city.

LaZar (LAH-zar)—a small city.

Lemnock (LAYM-nok)—a large city.

Osporivat (As-poor-IGH-vet)—a large city.

Prohothra (Pree-HATH-ra)—a large city.

ozmath (ROZZ-mith)—a medium-sized city.
talmize (STAHL-meez)—the Eastern high kingdom.

Bodies of Water

mirannak Sea (A-MEER-an-nak)—the Northernmost ocean.
runn River (BRUN)—a muddy river in the Northlands.
onus River (KONE-uss)—a shared river of the Eastlands and Westlands.
y River—a cold, Northern river.
ewel River—one of the rivers that flows to Trader's Lake.
erionyx River (Peh-ree-ON-ix)—a Western river.
outhern Sea—the southernmost ocean.
rader's Lake—a harbor for trading boats in Pudar.
rader's River—the main route for overwater trade.

Objects/Systems/Events

he Bards—a familial curse passed to the oldest child, male or female, of a specific family. The curse specifically condemns the current bard to obsessive curiosity but allows him to impart his learning only in song. A condition added by the Eastern Wizards compels each to serve as the personal bodyguard to the current king of Béarn as well.
ardinal Wizards—a system of balance created by Odin in the beginning of time consisting of four, near immortal opposing guardians of evil, neutrality, and goodness who were tightly constrained by Odin's laws. Obsolete.
he Great War—a massive war fought between the Eastland army and the combined forces of the Westlands.
arval—"the Gray Blade." The sword of balance imbued with the forces of law, chaos, good, and evil.
he Knights of Erythane—an elite guardian unit for the king of Erythane that also serves the high king in Béarn in shifts. Steeped in rigid codes of dress, manner, conduct, and chivalry, they are famed throughout the world.
olbladnir—"the Cold-bladed." A magic sword commissioned by Frey to combat Surtr at the *Ragnarok*.
jollnir—"Mullicrusher." Thor's gold, short-handled hammer so heavy that only he can lift it.
he Necklace of the Brisings—a necklace worn by the goddess Freya and forged by dwarves from "living gold."

The Pica Stone—a clairsentient sapphire. One of the rare items with magical power.

Ragnarok (ROW-na-rok)—"the Destruction of the Powers." The prophesied time when men, elves, and nearly all of the gods will die.

The Sea Seraph—the ship once owned by an elf known only as the Captain.

The Seven Tasks of Wizardry—a series of tasks designed by the gods to test the power and worth of the Cardinal Wizards' chosen successors. Obsolete.

The Trobok—"the Book of the Faithful." A scripture that guides the lives of Northmen. It is believed that daily reading from the book assists Odin in holding chaos at bay from the world of law.